Praise for Lesley Lokko

SAFFRON SKIES

'This is everything you'd expect of a blockbuster – glamorous locations, ambitious female protagonists and a singing, gliding narrative – but with a little more intelligence'   *Glamour*

'With five decades of family feuds, sibling rivalry and love affairs . . . an exciting, intelligent blockbuster'   *Eve*

SUNDOWNERS

'A very 21st-century blockbuster . . . Much more than a coming-of-age tale, this creates a glamorous and exciting world that is so contemporary and convincing you'll feel like a special fifth member of their group'   *Cosmopolitan*

'A novel where Glamour with a capital "G" is the entire raison d'être . . . refreshingly, wonderfully unpretentious . . . Lokko has the skill to make you care about what happens to the characters . . . this is her first novel. I'm looking forward to her next one already'   Wendy Holden, *Sunday Express*

BITTER CHOCOLATE

'So engrossing, you'll want to read through your lunchbreak'
New Woman

'A blockbuster with brains . . . the ultimate guilty pleasure'   *Bella*

'A bittersweet story of love, pain and three feisty women'
Woman

After a lifetime spent between Ghana and Britain (and quite a few other places), Lesley Lokko finally put her long years of architectural training to good use and designed her own home in Ghana. As soon as it was finished, she turned straight round and went to live in Hackney.

Rich Girl, Poor Girl is Lesley's fourth novel and she's hard at work on the fifth. Her previous three novels, *Sundowners*, *Saffron Skies* and *Bitter Chocolate*, are available from Orion. If you'd like to find out more about Lesley (or to see pictures of her house), visit www.lesleylokko.com. She really does answer her emails.

Rich Girl, Poor Girl

Lesley Lokko

An Orion paperback

First published in Great Britain in 2009
by Orion
This paperback edition published in 2010
by Orion Books Ltd,
Orion House, 5 Upper St Martin's Lane
London WC2H 9EA

An Hachette UK company

3 5 7 9 10 8 6 4

A CIP catalogue record for this book is available
from the British Library.

ISBN 978-1-4091-0351-6

Typeset at the Spartan Press Ltd,
Lymington, Hants

Printed and bound in Great Britain by
Clays Ltd, St Ives plc

The Orion Publishing Group's policy is to use papers that
are natural, renewable and recyclable products and
made from wood grown in sustainable forests. The logging
and manufacturing processes are expected to conform to
the environmental regulations of the country of origin.

www.orionbooks.co.uk

For Patrick. This is his book too, and is for him.

Acknowledgements

As always, heartfelt thanks are due to Christine and Kate, who took the raw material and pruned it into shape, and to Sophie Hutton-Squire who painstakingly copy-edited the unruly draft with such good grace! This time round, thankfully (!), it was more or less written in one place, Eastside Farm, and again, my thanks go to Alistair and Susie Cowan for having me there and for being such splendid company; to my sister Debbie for our late-night chats, diet tips and taking such good care of my UK home; to Vic for taking care of things in Accra, always, and to Elkin, for the generous use of his flat. For conversations around Zimbabwe in general and the Shona translations in particular, I'm very grateful to Keith Shiri, Brian Chikwava and Elkin Pianim; Peter Godwin's *Mukiwa: A White Boy in Africa* (Grove Press: 2004); Christina Lamb's *House of Stone* (Harper: 2007) and Alexandra Fuller's *Don't Let's Go to the Dogs Tonight* (Random House: 2002) were all useful in chronicling the lives of white Zimbabweans. Several biographies were also invaluable. Amongst those were: *Tiny Rowland: A Rebel Tycoon* by Tom Bower (Heinemann: 1993) and Chris Hutchins and Dominic Midgley's *Goldsmith: Money, Women and Power* (Mainstream: 1998). As ever, a big thank you to Jonathan, Ro, Rahesh, Henry, Dee and Samir, all in London; Marilí, Lorenz, Susi, Jörg and Suzanne in Basel and the Fantastic Four, Tash, Poem, Liz and Nana Amu in Accra, as well, of course, as the usual suspects, Vic, Sean, EP, Delta Kilo and above all, Patrick, best man and best mate *extraordinaire*, without whose help I'd never have managed to write this in the first place.

PART ONE

Prologue

London, England, 2007

Rain was falling in sodden, misty sheets from a darkly tearful sky; all the light seemed to have been sucked out of it. It was eleven o'clock in the morning but the December day felt as though it was already creeping to a close. The young woman sitting in the back of the car shivered, wrapped her pashmina around her shoulders and pressed her nose against the glass. They swept past the British Library and the interminable building works along the Euston Road. The old arches were still there, she saw as they turned left and drove under the bridge. But not the old gasworks. Everything had been torn down to make way for the new terminus. St Pancras to Paris in a couple of hours. She winced involuntarily. Thinking about Paris brought on the usual sharp stab of pain. That was where she'd seen her last – where they'd all seen her last. But it was better not to think about that. Especially not now.

Her stomach was in knots by the time the driver pulled up outside a small, rather shabby building on Camley Street. *Inner North London St Pancras Coroner's Court,* the building announced itself. *By Appointment Only.* She stared at the door. She'd never been to a coroner's court before. Or to an inquest, for that matter. She'd been called to attend as 'an interested party', the lawyer told her over the phone. Not as a witness or a suspect, of course . . . it was simply routine, something that had to be done. Nothing for her to worry about – for any of them to worry about. She'd wanted desperately to believe him.

3

'Shall I wait for you, miss?' the driver asked, turning his head.

She nodded slowly. 'Yes, please. I don't know how long it'll take. Will you park somewhere near? I'll ring you when I'm finished.'

'Very good, miss.'

She opened the door and stepped out, unfurling the umbrella. She looked up at the sign again. Behind her, the car pulled slowly away. She squared her shoulders, took a deep breath and walked up the steps. It was just over six months since the terrible events of that night. She couldn't believe the nightmare was about to begin again.

I

Why did they call it a 'garden', sixteen-year-old Caryn Middleton wondered crossly as she wheeled her bicycle across the forecourt of Baberton House. There weren't any flowers. There wasn't any grass. Just a bare patch of dirt that the council occasionally swept clear of discarded toys and the odd needle, left over from when the drug dealers from Gascoyne used to hang around outside the flats. But not any more. They were all gone now. She remembered the night her mum had gathered the residents of Baberton and Cheney and held a vigil to keep them out. She'd been so proud of her. Her mum, knocking on people's doors, organising things, explaining what she thought everyone should do and say. She'd sounded so proper. In charge. They'd sat outside for three nights – everyone, all the residents, even those who didn't talk to each other, holding hands, forming a tight protective cordon around the estate. The council sent the police round to watch out for trouble, but there hadn't been any. Not a single fight. The dealers had slunk off after the third night, deciding it was *too much fucking trouble.* She'd heard at school the following week that they'd moved to another estate further down the road. She'd watched everyone coming up to her mum, hugging her, laughing, thanking her for making them bother. She thought her heart might burst with pride. Her *mum*!

It hadn't lasted, of course. For a few brief, giddy days it looked as if Alice might pull herself together. She rushed around the flat, singing at the top of her voice, cleaning, polishing, dusting, a whirlwind of nervous, excited energy. There was food on the table, bubbling pots on the stove and when Caryn came home from school, her little brother Brian had been bathed and fed. She even helped Caryn with her homework. It was bliss; it made her feel normal, like everyone else. Although she'd never have dared say it out loud, least of all to Alice, it was tiring being the only responsible one in the whole family. It felt wonderful to know that *she* didn't have to make sure Brian had eaten or that there was enough milk in the fridge or that the electricity meter was topped up. For a few days, she was just another normal teenager with normal concerns.

Then Alice crashed again, of course, and it all came to an end. Soon she was back in her dressing gown, spending most of her time in bed. There were days when she came out of her room only for food. It was hard to tell what was wrong with her. *Depression*, everyone said knowingly. The bathroom was full of little orange containers with white lids. The pills were supposed to make Alice feel better. They never did. Watching her, it was clear to Caryn that the problem wasn't just that Alice sometimes felt sad. It was much more than that. One of those deep, unsolvable, grown-up problems. Alice was different; she was lonely. Although she occasionally spoke to a few of the other women in Baberton, she was like a fish out of water on the estate. She'd been an art teacher once, long ago, before they all moved to London. They'd lived in Colchester then but Caryn couldn't remember any of it. She couldn't even remember her father. He'd run off with the sixteen-year-old daughter of the couple who owned the pub around the corner. 'Can you imagine . . . sixteen years old! Same age as you, darling,' Alice often said until Caryn begged her to stop. It made her uncomfortable to even think about it.

Her eldest brother, Cameron, left home as soon as he could and there wasn't anyone else to ask what life had been like before. Her middle brother Owen technically lived with them, but was barely ever at home. She minded, but in a funny, distant sort of way. She felt as though she didn't really know them. She didn't think of them the way she thought about Brian, her little brother. She loved Brian more than anyone else in the world. Brian was born after they had moved to London. He had a different dad – Mike. Mike was a builder and came round occasionally. Caryn liked Mike. He was funny and smiled a lot and gave her a fiver every time he came to see Brian. He was brown, even in winter. His dad had come over from Jamaica, he'd told her. That was the reason everyone said Brian looked Italian, or Spanish . . . or Greek. Not quite as pale and English as the rest of them. Caryn loved the look of him: golden skin, curly brown hair . . . everyone said he'd be a heartbreaker, just like his dad. But Mike couldn't do much about Alice, unfortunately. He said she needed proper help. He said she was 'gone in the head'. 'Gone where?' Caryn longed to ask. There were days she wanted to go there too. But she couldn't, of course. Who would look after Brian? It was a good job Caryn had learned how to cook and take care of the house, she'd heard Alice say to Mrs Fields, their neighbour, once, on one of her better days. *My darling little Caryn. I don't know what I'd do without her.* Hearing it ought to have made Caryn feel proud, but it didn't. It just made her feel uneasy, as though she was being given something she didn't want.

She pushed open the door to the lobby and dragged the bike in. The lift was broken. She kicked open the door to the stairwell and began the long climb to the eighth floor, the bike grinding along on the stairs behind her. She sighed. There were weeks when nothing seemed to go right.

2

'Avonlea', Chinhoyi, Zimbabwe, 1993

The wind dropped to a gentle whisper as Nic Harte quietly led her horse away from the stables and across the dirt track, heading towards the road. The msasa trees that lined the driveway had stopped their frantic midday shimmer. Now, in the cooler late afternoon, everything was still, quiet, waiting for dusk when the temperatures dropped and the inky darkness rolled in. Beyond the track and the dreamily swaying trees lay rolls of corrugated white-blonde maize fields, stopping just before the swell of the hills. As soon as she was past the end of the driveway and out of sight of the main house, she vaulted easily on to Simba's back and kicked her heels into his flanks, feeling his immediate response under her thighs as he surged forwards and broke into a canter. Away from the house and the thick, angry air of the argument with her stepmother, Nic felt the tightness inside her chest finally begin to ease.

They galloped alongside the narrow track, still in the shade of the msasas, sending up a cloud of sandy dust in their wake. At the edge of the maize fields she turned left, heading towards the hills, cutting through the long, dry-season grass. The stalks rushed at them as they followed the winding, two-lane path along which the villagers walked, their heads occasionally breaking through the thick yellow bristles as they moved between the farms and the outlying villages.

Then, just as suddenly as they'd plunged into it, they emerged from the grass and started to climb. Simba slowed down and began to pick his way through the rocks and small boulders that marked the beginning of the hills. They climbed steadily for a while, the only sound in the world their breathing; hers soft and shallow, Simba's deep and impatient. His neck was flecked with ridges of foamy sweat where the bridle rubbed against the swell of his muscles. Of the six horses stabled at the edge of the farm, behind the servants' quarters, Simba was her favourite.

Halfway up the hill she reined him in and turned to look back at the house, half hidden in the rolling yellow grasslands that lay prostrate before the ridge of white stone hills. To the left of the house and the farm were the scattered mud huts and flimsy lean-to shacks of the workers; tiny, insignificant dots in a landscape that had been tamed, swept and cleared to make the huge, ten-thousand-acre farm that her father had started, almost as a hobby, some thirty years earlier. It was the biggest estate in the area – Avonlea, named after the green fields beside the river Avon, which was presumably where her father had spent most of his childhood. Nic wasn't exactly sure where he'd grown up. Jim Harte wasn't the sort of man to say. She – and most other people – knew next to nothing about him. Except, of course, that he was one of the richest men in Zimbabwe. RhoMine, the sprawling network of companies her father owned, was the country's largest private employer. A powerful, driven and utterly ruthless man with a fierce and notorious temper, he was an easy target, the sort of man everyone loved to hate. Not that Jim Harte would even notice, or care. He didn't give a damn what other people thought of him.

Still, as everyone would say (behind his back, of course), success had come at a price. Even Jim Harte wasn't immune to tragedy. His first two marriages had ended in deaths. Jane, his first wife, had committed suicide. It was rumoured he'd driven her to it; whispers of affairs; an illegitimate child; a broken heart. Nothing was ever proved; no bastard child ever surfaced. Shaun and Patrick, Nic's older half-brothers, were the only sons to carry his name. Eventually the rumours died away. Jane was buried at the bottom of the estate in the pretty rose garden that the gardeners tended every day. Nic had never once seen her father visit her grave. Shortly after her death, he married Sarah Parker, Jane's best friend from boarding school in England. Jane and Sarah had been inseparable at school and when Jane left England, Sarah had come out to Rhodesia as often as she could. She was present at Jane's funeral – inconsolable, Nic had heard people say. But she never returned to England. Six months after Jane was buried, she married Jim Harte. Three years later, she too was dead, killed in a hunting accident. She left behind a two-year-old baby girl as well as the two stepsons she'd inherited. Jim never mentioned her name, either. All traces were carefully removed from his various homes.

Molly, his third and current wife, was practically a teenager when she married the forty-six-year-old, twice-widowed businessman. The insecure, mousy daughter of an English aristocrat, whom Shaun, Patrick and Nic detested on first sight, she seemed bent on dividing the already fractured family even further. Almost as soon as she moved in, she packed Shaun, Patrick and Nic off to boarding schools – first in Harare, then, further away, in England. As far away as possible. She and Jim had a daughter, Jessica, who was now four, on whom Molly absolutely doted. Nic liked Jessica; or at least she *would* have liked her if she'd been given half a chance. Molly never left Jessica alone with her. She claimed she didn't trust Nic with her precious daughter. Nic overheard her telling her father one day that she was afraid Nic would hurt Jessica. Nic's mouth had dropped open incredulously. Hurt Jessica? Why on earth would she do that? She'd waited outside the kitchen, her anger mounting, for Jim to defend her – and of course, he hadn't. He'd grunted something Nic couldn't hear and walked out.

All in all, Molly's presence didn't exactly make for a harmonious home. But Jim wasn't the kind of father to whom you could complain – after all, he was hardly ever there. And when he was, they'd all learned to keep their mouths shut. All three were terrified of him. Especially Nic. She knew, somehow, that she reminded him of Sarah, her mother. Something about the way his lips tightened involuntarily when she walked in the room; a look of exasperation and something dangerously close to contempt when he met her eyes. He couldn't help or hide it and Nic had long since taught herself not to care.

She nudged Simba up the last section of the path and stopped in front of the enormous smooth-faced boulder that jutted out from the bluff. It was almost four-thirty in the afternoon and the shadows were elongated and inky black against the ground. She threw the reins around a nearby tree stump and scrambled up on to the boulder, keeping a wary eye out for snakes. They too liked the warmth. The heat of the day had warmed the white, lightly speckled surface of the boulder and she lay back, palms down, lightly touching it with her bare arms. The late winter sky was a deep, luminous shade of blue. She closed her eyes briefly, feeling the sun pleasurably on her eyelids. She fished in her pocket for her cigarettes. In a few days' time she'd be packed off back to school in London. Shaun and Patrick were so lucky. They were older than her, and freer too. They'd long since left Eton, where Jim had sent them more for the social contacts he seemed to think they'd develop than anything else. They both now worked for RhoMine. University wasn't an option. A complete waste of time, Jim had decided. What was the point of having sons if they didn't follow in your footsteps? There was nothing said about daughters. No one seemed to know what Jim had in store for her, least of all Jim. She had another two years to go at the exclusive girls' day-school he'd sent her to in London . . . but then what? No one seemed to know or care. That was what the argument had been about. What Nic was going to do afterwards. Molly couldn't have been less interested if she'd tried.

'What d'you mean, "afterwards"?' She'd glared at Nic whilst continuing to bang pots and pans around the kitchen. She was in a rage with the servants, as usual.

'When I finish my A levels. I was thinking about doing—'

'You'd better start thinking about your behaviour *at the present moment*, my girl,' Molly said dismissively. 'I'm sick and tired of getting letters from your headmistress about how rude you've been in school. Why are you always such a problem?'

'I am *not*!' Nic glared straight back at her. 'Besides, what do you care?'

'I don't.' Molly spat the words out decisively. 'I *don't* care. That's the point. Oh, go ahead and get yourself expelled yet again, Nicola. I don't know why we bother, honestly I don't.' She turned away to scold the maid who was holding out a pan. 'No, Mary . . . not the red pot. The *blue* one. Jesus Christ. Don't you understand English? *Blue*, not red. Give it here!' She turned her back on Nic and bore down upon poor Mary, the latest trainee cook in a long list of servants whom Molly sacked every other week.

Nic stared at the back of her head for a moment, thick angry tears forming behind her eyes. It was always this way. 'Go to hell!' she said angrily, turning on her heel.

'Nicola! How dare you speak to me like that!' Molly's shrill voice followed her into the hallway. 'Come back here, you ungrateful wretch!'

'Fuck you,' Nic muttered under her breath, slamming the front door behind her.

'Nicola! Come back here this *instant*. Just you wait—' But Nic was already gone. She ran towards the stables – anything to get away from Molly's semi-hysterical voice and the list of threats that would surely follow. *Just wait till your father hears about this! I'll make sure he sends you back to England without a penny! Let's see how you get along without any pocket money!* And so on and so forth. But what the hell had she done wrong, anyway? All she'd wanted to know was whether there was any chance – even the *smallest*, slimmest chance – that she'd be allowed to do what she'd always longed to do. She wanted to be a writer. Go to university and do nothing but read. And write, of course. But the likelihood of that happening seemed more and more remote by the day. Was this what it would be like for ever?

She lay in the sun, smoking, watching the blue smoke rise lazily away from her, dissipating quickly in the warm, late afternoon air. Just like her future. Gone before she could catch it.

3

34 Hortensia Road, Fulham, London, England, 1993

'To*ry*!' Her mother's voice floated up the stairs. 'Are you there? Supper's ready.'

Tory Spiller was silent for a moment. Then she swung her legs out of bed and stood up. 'Coming,' she mouthed to her reflection in the mirror on the opposite wall. She opened her door.

'Tory?'

'Coming . . .' Tory repeated, louder this time, walking slowly down the stairs. She could hear her father clearing away his papers in his study. He always left the door open. He appeared just as she reached the bottom.

'Hullo, darling,' he said, taking his pipe out of his mouth. Tory looked warily at him. She was still learning to read the signs. There were days – even now, over a year later – when all the light was gone from his eyes and his fingers shook. 'Finished your homework?' he asked, giving her a quick smile.

'Yes,' Tory said cautiously. His voice was steady, usually a good sign.

'Smells good, doesn't it?' He followed her down the hallway to the dining room. Tory nodded. All things considered, they'd had a pretty good week, she thought to herself as she pushed open the door. It had been Susie's nineteenth birthday on Saturday. Would have been, she reminded herself. Her mum had baked a cake. Tory had watched her face anxiously, hoping she wouldn't cry. She didn't.

'There you are!' her mother smiled at her, a little too brightly. 'Hope this tastes all right. It's a new recipe.'

'Some wine, Gilly?' her father asked, picking up a bottle from the sideboard.

'Just a drop,' her mother said, bringing the casserole out of the oven. Tory frowned. It was all a bit too cheery – now, that *wasn't* a good sign. She'd learned from bitter experience that a few days of bright, polite conversation usually signalled a breakdown of some sort, from either of them. She'd come upon her father once, his face pressed against Susie's coat, which still hung in the cupboard under the stairs, making the sorts of animal noises she'd heard on wildlife programmes. It had frightened her so much that she turned and fled back up the stairs, wishing desperately that there was something she could do to lessen the pain. There wasn't. 'It'll pass,' the school counsellor told her in one of their infrequent sessions. 'Just be patient with them. And kind.' She was, but sometimes it felt as though she was being asked to be patient and kind and strong for everyone else. No one seemed to take much notice of her. She winced. She hated herself for even thinking that way.

'How about you, Tory?' her father turned to her, a bottle of red wine in his hand. 'Would you like a glass, darling?'

'Oh, John . . . no,' her mother murmured automatically. 'She's only—'

'I'm seventeen, Mum, not twelve,' Tory said, regretting the words as soon as they were out. Susie was seventeen – *had been* seventeen. When it happened.

There was a short silence. Her parents looked at each other. Then her father slowly poured her a glass. Tory couldn't drink it.

The rest of the meal passed in almost total silence. As quickly as it had emerged, the cheeriness was gone. That was another thing the counsellor told her to watch out for – quicksilver changes in mood. *It's only to be expected.* Everything, it seemed, was to be expected. As soon as she could, Tory excused herself from the table and went up to her room. She leaned across the bed and picked up the phone. She *had* to get out of the house.

Ten minutes later, she ran quickly downstairs and stuck her head round the door. 'Mind if I just pop out for a bit?' she asked. 'I'm going to meet Jenny.'

'Oh, gosh . . .' Her mother slowly shook herself awake. 'No, but don't be late, will you? Will you phone if—'

'Gilly, she's only going round the corner,' her father rebuked her gently. Tory squirmed.

'I won't be late,' she said, and closed the door. She leaned against it for a moment and closed her eyes. *When* would it pass? The sight of the two of them, staring at the empty place where Susie used to sit, chewing their food without really tasting it, despite her mother's attempts to throw herself into cooking as a way to forget – how much longer could it go on?

Jenny was waiting for her on Fulham Broadway. Tory pulled up the hood of her anorak as she ran across the road. It was drizzling lightly; she'd forgotten to bring an umbrella.

'Hi,' Jenny said as she drew near. 'You're late.'

'Sorry,' she shrugged. 'Long dinner.'

'Gloomy?'

'A bit.'

'Well, I've got just the thing to cheer you up,' Jenny said, slipping an arm through hers. 'Come on. You'll see in a minute.'

'Where're we going?'

'The Lamb and Flag.' She stopped and peered at Tory in the drizzle. 'Haven't you got any lipstick with you? You don't *look* eighteen.'

'I forgot. Sorry.'

'Here.' She fished a lipstick out of her coat pocket. 'Slap a bit of this on.'

Five minutes later they were safely in the pub. With two half-pints of lager and a bag of crisps in hand, they made their way to the back. 'So how's this supposed to cheer me up?' Tory asked, looking around the smoky room.

'Look over there,' Jenny said, nodding in the direction of the jukebox. 'D'you see who I see?'

Tory looked. Her heart sank. Julian Hill and Chris Parker. Jenny had a massive crush on Chris, although quite how *that* was supposed to cheer Tory up was lost on her. 'You could've *told* me,' Tory whispered as they made their way over to them.

'Why? You'd've just changed your mind about coming out.'

'I wouldn't.'

'You would.' Jenny walked over to Chris. 'Oh, *hi* . . .' she gushed, pretending to be surprised to see him. Tory stifled a yawn. It was always the same. Both sides played a funny little game in which each tried to pretend they had very little interest in the other. It seemed pointless. She'd asked Susie about it once, a long time ago.

'Why don't you just say you like him?' she asked, watching Susie apply eyeshadow, mascara and lip gloss before meeting her boyfriend Rob. Tory liked Rob. A lot. He was good-looking and cool, and all of that, but he was also clever and funny and he was always nice to her. He

and Susie made the perfect couple, everyone said so . . . even their parents.

''Cos,' Susie said firmly.

''Cos what?' She'd been genuinely puzzled. It all seemed ridiculously complicated.

'Just because. You'll find out one day. Now, scram, will you? I've got five minutes to get dressed.'

'Sorry?' She blinked at Julian, coming slowly back to the present. Had he said something to her?

'What d'you want to listen to?' he repeated, watching her closely. She recognised the look. The Look. It was The Look that everyone gave her whenever she appeared a little withdrawn or preoccupied. She knew exactly what they were thinking. *Imagine what it must be like to have a sister who's been murdered.* They all did it. Teachers, relatives, friends . . . even people she didn't know.

'Oh, I don't mind,' she said mildly. 'Anything. Whatever you like.'

'Um . . . wh . . . what about Simple Minds?' he asked, a little uncertainly. That was the other thing. Everyone still walked on eggshells around her.

She shrugged. 'Yeah. Whatever.'

Don't You Forget About Me. The haunting music flowed over them. Bad choice. They listened to it in silence, each not knowing quite what to say. She looked across the table at Jenny and Chris, who were holding hands under the table and talking softly to each other, oblivious to everyone else. *Don't You Forget About Me.* The pain that hovered just underneath her ribcage intensified for a moment, bringing a film of tears to her eyes. Suze. Sometimes she missed her so much it hurt to even breathe. She turned her head carefully away from Julian. She couldn't bear to see The Look.

4

Estelle Mackenzie put down her hairbrush and stared at her reflection in the mirror. She'd blow-dried her hair until it hung over her shoulders, falling halfway down her back. It was fine and silky, not a split end in sight despite her almost daily sessions with a hairdryer and – thank God – not in the least bit frizzy. Not even when it rained. She looked at her watch. It was nearly nine o'clock. Nearly time to meet Thandie. Through the bedroom door she could hear the steady drone of prayer. She rolled her eyes in irritation. It was her mother's turn to host the members of the Kingdom of Christ Prayer Army. It was a bit of a joke, really. How on earth did a group of middle-aged domestic workers constitute an army? Try asking Gloria Mackenzie *that*, though. She'd given up waiting for her rewards in this life (other than Estelle, of course) and had decided instead to concentrate her efforts on the next. Privately, Estelle thought she was mad. She wanted her rewards right here and now, as quickly and as often as possible, thank you very much. What on earth was the point of waiting?

She turned back to her image in the mirror and picked up a tube of lip gloss. She applied a little with her forefinger and then quickly slipped all the products into her bag. It was likely to be a long night ahead. She held her new dress against her. It was too risky to try it on in her bedroom. At any moment Ma, or one of the other 'soldiers', might come marching in through the door. No one in Arcadia ever knocked on a door. The dress was white, made of a thin, jersey fabric that clung to her hips and thighs before falling in a swirl to just below the knee. She stuffed it into her bag and opened her bedroom door cautiously. The monotonous drone coming through the living-room door was intensifying. In a few moments, one of the 'soldiers' would get up from her knees and start circling the room, sending the rest of them into a trance of clapping, crying, cajoling. She could hear someone starting to wail. 'O Lord, help me to make this crooked way straightened. I give thanks to thee, O Lord, for helping me to overcome the night. O Lord . . .' Estelle shook her head. Didn't they *know* how ridiculous they sounded? She opened the front door and stepped out, relieved to be away from it all. The evening air was cool. She wrapped her cardigan around her and pushed open the small gate. She bent down and quickly slipped off her school sandals, sliding her feet into the black satin pumps she'd bought at the weekend. She hid her sandals behind the dustbin and stood up. The high-heeled shoes were new and the short walk to Thandie's house would help her get used to them. There was nothing worse than hobbling across the dance floor in unfamiliar, too-tight shoes.

'*Sis*, man! How much longer you gonna be?' Thandie sucked her teeth at her as she stood outside the toilets, waiting impatiently for Estelle to finish adjusting her dress. She took a drag on the joint she'd rolled and passed it over.

'Gimme a sec, will you?' Estelle carefully retied her dress to reveal just the right amount of cleavage. She took a quick puff, hoping it would calm her down. Her heart was thudding. It was only her fourth or fifth time. Nadine, Thandie's older sister, had shown them how to do it. Estelle had been nervous at first but it was so *so* easy. There wasn't a single man in the bar who wouldn't have given his eye-teeth to be with her – that first time, they'd practically knocked each other out to buy her a drink . . . and more. The first time, she'd been too shy and embarrassed to do anything other than perch on the bar stool, sipping one pina colada after another. Nadine had laughed at her. Nadine had gone home that night with a hundred bucks in her bag – *American* bucks, too, not near-worthless Zim dollars. The following weekend, Estelle was more than ready. She made double that and she hadn't even had to go all the way. She'd done that the following weekend, and walked home with almost three hundred dollars in her pocket. After that, it was easy.

'Come *on*. The place'll be full of other girls soon,' Thandie moaned.

'OK, OK. I'm coming.'

'You look good,' Thandie nodded approvingly at Estelle's red lace bra peeking out from the folds of her dress. 'You'll pick someone up in no time, you'll see.'

'Ready?' Estelle asked, sweeping past the jealous looks of the other girls in the powder room. She knew why they hated her – they couldn't stand her pale, almost-white skin and her long, nearly blonde hair. Everyone, including Estelle herself, wondered how on earth she'd been born to someone as dark-skinned and plain-looking as Gloria. Where Gloria was short and squat, bulky around the middle with graceless legs, Estelle was tall, long-limbed, perfectly proportioned. Her skin was the colour of buttermilk; big, blue-green eyes with thick, dark lashes; a cute, tip-tilted nose and lusciously full lips. *It must've been the father*, they whispered in amazement. Estelle had no idea. She'd never seen her father. There wasn't a single photograph of him in the little two-bedroom house she and Gloria shared. All Estelle knew was that he was Scottish, that he'd worked on the mines somewhere in the Eastern Highlands. Gloria had been a domestic worker in his house. From the little Estelle had gleaned growing up, he'd disappeared back to Scotland even before she was born. As a child, Estelle's pale skin and straight hair had been the source of some pain. Back then, she'd longed to be just like everyone else. A little darker, frizzy-haired. Coloured, as opposed to *almost*-white. Not now, though. Now her golden skin and silky-straight hair were the envy of everyone she met. Far from wanting to look like everyone else, she knew her looks were the only asset she had and the only way she would ever get the hell out of Arcadia.

She swept out of the toilets and strode into the bar. They walked over to a spare pair of bar stools, aware that every eye in the room was upon them.

'Good *evening*, ladies . . . can I offer you anything? Something to drink, *ay*?' It had barely taken a minute.

Estelle turned her head slowly. A tall, ruddy South African.

She summed him up quickly. Businessman, early thirties, a wife and maybe a kid or two back in Bloemfontein. A bit flash, slightly nervous, eager to show her off. 'Thanks,' she said with a slow smile. 'I'll have a cosmopolitan and she'll have a martini.'

'A cosmopolitan? *Very* sophisticated!' He smiled patronisingly at her before turning and snapping his fingers at the barman. Estelle didn't bother to reply. Fucking Boer. Wouldn't know 'sophisticated' if it hit him on the head. 'Here we go, ladies . . .' He brought their drinks over and sat down. 'So . . . are *all* you Zimbabwean girls this pretty, *ay*?'

'Sure we are,' Estelle murmured lazily. 'But I'm prettier than most.'

5

The doorbell interrupted Caryn's frantic search for a blank piece of paper. Her history essay was due the following morning and she hadn't even started it yet. She straightened up, frowning. Owen was out, as usual. Alice was probably out cold. She sighed and ran down the stairs. 'Who is it?' she yelled as she reached the bottom.

'It's only m–me.' It was Mr Humphreys, the neighbour. Caryn opened the door. 'Oh, hu–hullo, Caryn,' he stammered, twisting his cap in his hands. 'S–sorry to ask you so late but I was just w–wondering if you could l–look after Timmy for a bit tonight? I know it's a bit sh–short notice and all that . . . only there's a leaving do on at the union tonight and I was . . . well, I just w–wondered if you c–could . . . I'll pay you d–double?' He was the most timid man Caryn had ever met. She felt terribly sorry for him. She'd been babysitting for him for almost a year, ever since his wife had left. Caryn's best friend, Lisa, heard she'd run off with someone else. Nearly everyone on the estate had a parent who'd 'run off'. Caryn sometimes wondered where exactly they'd all 'run off' to. 'P'raps your dad and my dad and Mrs Humphreys are in the same place together,' Lisa speculated once, when they were much younger. Caryn doubted it, although she didn't like to say so. Her dad was with his sixteen-year-old – although by now she'd be twenty-five or thereabouts – and from the little she'd heard of her father, she somehow didn't think he would like Mrs Humphreys with her dyed black hair and carefully painted face. She didn't look anything like Caryn's mum, assuming he'd liked *her* at one point, of course. Alice was blonde, like Caryn, but perhaps that was the whole point? Perhaps you *did* run off with someone who looked nothing like the person you'd chosen before?

'Oh, you don't have to do that.' Caryn tried to smile encouragingly at him. His stammer really was dreadful. 'You don't have to pay me double. I'll just do my homework at yours. I'll bring Brian with me.'

'Oh, th-thanks, Caryn. Th-that's awfully g-good of you. 'Bout seven, if th-that's all right?'

'Seven's fine. See you then.' She closed the door.

'Who was that?' Alice asked, opening her door. Caryn glanced at her warily. Her hair was sticking on end; she looked rather wild-eyed.

'Only Mr Humphreys. He needs a babysitter tonight. I'll take Brian with me.' Alice yawned suddenly, running her fingers through her hair. 'I went to the shops this morning . . . will you help me make the tea?' she asked, patting her dressing gown pocket for her cigarettes.

Caryn sighed again. Going round to Mr Humphreys' was probably the only way she'd get her blasted homework done. She followed Alice into the kitchen, eyeing the bag of groceries that had been left on the table. Alice started carefully laying out the items. Caryn's heart sank. Alice was always buying the oddest combinations of things – things Caryn couldn't work out what to do with. A bottle of vinegar and a dozen eggs. Or cigarettes and half a pint of whipping cream. Things that just didn't go together, no matter how hard she tried. 'What's that?' she asked, pointing to a glass jar of greenish paste.

'It's curry sauce, darling. I bought it at the corner shop. Mrs Khan says it's *delicious*,' Alice said dreamily.

'But Brian doesn't like curry,' Caryn said worriedly. It was nearly teatime and she'd have to feed and bathe Brian before going next door.

'Doesn't he?' Alice sounded surprised.

'No, he doesn't. Plus we haven't got any rice. Will it go with potatoes?'

Alice looked at her dubiously. 'Well, I don't see why not,' she said finally. 'We could mash them.' They looked at each other warily. For a split second Caryn thought Alice might burst into tears. Luckily she began to laugh instead. Caryn hurriedly joined in.

'What're you two laughing about?' Owen asked, slamming the front door behind him. He glowered at them. 'What's so funny?'

'Curry and mashed potatoes, darling!' Alice gasped, wiping the tears from her eyes. 'Can you imagine? Curry and *mashed potatoes*!'

Owen looked quickly at Caryn. He shrugged. *What the fuck's wrong with her?* he mouthed at her. Caryn turned away. It was too complicated to explain.

'Is it teatime yet?' Brian wandered in. 'I'm *hungry*.'

'We're going to Timmy's for tea,' Caryn said quickly. 'We'll have beans on toast. And I'll let you watch the telly.'

'Television,' Alice corrected automatically. 'Or TV, if you must.' She was fumbling with her cigarettes. She'd stopped laughing as abruptly as she'd started. With any luck, she'd go straight back to bed. Sure enough, a few moments later, she walked out of the kitchen. Caryn heard her bedroom door shut quietly behind her. She bit her lip. It looked like being a bad week ahead. She collected Brian's pyjamas and his favourite bedtime book and together they left the flat.

Dave Humphreys' flat was smaller than theirs; there was no upstairs. Just two tiny bedrooms, a small living room that over-looked the garden-that-wasn't-a-garden eight floors down, and an even smaller kitchen. It was scrupulously clean; something that couldn't always be said about *their* flat. She fed the two boys, let them watch TV for half an hour and then put them both to bed. She'd simply carry the sleeping Brian back to his own bed when Mr Humphreys came back. She closed the bedroom door behind her and wandered back into the living room. Even though the flat was tidy, it was bare and empty, in an undecorated, unloved kind of way. There weren't any pictures on the walls; no photographs of Mrs Humphreys or even Timmy. Mr Humphreys had obviously taken pains to make sure there were no reminders of the wife he'd once had. Alice had done the same thing. There were still photographs lying around their flat in which Pete Middleton had been carefully removed with a pair of nail scissors, or so Owen said. The photographs looked odd; large blank circles where her father ought to have been. After a while, Alice put them away. Oh, well, Caryn thought to herself, wherever Pete Middleton and Barbie Humphreys were, she hoped they were happy. No, that wasn't true. She hoped they were as unhappy as all hell, considering the mess they'd left behind. She pulled her homework out of her bag. She'd finish it as fast as she could and settle down on the sofa to watch TV. It was nice to have the living room to herself, she thought, chewing the end of her pen. It would be brilliant to have sole control of the remote and no arguments over what to watch.

She was dozing, a rerun of *The Tube* flickering silently in the background, when she heard the key turn in the lock. She sat up, rubbed her eyes and glanced at the clock. It was just after eleven. The living-room door opened and Mr Humphreys popped his head round. He smelled strongly of beer.

'A-all right, Caryn?' he asked, smiling at her. 'Everything all r-right?'

'Yes, Mr Humphreys,' Caryn said, quickly tucking her hair behind her ears. He seemed even sadder and quieter than usual. He rarely raised his voice and was never seen talking to any of the other single dads on the estate, of whom there were a few, Caryn had noticed. He never played football in the dirt patch in front of Baberton and apart from the weekly Saturday-night trip to the pub when she usually looked after Timmy, she'd hardly ever spoken to him. At first he'd tried to insist she call him 'Dave' but Alice disagreed. 'He's not your uncle,' she said sternly, 'and he's certainly not your friend. Mr Humphreys will do.'

'Timmy fall asleep a-all right, d-did he?' he asked, walking into the room. The smell of beer was overpowering. Caryn wrinkled her nose.

'Yes, Mr Humphreys. Brian's in with him. I'll take him back with me now.'

He shrugged off his jacket and laid it over the arm of the sofa. 'That's g-great,' he said, sitting down heavily next to her. He reached into his pocket for her money and brought out a ten-pound note. 'H-have you got ch-change?' he asked. 'Or I c-could g-give you ten pounds? W-w-would you like a t-tenner?' He was slurring his words and his eyes were drooping.

Caryn looked at him uncertainly. It was a fiver for an evening. She shifted a little. 'I thought . . .' she began hesitantly. 'It . . . it's always a fiver, isn't it?' she asked, wondering if it would be rude to stand up suddenly.

'Well, y-yes,' he said, turning to look directly at her. Caryn felt the sweat begin to prickle under her arms. 'B-but I could always give you a b-bit extra,' he said, a strange, slow smile beginning to spread across his face. Caryn stared at him. She'd never seen him like that before.

'No, five's fine, Mr Humphreys,' she said, leaning forward to pick up her bag. He was obviously very drunk. He held the crisp, new ten-pound note between his soft, podgy fingers. And then he laid a hand on her bare knee.

Caryn stared at his hand, the money sticking up stiffly between his fingers. She swallowed. Her throat was completely dry. She could hear his raspy breathing; the sour scent of alcohol wafted over her. His sweaty palm moved slowly across the tender skin of her knee then lifted her skirt very, very slowly. She was frozen to the spot. His hand slid up her thigh, nibbling gently at her skin until he reached the thin white line of her panties. She felt the pressure of his fingers against the cotton; his hand was shaking slightly and his breathing quickened. Revulsion spread over her like a stain. Bile suddenly flooded her mouth, as though she were about to vomit. She drew in a deep breath, her heart beating wildly against her ribcage. She brought her knees together, trapping his hand between her thighs. 'I . . . I'd better go, Mr Humphreys,' she whispered, edging herself away from him. He had no option but to remove his hand. She felt it slide across her thigh, still trembling. She stood up carefully, taking care not to move too fast. There was complete silence in the room. His heavy-lidded eyes looked up at her. 'My . . . my mum'll be waiting for me,' she said quietly, using both hands to smooth down her skirt. He appeared not to have heard her. She turned and quickly walked out of the room. She closed the living-room door firmly shut behind her, pushed open Timmy's door and grabbed Brian, dragging him out of bed. He began to cry but she didn't care. She just wanted to get out of the flat as fast as she could. She kicked the front door shut behind her and ran down the corridor. She burst into her own home and slammed the door shut, leaning against it. Brian started to howl.

'What the hell's going on?' Owen came out of the living room, his face twisted in an ugly scowl.

'Nothing,' Caryn muttered, dragging the crying Brian in behind her. 'Just take him, will you?' she said, shoving Brian in front of her. She could feel her throat beginning to thicken. She ran up the stairs to her room and slammed the door shut. The last thing she wanted to do was burst into tears in front of Owen.

'For fuck's sake, Caryn!' Owen shouted up the stairs at her. 'I'm watching telly! That's your fucking job!'

Caryn ignored him. She sat down on the edge of her bed, her knees shaking. She didn't know what to think or do. She couldn't get the sight of the ten-pound note, bent stiffly between the fingers that lay heavily on her skin, out of her head. She grabbed a tissue from her dressing table, wet it quickly with her tongue and wiped her thigh. She scrubbed at it until the skin was pink and raw-looking. It hurt, but nowhere nearly as much as the pain in her head.

6

The surface of the pool, which had lain dormant and shimmering all winter, was broken abruptly as Justin, Shaun's friend from Eton, ploughed steadily through it, sending streamers of silvery, frothy bubbles up and down its length. Nic watched in admiration from the balcony outside her bedroom as he swam up and down in a dozen powerful strokes. Shaun lay on the grass, reading, looking up every once in a while as Justin tucked himself over into the turn and began again. They couldn't see her; she'd been sent to her room – like a bloody child! – for arguing with Molly. She couldn't even remember what had started it, but it ended abruptly when Nic called her a jealous bitch and Molly's temper exploded. 'Get *out* of my face,' Molly screamed at her. 'Just get out! If I could send you away for the rest of your bloody life, I would! Believe me! You're to stay in your room till your father gets back!' Nic turned and sauntered up the stairs, her back ramrod straight but her heart pounding like hell.

She lit a cigarette and watched the gorgeous Justin swim another length. Only two more days of holiday and she was locked up in her room. Could life possibly get any more unfair? Suddenly, Patrick's dark brown head appeared below, breaking up her view. He squinted up at her. 'Dad wants to see you,' he shouted. 'In his study.'

Nic's heart started to race. 'Now?' He nodded. 'What for?' He shrugged and held out his hands. No idea. She felt her stomach twist nervously. Molly had obviously made good on her threat and reported her as soon as Jim came home. She stubbed out her cigarette and stepped back inside the room. She pulled her hair into a knot and quickly brushed the strands out of her face. Her father hated untidiness, especially in women. He was always commenting on her torn jeans, her hair, the red dirt under her nails, scratches on her knees . . . everything about her was unladylike and unrefined. What on earth was the point of sending her to England if she couldn't even manage to master a few manners? he often asked aloud, to no one in particular. She opened her bedroom door, cast a quick, nervous glance around and hurried down the stairs, praying he wasn't in a bad mood. Whatever punishment she was about to receive would only be made worse. She knocked on the closed door of his study.

'Come in,' he barked. He didn't even look up.

She cleared her throat. 'Um, Dad,' she began nervously, thinking it might be a good idea to get an apology in before anything else was said. 'I'm sorry about talking to Molly like that. The thing was—'

He looked up at her and scowled. Her heart sank. He *was* in a bad mood. 'What're you talking about?' he interrupted her irritably. He held out a letter. 'Look, I need you to take this with you tomorrow night. It's for someone in London. He'll come straight to the plane to collect it.'

Nic blinked. 'I'm leaving on Sunday,' she said warily. 'Not tomorrow.'

'No, I've changed my mind. You're leaving tomorrow night. I need to get this to London by Sunday morning.'

'But Dad . . .' Nic's face fell. She'd been looking forward to going to Harare with Shaun and Patrick – and the gorgeous Justin, of course. They'd had it all planned – a party at someone's house in Borrowdale, and then they'd promised to take her to a nightclub in downtown Harare.

'But Dad . . .'

Jim frowned. '*What*?' He was obviously itching to get back to more important things.

Nic hesitated. What could she say? 'Nothing,' she muttered.

'Put it in your hand luggage,' he said, turning his back on her and swivelling round to pick up the phone. 'Make sure you don't lose it, for Christ's sake.' And that was it. She was dismissed. Just like her plans.

The following evening she was driven in almost total silence by a chauffeur from Avonlea to the airport just outside Harare. No one saw her off. Manning, her father's pilot, was waiting for her at the private airstrip at Harare International. She handed over her bags miserably. After the departure formalities were over, she followed him on to the tarmac, steeling herself not to cry. She settled herself into the seat, stony-faced, doing her best to look as though she didn't give a damn. Not that Manning would notice, or care. It wasn't his job to care.

As Manning lifted the plane smoothly into the sky she looked out of the window at the twinkling lights of Harare – it would be four long, lonely months before she saw them again.

7

Tory's parents stopped talking as soon as she walked in the door. It was obvious they'd been discussing her. Her mother forced a smile of welcome on her carefully composed face. There was a brochure lying on the table which she quickly shoved under a pile of letters. 'Hello, you're back early,' she said brightly, trying to sound pleased.

'Yeah, I didn't feel like staying on for games,' Tory said, slinging her bag over the back of the chair and going to the fridge.

'Had a good day?' her father asked. Tory nodded. It was a Thursday. On Thursdays, he usually stayed at home to do his marking. He was a professor of medieval history at Goldsmiths. 'Professor's Daughter Found Dead' – that was how one of the newspapers had reported it. Tory supposed she was also a professor's daughter. Alive, though. 'What sort of homework have you got, poppet?' he asked.

Tory shrugged. 'Not much.' She didn't like being helped with her homework. It made her acutely conscious of the fact that she wasn't very bright – at least, not in the way her parents expected or hoped. English, French, geography, history . . . those were the subjects they'd chosen for her, mostly because those were the subjects Susie had been good at. Correction: Susie had been good at everything. Unlike Tory. She wasn't good at anything except art and that didn't really count. She managed, of course – she couldn't *not* manage. There wasn't a single teacher who didn't 'take it into account'. Where others got back essays with huge, scrawling red lines and acidic comments scribbled in the margins, all she ever got was 'well done' or 'nicely put' or even 'good attempt'. It was bollocks and everyone knew it – but no one dared say. Sometimes she wondered what they thought she'd do if they told her the truth. Kill herself? No, one dead professor's daughter was quite enough, thank you.

'Tory,' her mother began, looking nervously at her father. 'We wanted to discuss something with you . . . we were just talking about it. Before you came in.'

'Got a minute?' her father asked, a touch too heartily.

It wasn't going to be One of Those Talks, was it? 'What about?' Tory asked nervously.

'Well, it's about school,' her mother said, looking equally nervous. 'We've been thinking about it for a while. How . . . how would you like to change schools next year? Do your A levels somewhere else?'

'Change schools? Why? What's wrong with Queen Anne's?'

'Oh, there's nothing wrong with Queen Anne's,' her father said hurriedly. 'It's a perfectly good school – a *great* school, in fact, but—'

'So why do I have to change?' Tory interrupted him.

'You don't *have* to,' her mother said, a touch sharply. 'We just thought you might *like* a change, that's all.'

'Why would I want to change?'

'Well . . .' she saw her parents exchange an uncomfortable look. 'It's just . . . just . . .' Her mother stopped, swallowing painfully.

'Because of Susie?'

No one spoke for a moment. Her mother's eyes filled with tears. She nodded wordlessly. Across the table, Tory saw her father reach for her hand. 'We just thought you might do better next year with . . . well, with a fresh start,' he said.

Tory's stomach twisted into a painful knot. 'You're afraid I'll fail my exams, aren't you?'

'Of course not!' Her mother was quick to protest. 'Don't be silly. Of *course* you won't fail. But . . . it was Mr Barrington who brought it up. He wondered if all the attention wasn't, well, getting to you a bit, that's all.'

'We'd never make you do *any*thing you didn't want to,' her father said. 'You know that. Just have a think about it, will you, darling? Just think about it.'

'Wh–where would I go?' Tory asked.

'Well, we've been thinking about St Augustine's – it's a sixth-form college in Chelsea,' her mother said eagerly. 'It's just round the corner, in fact. We've already been round to see the head-mistress. Look, I'll leave the brochure out for you. There's no hurry. No hurry at all. Just have a think about it, like Dad said. We can talk about it another time, if you like.' She slid the brochure out from under the letters and pushed it across the table. She stood up. 'Right,' she said, 'who wants a cup of tea?'

Tory eyed the glossy brochure. 'No thanks,' she said slowly, picking it up. 'I suppose I'd better see what it's like. You've already decided, haven't you?' She ignored the look of hurt on both their faces as she walked out of the kitchen.

8

'You are so fucking *beautiful*.' The hand trailing across her shoulders stopped just at the point where her collarbones met and paused for a second, fingers lightly touching the soft hollow. 'But you know that, don't you?' Estelle shrugged as nonchalantly as she could manage. 'How old are you?' he asked suddenly.

'Old enough.' She hoped he couldn't feel the steady thump of her heart.

'You sure? I don't want any trouble, *ay*? You're over eighteen, aren't you? You must be . . .'

'Of course. I'm *way* over eighteen.' The man whose name she'd already forgotten, relaxed. He put his hands on her hips and pulled her forwards so that she was almost sitting in his lap. She could feel his hard-on pressing uncomfortably against her thigh. Across the bar counter, she saw the barman's eyes flicker slowly over her, though whether in admiration, lust or disapproval she couldn't tell. Not that she cared. She leaned towards him, aware that her breasts were spilling out of the deep 'V' of her dress. She looked up at him. There was a glazed expression in his watery, pale blue eyes. 'Haven't you got a hotel room somewhere nearby?' she asked.

He couldn't get off the stool fast enough. He fumbled for his wallet – nice and thick, Estelle noticed – peeled off a few Zim dollars and crammed it back into his pocket. 'Come on, you little minx. It's just across the street.'

Estelle slid obediently off the stool and followed him. She looked around for Thandie but she was no doubt occupied doing something similar. They'd been doing it for almost four months now. Good girls by day; good *time* girls at night. Thandie's mother was also a cleaner, like Gloria, but she had seven children to look after and the money that Thandie brought home from time to time forbade too many awkward questions. She didn't ask what her daughter was up to and

Thandie didn't tell. Gloria was harder to fool but Estelle was an old hand at showing her mother what she thought she wanted to see. It helped, of course, that Estelle was a grade A student, the sort of thing that made Gloria's chest fill up with pride at the few parent-teacher meetings she managed to attend. She often stared with delight at the tall, effortlessly beautiful girl she'd somehow given birth to. Estelle was a credit to her mother; everyone said so.

'You know,' she'd said to Estelle one afternoon after one such meeting, 'Father Richards says you could easily go to university. You could get a scholarship. Just like that!' She snapped her fingers.

'You need money to go to university, Ma,' Estelle said dryly.

'Of course. But I'll *get* the money. We will all pray for it. When haven't I been able to provide for you, eh? You tell me—'

'Yeah, I know, but it's a long way off, Ma. Plenty of time to think about it later.'

'No. We should start to think about it *now*. University!' University. Gloria's accent was much more pronounced than Estelle's. Estelle's was nice and soft. An *educated* accent, thanks to the elocution lessons Gloria had scrimped to provide. She wasn't about to have her only daughter held back by those thick, impenetrable township vowels.

The man's arm was draped heavily across her shoulders. He was more than a little drunk. She liked it better when they were drunk. Sex was much quicker; no need for foreplay or any of that nonsense – and then, of course, they fell asleep afterwards that much faster. But not before she'd been paid. She'd made *that* mistake the first time and had walked home empty-handed and furious. Thandie laughed at her. Why didn't she just take it from his wallet? Estelle nodded, annoyed with herself. She'd never made that mistake again.

He was overweight, she noticed, as he pulled off his trousers, almost losing his balance. A large belly and fleshy, overripe chest like most of the men she'd slept with. He – what the fuck did he say his name was? Coen? Steyn? – was number eleven. Thandie was already on number fourteen. 'Hurry up, you've got some catching up to do,' she'd laughed as they were coming out that evening. But Estelle was in no hurry. Numbers eight, nine and ten had paid almost a hundred US dollars for her company each time, bringing her earnings close to the thousand-dollar mark. A thousand US dollars! Almost three thousand Zimbabwean dollars. It was a fortune. More than Gloria earned in half a year. It was July; another three to four months of this and she would have more than enough for her one-way ticket out of Arcadia.

'Hey, gorgeous . . . c'mere.' Coen/Steyn placed a heavy hand on her thigh. 'Can't you take this off, *ay*?' he mumbled petulantly, pulling back the covers and trying to take off her dress at the same time.

'Hang on a minute,' she said, standing up gracefully and unbuckling the side-belt that kept the whole outfit together. There was a whisper as the jersey material slid down her body. She stepped out of it, wearing only her tight black lace panties and the string of silver and amber beads around her waist. Coen/Steyn gave a strangled gulp.

'It's two hundred dollars. American,' she said firmly, running her hands up the side of her smooth waist and cupping her breasts. She let her thumbs graze over her own nipples. Coen/Steyn grabbed his wallet with both hands and shoved the money at her. 'Thanks, hon,' she said with a little smile. She picked up her purse, which was lying on the side-table, slid the notes in and closed it with a snap. Then she hooked her thumbs into her underwear and pulled. Naked, she lifted the sheets and slid in next to him. He was on top of her in seconds. He'd never seen anyone as beautiful, he kept mumbling as his hand slid between her legs, readying her. He wasn't as drunk as he looked, she thought, as he began his relentless hammering against her. She'd been hoping it would be over in seconds. She remembered what Thandie had told her. She parted her legs further, reached down, felt for the thick, sensitive base of his penis with her fingers and pushed hard. Thandie was right. Over in seconds.

He collapsed, utterly spent. She waited a few minutes then rolled herself out from under his dead weight. Two *hundred* fucking dollars!

9

'Caryn Middleton?' The school secretary stuck her head round the door, interrupting the class. 'Mr Tooley wants to see her in his office. Can she be excused?' The French teacher nodded reluctantly. Caryn got up with a sinking feeling in her stomach and followed her down the long, gloomy corridor. What now? 'Just wait here,' the secretary said as they reached the headmaster's offices. She disappeared through one of the doors.

Five minutes later she was summoned in. Mrs Bradley, her English teacher, was perched rather awkwardly on the edge of the small sofa. There were two women whom she didn't recognise sitting by the window. Tooley was standing by the window; all three of them held cups of coffee and the atmosphere was relaxed, almost cheery. Caryn swallowed nervously.

'Ah, there you are, Caryn.' Tooley walked over, balancing his coffee cup in one hand and extended the other to her. Caryn shook his hand incredulously. In the six years she'd been at John Featherstone Comprehensive, she'd never shaken anyone's hand, least of all Tooley's. 'Come in, come in, my dear. Cup of tea?'

'Er, no, thank you, sir.' Now she was *truly* bewildered.

'Let me introduce you, Caryn. Dr Walsh and Miss Lowe, from St Augustine's in Chelsea. I'm delighted to say we've been asked to put forward a couple of names and—'

'Mr Tooley, if I may?' Dr Walsh interrupted him with a smile and turned to Caryn. 'We're here on behalf of the Board of Trustees of St Augustine's, Caryn. We've been in correspondence with Mr Tooley and several of your teachers for the past few weeks. We're looking for a bright, ambitious young student to be put forward for an awarded place at St Augustine's. Your name has come up several times. My colleague, Miss Lowe, and I are here to have a little chat. Is something the matter, my dear?'

'I'm not sure I understand—'

'A scholarship, Caryn,' Tooley couldn't stop himself from butting in. 'A full scholarship. You would do your A levels at St Augustine's. *If* you won the scholarship, of course.'

'*Me?*' Caryn stared at them, amazed.

Half an hour later, her head still reeling, she walked back down the corridor, clutching the brochure Dr Walsh had given her. A *scholarship*! To a school she'd never heard of. St Augustine Girls' College, a private, sixth-form college in Chelsea. She'd been to Chelsea once, a couple of years earlier, with Lisa; a place full of elegant white houses and beautiful shops out of which beautiful girls drifted, bags in hand. They'd walked up and down King's Road several times one Saturday afternoon because it was something Lisa said Had To Be Done – Caryn had no idea why. She'd found it beautiful, but utterly alien. She glanced down at the brochure again. 'We place great emphasis on the intellectual, moral and social development of our girls.' *Our* girls. Were they seriously telling her she had a chance of becoming One of Their Girls? They actually thought she had a chance of winning a scholarship? She'd never won anything in her life. Well, that wasn't quite true. She'd won a spelling competition when she was about eight, and once she'd won a flask in a fairground shooting gallery.

Alice turned the brochure over carefully, as if it might bite. They were sitting together at the kitchen table. Caryn had just finished speaking and her stomach was wound into a tight, nervous knot. There was an uneasy silence for a few minutes. 'Wh-what d'you think, Mum?' Caryn finally burst out.

Alice was quiet. She lit a cigarette and Caryn saw that her fingers were shaking. She drew a deep breath and then looked at her. There were tears in her eyes. 'I think,' she said carefully, blinking rapidly, 'that I'd be the happiest person in the whole fucking world if you got in.'

Caryn swallowed. It wasn't like her mother to swear. At least not *that* word. 'Bloody', yes, and sometimes 'bugger'. But not 'fucking'. Not ever. Caryn felt her eyes begin to prickle. She got up to fill the kettle, not wanting to cry in front of her. Alice reached out as she passed and grabbed her round the hips. She pulled her close, pressing her face into Caryn's stomach. 'You're the tops, Caryn, d'you know that?' she murmured, holding her cigarette away from her. 'You're the absolute tops. I swear I don't deserve you. I don't.'

'Don't be silly, Mum,' Caryn whispered, wiping her cheeks. 'I haven't got in *yet*,' she said, trying to laugh.

Her mother tightened her grip on her. 'But you will, love. I know you will. You can do anything you put your mind to. Not like your old mum. You're a winner, Caryn. Don't you ever forget that.'

10

By mid-September, the pile of money Estelle kept in the top drawer of the dresser in her room had grown. Over five thousand Zimbabwean dollars. About one thousand, seven hundred US dollars. More than enough for a plane ticket and a couple of months' rent when she got to London. She drew her legs up under her and began the highly pleasurable process of counting it all over again. She had her escape all planned, right down to the last detail. She already had her visa, thanks to a 'friend' in the British High Commission; she had somewhere to stay for the first few weeks when she arrived courtesy of another 'friend'; she'd been given the addresses of a couple of men whom she'd met recently who'd promised to help her get on her feet. All she needed to do now was to buy her ticket.

She would have to do it in secret, though. Telling Gloria was out of the question. She would simply collapse on the spot. She would leave a letter, of course, something along the lines of how much better things would be in Britain, or even America; how she would be able to take care of Gloria, send money every month, make a life for herself, for both of them. She would have to impress upon her how she could finally *be* somebody, away from Zimbabwe. If she stayed in Arcadia, she would never amount to anything. She'd always be just another pretty, fair-skinned girl, no matter how long and shiny her hair was or how many As she collected at school. She wanted more than Arcadia could ever provide. There was a whole *world* out there – why shouldn't she be the one to see it? Yes, a letter was the way to do it – with a little something extra tucked inside to help ease the blow. She folded the notepaper she'd been scribbling on for weeks and tapped the pen against her teeth. In London, everything would be different. She could finally begin her glamorous, glittering new life. She could be a model or an actress – maybe even a singer. Everyone said she had a good voice. In London, she could be whatever she wanted to be. She snapped the flap of her satchel shut and picked up her bag. Her new life was waiting for her, calling out, beckoning her. All she had to do was get there – and *live* it.

I I

Nic walked into the classroom, her head held high, stiffly avoiding the glances that were thrown her way. Scorn or pity – either way, she didn't give a damn. She knew exactly why they were staring. Her father was in the news again. He and Molly had arrived unexpectedly that morning from Harare. She hadn't read the papers but she'd overheard Ogilvy, her father's lawyer, telling him to expect the worst. She had no idea what he'd done but from Ogilvy's nervous comments, she gathered he hadn't exactly played by the book – no surprise there – and that somehow the media had got hold of the story. 'Expect the worst, Jim,' Ogilvy had said gravely. 'But we'll ride it out.'

Now, from the sudden lull in conversation as she walked in, she gathered that Ogilvy's prediction had come to pass. Bloody typical. Her first day back at St Augustine's and he'd managed to overshadow it. She stole a quick look around her. There were two new girls, one of them sitting directly in front of her and one to her right. She felt an odd tug of sympathy for the girl in front of her. She was very, very nervous, sitting on her hands to stop them shaking. Nic remembered doing exactly the same thing the first year she'd arrived. The girl was small and blonde with badly fitting shoes. Brand new, Nic noticed – the labels were still sticking to the soles. Burgundy, pointed shoes . . . not at all like the shoes everyone else wore, including Nic. Her outfit was a little odd, too. A thick, cable-knit cardigan, even though it was a warm September day, with a starched white blouse and a tartan pleated skirt. *Very* odd. Sixth-form girls didn't have to wear a school uniform. Someone had obviously forgotten to tell the new girl that first impressions were almost impossible to overcome and that she'd blown it already.

She turned her head sideways. The other new girl was sitting to her right; Nic could see only her profile. She was tall and willowy with long, wavy dark brown hair, hazel eyes and full lips. Very pretty, but in a cool, disinterested sort of way. Probably not the sort of girl who would be friends with the girl everyone loved to hate. One nervous; one cool. *Great*. It looked like another long, lonely year ahead.

The form teacher swept in suddenly, and for the next twenty minutes droned on about how welcome they all were, how good it was to see everyone back looking so fresh and tanned, having been on exotic holidays, etc, etc. Nic's attention wandered. She wondered what Shaun and Patrick were up to at that very moment – would they be in the pool, or out riding, perhaps? Or maybe they'd have taken one of the pick-up trucks and driven into Harare?

'If it's not too much *trouble*, Nicola Harte, perhaps you could drag your attention away from whatever it is that's occupying you and do me the courtesy of listening?' Miss Milligan's scathing voice rang out suddenly. Nic blinked. There were titters from the rows around her. Someone whispered something to the girl sitting next to her. Nic felt her face begin to burn. Bitches. Every last one of them, including the new girls.

Caryn listened to the muted giggles with growing unease. It was all rather unnerving. Her first day hadn't begun well. She'd barely slept a wink the night before. She kept getting up to look at her new tartan skirt and the shoes her mother had found in a second-hand shop just off Roman Road. They were burgundy leather shoes with a small heel and a pointy toe. Caryn thought they were gorgeous. She'd spent ages in the bathroom, despite Owen's persistent banging on the door, and emerged feeling sicker than ever. Alice's silly, bolstering chit-chat didn't help, either. She went on and on about the opportunity Caryn had been given; the chance she'd now have to get out of the estate and the sort of life she could have with the education she was about to receive. Caryn, sitting in silence beside Brian and trying to make sure his porridge didn't wind up on her skirt, was fuming. She hadn't been *given* the opportunity, she wanted to fling at Alice – she'd bloody well earned it. She'd exhausted herself working to pass the scholarship exam and if the estate was so bloody awful, how come they'd ended up there in the first place? But she knew better than to argue with her mother when she'd had one Valium too many. She wished *she* could take one – she felt like throwing up.

She left the flat at seven a.m., her feet already beginning to rub uncomfortably in her new shoes. They were half a size too large and the small wedge of tissue Alice had shoved in to pad them out was starting to disintegrate. It was an hour's journey on three different buses to Chelsea and she desperately didn't want to be late. She walked to Kingsland Road that morning, her heart sinking lower with each step.

St Augustine's was six miles and yet a whole other world away from Hackney. Set in the grounds of a small palace just off Whitfield Street, a few blocks from the river, it was huge and elegant and, to her at least, terribly imposing. The classrooms were bright and sunny; there were lawns with carefully trimmed hedges and beautiful flower beds; the school canteen looked like something out of a space-age film with shiny metal counters, gleaming white surfaces and a glossy, squeaky floor. There were music rooms; reading rooms; rooms full of computers; special airy, light-filled rooms called studios where 'art' took place. The girls were unbelievably posh, even the studious-looking ones who sat at the front. They wore long simple skirts in lovely materials, pastel-coloured sweaters and snow-white shirts with beautiful lace collars – in her stiff, plain white shirt and her tartan skirt she looked like a complete frump. No one else was wearing pointy-toed shoes, she noticed immediately, sliding as quickly and quietly as possible into a spare seat. Lovely suede slouchy Chelsea boots, yes. Flat-heeled patent ballet shoes with bows, yes. Burgundy shoes that were clearly a size too big with a small heel – *no*. She'd never been to a school where uniforms weren't compulsory; the thought of agonising each morning over what to wear was daunting. Not that she had much choice. There weren't many clothes in *her* closet. And those that she did have, she realised miserably, staring down at her hands, were wrong. Plain wrong. She sat on her hands to stop them shaking. It wasn't a good start.

Tory looked around her indifferently. It wasn't all *that* different from Queen Anne's. There were ten or eleven girls in the class – best friends, no doubt – loud, confident, mostly very, *very* pretty. Tory knew the type. Golden girls, like Susie. As a child, she'd often wondered whether she and Susie really *were* sisters – they were so different. Susie was petite and blonde with lovely big blue eyes and fair skin that went gold in the sun. Tory was five foot ten, olive-skinned and boyish. In fact, she'd often wondered whether she belonged to the Spiller family at all. Perhaps she'd been dropped on the doorstep at birth and every-one was too kind to admit it? Susie looked just like her parents, a golden combination of both. Tory looked like neither, like nobody. And now here she was, a brand-new girl in a brand-new school where she really *was* a nobody. She would only be there for a year – not nearly enough time to turn from being a nobody to a somebody. Might as well give up from the start.

She turned her head and looked at the girl sitting a couple of seats in front of her. She looked dreadfully uncomfortable; you could see it in the way she sat on her hands – to stop them shaking, Tory supposed. She'd done that herself for quite a long time after Susie died. She could see that her shoes didn't fit, either. Funny shoes – pointy and quite grown-up, not really school shoes at all. She felt a sudden pang of loneliness. What would Jenny be doing right now? And Belinda and Caroline? She stopped herself. Soon, Jenny and Belinda would become friendly with someone else; Caroline would find another best friend and she'd be forgotten, of course. That was how it worked.

The new girl turned suddenly and looked straight at her, catching her off guard. Tory felt her cheeks turn red. It was rude to stare but she didn't quite know how to explain that she hadn't actually been staring – she'd simply drifted off whilst looking in her direction. But before she had a chance to even gather her thoughts, the girl had turned away again, her own cheeks reddening. Oh well, Tory thought to herself miserably as she gathered up her bag and her books, start as you mean to go on. Friendless. Might as well get used to it.

They were all taking the same subjects, Nic noticed as they trooped from one classroom to the next. English, French and history. The blonde girl, whom she'd quickly learned was called Caryn, was taking art history as well. Four A levels. So she was brainy, then. She was a scholarship student from the East End or so she'd overheard someone say. 'God, no wonder her clothes look so second-hand,' someone else said cruelly, sniggering. Nic shook her head. For the life of her she couldn't understand why her father had been so keen to send her to school in England. The anguish the girls inflicted upon one another was far worse than anything she'd ever heard anyone back home hand out – and *that* was saying something. Who *cared* if the bloody girl was on a scholarship, or if her shoes didn't fit properly? She felt a hot flush of anger towards them all. Just then, she caught Caryn's eye as Mr Hayes, the English teacher, handed out the reading lists for the first term. Caryn gave her a quick, timid smile. Nic stared at her coolly. It just wasn't worth making the effort to be friendly. Within a couple of days, Gemma or Monica or someone would pull her to one side, explain who was who in the class and that Nic Harte was definitely not worth talking to . . . and that would be it. Corinne might even enjoy taking the new, obviously poor girl under her wing – it was just the sort of thing Corinne enjoyed doing. The Four Bitches would slowly let her into their group, lend her clothes, show her what to do with her hair and make-up, thereby earning themselves her undying gratitude. The poor girl would then spend the rest of the year taking notes for them, running errands, doing their prep duty when they didn't want to do it . . . Nic had seen it all before. She bent her head, allowing the thick, dark curtain of her hair to fall across her eyes, shielding her from their beady, never-miss-a-thing eyes. She looked at the reading list they'd been given and sighed. Shakespeare, Dickens, Chaucer, Byron . . . the usual bloody suspects. Old. Boring. And a million miles away from anything she knew or cared about.

'Care to share the source of your distraction with us, Miss Harte?' Mr Hayes, the English teacher, enquired frostily. Nic's face was on fire again. She shook her head mutely. 'What a *pity*,' he murmured sarcastically to the rest of the sniggering class. 'I do *so* look forward to hearing your thoughts.' Nic bit down on her tongue to stop herself answering back. Mr Hayes had been on the receiving end of Nic's sharp tongue twice in the previous year, incidents for which she'd been threatened with yet another suspension. She'd explained angrily to Miss Lowe that he'd been rude about Zimbabwe and her family's connections to what he called 'undesirables' – what the hell did *he* know? Miss Lowe, of course, was unsympathetic. She'd had to stay behind in detention until seven p.m. all week for her little outburst and had earned herself Hayes's undying contempt. Too bad – the feeling was mutual. She *loathed* him. She caught Caryn's eye again as she lowered her head. Caryn gave her another quick, sympathetic smile. Nic was so astonished she forgot to let her hair drop and her look of pained surprise was caught by all. Someone giggled again.

12

'So? How'd it go?' Alice pounced on her as soon as she walked into the flat.

'All right,' Caryn said shortly, pulling out a chair and collapsing into it. Her new shoes would have to go. And not just because they were so obviously the wrong sort.

'Just "all right"? Did you make any new friends?' Alice said anxiously.

'It's only the first day, Mum,' Caryn sighed. 'They all know each other. There's only one other new girl.' She eyed Alice nervously. Had she been drinking?

'Why don't you invite a couple of the girls to tea . . . maybe on Saturday? That'd be nice, wouldn't it? I could do a cake,' Alice went on dreamily. 'A chocolate cake. Could have a bottle of wine, as well. Now, there's an idea. A cake and some wine. Very grown-up, don't you think?'

Caryn hesitated. 'Maybe a bit later, Mum, when I've got to know a few people a bit better.' She *had* been drinking. Blast. She was in one of her odd, glittery moods. In the circumstances, escape would be prudent. 'I'll . . . I'll ask them tomorrow. They might be busy, though,' she said as noncommittally as she could.

'Don't you take that tone with me, young lady,' Alice said sharply. 'Don't think for a second I don't know what you're up to.'

'Mum, I'm not up to anything. I'm *tired*. I've been on the bus for the last two hours and I've got homework to do. Have the boys had supper?' She looked around the kitchen.

'*Have the boys had supper?*' Alice mimicked her sarcastically. 'Of *course* they've bloody had supper! *I'm* their mother, not *you.*' She glared at Caryn, daring her to say something, anything.

Caryn looked around. There were no dishes in the sink and no smell of food in the air. Of course they hadn't eaten. She sighed again. 'I . . . I'm just going upstairs for a bit,' she said, picking up her bag. With any luck Alice would soon retire to her room. She and Owen could nip out later and get a couple of bags of chips to share. Luckily Brian loved chips. She turned and fled up the stairs.

Both Tory's parents were waiting for her when she got home. The air was sweet with the scent of baking and her mother came towards her with floury hands. She held them up as Tory came into the kitchen. 'Jam roly-poly . . . thought you might like something sweet after your first day. How was it?'

Tory hung her bag on the back of the door. 'All right.'

'What're the teachers like?' her father asked cheerily.

'All right,' Tory shrugged. 'Same as the ones at Queen Anne's, really.'

'Any other new girls?' her mother asked.

'Only one.'

'Well, you'll soon make friends, I expect,' she said in a tone that suggested the opposite.

'Of course she will,' her father said, walking to the sideboard and picking up a bottle of wine. 'She'll make friends in no time. No time at all.' They both began talking hurriedly about *their* first day at school, desperately trying to show her they'd made the right decision. Tory sighed. It was silly. They all knew why they'd sent her there.

'Tory?' her father's voice interrupted her a few minutes later. 'Tory?' he said again, gently this time. She blinked and looked at him.

'Sorry. I was just . . . thinking,' she said, watching the shadow of pain quickly flit across his face. Whenever she drifted off like that, it meant only one thing. She was thinking about Susie. She knew it and they knew it. It couldn't be helped. That was just the way it was.

Nic pushed open the front door of the house on Eaton Square and walked in. It was deathly quiet. She remembered hearing Molly say something to Mrs Jenkins, the housekeeper, about the two of them going down to Studgrove, their country estate, later that afternoon. Typical. No one thought to tell *her* anything. She tossed her keys and her bags onto the sideboard in the hallway and wandered into the kitchen. She looked at her watch. It was almost six. She wondered where Mrs Jenkins had got to. Sometimes Nic ate with her in the large kitchen on the ground floor; at other times she carried her supper through to the living room on the other side of the hallway, and watched TV whilst she ate alone. It was a world away from the bustling, busy kitchen at Avonlea where there was always someone to talk to; there were half a dozen cooks and servants wandering in and out of the kitchen and dining room to whom she chattered almost non-stop, despite Molly's glowering disapproval.

She walked back into the hallway, wondering what to do. She pushed open the door to the living room, kicked off her shoes and flopped down on the sofa, reaching for the remote control. There was nothing on, only the news – and the last thing she wanted to see was her father's face on the screen. She got up, suddenly restless, and walked upstairs into the large, formal living room, her feet sinking into the soft cream carpet that ran throughout the house. The room was decorated in the pale cream and light green washed-out colours that Molly liked. Molly had obviously told the decorator she wanted an 'English' look – insipid colours, heavy velvet curtains, gold-tasselled ropes, antique furniture . . . it looked ridiculous, thought Nic. She pulled back one of the heavy drapes and stared down at the square. Dusk was falling; the gardens were bathed in a soft, pale, late summer light. A couple strolled past on the street below, hand in hand. She saw the girl smile as she walked past and turn her face upwards, laughing at something her partner had said.

Nic swallowed. She longed to have someone to talk to about her first day back at St Augustine's but there was no one. She stared at the phone for a moment, struggling to contain the waves of loneliness sweeping over her. Then she picked it up and dialled Shaun's number in Harare. *Somebody* was going to hear about her first day back at school, like it or not. But the lines to Zimbabwe were either busy or down. She dialled again and again, fighting the tears that kept rising in her throat every time she heard the operator's perky, recorded voice. 'The lines to the country you have just dialled are—' *Oh, fuck you*, she mouthed silently, slamming the phone down after the fiftieth attempt. A tear slid down her cheek. She got up quickly and made her way upstairs. The last thing she wanted was for Mrs Jenkins to come upon her, clutching the silent phone and crying in the dark. She couldn't bear the thought of anyone feeling sorry for her.

13

'So — where've you just come from, then?' The taxi driver looked her up and down.

'Harare,' Estelle said shortly. She was tired and nervous; the last thing she wanted to do was chit-chat with a balding, overweight taxi driver.

'Where's that, then?' he asked, obviously clueless.

'Africa.'

'Oh. Well, you don't *look* very African,' he chuckled, peering at her again as if to be sure. He opened the cab door with a flourish. 'Hop in, love. Where're you going?'

Estelle fished the piece of paper out of her pocket. 'Brighton Road. Stoke Newington?'

'Stoke *Newington*?' He scratched his head. 'Blimey, love. That's a helluva way. You sure you want to take a cab?'

'How far is it?' Estelle asked, alarmed. She had no idea where Stoke Newington was and even less idea how to get there.

He scratched his head. 'This time of the morning? 'Bout an hour and a half, I'd say.'

'H-how much will it cost?'

He scratched his head again. 'Dunno . . . depends on the traffic, love. Thirty, thirty-five quid . . . mebbe a bit more? It'll be something like that.' He looked at her suddenly downcast face. 'Tell you what, I'll make it an even thirty. How's that sound?'

'That's fine.' Estelle climbed in. He stowed her suitcases behind her and closed the door. She had the address and telephone number of a friend of one of Thandie's brothers – Jonathan Marimba. He was a journalist, or so the friend said. He'd agreed to put her up for a couple of weeks. So far, despite the exorbitant taxi fare, everything was going according to plan. She leaned back in the seat as the cab pulled away from the kerb and tried not to think about Gloria. She would have found the letter by now. And the three hundred dollars, of course. That would help lessen the blow.

'On holiday, then, are you?' Having established he'd done her a favour, the driver was keen to make conversation.

Estelle wasn't. 'No,' she said curtly. She pulled out a packet of cigarettes. She lit one, meeting his eye in the rear-view mirror. Stop me if you like, she dared him with her eyes. They drove on in silence.

'Here we are,' he said, about an hour and a half later. He hadn't been joking. It *was* far. 'What's the number again?'

'Twenty-two,' Estelle said, glancing again at the piece of paper.

'Eighteen, twenty . . . right, that's it. Here we go.' His tone was a little less friendly. If he'd been hoping to strike up some kind of friendship along the journey, she'd dashed his hopes.

She carefully counted out the money and pushed it through the window. 'Thanks,' she said quickly and opened the door. It was late October and the wind was colder than anything she'd ever experienced. She hauled her cases out, slammed the door shut and watched as the cab pulled away. Number twenty-two was identical to number twenty and number twenty-four. She pushed open the small wooden gate and walked up the path. It was nothing like she'd imagined. A long street full of joined-together identical houses, stretching up and down in both directions. A blue front door here, a yellow one there. Jonathan Marimba's was black. Peeling, too. An empty beer can rattled around on the concrete path in front and there were no curtains at the front window. She shivered and pulled her coat around her. She pressed the bell and waited. Presently she heard the sound of footsteps and then the door opened. A woman stood in the doorway, looking enquiringly at her.

'Yes?'

'Hi. I'm Estelle.'

'Estelle?' She looked her up and down. There was hostility in her gaze.

'Yes . . . does Jonathan Marimba live here?'

The woman gave her another piercing look. She turned and yelled up the stairs. 'Jonathan!' Behind her, Estelle could make out a rather dark, narrow corridor with a single flight of stairs disappearing overhead. The woman turned back. 'Who're you?' she asked suspiciously. 'A friend?'

Estelle met her gaze coolly. She was used to the suspicious looks of others, especially women. 'No. Who're *you*?' She saw, with satisfaction, that she'd scored.

'I'm his wife.'

'Who is it?' A man's voice came from somewhere in the gloom behind her. 'Shikedé?'

'I'm Estelle Mackenzie. I'm a friend of David's. David Gono. He said . . . that I could stay with you for a bit. He said he'd spoken to you?'

'Oh, yeah . . . yeah, right.' He scratched his head. He'd obviously clean forgotten. 'OK, yeah. Well, come in . . . those your bags?'

'Yes. It's just for a couple of weeks.'

'It's no problem, no problem, man. There's always room.

Sylvia . . . show her upstairs, will you? She can sleep in Corinne's room.'

'And where's Corinne gonna sleep?' Sylvia's tone was aggressive.

'In with Matthew. It's fine, Sylvia. It's only for a couple of weeks, right?' He glanced quickly at Estelle.

'Yeah. That's what they all say,' Sylvia said sulkily. She switched to Shona. Estelle couldn't follow her but the tone of her voice needed no translation. Sylvia led the way up the narrow stairs, still grumbling to herself, and showed her into a tiny box-like bedroom directly off the landing.

'Look, I don't mean to put anybody out . . .' Estelle began stiffly, annoyed at the turn the conversation had taken. It was a far cry from the welcome David had promised.

Sylvia ignored her. 'You can put your things in there.' She pointed to one of the drawers. 'But don't use the wardrobe. It's full. The last person who stayed here left all his stuff.' It was obviously a frequent occurrence.

'Don't worry, I won't,' Estelle said shortly.

'It's thirty pounds a week. And if you want to share meals, it's another fifteen. Plus you share the bills.'

Estelle blinked. David hadn't said anything about *paying* to stay here. 'David didn't mention—' she began.

'Well, I'm mentioning it now. It's not a free hotel, you know.'

Estelle's lips tightened. One night. That was it. She wasn't going to stay more than a single night in this tiny little room in the damp, fusty-smelling house with a hostile wife and a husband who looked as though he couldn't say boo to a goose. She shut the door as soon as Sylvia had gone and sat down on the bed. Her arrival in London wasn't exactly the way she'd pictured it. Where were the lovely, elegant old buildings? Buckingham Palace and the Houses of Parliament? The narrow cobbled lanes and the leafy avenues beside the river that she'd spent most of her life hearing about? This . . . she looked around her in open disgust . . . wasn't much better than Arcadia. In fact, it was worse. It was *cold*. She pulled up her handbag and took out her little yellow notebook. In it, she'd listed every telephone number, every name, every contact she'd come across in the past six months who might be useful to her, however remotely. She opened it and began to go down the list. Someone was going to have to help her to get out of here. She didn't care who.

14

Caryn's first few weeks flew by in a blur. There was so much to learn – and quickly. No sooner had she handed in an essay than she got it back and another was set. She had to run just to keep up. Her fellow students were no friendlier on the third or fourth day than they had been on the first but, after a week, she finally got a rather reluctant 'hello' out of the tall, dreamy new girl called Tory. She'd tried to say hello a couple of times to Nic, the girl everyone seemed to dislike, but she'd just looked at her blankly and turned her head. Stuck-up cow!

She was running from her art history class to French one morning, about a month after she'd started, when she accidentally tripped going through the doors and dropped her file folder. It burst open, and half a dozen sheets spilled out. She bent down to retrieve them, conscious of a group of girls coming down the stairs behind her. They walked straight past, giggling, and pushed open the doors – the gust of wind immediately sent the sheets flapping across the floor. It was Gemma Kinnaird and her gang. Bitches, she thought to herself as she knelt down and tried to gather them up. They let the door swing shut behind them, still sniggering, and sauntered out. She scooted around on her knees, trying to pick the sheets up before someone else walked in.

'Here,' someone spoke.

She looked up. It was Nic. She was holding a couple of sheets. Caryn hadn't seen her come down the stairs. She stood up. 'Thanks,' she said awkwardly, taking them from her. 'I . . . I must've tripped . . .' she stammered.

Nic looked down at Caryn's shoes. 'I'm not surprised,' she said dryly. And then suddenly, they both giggled. 'I'm sorry,' Nic said finally, trying not to laugh. 'But they're just the—'

'. . . most awful shoes,' Caryn finished for her, shaking her head ruefully. 'I know, believe me.'

'Well, why d'you wear them then?'

'Because I haven't got any others.'

'Oh.'

'Well, thanks for helping me,' Caryn said finally. 'I'd better run. I've got French . . . well, so've you.'

'Oh, I don't think I'll bother today,' Nic said nonchalantly. 'I'm not in the mood.'

Caryn stared at her. Not in the *mood*? 'Er, OK. Well, thanks again.' Nic nodded and turned away. Caryn hesitated. 'You . . . you can borrow my notes, if you like. If you're not coming.'

Nic stopped and turned round. It was her turn to look surprised. 'All right. Thanks.'

'Bye.'

'Bye.'

All through French Caryn thought about Nic. She'd seen something in Nic's eyes when she'd offered her notes – a small spark of something other than the sullen defensiveness that normally defined her face. She was incredibly beautiful, despite her habitually closed expression. High cheekbones; startlingly blue eyes. She was tanned, too – the sort of colour that Caryn had always associated with Italians and Spaniards, a bit like Brian, actually. She wasn't quite sure where Nic was from – somewhere in Africa, she'd overheard people saying. But she certainly didn't look African. From the little she'd heard about her, she gathered that her father was one of the biggest crooks in Zimbabwe, wherever that was. Caryn had no idea. She made a mental note to look it up. But when Nic smiled – which wasn't very often, granted – her whole face was transformed. She was awfully prickly, but after a month at St Augustine's, Caryn understood why. Featherstone's had a reputation for being one of those tough, inner-city schools that no one sent their kids to unless there was no choice – which was pretty much the situation of everyone who went there. But Featherstone's was *nothing* compared to St Augustine's. At least Featherstone's was *fair*. No one was really picked on for having a funny accent or the wrong shoes or a father who drank. Or if they were, the issue would quickly be settled by a fight and as long as you held your own, things would generally improve.

St Augustine's was different. There was a secret language spoken amongst the three or four tribes in the school, as she called them, to which everyone else was deaf. Newcomers, of course, didn't understand the codes and membership appeared to depend on factors that were largely beyond your control. Such as where your father went to school, or where you lived, or how you pronounced your words. Or even stupider little things like whether you wore opaque tights or not, or whether your ears were pierced. Caryn realised from the very first day that she didn't speak the right language, live in the right part of London or have a father who'd been to Eton. In fact, after a week, the most oft-repeated question she heard wasn't where *she'd* been to school before arriving at St Augustine's, but where her father had been. 'Don't know,' she told them, puzzled by their shocked expressions. 'I don't have one.'

'You don't have a *father*?'

'No.'

'Is he dead?'

'Dunno.'

And that was the end of that.

About a week after their brief encounter in the hallway, Caryn somehow found herself walking in step with Nic and Tory. The three of them walked down the corridor in uneasy silence for a few moments. Finally Caryn plucked up enough courage and asked if they'd found the lesson as hard as she had.

'Yeah,' Nic said. 'I *hate* Molière.'

'Me too,' Tory said suddenly.

'So do I,' Caryn said, although it wasn't strictly true. The three of them looked at each other warily.

'So, where did *you* go to school?' Nic asked, pushing open the swing doors. 'Before here, I mean.'

Caryn breathed a silent, cautious sigh of relief. For once, it wasn't a question about her bloody father. 'John Featherstone's,' Caryn said, wrinkling her nose. 'It's in Hackney. It's . . . well, it's a bit different from this.'

'And you?' Nic asked, looking at Tory.

Tory shrugged. 'Queen Anne's. Pimlico. And it was exactly the same.'

'How long've you been here?' Caryn asked Nic, emboldened by the unexpected exchange.

'Three years. I hate it.'

'Why?' It was the first direct question Tory had asked either of them.

Nic went red. 'Because they hate *me*,' she said finally.

'Why?' Caryn was curious.

Nic shrugged. 'Dunno. Ask them.'

Tory and Caryn looked at each other quickly. 'Oh, well . . . who gives a shit what they think,' Caryn said finally. 'I can't *stand* them.' It was Nic and Tory's turn to look at Caryn in surprise. 'They're so snobbish,' Caryn said, colouring, embarrassed by her little outburst. But it was true. She'd overheard them talking about her the day before in the toilets. Someone – Caryn didn't recognise her voice – had made a comment about the school letting in too many NOCDs. She was still in the stall when she heard her name being mentioned. She froze.

'Especially that new scholarship girl; what's her name?'

'Caryn. D'you see how she spells it? God, the working classes are just *too* dreadful for words.'

'I know. I practically have to hold my nose every time she walks by. I can't stand cheap perfume, can you?'

'No. Ooh, look what I bought yesterday . . .'

Caryn put her hands to her ears. Her face was on fire. Alice had given her a small bottle of Avon perfume the other day. *Something to cheer you up*, she'd told Caryn, guiltily noticing the dark circles under Caryn's eyes as she struggled with her homework, looking after Brian and keeping the house in reasonable order. Alice occasionally did little things like that which filled Caryn with remorse for all the awful things she thought about her mother. She'd dabbed a little of it on her wrist before rushing off to catch the bus. It was a little floral for her tastes but, still . . . it was a nice gesture. She'd waited until the toilets were empty and then tried to scrub it off.

'What's an NOCD?' she asked Nic and Tory, suddenly emboldened.

Tory hesitated. 'It's not very nice,' she said slowly.

'I don't care. What does it mean?'

'Er, it's short for . . . Not of Our Class, Dear,' Tory said, glancing at Nic.

'Oh. Thanks.' Caryn's cheeks turned even redder.

'D'you know . . .' Nic said slowly, looking at both of them. 'You're absolutely right. Who *gives* a shit?' The three of them looked at each other. Nic looked at her watch. It was almost lunchtime. 'I'm going to the canteen,' she said, hoisting her bag on to her shoulder. She started to walk away and then turned. 'Well, are you two coming or not?'

A fortnight later, Caryn sat gingerly on the flowered sofa, looking around her in ill-disguised awe. She made a solemn vow. She would never, *ever* bring Nic Harte round to her own home. Never. Ever. She glanced quickly at Tory to see if she was similarly impressed. Nic's house was like something out of a film set. A uniformed housekeeper had shown them into the living room on the first floor whilst she'd gone off to find Nic. The room in which they both sat was almost twice the size of her entire flat! She looked down at the richly patterned rug. It was so intricate she felt dizzy just looking at it. On the gleaming table in front of the window was an enormous bunch of lilies, their rich, potent perfume gently wafting through the air. She caught Tory's eye but before either of them could say anything, they heard Nic's hurried footsteps. She burst into the room and then immediately slowed down, trying hard not to look *too* pleased. Caryn smiled to herself. Nic was so funny. Desperate to show that she didn't need anyone and yet obviously dying for company. Living alone in such a beautiful house, despite its elegance, couldn't be much fun. She wondered where Nic's parents were. From the little she'd managed to glean, her father spent most of his time in the air and her stepmother trotted around the world after him, constantly decorating and redecorating his various homes. Depending on whom you believed, he was either the most exciting businessman the world had ever seen – or the most crooked. Nic hardly ever spoke about him. She seemed rather frightened of him.

But, as Caryn was beginning to discover, talking to Nic wasn't always the easiest way to the truth. More often than not, it lay in the things she *didn't* say. Like why no one in her family had remembered her seventeenth birthday. She'd celebrated it alone with a cake – with the housekeeper, she told them, pretending to be surprised at their obvious sympathy. There was something so desperately vulnerable about Nic that Caryn sometimes longed just to put her arms around her. Not that Nic would ever have allowed it. Caryn had never met anyone quite so determinedly self-sufficient. *I don't need anyone.* It was a statement she seemed to live by. Yet all you had to do was scratch the surface – and even then, not very hard. In that way she was completely different from Tory, Caryn thought.

Tory wore her inexplicable sadness on her sleeve, right on the surface of her skin. There were times when it hurt just to look at her. She was talking to Nic at that moment but you could see that only half her attention was on her. That was Tory through and through – no matter where you were, or what you were talking about, Tory always seemed to be carrying on a different conversation with someone you could neither see nor hear. She had an older sister, Susie, who was at Oxford, and her father was a professor at one of the London colleges. She didn't say much about either of them.

In fact, Caryn suddenly thought to herself, perhaps that was one reason why they all got along so well. For various, unspoken reasons they were each reluctant to talk about where they came from. Caryn would sooner die than take either of them back to Milton Gardens, and Tory kept saying her mother was always too busy to have people over. For the foreseeable future, at least, it looked as though they'd be meeting up at Hotel Harte, as Caryn had quickly dubbed it. It certainly felt more like a hotel than a home. As if to confirm her opinion, the housekeeper suddenly popped her head round the door and asked them to come into the kitchen for lunch.

They stayed for the rest of the afternoon, sprawled out on the soft rug in Nic's own little sitting room at the top of the stairs, listening to music and gossiping about school. At five, reluctantly, Caryn got up to leave. It was the first Saturday she'd had off in months but she still had to make sure Brian was bathed and fed before bedtime. She and Tory walked downstairs, Caryn still reeling from the sheer opulence and glamour of the afternoon they'd just had. They left Nic alone in her living room with the television on for company and her unfinished homework spread around her like a web.

15

By the middle of the first term, to everyone's astonishment, it had firmly been established that Nic Harte, Tory Spiller and Caryn Middleton were best friends. No one could quite believe it. Neither, it seemed, could they. Suddenly Nic had someone to talk to in and on the way to classes; Caryn's dress sense was slowly being improved under their influence and even Tory wasn't quite as odd as she'd first appeared. She spent less time staring out of the window and seemed a little more forthcoming about the seventeen years she'd spent before coming to St

Augustine's. She idolised her older sister, Nic noticed almost enviously. Susie sounded like the perfect sister – she was always sending Tory little gifts, extra bits of pocket money, a new record or two or the odd new piece of clothing. The close relationship between Tory and Susie bore no resemblance to her own relationship with her half-sister, Jessica, or to the horror stories Nic remembered from her friends back home. Susie seemed perfect. She was studying history at Oxford, just like Tory's father. She was going to be a professor or an actress, Tory said blithely. Caryn and Nic were equally impressed. Nic wasn't sure if anyone in her family had even been to university. Her father never spoke about his past. She knew nothing of where he'd grown up, who his parents were, where he'd gone to school. Both sets of grandparents were dead. She couldn't even remember if he'd told her that. It seemed to be something they all knew, had always known.

'Where're you thinking of applying for university?' Caryn asked them both one frosty morning in December as they were crossing the lawn to the library.

'Oh, I don't think I'll bother with all that,' Nic said airily.

''Course you will,' Caryn grinned. It might have worked a few months ago but she was no longer fooled by Nic's nonchalance. 'Come on, you know you want to.'

'I don't actually. I haven't really thought about it,' Nic said, almost truthfully. She hadn't dared think about it. 'I . . . I'll decide later.'

'I'm not,' Tory said suddenly. Caryn and Nic looked at her.

'Not what?'

'Not going.'

'What about your parents? Won't they want you to go?' Caryn asked, interested. She and Alice hadn't spoken about it – she was dreading bringing the subject up, mostly because of what it would cost. Not to mention the thought of leaving Brian alone with her.

Tory shrugged. 'Oh, Susie's doing so well . . . she can be the brains for both of us. I just want to get as far away from here as I can.'

'Where to?' Both Nic and Caryn were taken aback by the sudden bitterness in her voice.

'Dunno. Anywhere. Anywhere'd be better than here.'

Caryn hesitated. She looked quickly at Nic. There it was again. That same, odd note of desolation. Neither knew quite what to say. They passed The Four Witches, walking in the opposite direction. For once, nothing was said. It was the one supreme advantage of being a group, Caryn noticed. Alone, you were a sitting target, easy prey. With three of them, it was harder and Gemma Kinnaird was nothing if not a coward.

'Fucking cow,' Nic muttered as they reached the library building. 'Did you see the look she gave us?'

'Well, better that than hearing something awful come out of her mouth,' Caryn said dryly, pulling open the door. 'D'you notice how quiet she's been lately?'

'Just you wait,' Nic said gloomily. 'She's gearing up.'

'Who cares?' Tory said suddenly. 'What's the worst thing she can say? I think she's already said it, actually. She's run out of things to say. That's why she's quiet.'

Nic and Caryn looked at her in surprise. Just when you thought Tory had completely switched off, something sharp and true would come singing out of her mouth. It was true – what could Gemma say about them that hadn't already been said? It was an immediately cheering thought.

16

Estelle looked around the room quickly. It was clean, of reasonable size and it had a rather nice bay window overlooking the garden – well, what *would* have been a garden had anyone bothered to weed it. She turned back to the two girls who were standing in the doorway, obviously still overawed by her. 'Yeah. It's fine. I'll take it.' The red-haired one, Rebecca or whatever her name was, smiled in relief.

'Great! I'm glad you like it. We've had some real weirdos, I can tell you—'

'Yeah, there was this *one* girl . . .' The other one, Amanda, immediately started wittering on about someone who'd come the previous Monday.

'And the bathroom?' Estelle broke in quickly. She had no desire to stand there chatting to either of them.

'Oh, er . . . it's just here, down the hall.'

Estelle walked down the hallway. She opened the door to the tiny bathroom. Like the rest of the house, it was clean, if hardly luxurious. But after a week in Jonathan and Sylvia's home along with half a dozen other expatriate Zimbabweans who dropped in and out at will, followed by two weeks in an absolutely filthy bed-and-breakfast place she'd found near Victoria Station, she'd had enough. Her money was dwindling at an alarming rate and none of the leads she'd arrived with had quite panned out. After the fifth embarrassing phone call when she'd rung a man who'd said 'ring any time' – and found that he had no intention of admitting having met her, especially not in front of his wife – she hung up and ripped the contacts sheet out of her notebook. It was clearly one thing to give a girl you'd just met in a bar in Harare your phone number and the casual invitation to call 'whenever you're in town' – and quite another to actually mean it. She wasn't even sure his name was really Frank. Or Jim, John, Dave . . . what difference did it make? None of them were prepared to help her in *any* way, never mind the way they'd promised – and that was that.

'When can I move in?' she asked the two girls who were standing, rather dumbstruck, still looking at her.

'Oh, any time. I mean, as soon as you've . . . you know . . .'

'The . . . er, deposit . . . ?' Rebecca said, looking pained.

'Can't I pay you now?' Estelle couldn't quite get to grips with the silly embarrassment that talking about money seemed to provoke in the British.

'Now?'

'Yes. I've got it with me. In cash.'

'Oh, well . . . yeah . . . absolutely.'

'Here. It's thirty a week, you said. And a month in advance?'

'Er, yeah.'

'OK. So, that's all of it.' Estelle counted out the notes. 'I'll just go back to the hotel and get my stuff. Anything else?'

'Er, no . . . no, I suppose that's it, then,' Amanda smiled timidly at her.

Estelle ignored her and picked up her bag. She was being rude but the last thing she felt like doing was making friends. She wanted a place to live; she'd seen their advert in a newsagent's window. *Female, non-smoker, sought to share comfortable flat. One-third share of bills.* She met the criteria; the flat met hers. End of story. She had business to attend to and she hadn't come to London to make friends, especially not with those two. She would be perfectly polite to them but she had to make it absolutely clear – she wasn't on the lookout for a new best friend. And if she were, she thought to herself as she closed the front door behind her and turned her collar up, she certainly wouldn't pick either of them. Students – Estelle couldn't remember where or of what. Rebecca's father owned the flat or something. They'd had a third flatmate who'd dropped out of the course they were on and it had taken them almost a month to find her replacement. 'You wouldn't *believe* the kinds of people who've called,' Amanda had said as they opened the door to show her the room. Actually, she probably would. In the month she'd been in London, she'd met them all. Like a giant, unfiltered dustbin, the city seemed to attract the jetsam and flotsam of the rest of the world. In the bed and breakfast she'd been staying at she'd met more actresses, models, singers and stars than she cared to remember. Everybody, it seemed, wanted to be somebody. Well, nobody wanted it as badly as Estelle Mackenzie. And that was a fact.

17

'It's parents' evening at your school next week,' Tory's mother called out as she walked in the kitchen. 'We got the invitation this morning. It looks like your year are organising the Christmas buffet. That'll be nice. We might even get to meet your new friends.'

Tory stopped in the doorway. 'You're not going to come, are you?' she asked, alarmed.

Her mother frowned. 'Of course we're going to come. What a question!'

'It'll be *boring*,' Tory said, trying desperately to think of a better reason. 'No one else's parents are coming.'

'Don't be ridiculous, Tory. We've always gone. At Queen Anne's, don't you remember?'

Tory let her bag drop. 'It'll just be a waste of time,' she said lamely, aware that her cheeks were suddenly flaming. 'Who wants to meet the stupid teachers anyway?' She turned and walked out of the kitchen.

'Tory!' her mother called after her. Tory ran up the stairs two at a time, her heart pounding. She couldn't tell her mother the real reason she didn't want them to come. How could she? How would she explain she was afraid someone would say something about Susie and then the whole game would be up? She'd have to find a way to make sure no one said anything – but how? It had all started off so innocently. She'd made a slip of the tongue once, when she first got there. She'd been talking about maths or something and it had just slipped out. *My sister's good at maths.* Not 'my sister *used* to be good at maths. My sister-who-was-murdered.' Neither Caryn nor Nic had said anything and with relief, Tory realised they didn't know. No one at St Augustine's seemed to know. The teachers didn't refer to it; no one asked her how she was, how she was coping, how her parents were. It was – for one, brief, giddy second – as if it had never been.

She pulled back the duvet and crawled into bed, fully clothed.

How was she going to get out of this one? She'd just have to make sure neither Caryn nor Nic spoke to her parents all evening. How long did those things last? An hour or two? She'd just have to stick beside them the whole time and make sure they didn't meet. She felt sick. The euphoria of the past month had suddenly evaporated.

'This came for me,' Alice said as soon as Caryn walked in the door. 'This morning. Wh-what d'you think I should do?'

Caryn took the little white card from her. An invitation to the Christmas parent-teacher evening. She bit her lip. 'I don't know,' she said slowly, wondering how on earth to tell her mother that she would simply *die* if Alice showed up. 'D'you want to go?'

'Oh, I don't think I can, darling,' Alice said nervously, fingering her throat. 'I mean, what'll I wear? I'd have to get a new dress or something.'

'Well, I won't mind if you don't come,' Caryn said, guiltily relieved.

'But I ought to go, shouldn't I?' Alice said again. 'It's important, isn't it?'

'Well, you've never been to one before, have you?'

'No.'

'Well, then . . . maybe next year?' Caryn said warily. She could see the wheels of Alice's mind beginning to turn over.

'No, I think I ought to make the effort, love. I mean . . . I could get a new dress, couldn't I? There's the twenty I put aside for Brian's bike, you know . . . the one he wants for Christmas. I can always replace it later, can't I? You've got a bit spare, don't you, love?'

'Mum . . . no, not really. I—'

'But what about your money from your Saturday job? You can't have spent it all, surely?' Alice's voice rose.

Caryn's heart sank. She could see what was about to happen. Alice was always complaining she had so little to look forward to; she was beginning to get excited at the prospect of having somewhere to go. 'I've got a bit,' she admitted warily. 'But not much.'

'I won't need very much,' Alice said, lighting a cigarette. 'I've got that blue top . . . you know, the one with the sequins across the bust . . . and I could just get a skirt. Get my hair done. Oh, it'll be *nice*, Caryn, won't it? Won't it, love?'

'What's going to be nice?' Owen walked into the kitchen, scowling.

'I've been invited to meet Caryn's teachers,' Alice sang, her mood escalating by the second. Caryn felt ill. She knew exactly what would happen. Alice would spend the next few days and fifty quid on a new outfit, a haircut and a bottle of something to keep her spirits up and then, a day or perhaps even hours before the big event, she'd come crashing back down to earth; she'd be sick and unable to go and it would take them weeks to lift her out of the hole into which she'd sunk. It happened every time. Every fucking time. She wanted to scream.

'Oh, going to see Miss La-di-da's *teachers*, are you?' Owen sneered. 'Going to tell them what a *good* little girl your precious Caryn is?'

'Shut up, Owen,' Caryn snapped angrily at him.

'Why? You gonna make me?' Owen laughed nastily, opening the fridge. He peered inside at its meagre contents and then slammed it shut. 'Why is there never anything to fucking eat in this house?' he fumed, grabbing his jacket from the back of a chair.

' 'Cos you never fucking buy anything!' Caryn shouted, pressing her hands to her ears.

In the corner, Alice was going on dreamily about the dress she was going to buy. 'A nice dark colour, I think. Dark blue. Or no, maybe black. Black suits me, you know, Caryn. I could get my hair coloured as well, get rid of the grey. Oh, you never know . . . I might even meet someone . . . wouldn't *that* be something?'

'Will you be *quiet,* Mum. *Please*,' Caryn said, clenching her fists. In the living room Brian had turned up the television to drown out the sound of the squabble going on in the kitchen.

She shook her head to try to clear it. Everything was beginning to get on top of her. Owen gave her one last jeering look and walked out, slamming the door behind him so hard that the knives and forks in the draining rack jangled. Alice blinked. Caryn picked up the invitation card and slid it into her pocket. So much for a pleasant 'meet the parents' evening. Not all parents were the same; that was the problem.

18

Nic looked round at the thirty or forty parents and teachers who were gathered in the assembly hall. Her father and Molly hadn't arrived yet. She didn't know whether to be pleased or annoyed that they'd decided to come. Not that they'd come to London specifically for this, of course. They'd arrived the week before and had spent most of it at Studgrove, only returning to Eaton Square that morning. Nic had reluctantly shown them the invitation. It was Molly who wanted to go, of course, not Jim. 'Isn't Lord Palmer's daughter in your class?' she'd asked Nic before turning back to Jim. 'Now, darling . . . *I* think it would be *extremely* useful—' Nic turned and walked out of the room in disgust.

She could see Tory's parents talking to Dr Walsh with Tory hovering anxiously behind them. She'd been behaving oddly for the past few days, fretting in the most absurd way about the upcoming evening. Frankly, Nic couldn't see what she was worried about. As far as she could tell, Tory's parents looked like perfectly ordinary, perfectly nice people. Her father was tall and thin with a kind, slightly bemused expression. Exactly what she imagined a history professor would look like. Her mother was blonde and small and round, nothing like Tory. Apparently Susie, her older sister, took after them. Tory obviously didn't. She looked away from the Spillers towards the door. Still no sign of her father. Suddenly she spotted Caryn and her mother in the far corner of the room. She walked up to them, relieved to have someone to talk to.

Caryn's mum looked like an older, slightly faded version of Caryn – wavy blonde hair falling to her shoulders, slim, with a small, pointed chin and large blue eyes. She was dressed a little oddly, perhaps, with a sparkling blue top and a pair of too-big trousers belted tightly at the waist – pretty, but in a strange, almost vacant sort of way. Nic stared at her. Caryn looked uncomfortable – funny, wasn't it, Nic mused. They were all anxious in one way or another about their families.

'Mum, this is Nic,' Caryn mumbled as Nic joined them. Nic held out a hand.

Alice stared at it for a moment, then looked up. She was a good head shorter than Nic. 'Nic. Oh. Goodness me . . .' she said, a quick smile suddenly breaking across her face. She seemed about to continue, but nothing further came.

Nic waited for a second, then withdrew her hand, baffled. Caryn looked as though she wished the ground would open up and swallow her. 'Shall I get you a cup of tea, Mum?' she asked hurriedly.

'No, don't worry, I'll get it,' Nic said quickly. 'Milk and sugar?'

'Vodka, if you've got any,' Alice giggled.

'Mum . . .' Caryn's expression was pained.

'I'm not sure that's on offer,' Nic said, smiling at Alice. 'But I'll have a look.' She flashed Caryn a sympathetic look and headed off towards the buffet. She collected two cups of tea and was just about to turn and head back when someone spoke behind her. She turned around. It was Tory's father.

'You must be Nic,' he said, smiling at her. 'I just overheard you talking to those two.' He looked back in the direction of Caryn and her mother.

'Oh, hello, er . . . sir,' Nic said, a little self-consciously. She was never quite sure what people thought of her; what they might have heard.

'You must come and say hello to Gilly, my wife. She's been dying to meet you, and the other young lady – Caryn, is it?'

'Er, yes. I'm just taking them a cup of tea—'

'Here, let me help you. I'll take that one, shall I?' He took the cup from her. He signalled to Tory and her mother to follow them and descended purposefully on Caryn and her mother. Nic could see Caryn's look of alarm as they approached.

'Hullo, I'm John, Tory's dad. You must be Caryn. We've been wanting to meet you for absolutely ages! Tory's been keeping you quite hidden. And you must be Caryn's mum. This is my wife, Gillian . . .' John Spiller made the introductions whilst the three girls stood silently by, two of them squirming in agony, though Nic couldn't quite work out why. There was an awkward pause as Alice struggled to take it all in.

'Well,' John said heartily when the introductions were finally over. 'That's it, then . . . we've finally met everyone. Gilly and I were saying only the other day how nice it would be to have you round for supper. We must arrange it. Christmas'll be on us before you know it,' he said, smiling at everyone.

'Christmas,' Alice said dreamily. 'Is it Christmas already?'

'That would be lovely, sir,' Caryn broke in hurriedly. 'We'd really like that. Will Susie be back? It'd be lovely to meet her as well,' she rushed on, trying to fill the awkward pause that followed Alice's words. Alice wasn't coping well with all the new faces, she could see.

There was a second's stunned silence. 'S–Susie?' Gilly Spiller finally croaked. She looked wildly around her.

Caryn stared at her, confused at the sudden change in mood. 'Er, yes. She's at Oxford, isn't she?'

Gillian's hand holding the tea cup started to shake. The rattling sound was awful. Nic looked at Tory. She was staring at the ground. John Spiller ran a hand through his hair. His face was contorted in genuine anguish. Nic stared at him. She had a strange sense of foreboding, as if she somehow knew what was coming next. 'Is . . . is this some kind of joke?' he asked finally, his voice breaking.

'N–no,' Caryn stammered, bewildered. 'I–I just thought . . .'

She flashed a desperate glance at Tory. Had they had a fight or something? There was another pained silence.

'Who's Susie?' Alice asked brightly, breaking it.

'Susie was our other daughter,' John said through gritted teeth. Tory was still staring fixedly at the ground. 'She's dead. She was murdered two years ago. I thought you . . . I'm surprised Tory hasn't told you.'

Gillian Spiller let out a soft moan. There was a sudden intake of breath and then the awful sound of china hitting the floor. Nic had dropped her cup. Seconds later, Gillian Spiller slumped to the ground. There was a flurry of voices and movements as everyone rushed to her side. Tory walked off in the direction of the toilets. Caryn and Nic remained rooted to the spot. Suddenly, there was an even greater commotion at the other side of the room. Nic looked over the heads of teachers and parents crowded around them and saw that her father had arrived. He stood in the doorway, filling it, his tanned, handsome face looking in her direction, frowning, as usual. She saw him turn to Molly. *What the hell has she done now?* The murmur around him grew louder. *Look, isn't that Jim Harte? Good God, yes it is. Gosh, it's Jim Harte.*

She turned her back on them and followed Tory into the toilets. What the hell had just happened? Tory's sister was *dead*? Murdered? She shivered. Suddenly a lot of things about Tory made sense.

19

Alone in her room with the fuzzy white light of the television screen playing silently in the background, Nic pressed the receiver to her ear and listened to Molly outlining the reasons why she wouldn't be returning to Avonlea at Christmas as had been planned. God, she *hated* her!

'Your father's got an important meeting in Verbier,' Molly said, injecting everything she'd ever learned about French pronunciation into the word.

Nic rolled her eyes. 'But I'll be *fine* on my own in the house,' she said, resentment clawing at her throat.

'Out of the question. *Absolutely* out of the question.' Molly was positively revelling in her role as boss.

'But what about Shaun and Patrick?'

'They'll be in Harare. Look, Nicola, this isn't up for discussion. Manning will bring you to Verbier on the twenty-third, you'll spend Christmas and New Year with us and then we'll all return to London on the fourth. Now, we'll be entertaining a number of your father's friends so I want you to—'

Nic slammed down the phone. She couldn't bear to hear another word. A second later, it began to ring again. She stared at it, too angry to think. The shrill, insistent ring punctured the air rhythmically until it finally fell silent. She closed her eyes. She wasn't going to shed a single further tear – she'd promised herself. Easier said than done. After four long months at that dreadful school, all she wanted to do was take Simba up into the hills and lie against the burning rocks. She felt a tear begin its slow journey down her cheek.

Caryn walked along Essex Road, her collar turned up against the wind, hands shoved deep into her pockets. She was pleased with herself. She'd found a holiday job at Top Shop on Upper Street. It didn't pay much but it did give her a twenty-five per cent discount on clothes, including those in the January sale racks. That alone would have been incentive enough! She desperately needed a new winter coat, not to mention a pair of boots and a couple of jumpers . . . anything, in fact. Tory and Nic had been brilliant over the past couple of months; both of them had given her a few things they claimed were too small. Nic was five foot seven and Tory was a staggering five foot ten so, yes, in truth, they were both at least a head taller than Caryn who was only five foot four, but still, it would be nice to be able to buy something of her own every once in a while.

She thought about them as she turned up Islington Green. Nic had gone off to Switzerland the day before, sulking furiously. Caryn couldn't understand why she was so angry. Neither a summer in Zimbabwe nor Christmas in Switzerland seemed particularly dreadful choices. God, she'd have given her front teeth for either. Both beat working in Top Shop hands down, with or without a discount! Tory was spending the holidays at home in Fulham with her parents. She'd said very little about the counselling sessions she'd been forced to attend every Thursday morning – it was almost as if the incident hadn't really happened. She'd stopped talking about her sister, though, which Caryn supposed was a good sign.

It was funny how things had steadily become more complicated, she thought to herself as she hurried along the road, her breath scrolling out before her as she went. Winning the scholarship to St Augustine's had seemed to her to be the most important thing, ever. At the time, she'd imagined everything else would simply fall into place. But getting into St Augustine's was only the start of something, she saw now. It would change her in ways she couldn't yet describe. It had already changed her. At Featherstone's she would never have come across anyone like Nic. Nic's world was wide and free in a way that she knew hers could never be. And yet . . . for all that, Nic was no happier than she was. In fact, half the time, she was a lot *un*happier. And Tory, with her warm, supportive parents – the sort of family that Caryn dreamed of having – look at her! Stuck in a weekly session with a stranger, forced to talk about something that, to Caryn, was so horrible and mind-bogglingly awful as to send shivers down her spine. Poor Tory.

She could see why everyone at school was mystified by their friendship. One rich, one damaged, one poor. What a trio! And yet, somehow, in ways that others perhaps didn't see, they complemented each other. Nic, for all her money and the freedom it brought her, was lonelier than anyone could ever guess. Tory was still bleeding from a wound that no one saw and Caryn . . . well, she was the glue that held the three of them together. It was Caryn who looked beneath the surface of things, just as she'd always done, and saw things there that others somehow missed. She saw something else in the arrogant, touchy Nic and the dreamy, absent Tory that drew her to them, and perhaps even vice versa. Although it was something she was only just beginning to grasp, Tory and Nic gave *her* something that Alice had spectacularly failed to provide. Ambition. Without ambition, she understood, she would wind up just like Alice, or worse. It wasn't a question of talent; Alice had that, plenty of it. But she'd squandered it. Caryn didn't fully understand the reasons why Alice had given up on everything – yes, her marriage hadn't worked out but was that a reason to spend every day in bed? She didn't know. She'd never had a boyfriend, never even really fancied anyone. Any time she thought about it, a queer, sick feeling came over her; the same feeling she'd had when she saw Mr Humphreys' hand on her knee.

20

Nic slung her skis over her shoulder and trudged to the back of the queue. Even at nine in the morning the lift was packed. The air was bitingly crisp; it stung her cheeks and forehead, the only parts of her that weren't muffled against the cold. Ahead of her, the mountains were silhouetted magnificently against the early-morning powdery sky, a sharp line of petrified graphite running jaggedly across the valley. She steadied her skis with a gloved hand. London seemed very, very far away. Around her were voices in French, German, Swiss-German, English, Italian. Everybody was with somebody; they stood around in groups of twos or threes, chatting and laughing, waiting for the swaying bucket seats to come past. Everybody except her, that was. She'd been in Verbier for just over a week and from the very first day it was clear that most of the time she'd be on her own. She'd barely seen her father since her arrival and Molly and Jessica were always out visiting other people or shopping. The villa he'd rented for the month was positively palatial, spread over several acres of snowy white gardens adjacent to the Verbier Country Club and hidden behind an extremely large stone wall. Her room overlooked the small, frozen lake at the rear of the house. At night, the birch trees creaked gently and every once in a while an owl hooted as it flew across the dark landscape and disappeared into the night. In the mornings there were huge bowls of milky coffee and croissants bought from the village bakery. Nic ate most of her meals with the Swiss housekeeper, Marianne, who spoke slow, lilting French and smiled a lot. In that way, it wasn't much different from any of her other homes. She spent most of her time alone.

She inched her way forward in the queue, still feeling a little self-conscious about being alone when she caught the eye of someone standing a little to one side of the group in front of her. She couldn't see much of him under the woollen hat and scarf he wore but she was aware of a pair of dark brown eyes and tanned, slightly sunburnt cheeks. She looked away quickly. The group in front of her, including him, took the first four seats amidst much laughter. She positioned herself as the bucket seat came up quickly behind her. There was the strange, falling sensation as her skis left the ground and then they were up, creaking and swaying above the pristine white expanse below.

At the summit of the blue run, she slid off the seat smoothly, turned away from the direction of the lift and ploughed to a stop. She gazed down the long length of the mountain. She was a good skier. She'd taken to it exactly the same way she'd taken to water as a child, thrilled by the feeling of weightlessness and speed and the way you had to trust your body, intimately attuned to its strengths and weaknesses. She was just positioning her skis and adjusting her goggles when a figure loomed beside her, coming to an expert halt and sending a shower of fine snowy powder over both of them. She looked up, annoyed. It was the young man who'd glanced at her in the queue. He pushed the goggles up over his forehead. He had the tell-tale

T-bar of sunburn across the forehead and nose, and a curl or two of dark brown hair escaped from under his woollen ski hat.

'Hi,' he said cheerfully. 'Mind if I take the run down with you?' He pointed to the run below with his pole.

Nic stared at him. He was rather good-looking, she noticed straight away. Brown, friendly eyes; an easy, confident air; a nice smile. Her own face was muffled tightly against the wind. She lifted a gloved hand to pull down her scarf. 'Sure,' she said cautiously. He was English – how did he know she was?

'I heard you talking to someone the other day,' he said, quickly reading her expression. 'I'm Will, by the way.'

'Er, Nic,' she volunteered a second later.

'You're a pretty good skier,' he said, adjusting his goggles and looking down the length of the slope. 'Helluva lot better than me.'

Nic blushed under her scarf. 'A bit out of practice,' she mumbled. How did he know? Had he been watching her?

'Yeah, I've been watching you,' he said, reading her expression for the second time. 'You passed me on the run down a couple of times yesterday,' he said with a grin. His smile was wide and generous. Nic felt her cheeks get even hotter. 'So . . . shall we?' He planted his poles firmly in front of him. 'Winner buys the *glühwein*.'

'But it's only ten o'clock,' Nic called, her voice whipped away by the wind as they fell away from the slope together.

'Tonight,' he yelled back. And then he was gone.

Fifteen minutes later she skied up to him, grinning in spite of herself. 'You said *I* was better than you,' she exclaimed, coming to a sideways halt in front of him.

'*Better*, I said, not faster.' He pulled off his hat and ran a hand through his thick curls.

'Same thing.'

'Not at all. You've got great form but you hold yourself back. If you let yourself go a bit more, you'd be much faster.'

'Oh, really? And who are you? An instructor?' Nic scoffed, her face on fire. She had the distinct impression he wasn't only referring to her performance on the slopes – ridiculous, really. He'd only just met her!

'Actually, yeah, I am.'

'Oh.' Nic didn't know what to say.

'Look, why don't we go up again? I can show you what I mean. About your form,' he added, looking her up and down.

Nic hesitated, then nodded. The depressing prospect of another solitary afternoon suddenly vanished. 'Oh, all right,' she said, replacing her goggles. 'Why not?'

'Excellent,' Will said, grinning as he replaced his own. 'By tomorrow I'll have you on Tortin. It's the toughest run.'

Nic smiled to herself. He was subtle as well as funny. With a couple of words – 'tonight', 'tomorrow' – he'd let it be known that he wanted to see her again. After just half an hour in his company, so did she. Unusual. For her.

'You're incredible,' he said, as he came up to meet her at the bottom after a jaw-dropping, adrenalin-fuelled slide down the steepest slopes she'd ever tried. Her heart was pumping so loudly she was sure he could hear it. 'Amazing. I just had to say it and you were off. Where did you learn to ski, by the way?'

'Oh, here and there. We used to come to Europe every summer,' Nic said, blushing. 'Mostly to Switzerland.'

'Every summer?' Will looked confused. 'Bit of an odd time to learn how to ski.'

'I meant winter. Summer for us.'

'Are you Australian?' he asked, pushing open the gate at the side of the run and letting her through.

'Er, yes,' Nic said quickly. She had no intention of telling him who she really was. 'But I've been at school in England for ages.'

'Ah. I'm from Croydon.'

'Where's that?'

'Well, exactly.' He turned and looked down at her. 'Look, I don't know about you and I swear I'm not being pushy or anything . . . but I could eat a horse right now. I'm absolutely *starving*. D'you have to be anywhere soon?'

Nic shook her head. 'No, not really. I don't have to be back till supper.'

'Well, shall we have lunch?'

'Why not?'

Over lunch at a tiny café near the town centre, she found out he was twenty-three, that he'd been coming to Verbier with two other friends who were also instructors every year for the past three years and that he generally stayed for the whole season. They worked in a rota, which gave him enough time to enjoy the slopes and enough money to last until the summer when he went to the south of France and taught rich women and their children how to water-ski. Nic was already in awe of him. 'Better than sitting in an office,' he said, draining his beer. 'That's what most of my friends back in Croydon are doing, anyway. How long are *you* here for?'

'Until the week after New Year, I think,' Nic said, sipping her own beer. 'My dad's rented a villa, just behind the Country Club.'

'Oh-ho. The Country Club. You're posh, aren't you?'

'No, I'm not.' She bent her head to her plate so he wouldn't see her reddening cheeks. She was beginning to feel slightly out of her depth. She hoped he wouldn't ask her how old she was. Eighteen would sound awfully childish.

'So . . . you at uni?' he asked.

'Uni?' Nic swallowed a mouthful without chewing and almost choked. 'Er, yes.'

'What are you studying?'

'English.'

'Ah. Thought so. Whereabouts?' He seemed interested rather than prying.

'Er, London,' she said, desperately hoping he wouldn't ask her anything more.

'Croydon's in London, by the way,' he said, smiling at her. 'Well, sort of. Only two important people ever came out of Croydon. Kate Moss is one of them.'

'Who's the other?' Nic asked, relieved to have changed the subject.

'Me, of course. Silly.'

Nic laughed. She liked him. She liked his quick, easy wit and his charm. There was none of the posturing or the unmistakable air of entitlement that characterised almost every young Zimbabwean male she'd ever met. He was subtle and self-deprecating, his voice permanently tinged with humour. She smiled at him. 'I didn't recognise you. It was the goggles.' Their eyes met; he grinned. A kind of ease was established between them.

It was almost four and the sun was beginning to sink by the time Nic reluctantly got up to leave. 'I'd better get going,' she said, her head feeling distinctly woozy from the effects of the morning's hard exercise and three glasses of wine. Will jumped up.

'So I'll see you tonight?' he asked, his eyes creasing at the corners.

Nic's heart did a quick somersault. 'Tonight?'

'Yeah. *Glühwein*. You're buying,' he grinned.

Her heart continued to turn. 'Um, where?'

'How about Bar Jo's? Near Place Centrale. It's the only one in the square. You can't miss it. Just before the church.'

'I'll find it,' Nic said, picking up her poles. 'What time?'

'Whenever you like. Nine?'

She nodded happily. 'I'll see you there.' They looked at each other. There was a second's hesitation then he bent his head and kissed her lightly and swiftly on the cheek. Nic was having difficulty breathing. 'I . . . well, I'll . . . I'll see you later,' she stammered, turning away rather clumsily. She walked out, her head swimming, and went back to the villa in a daze. What would Caryn and Tory say?

21

There was a young man who'd been sitting squashed up next to Tory on the sofa but he'd said nothing to her all evening. She didn't recognise him and no one had introduced them. She stifled an irritable yawn. The party was boring in the extreme. She looked around for Jenny. It was Jenny's eighteenth birthday. She'd been staying at Jenny's for five long, drawn-out days; in another two, she'd be going home. She couldn't wait. Not to get home, *per se*, but to get away from all her old school friends who treated her just as they'd always done – cautiously. It was as if she'd never escape their concern. She longed for Caryn and Nic. It had been the bloody counsellor's idea to send her away for a few days – just went to show how little he understood her, she longed to tell her parents. But her mother was strangely insistent. 'You're not the only one who's suffering, young lady,' she'd said to Tory a few days before she'd been packed off to Jenny's for a week. Tory had just looked at her, speechless with hurt. Ever since the disastrous parent-teacher evening, her relationship with her mother, never comfortable even at the best of times, had deteriorated. Buried way below the surface of her mother's forced cheerfulness was a truth about their relationship that Tory dared not even think about.

The young man sitting next to her spoke suddenly, interrupting her unpleasant thoughts.

'What?' Tory could hardly hear him above the music.

'Dance? D'you want to dance?' he repeated.

'I'm not a very good dancer,' Tory said, shaking her head.

'It's easy,' he said, pulling her to her feet. At least he was tall, Tory thought, as he pushed his way through the couples who were glued together on the narrow patch of carpet. At five foot ten it was difficult to find boys who were taller than her. He cleared a tiny space for them and hesitated. Then his arms went round her and she found herself pressed against his chest. It was disconcerting at first. She hadn't been that close to anyone in a long time. Her face was pressed against his neck; he smelled of mild aftershave and cigarette smoke; she opened her mouth slightly and then, suddenly, for no particular reason that she could think of, she stuck her tongue out, grazing the skin with its tip. He pulled back for a second, startled, then his arms quickly tightened around her. One hand came up to touch the nape of her neck, pressing her head against him, and the other slid down her back.

The music stopped suddenly as the DJ fumbled with another record and in the dazed, deafening silence, he kissed her. His tongue was warm and heavy, surprisingly firm. It pushed its way into her mouth rudely, but she found, to her surprise, that she liked it. It wasn't as though she'd never been kissed before, but after Susie's death, boys had avoided her like the plague. Everyone had avoided her at first, not knowing what, if anything, to say. She'd gone from being a normal, carefree teenager to a leper overnight. And at St Augustine's, of course, there wasn't a boy in sight.

'Let's get out of here,' he said against her ear. Tory nodded. She wanted that feeling again.

Slowly, dreamily, she led him upstairs. Past the first floor where Jenny's room was; up the next flight of stairs to the spare bedroom where she was staying. Jenny's parents were out; they'd promised them the party would be over by one. They'd also had to promise to do the clearing up in the morning. She pushed open the door to the room. Her bag was on the bed, along with the jeans she'd thrown off earlier. She reached out to switch on the light but he caught her hand. 'Leave it off,' he said, sounding rather nervous. Tory smiled. Funny, she didn't feel nervous at all. All she wanted was the heavy, reassuring feel of his arms around her and the taste of his skin in her mouth. She turned to him.

It was very dark in the room; the bass from downstairs thumped gently against the floorboards. He sat beside her on the narrow, single bed and kissed her. She pulled her head back but his mouth was sweet and insistent and she allowed herself to be coaxed back. His hands were slow and steady, even though she could feel his heartbeat through the thin fabric of her shirt. He touched the buttons on the front of her shirt, fingers working each one until he pushed it slowly from her shoulders. She felt herself floating away as she sometimes did when memories became too painful or the ache in her side unbearable. She watched herself with a surprised air as she pushed her hands under his sweater and helped him wriggle free.

'Tory,' he mumbled against her hair. She couldn't remember his name so she said nothing. There was the sound of his zipper, and then hers. She could feel him sliding her new jeans down her legs and the slight chill as the air hit her bare skin. She protested faintly, pulling back the bedspread and climbing underneath. He finished undressing and then climbed in after her. It was all touch; very little sound, no light. His skin was warm and slightly rough under her fingertips. He shuddered when she touched him; trailing her hands down his trembling stomach brought sounds from him that made her think of a boiling hot summer's day and the exquisite relief of ice-cream on her tongue or the first, delightful shudder of running into the ice-cold sea. She heard him fumble with something that made a sharp, tearing noise and felt something cold upon her thigh. He was heavy, she thought, as he raised himself over her, although for some reason she felt as though he could never be heavy enough. The sensation, as he entered her, was one of surprise. For those brief, few moments as he slid his way inside her, everything else was pushed out of the way. Everything. He seemed to fill her with something other than the sadness that had settled on her like dust, ever since the day the police came and she felt herself pressed against the inspector's chest. That was the last time she'd been held. Somehow, in the days and weeks and months that followed, she understood that if her father had so much as hugged her, he'd have fallen apart.

22

Caryn let the curtain drop, biting her lip nervously. It was nearly eleven and Owen still wasn't home. He'd been out all day. She was worried. A new wave of dealers had moved on to the estate recently and Owen, Caryn knew, was one of them. He was twenty-two, unemployed, without a single qualification to his name – not even a GCSE – what else was there for him? Their relationship had taken a turn for the worse after she'd won the scholarship and Alice kept proudly announcing that 'at least one person in the family's done something worthwhile'. Every time she said it, she could see Owen's tense, resentful face staring at her. *It's not my fault*, she wanted to say, but couldn't.

She pulled back the curtain yet again. There were a few young men hanging around by the entrance to Baberton. She could just make out Owen's hooded sweatshirt and ridiculously baggy trousers. *Los Angeles*, it read. Owen was obsessed with going to LA. She sighed. The only way he'd ever make it to LA was to get a job, save his money and buy a plane ticket. Simple as that. She'd tried telling him that the other day but he'd just laughed at her. Called her a 'fucking moron' for believing all that crap about hard work and passing your exams. *Too fucking gormless to see the truth.*

'And what, pray tell, is the truth?' she'd asked him acidly.

He laughed out loud. 'Pray who?' He'd turned to Digby, his best mate whom Caryn detested, who was lagging behind, pretending not to hear. 'Can you believe her? Uptight fucking little *bitch*.'

Caryn had to walk off, tears of anger forming in her eyes. What had she ever done to him to make him talk to her that way? And in front of that idiot Digby? And yet . . . at times when she least expected it, he'd say something to her, something sweet and kind and her heart would just melt. She worried for him, just like she worried for Brian and her mum. In fact, in between working at Top Shop and struggling to keep up with her schoolwork, that was all she did – worry. About everyone else. She worried for England, Nic told her in exasperation one day.

She could hear the dull whine of the lift descending to the ground floor. She held her breath. Yes, down the gangway she could hear the doors opening. A few seconds later, she heard his key in the lock. He was home. Safe. She could breathe again.

'Psst! Caryn? You awake?' It was Owen, tapping lightly at her door. She sat up with a start, her heart hammering. She peered at the clock on the bedside table. It was almost one a.m.

'What is it? What's the matter?'

'Can I come in?'

'Hang on.' She pulled her dressing gown off the chair and slipped it on. She padded to the door and opened it. 'What's wrong?'

Owen giggled softly. 'I wanna show you something,' he said, tugging at her arm.

'Stop it,' she hissed. 'You're pissed. Go to bed, will you? I've got to be up early in the morning. Some of us have jobs, you know.'

'Oh, come on . . . don't be such a spoilsport. I've got something to show you. It won't take a minute, honest. Get dressed.'

'Owen, are you mad? It's one o'clock in the morning. I've got to go to work tomorrow. What on earth are you talking about?'

'Oh, *Jesus*, Caryn. I always listen to you when you're going on about your bloody school . . . you're not the only one with plans, you know.' Owen looked at her sulkily. 'I just thought you'd be interested, that's all . . .'

'All right, all right.' Caryn felt immediately guilty. 'What is it?' she asked, more softly this time.

'Get dressed and I'll show you.'

Caryn shut the door, shaking her head. What on earth was he up to? She hurriedly pulled on a pair of jeans and a sweatshirt and fished her tennis shoes from under the bed. She opened the door again and ran down the stairs. Owen was standing in the hallway, smoking.

'Put that out,' she hissed. 'You're stinking the whole place up.'

'Car . . . you need to take a fucking chill pill,' Owen said, blowing rings into the air. Of late he'd started affecting an American accent. A bad one.

'Shhh! You'll wake everyone up!'

'Let's just get out of here. Come on. Digby's waiting downstairs.' Owen opened the front door. Caryn felt a sharp stab of fear.

'Digby? What's he doing here? What's going on, Owen?'

'Just follow me, will you? And be *quiet*.'

She followed him out to the lift, her heart thumping. She was torn between wanting to run back to her room and not wanting to appear dismissive. She had no idea what he was doing but two things were clear – one, he was more than a little tipsy and two, if Digby was involved, it would undoubtedly mean trouble.

They reached the ground floor. 'All right, Caryn?' Digby mumbled as they stepped out of the lift. She nodded curtly.

'What's *she* doing here?' she heard him hiss as Owen led the way.

'Shut up,' Owen said, glaring at him. 'I just wanna show her, all right?'

They walked quickly over to Cheney House but instead of going in the front door, they went round to the back of the building. Caryn's heart started to pound. There was an old caretaker's lodge to one side. It had been boarded up and abandoned for as long as Caryn could remember. 'What're you doing?' she hissed as Owen lifted himself over the wall and disappeared. Seconds later, she heard one of the side doors creaking open.

'Come on,' said Digby. 'Quick!'

It was too late to do anything else. She slipped into the dank, musty building, silently cursing the pair of them, her heart thudding. Owen lit a match. In the sudden yellow flare she saw them. Plants. Hundreds of plants. He lit another match and this time held it in front of him. Caryn's mouth dropped open. Dope. Row upon row of cannabis plants in their neat, black plastic containers. Thin rubber hoses ran over and under the boxes, connected to several large blue plastic tanks stacked against the wall.

'Sprinklers,' Owen said proudly. 'An' lights. We've got it all, man.'

'Yeah,' said Digby happily. 'That's about five grand's worth of shit you're lookin' at!' The two of them high-fived each other, giggling. Caryn's heart dropped to the bottom of her stomach. They were both looking at her expectantly. The match burnt out suddenly, plunging them into darkness.

'So . . . what d'you think?' came Owen's excited voice. 'You'd never guess, would you? When the plants are ready, there's about ten grand in here, Caryn. Can you imagine? Ten fucking grand! We'll be *loaded*!'

Caryn's heart gave another wrench. It had been years since she'd heard such optimism in Owen's voice. She had no idea what had persuaded him to show his latest venture to her but one thing was suddenly – painfully – clear. If she hoped to have any sort of relationship with her brother, now or ever, this was not the time to tell him what she really thought. She swallowed. 'It's . . . it's an awful lot of dope, Owen. Don't get caught, will you? Promise me you'll be careful?' she whispered.

Owen laughed. A silly, high-pitched laugh. He was stoned, as well as drunk. He cuffed her lightly on the shoulder. ''Course I'll be careful. Me 'n' Digs, we're the fucking dogs bollocks, we are!'

'Come on, we'd better scram before someone sees,' Caryn said nervously.

'Relax, will you? The windows are all boarded up – no one can see a thing.'

'Still . . . I'd . . . I'd better go. I've got to go to work in the morning.'

'Yeah, well, when this lot's sold, you won't have to do *that* any more.'

Caryn turned to peer at him. 'Why?'

''Cos we'll be *rich*, you eejit. Fuckin' *loaded*! I'll fucking *pay* for you to go to university, Car. You won't have to worry about getting a fucking scholarship! They can shove it up their arses!' He and Digby giggled.

Caryn said nothing. There was a lump in her throat. She wrapped her arms around her waist and followed them out of the darkness. Despite being desperately touched by Owen's sudden show of affection, however misguided, she had a horrible, sinking feeling in the pit of her stomach. Something was going to go wrong. Things generally did where Owen was concerned.

23

Holding her beer, her stomach taut with excitement at the feel of his arm around her waist, Nic still couldn't quite believe where she was. She'd mumbled something to Molly about meeting a few girls in town and was relieved to see she was neither worried nor interested. Her father, of course, was out. 'Fine,' she said curtly, not even looking up from her magazine.

'I'll be back late . . . probably around midnight,' Nic said and held her breath.

'Fine.' And that was it. She'd walked the short distance from the villa to the centre of town, her stomach churning with nerves. It had taken her nearly an hour to get dressed – not usually her style – but she really, really, *really* liked Will. She couldn't remember the last time anyone had looked at her with such searching interest – except for Caryn and Tory, of course, and they didn't really count. She'd thrown on and off half a dozen outfits before finally settling on a pair of jeans and a dark blue cashmere pullover. Her wedge-heeled boots with the rubber soles to prevent her from sliding around in the snow made her already long legs look even longer. Not normally the type to spend hours in front of the mirror, she'd checked herself carefully from as many angles as she could manage – it all looked good. Will obviously thought so – his whole face lit up as she walked into the bar, her hair tumbling around her face. Her heart was racing so fast she could hardly speak.

'Hang the bar,' he said, smiling into her hair as he bent to kiss her on the cheek. 'I know a hotel just round the corner that serves *glühwein* . . .' he broke off, laughing at her confused expression. 'Only joking. You look great, by the way.'

Nic let her hair fall over her face. Her whole body burned with pleasure.

'So . . . I don't want to sound too keen or anything, but can I see you tomorrow?' Will asked against her ear as he walked her slowly back down Chemin de la Morintse. 'I'm teaching in the morning, though. Can we meet for lunch again?' Nic nodded. She slipped a little on the icy pavement; his grip tightened around her waist. She took a deep, excited breath. The whole evening had an unreal quality to it.

'Yes,' she murmured. She'd had two bottles of beer followed by a tequila and her head was swimming pleasurably.

'Let's meet at Café Spitz; it's about halfway down Mont Fort.' He stopped and turned towards her. They were almost at the Country Club. She leaned back against the wall for support, veins electric and tingling. He kissed her, and the electric feeling began to spread slowly through her, carried along by a hidden, hot wetness that brought tears to her eyes. He was standing with one arm pushed against the wall and the other resting lightly on her stomach, the thumb sliding surreptitiously across the waistband of her jeans. She leaned her hips into him; he brought both hands up around her face and the kiss intensified, deepened. His fingers were hard and strong and she could feel the tension in him beginning to build. She pushed her hands underneath his jacket and up his back, her ears filled with the change in pitch of his breathing. A hand cautiously moved across her breast; sensing no resistance, he boldly slipped it under her sweater and she shivered, as much from the touch of his fingers on skin as from the cold.

Suddenly there was a blast from a car horn as three cars swung round the tight corner, their headlights picking them out in a wash of light and then plunging them back into darkness as they flashed through the gates of the club. Will lifted his head for a second as they passed, his eyes squinting against the light and the intrusion. Their red tail lights glowed in the dark. The last car screeched to a halt. They both looked up. Nic's heart almost stopped beating. The car reversed wildly, coming to stop just beside them. The rear door opened and she heard her father's voice.

'Get in.'

She didn't even have time to say anything to the astounded Will. She wrenched herself out of his arms and climbed in the open door. Her father's face was set in anger. They drove to the villa in stony silence. Nic sat beside him, her heart thumping in fear.

Nic wasn't on the ski slopes the following day, or the day after that. Will waited every day for her. Then it was Christmas and the slopes were almost empty. Will celebrated it with Mark and Tim and a couple of the French and Swiss instructors at Bar Jo's, although it was hardly a celebration. It was clear to everyone that he was sorely missing the tall, dark-haired beauty with the great legs he'd brought to the bar a few nights earlier.

'I wish I knew what was wrong,' he confided moodily to Tim, nursing his third or fourth beer of the evening.

Tim nodded, his attention on two blondes who'd just walked in. He nudged Will. No response. He looked at him in surprise. Man, he had it *bad*. 'Why don't you go round?' he asked, not taking his eye off the duo. 'You know where she lives, don't you?'

'If you'd seen the Merc he pulled up in,' Will said morosely, 'you'd think twice. You should have seen it. Plus there were two of the biggest guys I've ever seen sitting in the front. I think they were his bodyguards.'

'Bloody hell. Who is she again?'

'Dunno. She's Australian. I don't know who her father is.' Will shrugged. 'She's obviously loaded. Maybe they've left already,' he added, sounding even more morose.

'Look, you can't sit here for the rest of the season like this, mate,' Tim said, ordering another round. 'Go round tomorrow. Take a bunch of flowers or something . . . put yourself out of your misery. Give the flowers to her mum. Charm the pants off them. You're good at that. Or at least you *used* to be . . .' he grinned.

Will nodded glumly. 'Yeah, maybe.'

Which was how he found himself at ten o'clock in the morning on Boxing Day, walking up the long drive to the Country Club, an expensive bunch of dahlias in hand, sweating nervously despite the cold. He found out from the pretty receptionist that there was an English family staying at the chateau behind the golf course, but she warned him that if he didn't have an invitation to visit, it might be prudent to obtain one. Will looked at her uncertainly.

'I . . . I'm a friend of Nic's,' he said. 'The . . . er, daughter. I'm sure it'll be all right.'

She shrugged, unimpressed. 'Don't say I didn't warn you,' she said, turning back to the phones.

He left, clutching the flowers even more tightly. It was a short walk from the main clubhouse. In the wintry landscape, snow crunching underfoot, the whole place had the air of a silent film set, the elegant homes with their shuttered, pale façades staring blankly back at him as he approached. At one side of the short, circular drive were the three black cars he'd seen before; polished hourly, it seemed – not a speck of dust or a snowflake on their sleek exteriors. He walked up to the front door and pressed the bell. He could hear it echoing in the hall on the other side of the door. A few minutes later he could hear footsteps coming towards him. He swallowed nervously.

The door opened and a young girl, obviously a maid, looked at him blankly. '*Oui?*'

He coughed and began to explain that he'd come to see Mademoiselle Nic . . . he hoped it was the right house?

'Who is it?' he heard an English voice call out. A woman appeared in the doorway. 'Can I help you?' she asked frostily, sizing him up. The maid quickly disappeared.

She didn't look old enough to be Nic's mother. Will wondered who she was. 'Um, yes. I was just wondering . . . this is Nic's house, isn't it?'

'Yes, it is but she's not in,' the woman said quickly – a little *too* quickly.

'Oh. D'you know when she'll be back?' Will asked, sensing that she wanted to get rid of him as fast as possible.

'No, no . . . sorry. I'll let her know you came round,' she said, making to close the door. She hadn't even asked his name. Obstinacy began to rise in him.

'Look, I just wanted to—'

'Who the hell is it?' He heard a man's voice in the background.

The woman tried to shut the door. 'I'll tell her you came,' she hissed, 'but please just leave!'

'Molly?' Will caught a glimpse of a tanned, angry face before the door was slammed shut in his. He stood there for a second, blinking in surprise and mild embarrassment and then the door was flung open again.

'Get lost,' the man said angrily, jabbing the air in front of his face. Will took a step backwards. 'Go on, bugger off. If I catch you anywhere near this place I'll call the police, d'you understand? And if you so much as come within ten yards of her, I'll see to it that you wish you'd never been born. Do I make myself clear?' Will nodded, too terrified to speak. 'Now get lost. Go on. *Move!*'

He turned and fled. The man looked as though he wouldn't think twice about calling for back-up and Will had seen the bodyguards in the front seat. He tossed the flowers over the hedge and practically ran all the way back to the chalet. He would most definitely not be seeing Nic again.

★

Three days later, as soon as Jim left with his guests for Zurich, Nic scrambled out of the window and shinned her way down the wall. She rushed to the slopes with her heart in her mouth. She found Will at the bottom of the beginners' run, patiently coaching a group of giggling teenagers. When he saw her, he lifted his hand in a half-hearted salute and then slowly turned away. She stood there, tears springing to her eyes. He did not look around. After a few moments, she turned away and trudged disconsolately back to the villa, tears freezing on her cheeks. Her brief holiday romance was well and truly over.

24

Caryn was speechless as she listened to Nic on the first day back at school. She'd never been on holiday, let alone a skiing holiday, in her life. 'So what happened?' she whispered. The three of them were in the library.

'Nothing.'

'You didn't even say goodbye?'

Nic shook her head miserably. 'I couldn't. He wouldn't even turn around.'

'It's like a film or something,' Caryn said, impressed, despite Nic's unhappy face. 'Poor you, though,' she added quickly. Nic looked heartbroken.

'I really liked him,' Nic said plaintively. Caryn was silent. She'd never had a boyfriend before. Three snogs with Jimmy Paul, who was in her class at Featherstone's, before he'd settled on Felicity Wright; a single, forgettable grope at a school dance with Tim Knight and then Mr Humphreys' hand on her thigh. Not much to boast about.

'Haven't you ever had a boyfriend?' Nic asked her suddenly.

Caryn reddened a little. 'No,' she said in as off-hand a manner as she could manage. Nic had the grace to look embarrassed. It was one of the things she liked most about her, Caryn thought. Despite her outward toughness, Nic really cared about other people's feelings.

'I've got one,' Tory said suddenly. The other two stared at her.

'What?'

'A boyfriend. Well, sort of.' Tory shrugged.

'Who?' Caryn whispered.

'Really?' Nic said disbelievingly. 'When did *that* happen?' Around them someone said 'shush'. They lowered their voices immediately.

'His name's Jonathan. I slept with him at a party. I only found out the other day. About his name, I mean,' Tory whispered.

Caryn looked quickly at Nic. She didn't know which piece of information to be more surprised about – the fact that Tory had slept with someone or the fact that she'd done it without knowing his name. She had no idea what to say.

'Wh . . . why didn't you say something?' Nic said. 'Here I am, going on about a couple of kisses and you . . . you've *done* it? What was it like?'

'Um, it was . . . nice,' Tory said after a bit. 'Yeah, it was nice.'

It wasn't much of a description. 'So are we going to get to meet him?' Nic asked finally.

Tory looked away. She was quiet for a moment. 'Dunno,' she said, shrugging her shoulders. 'Maybe.' She pushed back her chair. 'I'm going outside for a fag. See you later?'

They both watched her go, long dark brown hair swinging as she walked. Nic turned to Caryn. 'Is she all right, d'you think?' she said carefully.

Caryn bit her lip. 'I don't know.' She forgot all about Nic's glamorous, tragic holiday as she picked up her books and the two of them made their way to English. She wondered how to help Tory. But how could you help someone if you didn't know quite what was wrong in the first place? Wasn't that what the counsellor was supposed to be finding out?

25

Caryn no longer slipped her hands under her thighs when she was nervous but that morning, she had the irrepressible urge to sit on them again. Dr Walsh was smiling at her in that expectant manner that meant she was supposed to say something. 'Th-thank you, Dr Walsh,' she stammered eventually, still too dazed to think properly. For the second time in her life, something extraordinary was being offered to her. Cambridge. A scholarship place to Cambridge to read English. What would her mother say? She felt the hot prick of tears behind her eyes. 'Can I go?' she asked, not wanting to burst into tears in front of Dr Walsh.

Dr Walsh nodded. 'Of course. We'll talk about it further, what it'll mean in terms of extra coaching for the exam and so on, but . . . well done, Caryn. This really is a tremendous opportunity for you.' Caryn let her hair fall over her face as she picked up her bag and books and fled the headmistress's study. *Cambridge*. The name rang in her ears. *Cambridge. She was going to attempt to win a place at Cambridge.* The rest of the afternoon passed in a blur. *It's a marvellous opportunity.* Dr Walsh's words ran round and round in her head. She couldn't wait to tell Alice. She sat in the bus going home that evening, trying to recall anything and everything she'd ever heard about Cambridge, her stomach twisted in a tight knot. What would Alice say?

'Cambridge?' Alice repeated, sounding, if anything, even more dazed than Caryn. 'You're joking, aren't you?'

'No, I'm not. Honestly. Dr Walsh called me in this morning. It depends on what I get in my A levels. If I get two As and a B, I'll get a place automatically but if I don't, there's a separate exam that I can sit in November and—'

'November? *Another* term?' Alice said anxiously.

'Yes, but the board'll pay,' Caryn said quickly. 'You wouldn't have to—'

'Oh, Caryn, love,' Alice said, her face lighting up. Caryn thought her heart would burst. At that moment, everything was worth it – the Saturday jobs, putting up with the snobbish girls and their hurtful remarks, never bringing any friends home – everything seemed worth it just to see the look on her mother's face. 'I'm just so *proud* of you! I can't believe it. I just can't believe it!' Alice laughed giddily. 'Just wait until bloody Margaret Fields hears this!' She put her hands to her face. 'D'you think . . .' she hesitated, the smile suddenly dropping from her face. 'D'you think I should tell *him*?'

'Who?'

'Your granddad. Oh, it'd stick in his throat! God, I'd give anything to see his face!'

Caryn looked at her in surprise. 'I haven't got in yet, Mum,' she said hesitantly. 'Maybe wait a bit? I might not get in, you know.'

'You will, darling. I just know you will,' Alice said simply. 'You can do anything you put your mind to, Caryn. That's the way you've always been. Always. Right from the start.'

The news went round the school in a flash. Caryn Middleton, NOCD, was being put forward for a place at Cambridge. She found the attention both excruciating and bewildering. Teachers, some of whom she'd never even seen before, stopped her in the corridor and offered their congratulations. She mumbled her thanks each time, genuinely puzzled by the enormity of the response. She hadn't even sat her exams yet! She might fail!

'Rubbish,' Tory said loftily, as though she were on the examinations board herself. 'You won't fail. You can't.'

'You've never failed anything in your life,' Nic said loyally. Inside, Caryn squirmed. She hated being the centre of attention.

'Don't say that,' she implored. 'Please!'

'Why not? It's true, isn't it?' Nic said, surprised. She studied Caryn's embarrassed face. Though she'd never have admitted it, she was just the teeniest bit jealous. She longed to have strangers come up to her in the corridors and say 'well done' for something she'd achieved on her own without her father's help or interference. How gratifying it must be to hear your name in the morning assembly hall – and not in connection with anything RhoMine might or might not have done. It would never happen to her, she thought glumly. She was an average student with what everyone else assumed was an extraordinary background. Unbelievable wealth, fabulous homes around the world and a swashbuckling, glamorous father, even if he did seem to cross the line of legality with impunity. She didn't seem able to explain that it wasn't like that at all. Living with Jim Harte was like living on top of a smouldering volcano, prone to eruption at the slightest provocation yet full of the kind of fiery dynamism that made everything and everyone else look tame by comparison. The worst thing about her father wasn't his gargantuan ego or his blatant disregard for the conventions that others seemed to live and die by – no, the worst thing about being Jim Harte's daughter was that it seemed to matter more to everyone else than it did to him. He didn't seem to care who or what she was so long as she stayed well below his irritability radar. Disregard, she'd discovered, was the worst punishment of all. And whatever else anyone had ever said about Caryn Middleton, *that* was no longer her fate. No wonder Nic was envious. Caryn had the one thing she longed for but was sure she would never have. Respect.

Tory listened to the two of them with half an ear. She was pleased for Caryn and especially pleased that she seemed so happy about it, but Tory honestly couldn't understand what was so great about having the rest of your life planned out for you before it had even begun. She thought back to the uncomfortable conversation – as most of them were – between her and her parents a couple of days earlier.

'Now, how about your UCCA forms,' he'd asked cheerfully. 'We'll need to start filling them in soon.'

'My UCCA forms?' Tory said, alarmed.

'Yes, they'll be due in fairly soon. What're you thinking of studying? We thought English or history might be good choices, given—'

'I'm not sure yet,' Tory said, bending her head to her plate. 'I haven't thought about it.'

'But what are you waiting for?' her father asked, irritation beginning to creep into his voice.

Tory put down her knife and fork carefully. 'Nothing. I'm not waiting for anything. I just don't want to think about it yet, that's all.'

'Tory, please don't take that tone of voice,' her mother said, getting up from the table to fetch dessert. She came back and put the pudding down heavily. 'We're just concerned, that's all.'

'But what's there to be concerned about? I don't understand it. It's my decision. I just want to take my time about it. What's the bloody rush?'

In retrospect, perhaps swearing was the wrong way to go about it. Within seconds, the discussion had escalated into an argument which ended, as such arguments tended to do, with her mother's tears, her father's set, stony expression and Tory's escape up to her room where she sat on the window sill, smoking, waiting for the pain and anger in her chest to die down.

Now, listening to Caryn talk about Cambridge, she was even more acutely aware of her own lack of ambition. She didn't really care what she did as long as it involved leaving Hortensia Road, St Augustine's and the prying eyes of her parents, teachers, old friends, paid counsellors and Jonathan, the boy she'd slept with. At first he just wouldn't leave her alone. He'd called her incessantly for almost three months. Every time the phone rang she'd begged her mother to say she was out. She didn't want to see him again. It wasn't that she was being horrible or mean to him or any of the things Jenny accused her of – no, it wasn't that. She didn't know how to explain it. Whatever it was that they'd shared that night, that was it. It was enough for her. She didn't want any more. She didn't want to hold hands with him and walk down the street or listen to his stories about his family and his friends, forcing herself to laugh at the appropriate moment or drop her face when he did. She didn't want to wait by the phone for hours, hoping he'd call, or wonder where he was when he didn't. No, she didn't want any of that. She'd seen it all with Susie and Rob. Perfect as they were, there was always something to fight over, row about . . . the endless, monotonous cycle of peace, argument, reconciliation, kiss-and-make-up . . . it was *boring*. It took too much effort and she had precious little to waste. No one seemed to understand quite how much effort it took just to get through the day; to finish her lessons, avoid her parents' searching eyes, not think about the past. Once she was done with that, there just wasn't much left over. That was why she liked Caryn and Nic so much. They just let her *be*. They weren't constantly trying to make her over into the image of something – or someone – that they carried in their heads. They were content with her as she was. Everyone else wanted her to be Susie. Or close enough. Even, she suspected, Jonathan. Jenny had told her he'd had the biggest crush on Susie for ages. It certainly wasn't what she needed to hear. It just made her want to see him even less.

No, she wanted to be rid of them all. Everyone. Except Caryn and Nic, of course. That was the tricky part. How would she manage her escape without losing them as well?

26

Panic, Estelle discovered, was an emotion one could learn to live with. She'd grown used to its banked-down, bubbling presence. She realised that no matter how bored or restless she'd been in Harare, London was a whole different universe. Growing up in Arcadia was absolutely no practice at all. In Arcadia, believe it or not, she'd been *spoilt*. Everyone knew her; in the tight little confines of the community in which she'd been raised, she was safe. Poor, maybe, but safe. In London, things were different. She was only as safe as the pile of notes in her bag and it was almost gone. When she'd first arrived in Ladbroke Grove and looked round the small room with its narrow little bed and not much else, she was filled with anger, not panic. This wasn't what she'd planned.

She looked at her purse. It was pointless opening it – she knew exactly how much was left. She was broke. Stony flat broke. She sat on the edge of the bed and lit a cigarette. Come *on*, she admonished herself severely. She had to get her shit together otherwise she'd be using the return half of her ticket – and there was no fucking way she was doing *that*. Such was her determination to get out of Arcadia that she'd have bought herself a one-way ticket if the conditions of her visa hadn't said otherwise. She tossed the half-smoked stub out of the window and looked at herself in the mirror. She'd lost weight since coming to London; she was longer, leaner, older. Her cheekbones stood out, giving her face a new maturity. The last traces of puppy fat were gone – now she was properly grown-up. Grown-up and *desperate*. She winced. It wasn't what she'd planned.

Rebecca and Amanda were arguing half an hour later when she walked into the kitchen. She couldn't stand being alone any longer. Even half a dozen words exchanged whilst she made herself a cup of tea would do.

'She's not,' Rebecca said, looking up in surprise as Estelle walked in. 'Rubbish. There's no way—'

'She *is*, I'm telling you,' Amanda said primly. 'How else would she be able to afford all those things? D'you see the clothes she wears? And the car that was parked outside last night? I know she is; I just know it.'

Estelle couldn't help herself. 'Who're you talking about?' she asked, her curiosity piqued.

Rebecca rolled her eyes. 'The girl who's just moved in upstairs – you know, the top flat. Dunno what her name is. Mandy thinks she's a . . . a—'

'Prostitute,' Amanda said, pursing her lips disapprovingly. ' 'Course she is.'

'A prostitute?' Estelle murmured. She stirred her cup. 'How d'you know?'

'She doesn't,' Rebecca giggled. 'She's making it up!'

'I'm not! I'm telling you. I bumped into her on my way in last night – she was wearing a mink coat and—'

'Oh, Mandy, wearing a mink coat doesn't automatically make you a prostitute,' Rebecca laughed. 'You've got too much imagination, that's your problem.'

Estelle had stopped listening. She had no idea if Amanda's assumptions about their neighbour were correct but she didn't really care. She had less than a hundred pounds left in her wallet. She carefully spooned some sugar into her tea and left the kitchen. As reluctant as she was to go back to that sort of life, there was no other option. It was time to go back to what she knew how to do. So much for coming to London to become rich and famous.

27

Tory held the envelope between her fingers, loosely turning it over. Once, twice, three times . . . she stared down at her hands. All she had to do was insert a finger under the flap and open it – but she couldn't. She was aware of the slow, steady drumbeat of her heart and the sound of children playing across the road. In a few minutes, once she'd plucked up the courage to open it, she'd know. They'd *all* know. Victoria Spiller had failed her A levels. Or damned near as close as. Finally, everyone would know what Tory had known all along – that she wasn't Susie. Wouldn't ever be. She took a deep breath, slid her finger under the flap and drew out the thin white slip.

Her mother looked up anxiously as soon as she entered the room. Her father was standing by the sideboard, trying not to follow his wife's lead. He busied himself with something – screwing and unscrewing the top of the whisky bottle, she noticed – until Tory cleared her throat, and spoke. 'One D and two Es,' she said quickly, not looking at either of them. There was a moment's stunned silence. Her mother's hand went to her throat.

'A D and two Es?' she repeated. The disappointment in her voice was palpable.

'Yeah.' Tory's voice was as neutral as she dared make it.

'Well, it's not *quite* as good as we'd hoped,' her father began, trying – and failing – to inject a more positive tone into his voice. 'But it's a pass, isn't it? That's the main thing.'

'Dad, it's *barely* a pass,' Tory said, shamed by his false heartiness. To her horror, she felt tears begin to well up in her eyes. She looked away, blinking furiously. Out of the corner of her eye she saw her father put out a hand to cover her mother's where it lay resting slackly on the gleaming surface of the table. He patted it gently. It was a classic gesture. She turned and walked out of the room. Neither asked her where she was going. That, too, was classic. She went back up the stairs to her room, changed into a pair of jeans and threw on a jacket and quietly left the house.

She emerged into the sunlight out of the banked-up heat of the Underground at King's Cross. It was a hot summer's day; she shrugged off her jacket and tied it around her waist. There was a flower stand just outside the station, bursting with colour. She bought a small bunch of purple and red peonies and watched as the girl deftly tied them with a purple ribbon. It hung loosely from her hand as she walked up St Pancras Way, past the gas works until she came to the nature reserve that ran alongside the canal. She pushed open the gate and walked up the towpath. A family of ducks floated past; the surface of the water was dark and still and glassy. She walked along until she came to a wooden bench and sat down. The towpath was almost deserted; she could hear a dog barking somewhere in the distance. Some- one was coming towards her on a bicycle; the image wavered and then broke up as he sailed past. She sat quite still for a few moments, not doing anything, not thinking. The air was heavy with the sound of wasps and the occasional, high-pitched drone of a bee. The flowers lay beside her, wilting a little in the heat. After a few minutes, she got up and walked over to where the wall of the buildings behind the reserve began. She knelt down, brushing away the soil and laid the peonies gently against the wall. That was where the police said it had happened. Right there. He'd pinned her against the wall – it was a detail that shouldn't have been let out but it had, somehow. Tory didn't even remember who'd said it – the police? Three of them had come to the house that night, two men and a young police-woman whose face was pinched with anguish. Tory had seen her from the top of the stairs before her dad roared at her to go back to bed. Impossible, of course. She'd known as soon as they walked into the sitting room that something awful had hap-pened – only she couldn't have said then just how awful it would turn out to be.

She rocked back on her heels and looked around her. An elderly woman with a small, shaggy-haired dog was walking towards her, a sympathetic smile already fixed on her face. Tory had seen her before – several times, in fact. Back then, right after it had happened, she'd come almost every day to lay a flower, touch the earth, think of her sister's last moments. It was also where she'd last seen Rob, Susie's boyfriend. She'd walked up the path one evening, perhaps three or four weeks after the funeral, and seen him standing there, looking out over the water, his hands thrust in his pockets. She'd stopped and looked away, not sure what to say. She hadn't seen or spoken to him since the funeral, when he stood silently beside his mother, his face carefully composed, like a painting, as though it might crack. Tory recognised the look – she, too, wore it. After a few minutes, he'd turned and walked off in the other direction and that was that. She'd never seen him again. What was he doing now? she wondered. She'd heard from her mother that he'd left Britain . . . she'd bumped into *his* mother somewhere, in town. Vietnam? Thailand? Somewhere like that. Well, he was getting on with his life, just as she had to. *I miss you, Suze,* she whispered, touching the patch of earth where she'd laid the flowers. *I wish you were still here.*

The woman with the dog was standing by the water's edge, looking at her. She got to her feet, dusted her knees and turned away. Her cheeks were wet; the last thing she wanted to face was some stranger's pitying gaze. She hurried off, not looking back. Maybe it was time for her, too, to leave?

28

She ought to take the little white slip of paper downstairs to her mother who was sitting at the kitchen table, smoking one cigarette after the other, waiting for Caryn to break the news. She'd glanced at her nervously as soon as the envelope had come flying through the letterbox. Caryn took it without a word and ran upstairs to her room. She looked at the slip again. She *ought* to go downstairs and put Alice out of her anxious misery, but she didn't. She sat on the edge of her bed, smoothing it out, running her fingers across the crinkled surface, staring at the four little letters that were the culmination of everything she'd worked for over the past two years – four little letters that were about to change her life. A. Not one, but four. *English: A; French: A; History: A; Art: A.*

There would be no coming back to St Augustine's for that extra term. No cramming for the Oxbridge exam in November. No need for any other exam, in fact. She was in. She'd done it. Her life was about to change. She buried her face in her hands, knocking the little bedside clock off the table, clumsy with emotion. In three months' time, she would be 'going up' to Cambridge. She had only the foggiest idea of what it actually meant. She'd made only one trip to Magdalene College for her interview, going by train with Dr Fox at her side, and she'd had difficulty believing that the future everyone talked about in such reverential tones could, if she worked hard enough, actually be hers for the taking. A room in the beautiful old red-brick building could actually be *hers*. Together with some of the nervous young men and women she'd seen that day, she would walk around the immaculate grass quadrangle on her way to lectures . . . the reading list they'd shown her would be pinned to her wall; the row of books on the shelf above the bed would be hers. She stopped herself, almost unable to take it all in. She, Caryn Middleton, had done it. Surpassed everyone's expectations, including her own. She wiped her cheeks slowly.

In the kitchen downstairs, she could hear Alice pacing nervously up and down. She got to her feet. There was a sudden glorious lightness about her movements, as if something had been lifted from her, freeing her. As she descended the stairs, the feeling intensified. She saw in Alice's face the same tremulous expression – had she? Was she . . . ? She nodded, not trusting herself to speak. The moment caught and held; they stared at each other, no sound in the kitchen other than the slow, measured ticking of the clock above the dresser and the rise and fall of Alice's chest. She stubbed her cigarette out in the sink and when she turned back, Caryn saw there were tears in her eyes.

Alone in her room, alone in the house, alone with the same little white slip of paper, Nic looked at it again and again. She'd passed. Probably not as well as either Caryn or Tory, but she'd passed. That was the main thing. The other thing – the thing she'd told no one about, not even her two best friends – was safe, assured. Unbeknown to anyone except one or two members of staff at St Augustine's, she'd applied to UCL at the very last minute to read English. With an A and two Bs, she was in. And there was no one to tell. She leaned back against the headboard, her mind racing. She wasn't even sure how it had come about; why she'd decided, two days before the deadline for applicants expired, to walk up the stairs to the library, turn left at the top and tap on the door of the careers counsellor. June Whitby listened to her carefully, pushed the forms across the desk and made no comment as Nic filled them out. A month later, she'd sat across the desk from the admissions tutor in a sunny room off Torrington Place and answered their questions as truthfully as she could. In due course, a letter arrived for her. 'Dear Ms Harte, we are pleased to inform you that you have been offered a place to read English at UCL conditional upon . . .' She'd buried the letter at the bottom of one of her drawers and said nothing. Not to anyone. And now the final piece in the jigsaw had slotted neatly into place and she was in. Now what?

The house was quiet. A shaft of sunlight sharpened slowly on the carpet at the foot of the bed. Midsummer in London; midwinter in Harare. She was due to fly back in a few days' time, although nothing had been said about what she might do once she got there. In fact, aside from the occasional, muttered conversation in passing when her father and Molly were in town, nothing much had been said about anything. It was hard to fathom. Jim Harte was the sort of man who absolutely thrived on control – of everything. His businesses, his properties, his sons, his wife . . . everyone, in fact, except Nic. He prided himself on his meticulous attention to detail: *no one will ever do anything for you as well as you'll do it for yourself.* It was a mantra he seemed to live by and yet he seemed unable to pay her anything more than the most perfunctory attention – she was fed, clothed, housed and schooled . . . and that was it. The sum total of his parenting. So long as she stayed out of trouble and didn't impinge on his consciousness, everything was fine. But Nic wanted more. She saw what it was like for others to be bathed in the full light of Jim Harte's gaze. She saw how hard Shaun and Patrick worked to please him, make him proud. She noticed the subtle change in pitch whenever he entered a room; there was a space around Jim Harte that those in his orbit constantly sought to fill. No one was immune – even little Jessica, all of six years old, fell under his spell. It was a mark of his special attention to detail that he noticed their devotion, thrived on it, occasionally letting slip the tiny gestures of unexpected affection that kept everyone around him on their toes, hungry for more. And there was no one hungrier than Nic.

She heard the front door open and close downstairs, then a few seconds later, the static buzz of the kitchen radio; Mrs Jenkins had arrived to cook the evening meal. She sighed. In a few minutes she would wash her face, brush her hair and go downstairs, clutching the little white slip in her hands. She would slide onto one of the breakfast stools, push the slip across the table and watch Mrs Jenkins' face. As always, it would be Mrs Jenkins who would offer a few words of congratulation, smile at her, perhaps even open a bottle of wine . . . in the absence of anyone else, it was Mrs Jenkins to whom she turned. But it wasn't the same. Anne Jenkins had her own children to care for, worry about, make a fuss over. At times like these, the desire for Jim's approval threatened to overwhelm her. A dangerous longing. But Nic was nothing if not practical. It was a desire she kept firmly in check. After all, she reasoned, there was very little point in hankering after something you were never likely to get. Still, wouldn't it be lovely – just once – to be the centre of his attention for reasons other than annoyance? Wouldn't it be magical to have the full weight of his steely blue eyes turned on her in pride? She flicked away the blasted tear that had suddenly spilled out of the corner of her eye and wiped her cheeks angrily. Jeez, what was the point in crying? The source of her anxiety was six thousand miles away and if there was one thing she could count on with absolute certainty, it was that *he* certainly wouldn't be thinking about *her*.

Caryn looked at Tory and then back at Nic again. 'But why didn't you *tell* us?' she asked, aware that her voice sounded plaintive, even to her own ears.

Nic shrugged. Her face was unusually high in colour. 'Dunno. It . . . it just sort of came to me,' she said lamely.

'Came to you?' Caryn repeated. 'Here I am, banging on and on about Cambridge for *months* on end, and you never said a word?'

'Look, I wasn't sure I'd get in. Anyway, it's done. We're both in and *you* . . .' Nic turned to Tory, eager to deflect their attention, 'when are you off again?'

'Couple of weeks,' Tory said nonchalantly. She lit a cigarette. 'They're not exactly thrilled about it, but—'

'A writer?' Nic pulled a face, impressed. 'What sort of books does he write?'

'I'm not sure,' Tory said, blowing out a cloud of smoke. 'He's a professor of some sort. Philosophy. My dad knows his wife.'

'It sounds so . . . grown-up,' Caryn said, a touch of envy in her voice. 'A flat of your own in Paris!'

Tory shrugged. 'I've never met either of them. They could turn out to be complete wankers.' She grinned suddenly. 'Who knows?' She stubbed out her cigarette and propped her face in her hands. 'The important thing is that it's away from here, that's all. I don't think I can bear another month with my parents. I don't think they'll ever get over it – me not going to university. It's the end of the world, for them.'

'But you might, later on, I mean,' Caryn said anxiously. 'When you come back.'

Tory shook her head firmly. 'You sound just like Foxy. I won't. That's the whole point. I don't want to spend three years studying something just because my parents want me to. I don't *care* what they want.'

'But what about your future?' Caryn said timidly. 'What sort of future'll you have if—'

'My own.' Tory's voice was quiet. She looked away. 'That's the whole point, don't you see?'

The air was pulsing softly with heat. Caryn's hair was a heavy coil around her neck. She lifted it and felt the damp, cool air against her skin. Tory was right. Just as going up to Cambridge meant everything to her and getting into UCL meant the world to Nic, for Tory, doing things her own way *was* the right thing to do. She took a long, ice-cold sip of her drink. 'Let's make a promise,' she said suddenly, looking at them both, her eyes shining. 'What's today's date?'

'August fourteenth,' Nic said, looking at her watch.

'Every year,' Caryn said, reaching across the table and

grabbing both of them by the hand. 'On August the fourteenth every year – doesn't matter where we are – let's meet. I couldn't bear it if we all just went our separate ways, if I didn't see you again.'

' 'Course we'll see each other,' Nic said, suddenly blinking rapidly. 'We'll always be friends. Always.'

'Promise?' Caryn looked at them both.

'Promise.'

'Promise.'

PART TWO

29

As soon as the hammering began, Caryn knew exactly who it was, and worse, why. 'Police! Open up!' The shouts shattered the early-morning calm. She flew out of bed, grabbed her dressing gown from the back of the door and ran downstairs. Brian was already up; she could hear him crying. Alice had taken two sleeping tablets the night before – nothing would wake her. Caryn stumbled to the front door, groping for the light. She opened the door a crack. There were four uniformed officers and a man in a dark grey overcoat standing outside. One of them held up a badge. Caryn's heart fell straight to the ground. She'd seen enough police dramas to know what happened next. Across from Baberton she could see people opening their curtains to see what the hell was going on.

'Special Branch. Owen Middleton's house, is it?' the man in the trenchcoat asked. Caryn nodded and held the door wide open. She stood aside as the four of them trooped in. She could hear Brian's wails intensify. Owen would no doubt be up. It was lucky they were on the eighth floor, she thought to herself as one of the policemen said something into his walkie-talkie, otherwise Owen might well have jumped out of the window. 'Is he in?' the policeman asked.

Caryn nodded dumbly. 'Can I . . . can I just get my little brother?' she asked. 'I'll take him into my room. I don't want him to see . . .'

'That's fine, love,' the same officer said, not unkindly.

Caryn's eyes filled with tears. She ran up the stairs and tapped on Owen's door. He opened it, unable to meet her worried gaze. He was already dressed. She grasped Brian's hand as he wailed in fear, and hurried into her own room with him. 'Stay here,' she whispered, tucking the duvet in around him. 'I'll be back in a minute.'

'Where's Owen going?' Brian wailed. 'Is it the police?'

Caryn's heart contracted. 'He's just going to help them find something,' she whispered soothingly. 'He'll be back before you know it. Stay here, all right?'

Brian nodded, still sobbing under the duvet. Caryn took several deep breaths, steadying herself. Then she closed the door behind her and went downstairs.

It was all over in minutes. There was none of the drama of the TV shows. It was all quite mundane, really. Owen stood with his legs slightly apart, hands held behind his back, waiting for the cuffs. Caryn stood at the foot of the stairs and felt an enormous lump rise in her throat. Where had Owen learned all that? How to stand, legs slightly akimbo, patiently awaiting the cuffs, his head lowered? His whole body emanated defeat. Almost without a word, the five of them disappeared. She could hear doors closing all the way down their corridor. Just another arrest. Something to gossip about in the morning, perhaps, but no real cause for alarm. She sank down on to the stairs. Her mother still hadn't woken up. Her heart was slowly sinking to the pit of her stomach. She was due to go up to Cambridge in six weeks. If Owen didn't come home, she wouldn't be going. It was as simple as that.

Dr Fox stared at Caryn. She still couldn't believe it. The girl had come in that morning to say that she wouldn't be able to take up her place at Cambridge. *A family problem.* What sort of a family problem? She'd listened, unable to stop her jaw dropping, as Caryn explained. Well, there it was in front of her, in all its sordid ugliness. Older brother in jail, mother unable to cope and social services threatening to place the youngest child in a foster home. Yes, that certainly constituted a family problem in Dr Fox's book and the saddest thing was, there wasn't a damn thing anyone could do about it. She sighed, close to tears herself. No matter how hard they tried with the scholarship girls, it remained an unalterable fact – it seldom worked. Desperately sad, but true. Caryn Middleton had been one of their brightest hopes; the sort of student you were able to point to at staff meetings with justifiable pride. The sort of student who made everyone feel good, especially the board of governors. They loved a successful rags-to-riches story, just like everyone else. Each year they spent a considerable amount of money trying to persuade everyone around them that they weren't just catering to the elite, that they had a strong sense of duty to help those less fortunate, and so on. In the race to appear egalitarian, students like Caryn Middleton were a rare and valuable asset. Universities like Oxford and Cambridge were particularly indebted to schools like St Augustine's, especially now that the pressure was on them to accept more students from state schools. Oh, dear. What a bloody shame. She looked at Caryn again. The girl was doing her level best to appear composed. She certainly wasn't the type to allow anyone to feel sorry for her, but dammit, she *did*. She felt *terribly* sorry for Caryn. 'This really is most unfortunate,' she said finally, wincing at her own understatement. 'Dreadfully unfortunate.'

Caryn nodded. 'I'm really sorry to let everyone down like this,' she began simply.

Dr Fox put up her hand, interrupting her. 'Don't worry about everyone else, Caryn. It's you I'm concerned about. Do you think . . . might you be able to go up next year? Take a year off? Many of the girls do, these days. A gap year . . . it might be . . .' She stopped. The notion of someone like Caryn taking a gap year to trek around Patagonia was about as unlikely as her taking up croquet.

Caryn spared her the embarrassment. 'That might be an idea,' she said, desperately trying to sound matter-of-fact. 'I'll . . . I'll let you know how things are.' She got to her feet. Dr Fox saw that the girl had the good manners to sense that the short meeting ought to be drawn quickly to a close. She was right. There really wasn't much to say. Yes, it was unthinkable that the younger brother should be left in the care of a mother who sounded so unstable, and even more unthinkable that the boy should be taken into care. The hopelessness of the situation was overwhelming. She watched as Caryn walked quickly to the door. 'Um, Dr Fox . . .' Caryn said suddenly, just before she reached the door. 'I was just wondering . . . I'll need to find a job quite quickly. I was hoping you or Miss Lowe would write me a reference.'

'Of course I will, Caryn,' Dr Fox said, relieved to have something practical to do. 'Absolutely. I'd be very happy to. Least I can do.'

And that was that. The door closed behind her. Another scholarship pupil gone, with dreams unfulfilled. Four straight A grades and all that hard, hard graft gone to waste. What a sad, bloody waste.

Caryn walked quickly down the corridor, ignoring the questioning looks of the administrative staff. She was crying; she could feel the tears slide hot and silky down her cheeks. She pushed open the doors and walked across the lawn. In all likelihood it was the last time she would come to St Augustine's. She'd done the maths. It was eleven days since the police had come round; nine days since Alice had been admitted to the Homerton after her 'accidental' overdose and three since she'd been back at home; a week since the two women from social services had come to assess the situation and two days since they'd come back and said Brian ought to be placed in care. At breakfast, she'd looked at Brian carefully spearing Hula Hoops in tomato sauce – his *breakfast!* – and he'd smiled at her through a mouthful of rings. Right there and then the decision was made for her. How could she even *think* of leaving? For almost all of Brian's life, she'd been the one to feed him, clothe him, bathe him, read him to sleep at night. He wasn't a baby but it didn't mean he needed her any less. She'd been so caught up in the excitement of going up to Cambridge that she hadn't really stopped to think about what leaving would mean for him *or* for her. What would she be abandoning him to? In a few years' time he'd be out on the streets in the evenings, just like Owen, hanging around with losers like Digby, waiting for trouble to find him. In another three or four he'd be headed for Penton-ville – which was exactly where Owen was headed. Three years for possession with intent to sell; living on the estate, Caryn knew the score. Out in two for good behaviour, not that *that* was a likely outcome. Losing one brother was bad enough, but she couldn't afford to lose two. She realised she no longer even thought about Cameron; she had no idea where he was. She wiped her cheeks, squared her shoulders and walked quickly to the Tube. No use looking back on what might have been, she told herself sternly. That would just make it worse.

Fortunately, the flat was silent when she got home. Brian was out playing and Alice was still out cold. She ran quickly upstairs and flung herself on her bed. There, and only there, huddled in the familiar scent of her pillows, surrounded by books she would no longer open, did she give in to the pain.

That evening, her eyes still swollen from the storm of weeping that had overtaken her, she made supper for her and Brian. If he noticed, he didn't say anything. 'Can I have some more?' he asked her, holding out a licked-clean plate. Caryn had to smile.

'You know you're not supposed to do that,' she said, taking the plate from him. 'You're not a dishwasher.'

'No, I'm a *plate* washer,' Brian announced, pleased at his own wit. He grinned at her. Caryn spooned some more pasta and sauce on to his plate and set it down in front of him. 'I'm *hungry.*'

'What did you have for lunch?' she asked, fearing his answer before it came. Alice had probably forgotten to make him any.

'Nuffink,' Brian said matter-of-factly. 'Mum was sleeping.'

She bit her lip and looked away. When Owen was here, at least he'd made sure Brian ate more or less regular meals whilst she was at school. Now that he was gone, on those days when Alice barely surfaced from her room, there was no one to check if he'd had something to eat, no one to ask if he wanted to go out and play. She looked out of the kitchen window at the vandalised face of Cheney House opposite. Yes, she wanted to leave Milton Gardens, but not like this. She couldn't turn her back on the people she loved most in the world. Going to university wasn't the only way to get on in the world – hard work, a good attitude, being in the right place at the right time . . . those were also legitimate ways to succeed. In the *real* world – not the fairytale world of Nic and Tory and the girls at St Augustine's like them – people made their own luck. Helping someone else, she suddenly realised, was sometimes more rewarding than helping oneself. She wanted something else for Brian, something more than Owen had been given.

'I'm *full*,' Brian announced, interrupting her thoughts.

'Good. You can watch telly for ten minutes, no more,' Caryn said automatically, pouring washing-up liquid into the bowl. 'Ten minutes, all right?'

'OK.' Brian gave an exaggerated sigh as he slid off his chair. She looked at him and couldn't help but smile. Painful as it was, she'd done the right thing, hadn't she?

30

Clutching the address and with her suitcase banging awkwardly against her legs, Tory got out at Odéon, just as her father had instructed. She crossed the street and walked down Rue Saint Sulpice, turned left on to Rue Bonaparte and there . . . she squinted at the street name . . . yes, there it was – Rue de Mézières. She gulped. Number seventeen, rue de Mézières, was an imposing, pale stone building with the intricate wrought-iron balconies, tall, elegant shutters and the closed-off, wary look of the very, very wealthy – she'd been in Paris all of an hour and it was already clear what sort of company she was in. She struggled to remember what her father had told her about Inès de Courcy and her husband, Thierry. She knew they'd met at a conference fifteen years or so earlier and that an unlikely friendship had been struck up between the glamorous Parisian academic and her father, the slightly dishevelled English professor. They'd stayed in touch over the years; Thierry was Inès' second husband; Tory dimly remembered her parents going to Paris for their wedding. For Susie's funeral, she'd sent the most enormous bunch of scented white lilies; she could remember them sitting in their stiff, clear cellophane wrapping on top of the piano. Later, her mother had laid them to rest on the coffin. Tory stopped her thoughts from going any further down that route. She was here, at Inès' home in Paris. Now it would be her home for the next few months. That was all that mattered.

She still couldn't believe she'd done it. Found a job, somewhere to live, found a way to get out of the stifling atmosphere of disappointment that permeated every square inch of 34 Hortensia Road. Although, truth be told, it was mostly her father's idea – she'd announced at breakfast one morning that she was thinking of moving out and her alarmed parents had immediately sprung into action. Within a week, it was all sorted out. Thierry de Courcy's new book was coming out in English; he needed someone to type up the translator's notes – Tory could type (more or less) and file, which was mainly what the job seemed to consist of, so why not? Tory accepted the proposition with alacrity.

She pressed the bell. Her arms ached from lugging her suitcase around. The journey had taken practically the whole day. Her father had driven her to Heathrow that afternoon, full of advice about Paris and things to do and see, which she'd listened to with half an ear. She couldn't see much beyond getting away from London. She rang the bell again. The lovely, pale green shutters stared blankly down at her. The sound of the traffic on the Boulevard St Germain, a few streets away, was filtered, like the late afternoon sunlight coming down through the manicured trees. A bird sang somewhere above her head; she heard the raspy stutter of a motorcycle accelerating up the road. It was extraordinarily peaceful.

'*Oui*?' a voice rang out imperiously from the small speaker set into the wall.

Tory jumped. 'Ma . . . Madame de Courcy?' she asked in her best French accent.

'*Entrez, s'il vous plaît.*' The buzzer sounded. She pushed open the heavy wooden door and stepped into a small, perfectly ordered courtyard of large terracotta pots full of flowering plants and neatly trimmed young trees. She looked up; the building rose dizzyingly around her on all four sides.– surely it wasn't one house? There was another, inner door to one side; as she approached, it clicked open. A graceful, curving staircase led away from the courtyard. She dragged her case up the last flight of stairs and stopped in front of the partially open door, not sure if she should enter. She could just see a gleaming wooden parquet floor and the edge of a richly patterned oriental rug and then the door was flung wide open. A handsome man with dark hair silvering at the temples looked down at her. He was very tall. Not many people peered down at her.

'*Edith? Veuillez prendre la valise de M'selle Spiller, s'il vous plaît,*' he said, speaking to a uniformed maid standing behind him. 'Victoria, I presume? You should have phoned us,' he said in good, if heavily accented English. 'We'd have sent a car to pick you up.' His tone was abrupt, his voice quiet. Tory was rather taken aback. It sounded almost like a reprimand.

'Well, I . . . I didn't want to impose,' she said quickly, surrendering her suitcase. 'It's not far, anyway. The Métro was perfectly—'

'Yes, well . . . *entrez,*' he interrupted her, holding open the door. 'I am Thierry de Courcy,' he said, a touch pompously. 'Inès isn't in at the moment. Edith will show you to your apartment. Dinner is at eight prompt. We dress formally.'

Tory stared at him. She opened her mouth to reply but couldn't think of a single thing to say. Thierry de Courcy nodded curtly at her and disappeared.

She followed Edith up two flights of stairs to her 'apartment'. It wasn't a slip of the tongue, she saw as soon as she opened the door. It really *was* an apartment. Small, perfectly formed with its own tiny kitchenette, bathroom, living room and bedroom. She gulped. Her father had said the de Courcys were wealthy but she hadn't quite expected *this*. Edith put her suitcase down and disappeared. Tory walked into the bedroom, still dumbstruck, and sat down on the bed. *This* was to be her home for the next few months, perhaps even longer. A small thrill of excitement mixed with relief ran through her. She got up and opened one set of French doors that led to a tiny balcony outside. The pungent smell of bitumen floated up from the streets, which were baking in the late August sun. In a week, her father had said, Inès and her husband would depart for their second home in Biarritz, leaving Tory alone to get on with work and settle in whilst they were gone. She lit a cigarette, leaning against the wrought-iron balustrade, and watched the clouds drifting past in an endlessly blue sky. The sound of car horns and the accelerating buzz of motorcycles came and went. It was the first evening of the first day of the rest of her life. It felt good.

At a quarter to eight, mindful of Thierry de Courcy's edict, Tory checked her reflection one last time and sighed. She'd spent half an hour going through her rather workaday wardrobe wondering what to wear. It simply hadn't occurred to her that she might be expected to eat with them, or dress up for dinner. She looked at the pile of clothes on the bed. Six pairs of jeans, a dozen T-shirts, a few cotton sundresses that would hardly qualify as 'formal' – there was nothing in her wardrobe that seemed even remotely suitable. She'd chosen the simplest pale yellow and white flowered dress, put a white cardigan around her shoulders and slid her feet into the new white plimsolls that Nic said made her look very French. It would have to do, she thought to herself, switching off the light. She was here to work. So long as she did that, who *cared* what she wore to dinner?

She ran down the stairs and knocked on the door. It was opened immediately by Edith, who did little to conceal her surprise at Tory's casual outfit. She looked her up and down without saying a word, and then turned and showed her through to the dining room. As soon as they entered the room with its high ceilings, immaculate furniture and equally immaculate guests, Tory's heart sank. There were eight or ten people standing around the gleaming, beautifully laid table. The women were marvellously glamorous in the way only French women could be – stick-thin, not a hair out of place with tanned, cared-for skin and hyper-fashionable, sleek haircuts. The men were in expensive linen jackets or pale, pastel-toned shirts – they simply reeked of money and taste and sophistication, the polar opposite of Tory in her beach-girl sundress and flat, too-white shoes. Everyone stared at her, including Thierry de Courcy. She suddenly wished the floor would open up. Her face began to burn.

'Ah, *voilà*! You're here at last!' A slender, petite woman in a sheer black blouse and a green flared skirt came to the rescue. She walked over to her, arms outstretched. Tory caught a whiff of expensive perfume and cigarette smoke as she was kissed on both cheeks, her shoulders touched ever so lightly. 'Victoria, welcome, *ma p'tite*. Welcome to Paris. Thierry told me you walked here from the Métro. Silly girl . . . next time you must tell us you're coming and we send the car for you. Oh, *les Anglais*!' she said, shaking her head indulgently and turning towards her guests. It was obvious from their smiles they'd been talking about her. Tory mumbled something incoherent in reply. Her father had told her Inès de Courcy was in her late forties, but she looked at least a decade younger. Tiny, perfectly proportioned and exquisitely dressed – simple, elegant jewellery, a large silver-and-jade necklace that complemented the rich green of her skirt; bare, tanned legs . . . perfectly manicured hands with a loose, heavy metal watch on the left wrist and a large, fiery diamond on her finger. She was groomed to perfection – brows, eye make-up, lips, skin . . . the works. Tory had to drag her eyes away. She was about as far from Tory's image of a history professor as anyone she could think of. Her father and his colleagues favoured dull, colourless pullovers and corduroy trousers that invariably sagged in all the wrong places.

Inès beamed at her, obviously appreciative of Tory's admiration, and then turned back to her guests, all of whom were still eyeing Tory curiously. 'Allow me to introduce the youngest daughter of my very dear colleague, John Spiller,' she said charmingly, 'whom many of you already know from his *exquisite* work on the court at Versailles. It's a pleasure to have her with us. She will be staying here for a few months; she will be helping Thierry with the translation of his new book – the first into English . . . yes, yes . . .' she gracefully acknowledged the nods and soft murmurs of congratulations. 'Yes, we are *very* proud,' she said, turning to look meaningfully at her husband. Someone applauded, very slowly, in the background.

It was all so staged and absurd Tory was afraid she might burst out laughing. 'You will sit next to me, *chérie*,' Inès murmured, placing a hand on Tory's arm. 'Don't worry, I will protect you!' she laughed.

Tory was momentarily baffled. Protect her from what? She sat down quickly, mostly because she couldn't think of anything else to do. There was a general scraping back of chairs as everyone followed suit. Edith and another uniformed maid quickly rushed to remove the pre-dinner drinks and glasses. New bottles were brought from the sideboard; wine was splashed gently into bulbous glasses, toasts were made – to Thierry's new book; to Inès' recent lecture trip to the United States – someone else added a welcome to the young English girl. Tory barely tasted her wine. All she could think about was the trauma of having to sit with the de Courcys every single night. Please, God, no!

Inès suddenly leaned over, placing a hand gently on her arm again. 'No, you won't have to do this every night, I promise,' she said with an indulgent smile. Tory blushed fiercely. How the hell had she read her mind? The woman on the other side of Inès looked at Tory.

'Does she speak French?' she asked rudely.

'*Oui . . . enfin, un peu.* She's helping Thierry with his new book.'

'Really?' The woman raised an arched eyebrow.

'It's all been arranged,' Inès said hurriedly, smoothing over the woman's obvious surprise. 'It's a very good exchange. Tory gets to see a little of Paris – and the French, of course – and we have the pleasure of a young person in the house! So, you see, it's all worked out beautifully. Ah, *chéri* . . .' she murmured, looking up at her husband as he stopped behind her chair. 'Will you ask Edith to bring the first course?'

Thierry nodded and turned, catching Tory's eye for a fleeting second. Tory frowned. She'd caught sight of something on his face – an expression of something . . . anger? But it passed so quickly and before she could ponder it further, he was gone. She stared after him. Inès claimed her attention again. 'You're not vegetarian, I hope,' she said in her delightfully low voice, making it sound like a disease. Tory shook her head. Inès smiled in mock-relief. 'Thank God for that,' she said archly. 'One never knows with young people these days.' Her tone was both condescending and predatory. Tory said nothing. She didn't know what to say. She'd been in the de Courcy household only a matter of minutes and already she could sense there were undercurrents that she couldn't quite place. She lifted her glass of wine and took a large gulp. Thank God she'd be dining alone for most of the rest of her stay. The thought soothed her immediately.

31

Estelle strode into the lobby at the Hilton on six-inch heels. She was looking good – *better* than good. Drop-dead gorgeous, in fact. She knew it. So too did every red-blooded male over the age of fourteen. Even the bellhops stopped for a second to watch her as she strode past. Those heels; a short navy-blue skirt and a crisp, white shirt buttoned just low enough for the black lace of her bra to glide in and out of view. Her hair was silky and shiny, bouncing around her shoulders in luscious waves, skin gleaming with make-up, nails immaculate and carefully painted, Caitlin's new, shiny red leather bag slung casually over one arm. She and

Caitlin had spent a good three hours on her appearance before she left the flat and it showed. 'Just head for the bar,' Caitlin had advised her. 'You'll pick someone up in a heartbeat. You'll see. It's so fucking easy.' Two of them together wouldn't work, Caitlin said, eyeing her through a cloud of smoke. They'd agreed to work separate nights; London wasn't Harare – there were *laws* against doing what Caitlin had done for the past two years. She'd passed the joint to Estelle, 'to help get you in the mood', she giggled, looking her up and down approvingly. She was right; the pungent, acrid-tasting smoke seeped slowly through her veins, warming and calming her at the same time. When it was time to go, Caitlin looked up at her from her curled-up position on the sofa and whistled. 'Knock 'em dead, screw his brains out and take all the cash you can get,' she grinned, taking a long, slow drag. 'And wake me up when you get back.'

Estelle giggled. She liked Caitlin. Prissy Rebecca and Miss Goody Two Shoes Amanda belonged to the past. She'd seen something in Caitlin almost as soon as she set eyes on her that reminded her a little of herself. A certain cold, glittering hardness around the eyes; a glint of determination; the tiny, outward thrust of her chin. Caitlin was tough, just as she, Estelle, was. Less than a fortnight after marching up to her door that Sunday evening, she'd cleared her belongings out of the downstairs flat and moved in. 'We split everything fifty-fifty,' Caitlin had declared lazily, 'including drugs.' She grinned. 'I'm partial to a bit of blow every now and again. You?' Estelle simply nodded, too impressed to speak. Cool as ice, tough as nails and casual as all hell. Caitlin seemed too good to be true.

Amanda and Rebecca had got one thing right, at least – Caitlin Harries *was* a hooker, but definitely of the classier kind. She'd come down to London from Leeds at the tender age of seventeen, hoping to get into modelling or acting, which of course hadn't happened. She'd fallen in with the wrong crowd, gone from smoking pot occasionally to regularly doing lines at the clubs she and her new friends hung out at and wound up flat broke and homeless several months later. One of the girls she'd become friendly with introduced her to a couple of men – and that, she declared breezily, was pretty much it. Three years in and she'd saved up enough to pay her rent six months in advance, take the odd holiday and have her hair and nails done every week. It wasn't quite what she'd imagined when she thought about leaving home and moving to London, but fuck it . . . it beat working in McDonald's for a pound an hour and besides, it wasn't like she had a whole range of options, either. She wasn't exactly a beauty, but, as she explained patiently to Estelle, that wasn't the point. Presentation, grooming, make-up, expensive clothes . . . it was the overall *package* that counted, not the details underneath.

Estelle had sat on the end of the bed, chin in hand, listening intently. Caitlin looked her up and down enviously. 'You're so fucking *lucky*,' she said with feeling. 'You could be a fucking model or something. Honestly.' Estelle gave a wry smile. At that precise moment becoming a model seemed about as likely as returning to Arcadia – and *that* simply wasn't an option. Meeting Caitlin was the smartest thing she'd done since she'd arrived in London. It was up to her to get what she could out of it – and move on. On and up. She certainly didn't intend to be a prostitute for ever. It was a temporary measure; a stopgap. Something to do whilst she prepared herself for bigger and better things.

There was a woman sitting alone in the far corner of the bar; she looked up as Estelle walked past. It was the third or fourth time she'd seen her in here, Estelle noticed as she found herself a seat nearby. She was in her late forties or early fifties – hard to tell. She was beautifully dressed – a long, low-cut linen dress with crocodile stiletto slingbacks and a matching purse. She was having afternoon tea, leisurely leafing through a stack of newspapers and magazines. She looked wealthy, cared-for, independent. Exactly how Estelle wanted to look one day. As though she didn't give a damn what the bill came to. As though she could afford to *live* in the Hilton if she chose.

'Madam?' One of the pompous little waiters suddenly

appeared in front of her. She wondered if he'd been the one serving a couple of weeks ago when she'd come in for the first time. There was an unmistakable air of snobbery about him. 'Would you care to order something?'

Estelle let her eyes flicker slowly over him. Arrogant little prick. 'I'll have . . . some tea, please. Afternoon tea.' She looked back down at the cream and gold menu card and blinked: £7.50 for a pot of tea and a scone? Shit, too late.

'Very good, madam,' he smirked at her, reading her mind. He turned smartly on his heel. Estelle leaned back in the leather seat, opened her handbag and took out her cigarettes. She picked up her lighter but after several attempts, realised it was empty. She was just about to raise her hand and attract the little prick's attention when the woman she'd been looking at leaned forward.

'D'you need a light?' she asked. Her voice was low and husky with beautifully modulated vowels.

'Oh, thanks,' Estelle leaned towards her. The woman's hand touched hers briefly as she cupped the cigarette. Beautiful nails, Estelle noticed, and a weighty, sparkling diamond. 'Thanks,' she said again, leaning back against the plush upholstery.

'My pleasure.' She regarded Estelle frankly. Estelle felt the heat begin to rise in her cheeks. There was something slightly odd about the woman's stare. Was she . . . *flirting* with her?

'Your tea, madam?' The waiter reappeared.

'Just put it down,' Estelle snapped. She'd had enough of his snotty attitude.

'Very good, madam.'

'Scones are absolutely scrumptious,' the woman said, smiling pleasantly at her. 'I'm Mrs Devereaux,' she said, extending a hand. 'Are you staying here at the hotel?'

'Er, no. I was just . . . just passing,' Estelle said, extending her own. 'I'm Estelle.'

'Lovely name. Suits you.' There was a second's pause then Mrs Devereaux leaned forward again. Her smile was still pleasant; she dropped her voice a fraction. 'Are you on the game?' she asked, looking directly at her.

Estelle blinked. She had no idea what to say. She looked nervously around her. 'I–I'm not sure I understand . . .' she stammered, almost spilling her tea.

'I think you know what I mean.' Mrs Devereaux continued to regard her pleasantly. 'I saw you here the other night. And the night before that. Don't worry. I'm hardly about to report you.'

Estelle's face had gone a deep crimson. 'I—'

'Come up to my suite,' Mrs Devereaux said crisply, ignoring her obvious embarrassment. 'When you've finished your tea, of course. Suite 1300.' She smiled at Estelle again and stood up. 'It'll be worth your while, I promise. You're far too stunning to be doing it this way.'

Estelle could only watch, open-mouthed, as Mrs Devereaux clipped her way across the marble floor in her four-inch heels. She lifted her cup with a shaking hand. She couldn't even eat the scone. Her stomach was taut with a mixture of apprehension and embarrassment. Was it really that obvious?

'Only to those who know what to look for,' Mrs Devereaux said, twenty minutes later as she and Estelle sat in the living room of what was without a shadow of doubt the most sumptuous, most elegant, most expensive room Estelle had ever set foot in. 'How long have you been at it?'

Estelle cleared her throat. 'About a month,' she said, hoping her voice was steady. For the first time in her life she felt completely out of her depth. 'I have a friend . . . she's been doing it for ages. She works at the Dorchester, mostly.'

'How old are you?'

'Twenty-one,' Estelle lied. Mrs Devereaux smiled. 'Nearly,' she added. She could see already that there wasn't much Mrs Devereaux didn't catch.

'I have to say, Estelle, you're extraordinarily beautiful.' She continued to regard her thoughtfully through a cloud of smoke. 'Far too beautiful to walk in off the street. Look, this is all a bit sudden and you're probably wondering who the hell I am,' she smiled. She stubbed out her cigarette decisively. Her voice was suddenly serious. 'I run a *very* successful business. I've got twelve girls on my books and another twenty-five desperately wanting to join. We make an awful lot of money, I don't mind telling you. I'm assuming from the way you're dressed and the place you've chosen to work that you're also interested in making money, even if you're going about it the wrong way. Am I right?' Estelle nodded vigorously. 'Good. You're ambitious. I like that.' She stood up. 'There are several levels to the business we're in, Estelle. You're obviously a couple of steps up from street-walking, don't get me wrong, but you'll never make the sort of money *I* think you're interested in. I rarely take on anyone new. Most of the girls who work for me have been with me since the beginning. I like the look of you – I very much doubt you were born into money but you've got class, which I like, *and* you're gorgeous. Which I also like. And don't worry,' she added with a smile. 'I'm interested in *money*, Estelle, not girls. Relax.'

Estelle reached for a cigarette with a shaking hand. 'So what exactly are we talking about?' she asked, lighting up.

'I take care of the needs of a certain kind of man,' Mrs Devereaux said, walking across to the windows. She looked down at the traffic rushing past on Park Lane and then turned back to Estelle. 'I'm very discreet and *extremely* exclusive and my clients know it. I deliver the best possible service with the best possible girls. If I decide to take you on – and it's still an "if", mind you – you'll be given your own flat, you'll have a driver at your disposal, your bills will be taken care of . . . everything. In short, Estelle, you'll have everything you've ever dreamed of.'

Estelle stared at her, her cigarette frozen halfway to her lips. 'What's the catch?' she asked.

'None. I get fifty per cent of what you earn. I handle everything – cash, expenses, travel, the works. You'll be on call twenty-four hours a day, seven days a week, three hundred and sixty-five days a year. You'll have some of the most powerful men in the world eating out of the palm of your hand. You'll fly first-class everywhere you go, be treated like a royalty . . . as I said, you'll have everything you've ever dreamed of.'

'And all I have to do is . . . ?'

'Whatever the client wants. Don't worry, they're all perfectly normal, give or take a few predilections. Nothing awful, I assure you. Most of them are married. They're just filthy rich.'

Estelle blew out a cloud of smoke. 'When can I start?'

Mrs Devereaux chuckled. She walked over to the sideboard and pulled open a drawer. 'Call this number,' she said, walking back towards her and holding out a small, gold-embossed card. 'Make an appointment with Dr Bowens. When I get the results, I'll call you. Have you got a phone number?'

Estelle took the card. It was a Harley Street address. 'How do I pay for this?' she asked, thinking that there had to be a catch. It sounded too good to be true.

'You don't. Just turn up for your appointment on time and wait for me to call. That's all. Simple.'

Estelle looked at her. Everything about the woman screamed wealth, from the tip of her immaculately polished shoes to the discreet diamond studs flashing in her ears. She had thick auburn hair that fell in a perfectly groomed bob to just below the chin; no jewellery apart from the diamonds in her ears and the baguette on her finger. A Cartier watch. Yes, she looked like the real deal. She stared at the card again. What did she have to lose? She got to her feet. 'Thanks,' she said, not sure whether to offer her hand or not.

'Be sure to call that number, Estelle.' Mrs Devereaux turned away and looked out of the window again. 'Think of it as your lucky day. Oh, and one other thing.' She turned to look at her. 'Nice as Caitlin is, keep this to yourself, won't you?' Estelle could only gape at her; how . . . ? 'I've been watching you for a while, dear,' Mrs Devereaux continued smoothly. 'There's not much I don't notice. You'll find that out soon enough.'

32

Caryn took a deep breath, fought the rising tide of disappointment inside her and pushed open the door. Inside the cramped little office, chaos reigned. Phones were ringing, the fax machine sang, the photocopier buzzed. Half a dozen girls were talking at once – to each other, down the phone, across the room.

'Oi! Take a seat!' someone shouted at her. She looked at the row of chairs behind her; every single one was taken. Take a seat? Where? She joined the queue of girls standing against the wall, waiting self-consciously for further instruction. Slowly, they inched forwards to the desk where a bossy-looking girl in a black suit fired questions at them. Some were dismissed immediately; others were told to stand to one side and a few were shown to a row of computers at the back of the office. There appeared to be some sort of test to pass. Caryn bit her lip nervously. She'd spent the past three weeks teaching herself how to type, but she was hardly fast or proficient. She'd explained as much over the phone the day before but she'd been told to come in anyway.

Presently, her turn came. 'Name?' the girl asked, simultaneously chewing gum, flicking through a Rolodex and tapping out a number on the phone with impossibly long, red fingernails.

'Caryn. Caryn Middleton. I rang yesterday. I spoke to someone called Vanessa, I think. She said I should—'

'Van!' the girl cut her off, turning and yelling behind her.

'What?' came a shout from the tiny office behind the staircase.

'Someone to see you. Carol? Karen?'

'Send her in.'

Half an hour later, her head spinning, she was on her way to her first job. Vanessa had sent her off to the typing pool at Standard Life Insurance Company on Fenchurch Street, just round the corner from the temp agency. 'I like the way you speak,' she told Caryn with a wink. 'Posh-like. Doesn't matter about your typing. You'll pick it up in no time, bright girl like you. *Four* A levels . . . clever little thing, ain't ya?' Caryn looked at the ground.

She walked up the steps of the dull grey building and slipped unnoticed into the steady stream of people going in and out of the enormous revolving door. She was disgorged into a cavern-ous hall, hundreds of footsteps clacking in unison on the cool, marble floor as men and women in black and grey suits rushed past, frowns etched on to their faces like tribal marking. No one spoke, no one stopped or held open a door, smiled or caught another's eye. She clutched the piece of paper Vanessa had shoved at her and made her way to the lifts. For six whole months she'd dreamed about a room in a building made of creamy yellow brick with gnarled wooden doorways and creep-ing roses; discussions that went on deep into the night; warm beer and warm days spent punting on the river. Strawberries, seminars and silence. *Stop it*, she said to herself fiercely. That was then. This is now. She squared her shoulders and pushed her way through the crowds to the lifts. She looked at the paper in her hand. *3rd Floor. Mrs Banks, Human Resources* and firmly pressed the button marked '3'.

33

Tory woke every morning with the first rays of light, listening to the sound of pigeons strutting about on the small terrace outside and the occasional honk of a horn far away. The walls of her room sloped steeply upward, following the pitch of the mansard roof – for the first few days after her arrival, she'd regularly bumped her forehead until she'd learned how to slide in and out of bed. She would lie in bed for a few minutes, luxuriating in the stillness, still bowled over by the fact that here there was no one to chivvy her to come downstairs, have breakfast, make conversation . . . she was completely and utterly alone. Sometimes she made herself a coffee, drinking it out of a bowl the French way, sitting at the little table by the window. She would reach for her cigarettes and lean back, watching the lazy, drifting path taken by the smoke as she exhaled. Then she would get up, take a shower and get ready for work. By eight forty-five a.m. she was ready; a final cigarette or a mouthful of coffee, then she closed the door and walked downstairs.

Thierry de Courcy worked in a large, sun-filled study at the rear of the enormous apartment. Parisian apartments were very different, she noticed immediately. Everything in Paris was bigger, more expansive, more gloriously spacious. The elegant halls and wide, high-ceilinged corridors of the de Courcys' home were practically rooms in their own right. She thought of her perfectly nice, perfectly ordinary three-bedroom house in Hortensia Road – now it seemed tiny and cramped by comparison, not to mention chintzy and, quite frankly, rather cheap. Everything in the de Courcy household was chosen with care, from the beautifully worn and polished parquet floors to the tasteful mix of antique and modern furniture. Thierry was usually already at his desk by the time she came in. His graceful, leather-topped desk faced the window overlooking the inner courtyard. He liked to keep the French doors open, allowing the occasional puff of sharply scented air from the citrus trees below to waft upwards. Tory's desk was opposite, facing away so that the two of them could work in almost absolute silence, neither distracting nor disturbing the other. Occasionally the phone rang and he would disappear into rapid, quick-fire French that Tory had difficulty following, despite having taken it for almost ten years of her school life.

The work was easy enough. It was her job to look over the translations of his texts, checking them for mistakes before transferring the hand-typed manuscript to the computer. Thierry still wrote by hand, she noticed, watching his pen fly across the pages of the thick, creamy-white paper he favoured.

She could barely make sense of the subject matter. She knew nothing of philosophy when she started the job, and, after a week or so, found she knew even less. Not that it bothered her. There was something calm and soothing about following someone else's directions, page after page, line by line, one pile of sheets after another. She wasn't a particularly fast typist but Thierry didn't seem to notice. He was vague about the delivery date of the manuscript. From Inès' slipped comments, Tory gathered that the job was more about finding *her* something to do rather than her husband's need to put his manuscript on to the computer, but she didn't really care. That was their problem, not hers. All she wanted was a little corner of solitude where she could put her head down and not have to think. This arrangement seemed to suit everyone perfectly.

At first, although he was at pains to conceal it, Thierry didn't like Tory's presence in his study. Not one little bit. The whole bloody thing had been Inès' idea, of course. His objections, such as they were, had very quickly been overruled. Inès was outraged. How *could* he be so selfish? Did he have any idea what that poor girl had been through? What the *family* had been through? 'What if it were your daughter?' Inès demanded, eyes flashing angrily. 'Or your sister?'

Thierry shook his head impatiently, unable to conjure up such a scene since he had neither daughter nor sister. 'That's not the point,' he said acidly. 'You barely know this man. I'm sorry for what happened to his child and to the rest of the family but . . . a whole summer? In *my* study?'

'What's a few months compared to the rest of that poor girl's life?' Inès shouted.

'Nothing, but I just don't understand why this has become our problem,' Thierry said, his own temper beginning to rise. '*My* problem,' he corrected himself quickly. '*You're* going to be gone in a week. Aren't you going to the States as soon as we come back from Biarritz?'

'Oh, for goodness' sake, Thierry. Try thinking of someone else for a change,' Inès said in her most exasperated tone of voice. She picked up her bag and her car keys. 'If she disturbs you so much, move her into the other room. Or upstairs. Simple.' And then, of course, she'd disappeared.

And now here he was, sitting opposite Tory, seeing the long, thick rope of her pony tail every time he turned around. Despite the careful positioning of the desks, her presence *was* a distraction; he didn't quite understand why. It was nothing to do with *her*, per se . . . she was actually easier to be around than he'd feared. She was very quiet. Watchful, but not unpleasantly so. Discreet. She went about her work with a detached, very faintly bored air. After a while, to his great surprise, he found he rather enjoyed it. He was so accustomed to the exaggerated fawning that accompanied his every pronouncement that this . . . this . . . *English* reserve was curiously rather appealing. Take that morning, for example. She'd been typing away quietly, the only sound the steady lifting of papers every half an hour or so as she turned the page, and then she'd stopped. He slowly became aware of the growing silence, louder in its way than words. He turned in his chair and looked at her questioningly. She blushed and he found he rather enjoyed the sight. 'Something the matter?' he asked gravely, peering at her from over the top of his frameless glasses.

'I . . . I was just thinking,' she said, slowly swivelling round to face him. She pulled a sheet out from the stack in front of her and got up. She crossed the floor and handed it to him. He was uncomfortably aware of the faint trace of perfume on her hands. 'This word, here . . . where she's put "closeness" – I think it reads better if you say "proximity" instead. "Distance and proximity."'

He frowned and took the paper from her, studying the words. ' "The central question of the presence and absence of God, the circular journey between distance and closeness, between mystery and clarity lies at the heart of the Christian endeavour."' After a few seconds' deliberation, he handed it back. 'Yes, you're right,' he acknowledged gravely. ' "Proximity" *is* a better word. Has a nicer sound to it.' He glanced at her quickly. 'Thank you.' And then he turned back to his own papers, impressed, in spite of himself. Inès had said something about the girl not being very bright – utter rubbish. He heard her cross the floor back to her own desk.

He got up suddenly, irritated by the direction of his thoughts. This was exactly why he hadn't wanted anyone in the study with him. Without intending to, she'd crept into his peripheral thinking and, once lodged, she was proving difficult to dispel. It wasn't the poor girl's fault. It was just so typical of Inès. Organise a situation to everyone's maximum *disruption* – save hers, of course – then disappear. 'I'm going out for a while,' he muttered. She nodded but didn't look up. He left, mildly annoyed, though he couldn't exactly say why.

A fortnight later at the beginning of September, Tory stood at the window and watched the silver Citroën disappear around the corner. She gave a deep, luxurious sigh. Alone. She was completely, utterly alone. Downstairs, in the de Courcys' apartment, shutters had been closed, curtains drawn, dust covers thrown over the raw silk settees, everything polished, put away, protected. She'd never seen such chaotic preparations for a fortnight's holiday – the staff rushed around cleaning anything and everything they laid eyes on whilst Inès stood in the middle of the room, directing operations with the skill and precision of a conductor. She and Thierry were going to Biarritz, to their villa for two weeks, then she was flying on to Boston, where she was due to give a paper and had accepted an invitation to holiday with the dean and his family at their Hamptons home. It was all so different from the world Tory's father inhabited – all she could remember of summers in Fulham was the sound of her father's typewriter clacking away and the strict edict that *he was not to be disturbed under any circumstances*. She and Susie saw less of him in the summer than during term time, or so it seemed. Afterwards, of course, summers were especially hard; all that time on their hands without the routine of term and school to distract them – the very air seemed to shimmer with sadness as well as heat.

She leaned out against the wrought-iron rails, stretched her hands above her head and turned her face towards the sun, basking in the heat. It was September but Paris was still baking. Inès had told her they preferred to leave in September when Paris filled up with everyone coming back from their August holiday – the city, she declared dramatically, was unbearable. So crowded! Looking down on to the street below, she saw it was true. She'd taken a walk along the Seine the previous evening and could barely move for the cyclists, pedestrians, roller skaters, skateboarders and gawping tourists, not to mention the cars.

Yes, coming to Paris had been a good idea, no matter how boring she found the work at times. Since arriving, she'd felt the tight noose of her parents' disappointment ease and a lightening of her head and heart that surprised her. It wasn't that she didn't miss Susie, or that she no longer thought about her. It seemed as if she would never stop thinking about her. But something had changed over the past few weeks that she couldn't exactly put her finger on. Thinking about Susie no longer produced the same, gut-wrenching pain. Instead of relentlessly trying to im-agine Susie's last moments or exactly, precisely how she'd died, she began to remember other things. The sound of her laughter, the way she smiled, the jokes she liked. She remembered the look of her hair when she'd just come out of the shower, curling round her face and hanging down her back; the time she'd cut her knee on the swings at the back of the first house they'd lived in, before coming to London. Or the time she'd painted her nails for the first time and Tory had been so in awe. She even caught herself smiling once or twice, remembering something unexpected. Little by little the dark, angry cloud that had settled on her the day Susie died was beginning to lift. She even found herself thinking warmly of her father. Yes, coming to Paris had been the right thing to do.

34

Caryn listened to Michael Baxter's monotonous, faux-posh voice droning on in her earphones and felt like hurling herself out of the window. She'd been at her job for just under a month – the longest month of her life. During the eight or so hours that she was at her desk each day, time practically stood still, the hands of the clock on the wall in front of her desk inching their way towards five with agonising slowness. She looked at it for the hundredth time that morning. It wasn't even noon. She sighed. Vanessa was right about one thing, she thought as her hands moved quickly across the keyboard. Typing wasn't *that* difficult. She'd picked it up quickly, just as Vanessa had said. In fact, the job was ridiculously easy. Come in, sit down, slide on headphones, switch on computer, listen and type. Simple. Granted, it was made infinitely more complicated by the ridiculous accent Michael Baxter put on every time he opened his mouth, but that quickly became a source of private amusement. 'Plastic' became *plar-stic*, 'maths' became *mar-ths*, 'decision' became, inexplicably, *dur-si-sshyun*. She longed to be able to laugh about it with someone, but there was no one amongst the temps and regular secretaries on the sixth floor whom she felt comfortable enough to approach, let alone giggle with. As the latest in what she gathered was a long line of temps who'd worked for Michael Baxter over the past couple of years, she was the most junior, most lowly employee on the corporate ladder, certainly not worth anyone's attention or effort.

She typed on for a further five minutes, then pulled the earphones off impatiently. She'd had enough of his voice for the time being. She pushed back her chair and walked quickly to the bathroom. Even going to the loo was a welcome distraction.

She came out of the stall a few minutes later and looked at herself critically in the mirror. She could hardly recognise herself. She looked awfully . . . well, corporate. A plain black jacket, black skirt, white shirt and black, low-heeled shoes. All bought with her first week's pay. It was what all the typists at Standard Life wore – just cheaper, shinier versions of the suits worn by every other woman in the company – even the fund managers, of whom there were precious few. Pension-schemes fund management didn't seem to attract many women – corpulent, red-faced men with bad haircuts were much more the norm. They all seemed to have the same annoying little habits, like speaking to her at chest level and patting her on the behind if and when they could. She was convinced Michael Baxter didn't think of her as anything other than a pair of legs in perpetual motion between his desk and the coffee machine.

The door opened and someone walked in. She recognised the woman; one of the older PAs on the same floor. Caryn smiled at her hesitantly. The woman ignored her and walked into an empty stall. Caryn sighed. That was another thing she'd learned about the City. The Rules. No one seemed to deviate from them, though Caryn found it almost impossible to figure out how and when you learned them. As a rule, PAs didn't speak to typists. Secretaries, however, were a cut above typists and could therefore be addressed but PAs still lorded it over them. Typists, truly those on the lowest rung, were generally referred to as 'girls'; secretaries were sometimes 'ladies', occasionally 'girls' and even sometimes 'temps', but they tended to be posh blondes with Sloaney accents who were simply whiling away time until they found a man who worked in the City (just like Daddy). There would be a flashy wedding and a honeymoon somewhere exotic and occasionally a picture in *Tatler* of *Hermione and Biffy* or *Squiddy and India* or some other such equally ridiculous names . . . and then another 'girl' or 'lady' would enter the ranks on the sixth floor and take her place. It was all very bewildering. Caryn had considered St Augustine's the apogee of class sensitivity until she'd come to work in the City. *Each according to his rank* might well have been the motto of the Square Mile. Problem was, it was hard to distinguish who exactly was of your rank and who wasn't.

As usual, Caryn didn't quite fit the mould. Once, about a week after she'd started, a female manager had come by to see

Michael and had picked up a book Caryn had left on her desk – *Midnight's Children*, by Salman Rushdie. She'd looked at Caryn and raised an eyebrow. Nothing was said, but her look implied a question. *What're you doing here?* There was obviously something about Caryn that made the other girls hesitate to approach her – her 'posh' voice and the way she kept to herself, perhaps . . . sitting at her desk at lunchtimes with the little white plastic lunchbox, a meagre sandwich and an apple instead of the expensive baguettes, exotic crisps and canned drinks the others brought in from the deli counter at Leadenhall Market. She was a bit odd, a little out of place. Best to leave her alone. She read the confusion in their eyes but didn't know what to say.

The woman who'd gone into the cubicle next to her emerged, unsmiling. She too raised her eyebrows at Caryn, but for a different reason. *What are you still doing here?* her expression read. *Haven't you got work to do?* Caryn hurriedly dried her hands and left.

35

Nic walked up the steps of UCL, enjoying the cool damp of the portico, and then pushed open the heavy wooden doors leading to the library. Her bag was heavy; she'd just come from a lecture by the renowned academic Frank Kermode, and his words were still ringing in her ears. 'English shouldn't be a soft option. It should be a severe option, restricted to those who are qualified to do it. Remember, one of the great benefits of seriously reading English is you're forced to read a lot of other things. You may not have a very deep acquaintance with Hegel but you need to know something about Hegel. Or Hobbes, or Aristotle, or Roland Barthes. We're all smatterers in a way, I suppose. But a certain amount of civilisation depends on intelligent smattering.'

It was highly unlikely Professor Kermode could even see Nic Harte amongst the eager, first-year faces clustered in groups of two or three in front of him, but she felt as though he'd singled her out, spoken to *her*, for her ears alone. After Jim's disparaging remarks about reading English when 'you clearly haven't got the brains to think of or do anything else', Professor Kermode's words were an unexpected and soothing balm to her injured pride. *English?* Jim's expression had conveyed even more accurately than his words precisely what he thought of that idea. *What the hell for? No daughter of mine's going to sit on her arse for three years learning how to do something she ought to bloody well know already. Jesus Christ! Haven't I spent enough on your damned education as it is?*

She ran up the short flight of steps to the library, the heat surging back into her cheeks. Well, he was right about one thing. *No daughter of mine.* She'd changed *that* little fact before she'd even started her course. She'd taken her mother's maiden name. So simple. Nicola Harte became Nicola Parker. She explained to the registrar who'd taken her photograph that Harte was her middle name; someone must have made a mistake. He shrugged, took her photograph and duly typed in 'Parker'. Nic Parker. And now, after hearing Professor Kermode, after having been at university for less than a week, she finally knew exactly what she wanted to do with the rest of her life. She wanted to be a journalist and the strangest thing was, she couldn't have said why. She just *knew*. She'd looked at the first-year prospectus and her heart started to race. *Narrative texts. Intellectual and Cultural Studies. Introduction to Critical Theory.*

But coupled with the thrill of pleasure, of course, was the savage stab of disappointment she felt every time she thought about Caryn. The thrill of being at university should have been Caryn's too – and of course it wasn't; it couldn't be. Caryn tried to pretend that it was no big deal, really. She could always go to university later, after . . . after what? It was on the tip of Nic's tongue to shout it out but she stopped herself just in time. Caryn was wrong. It *was* a big deal. She tried to think of what *she* would do in Caryn's place, but she'd never been asked to make anything even remotely resembling the sort of decision or sacrifice Caryn had made. Nic never had anyone to consider other than herself, really.

She'd gone home that evening after going round to Caryn's home for the first time ever, utterly humbled. Caryn had guts. She was the bravest person she knew. Nic, who could fix a car, shoot an antelope, ride any kind of horse, travel halfway across the world without blinking, suddenly understood that there was another kind of courage to be had, one that she'd never had to call upon. Something deeper and tougher and much more precious. Caryn knew it. Maybe Tory did, too, after what had happened to her sister. Another kind of life. Suddenly Nic was the one who was unprepared. She, who had everything money could buy. It would have been too easy, too glib, to pretend that it was thinking about Caryn that had prompted her to choose journalism, but the fact stubbornly remained – after seeing what had happened to Caryn, despite the brave face she put on it, she couldn't even contemplate returning to Zimbabwe and simply waiting around suburban swimming pools to get hitched, as Shaun put it. *That* would have been much more in line with Jim's plans for her. Shaun and Patrick hadn't bothered with university, naturally; there were far more important things to do – namely *life*. But Nic was strangely adamant. In the end, giving in and agreeing to pay her fees was the less onerous of two options and Jim had grudgingly – and somewhat mockingly – given his consent. She'd endured a summer of ribbing from the few friends she had left in Zimbabwe – debutantes all, clinging on to the last vestiges of a lifestyle that was no longer really theirs to enjoy, desperate to marry and 'get the hell out of here', as they put it – and then in September, she'd flown back to the UK with Manning. Only this time, she was flying back *to* something – to her own life. Or the beginnings of it, at least. And now, after a week spent in a room that was barely larger than the shoe-cupboard at Eaton Square, she was very firmly living it. Her own life. Now that it was here, she couldn't quite get over it.

36

After almost a month in Paris, Tory was slowly beginning to settle in. She knew which buses ran where; where to shop for buttery croissants and the most pungent, softest cheeses; how to get to the major museums and galleries and, now that she'd met Saskia, a young German au pair who lived at the end of the road, whom to call on if she felt like a coffee or a walk by the river. Her favourite place of all was the flower market at Place Louis Lépine, on the Île de la Cité; she could wander for hours amongst the stalls selling everything from tiny, delicate white spray roses to gigantic, waxy bird-of-paradise flowers flown in that morning from the Far East. The city was beginning to work its charms on her and was starting to feel like home.

Thierry came back in the middle of September, without his wife. He was already at his desk the following morning when she walked in. He looked tanned and relaxed; the permanent frown between his eyes was gone and there was even the faintest hint of a smile behind his habitually stern expression, especially when looking at her. She hurriedly looked away, aware of the heat in her cheeks. He was far too old to be thought of as attractive, surely? It came as something of a shock to find herself looking at the sweep of hair that fell away from his forehead and appreciating the colour of his eyes in his newly tanned face.

'You had a restful time?' he asked, turning partially towards her.

'Yes, thanks,' Tory said, still looking intently at her nails. 'Er, did you have a nice holiday?'

'Oui.'

And that was it. He pulled a sheaf of papers towards him. The translator had nearly finished the manuscript and had left a large stack of sheets for him to go through. They worked in silence for a few minutes. Then he looked up suddenly and caught her eyes. She blushed crimson and quickly bent her head. She stared at the sentence she'd just typed. 'The play between loquaciousness and silence is characteristic of Judeo-Christian religions. At times the word of God is luminous – it is the miracle of illumination. At other times, darkness and enigma prevail.' OK, so she wasn't exactly a brain-box, but there was something about the words that appealed to her. *Illumination and darkness. Clarity and enigma.* Well, Thierry de Courcy was certainly an enigma. She sighed. What was going on?

'Something wrong?' he enquired.

Tory shook her head, not daring to look up. 'No, nothing. It's just . . . well, it's just interesting . . . what you've written . . .' she added lamely.

He didn't respond but she felt his eyes on her. It took all of her self-control to carry on typing. Eventually she heard him push back his chair and get up. She continued typing, her whole body suddenly tense. He crossed the floor to her desk and then, to her horror, walked round it so that he was standing beside her, his eyes following her words across the screen. 'You are interested in religion?' he asked her suddenly.

'*Me*? Oh, no . . .' Tory exclaimed, embarrassed. She didn't even understand his question. Was she religious? 'I mean, no, not really,' she corrected herself quickly.

'Ah.' He stood by her side for a few seconds more then walked away.

Her face burned. She felt like an idiot. For the rest of the morning she was quiet. Just before lunchtime he got up, put on his jacket and left without saying anything. She watched the door close behind him and put up a hand to her face, unnerved. She'd noticed things about him that disturbed her. The colour of his hair, the texture of the sunburned skin at the nape of his neck, the shape of his hands. Christ. He was old enough to be her father. When had *that* happened?

37

The euphoria following her meeting with Mrs Devereaux was short-lived. The very next day, just as she'd been directed, Estelle made an appointment with Dr Bowens at his Harley Street clinic. The practice nurse skilfully withdrew the tiny needle from her arm, capping the lid on the vial of blood they'd extracted – and that was it. Mrs Devereaux would receive the results in a few days' time. Estelle went home in a state of pleasurable anticipation. A week passed without a call from her, and then another, and still there was no word. After the third week, she began to wonder if she'd dreamed the entire thing. She hadn't worked since their meeting, and her savings were again dipping dangerously low – it was time to give up the pipe dream, no matter how exciting the whole thing seemed, and get back to work. Caitlin was no fool, either.

'What's going on?' she demanded at the end of the second week. 'You haven't left the house in ages. You sick or something?'

'No,' Estelle shrugged as nonchalantly as she could. 'Just don't feel like it.'

'Well, you'd better start feeling like it again pretty sharpish,' Caitlin said, snapping her bag shut. 'You still owe me for last week, remember? And we've got rent coming up next week.'

'I know, I know . . . I'll start again tomorrow, all right?'

'I don't care when you start, love. Just make sure you can keep to your share of things, that's all. The last girl—'

'Look, I said I'll pay you back, OK?'

'Keep your hair on. God, what side of the bed did *you* get out of this morning?' Caitlin rolled her eyes at her. 'See you later.' She disappeared in a cloud of perfume and cigarette smoke. Estelle groaned and leaned back against the cushions. She'd landed back down on earth with a bump. What had she been thinking? She knew almost better than anyone that things never just fell into place. Nothing was ever as good as it sounded –

she'd known that almost all her life. From the father who never came to visit, to the future that Gloria always promised would be hers . . . nothing was ever easy; nothing ever panned out; dreams just didn't come true. She knew it. She grabbed a cushion and bit down on it, hard. Why had she been such a bloody fool? She'd lost almost a month's worth of earnings, sitting around moping all day, waiting for the phone to ring. It did, but it was never Mrs Devereaux – it would *never* be Mrs Devereaux; that was the point. It was time she got that little message into her head. Why was she being so dense about it? There was only one person in the whole fucking world she could count on and—

The phone rang again, interrupting her. She stared at it. It would be one of Caitlin's clients, no doubt. Why the hell couldn't she just get an answering machine like everyone else? She yanked the receiver up after the fifth ring and barked out a surly 'Hello?'

'That's no way to answer a phone, Estelle,' a woman's soft, polished voice rebuked her. 'Surely you can do better than that?'

A cold wave of shock flowed over her. 'Mrs Devereaux?'

'How are you, my dear?'

'I–I'm fine. I—'

'Will you come and see me tomorrow morning?' Mrs Devereaux continued briskly. 'Nine. Don't be late. I can't stand tardiness.' She offered no explanation as to why it had taken her almost a month to call.

'At . . . at the Hilton?' Estelle stammered.

'Where else?' Mrs Devereaux chuckled and hung up the phone. Estelle slowly replaced the receiver, too stunned to speak. Her heart was racing. She leaned back against the cushions, her head spinning, all sorts of possibilities suddenly opening up again in her mind.

'Business was good,' was all Mrs Devereaux said the following morning when Estelle – on time, for once – dared to raise the question of why it had taken her so long to call. 'I've been busy.

Now, there's someone I'd like you to meet,' she went on briskly, selecting a cigarette from her silver case and lighting up. 'Someone *quite* special. I think he'll like you. You'll be meeting him at his club. It's somewhere in the City, I think. But first we'll need to get you something to wear.' She stood up and regarded Estelle critically, arms folded. 'You'll need a good haircut, too. I'll take you round to see Nicky. A few highlights wouldn't hurt, but let's see what he says, shall we? Nails?' she went on before Estelle had a chance to open her mouth. Estelle held out her hands mutely. 'Not bad. We'll get you a quick manicure at the same time.' She stubbed out her cigarette and looked down at Estelle. 'Well? What are you waiting for? I haven't got all day. I've got two other girls to see to, you know. Let's get moving.' Estelle jumped to her feet and followed Mrs Devereaux out of the door. Now her head really was spinning. Where the hell were they going?

She walked out of the tiny cubicle and turned slowly. Even the sales assistants gasped. The halter-neck dress, made up of a thousand delicate slivers of silver and black silk stitched together, clung to her skin, fitting tightly across the bust, following the slender line of her hips before bursting into a shimmer of light and movement at her feet. She stood in her bare feet, unable to breathe. She'd never in her life been so close to anything quite so gorgeous. Across the room Mrs Devereaux regarded her thoughtfully. It was the third outfit Estelle had tried on. The previous two had been dismissed with a tiny, almost imperceptible flick of her wrist.

'Yes, that'll do,' Mrs Devereaux murmured finally to the personal shopper standing next to her. Two assistants rushed forward immediately. As the zipper slid down her back, Estelle was finally able to breathe again. She quickly pulled on her jeans and slid her shirt over her head as the dress was lovingly folded between layers of tissue paper in an enormous white box cover-ed in gold lettering. She didn't even dare enquire about the price. Mrs Devereaux was busy looking through the piles of garments the assistants had laid out in front of her – she pulled out a pair of the skimpiest white panties Estelle had ever seen. Five minutes later, clutching a second bag with a pair of high-heeled black patent pumps, she followed Mrs Devereaux out of the shop. The driver was on hand to relieve them of their packages. Estelle clambered into the sleek black Jaguar after Mrs Devereaux, still speechless. In less than twenty-four hours, her entire existence had been turned upside down.

If she'd had any doubts at all about Mrs Devereaux's authenticity, three hours spent in her company inside the small, obviously exclusive Bond Street boutique had dispelled them all, every last one. Not only was Mrs Devereaux *known*, she was quite clearly respected. Estelle wasn't fooled by the obsequiousness – she was from Arcadia, after all . . . she knew *all* about bowing and scraping. No, all the little pleasantries and the over-the-top flattery she'd witnessed that afternoon simply pointed to the fact that Mrs Devereaux, whoever she was and however she earned her money, earned *lots* of it. It was blindingly obvious. Mrs Devereaux was the real McCoy – and if Estelle Mackenzie wanted some of it (which she did, make no mistake) then she too had to learn how to bow and scrape, and do exactly what the woman wanted. It didn't sound *so* bad, she mused to herself as the car pulled away from the kerb and purred silently up the road. Christ, she'd done a lot worse . . . *without* a beautiful black and silver dress that undoubtedly cost a small fortune *and* matching shoes to take the sting out of it. Was the dress hers to keep? she wondered. And what was it Mrs Devereaux had said about her own flat and a driver? She hugged the box to her chest, too excited to speak – or think. For the first time in her entire 'professional' life, she was looking forward to the evening ahead.

38

'What made you choose to come to Paris?'

Tory looked up in surprise. Thierry was looking at her. He had taken off his glasses, dangling them from his mouth as he regarded her astonished face. 'I didn't, actually,' she said, hoping her face wasn't quite as red as it felt. 'It was my father's idea, really. He and Inès thought it would be a good idea . . . because of what happened.'

'What d'you mean?'

She looked at him uncertainly. 'You know that . . . that my sister died?' she asked, her throat thickening suddenly.

'Yes, I do. But it's not the only thing worth knowing about you,' he said mildly. He slipped on his glasses. 'Is it?'

The statement, and the question that followed it, was so unexpected it knocked her sideways. She stared at him, unable to respond. Finally she shook her head. 'N-no, I suppose not,' she mumbled. 'I never . . . I've just never thought of it like that.'

'Perhaps you should.' It wasn't a question. Tory stared at him. To her horror, she felt tears begin to well up behind her eyes. She turned away, back to the computer, determined not to cry in front of him. Without knowing it, he'd touched a raw, aching nerve. If she wasn't the sister of a girl who'd been tragically murdered, who was she? And if she *was* only Susie's sister, why did she sometimes feel so angry with her? The screen began to blur in front of her. She lifted a hand surreptitiously to wipe her cheeks and then she felt his hand on her shoulder. Her whole body stiffened. He turned her round gently to face him. '*Ça va*,' he said softly. 'Shh.'

'I . . .' She struggled to speak.

'I know. Here.' He pulled a handkerchief out of his shirt pocket and handed it to her. 'It's OK. You can cry. But not for her, hmm? It's over for her; it's finished. But you . . . you have to get on with the rest of your life.'

'B–but how?' Tory sobbed, feeling as though her heart would split in two. 'I can't forget . . . I . . . j-just *can't* . . .'

He crouched down until his face was level with hers. Nudging her arms gently aside, he rested his hands on her knees and looked up at her. Tory was struck by the absurdity of the pose – Thierry de Courcy, almost kneeling at her feet? He put up a hand to push away a strand of her hair that had stuck to her cheek . . . his fingers grazed her cheek . . . and then, of course, he kissed her. Chastely, at first, as though he were aiming for her cheek or forehead, but she turned her face at the same time so that she received him not as a child, but as a woman. There was a second's hesitation, then he stood up, pulling her up with him. She felt his grip change – no longer gentle or comforting; there was a hunger and tension in him that she quickly responded to, matching it with her own. *How did this happen?* She asked herself the question again and again as he began to unbutton her shirt and she found her own fingers busy at his. He kicked the door shut, remembering to turn the key before coming back to show her, in the most direct way possible, that no, it wasn't the only thing worth knowing about her. Not by a very long shot.

PART THREE

39

London, England, July 1997

It was hard not to stare at her own image, seated as she was only inches away from it. Behind her, frowning in concentration as she worked, the stylist snipped and cut, stopped, tilted her head this way and that, ruffled her hair and snipped away again. And again. The pile of dark brown hair on the ground grew larger and messier; the hair on her head got shorter and shorter and yet shorter still. By the time the scissors finally stopped, she was practically unrecognisable, even to herself.

'Looks great, doesn't it?' the stylist said cheerfully, grinning at her in the mirror.

Nic swallowed. She'd had long, straight dark brown hair for as long as she could remember. She was in possession of a hundred and one mannerisms that relied on it; from twisting the ends when she was nervous to curling strands around her little finger when she read. She stared at the image of a stranger in the mirror again. 'It looks . . . different,' she said finally.

''Course it's different – that's the whole point! It'll take a bit of getting used to, but it suits you, it really does.'

Nic put up a hand to touch it. 'I've never had short hair before.'

'Well, you should. You've got the cheekbones for it, darling. Wish *I* did,' the stylist smiled at her as she whipped off the cape. 'There you go: a whole new you.'

Fifteen minutes later, Nic walked out on to the street, still putting up a self-conscious hand every now and again to touch the bare skin of her neck. She crossed the road, enjoying the unfamiliar feeling of lightness, and caught a startled glimpse of herself reflected in a shop window as she passed. In a few hours, she would meet Caryn and Tory – what would they say? Her stomach gave a little lurch. Before that, however, she would have her father and Molly to face. The house was still reeling from the unexpected row that had blown up. It had started with the invitation to her graduation ceremony. Of course. The envelope came sailing through the front door, addressed to Nicola Parker. Molly picked it up on her way into the kitchen and showed it to Jim. And then all hell had broken loose. Nic was completely unprepared for the storm that followed; Jim bellowing at her, Molly's tight, angry face, Jessica, home for the weekend from her private school, peering at them through the banisters – what was all the fuss about? So she'd used her mother's maiden name . . . so what? For the first time in her life, she answered back. She thought he might strike her. In the end, Molly had intervened and shoved Nic into the TV room and then turned to her husband to try to calm him down. *Spoiled, ungrateful wretch!* She heard him calling her names as he marched into his study, slamming the door so hard that the clock on the wall in the hallway fell off its perch.

The house was quiet for the rest of the day. Jim barely surfaced; Nic spent most of it in her room. There was an angry, tight knot of resentment in her chest that refused to budge. How dare he shout at her like that? *Spoiled*? If there was one thing she was proud of, it was that she'd taken just what she needed from him to survive at university – and not a penny more. Three years of slogging her guts out, living in student digs, holding down a series of mundane bar jobs just like all her fellow students, despite the fact that she could have lived in palatial comfort at Eaton Square if she'd chosen. But she hadn't. She'd done it the hard, hard way, desperate for the chance to prove – if only to herself – that there was more to her than being Jim Harte's daughter, that she could and would make it on her own. For three years she'd learned to shut her mouth at the odd family gatherings in London, Studgrove or in Harare and keep the details of her life to herself. No one asked how her course was going; no one asked if she was enjoying herself, or what she planned to do when she'd finished. Shaun and Patrick were so caught up in the waves of scandals that seemed to be hitting RhoMine on a weekly basis that there was precious little time or energy left to worry about a younger sister who'd made it abundantly clear that her future lay outside the family firm, not within it. No, the stark truth of it was that *no one cared*. Least of all her father. Well, she'd coped with it; she hadn't complained, not once – how *dare* he call her spoiled?

As she rounded the corner into Eaton Square, she saw Jim's enormous silver BMW was parked outside but the chauffeur was nowhere to be seen. There was another car, sleek, black, parked next to it. Visitors, no doubt. She turned the key in the lock and pushed open the door cautiously. There didn't seem to be anyone about. She looked into the dining room. There was a centrepiece of flowers on the gleaming mahogany table. A few drops of water still beaded its surface; someone had been in quite recently. She heard a noise and looked up. Raised, muted voices were coming from her father's study on the first floor. She left the dining room, walked up the stairs and was just about to climb the second flight to escape to her room when she heard someone speak.

'You can't just leave him there,' she heard a man say, his voice rising in anger. 'You've got to get him out.'

'How? What d'you expect me to do?' Her father sounded irritated. 'Send in the army? Whose army? Yours?'

'He did this for *you*, Harte. He's your responsibility. You sent him in; you get him out. I don't want Simon Carter's blood on my hands.' Nic felt a cold hand creep up her spine.

'He's a big boy. He knew what he was getting into.' She recognised the tone in her father's voice. Final.

'Jesus *Christ*, Jim! Have you no fucking conscience? How old is the guy? Thirty? Harold's right. You can't just leave him there.' Someone else joined in the conversation in a disgusted tone.

'Gentlemen,' Jim said briskly, speaking over the objections. 'Do we have an agreement or not?' There was silence for a few minutes. Nic felt the hairs on the back of her neck stand up.

'But—' someone else's voice fell into the silence.

'Enough already!' her father suddenly shouted. 'You just don't get it, do you? We've *all* got AK47s now, you idiots. The only question is – who's gonna shoot first? I'm not about to walk away from this, not after all this time. Carter knows what he has to do. He's done it before. He'll do it again. He knows how to take care of himself. End of story. Now, for the fiftieth fucking time, do we have an agreement or not?'

Nic had no idea what or who the conversation was about but she was clearly not meant to hear it. She wished she hadn't. She continued up the stairs quietly, wondering who the hell they were talking about. Whoever it was, it sounded ominous.

Caryn glanced at the clock for the umpteenth time that afternoon. Another hour and a half to go. The minutes were dragging past, slower than ever. She was *dying* to pick up her bag and leave. It was August the fourteenth on one of the hottest days of the year. She, Nic and Tory were meeting up at Blushes on the King's Road, their favourite spot. It had been a couple of months since she'd seen Nic – what with her final exams and a last-minute trip back home to Zimbabwe, she'd been so busy they'd missed each other. Tory had been gone for almost three years, hard as it was to imagine. She'd written from Paris, of course, but she'd missed the reunion twice; something wasn't quite right, Caryn and Nic agreed, but neither knew quite how to broach the subject, especially not in a letter.

She looked at the clock again. In a couple of hours she would see them both. Her stomach gave a lurch of pleasurable anticipation. So much had changed for the two of them – in comparison, nothing much had changed in *her* life. Well, that wasn't quite true. She'd been at Metropolitan Life Assurance for almost a year; still working in a typing pool and still employed on a temporary basis, but she'd come to tolerate, if not actually enjoy, the work. At least the other typists were friendlier than they'd been in her previous jobs. Brian was doing well in school – against the odds, he'd developed into a sunny, bright, inquisitive boy who everyone said was just like his older sister. That, she kept reminding herself, was the main thing. And hard as it was to believe, in less than a year Owen would be out of jail. In no time at all, things in the Middleton home would be back to normal. Or as close to normal as they would ever be. Only Alice hadn't changed. Wouldn't ever change.

'Off somewhere special, then?' Angie, one of the secretaries on her floor, peered over Caryn's cubicle, a teasing note in her voice. 'You've been looking at that blasted clock every other minute. Got a date, have you?'

Caryn blushed. 'No, nothing like that. I'm just meeting my . . . two of my friends, that's all. One's just finished her degree and the other's coming back from Paris. She's been away for ages. I can't wait to see them.'

'School friends, are they?' Sometimes the secretaries teased Caryn about her 'posh' voice and the fact that she'd been to private school – Caryn often wondered how they knew – but at MetLife it was good-natured, not bitchy.

'Yeah.' Caryn smiled shyly.

'Look, why don't you just finish up for the day,' Angie suggested, eyeing the pile of letters in Caryn's in-tray. 'I'll finish those off for you. You can do it for me next week, if you like. I've got a hot date on Friday night.'

Caryn hesitated. It was a tempting offer. She couldn't concentrate in any case. 'You sure?' she asked dubiously.

''Course I'm sure. Go on with you. Enjoy yourself. Can't stand watching you watch the clock! Go on. I'll clear these in no time.'

'Thanks, Angie,' Caryn said gratefully, saving the file she'd been working on. 'It's awfully kind of you.'

'Not at all. Just make sure you stay behind on Friday night. Unless *you've* got a hot date . . .' she grinned.

Caryn blushed again. The other girls teased her endlessly about her love life – or the spectacular lack thereof, as Chrissie put it. None of them could believe she didn't have a boyfriend –

hadn't *ever* had a boyfriend, come to that. *Pretty little thing like you!* Caryn never quite knew what to say. It was as if the memory of what had happened that night at Dave Humphreys' flat would never leave her. There was a queasy, nauseous feeling in the pit of her stomach that made the thought of a boyfriend almost unbearable. 'No, nothing like that,' she repeated shyly.

'Didn't think so.' Angie laughed. 'One of these days, Caryn, we're going to take you out, get you absolutely plastered and—'

'Oh, leave the poor thing alone,' Chrissie piped up. 'Look at her! Red as a beet!'

Caryn hurriedly switched off her computer, aware the others were staring at her. She bent down and grabbed her bag. 'Thanks,' she said again, picking up her jacket from the back of the chair. 'I'll finish up for you on Friday, I promise.'

'Enjoy yourself.' Angie waved her off. 'We're only teasing you, you know.'

'Yeah, I know. Bye!' Caryn fled before anyone could say another word.

Tory twisted her hair into a loose plait, pulled it on top of her head and secured it with a clasp. She turned sideways and looked at her reflection. Too grown-up? Too French? Dark blue jeans, a pale blue shirt rolled up at the sleeves and a pair of black, low-heeled sandals. And the silver necklace Thierry had given her. She fingered it gently. She frowned at her reflection. She was only going to meet Caryn and Nic, for Christ's sake – why all the fuss about what she was going to wear? But the memory of dressing with such care and attention to detail was too fresh to be brushed off, and she spent the next few minutes in silent contemplation of her image, just as Thierry had done, and in turn, of course, coaxed her into doing. He was exceedingly particular about his tastes. Pretty underwear, of the complicated, fancy sort she'd never worn. He liked the surprise of finding a pair of silk lace-edged shorts under a pair of jeans, for example – the elegant, sensual contrast between the rough, workaday denim and the soft, luxurious silk. Or a lace bra with tiny flowers and ribbons under a plain cotton shirt – he liked the unexpected, he told her. In time, so did she. That, too, had to change. But not yet. Not quite yet.

She looked at her watch. It was nearly time to leave. She felt her stomach give a lurch. As much as she was looking forward to seeing Nic and Caryn again, she was also dreading it. Nic, in particular, wouldn't be easily fobbed off. She would want to know everything. How could she explain that she wasn't ready to tell, to explain? That even thinking about it brought on the sort of pain that thinking about Susie wrought? It seemed to her sometimes that the experience was simply another in the chain of things that had happened after Susie. A particular kind of dread that lay just beneath the surface of her everyday life. She stopped herself from thinking any further. There would come a time when the mention of his name, even silently, in her mind's eye, wouldn't produce a sharp, sweet stab of pain. But not yet. For now, it was better to shut it off, block it out, stop herself from thinking, dreaming, feeling. Thierry was back with Inès. Where he should be. He was no longer with her, if he ever had been – and that was the end of it.

She picked up her keys abruptly and closed her bedroom door. More pressing than reminiscing about Paris was the need to find herself somewhere to live. After three years on her own, living with her parents was proving impossible to take. She ran quickly down the stairs and out the front door before her mother had a chance to ask her where she was going.

'*Nic*!' Caryn's uncharacteristically loud shriek nearly caused the waiter to drop his tray.

'Your *hair*!' Tory's mouth hung open before she realised she'd a mouthful of half-chewed peanuts on display. She promptly shut it again. 'Your hair!' she mumbled again indistinctly as Nic waltzed up to them, grinning.

'Like it?' she pirouetted.

'I *love* it! It's so . . . cool,' Caryn cried, getting up to hug her. 'You look great!'

'When did you get it done?' Tory asked, hurriedly swallowing the last of her peanuts.

'About two hours ago. Oh, God, it's *so* good to see you two!' Nic grabbed both of them at the same time, squeezing them to her. 'I've missed you *so fucking much*!'

'Mind your language!' Caryn squealed from underneath her arm. Although the bar wasn't full, they were already the centre of attention.

'Why? It's true.' Nic gave her another squeeze. 'How *are* you both? God, I've missed you!' She looked at Tory searchingly. 'You look so fucking *sophisticated*! I want to hear everything, OK? Every last detail!'

Tory turned bright red. By now everyone in the bar, including the waiters, was staring at them. 'Shh!' Tory said, putting a finger to her lips. 'Everyone's looking!'

'So?' Nic flopped into the seat beside her, shrugging off her jacket. 'Hope they like what they see. Now, what're we drinking?' She turned to the waiter who'd appeared magically at her elbow. There was something about Nic Harte's presence that said she was very definitely in charge. 'And before you two even start . . . this is on me. Champagne?' Caryn and Tory looked at each other and smiled. Well, why not? It wasn't as if they saw each other every day. And today *was* special. August the fourteenth. An anniversary, of sorts.

Five minutes later, a freezing-cold bottle of Krug nestling in a bucket of ice beside them, they raised their glasses. 'Cheers,' Nic murmured, taking a sip. She shivered dramatically. Caryn stared at her. Something else had changed in Nic alongside the haircut. She seemed . . . freer, somehow. Lighter. An image of the very first time she'd seen Nic suddenly popped into her head. Sitting a row behind her on their first day at St Augustine's, her face a mask of barely controlled anger, mouth obstinately set against the row of faces surrounding her, all of them. She'd held her head high, but there was pain there, burning below the surface of her skin like a fever. Caryn had sensed it somehow. Perhaps that was why Nic had spoken to her that day when she dropped her files and the two of them had finally talked to each other. If that hadn't happened . . . what then? Would they still have become friends? As odd as it seemed, Caryn couldn't quite remember what life had been like before Nic and Tory. It seemed to her as though she'd known them all along, as though they'd always been there, right from the start.

If Nic seemed lighter, Tory was the opposite. There was a brittle hardness to her that made Caryn think of a mirror about to shatter. She knew only the vaguest of details – Tory had had some sort of relationship with Thierry de Courcy, the man she'd gone to Paris three years ago to work for. From the postcards and the odd letter or telephone call, she'd gathered that his wife had found out and that he'd returned to her – if indeed he'd ever intended *not* to. All things considered, Tory seemed to have taken the news well. Now, looking at her, Caryn realised she hadn't. Her heart sank as she noticed that Nic was looking at Tory expectantly; she was looking for details, answers, a story . . . Nothing, Caryn was sure, could be further from Tory's mind. She could read the signs, even if Nic couldn't.

'Well?' Nic looked at the two of them, her eyes shining. 'Who's going to start then?'

'With what?' Tory's voice was mild.

'With *every*thing. I haven't seen either of you in bloody ages. And if you think a scribbled postcard is going to cut it,' she looked meaningfully at Tory, 'think again. It won't. I want to hear it all. Every last detail.'

Tory gave a slight smile. 'Nothing to tell,' she said carefully. She held the stem of her champagne glass between finger and thumb. 'It's over.'

Nic stared at her. 'But—'

'But nothing. It's over. He went back to his wife.'

'*Jeez*, Tory, you can't just—'

'Nic . . .' Caryn laid a hand on her arm, restraining her. She turned her clear, blue-eyed gaze on Nic. There was a warning in her eyes. 'What about you? Have you got your results yet?'

Nic hesitated. The atmosphere had slipped a gear suddenly, and she was conscious again of the great gulf of experience that occasionally sprang up between her and her two best friends

– nothing in her life could have prepared her to follow Tory in those moments when the protective veil of silence closed off her face and there was nothing more to be had. She glanced away. The petty argument over her name and the fact that her father had called her a spoiled wretch . . . what was that compared with the sacrifices Caryn had been called upon to make, or what Tory had gone through after the man she loved had returned to his wife? She shook her head, unable to grasp it. How had it happened that things had turned out so differently for each of them? As always, it was she who felt most unprepared – she who'd had everything money could buy.

40

Tory woke early the following morning with a mild hangover after a night of restless dreams. It took her a few seconds to realise where she was. No longer in the bedroom with the pale green shutters and the view over the rooftops. She was back in London. At home. She rolled sideways out of bed and almost tripped over the pile of brochures that had been lying at the foot of the bed since her arrival a week before. She bent down and picked one up, studying the cover. *The Cecilia Fry School of Flower Arranging*. She flicked it open to the first page. 'Welcome to the wonderful world of Cecilia Fry. Beautiful flowers, fine food and an elegant lifestyle are our expertise.' She winced and put it down again. Her parents would have a fit. A three-month, two-days-a-week course at the Cecilia Fry School in Chiswick in *flower arranging*. She could almost hear her mother's voice. *Flowers?*

The alternative that her parents had chosen, of course, left her absolutely cold. The mere thought of university made her feel distinctly queasy – there was nothing amongst the carefully laid-out prospectuses and course descriptions that they left lying not-so-discreetly on the breakfast table every morning that even remotely interested her. 'Ancient Greek?' her father had asked hopefully one morning. 'How about Medieval European history? Modern languages? Anthropology? *Any* kind of "ology"?' No, nothing like that, Tory shrugged. She wasn't sure yet . . . she'd give it some thought. She managed to slide from the table without further questioning, but she'd seen their look of panic. What was to be done with her?

It was Inès who'd sparked it all off. She'd noticed the bunches of fresh irises and sweet peas Tory brought home from the market nearby. At first she'd made no comment, but one morning, out of kindness, perhaps, she'd asked Tory to pick up 'whatever took her fancy' and to try her hand at arranging the enormous bunch that always stood on the dining table. Those first few times, Tory hadn't had the nerve to try anything different. Inès abhorred what she called 'arrangements' and the giant bunches of blood-red roses or fuchsia geraniums that dotted the apartment were ostentatiously simple, never mixed. But Tory came back the third or fourth time with armfuls of pale lilac sweet peas and delicate lemon-yellow carnations, and she'd tentatively mixed the two, adding sprigs of purple flowering rosemary, and the effect was pleasing. Even Inès had to admit it brought a certain freshness to the hallway, which had only ever known her preferred stark, imposing displays. After that, Tory was hooked. She looked forward to her weekly visits to the flower market. She loved the sights, smells and sounds: the cries of the vendors, the air thick with the perfume of flowers, freshly brewed coffee and the occasional whiff of cigarette smoke; giant buckets of blooms flown in from almost every corner of the globe. She stopped to chat to the sellers, learned the names of flowers she'd never seen before, learned to tell the difference between waxed and unwaxed bulbs, how to tell the three-hundred-odd varieties of roses from each other, what flowers were likely to last and which would wilt and die . . . she could have spent the whole day wandering in and out of the stalls.

She looked down at the brochure again and sighed. Going to

the market once a week to choose a single display and trying to make a career out of flowers were two very different things. How would she ever persuade them that this was what she'd set her heart on? She could hear her mother moving around downstairs. Their conversations had been polite, but strained. Tory had chosen to say very little about Paris, but of course they knew. Everyone knew. After Inès found out and asked her to leave, it was clear to everyone what had happened, even if no one said a thing. And here, now, there didn't seem to be an easy way to bring it up. So she said nothing and they said nothing, and the uneasy balance that had characterised relations between them before she'd gone, remained.

She sighed and picked up the brochure. Might as well get the ball rolling, she thought to herself as she walked downstairs. She had a feeling it would roll for a while.

'*Flower* arranging?' Her mother put a hand to her throat. Tory looked at the ceiling. She might as well have said knitting. Or macramé. Even cookery would have been a more respectable choice. 'You mean . . . arranging *flowers*? For a *living*?'

'Mum, it's not like that. It's a proper course. It's . . . you get a diploma—'

'In arranging *flowers*?' Her mother started to laugh, but without humour.

'Yes. No. It's more than that. It's like . . . horticulture. You learn about plants and soil conservation and the environment, stuff like that. It's like getting a degree,' Tory said, making it up as she went along.

'A degree? In what . . . three months? Oh, come off it, Tory. What'll your father say?'

'What's it got to do with him? It's *my* choice. I'm the one who wants to do it,' Tory said, her temper starting to rise.

'Not if you're asking *us* to pay for it,' her mother replied tartly. They looked at each other. Tory was aware, as her mother was, no doubt, that an argument would take them both into dangerous, uncharted territories. Fuck it, Tory thought to herself angrily. What did she have to lose?

'Why won't you ever let me do what *I* want to do?' she asked, feeling the sudden, sweet rush of release as the words she'd been longing to say for months, years even, came tumbling out. 'You *never* listen to anything I have to say. It's always what *you* want, what *you* think is right and proper and suitable. I'm sick and tired of being told what's suitable for me.'

Her mother stared at her in astonishment. 'What *we* want? *Us*? Your dad and me? All *we* want, Tory, is for you to stop acting as if you're the only person in the world with *feelings*,' she spat out angrily, 'and to buckle down like the rest of us—'

'Buckle down? To what?' Tory was shouting now.

'To *life*! To getting on with your life like *we've* had to do. Don't you think that I didn't *long* to escape like you did? Don't you think I'd have liked to run off to Paris after . . . after . . .' She swallowed, unable to bring herself to say the words. She put up a hand to furiously wipe away her tears. 'But running away wasn't enough . . . no, not for you – nothing's *ever* enough. You had to go and disgrace us, on top of it all. How d'you think it made us feel?'

Tory could only gape at her in disbelief. 'What are you t-talking about?' she stammered, fear rippling over her.

'You know exactly what I'm talking about,' her mother said, turning away. She walked over to the kitchen sink, her shoulders heaving. 'He's as old as your father, for Christ's sake. How could you? When I think of you living in that flat, all that time, with *him* . . . it's *disgusting*, Tory. Running after a married man. You . . . you *disgust* me.'

Tory's eyes narrowed. The hot, shameful sensation came at her in a rush. She opened her mouth to speak, knowing as she did that there would never be a return to the way things had been, before. '*I* disgust *you*? No, it's the other way round, Mum. At least I'm still *alive*! At least I can feel something! At least I'm still capable of feeling something, sleeping with someone, *any*one. Who cares if he's married? Who gives a shit? At least he can still do it! And that's more than *you* can do, isn't it? How long has it been since—'

'*Shut up!*' Her mother turned towards her, her face white with anger. 'How dare you talk to me like that? How *dare* you?'

'But it's *true*, isn't it?' Tory was sobbing now and the words just wouldn't stay put. 'That's what you can't stand, isn't it? You can't stand it that I'm still alive and she isn't. You can't stand it that *I* wasn't the one he attacked. That's what you've wished for *every single fucking day* since it happened!'

There was a sudden rush of air as the front door opened. 'Gilly?' It was her father's voice. The two women stared at each other, both white-faced with fear. Tory's heart was hammering so loudly she was sure her mother could hear it. 'Gilly?' her father called again, walking down the passageway to the kitchen. Tory swallowed. There was nothing more to be said. She turned and pushed past him, ignoring his bewildered look, and grabbed her bag. She had to get away. Away from the things that had been simmering inside her for as long as she could remember and that she'd spectacularly failed to suppress. But it was true. Every single accusation that she'd flung at her mother was true and there wasn't anything Gillian Spiller – or anyone else – could say in her defence. And the worst thing was, she realised as she let the front door slam shut behind her, that her mother hadn't even tried.

41

Estelle picked up the silky-soft brush and began dreamily to powder her face. Roberta Flack was crooning softly in the background. 'Killing me softly . . .' It was an apt metaphor for what she was about to do to Hans Berndt, the Swiss banker who'd become one of her regulars over the past year. She stared at her reflection in the mirror. She looked *hot*. Smoky, glittering eyes, a hint of green in the shadow that brought out the turquoise flecks in her irises; lips carefully drawn with pencil and then filled in with lipstick. A touch of blusher on the cheeks to accentuate her high cheekbones . . . she blotted her lips carefully, fastened the diamond studs Hans had bought her on their third date and stood up, swaying slightly. She'd had a joint or two that afternoon, then a glass of white wine whilst having her bath, and there was a little white tablet in its usual place on the bedside table. She looked at it, brimming with anticipation. She checked her reflection carefully. The dress, of deep, fiery orange crushed silk, fitted her like a glove; tight, all the way down to her knees. Smooth, caramel-coloured calves, tapered into slender, fine-boned ankles before disappearing into tan high heels – she looked like a dream. She *felt* like a dream, and she hadn't even taken the little tablet yet. She had Jody to thank for all that. Jody, the fresh-faced, peaches-and-cream Midwestern girl who lived in the apartment next door. Jody, who looked as though butter wouldn't melt in her mouth and who, after nearly five years, was Mrs Devereaux's highest earner. Jody, her newest best friend.

She pirouetted one last time, walked over to the bedside table and slid the tablet off the tiny lid. She looked at it for a moment, then popped it under her tongue, letting it dissolve, waiting exultantly for the rush. The first fizz like a shock of cold water against the skin . . . warming up, relaxing, sliding into pleasure. Within minutes, the world around her was transformed. She felt gorgeous, she *looked* gorgeous; she was going to have a gorgeous night. It was what she loved most about the pills – unlike coke, which she'd tried a few years back when she lived with Caitlin, there seemed to be no downside to ecstasy. Just happiness, a feeling of effortless, thrilling pleasure. Everything was softened, melting, sensual. Every movement, every gesture, every glance was accompanied by a surfeit of emotion. Jody called it the lovedrug. After her first few tries, Estelle understood why. And the other good thing about ecstasy, Jody said knowingly, was that you couldn't really tell. Mrs Devereaux couldn't really tell. Oh, she wasn't blind . . . she knew there was precious little chance her girls *weren't* smoking joints or taking the occasional line of coke – she said as much herself. But she drew the line at heroin and if anyone's little drug habit got so far out of control that she could no longer function, she was out. Simple as that. Estelle had been with Mrs Devereaux for almost three years – in that time, she'd seen twice as many girls come and go. The message was very, very clear. In the meantime, Estelle could see nothing wrong with a little white tablet that made the world a sweeter, kinder place. In their line of work, a good thing, surely?

She walked into the living room. It was a quarter to eight. In exactly five minutes' time, Rolf, the driver, would pick her up. Hans had booked her for three days, during which time she would stay with him in his suite at the Lancaster and be, quite literally, at his beck and call. Tonight she was to accompany him to the opera and then to a business dinner with some Japanese bankers. Hans was all right, all things considered. A quiet, taciturn man with rather conventional tastes and appetites, he treated her pretty well. In the seven or eight months she'd been seeing him, he'd bought her a couple of expensive gifts, always complimenting her on her appearance. About himself he said nothing. All she knew – and, as far as Mrs Devereaux was concerned, all she *needed* to know – was that he was phenomenally wealthy, married, of course, but despite that fact didn't mind paying over the odds for exceptionally attractive female company whenever the mood took him. And Estelle was, as he kept telling her, exceptionally attractive.

A car horn sounded discreetly outside. Rolf was waiting for her. She picked up her overnight bag, switched off the lights and closed the door. Leaving the lights on was another of Mrs Devereaux's pet hates – waste. The apartments in which six of the twenty girls on her books lived weren't exactly palatial. In fact, they were downright poky. Identical one-bedroom flats with barely enough room to swing a cat around in. But it was the address that counted, as Mrs Devereaux constantly reminded them: 24 Jermyn Street. A *Mayfair* address. There were days when, even now, Estelle would stand at the tiny kitchen window overlooking the square and pinch herself. She still couldn't quite believe it. She'd made it. She was on her own, living in the best part of London, simply light years away from the tiny, claustrophobic world she'd left behind in Arcadia and the shock of her arrival in London. Stoke Newington? She wouldn't be seen dead anywhere near Stoke Newington now. She was wined and dined every week in the best restaurants, with men who paid a small fortune for her company. The fact that she earned it lying flat on her back with her legs open . . . a small price to pay, surely? Christ, she'd done the same in Harare for one-thousandth of the price. It was nothing to be ashamed of. Just think of the money she sent to Gloria every month. Five hundred pounds, without fail. Since she'd started working for Mrs Devereaux, she hadn't missed a month. Not a single month. She hardly ever bothered to read Gloria's replies. Too saccharine by half, for one thing, and too far off the mark for another. She wasn't sure quite what Gloria believed; modelling, acting . . . something along those lines. Something she could brag about to her fellow Christian soldiers. Despite the ecstasy flowing swiftly and easily through her veins, Estelle grimaced. She hated thinking about who and what she'd left behind. Thinking about Gloria and Thandie produced an ache in her side that sometimes stopped her breath. Much better to focus on what lay ahead. For tonight, at least, Hans. And an evening at the opera.

The midnight-blue Mercedes was waiting for her across the road. 'Hi, Rolf,' she said as she slid gracefully into the back seat. The door seemed to close itself. Luxury. Pure luxury.

'Evening, Estelle.' Rolf nodded at her in the rear-view mirror. 'The Lancaster, is it?'

'Yep.'

'We'll be there in ten.'

She leaned back, opened her purse and took out a small bottle of perfume. A quick dab on the wrists, one at the base of the neck and a touch behind the ears. Not too much – just enough for Hans to smell her on his skin all through his meetings the following morning. It seemed to reassure him that his money had been well spent.

'Estelle . . .' Hans rose as she walked into the lobby. He was with two men, one Japanese, the other European or American.

He kissed her on both cheeks. 'You look lovely, my dear. Let me introduce you. Mr Moritako. M'sieur Roche.'

Mr Moritako bowed deeply. Estelle hesitated. What was the protocol with the Japanese? Should she also bow? She inclined her head a fraction. It seemed to work. Mr Moritako smiled as he straightened up. Mr Roche was also smiling as she turned and extended her hand. If he recognised her for what she was, he made no sign.

'*Enchanté, mademoiselle*,' he said suavely, bringing her hand to his lips. Estelle stifled the impulse to giggle. She inclined her head a second time.

Hans placed his hand on her elbow. 'Mr Moritako will be joining us at the opera, my dear. Will you have something to drink? A glass of wine, perhaps? The driver should be here in half an hour or so.' He was attentive and solicitous in a rather old-fashioned way that she liked. A waiter appeared silently.

'Martini, please. Dry,' Estelle said briskly, and sat down in the seat next to Hans, conscious of the men's appreciative glances as she crossed her legs. This, she'd come to understand – more than the sex, however good it was – was what men like Hans paid for: they liked the fact that others saw what they could afford. Hans was an average-looking, middle-aged man. All things being equal, not the sort of man able to attract a girl like Estelle. But he was rich, fabulously rich. And that made all the difference. He'd said to her once, the second or third time he'd asked for her, that paying a woman for sex was often more pleasurable than the act itself. He didn't expect her to understand it, he said – but she did. More often than not, sex was about power and Estelle, too, was interested in power. Money, she'd come to understand very quickly, was one route to power; sex and beauty another. She had the latter; Hans – or the men she routinely slept with – had the former. Soon she, too, would have money, and with it, all the power she wanted.

She sipped her Martini, listening with half an ear to Berndt talking to his guests. Real estate. Tokyo. Geneva. Manhattan. As he talked, Berndt reached out and put a hand on her knee, claiming her attention. Estelle smiled. She turned her head slightly and looked straight at M. Roche. He too was staring at her knee. Enviously. She felt the slow burn of desire begin to stir in her. At moments like these, she sensed the power of her own beauty, stronger in its pull than any sexual attraction she'd ever felt.

42

Fundamentals. Tory underlined the word several times. *Good floral design should be immediately attractive and yet appear effortless and natural.* Her pen hovered above the paper for a second or two. Then she quickly underlined the words 'effortless' and 'natural' for further effect. She stole a hasty look around at her fellow students. There were eight of them on the course; seven middle-aged women in tweed skirts, cardigans and sensible shoes – and Tory. She looked down at her striped jumper, old jeans and Doc Martens wondering what, if anything, the others made of her. Apart from the initial 'hello' they'd all exchanged on the first day, they'd pretty much left her alone. It was like being back at St Augustine's. Forever the odd one out. Not that she minded. She still couldn't believe she was here, at the Cecilia Fry School of Flower Arranging in Manor Park, Chiswick, in her second week. She'd expected to have the most monumental battle with her father, especially after the argument with her mother, but it hadn't happened. A few days after the outburst, she'd come home one evening and found a cheque on the dining table for the full amount of her fees. Her father looked up from his paper, mumbled something about wanting to make sure she was happy and her mother hadn't said a word. She'd picked it up, slipped it in her pocket and gone up to her room, her face wet with tears. A week later, she was enrolled on the course.

And it wasn't as easy as it sounded, either. Certainly not just a case of sticking a rose in a glass or choosing what foliage to put where. It was a weekend course, starting at nine o'clock sharp on Saturday morning and running straight through until six with an hour's lunch break and a short tea break at four. Sunday's classes began at ten and ended at five with half an hour's lunch and no tea. It was intense and densely packed with information, and by the end of her first weekend, Tory's head was splitting. There were history classes and horticultural lectures; classes on colour and texture; a seminar on someone called Linnaeus and his extremely complicated systems of ecological classification; there were talks about climate and colour; local and foreign varieties of plants; tropical plants; seasonal plants . . . line-form, line-mass, symmetry, parallel styles, deconstructed styles . . . balance, scale, proportion . . . it went on and on. The list of things she had to learn before even catching sight of a flower was daunting. But from the very first day, she loved it.

After the third weekend, she found herself a part-time job at a florist on the Fulham Road, not far from home. On the tiny salary it paid, moving out of her parents' wasn't an option, at least not yet. But it kept her out of the house for most of the day and the course kept her away all weekend. By the end of her first month, she'd almost forgotten her determination to move out and was fully, happily engrossed in her work. And then she discovered that the other women on the course weren't half as bad as she'd feared. Claire, one of the older women, was a hoot. They'd been given a short lecture on the 'four key principles of experimental design – movement, dominance, rhythm and repetition'. The tutor had asked them to demonstrate them in flower arrangements that incorporated the key aspects of each. Tory did well on her first attempt, 'movement' – she'd designed a pretty, trailing arrangement of pink orchids and twisted, dyed red vines and put it in a simple clear glass vase. The fat, curving petals of the phalaenopsis orchids lent themselves well to the idea of movement, spilling out over the lip of the vase and trailing downwards on to the surface of the table. Jane, their tutor, was pleased. Inspired by Tory's success, Claire attempted to do something similar with 'dominance' – except that her resulting mélange of green cymbidium orchids, upright palm fronds and mounds of green and pink bun moss looked a little . . . well, odd, frankly.

'It looks like . . .' Belinda, one of the other women struggled to put it into words.

'A rather large, pointy pink penis,' Claire muttered under her breath. 'Reminds me of my ex.' She was standing next to Tory, who almost dropped her own vase in surprise. Claire looked at her and winked. Tory put a hand to her mouth and giggled.

'Anything funny?' Jane asked, eyebrows arched. Tory shook her head. She couldn't look at Claire for the rest of the afternoon, however, without giggling.

43

Caryn looked around her anxiously. It had been a grave mistake to give Nic her work number. Nic didn't seem to realise that she was at work. She'd been on the phone for nearly ten minutes and the conversation was showing no signs of winding down. 'Nic?' she whispered into the receiver. 'Nic. I've got to go. I'm at *work*.'

'D'you think I ought to ask him?' Nic asked, a note of uncertainty in her voice.

'Yes. No. Look, I'd better go. I'll call you tonight, OK?' She put down the phone before Nic could say anything further and looked around her to see if anyone else had noticed. She sighed for about the fiftieth time that morning. She wasn't sure how much more of MetLife she could possibly take. She'd been there for over a year – but with all the advice she'd been dispensing lately, something had begun to nag at her. If she was so bloody good at sorting out the lives of others, she really ought to start sorting out her own. Starting with her job. Yes, it was time to move on. She had to find something a little more taxing than deciphering faux posh voices and making endless cups of tea or she'd literally go mad.

'I knew you'd get fed up,' Vanessa said to her cheerfully the following Friday. 'I'm surprised you stuck it out this long, to be honest. *I* wouldn't. Anyhow, what're you looking for next?'

'I don't know,' Caryn said slowly. 'Something a bit more . . . creative?' She held her breath.

'*Creative*? Blimey . . . this is the City, love, not the bloomin' West End. I could send you to Soho, though . . . there's all the TV and film stuff down on Wardour Street. Shall I ring up the Soho branch, see what they've got?' Caryn nodded eagerly. Soho sounded a lot more interesting. Why hadn't she asked Vanessa before? 'I'm only doing this as a favour to you, mind,' Vanessa said sternly as she reached for the phone. 'I'll be really sorry to see you go. You've been a good little earner for me, you know.'

'Thanks,' Caryn said, meaning it.

Ten minutes later, it was done. She was to report to Jackie on Monday morning at the agency branch just off Soho Square. She hugged Vanessa warmly, picked up her cheque and left. There was a faint fluttering of excitement in her stomach; something she hadn't felt in . . . well, years. Since St Augustine's, in fact. She'd fallen into a rut, she realised. Seeing Nic and Tory again the other evening had given her a bit of a jolt – Nic had her precious degree and Tory'd had three years of the sort of experience Caryn could only dream about. Well, the only person who could do anything about it, she realised as she fought her way on to the Tube, was her. Yes, it was time to move on.

Nic drew a deep breath, knocked on Jim's study door and pushed it open. He was sitting at his desk, wading through a mountain of paperwork, a lit cigar at his elbow. The acrid, pungent scent filled the room. He glanced up at her. She felt her knees begin to shake. There was something about her father's expression that could throw even the most confident person off guard.

'What is it?' His voice was short.

'I . . . I could come back another time if you're busy—' Nic said hesitantly.

'What is it?' Jim repeated, already irritable. Nic's heart sank.

'I just wanted . . . I was thinking about—' she stammered, the words suddenly sticking in her throat.

'Oh, for God's sake, spit it out – *what?*'

'About what to do after . . . well, now that I've finished—'

'Finished what?'

'College. I mean, I thought I'd try to get a job and—'

'A job? What on earth for?' Both his tone and his look were dismissive; the memory of their recent argument was still reflected in his eyes. Nic could feel her temper begin to rise. Was he deliberately trying to goad her?

'I want to earn my own living,' she said, trying not to sound plaintive, or worse. 'I've finished my degree – it's time to get a job. I just thought—'

'That I'd help you get one? After turning your back on your family?'

'I didn't turn my back on you!' Nic's temper was up. 'I just didn't want anyone to know who I was, that's all.'

'Why? What're you ashamed of? Not good enough for you now, are we? Now that you've got yourself a fancy college degree you've decided—'

'I haven't decided *any*thing!' Nic burst out, unable to stop herself. 'I just didn't want people thinking I was trading on your name, that's all. I wanted to know I'd done it on my own. I still don't understand what's so terrible about that!'

'But why *that* name? Why *her* name?' It was the closest she'd ever heard her father come to mentioning her mother's name. There was a sharp stinging of tears behind her eyes. 'Couldn't you have picked another, for Christ's sake?'

There was an awkward moment of silence in the study as they faced each other. The cigar glowed between his fingers but he made no move to smoke. A shaft of sunlight hit the desk suddenly and the room brightened momentarily. Nic was waiting for something from him – some sign, a gesture, a word – something that would cut to the heart of the tension that seemed to surround every single exchange she'd ever had with her father . . . but nothing came. He dropped his gaze, his attention claimed by the reports and files that were spread around him. In a heartbeat, she was dismissed. She stood uncertainly by the door for a moment longer, willing him to look up. He did not. She shut the door quietly behind her.

Jim swore under his breath as soon as the door closed. He hadn't meant to be quite so cutting but he couldn't help himself. He tried – Jesus Christ, he *tried* – but it was no use. Everything about her reminded him of Sarah. He drew a deep breath, steadying himself. It wasn't Nic's fault, poor girl. He saw how it hurt her, how wounded she was by his anger, without the comfort of knowing why. Yet he couldn't stop himself. Every time he looked at her, he saw Sarah's face in those last few dreadful moments. It took him a few minutes to bring himself under control. The worst part was, it was getting harder, not easier. Who was it who'd said time heals all wounds? Whoever it was obviously hadn't taken all possible circumstances into account. Especially his.

PART FOUR

44

Alone in the small Chelsea flower shop where she worked, Tory emptied the pails, lugged the plastic bags full of dead leaves and stalks out to the front for collection and picked up the broom. She pushed her hair out of her face impatiently; despite the cold outside, she was sweating. She'd been on her feet since eight a.m. and she was exhausted. It was nearly six, almost time to close up and go home. Katie, the teenager who came in after school twice a week, had gone home early with flu. It had been a busy week – two weddings, several office Christmas parties and a last-minute order from Great Ormond Street Children's Hospital – *something cheerful for the reception desk!* – and on top of it all, Jim and Catherine, the owners, were away on holiday in Spain.

Tory had been alone for almost the entire week – but she'd coped admirably and, in truth, had been grateful for the peace and quiet. And the chance to make the displays her own, too. Much as she admired Catherine's floristry skills, she'd relished the opportunity to try things out her way. The two weddings had been a success, she knew. The bride's mother had sent over a bottle of champagne and a *very* generous cheque shortly afterwards to express her thanks. Tory was secretly delighted. They'd unexpectedly run out of the rather fussy peonies and sweet peas that the bride's mother had chosen, and Tory had substituted a simpler, more elegant palette of winter colours – white lilac, white 'Bianca' roses and creamy vanilla-coloured ornamental cabbage leaves tinged at their edges with dark, vibrant green.

She'd thrown in some bronze-coloured 'Rubella' to complement the whites and creams and added several sprigs of dried cinnamon bark to the stems . . . she could still smell the spicy scent in the office downstairs. Fortunately for her, the last-minute changes had obviously gone down well.

She wiped down the counter, made sure the flowers that remained had enough water and was just about to switch off the lights when she heard someone rapping on the window in the shop. She glanced at her watch, frowning. It was a quarter past six. They were closed. She put down the cloth and walked through to the shop. A young man was standing outside, his face red with the cold and a look of panic that almost made her smile. 'We're closed,' she mouthed through the glass pane. She pointed to her watch. He lifted his shoulders beseechingly. He was young, good-looking . . . and desperate. She shook her head in mock exasperation and opened the door.

'I know, I know . . .' he said, immediately apologetic. 'You shut at six, I know. But I ran all the way—'

'We *are* closed . . .' Tory said, relenting. 'What d'you need?'

'Just something for my girlfriend. We've been going out for three months.' He grinned suddenly. 'Not that long, I know, but I'm taking her out to dinner and a mate of mine said I ought to get her some flowers . . . a bunch of roses, anything, whatever you've got.'

'I've got these,' Tory pointed to the blood-red Milano roses just beginning to open in a bucket by the door. 'Or the Coolwaters; they smell lovely. I could wrap you up a quick bunch.'

'Yeah, those look good. Anything. Whatever you say.'

'Or . . .' she said suddenly, cocking her head to one side. 'How about these?' She turned and picked up a large bunch of purple violets. She gave a short, almost embarrassed laugh. 'I read something this morning in one of the flower magazines. Did you know Napoleon's nickname was "Corporal Violet"? He used to send Josephine a bouquet of them every year. When he went into exile, he took a few petals from her grave in France and he died with them in a locket round his neck.' She smiled at him. 'Not quite what you think of when you imagine Napoleon, is it?'

'Er, no, I suppose not.' The young man looked at her uncertainly.

'Quite the romantic, apparently,' Tory smiled.

'Yeah, they'll do. I'll tell her the story. Thanks. You've saved my evening!' A few minutes later, he walked off whistling down the road, an enormous bunch of scented violets in hand. Tory stood at the window watching him, her mind slowly beginning to turn round. Four bunches of violets cost far less than a dozen red roses but the look of satisfaction on his face made it more than worthwhile. That was the marvellous thing about flowers. She didn't know anyone who wasn't moved by their beauty. A bunch of flowers never failed to put a smile on a customer's face – *any*one's face – and yet few people knew anything about them. Take the story she'd just told: imagine if every bunch she sold came with a little story attached, a small historical titbit, a little something that took the flowers out of the ordinary. Flowers with a story. Flowers with history. Her heart began to beat faster. Blooms with a story. Blooming stories. *Bloomin' Stories*. Suddenly she grabbed her bag, switched off the lights and set the alarm and ran all the way down Sloane Street to the Tube.

45

Caryn looked up at the building, looked back down at the scrap of paper in her hand and hesitated. Thirteen Charlotte Road, just east of Liverpool Street, resembled a derelict building site, definitely not the offices of the cutting-edge film producers Jackie had promised. Had she made a mistake? She stepped back off the pavement and squinted up at the building again. It was obviously a warehouse of some sort – or had been, once, long ago. There was a rusty bell to one side of the doorway. She pressed it gingerly. A few seconds later, much to her surprise, she heard a faint answering click. She pushed the rotting wooden door open and stepped inside. The tiny vestibule was dank and dark. There was a door to her right – locked – and a staircase ahead of her. She gripped the handrail and began to climb, wondering where the hell she was going. After the gloss and polish of the offices she'd worked at over the past few years, this felt distinctly odd.

Why on earth had she let Jackie talk her into applying for a permanent job? She *liked* temping. She liked the fact that she could leave with a week's notice if she got bored or fed up. After the rut she'd fallen into at MetLife, she guarded herself against making the same mistake twice – and the best way of doing that was to change direction every once in a while, try out new things, learn new skills. Just as she'd been for Vanessa, she was one of Jackie's favourites. In the three years she'd been with her, she hadn't once been without an assignment or somewhere to go. Not once. She *liked* it. So why had she let herself be persuaded? Even Jackie admitted she wouldn't normally suggest a permanent job to one of her best temps, but the job description had landed on her desk by mistake and she'd immediately thought of Caryn. 'Should've gone to Kelly; she does the permanents,' Jackie said, tossing it casually over to Caryn across the desk. 'It'd suit you down to the ground, though. Take a look. Won't hurt to look.' Caryn picked it up dubiously. *Personal Assistant to the director. Cutting-edge film production. Trendy East End offices.* 'Sort of thing you could do standing on your head,' Jackie said, smiling almost ruefully at her. 'Or asleep. Go on, you can't temp for ever, you know. And it's close to where you live, isn't it?'

Well, here she was, climbing the stairs in a building that smelled of years of neglect and – she wrinkled her nose delicately – other, dreadful things. Well, yes, it was certainly close to home but there was a very good reason there were few jobs in Shoreditch. She rounded the last bend and all of a sudden, the smell of fresh paint hit her nostrils. There was a newly painted grey door in front of her with a small sign. *Crystal Vision Films.*

So they *did* exist after all. She pushed open the door and stepped inside another world.

The open-plan offices ran the entire length of the enormous, light-filled room. She could see straight across the slate rooftops to the silver and grey-green glass-and-steel buildings of the City. The glossy-haired receptionist behind the sleek counter looked expectantly at her. Caryn gulped. Dressed in a pale green cardigan, a skintight denim skirt and a shiny crocodile-leather belt, she looked more like a model about to step on to the catwalk than a receptionist. Red lipstick, red nails. Pure glamour, in other words. In her sensible black suit, white shirt and low, practical heels, Caryn felt like fleeing.

'Hi,' the gorgeous creature said, opening her beautiful red mouth. 'Can I help you?'

'Um, hi. I . . . I'm here about the PA position. I've got an interview with Mr Keane. At ten a.m.?' Caryn stammered. Was Jackie mad? There was no way she would fit in *here*.

'Oh, right. Rowland's PA? Fan-*tastic*. Take a seat, babe. He's not in yet. Shouldn't be long, though.' She paused in her stream of chatter and smiled. Perfect teeth. 'Cup of tea?'

'No, I'm fine, thanks. Could I . . . is there a toilet anywhere?'

'Yeah, of course. Just there, the door on the right.' She pointed halfway down the corridor. Caryn fled. She caught a glimpse of perhaps half a dozen people behind shiny white computer screens in the minimally decorated space with its exposed brick walls and rows of snowy-white desks. No – definitely, absolutely, *unequivocally* not the sort of place for her. She shut the door behind her and walked over to the mirror. She examined her face anxiously – pale, tired and wan. The polar opposite of the sunny, confident creature behind the desk. She lifted her shoulders in a little gesture of dismay. There was *no way* she'd get the job. She was as out of place here as she had been at St Augustine's. The distant, uncomfortable memory made her even more nervous. She splashed a little water over her face, made sure her pony tail was secure and pulled a face at herself in the mirror. She ought to stick to temping – that was what she did best.

She opened the door, turned left and promptly fell over the bicycle that someone had left propped temporarily against the wall. The receptionist gave a little squeal and rushed over. 'Oh, gosh. I *am* sorry! It's Rowland's bike. I *told* him not to leave it there! Are you all right?'

'Yes, yes, I'm fine. Thanks,' Caryn said quickly as she staggered to her feet, her face on fire. Everyone was looking curiously in her direction. 'No, it's fine . . . honestly,' she tried to assure the girl, who had bent down to inspect her legs.

'No, look, you've ripped your tights. See?' She pointed at Caryn's knee. 'I'll give you some petty cash to get another pair. Rowland, you idiot. Look what you've gone and done. The poor girl's only just come through the door!' Caryn opened her mouth to protest, caught sight of a pair of twinkling blue eyes, a tanned face and a mop of curly, dark brown hair – and promptly shut it again. Rowland. Obviously.

'Oh, shit . . . I *am* sorry,' he said, glancing at her knee. 'My fault entirely. *Mea culpa.* You're all right, though, aren't you? No cuts, no bruises?'

'Oh, no, no, I'm fine. It's nothing. Really. You don't need to get me another pair of—'

'Of course we do,' Rowland said firmly. 'Charlie, be a darling and get the girl another pair, will you? What's your name, by the way?' he turned back to Caryn.

'Caryn, sir.'

'Sir?' He raised an eyebrow at her. His eyes were still twinkling. Caryn felt her stomach flutter. There was something about him that made her want to smile back. 'Rowland'll do just fine. Well, follow me, Caryn. You're the fifth person we've seen since yesterday but I rather think we owe you the job!' He grinned at her. Her stomach gave another lurch. She followed him down the corridor.

'Right,' Rowland said, opening the door to his office. 'Have a seat. I'll see if I can find your details in all this mess.' He gestured at his desk, which was covered in paper. The whole office was wonderfully chaotic in a hip, casually trendy sort of way. On the exposed brick wall behind him was a large red-framed poster with the words 'Keep Calm and Carry On!' Good-looking, hip, trendy *and* funny. She'd never met anyone like him. He rummaged around on his desk until he found her CV. He pulled it out of the stack, looked at it for a few seconds and then looked back at her. 'St Augustine's?' he murmured, almost to himself. 'In Chelsea?'

'Er, yes.'

'*Four* As at A level?' That eyebrow again.

'Er, yes.'

'But no degree?'

'Er, no.'

'How come?'

'I . . . I'd rather not say,' Caryn stammered. Her cheeks were on fire again.

Rowland looked at her closely. 'Fair enough. Right, when can you start?'

Caryn blinked. 'Start?'

'Yeah. When can you start work?'

'Oh. Does . . . does that mean I've got the job?'

'Well, by implication, yes,' Rowland said dryly.

Caryn flushed. She was being spectacularly dense. He was having the most unusual effect on her. 'Monday?' she said, thinking rapidly ahead. That would give her two days to find a more suitable wardrobe. There was *no way* she could come into *this* office in the plain skirts and shirts she'd been wearing. And, as always, it would be Nic to the rescue.

'Monday's fine. Nine on the dot. Charlie can let you know more or less what the job entails.' He flapped her résumé at her. 'You've got great references. *And* four A levels. You could do this silly job standing on your head. So . . .' he stood up, signalling the end of the interview, if it could be called one. Caryn hastily followed suit.

'Thanks,' she muttered.

'Great. See you Monday. And don't forget your tights.' He glanced down at her legs. Her stomach gave yet another lurch. She walked quickly to the door, hoping desperately that the confusion he'd thrown her into didn't show on her face. She thanked Charlie, picked up the tights and practically ran down the stairs. She walked down Charlotte Road, unnerved by the whole episode and unsure whether or not to be pleased that she'd got the job. Somewhere at the back of her mind, however, she was aware of the faint but unmistakable burn of pleasure every time she pictured Rowland Keane's face.

The following Saturday, she sat on Nic's bed in her underwear, looking on anxiously as Nic pulled pair after pair of trousers off their hangers and tossed them on to the growing pile of clothes on her bed. Across the room, Tory was lying almost comatose on one of the armchairs, staring into space. 'Here, try these,' Nic said finally, handing her a pair of navy-blue woollen trousers.

Caryn looked at them dubiously. 'But what'll I wear them *with*?'

Nic picked up a blue-and-white striped shirt. 'This. And this.' She tossed over a grey waistcoat. Caryn bit her lip. 'Trust me,' Nic said firmly.

There was nothing for it. Nic's face wore that grim look of determination Caryn knew only too well. She got off the bed and began to get dressed. 'The shirt's too big,' she said, holding out her arms. It was true; the cuffs reached her fingertips. 'And this . . .' she turned around. The waistcoat reached her bum. 'I look like a bag lady.'

'No, you don't. You look fine,' Nic insisted. 'We'll just have to take things in a bit, that's all.'

'What d'*you* think?' Caryn turned to Tory.

'Huh?' Tory turned her head slowly towards them.

'Tory. You're not paying attention,' Nic said sternly. 'What's got into you today? This is only the most important day of poor Caryn's life and you're—'

'No, no, it's fine,' Caryn broke in hurriedly. The last thing she wanted was an argument over her wardrobe – or lack thereof. 'What'll I do about the trousers, though?' She peered down at her feet, hidden by folds of material.

'Take them up, that's all. It won't take long, I don't think. Er, can either of you sew?'

'I can. Sort of,' Caryn said, wondering how long it would take. 'Not very well, though.'

'Well, rather you than me,' Nic said dryly. She frowned at Tory. 'What on earth is the matter with you? You've hardly said a word all morning.'

'Nothing. I'm just *thinking*,' Tory said, yawning.

'About what?'

'Stuff.'

'Yeah, but what sort of stuff?'

'Oh, this and that,' Tory said vaguely. She swung her legs off the bed and stood up. 'That's nice,' she said, pointing to a long floral skirt, obviously making an effort to get into the spirit of the event, a morning spent restructuring – or building from the ground up, depending on how you saw it – Caryn's wardrobe. She'd rung up the day she'd got the job, wailing about the complete and utter unsuitability of her wardrobe, such as it was. Nic, of course, bossy as ever, had promptly volunteered them both, which was how they all came to be sitting in Nic's bedroom on a cold, rainy Sunday morning, going through her collection of mostly too-big and unsuitable clothes. Now that Caryn had got – at long last – what Nic called a 'go-somewhere' job, it was imperative that her wardrobe went with her. Caryn wasn't quite as confident; she wasn't sure the job would lead to anything other than making tea for the gorgeous Rowland, but Nic was firm. 'At any rate,' she said cheerfully, pulling a pretty silk top from the pile of clothes on the bed, 'you'll stand a better chance of going *some*where with slightly trendier clothes. And that's a fact, darling. You can quote me.'

'Yes, but I'm not sure I *want* to go anywhere,' Caryn murmured. Anxious as she was to fit into her trendy new surroundings, there was a side to her that dreaded walking in on Monday morning in Nic's hand-me-downs, altered (badly) to fit.

'Oh, for God's sake, Caryn! Do you want a better job or not? You've been temping for bloody years – where's it going to get you?' Nic cried, her exasperation beginning to show. 'Come *on*. You're easily the brainiest of the three of us! It drives me crazy to see you just give up.'

'I haven't given up,' Caryn protested, her face suddenly crumpling. 'It's just—'

'Just what?'

'Just . . . well, my new boss, Rowland . . . he's going to laugh at me when he sees . . .'

'Caryn Middleton! You've gone all red. Who *is* this Rowland guy, anyway?' Nic's eagle eyes missed nothing.

Caryn felt herself go even redder. 'No one. My boss, I mean. I met him on Friday and—'

'You've got a crush on him? Already? You haven't even started the job!' Nic laughed.

'I *haven't* got a crush on him,' Caryn protested, wishing she'd never brought the subject of her new job up at all. 'He's just . . .'

'What?'

'He's . . . well, he's rather good-looking and—' To her absolute horror, Caryn felt the prick of tears behind her eyes. Surely she wasn't about to burst into tears? She quickly turned away from Nic. 'I need the loo,' she muttered, stumbling out of the room in her too-long trousers and oversized shirt before Nic or Tory could say another word.

Nic stared at her disappearing back, dumbfounded. She turned back to Tory. 'What the hell did I say?'

Tory shrugged. 'Well, it's pretty obvious, don't you think?'

'What is?'

'She's in love. With her new boss. Whatever his name is.'

'But she's only just met him!'

'Yeah, well . . . *coup de foudre* and all that,' Tory said mildly. 'Besides, it's about bloody time. Have you ever known Caryn to have even the mildest crush on anyone?'

Nic shook her head slowly. 'No, I suppose not. But that's why it's so strange. She's not like that. Not at all.'

'People change, Nic. We've all changed. Don't tease her. It's not fair.'

Nic stared at her. 'What on earth are you talking about?'

'Don't tease her, that's all. Look, it can't be that easy for Caryn. She's had a pretty tough time of it, you know. Living with that nightmare of a mother, having to give up going to university . . . it's different for her, that's all I'm saying.'

Nic opened her mouth to protest but the bathroom door opened at the same time. One look at Caryn's shiny nose and too-bright eyes and she promptly shut her mouth. As always, there was something in Caryn's proud, almost defiant gaze that put paid to any further probing, and the rest of the morning passed in rather uneasy silence.

When the two of them had gone, Caryn with at least four new outfits in a bag under her arm, Nic made herself a cup of tea and took it into the living room. She looked around her flat guiltily. Jim had tossed her the keys almost casually one afternoon, about a year after she'd graduated. Nothing as dramatic as a present – in his typical, off-hand way he'd said something about having to buy a second London property to offset taxes . . . if she didn't want it, Jessica could always have it when she turned eighteen. *She* had no such daft ideas about going to university. *Well, did she want it or not?* Nic, utterly fed up after two years of sharing a grotty flat with two other girls she'd met on her course, weakened. She'd taken it, a pretty, second-floor, two-bedroom flat in Primrose Hill, and then regretted it ever since. Jim missed no opportunity to remind her of his generosity, despite the colossal slap in the face she'd administered him by changing her name. Added to that, of course, was the matter of getting a decent job. It was all very well for her to lecture Caryn but what the hell had she done with her precious degree? She'd worked in a string of low-paid, low-grade editorial jobs for the first two years – hardly setting the journalistic world alight, more a case of making tea and changing the photocopy ink, not that she'd have admitted it to anyone. Then she'd found a job on a small, community-based newspaper which had folded approximately six months after she'd started. And now, six months into her present job, she was the lowest-paid member of staff at *Gossip!*, a celebrity chit-chat magazine whose existence relied solely on increasingly lurid stories about celebrities who'd fallen out of favour or were just about to fall. Jim, of course, had had a few words to say about that – *Three years of bloody university and this is all you can manage?* – but pride kept her at it. Pride and the inability to find anything else, of course. Being too weak to resist the offer of a free place to live was bad enough . . . accepting his nonchalant remarks about getting her a 'proper' job if she wanted it was a step too far. It didn't help that Jim had suddenly taken an unnatural interest in the media. For reasons Nic couldn't work out, he'd developed a desire to own a newspaper – any newspaper. If Murdoch and Maxwell could do it, she'd overheard him say more than once, why couldn't he? Nic bit down on her tongue to stop herself retorting.

Things were different for Caryn. As always, when she thought about Caryn, Nic felt a pang of sympathy mixed with awe. Since they'd left St Augustine's, she'd never once heard Caryn complain. Things at home seemed to chart an uneasy course between complete and utter disaster – her older brother's arrest, her mother's overdose, the threat of splitting the family up – and moments of almost unbearable pleasure. The year before, her younger brother had won a scholarship to Westminster, just like Caryn. Nic remembered the afternoon she'd met them both after taking him round his new school. He was a sunny, good-looking boy with none of Caryn's anxiety and all of her steady resolve. Tory, uncharacteristically insightful, said it was a result of the home Caryn had managed to provide, despite the odds. Nic just remembered how envious she'd been of the looks of love and pride that passed between them, younger brother and older sister, as they sat in the restaurant on Sydney Street that Nic had taken them to as a celebration. No one had ever looked at her that way.

She got up, feeling oddly out of sorts. The old feeling of inadequacy that sometimes came over her in Caryn's presence had resurfaced. It was hard *not* to feel inadequate. She, who had so much, had achieved so little. Caryn, on the other hand . . . *Oh, stop it*, she admonished herself severely. Nothing worse than a Little Miss Rich Girl drowning in self-pity. If she hadn't achieved much, it was entirely down to her. She walked over to her desk and switched on the computer. Zoë, her formidable and forbidding boss, had reluctantly given her an assignment at six thirty-five p.m. on Friday, just before closing. Bidina O'Connor − whose name meant 'little Bridget' in Gaelic, the Irish PR girl told her confidentially and irrelevantly − had checked into the Priory that morning. *So what?* was Nic's immediate − and erroneous − reaction before remembering that she was supposed to care. She'd been given a tiny article in the Features section.

'I can always put you on TV reviews,' Zoë said witheringly as Nic's face failed to show the sort of appreciation Zoë expected from junior staff members. 'Or is there something else you'd like me to say? Like, perhaps, goodbye and good luck with your *next* job?' Nic flushed in anger and embarrassment but managed to hold her tongue. She hated Zoë Williams-Dent more than anyone she'd ever met, including each and every girl she'd been to each and every school with − and that, as Caryn and Tory both knew, was saying something. But she was determined to stick it out, crawl up the journalistic ladder and claw her way on to the 'serious stuff', as she called it, one promotion at a time. Unfortunately for Nic, perhaps, so was every single other female journalist at *Gossip!*. The ladder was already overcrowded. Nicola Parker had just about as much hope of making it on to the payroll at *The Economist* or the *Guardian* as Tory did. That, too, was saying something. As far as she knew, Tory had never even picked up a newspaper.

Bidina O'Connor, whose name, incidentally, means 'little Bridget' in Gaelic − and there's nothing 'little' about Bidina after her recent two-stone weight gain, I don't mind telling you − checked into the Priory this morning under a halo of flashbulbs. Nic looked at the sentence she'd just typed and groaned. How was she ever going to claw her way out of the quagmire of celebrity gossip with sentences like *that*?

46

Tory followed her father into the restaurant. Luigi's was a small, family-run trattoria just around the corner from Hortensia Road. She'd been surprised to hear him suggest it. It had been a family favourite with the Spillers . . . before. 'It's the only place I know of that your mother won't look,' he said, smiling ruefully as they sat down. Giuseppe, their elderly waiter, was delighted, if a little surprised, to see them again after so long. He didn't mention Susie but something in his manner as he brought the menus to the table gave Tory to understand that she hadn't been forgotten. She listened to her father place the order – for a second, it was as if the blow from which they were all still recovering, even now, had never been.

'So, what's this *idea* that you have?' he asked gently, pouring wine for them both. He leaned back in his chair and looked at her, a finger pressed into the sag of his cheek as he waited for her to speak.

Tory took a deep breath. She'd rehearsed the speech so many times that she heard her own voice from a great distance, the words tumbling out, almost tripping over one another. She showed him the small folder that contained everything she'd been thinking about for the past few months; it took her almost ten minutes and when she was finished, she could feel her breath coming fast and laboured, as if she'd just run a mile. There was silence for a few moments. Her father's expression was hard to read. 'Does . . . does it sound mad?' she asked, hardly daring to hear his response.

'Mad? No, not mad. It's just . . .' he paused delicately, holding his wine glass between thumb and forefinger. 'Well, it's just not what we expected, Tory. I mean, what about university? You did say you'd think about it after Paris and—'

'Dad, I don't *want* to go to university,' Tory said, frustration beginning to well up inside her. 'Why can't you and Mum just accept it? Not everyone has to go to university, you know.'

'I know. It's just that with Susie gone—'

'Could we, *just for once*, leave Susie out of this?' Tory said bitterly. 'Just for once? This is about *me*, Dad. Not Susie.'

Her father glanced at her in surprise. 'Now, Tory, there's no need to get upset,' he said quickly. 'I'm just *saying*, that's all.'

'What *are* you saying, Dad? That it doesn't matter what *I* want to do with my life – just as long as it makes you and Mum happy?'

'No, of course not! It's just that this idea of yours . . . it's an awfully big step. It's a huge undertaking. You're barely out of your teens—'

'Dad, I'm twenty-four years old. I'm not a bloody teenager!'

'Yes, but running a *shop*?' He made it sound as though she'd suggested opening a brothel.

'It's a business, Dad. My own business. I've spent all this time working for other people and I know this business inside out! I know it'll work, I just know it.'

'But where on earth are you going to get the money to buy a shop?'

'I'm not worried about finding the money,' Tory said, sounding more positive than she felt. 'I can find the money. I just want . . .' She stopped, aware that her throat was aching.

'What *do* you want?' her father asked, more gently this time.

'I just—' Tory looked away suddenly, her eyes flooding with tears. 'I just want your *support*, Dad. That's all. I don't need your money to do this. I just want you—'

'Tory,' her father interrupted suddenly. 'Stop. I understand, all right?' His voice was kind. He reached across the table and placed a hand over hers. She was alarmed to feel it was trembling. 'I know what you're saying. Just . . . just give me some time to react, that's all. I *know* it's been hard for you. Believe me, I know. I look at you and I see all the things we didn't do for you after . . . after Susie died. I know it must feel as though we've forgotten about you but we *haven't*. I promise you we haven't. Now, will you let me look at this properly? Not over dinner?'

Tory nodded shakily. Her relationship with her mother had

never quite recovered from the argument they'd had when she'd returned from Paris; she couldn't bear the thought of it happening again with her father. She wiped her cheeks with the back of her hand and picked up her wine glass. It was the hardest thing in the world, she thought to herself miserably as she swallowed the last drop. No matter how hard she tried to pretend their approval didn't matter to her – it did. Of course it did. She wanted to hear them say they were proud of her. Just this once. That instead of being disappointed that she wasn't more like Susie, they were proud of her for being her.

'Give me some time. I'll need to prepare your mother for this,' her father said, his hand still covering hers. It was no longer trembling. He gave a short, shaky laugh. 'You know what she's like.'

Tory nodded glumly. 'Yeah. I do.'

'It's not like that,' her father said gently. 'I know it doesn't always seem that way, but you mean everything to her. To both of us.' Tory swallowed. She couldn't speak. 'Now,' he said quickly, clearing his throat and changing the subject, 'what'll you have for starters? How about the prosciutto?'

'Susie's favourite,' Tory whispered.

He gave her hand a quick squeeze. 'Yes, it was, wasn't it? She always left the melon.' Tory smiled at him through a thin veil of tears. For the first time since Susie's death, they were able to turn the emotion to a gentle, shared memory that belonged to the past but had somehow managed to survive it.

47

Caryn walked into her new job on Monday morning wearing Nic's trousers, her own plain, white shirt, a shiny black belt and, on Brian's expert advice, a pair of three-inch mock-crocodile stilettos. At the last minute, he'd dragged her down to the

Sunday market on Petticoat Lane. He'd chosen them and when she tried them on, he looked her up and down and said she looked 'fit'. Whatever he meant by it, Charlie certainly seemed to agree.

'Hi,' she said, smiling brightly. 'Ooh, I *love* your shoes!'

Caryn offered up a silent 'thank you'. She smiled back. 'These? Oh, thanks,' she said nonchalantly. 'I like your earrings.' Then, wondering if her response wasn't too underwhelming, added quickly, 'They really suit you.'

'Oh, these old things?' Charlie put a hand up to her ears. 'Thanks. Nice belt, too.'

There was a discreet cough behind them. Caryn turned round. Rowland Keane was standing behind them. Neither girl had heard him come up the stairs. 'Right, ladies, if we've *quite* finished? Caryn, follow me, please.'

Her face flushed with embarrassment, Caryn practically ran after him as he strode through the offices. It was nine o'clock and there were only a couple of people at their desks. They looked up as the two of them walked past, Caryn taking three steps to two of his.

He reached his office and stood aside for her to enter. 'Why is it,' he murmured, following her in and shutting the door, 'that women always go through that ridiculous mutual admiration society whenever they meet?' His blue eyes regarded her thoughtfully as though he expected an answer.

Caryn hesitated. 'Protection,' she said after a moment. 'You know, get in a compliment before the other person snubs you. Men do it too—' She stopped suddenly, wondering if she'd gone too far. It was only her first day – Christ, her first *hour*!

He looked at her, an eyebrow raised sardonically. '*Do* they now?' he muttered, taking off his jacket. 'How extraordinary.' His tone of voice implied the opposite. Caryn felt her cheeks redden even more. 'Right. Better get on with it.' He glanced at her hands. 'Haven't you got something to write with? I thought I'd better run through your tasks.'

'Oh, yes . . . yes, of course,' Caryn stammered. She hadn't even taken off her coat yet. 'Um, where will I be working?' she asked, looking around his office. Please God, not in here, she thought silently.

'Didn't Charlie show you?' he asked, clearly surprised.

She shook her head. 'No, she was busy with society matters,' she blurted out, unable to stop herself. It was nerves. He looked at her blankly. 'Er, the mutual admiration society . . .' she added lamely. For a second it looked as though he might bite her head off but then he smiled – a slow, sure, sexy smile that transformed his face completely. Caryn's knees began to wobble.

'Ah, a sense of humour,' he said, as if to himself. 'You'll need it, working here. You'll be out there, at that desk behind the door. I work in here most of the time, except when I'm travelling or we're on location. This,' he handed her a couple of typewritten sheets, 'was done by your predecessor. It's pretty self-explanatory . . . goes over most of the things you'll be asked to do.'

'Why did she leave?' Caryn asked. 'Just out of . . . er, interest.'

He looked at her, a smile beginning to play around the corners of his mouth. 'No sense of humour,' he said at last, and sat down at his desk. 'Now, unless you've got any questions . . . ?'

'No, no.'

'Great.'

Caryn looked down at the paper. *Daily Tasks. 1) Get Rowland's coffee. Milk, no sugar. 2) Open the post.* 'Well, I . . . I guess I'd better get started,' she said, glancing towards the door. 'I'll just get your coffee.'

'Good girl. There's a staff meeting at eleven. I'll introduce you to the rest of the team.'

She backed out of his office, her cheeks still flushed. *Good girl?* For all his sex appeal, the wide, heart-stopping smiles and the super-trendy offices, she could already see that this job wasn't going to be a huge improvement on the last. *Coffee-making, post-opening, phone-answering, general dogsbody Caryn.* Not bad for someone who very nearly went to Cambridge. It was enough to make you weep.

48

All of Manhattan glowed with fierce, twinkling lights. The streets were awash with late-evening shoppers streaming in and out of the stores in the last desperate few days before Christmas. A tall, broad-shouldered man with tousled dirty blonde hair, no hat and no gloves, exited the subway at Canal, walked quickly up the street and practically jogged the remaining few hundred yards to the corner of Hudson and Charlton, his duffel bag banging awkwardly against his thighs. He walked down Charlton, scanning the industrial-looking façades quickly, blowing on his hands to keep them warm until he found the number he was looking for. He pressed the buzzer impatiently and looked up the darkened front of the building to the eighth floor. A few seconds later, he heard the squeak of a window being opened. A man stuck his head out and peered down on to the street. 'Simon?' His voice was snatched up by the wind.

'Yeah. Open up, *bru*. It's freezing out here!'

'Watch out. I'm gonna throw you down the keys. Lift's bust, I'm afraid.'

'Shit.' The blonde-haired man pulled a face. Seconds later, there was a soft thud and the keys landed on the sidewalk, already covered in a fine dusting of snow. He bent down to pick them up. A few minutes later, only slightly out of breath from the climb, he pushed open the door and walked into a vast space. There was almost nothing in it save for a large fridge in one corner and an old, battered leather couch and a TV at the other end. Several filing cabinets stood in the middle of the loft like sentinels. He grinned.

'Simon . . . finally.' The man who had thrown down the keys turned from the window.

'Mat.' Simon went up to him. They gripped each other by the forearms, hard. 'Long time no see, *bru*.'

'Likewise.'

'Howzit?' They grinned at each other under the easy release of physical contact.

'Can't complain. And you? Everything OK?'

'Yeah. I'm good. Just got back.'

'From . . . ?'

'Er, Geneva.' Simon walked over to one of the windows, looked down at the street for a moment and then turned. 'So this is it? This is home? It's kinda . . . *empty, bru.*'

Mat shrugged. 'I like it. Suits me just fine.'

'I guess.'

Mat looked at him quizzically but said nothing. He yanked open the fridge door. 'Beer?'

'Thanks.' Simon walked across to the sofa and sat down, yawning. He leaned his head back, aware of the waves of fatigue slowly washing over him. He hadn't slept in almost twenty-four hours. The following morning he was flying on to Jo'burg, crossing the continent he'd only just left.

'You look tired,' Mat said mildly, handing him the beer. It was a question as much as a statement.

Simon opened his eyes. In the delicate way he'd always known Mat to have, it was left there in the comfortable silence between them, waiting for Simon to pick it up if he wished.

'Yeah. Long month. Lot of travelling.'

Mat said nothing for a moment. He didn't pretend *not* to be studying Simon. That was another thing about Mat: no subterfuge. 'Need to slow down, *bru,*' he said after a while.

Simon grinned. He closed his eyes again. 'Oh, please. Look who's talking. When was the last time *you* came home before one in the morning? Or took a weekend off?'

'Tonight, actually.' Mat took a swig of his own beer. 'So, business is good?' he asked in that calm, unhurried way of his.

'Yeah. Couple of new mines opened up last month. Things are moving. About bloody time. The war's brought the whole place to its knees.'

'Is it dangerous?'

'Yeah, in places. But I'm up-country most of the time, away from Maputo. Some places are so remote you'd never know there was a war going on. But hey, Africa's dangerous, full stop. If it's not, it ain't Africa, right?'

'Spare me the bullshit.' Mat grinned, getting up. 'I'm not one of your donors.' He pulled open one of the filing cabinets in the centre of the room. 'Speaking of donors,' he said, 'have you seen this? He tossed a newspaper at Simon. 'Sunday's. I kept it for you. You ever come across him?'

Simon unfolded the paper. Jim Harte's face stared impassively out at him. He felt the habitual tiny thrill of dislike. 'No, never,' he said, handing it back.

'Funny . . . I'd have thought you two would've bumped into one another, somehow. It's a good article. Must remember to show it to Dad.' He folded the paper in half.

'How is he?' Simon asked carefully. He was aware his hands were shaking slightly.

'They were asking about you,' Mat said, getting up from the sofa. 'Mum's mad at you. You haven't called in weeks.'

'*Ag*, I've been on the move,' Simon said wearily. 'You know how it is.'

'You know how *they* are,' Mat said mildly. There was a moment's silence. 'Is everything OK, *bru*?' he asked quietly.

Simon closed his eyes again. 'Yeah, everything's fine. Just tired, that's all.'

'What's your girlfriend say about it? All this travelling?'

'Dunno. Haven't got one. What about yours?'

'Dunno. Haven't got one either.'

'So. No change there, then.' He opened his eyes. Mat was grinning.

'Nope.' They looked at each other and began to laugh. Simon could feel the tension slowly begin to slip away from him. Mat always had that effect on him. Without trying, he somehow brought him back to himself. Back home. He relaxed even deeper into the couch. 'I'll get you a blanket,' Mat said, getting up. 'You're dead on your feet. What time's your flight?'

'Eleven,' Simon mumbled. He could feel the lassitude washing over him.

'You'll easily make it from here. Go ahead and use the

bathroom,' Mat called out as he crossed the room. 'I'll find you a spare pair of boxers. You still sleep in boxers, don't you?'

Simon was too tired to reply.

Five minutes later, he stood in front of the mirror in Mat's bathroom, brushing his teeth with Mat's toothbrush. He gave his reflection a faint smile. It wouldn't be the first time they'd shared a toothbrush. Probably not the last, either.

Mat walked in a second later, holding out a pair of tartan boxer shorts. For a moment the mirror held the two of them. Same height, same weight, same build. Perfectly matched, perfectly in tune. Closer than many brothers, they'd practically been brought up together. They'd lived in the same house, slept in the same bed, shared the same food and fought together in a way that few men ever had. They *could* have been brothers except for one, singular thing – Simon was white; Mat was black. Not biological brothers, then. Theirs was an unusual story. Those who knew them assumed one thing and were later astonished to find out that it wasn't so. Simon Carter. Mat Ndava. Two halves of an African story. They were both Zimbabwean but from entirely different worlds. Not, however, in the way most people expected.

Simon's parents were farmers – poor, unlucky, pig-headed . . . who knew? They'd come out to Rhodesia in the 1950s from Lancashire, lured by the promise of land and easy fortunes to be made. The Carters bought thirty hectares just outside the town of Chiredzi, on the banks of the Runde River, close to the border with Mozambique. For fifteen years, they tried to raise cattle, grow tobacco, cotton, tea, wheat, maize . . . anything. They failed, of course. The land was totally unsuitable for the type of farming that they'd chosen and by the time Simon was eight, he was already accustomed to saddling up one of the last remaining horses and riding across the dusty hills to the neighbouring farm to ask for food. The white farmers who lived on homesteads in the area around them pitied the Carters, especially the kid, Simon. Who'd want to grow up like that, hey? Like a bloody *munt*, they whispered amongst themselves. A *munt*, yes, but with a lot less to eat and no one to take care of him, the wives murmured. At least the *munts* had each other; Simon Carter had nothing, no one. That mother of his ought to be shot.

It wasn't strictly true, however. He *did* have somebody, though it wasn't someone their white neighbours would necessarily have approved of, or understood. Matari Ndava. Mat, as everyone called him. Mat's father, Gordon Ndava, owned the largest concessions store in Chiredzi. He was, within the confines of the economy in which he operated, one of the wealthiest men in the district. He was often away from home on business and in one of his absences, Matari, his only son, came home with a friend. A *white* friend. They'd found each other down by the river a few weeks earlier, Mat told them. Simon was teaching him to swim. Patience Ndava noticed that the white child her son had brought home was hungrier and dirtier than any of the children in the township. He ate the bowl of *sadza* and wild spinach leaves that she put down in front of him with gusto and came back for second and third helpings. He was a *mukiwa*, a white boy, but an unusual one at that. He spoke Shona as well as he spoke English, seemed completely at ease in their home with the endless stream of curious friends and relatives – a *mukiwa*, yes, but one for whom the differences between them did not exist. Patience was puzzled by him, but Mat was entranced. Whatever the reason, it was clear Simon Carter needed some looking after – Patience was shocked at his parents' neglect. There were weeks and months when all he ate was what she put in front of him. She became used to the sight of him winding his way through the crowded streets of the township after school, his uniform stitched where *she* had mended it, oblivious to the fact that the kids he went to school with didn't even know where Mkwasine, the Chiredzi township where blacks lived, was. He practically lived in Mkwasine these days. Without Patience and Mat, the boy would have starved.

Over the next few years, against the odds, he and Mat became inseparable. As the war for independence intensified, growing more bloody by the day, Mat and Simon simply disappeared into their own world, where 'it' – the question that was ripping the country apart – didn't matter, didn't even exist. They were brothers already, no matter one was white, the other black. When independence came and Rhodesia finally sank to the ground, the Carters, unable to turn on the blacks, turned on each other. Fourteen-year-old Simon was in Mkwasine when the news came over the crackling wireless. Another white tragedy – only this time, the farmer had carefully shot his wife and the dogs and then turned the gun on himself. Had Simon been there, he would have died with them. It had happened before.

No one seemed to know what to do with the fourteen-year-old boy, who, unbelievably, had more or less lived with the Ndavas for the past five years. He had no living relatives. None of the remaining white farmers wanted him; bad business with the parents and all that, but everyone was nervous. Mrs Blake from Creswell Farm across the valley made a half-hearted offer but Simon turned it down. He was fine where he was. What else was there to be done? Gordon Ndava paid the fees at the tiny, whites-only school in Chiredzi and sent Mat to join him, now that it was allowed. The following year, he sent the two of them to boarding school in Harare. When they were sixteen, he made the difficult decision to send them both to boarding school in England. ZANU, the party of liberation, rewarded those who'd assisted in the struggle but Gordon, ever the strategist, was wary. Zimbabwe's past had been one long, bloody struggle for power; he had no reason to believe its future would be different. He was already, even then, making contingency plans. Gordon was Shona; his wife was Ndebele. Neither wanted to live in a place where they might be forced to turn upon one another. A year after the boys left for Lancing College, he moved the rest of his family to London.

A shrewd businessman with contacts across the region, his fortunes began to rise. By the time Mat and Simon entered university, the Ndavas lived in a large and comfortable house in Hampstead. Ernestine and Adele, the two younger girls, were at

Bedales. Mat, the brighter of the two, went to Cambridge to study history; Simon did a degree in geology at Imperial. *These are my two sons*, Gordon liked to say to visitors when they came upon the two young men home for the holidays or – more generally in Simon's case – to drop off laundry. He enjoyed the widening of the eyes, the look of surprise, sometimes even suspicion . . . *no, really?* Were the two young men *gay*? No, no . . . Gordon enjoyed their confusion. He explained. A round of apologies immediately followed, astonished admiration – sometimes, too, envy. *What a wonderful story!*

Gordon was firm. 'As you know,' he told Simon right from the beginning, after the death of his parents, 'we don't have a word in Shona for "half-brother", or "foster son" or anything like that. You are my son, now. That's it.' It was, as they said, the African way.

It took Mat a while to fall asleep after the gentle rumble from across the floor told him Simon had no such trouble – he was asleep before his head hit the cushion. Not Mat. He lay awake for almost an hour, unable to put his finger on what was wrong. Something was bothering him. Simon seemed edgy, not tired; the expression in his face when he thought no one was looking was not one of exhaustion; there was a wariness in the green-brown eyes that Mat hadn't seen in a very long time. Something wasn't right. He knew Simon better than anyone, sometimes even better than he knew himself. It bothered him to think that something was wrong and that he had no idea what it was or how to help. He lay awake listening to the sound of his own breathing, to Simon's fitful snores and to the sound of Manhattan, eight floors down, still alert.

There was no time to talk the following morning. They both woke up late, showered quickly and left the apartment together. 'I'll call in a few days,' Simon shouted as he ran towards the subway with his duffel bag swinging out behind him. He turned at the last minute, grinned at him briefly, unhappily, and then disappeared, swallowed up by the crowd rushing down the subway stairs. Mat shook his head. Yes, something was definitely wrong. He pulled his lower lip into his mouth thoughtfully. No doubt Simon would tell him what was going on when he was ready. In the meantime, all he could do was wait. He stopped off at the coffee shop on the corner and bought his habitual double espresso. He was sorely in need of it.

'Hi, Mat,' the receptionist smiled at him as he walked through the lobby the next morning.

'Oh, *hi*, Mat,' – Gladstone's PA.

'Hey, Mat, how's it going?' – Monica, the legal assistant.

'Wassup, bro?' – Derrick, the Harvard intern who insisted on speaking gangsta-rap whenever they met, Mat couldn't work out why.

'Oh, *hi*, Mr Ndava,' – the bubbly blonde whose name he could never remember who ran the photocopier. 'How *are* you?' He smiled at each one in turn. By the time he finally made it into his office, he'd nodded to, smiled at and acknowledged almost two dozen people – if Derrick had his way there'd have been a high-five amongst the salutations as well. He closed his door with a sigh. As Simon had said to him once when he complained about the number of people he had to be nice to on his way in every morning, no matter how tired or irritable he might be, 'It's hard being everybody's favourite Negro.' He pulled a wry face. Well, that was one way of putting it.

He walked over to his desk, stunned by the view as he was every morning. He was on the fifty-fourth floor of Sixteen Hundred West Barclay, a few blocks from the World Trade Center and overlooking City Hall which, from this lofty height, seemed tiny, dwarfed by the titans of industry and finance that rose vertically all around. He stood in front of the plate-glass window, watching in fascination as the mid-morning mist clouds over Manhattan slowly began to dissolve. The cloud cover was below him, hovering somewhere around the thirtieth floor. It was strange to be up there, trapped between the carpet of wispy, thinning mist below and the brilliant streaks of blue above. Manhattan. How he loved it.

He turned from the window and looked at his desk. It too was covered in a thick carpet – of papers. Memos, letters, reports, printouts, Post-it notes, scraps, bits of envelopes and torn-out articles that he'd earmarked to read, drafts of his current story, copy-edits of his last. People who dropped by walked away bewildered by the chaos, wondering how on earth this – admittedly *exceedingly* good-looking and charismatic – man could ever have been described as the 'new face of African reporting'.

He sat down and switched on his computer. What everyone failed to understand, of course, was that there was method to the madness and an order to the chaos. At thirty-one, Mat Ndava was climbing steadily towards the top of his game. He'd left Cambridge with a First in history; worked briefly as a manage-ment consultant for a big investment bank and then defied everyone's expectations by changing tack completely and going into journalism. He'd always wanted to write – a summer's unpaid internship at the newly launched financial magazine *African Economist*, just off Northumberland Avenue in London, had paid off. He and the editor, a fiery Moroccan named Philippe, had got along famously. He'd sharpened his skills, learned the ins and outs of the trade and then moved on to the *Financial Times*, where he'd earned himself a reputation for his sharp, biting journalism and his ability to get under the skin of a story. A chance meeting with Robert Barron, the Canadian news and media mogul, had landed him a job in Toronto for a year. From there, he'd been sought out by the *World Economic Digest*, his current employers. Ten years out of Cambridge and he was doing what he felt he'd been born to do. How many people could say *that*, he wondered to himself only every other day. He loved his job; he loved New York. He still remembered his first day at *WED*, as it was affectionately known. Chuck Lauer, his new boss, had said something to him that he'd never forgotten. 'Welcome to Manhattan. You'll need to find three things: an apartment, a gym and a few good restaurants close to home. An oven in Manhattan is extra storage.' He understood the comment as Chuck intended. He was here to *work*.

He quickly read through the article he'd been working on, testing its rhythm and tone.

Share Markets for the Rich and Bored. Like the latter half of the high-risk equals high-return equation? Here's a quick exercise to see how up to date you are on global markets. Take a guess. Which region has had the best performing stock exchanges over the last four years? Asia, with its tigers, and China slowly coming out of communism? South America, suddenly sexy again? Not quite. The answer is, in fact, Africa. If you wanted a 109% US dollar return on the first eight months of the year, you should have invested in Malawi. If you have the stomach for it, these are the exchanges where you can cash in big – and even if you lose your shirt, you'll have great dinner party conversation for ever.

He tapped his pen against his teeth thoughtfully. Not bad. But it needed something else, something a bit harder-hitting. He began to type furiously.

49

Leonie Frith, the fiftysomething-year-old, formidably efficient office manager at *WED*, looked up as a group of young journalists passed in front of her desk, clearly on their way to one of their infamous Friday-night drinks sessions in the Sky Bar on the ninety-fifth floor. She noticed Mat wasn't amongst them.

She waited until the group had gone, noisily getting coats and jackets, and then walked over to Mat's desk. His back was to her; he was staring at something he'd just typed and didn't hear her come in. 'Aren't you going with them?' she asked, noting with a raised eyebrow the usual chaos on his desk.

'Not unless you come with me,' Mat said, not turning round. She could tell from his voice he was grinning.

'Oh, I'm far too old for that sort of caper,' she said firmly, lips twitching.

'Now, what sort of caper would that be, Frith?' he asked, swivelling round to face her.

'Go on with you. Now, is there anything else you need for tonight? I'm just about to lock up.'

'No, thanks, Frith. Have a good weekend.'

'You, too.'

She walked back to her desk, took her coat and scarf from the stand in the corner and pulled on her gloves. She looked at them for a moment. They were a Christmas present. From Mat. Calfskin leather in burgundy, a colour he knew she liked. She'd been quite overcome when he gave them to her, although he'd never have known it. She'd looked at the beautifully wrapped box and made a joke of it. 'Oh, my. If I were twenty years younger,' she'd said, shaking her head at him.

He hadn't missed a beat. 'Oh, boy. Then we'd both be in trouble.' He'd stumped her then. She hadn't known quite what to say. She'd mumbled something like, 'Thank you, it's very sweet of you,' or some such nonsense and then, when she was sure no one was looking, she'd gone to the toilets and allowed herself a little cry. She was fifty-one years old. Single, and childless. Her life hadn't quite worked out the way she'd expected it to – but, then again, whose had? She'd followed an American lover to the US when she was in her twenties – only to discover he was already married and had no intention of leaving his wife, but he'd wanted her to stay. So she'd stayed. She worked in the city, lived in a nice little apartment in Manhattan and he went home to New Jersey every weekend. They'd stayed like that for fifteen years. And then he died, quite unexpectedly, of a heart attack. She'd been in New York for so long by then and it seemed too much of a leap to return home to Battersea, where she'd grown up, so she stayed on. She found a job at *WED* and slowly worked her way up to being one of the most senior administrators in the company. Five years ago, she was assigned the Features floor and that was when she met Mat.

She'd been dubious of him, at first. Aged twenty-six with a degree from Cambridge, a glorious track record from the *FT*, three languages under his belt and the best damned body she'd seen on any man, young or old – she'd recognised his type as soon as he walked in the door. Mr Bigshot. An über-achiever. Twenty-one years her junior. Young enough to be her son. They'd got off to a rather prickly start. She was frosty and more than a little defensive. He was wary. She was a bit taken aback that he was black but honestly, within a few minutes of meeting him, it wasn't the thing you noticed. Any more than you'd notice someone had green eyes. Or blonde hair. Neither of which he had. What he did have, once you got to know him, was impeccable manners, a slow, easy smile that didn't come often and a calm, patient ability to sit out any storm, regardless of its intensity, which she very much liked. They were both English, sort of. At least he seemed to understand her in a way most Americans didn't, or couldn't. Nothing to do with language, although that did sometimes cause a bit of confusion. No, it was the other stuff, the unspoken stuff . . . the odd laugh over something, a gesture . . . the intonation in his voice and his sometimes very reserved, very discreet way of looking at things. They got on in a way she could never have anticipated.

By the time he'd been working with her for six months, she couldn't remember a time when he hadn't. By the time he'd been with her for a year – though she would have sooner *died* than hear anyone make the suggestion – Leonie Frith, aged forty-eight at the time, handsomely attractive in a rather austere, impeccably mannered way, was just the *teeniest* bit in love with Mat Ndava. And that was four years ago. She shook her head crossly. She was getting daft as well as soppy in her dotage, she smiled to herself. But, damn and blast it, he was *awfully* nice.

50

'Where the *fuck*,' Rowland asked, grinding the words out between clenched teeth, 'is the sound engineer?' No one spoke. It was nine-thirty on a Friday night and the six people, including Caryn, who were standing around had been there since eight o'clock that morning. Everyone was tired and irritable. No one, however, was more tired or irritable than Rowland.

'Look,' the assistant producer suddenly spoke up. 'Why don't we just call Anita Godwin on Monday morning and explain that the demo's going to be delayed. We can sort it out on Monday—'

'We are *not* going to call Anita Godwin on Monday morning and explain there'll be a delay because there won't *be* a delay,' Rowland said, slowly and sarcastically. 'But if you want to go home, sweetheart, then by all means do so. Just don't bother coming back.' The producer's face was crimson.

'Where does the sound engineer live?' Caryn asked suddenly.

'Bermondsey,' someone else said gloomily.

'Well, why don't I go round there and see if he's in?' Caryn said, looking anywhere but at Rowland. 'I mean, he's got to go home at *some* point. Even if it *is* Friday night.'

'What, right now?' Mark, one of the scriptwriters, looked at her.

'Why not? I'm the least important person here,' Caryn said matter-of-factly. 'It won't make any difference if I'm here or not. Might as well go over to his place and wait for him. As soon as I get the tape, I'll bring it back.'

There was silence for a few moments. Everyone looked nervously at each other and then at the back of Rowland's head. Rowland looked up. 'Yeah. All right. Most sensible suggestion I've heard all night. Take some petty cash from Charlie's desk.'

'I'll be back as soon as I can,' Caryn said, slipping away to get her coat. She was secretly relieved to be getting out of the tense atmosphere they'd been in since Rowland had discovered that the sound engineer, whom they'd hired for the documentary they were pitching the following week to Channel Four, had walked off with the tape – the *only* audio tape of the entire two-hour film – in his bag. They'd been waiting for him to pick up his messages ever since.

She took twenty pounds, grabbed her coat and ran down the stairs. Luckily she knew where the mini-cab office was on Kingsland Road. Five minutes later she was in the back of the cab speeding towards Bermondsey. She peered at the address she'd been given. George Row, just off Jamaica Road. She leaned back in the seat and sighed. Contrary to what she'd initially thought, there was one *major* difference between being a PA in the City or Soho and working for Rowland Keane. Hours. Lots of them. Late hours, early hours . . . *all* hours. But it was exciting. She loved watching the way a production came together, despite – or perhaps because of – the uncertainties and the stress. In two short months she'd learned a huge amount about the process, even though she'd never really been asked to do much other than type, file, answer the phones and make coffee. Tonight was the first time she'd done something out of the ordinary – and it had been her own suggestion. Oh, well. It beat standing around watching Rowland's face grow darker and angrier by the minute. It was a hugely important pitch; she'd overheard someone say that Anita Godwin only gave you one shot. All the more reason why she had to get that tape back to the studio, even if it meant waiting up all night.

George Row was exactly as the name suggested – a long row of nice-looking period houses. She rang the bell at number thirty-eight and waited. The house was in darkness; there was obviously no one home. She looked down the road. There was a pub on the corner. She hesitated. It was a bit of a long shot . . . he wouldn't be in there, would he? She belted her coat more firmly, asked the cab driver to wait for her and walked quickly towards it.

Inside, it was smoky and terribly noisy but not too crowded. It was obviously a neighbourhood pub. She leaned across the bar and beckoned the bartender over. 'I'm looking for someone called John Hastings,' she shouted over the noise of the jukebox. 'He lives around here. I was just wondering if you knew him, or if he might be here.'

'Who?'

'John. John Hastings.'

'Oh, John. Yeah, he's over there. By the window. Chap in the green leather coat.'

Caryn could have kissed him. She hurried over.

Fifteen minutes later she was back in the cab, speeding back to the office, three sets of audio tapes in her bag. They passed an off-licence on the way. On an impulse, she stopped the driver again and went in. She came out carrying two bottles of red wine and they continued their journey to Shoreditch.

'She's here!' Mark looked up as Caryn came through the door. 'And she's got the fucking tapes!' A cheer went up from the group huddled around Rowland.

'And she's got some wine!' Becky, one of the researchers, gave an excited whoop.

'You *star*!' someone else said, taking the tapes from her reverentially. 'Was he at home? We've been ringing him every five minutes since you left and he *still* won't pick up.'

'No, he wasn't at home. He was in the pub,' Caryn said, smiling.

'What pub?' Rowland asked, not looking up.

'There was a pub at the end of his road. I nipped in on the off-chance that he'd be there.'

'Quick thinking, Girl Friday,' Rowland murmured, sliding one of the tapes into the editing deck. 'Someone get her a glass of wine. She fucking deserves it.'

Caryn felt a warm glow of satisfaction. She accepted a glass from Mark, who held up the bottle admiringly.

'Good choice; good idea. All round good woman,' he said, laughing. The atmosphere had changed dramatically. They finished the editing, drank the wine and made plans to go out together the following Friday night to celebrate the completion.

'Sevenish suit you, Caryn?' someone called out as they were getting their coats. 'Next week?'

'Who? Me?' Caryn looked up. Were they asking her to join them?

'Yeah. Seven all right? We're going to the Cantaloupe.'

'Yes,' Caryn said happily. 'Yes, that'd be great.'

'Cool. Well, see you Monday, then.'

'Yeah. See you Monday.' She turned to pick up her bag, still smiling to herself, and saw Rowland standing in the doorway of his office, keys in hand.

'I'll give you a lift,' he said, shrugging on his jacket. 'Least I can do. Where d'you live?'

Caryn's heart sank. She couldn't possibly let Rowland see where she lived. 'Oh, no . . . please don't bother,' she said quickly. 'I just live up the road. I can get a cab, honestly.'

'Where d'you live?' he repeated, ignoring her protests.

'Milton Gardens,' she said hesitantly, hoping he wouldn't know where it was. He didn't. 'Just off Kingsland Road.' She could always get him to drop her off at the corner. She would sooner *die* than let him see the estate.

'Come on, get your things. It's two o'clock in the fucking morning. Can't believe we've been here all day.'

She picked up her coat and bag and followed him to the door. They walked downstairs in silence. Rowland's car, a flashy silver Audi, was parked outside the building. 'Um, look, are you sure about dropping me home? I can easily take a taxi.'

'Caryn, just get in the car, will you?'

'Which one?' he asked, turning into Nuttall Street. Luckily he'd put a CD into the stereo as soon as they got in the car and she was spared the effort of having to make conversation. It was beautiful, haunting music and by the time they pulled up in front of the first block of flats, she was feeling decidedly other-worldly. What with working so late, the mad dash across town in a taxi, the wine and the lift back home, she was almost completely disorientated.

She pointed vaguely in the direction of the flats. 'Here's fine,' she said, picking up her bag.

'Yeah, but which one? I'm not going to drop you on the corner of the road. Not at this time of the night.'

'That one.' She pointed out the hulking form of Milton Gardens. He made no comment as he swung the car into the half-crescent in front of the flats. 'I'll be fine,' she said, aware that she was blushing. 'Thanks for the lift.'

' 'Night, Caryn. I'll just make sure you get in all right.'

'Oh, no . . . no, you don't have to wait. It's late and—'

'Jesus, woman. Will you just go? You're the most stubborn little . . .' He shook his head. 'Just go in.'

She walked away from the car, cursing herself for being so gauche. She pushed open the entrance door and turned round. He was still waiting. She gave him a quick wave and then pushed open the door to the stairwell. As usual, the lift was broken.

51

There was a cough at the door. Tory looked up. Her father was standing in the doorway, a strange expression on his face and her folder in his hand. She swallowed. He cleared his throat and walked in. They stared at each other for a moment, Tory's heart beating so fast it hurt. He put the folder down on her desk, next to the piles of spreadsheets, brochures, magazine articles and frantically scribbled-on bits of A4 paper that she'd been working on for the past fortnight.

'I think,' he said carefully, his eyes not leaving her face, 'that this is brilliant.'

Tory felt relief flood through her. She was thankful she was already sitting down. She looked at the sheet on which she'd been doing her calculations. 'You mean it? You're not just saying that?'

'No, darling. I'm not. I don't know anything about flowers – other than the fact that they look nice and sometimes smell nice, too – but I do know a lot about history and you've unearthed some pretty interesting facts.' He sat down on her bed. Tory stared at him. It had been a long, long time since she'd heard anything close to the level of enthusiasm that his voice now held. 'Look,' he went on, spreading out the sheets she'd given him. They were covered in his small, precise handwriting. He'd been making notes. She felt a sudden uprush of feeling. 'I've been doing a bit of research,' he said modestly, pulling out another sheet, also covered in notes. 'Tulips. Did you know,' he asked, tapping the sheet with his forefinger, 'that tulips were essentially the first form of capital speculation? Now, I doubt that would encourage your average punter to buy a bunch, but there are some fascinating details about the weight and size of bulbs, not to mention all the cross-fertilisation techniques that were developed at the turn of the seventeenth century . . .' His voice took on the strong, confident tones of a lecturer completely at ease with his subject. Tory leaned back in her chair and let the words flow over her. She hadn't heard him speak like this since Susie died.

Three weeks later, she stood in the doorway of a small shop on Margaret Street, a narrow road running parallel to Oxford Street on its north side. It was small, very dirty and required a *huge* leap of the imagination to turn it into the sort of place she'd been dreaming about for the past six months, but the location was excellent and the price even better. Six thousand pounds a year. The letting agent, keen as mustard, was anxious to close the deal. The owner lived in Australia and wasn't likely to be back any time soon – if they wanted it, it was theirs. Tory was terrified. With two years' rent up front and the renovation costs, she'd be taking on twenty-odd thousand pounds' worth of debt at the age of twenty-five. It was a horribly sobering thought. Her father was surprisingly calm. It was a lot of money, yes, it was true . . . but what were parents for? If he and Tory were to be partners in the venture, then it would be agreed between them that she would provide the floral expertise and the creative direction of the business and he would provide the historical research – and the finance. He was as excited as she was. Her mother, somewhat predictably, was slightly less so, but by then Tory didn't care. They were going to do it! *They were really going to do it!*

The lease was signed on the twenty-third of October and she was handed the keys. The following evening they had a little party to celebrate in the uncleared space, to which she invited Nic and Caryn and her father invited a few of his university colleagues. Some of them clearly thought he was mad, but there were others in the small group of academics, most of whom she'd known in one way or another all her life, who came up to her, squeezed her hand with something that felt suspiciously like envy and wished them well. There was a moment's silence when John raised his glass and asked everyone to do the same in memory of Susie. A terrific daughter, he said, his voice thickening, whom they still missed every single day. One or two of the women blew their noses; someone stifled a sob. But it was also a toast to Tory, his other terrific daughter, who'd done the right thing and rescued him from the labyrinths of medieval history and shown him the route through to doing something *useful* with his knowledge. He grinned at them all. 'Hear, hear,' someone said quietly out of the silence that followed.

'To Tory and her bloomin' stories,' he said, raising his glass. Tory smiled through her tears.

But that, she reflected ruefully a few weeks later, was the easy bit. The *real* work had only just begun. She rested her arms on top of the vacuum cleaner for a moment and looked around. Three weeks of sweeping, chiselling, breaking, ripping up . . . and the place still looked like a derelict building site. There were three rooms in the shop; the larger upstairs room which led out on to the street and two small rooms downstairs, an office and a storeroom, as well as a small toilet at the end of the narrow corridor. The shop floor opened out on to a small courtyard; perfect for summer plants. The bare bones of the place worked; and that was about it. Everything had to be gutted and rebuilt, almost from scratch. Walls had to be stripped and replastered; the entire place needed rewiring. The floors were stripped and sanded; the courtyard was practically excavated and repaved. Square foot by square foot, the team of builders she'd hired stripped away everything and then square inch by square inch, they built it back.

By the end of November, they were all working at a feverish pace. Every day that Bloomin' Stories didn't open was a day of lost revenue. Even her mother had rolled up her sleeves. Christmas was looming; Tory was desperate to get it open at least a week before. As the building team busied themselves with the renovations, John Spiller buried himself in the basements of the university libraries. He was like a dog who'd caught a whiff of a scent; no reference was too obscure or too trivial. Every evening he left notes for Tory that he'd typed up neatly himself. She was slowly getting used to coming downstairs to breakfast every morning and finding an A4 sheet on which he'd typed his latest discoveries.

Variegated tulips, those with contrasting markings such as red or purple against a white ground, or those whose colour was displayed as thin feathers or flames that ran symmetrically along the centre of each petal and around the edges, were actually caused by a virus which infected the tulip, but also weakened it, and reduced its number of offsets. An infected flower was said to be 'broken' and there was no way to determine if, or when, a flower would break. This only added to its price. At the height of 'tulip fever', most transactions did not even involve the exchange of goods, becoming purely speculative. Everything was worth money and so current that one could get in exchange almost anything one desired. On 2 February, 1637, when a greater fool could not be found to make that one last purchase, the market collapsed. A Dutch merchant who had mortgaged his house, lamented – 'it has been a madness!'

Tory almost laughed out loud. How was she expected to

fit all of that on to the little green and gold cards she and the graphic designer had produced, which would accompany the bouquets? There were other, more esoteric nuggets: *In medieval England, bridal bouquets were originally made of herbs and bulbs of garlic. Different herbs had different meanings. Dill was known as the herb of lust. If a bride carried it down the aisle in a bouquet of garlic bulbs, she would lust only for her husband.*

She caught her breath suddenly, reading it. It came to her slowly that she hadn't thought about Thierry in a long, long while.

Miraculously, under the by now threatening command of Piotr, the new shop began to emerge. By the middle of December, with only ten days to go, she was able to stand in the middle of the shop floor and look round her in delight. They'd decided to keep the back wall in its original brick but the rest of the walls were covered in sheets of smooth, off-white plasterboard and the transformation was magical. Light bounced off the pale walls and illuminated the gloomy interior. One wall was painted a delicate pale lilac with the words *Bloomin' Stories* traced in a spidery, elegant font. The front of the shop had been taken down and replaced almost entirely with an opaque glass window on which the same words had been etched. From the outside, the effect was stunning – tiny slivers of flowers seen through the lettering, drawing the eye inward to the riot of colour and texture inside. The enormous oak table behind the cash register was delivered, along with the shelves and her tools. Secateurs, scissors, tape, wire, ribbons, glue . . . everything would be tidily housed in the deep drawers behind the table, neatly out of sight. For the past three years she'd worked in the comfortable jungle of Catherine's chaos – she was determined to do it differently *chez* Tory. There were nights when the place was full of workmen, noise and hammering, but Tory just didn't want to leave.

52

She still couldn't get used to it. Not even now. *Especially* not now. Being woken up by a handsome young man in a crisp, white uniform discreetly organising breakfast on a marble terrace at the far end of a hotel suite somewhere in the middle of the Caribbean . . . even now, after five years, she had difficulty believing it was actually real. That it was happening to *her*. That she'd made it.

The smell of fragrant, fresh coffee wafted through the air, carried along by the breeze blowing in through the muslin-draped windows above the bed. She struggled awake, her mind fuzzy, her head pounding from the champagne they'd consumed the night before, and stared down the length of the enormous room. Outside on the marble terrace, the handsome waiter finished his preparations and withdrew as quietly as he'd come. François was gone – probably already on the golf course. She pushed the crisp linen sheet aside gingerly and slid out of bed. She walked across the gleaming floor wearing nothing but her high-heeled mules and pushed open the bathroom door. The bathroom was the size of her living room back in London. She closed her eyes briefly. The sheer opulence of the place was overwhelming. She and François had been at the resort for three days and she still couldn't get used to it. Not that it should have surprised her; *everything* François did was elegant, opulent and expensive. It was principally why she liked him. Not the only reason, just the principal one.

She stopped halfway across the floor and looked at herself in one of the full-length mirrors. There was a very faint bruise on her left shoulder where François had bitten her, carried away by the potent mixture of cocaine and alcohol. She couldn't quite remember how many lines they'd done together – for once, she'd stopped before he had. Truth be told, she much preferred Es to cocaine and she rarely, if ever, smoked a joint. In drugs, as in all else, her tastes had been refined; memories of sharing the odd, illicit joint with Thandie and scoring a quick, furtive hit with – what was her name? Cathy? Carol? No, Caitlin – were hard to summon up.

Actually, it was hard to summon up anything about her previous life these days. Sometimes it was hard to summon up anything at all. The sweet, loving rush that had once accompanied the first tablet of the day just wasn't cutting it any more. There were nights when she found it almost impossible to feel anything, much less desire. Not that that surprised her. The majority of her clients barely roused a smile in her any more. She had six 'regulars', selected, vetted and approved of by Mrs Devereaux. Rich, middle-aged and overweight to a man. For almost two years now she'd been their exclusive property and, through them, she'd begun to live the sort of life she'd been dreaming of since her teens. She couldn't remember any more how or where she and Thandie had first heard of Hollywood or seen pictures of the mansions in which she now regularly made an appearance. She couldn't remember how her taste for the finer things in life had developed. When she thought about it – as she was doing now, sitting having breakfast on the terrace of a luxury villa somewhere in the middle of the Caribbean, a cigarette in one hand and a glass of champagne in the other – she had great difficulty believing that she was the same person who'd arrived on an Air Zimbabwe flight six years earlier with less money to her name than it cost to stay one night where she now was. Was it really only six years ago that she and Thandie had slipped out night after night to the bars in downtown Harare, looking for fat, rich South Africans in town on business with their pathetic, minuscule expense accounts? Christ, back then she'd practically done it for free!

Now . . . she took a drag on her cigarette, drawing the smoke into her lungs the way a drowning man might gulp at air, she was 'doing it' for upwards of a thousand dollars a fuck. She giggled suddenly. Yes, that was about right. François had had her for three days and nights. She had no idea what the resort cost. She'd never even heard of the Turks and Caicos islands until he'd tossed the tickets across the bed back in his suite at Claridge's.

She stared out across the infinity pool towards the sea. The water was turquoise, calm and still. The sky was a delicate shade of unbroken blue. The stretch of powdery white sand spread towards the horizon in a perfect, pristine arc. In strategically placed terracotta planters, dozens of species of wild orchids threw out vibrant splashes of colour. She breathed in deeply. She looked down at her plate. A beautifully balanced still-life of sliced banana, glistening kiwi fruit and slivers of orange peel. Life simply couldn't get any better. She picked up her fork and stabbed a perfect-looking strawberry straight through its heart.

53

It was Nic who insisted on throwing an opening party and also insisted on paying for it. It would be her gift to the new enterprise and she wasn't to be dissuaded. The three of them spent a very pleasant Saturday afternoon at a nearby café going over the arrangements. Simple canapés, fantastic wines, a small posy of flowers for everyone to take home (Nic's idea); specially printed discount vouchers for further visits (Tory's idea). They argued over the guest list – Tory wanted to limit it to forty or fifty people who'd had something directly to do with the business; Nic wanted to expand it to everyone they knew; Caryn secretly dreamed of handing an invitation to Rowland.

'Nic, that's over three hundred people!' Tory protested as the lists were being drawn up. 'It'll cost a *fortune.*'

'Oh, will you stop worrying about the cost,' Nic said, rolling her eyes. 'Let me take care of that. I won't even see the bills, I promise you. They'll go straight to my dad's accountant. Look, what's the point of having a trust fund if I can't access it every once in a while? And you know me, I *never* spend his money. Well, hardly ever.'

'Yes, but we won't even be able to *fit* three hundred people in there!'

'No, but there's the outside. I told you, the caterers are going to bring these fantastic outdoor heater-type things . . . we can open up the little courtyard at the back; people can spill out in there. It's not like it's going to go on all night, anyway.'

'Well, if you're sure,' Tory said, looking dubiously at the expanding list.

'I'm sure,' Nic said firmly. 'Absolutely sure.'

'What's this?' Rowland looked at the invitation Caryn had just handed him.

'It's a friend of mine. She's just opened a flower shop on Margaret Street, behind Oxford Street. It's the opening next Friday and I just thought . . . well, maybe some of you might like to come.' She stood nervously in the doorway to his office.

He turned the card over. '*Bloomin' Stories.* ✳ *Asters* ✳ *There are over six hundred species of aster. Ancient societies believed that the odour of its leaves, when burnt, drove away serpents. Whilst this might not be applicable today, perhaps its connotation is still relevant. Giving asters means, 'I am not sure you've been faithful to me.' Be careful who you send asters to! Bloomin' Stories – bouquets with a difference.*'

'Interesting idea,' he said, turning the card between his fingers. 'Asters, eh?' He looked up at her. 'Next week Friday?'

'Er, yes. It's a cocktail sort of party. I thought instead of going to . . . you know, the Cantaloupe . . .'

'Yeah, why not? A Christmas opening party. Nice. Asters, eh?' He looked up at her suddenly. 'Have you ever been unfaithful, Caryn?'

Caryn nearly dropped the papers she was carrying. 'Um, no,' she said, looking anywhere but at him. Her face was on fire.

'Just wondered,' he said mildly. And then he brushed past her and disappeared. She could almost *feel* the faint scent of him on her face. She turned and went back to her desk, her whole body tingling.

To her surprise – and pleasure – everyone wanted to come. Even gorgeous *I've-got-a-date-every-night* Charlie. 'How *exciting*!' she said to Caryn as they got ready to leave that night. 'Wish *I* could think of a business of my own – anything'd be better than doing a nine-to-five.'

'She'll be doing a heck of a lot more than that,' Caryn said, smiling. She held open the door. 'Twenty-four hours if the past few weeks are anything to go by.'

'Yeah, but it's *hers*. I'd give anything to be my own boss.'

'Yeah, like Rowland. It must be pretty satisfying, don't you think? Seeing all this, knowing it's all yours.' She waved her hand back in the direction of the office.

'Well, it isn't really his, of course.'

'What d'you mean?' Caryn asked, puzzled. Charlie turned back to look at her.

'It really belongs to Katie's dad. His father-in-law. He's the one paying our salaries, love, not Rowland. The business doesn't actually make any money. At least, not yet.'

'You're kidding. I thought . . . I thought Rowland was really successful. He's won an award and everything.'

'Takes more than one documentary to be successful. It's an *awful* business; there's so much competition. I reckon that's the only reason he puts up with her. She's an absolute bitch! Haven't you met her yet?'

'No. Gosh. I'd no idea.'

'I'm surprised. Clever thing like you – I'd have thought you'd have figured it out as soon as you got here. Or . . .' she looked at Caryn slyly. 'Am I missing something?'

'What d'you mean?'

'Oh, come on. He fancies you. Everyone can see it.'

Caryn stopped dead in her tracks. 'Can they?' she asked in a small voice.

Charlie nodded firmly. 'Oh, yeah.'

'Oh, God.'

Charlie surveyed her for a second. 'Do *you*?'

''Course not,' Caryn protested vigorously. 'He's married.'

'So?'

Caryn didn't trust herself to answer.

'Do I look all right?' Tory turned around anxiously, trying to catch a glimpse of her rear in the mirror.

'You look fabulous,' Caryn and Nic chorused.

'I'm going to force-feed you a Valium if you don't calm down,' Caryn threatened.

'Ooh, have you got some?' Nic asked, eyes lighting up. They both giggled.

'It's not funny,' Tory protested, still trying to size up her behind. She wriggled around in her tight black dress and high heels. She could barely walk.

'Come on,' Nic said, peering through the curtains. 'The taxi's here. Let's go. Yes, yes, you both look great. Charlie's Angels,' she giggled as they trooped noisily down the stairs. ''Cept there's no bloody Charlie.'

'I feel sick,' Tory muttered.

'No, you don't,' Nic said firmly, pushing her into the waiting cab. 'And if you do, *please* ask the driver to stop. Whatever you do, don't vomit over *me*.'

'You,' Tory muttered, holding her stomach, 'are evil. You're actually *enjoying* this.'

'You bet I am. Come on, girls, let's have a bit of fun! When was the last time we went anywhere together?'

'What if it's a complete disaster?' Tory turned an anxious face towards them.

'It won't be. Christ, with the amount of champagne and wine on hand, it can't *not* be a success. Relax. It's all in hand. Trust us, will you?'

Tory leaned back in her seat. Nic was right. Everything had been planned right down to the last detail. It was a side to Nic she'd never seen before. Utterly in charge, absolutely calm . . . she'd organised the entire event with all the precision and determination of a military campaign. Even her mother, who was normally the bossiest person in the borough, was secretly terrified of her. 'How . . . where did you learn to talk like that?'

Tory had asked her the previous week after hearing her dismiss the caterer's pleas for a change of menu at the last minute — she couldn't get hold of the Honduran freshwater prawns she'd promised. Nic wasn't having any of it: 'Find some.' End of story.

'Like what?'

'Like . . . like *that*? You just told her to get some. I bet she will, too.'

''Course she will. They always try and wriggle out of things. I've watched Molly deal with them for the past ten years — bunch of sharks, all of 'em.' Nic's smile was disarmingly dismissive.

Well, wherever she'd learned it, it had worked. Honduran freshwater prawns, lightly sautéed in chilli and garlic, were indeed on the menu. 'See?' Nic said as they trooped in an hour ahead of the guests. She pointed to one of the silver trays. 'Prawns. Honduran, too, I bet.'

Tory could only nod. Her stomach was tight with nerves. She looked around the shop. Her father's research into Christmas flower traditions had paid off. She'd decided against the usual reds and golds that everyone thought of as Christmas flowers and had gone instead for evergreens, silver and white, using the stubbly, nutty texture of pine cones, papyrus heads and large, waxy amaryllis leaves to fashion the baskets that hung from the ceiling. White tulips, tied at the neck with silver string; russet Leonidas roses in huge, clear glass bowls and dramatic white lilies gave the tables a beautiful, delicate air. The scent of hot, spiced mulled wine mixed with perfume drifted in and out of the space as the door to the courtyard opened and shut. The braziers were on in the courtyard, as were the tall church candles and tiny, glowing paper lanterns strung diagonally across, bobbing gently in the light breeze. The waiters were putting the finishing touches to the trays; opened red wine bottles stood to attention on the oak table . . . everything looked perfect, ready to go. The ache in her side was almost unbearable. She wished she hadn't chosen quite such a tight dress; she could scarcely breathe. Something would go wrong. It always did.

It was a quarter past nine. The party had been in full swing for over an hour. Caryn stood miserably to one side, nursing her third glass of red wine, trying desperately not to look at the door. Charlie and a couple of her co-workers had arrived at eight-thirty p.m. on the dot – but not Rowland. There was still no sign of him. Across the crowded floor she could just make out Nic's head above the crowd. She was being relentlessly pursued by two men in black jackets whom Caryn had difficulty telling apart. Tory, too, wasn't short of admirers. Despite looking so nervous she appeared almost ill, she'd been surrounded by men since the doors had opened. Caryn, on the other hand, had hardly spoken to anyone – or been spoken to. She wondered if she'd tried a little *too* hard to be stylish – a blue and green dress of some unidentifiable silky material (at £14.99, probably polyester); too-tight, too-high shiny white shoes and a clutch purse of a supremely ridiculous size – too small to put anything in, too large to hide. Brian, her style guide, had looked her up and down and grinned. His way, she thought, of telling her she looked all right. But as soon as she arrived at Nic's and saw her and Tory in sleek, sophisticated black, she'd panicked. Too late, of course. Nic made a tactful comment about the green in the dress bringing out the colour in her eyes . . . Nic's way of telling her she'd made a bit of a mistake.

So here she was, she thought to herself miserably, overdressed and underconfident, the wine already going to her head, waiting for a married man (her boss) to show up and . . . Someone spoke just above her ear. She almost jumped out of her skin.

'Hullo.' It was Rowland, looking gorgeously dishevelled, holding two bottles of beer by the neck in one hand. He smiled down at her. 'Want one?'

Caryn's heart did a slow double-flip. And another. 'Thanks,' she said, wondering what to do with her wine glass. 'I didn't think . . . didn't expect—'

'Me to show up?' he finished the sentence for her. His eyes

were twinkling. There was something about Rowland that made her want to smile, even when he wasn't. *If an Englishman could be descended from the gods it would be he.* Nancy Mitford's line came back to her suddenly. It was true. Rowland belonged to a class of English men and women that Caryn had only ever read about. Nic, although she was technically fabulously wealthy, wasn't quite English and therefore didn't count. Supremely confident without being arrogant, effortlessly witty, charming, at ease with one and all – the sort of person everyone liked and longed to *be* like. His casual, man-of-the-people air and easiness with everyone, even the cleaners, seemed utterly genuine. Not for him the steel and glass of the City, which was probably where his father – or his father-in-law – had made his money; no, he preferred the downbeat, scruffy, infinitely more *real* edges of the City because *he* was more real. That was how he seemed to her; there was a warmth about him that drew her steadily in.

She took the bottle from him with shaking fingers. 'Thanks.'

'Great party,' he said, looking around approvingly. 'Nice friends.' He looked in Tory's direction. She looked beautiful; her hair was tumbling around her shoulders and the tight-fitting dress showed off the lean, slender lines of her body. She looked incredibly grown-up, Caryn thought, looking down surreptitiously at her cheap, shiny outfit and silly patent shoes. Tory's father, clearly having the time of his life, was flitting madly from one end of the room to the other, unable to stand still for more than a second or two. Yes, the party was definitely a success. Even if she wasn't.

'Yes,' she said again, tipping back her head and swallowing a mouthful of cold beer. She took another swig, almost defiantly. She swayed a little. Three glasses of wine and a cold beer were definitely beginning to take effect.

'Whoa,' Rowland murmured, putting out a hand to steady her. 'Easy. You don't have to drink it all in one go, you know.'

She giggled. His hand stayed where it was, resting protectively in the small of her back. 'Sorry,' she smiled, hiding her blush behind the curve of her glass. 'I think I'd better slow down.'

'So do I,' Rowland murmured. His voice was very near to her ear. 'You smell nice,' he said. 'Of flowers.'

'Ah, but do you know which ones?' She looked up at him.

His eyes creased at the corners but he didn't take his hand away, nor did he move. 'Are you flirting with me?'

'Maybe.' She was astonished at her own boldness. 'Why? Does it make you uncomfortable?'

She felt his sharp intake of breath. He moved his hand from the small of her back to her elbow, gripping her tightly. 'Yes. But not for the reasons you think.'

She swallowed, suddenly unsure of what he meant. 'I . . . I think I need to . . . to use the bathroom,' she said, turning away. Her whole body was trembling with desire.

She could feel his eyes on her as she walked rather unsteadily towards the stairs, threading her way through the crowds of people packed inside the shop. She held on to the handrail tightly and descended into the basement, her high heels clacking loudly on the metal stairs. Thankfully there was no one in the toilet and she slipped in, her heart still beating wildly. She stared at her reflection in the mirror; she looked the same. Cheeks a little flushed, perhaps, but there was no outward indication of the stomach-churning, freewheeling butterflies that sprang to life every time Rowland Keane appeared. She splashed a little water on her face, careful not to smudge her make-up, and patted it dry. That's better, she thought to herself, the cool water suddenly sobering her up. She fluffed out her hair, smoothed down her skirt and opened the door.

It took her a second or two to work out that the body she'd run into as soon as she stepped away from the toilet was Rowland's and that he was going to wind up kissing her either in the toilet or in the corridor *leading* to the toilet, neither of which seemed to her to be suitable locations for a variety of reasons, not least of which was the fear of being seen. They were leaning against the door to Tory's office. She took a deep breath, slid a hand up behind her back and grabbed hold of the handle. The door opened immediately; it was dark inside. She shut the door, breathing fast. She heard a hoarse, whispered voice; her own. 'Lock it.' He reached behind her and turned the key in the lock. He took hold of her hand and raised it above her head, pinning her arm against the door. He began to kiss her; the feeling was one of delicious helplessness as he teased and nuzzled his lips against her neck, cheek, mouth . . . sliding down. In the thick, black quiet of the empty office with the muffled sounds of the party upstairs and the intermittent shuffle of others going up and down the corridor to the toilet, he undressed her, piece by careful piece. He slid her dress down her thighs with both hands and then worked his way back up her body with his mouth. Without her even realising, he had manoeuvred her against the desk. As if in a dream, she felt herself being hoisted up on to it, the edge cutting painfully into her bare thighs. She was being lowered and then his hands grabbed her hips and slid her forwards again, not much . . . an inch or two. And then everything slowed to a single point in her flesh as he quickly finished what someone else had started, long before. She gasped; she felt his own surprise, lost seconds later in that other, more urgent thrusting that brought tears of pain to her eyes . . . and yes, relief. She clung to him, her head banging gently against the surface of Tory's desk, hands clenched tightly as she waited for the agonised shuddering to subside.

'But why didn't you say something?' Rowland asked in a low voice, several minutes later when they both could speak again.

Caryn was silent. She reached for her dress and began to wriggle her way into it, suddenly mortified by her nakedness. 'I . . . well, what would I have said?' she asked, smoothing the skirt over her legs.

'Jesus, Caryn. It's . . . I mean, I'm *flattered*, don't get me wrong. But I just never expected . . . you know. I just thought you'd have had loads of boyfriends.' He pulled his jeans up and buttoned them, reaching into the pocket for a packet of cigarettes. He lit up. The flare was sharp and unexpected in the darkness. 'Want one?'

She shook her head. 'Wh–what happens next?' she asked after a moment.

'What happens? Nothing. You go first. I'll follow in a couple of minutes.' He blew out a ring of smoke in a rather satisfied, satiated way. 'Was it all right?' he asked, his voice suddenly tender. She nodded, embarrassed. 'It'll be better next time,' he said, reaching across and touching her chin. 'First time's always crap.'

Caryn stood still, rooted to the spot. Next time? There was going to be a next time? Everything else was eclipsed by the surge of relief that washed over her.

54

'D'you think we should say something?' Nic looked uncertainly at Tory as soon as Caryn left the room.

'Like what?'

Nic blinked. Tory's tone was unusually sharp. 'I don't know. That she ought to be . . . careful?'

'Define what you mean by careful.'

'Tory, is something wrong?' Nic asked, puzzled.

Tory put down her pen. They were sitting in Nic's living room; Caryn had been reading the paper on a rug on the floor, absent-mindedly rubbing the instep of one foot with the other as she read. She'd got up to make a phone call. Tory was toying with a sketch for a bouquet she'd been thinking about and Nic was writing and rewriting the weekly horoscopes, for about the hundredth time. Zoë had obviously thought it a joke. 'She's having a good time,' Tory said slowly. 'Just leave her alone.'

'What's the matter with you?' Nic said, frowning. 'I'm only saying . . .'

'Don't. Leave her alone.'

Nic stared at her. 'What's got into *you*?' she asked angrily.

'Not everyone's as lucky as you are, you know. He's her first boyfriend. Who cares if he's married?'

'What are you *talking* about?' Nic asked, her heart starting to race. 'I'm not lucky! I don't have a boyfriend either.'

'This is about Caryn,' Tory said, refusing to look up. 'Not everything's always about *you*.'

'Look who's bloody talking,' Nic exclaimed, throwing down her pen. 'You of all people!'

'And what's *that* supposed to mean?'

'What's going on?' Caryn suddenly appeared in the doorway. Neither Tory nor Nic had heard her come in.

'Nothing,' Nic said curtly, picking up her pen again.

Tory was silent. She got up suddenly, picked up her pencils and paper and without a word to either of them, walked out of the living room. Seconds later, the front door slammed.

'What on earth was all *that* about?' Caryn asked, bewildered. In all the years they'd known each other, she'd never felt such tension erupt between the three of them. They'd had their little disagreements, of course, but nothing like this. 'What did you say to her?'

'Nothing,' Nic protested, bewildered. She stared at her notebook for a few moments and then sighed. 'Well, if you must know, we were arguing about you. At least, that's what started it.'

'About me? What've *I* got to do with anything?' Caryn asked, her cheeks reddening.

'You know. You and Rowland. I just said I thought you ought to be careful, that's all. And then *she* got pissed off because—'

'I *am* being careful,' Caryn said quickly, interrupting her. Her face was flushed.

Nic looked at her. 'That's what I thought,' she said slowly. 'You are, aren't you?' Caryn nodded and then looked away. There was an uncomfortable silence.

'I'd better get going,' Caryn said at last, picking up her bag. 'I'll see you later.'

Nic sat at her desk after they'd both gone, bewildered by the sudden turn of events. What the hell had she said? One minute they'd been sitting there in total harmony, the next she was alone, two door slams one after the other. What was going on? Tory's business wasn't going as well as she'd hoped; they all knew that. She'd underestimated just how much hard work it would be. She and Caryn barely saw her any more. Getting up at three a.m. to drive to Covent Garden twice a week wasn't Nic's idea of fun, and there'd been that almighty cock-up with someone's wedding the other week . . . no, it wasn't easy, Nic could see that – but it was Tory's choice, wasn't it? All she'd ever done was be supportive, lend a hand when she could; she'd listened patiently to Tory's tales of wilting flowers, lost orders and competitors stealing her ideas, and *this* was how she repaid her? She began to fume. Tory was being unfair. She wasn't self-obsessed, not at all. If anything, it was Tory who'd been unable to see beyond the tip of her nose over the past couple of months. She tried to push her comments away but couldn't. She was angry now – but more than that, she was hurt.

It was past midnight when she finally fell into an exhausted, miserable sleep.

Rowland stirred just before midnight, waking Caryn in the process. He yawned, stretched his arms above his head in that lazy, contented way of his that held her spellbound, and swung his legs out of bed. He dressed quickly in silence. Caryn lay in the tangle of the sheets, her blonde hair spread across the pillow, sleepily watching him put away the strong, tender body she had just taken into her own and emerge, a few minutes later, into another, anonymous body in men's clothes. He bent down and kissed the tip of her nose. 'See you tomorrow,' he murmured, the bed creaking as he straightened up. 'I've got a meeting with BSkyB at ten. Will you make sure the material's ready and on my desk?' She nodded. 'Are you going to stay?' he asked, picking up his bag. 'Might as well. It's paid for. Or d'you want me to run you home?'

She shook her head. 'I'll stay,' she lied quickly. As soon as he was gone she would get a cab.

'Good girl. Don't forget to type up my notes, will you?' he said as he closed the door. And then he was gone. The room was even quieter without him. She listened to the sound of her breathing and the steady thump of her heart. She was lonely, she realised. Apart from a single weekend when Katie and the children had gone to Paris with her parents, they'd never spent more than four consecutive hours alone together. In the office, though she was given to understand that everyone knew exactly what was going on, they went through an elaborate pretence – never leaving the office together; never having lunch together; not touching, apart from the odd, snatched caress made all the more precious since she had no idea when, or if, it was coming. Some part of her dimly recognised that the relationship was being conducted almost entirely on Rowland's terms but another part of her didn't care, couldn't resist. He was thoughtful, though, that was the thing. He left small notes for her under her keyboard; the odd gift of a bottle of perfume that he liked or a CD he'd been listening to and for which she'd shown appreciation. In the very beginning when they'd first started going to the small hotel in Soho that he liked, he'd left a bunch of tulips for her on the pillow when she came out of the shower. Little things, small touches . . . she was hugely appreciative. He wasn't overly demonstrative and certainly never in public, but she'd had so little experience and was moved.

Nic had asked her once if she ever thought about the future – about what would happen next; if he would ever leave his wife and children. She couldn't really explain that the reason she didn't was because she couldn't. She couldn't bring herself to think about what would happen in six months' or a year's time. It was that simple. With Rowland, everything was about the present, the snatched little moments of now – not the future. For him, at least, the future didn't exist. He had a way of turning away from her if she ever dared bring it up, stifling a yawn, indicating without saying that there was nothing to be got out of him other than what she already had. She was nothing if not a quick learner. She stopped trying to ask.

She got up, showered quickly and picked up her own bag. Ten minutes later she was in the back of a cab. Staying the night alone in a hotel room that had been paid for by her married lover was a step too far.

Back in her own room, with her own, worn duvet pulled over her head and the familiar sounds of the estate rumbling quietly outside the window, it was somehow easier to pretend that theirs was a relationship, not an affair. An affair, by its very definition, could not last.

55

Nic was still feeling miserable and out of sorts when she walked into work the following morning. She'd barely sat down when the phone rang. It was Zoë. 'In my office in five. I've got something for you.'

Nic put down the phone, her heart hammering. Where were they about to send her now?

She stared at Zoë, bewildered. 'Human interest? Me? I don't know any . . .' she faltered. Weren't all stories "human"? By definition?

Zoë looked at her crossly and pursed her lips. 'Human *interest* – rags to riches, everyday problems, the death of a child, overcoming adversity . . . come *on*, Nic. I'm giving you one hell of an opportunity here. You're always bloody moaning about the assignments I give you. Look, go through these,' she said irritably, pointing to a pile of back issues. 'Read Davinia Irvine's column; that's exactly what I want. Do me a decent story by tomorrow lunchtime, will you? It doesn't even have to be *true*.'

Nic picked up the pile, cheeks flaming, and beat a hasty

retreat. She read as many of Davinia's columns as she could stomach. Rags to riches? She didn't know anybody who'd taken that journey. Death of a child? Overcoming adversity? Tragedy? She chewed her pen in desperation. Nothing like that had ever happened to her or to anyone she knew. And then it hit her. She stopped chewing and the pen almost fell out of her mouth. Tory. Why hadn't she thought of it before? Tory's story! What an article that would make. It had everything. Tragedy, despair, grief, hope . . . the works. She shot out of her chair, grabbed her notebook and pen and ran down two flights of stairs to the archive where the junior researchers worked and begged one of them to look up everything she could find on Susie Spiller.

Three hours later she was handed a folder in which the researcher had found more than a dozen newspaper articles on the brutal murder of a seventeen-year-old schoolgirl as she walked along the Regent's Canal in Camden. She thanked her, took a deep breath and opened the file.

It was after midnight when she finally finished typing the last words and pulled the sheets from the printer with a flourish. *Flower Power. The healing power of flowers.* She hadn't been at Susie's funeral, of course, but a reporter from the *Sunday Times* obviously had. She'd even managed to identify the white arum lilies that were placed over Susie's grave. Thanks to Bloomin' Stories and their cards she knew that lilies had once been symbols of chastity and fertility but they'd also been placed on the graves of children in Ancient Greece. *Just one of the many fascinating things to learn when you buy a bunch from this most unusual of flower shops, shaped, as it were, by Tory Spiller's own story of triumph and despair.* The sentence had brought tears to her eyes as she wrote it. Surely Tory would see how much she meant to her?

She tidied away her clippings, printed it out one last time and slid the two A4 sheets into the folder. Zoë would have it on her desk by nine, not lunchtime. She brushed her teeth and got ready for bed.

Zoë finished reading it, looked up at Nic and pulled an incredulous face. 'It's brilliant,' she said firmly. 'Really. Just what I wanted. We'll run it on Monday.'

Nic was rooted to the spot. For once, she was at a loss for words. She'd waited half her life to hear someone say those words about something she'd done. Brilliant. Great. The warm glow of satisfaction that had begun the previous night began to spread its way through her. She looked at her shoes. 'I enjoyed writing it,' she mumbled, aware her face was bright red.

'Send a photographer round this afternoon. Just a couple of exterior shots. This photo of her is great,' Zoë said, tapping the photocopied image of Tory that Nic had included. 'Where did you get it? Do you have rights?'

Nic hesitated. Something told her that admitting to her friendship with Tory wasn't quite the right thing to say at that particular moment. She felt a little twinge of guilt at not having said that she and Tory were best friends. It wasn't *lying*, exactly . . . just not quite telling the whole truth. She guessed it would somehow diminish her efforts if Zoë realised that they'd been friends since school − as if she hadn't worked all that hard to come up with the story. She swallowed. 'Oh, I found it. In . . . in one of the newspapers.'

'OK. Get Paul or someone to clear it before we use it. Good work, Nic. Now, I've got something else I want you to think about.' She pulled a folder on to her desk. 'Get an interview with this woman as quick as you can. She won the lottery on Monday night. She's a hairdresser, or something, but doesn't want to give up her job. Madness, I call it. But it'll make a good story. She's in Liverpool; get there as quick as you can.'

Nic offered up a silent, heartfelt prayer of thanks and practically ran from the office. At last. Finally. She'd been given a break. At long fucking last.

Tory mentioned it in passing to Caryn on the phone that evening, but since neither of them had spoken to Nic, there was no answer for what the photographer who'd taken a couple of pictures of her shopfront that afternoon was actually doing. She'd been busy with three customers simultaneously – something of a rarity – and hadn't had time to step outside and ask what was going on. By the time she remembered and looked up, he'd gone.

'He wasn't a tourist, was he?' Caryn asked automatically. Her mind was elsewhere. It was a Tuesday night and Rowland had mentioned, casually in passing, that he might drop by the office later, after dinner with his family. It was already eight-thirty and she was debating whether to go home, or continue doing the filing she'd started earlier. Or wait. Of course.

'Well, he had a couple of cameras round his neck,' Tory said. 'He didn't look like a tourist. Oh, well. Who knows? Where are you? Still in the office?'

'Er, yeah. Just finishing up, actually.' Caryn blushed violently. 'What time is it?'

'Nearly nine,' Tory said dryly. 'You sure he's coming back?'

'Who? Oh, you mean Rowland? No, no . . . I just had some stuff to do. I'll leave in a minute.' There was a second's hesitation. Caryn kept having to remind herself that Tory had been in exactly the same situation she was in. Not that Tory ever spoke about it. Staying in the office most evenings until nine on the off-chance that Rowland would ring and say he was coming back; putting her weekends completely on hold *just in case* – yes, Tory knew what it was all about. She looked out of the window at the gradually darkening sky. It was almost nine and the bars along Charlotte Road that had slowly begun springing up over the past few months were filling. In the open-plan office, two or three of the film researchers were still working; Mark, the scriptwriter, was talking on the telephone. She wondered sometimes if it wasn't just Rowland's way of making sure she was always on *his* watch; by constantly making loose, unspecified arrangements he kept her on tenterhooks, waiting for him. But she dismissed the thought – no, it wasn't his fault. He was the married one; he had commitments that were neither easy to break nor always predictable. She ought to be pleased, not cross, that he wanted to spend every possible moment with her. She picked up her bag and said goodnight to the others who were still working.

As she made her way down the stairs, it came to her slowly that it was getting harder, not easier and that telling herself not to be cross was one thing, feeling it was quite another. She *was* cross. She'd spent yet another evening waiting by the phone when he'd probably had no intention of returning to the office at all. *And whose fault is that, you silly cow?* She could almost hear Tory and Nic speaking to her as one.

The phone rang loudly in the empty shop. Tory slid off the stool, half-relieved to have something to do, and went to answer it. She hadn't had a single customer all day. It was her mother. 'I suppose,' she said, her voice strained and breathless, 'that this is your idea of a joke?'

'What is?' Tory asked, rolling her eyes.

'How could you?'

'How could I *what*?'

'I never liked that girl,' her mother said with feeling. 'Doesn't matter what she calls herself – Harte, Parker . . . I've never liked her. To think that—'

'What the hell are you going on about?' Tory interrupted her, genuinely puzzled. 'What's Nic done?'

'As if you don't know! You must have put her up to it. I can't believe you and your father could do this to—'

'What the hell are you talking about?' Tory almost shouted down the phone. 'What's going on?'

'It's in today's magazine. Imagine, I had to hear it from Belinda Taylor! *Gossip!* or whatever it's called. Cheap, nasty—'

Tory slammed down the phone, grabbed her purse and ran out of the shop. There was a newsagent on the corner. She scanned the shelves quickly, picked up a copy and tossed the money on to the counter. She flicked it open, her heart racing. She'd never read an issue before – from the disparaging remarks Nic always made, she knew it was generally full of tawdry stories about tawdry stars, the more outrageous the better. It was a source of complete mystery to her why Nic stayed at *Gossip!* if she despised it that much, but she and Caryn had given up asking. Yes, the stories were there . . . one Spice Girl or another caught without her underwear, a TV presenter caught with someone else's husband . . . the usual fodder, and then the magazine fell open at the centre and she saw it. Susie's face was staring back at her; the same image that had been on the news and in the papers – she felt as though she'd been punched in the stomach. *Flower Power. By Nic Parker.*

She'd never felt fear like it before. Not when Simba reared on seeing the slithering black mamba and she'd fallen from the saddle; not in front of her father; not ever. None of those earlier fears seemed even close to the cold, trembling feeling that kept rising and falling in her as she listened to Caryn's voice.

'But I . . . I didn't mean to . . . I didn't think . . .' she stammered, her throat thickening painfully.

'You never do, Nic. You just rush right in. How *could* you – without telling her?'

'I-I don't know,' Nic couldn't get the words out fast enough. A swell of tears was building up behind her eyes. 'I didn't think it would . . . Zoë was pushing me for a story and I thought—'

'Look, let's talk about it later,' Caryn interrupted her. 'I'm at work. I'll ring you later.'

'B-but what should I do?' Nic asked, her breath coming in gasps.

'I don't know. Just leave her alone for a bit. She'll . . . she'll come round.'

'She won't,' Nic started to cry in earnest. 'You know what she's like. She won't come round—'

'I'd better go. I'll ring you tonight.'

Caryn put down the phone and tried to concentrate on her work. She'd never seen Tory so angry – it just wasn't her way. She was usually the quiet one. It was Nic who blew up and down with the bewildering speed of summer storms. But Tory was angry, all right. Nic didn't seem to understand she'd overstepped the mark, not that it would have made any difference.

Tory refused to speak to her. The fact that the article had suddenly brought in a rush of customers just made it worse. Tory couldn't bear to think she was profiting off the back of a cheap, sentimental little tale of her murdered sister and how flowers had helped put things right. 'What right did she have?' she spat down the phone at Caryn. 'What does *she* know about grief?' The awful thing was, it was true.

'Caryn?' She spun round in her chair. Rowland was standing in the doorway to his office, a frown on his face. His voice was impatient, as if it wasn't the first time he'd tried to get her attention.

'Sorry . . . I was just lost for a moment,' she said, wondering what the problem was.

'You're not paid to get lost, Caryn,' he said pointedly. Someone giggled quietly in the background. 'I need these to go out this afternoon, not tomorrow or the day after. They need to go out *today*.' She took the documents from him, stung to the quick.

'I'll do it straight away,' she muttered, walking over to the reception area. She was bewildered, as well as hurt and angry. All he'd had to do was ask Charlie to call for a courier. She had no idea who'd giggled. It dawned on her suddenly, uncomfortably, that it had been ages since she'd been out with the rest of the team. Rowland rarely came to the early-evening drinks on Fridays, and she'd been so preoccupied with being available should he call or drop by that she'd begun making excuses not to go with them. It had been almost two months since she'd last gone out. The thought shamed her as she handed over the package to Charlie. She was rapidly becoming one of those women who gradually whittled away at every other existing relationship until it – the affair – was the most important thing in their lives. The *only* thing in their lives. She swallowed, suddenly nervous. That wasn't her, was it? Was that what she was turning into?

'Um, Rowland asked if you could get a courier,' she mumbled, putting the package on the counter.

'Yeah, I heard. Why didn't he just come and ask me?' Charlie said, looking pointedly at her. Caryn shook her head. She didn't know what to say. 'You all right?' Charlie asked, looking at her more closely.

'I'm fine. Why?'

'Nothing. Right. I'll get this sorted out,' she said, picking up the envelope. 'You can tell *His Royal Highness* that someone'll come for it before lunchtime.' It occurred to her suddenly that Charlie was trying to tell her something, but she wasn't sure what. She turned to go back to her desk. It was all threatening to overwhelm her – Rowland, Tory, Nic . . . and now Charlie. A silent rebuke from someone whose opinion shouldn't really have mattered. But the truth of it was that the number of people whose opinions *did* matter was steadily shrinking.

Nic cried; Tory refused to listen. Caryn pleaded; Nic cried even harder and still Tory was adamant.

'I don't want to see her,' Tory said quietly, expertly wrapping a bouquet with a long piece of twill.

'She's really sorry, Tory . . . really. She's sick with worry over the whole thing.'

'Yeah, well, she should've thought about that before she decided to go digging up *my* past to further her fucking career.'

'It wasn't like that,' Caryn said, lifting her shoulders helplessly. 'I know she's a bit impulsive and she just doesn't think things through . . . but I swear, hurting you's the last thing she wanted to do. I know her. *You* know her.'

'Caryn.' Tory put down a bunch of blood-red freesias. 'Can we just drop this? Please? I'm tired of talking about Nic. It's about time she took responsibility for the things she does instead of this pathetic "I didn't mean it" crap she's hiding behind. I'm angry – of course I'm angry. You would be too, if she'd done it to you. Now will you both just leave me alone?'

Caryn looked at the obstinate set of Tory's mouth and decided she was right. She was hurt and angry and that wasn't going to change overnight. She nodded slowly.

'All right. I *know* you're right. It's just that she's in such a state about it and—'

'Yeah, well, so am I. But I haven't just snapped my fingers and tried to get everyone else to sort it out for me.'

'Oh, but Nic didn't ask me to—' Caryn stopped. Tory wasn't listening. She *was* right. This was one mess that Nic had to figure out how to get out of by herself. She grimaced. She'd no idea why Nic thought *she* could help – she couldn't even sort out her own life.

What had happened to them all? she asked herself as she walked back down Oxford Street, oblivious to the spring sunshine or the throng of people jostling and brushing past. She thought back to the summer before they'd left St Augustine's. It seemed a million years away. Nic had managed to persuade her father to let her go to university; Tory was leaving for a year in Paris . . . and her? She'd been getting ready for Cambridge. The future seemed so full of possibilities, of optimism. So what the hell had happened? Where had all that spirit and joy gone? She walked all the way down New Oxford Street, heading towards Holborn, and the answers continued to evade her.

56

It took weeks for Tory to calm down. Nic tried everything. She stood outside the shop for ages, trying to summon the courage to go inside, and failed. Finally, in desperation, she bought a gigantic bunch of alstroemeria lilies and took them round to Tory's house, leaving them on the doorstep with a little note: *Named after the Swedish botanist Baron Klas von Alstroemer, the Peruvian lilies or alstroemeria symbolise friendship and devotion. I'm so, so sorry. Please forgive me, Nic.* She ran all the way back to the Tube station, her heart thudding inside her chest. She couldn't stand the thought of having hurt her best friend so badly that she'd never talk to her again. Finally, just when she thought she couldn't stand the silence a day longer, Tory rang.

'Hi, it's me.' Nic's chest tightened uncomfortably. She clutched the phone, wondering what Tory would say next. 'D'you want to meet me for a drink this evening?'

Nic felt tears springing into her eyes. 'Yes,' she whispered into the phone. 'Yes, please.'

'Look,' Tory said as soon as they'd made it back to the table with their drinks. 'I need to say this, Nic. I was pissed off about what you did. I can't remember the last time I've been that hurt about anything. No, let me finish,' she said, shaking her head. Nic was about to protest. 'I suppose I was . . . I've always been . . . I don't know, jealous of you, in a funny way.'

'Why?' Nic's voice was barely audible. She knew why.

Tory shrugged. 'Everything just seems so bloody easy for you, Nic, you know? There's poor Caryn, slogging her guts out in that crappy job with that asshole Rowland taking complete advantage of her—'

'But why doesn't she just get rid of him?' Nic couldn't help herself from butting in.

'It's not that easy. That's what made me so upset. You think everything's easy; you see everything in black and white. Caryn's never had a boyfriend before. She's never had anyone.' She paused and looked out the window. 'I started this business partly to get away from my parents. Don't get me wrong, it's great working with my dad and it's helped both of us. But it's difficult, you know. I . . . I don't know if I've bitten off more than I can chew. I look at my dad's face and I know he's worried. We're not getting the number of orders we should be getting; it's hard. And then you come along and it's like you exploited all of that, just for yourself. Just so you could get a better byline, or whatever you call it. I just got sick of it. You using other people's sadness so you can feel better about yourself.'

Nic blew out her cheeks slowly. Whichever way you looked at it, it was a pretty harsh blow. She said nothing for a minute.

She'd never ventured into this kind of territory with a friend – with *any*one – before. 'I know that's how it must seem,' she said carefully. 'To everyone. That I've got this easy, perfect life where nothing ever goes wrong, just because my dad's rich and—'

'I'm not saying it's perfect, Nic. No one's life is. I'm just saying that you see everything from your perspective – the way the world is for *you*. You never try to put yourself in anyone else's shoes.'

'But doesn't everyone?' Nic asked, genuinely puzzled.

'Yeah, but sometimes you have to think of how it is for someone else before you open your mouth.'

Nic looked down at her hands. 'I'm sorry,' she said again. 'I should never have written the article.'

'No, you're missing the point. Look, it's been good for business – turnover's tripled in the past three weeks. From that perspective an article's good for us. It's just that you should have talked to me *before*hand, not once you'd done it. That's all.'

Nic nodded. She suddenly reached in her bag for her cigarettes. If she'd ever needed one it was right now. She offered one to Tory. They both lit up shakily. 'Is it . . . are we . . .' Nic hesitated for a moment, then continued. 'I need to know . . . am I forgiven?' she said, rolling the cigarette between her forefinger and her thumb as she'd always done in Zimbabwe. That was one thing she would never do naturally – the elegant way European girls smoked with the cigarette between their index and middle fingers. She turned her brilliant blue eyes on Tory, brimming with tears.

Tory sighed. 'Yeah. Well, what else can I do? You two are practically the only friends I've got.'

'Me too.'

'Sad, aren't we?' Tory drained her glass of wine. 'Another?' she asked, the light slowly coming back into her green eyes. Nic nodded, relief flooding through her along with the wine. She held up her glass.

'A large, please.' She felt as though the death sentence she'd been handed down had just been lifted.

57

An uneasy symbiosis was beginning to emerge between the state of her relationship with Rowland and the nature of her working day. If things had gone well – a few hours a week of uncomplicated, fuss-free sex, which, if Caryn were being entirely honest, was increasingly coming to mean quick and bland – then there would be a little reward for her at work. A task or two a cut above the routine administrative stuff she normally did. 'Listen to this,' he'd say, coming into the office and tossing her a tape. 'It's the soundtrack to the film about the peacekeeping soldiers in Bosnia. What d'you think? Overdramatic?' And she'd spend the next hour comparing tracks. Or, 'Here, Caryn. Come over here a minute. What d'you think of the dialogue here? Too forced?' And then there would be a conversation in his office with the scriptwriter and every so often they would both turn their attention to her.

If things *hadn't* gone well – and often that had nothing to do with her – then he would ignore her. Once he'd tried to make her give him a blow-job and she'd squirmed away, embarrassed; but afterwards for a week, she'd found herself typing letters he would normally have done himself, almost totally ignored. The following Tuesday evening, in the hotel room in Soho, she did as he asked without comment. Two days later, he took her along to a production meeting in the City and then out to dinner as well. She knew what was happening but seemed unable to stop it. She tried to explain to Tory and Nic just what it was that she saw in him; why she couldn't bring herself to quit. They listened but shook their heads. He was a creep, Nic declared, taking advantage of Caryn's momentary weakness. Caryn shook her head. That wasn't it. Neither of them seemed to realise that however unreliable and manipulative Rowland might be, it was still better than what she'd had before.

'What d'you mean? What *did* you have before?' Tory asked,

frowning. She was nonplussed. As far as she knew, Caryn had never had a boyfriend before.

Caryn looked at her and spread her hands. 'Nothing,' she said, palms opening outwards in a gesture of gentle defeat. 'Anything's better than that.'

But was it really? A few weeks later, Charlie announced she was leaving. She'd found another job – a film-maker with a group of studios just up the road in Hoxton Square. Instead of being the receptionist, however, she was going to be an assistant floor manager. Quite a step up, she told Caryn at lunch. Caryn had an image of her in her wildly trendy outfits, marching around the set with headphones on, talking to the director and tossing out orders as she went. Charlie giggled. 'Oh, it won't be quite like that. I'm only the assistant to the guy who does that, but I won't be answering the phones or getting Rowland his bloody coffee – sorry. But anything's better than that!' Caryn was quiet. It was absolutely true.

'Don't you need . . . well, qualifications or experience to do a job like that?' she asked when their coffees came.

Charlie leaned forward conspiratorially. 'I told them I had a degree,' she said, giggling. 'They'll never find out.'

'But in what?' Caryn was genuinely shocked.

'Spanish. My mum's Spanish, though you wouldn't think it, would you?' she said, touching her light brown hair. 'My name's actually Carla, not Charlie, but everyone's always called me Charlie. Anyhow, the point is, I'm moving out of admin into a proper career and if I've got to tell a little lie to make it happen . . . well, I'll lie. I'm sick of typing and answering the phone, aren't you?'

Caryn nodded glumly. That wasn't all she was sick of – tiptoeing around Rowland, judging his moods, steeling herself for little disappointments and putting her life on hold were also pretty high up on the list. 'I'll miss you,' she said suddenly, stirring her coffee and looking down at the table.

'Me too. But I'll only be up the road,' Charlie said cheerfully. 'We can still have lunch and stuff.' Caryn nodded, but in her heart she knew it probably wouldn't happen. Charlie was moving on, in all senses of the word. She was standing still. In a few months' time, they'd have almost nothing left in common. 'Look, Caryn . . .' Charlie's voice, usually so bubbly, was hesitant. 'I shouldn't say this but . . .' She bit her lovely lip.

'What?' Caryn's stomach gave a lurch.

'Well, Rowland's hired the girl who's going to take over from me. He interviewed her yesterday. She's . . . she's awfully pretty and I overheard him and Mark talking about her this morning. I know this isn't really any of my business but—' She stopped, grimacing.

Caryn looked up at her. 'What?'

Charlie's face was genuinely anguished. 'There's . . . there's a bet on. Between them. Caryn, wait—' she put out a hand to stop her.

It was too late. Caryn threw down a tenner, grabbed her bag and walked out, her chest tightening to the point where she almost couldn't breathe.

It took her ten minutes to type out her resignation letter and a further ten minutes to summon up the strength to put it on Rowland's desk. When he came in later that afternoon, flushed with self-importance and the after-effects of a successful pitch to the BBC, she didn't look at him. He went into his office and came out a few minutes later, her letter in hand. He looked at her without saying anything, but she knew him well enough to understand that the light in his eyes was neither anger nor pain, nor was it disappointment. It was relief. It had been going on for almost six months. It was no longer naughty and it wasn't any fun. It was time to move on. And, thanks to Charlie, she had an idea just how to do it.

PART FIVE

58

In the pause between placing their orders and the arrival of a good bottle of wine − Montepulciano, '92, from Abruzzo, Richard DiAngelo's ancestral home − the older man reached into his briefcase and slid three buff manila envelopes across the table. Outside, sloshing wetly against the glass, the snow kept up a steady tempo. The sky was bruised and dark; the Christmas shopping season was in full swing. Mat looked down at the envelopes. 'What's this?' he asked, intrigued.

DiAngelo shrugged. 'Read it and see. Let's talk again on Monday morning. Oh, and keep this to yourself,' he added, almost as an afterthought. 'For now.' Mat raised his eyebrows but said nothing. He slid the envelopes into his own briefcase. They finished their dinner chatting about other things. The report, or the reason he'd been asked to meet DiAngelo for dinner, outside the office, wasn't mentioned again.

He began reading the reports the next morning after breakfast, settling himself down on the worn leather couch, a cup of black coffee in his hand. The first envelope contained a stack of papers entitled 'Background'. Simple enough. An outline of the current global economic climate − the sort of thing Mat knew about anyway. Markets around the world were becoming increasingly sensitive to global economic dips and bumps; Asian markets in particular were unusually volatile. Investors were growing wary of concentrating their activities and assets in one region. South America was showing signs of recession − people were looking for other markets, other opportunities. He skimmed through the reports, made a few notes and then opened the second envelope. Slimmer, it contained some of his own reports on the emerging markets in Africa. He frowned. Why was DiAngelo giving him his own stuff to read? There wasn't much about the economic potential of his own continent that Mat Ndava didn't already know. He hadn't spent the past five years reading, thinking and analysing almost anything and everything that had ever been written on the subject *not* to know what was going on. He settled himself back on the couch. He picked up the third envelope, slit it open and looked at the title. *Baseline International: Company Profile*. He frowned again. He'd never heard of them. He continued reading. By the time he got to the bottom of the first page, he could feel his heartbeat begin to accelerate.

An hour later, having gone through it for the second time, he put it down. There was a small, handwritten note attached to the last page. He prised it off and read it. He stayed where he was for a few minutes, catching his lower lip with his teeth, lost in thought.

Twenty minutes later he got up, went into his bedroom and emerged carrying a sports bag. He threw a coat on, ran down the eight flights of stairs and hailed a cab. It was still snowing but the streets had been cleared. It wasn't far to the health club on Riverside Drive. He got out, paid the driver, and ran lightly up the stairs.

The lane pool in the basement of the club was almost empty. In the dim aquamarine light its surface shimmered gently. He stood at the edge, breathing calmly, his body poised, waiting for the moment of release. He broke through the surface tension of the water, enjoying the smooth, warm rush as he entered, barely causing a ripple. There was a momentary lull as the water received his weight, held him, and then the surge of power as he pushed against it, propelling himself forwards. There was nothing like it – within minutes he'd settled into a steady, powerful rhythm, his tension dissolving in the fluid he dispelled in his wake.

An hour later he walked out of the gym. He turned his collar up against the biting wind. His head was clear; the slight headache brought on by the report was gone. It had stopped snowing and he began to walk, enjoying the easy coordination and balance in his body that the swim had restored. His mind returned to DiAngelo's note. He put his hand in his coat pocket and drew the folded piece of paper out. He opened it, the single sheet of paper flapping wildly against the wind. *'For the next two months find out everything you can about Jim Harte. Report your findings to me alone. Regards, DiAngelo.'* The word 'everything' had been underlined twice. He slid the note back into his pocket and picked up his pace.

59

Estelle let the perfume trickle slowly between her breasts and then dabbed it quickly on her wrists. She stood up, swaying slightly, and adjusted the too-tight bodice of her evening gown. Her head felt distinctly woozy – the after-effects of the previous night's drinking – and she was having difficulty focusing. When had she taken the temazepam? Last night? Early morning? She couldn't remember. It was getting increasingly hard to remember anything. Perhaps it was the tablets. She'd been having difficulty falling asleep at night, especially after a working night. Sometimes she lay in bed tossing this way and that, her mind roaming helplessly. Things she never once thought about when she was awake and in control – the neat little township house in Arcadia; the greasy, metallic smell of Gloria frying eggs in the morning; the varnished table in the living room with the pink silk cover and the green cushions with the tasselled fringes that had long since worn off. The more she tried to stop herself, the more the memories flooded in. It was Sue-Anne, the gorgeous redhead from Chicago who lived in the apartment above hers, who'd given her the tablets to help her sleep. She couldn't bring herself to explain – it wasn't just sleep she craved. She wanted to forget. Everything. Sue-Anne was blithely confident. She couldn't live without her temazepam, she'd confided in Estelle, giggling. *Easiest thing in the world – take one about fifteen minutes before bedtime . . . it'll knock you out till morning.* Sue-Anne was right. It was getting harder and harder to remember anything. But that was what she wanted, right?

She picked up her gold lamé clutch purse, adjusted the bodice of her dress once more and switched off the lights. She was about to meet a new client, someone worth keeping, Mrs Devereaux said briskly over the phone. 'I want you looking your absolute best, Estelle. He's been introduced to us by a very dear friend and I've promised him something special. He wants two of you, darling.'

Estelle shrugged. She'd done it before. 'Whatever he wants, right?'

'Good girl. I think I'll send Jody along with you – the two of you always look so striking together. It's a private party but you're not obliged to entertain any of the others, of course. Let me know if anyone makes any special requests.'

'I will.'

''Bye, darling.'

She checked her watch. Five minutes to eight. She collected her fur stole and her bag and walked to the door. Petko, the driver who'd taken over from Rolf, was always early, never late. Sure enough, the tail lights of the Mercedes were glowing in the dark. She locked the door and walked a little unsteadily across the cobblestones.

'Evening, Estelle,' Petko murmured as she slid into the back seat.

'Hi, Petko,' Estelle said, forcing a little smile into her voice. She liked Petko. It sometimes crossed her mind to wonder what, if anything, he thought about what she did. What they *all* did.

His job was to ferry the dozen or so girls that Mrs Devereaux had on her books from home to their various assignments. He never commented; not once, not ever. He was a good-looking young man, reserved and quietly spoken and always courteous. From Serbia, he told her once. Belgrade. She had only a hazy idea where that was. 'We're picking Jody up first,' he said, pulling out into Park Lane. 'And then straight to St John's Wood. There's a little traffic . . . should have you there by nine.'

'That's fine.' She leaned back and looked out of the window.

'You seem a little sad,' he said unexpectedly as he swung the car smoothly round Marble Arch.

Estelle blinked. He rarely commented on anything, let alone her mood. She sighed. 'Yeah . . . well, just a little. I don't know. Tired, I guess.'

'Ah.'

She looked out of the window at the Thursday late-night shoppers rushing up and down Oxford Street. 'It's nearly Christmas,' she said suddenly. 'Again.'

'You have family, Estelle?' he asked, again taking her by surprise.

She hesitated for a moment. 'No.'

'That's too bad. Christmas is time for family.'

'What about you?' she asked, opening her purse and taking out a cigarette. She had to do something with her hands. His question – and the oddly sad mood she was in – had unnerved her.

'No. Also not.'

'Well, we should spend it together. We're orphans.'

'Orphans?' His English, whilst good, sometimes ran aground. Estelle forced a smile. 'You know. Children without parents.'

'Ah. But we are not children.' His eyes met hers in the rear-view mirror. He was smiling faintly.

Estelle looked away. She couldn't bring herself to answer.

'Hello, gorgeous.' Jody opened the door and slid into the back seat next to her. 'You smell divine,' she grinned at Estelle. 'Doesn't she?' she asked Petko archly.

'Absolutely.'

'Here.' She opened her purse and took out a joint. 'Have some of this. You look like you could use it,' she said, handing it to Estelle. 'Cheer up. It'll be fun! Mrs Devereaux said he's absolutely *loaded*.'

Estelle took the joint she offered, but was quiet. Suddenly, 'fun' seemed an awfully long way off. It felt like a lifetime since she'd had any.

The new client turned out to be a portly, middle-aged man with greying hair and an old-fashioned, faintly pompous air. His accent was difficult to place. He kissed both their hands as he ran an appraising eye over them both. 'So lovely,' he kept murmuring as he instructed the maid to take their coats. 'So very, very lovely.' He led them into a large living room, stuffed with gilt and plushly upholstered furniture, ornate chandeliers and the lingering sweet scent of cigar smoke. There were two men sitting at one end of the room; they stood up as he entered with the girls. Drinks were brought, cigarettes lit, smiles all round. Estelle and Jody slipped seamlessly into the routine: a steady patter of inconsequential, charming chit-chat; the stretching out of a well-placed leg; bending down lower than was necessary to accept a light . . . within five minutes, the atmosphere was sexually charged. Estelle caught Jody's eye – wordlessly, they established that Jody would make the first move. She had on her burgundy silk dress, the one with the thigh-high slits. Any moment from now she would stand up, gracefully unhook the collar and let the whole thing slip to the floor. It was up to the client what happened next. Estelle smiled to herself behind the cloud of cigarette smoke. The men were eating out of their hands.

Suddenly, there was a knock at the door. 'Ah, our last guest.' The client who'd led them in jumped up. 'Wonderful, wonderful . . . we can begin now. Take it off,' he instructed Estelle, hurrying as fast as his short, fat legs would take him to the door. Estelle caught a glimpse of a tall, grey-haired man in a suit turning his head away from them as he reached behind and slammed the door shut.

Jim felt a powerful wave of irritation wash over him as soon as he saw the girls. Why did Arabs feel it necessary to go to such lengths? An African wouldn't. In the thousands of deals he'd made up and down the continent, *money* was what most Africans sought. Clean, simple. Not women and certainly not whores. He reached behind Khoury and shut the door. He'd come to his St John's Wood flat to celebrate their deal, not to be serviced by a couple of teenage hookers. Well, perhaps not *teenagers*, but too bloody young, whatever their age. He'd caught a glimpse of one of them as the door swung shut. Beautiful, of course, but still.

Estelle sensed all was not well behind the closed door. Even though she'd barely seen him, she could tell the newcomer was annoyed. She was adept at reading people; always had been. That was what made her so good at her job. She could tell, without being asked, what her clients wanted, how they wanted it . . . who, in effect, they wanted her to be. She got up suddenly and crossed the room to the window, aware of four pairs of hungry eyes following her. She looked down into the garden. The trees were bare; their spare, spiky branches were silhouetted against the yellow sulphate glow of the street lights. She could hear voices in the hallway.

'You don't understand,' she heard the newcomer say. His voice had an edge of controlled anger to it that excited her. 'I'm not interested.'

'But . . . but they are so *beautiful* . . .' her client whined. 'Come in, come . . . a Christmas present,' he wheedled. The door opened again as he tried to coax him back into the room.

'Khoury,' the man snapped angrily. 'Understand something.'

'Yes, of course, anything. Whatever you say.'

'If I want to have sex, a whore's the last person I'd choose.' There was silence for a few seconds, then she heard another door being opened and banged shut.

A minute or two later, a red-faced Khoury entered the room. He snapped his fingers at her. 'Take it off,' he commanded. 'Come here.' Estelle unhooked her dress as she crossed the floor again. He said something to his friend in a language she didn't understand. She knelt in front of him as he directed, aware of the uncomfortable and unfamiliar prick of tears behind her eyes. The statement of contempt rang in her ears. *If I want to have sex, a whore's the last person I'd choose.* He grabbed her by the hair, pushing her face into his lap. He was angry; he'd been embarrassed in front of his friend and someone was going to pay. It didn't take a genius to work out who.

60

It took him a few seconds to work out where he was. He was sweating heavily. There was a strange gusting sound coming from over his head and, every other minute or so, a blast of air. A fan. Circling above his bed. He was in a small hotel in Freetown. It came to him suddenly. He was back at home. In Africa. He pushed the crumpled sheet away from him and got out of bed. Naked, he crossed the floor to the window and opened the shutters. Storm clouds were gathering out at sea, hanging dark and grim against the sharp line of the horizon. The wind skimmed across the heaving skin of the ocean, racing down the crooked alleyways around the hotel. The loose, corrugated roofs of the houses began to flap against each other. In the street below he could see chickens running around in frenzied haste. Across the road, the roast plantain sellers were gathering their pots, clucking dismally over the unsold produce, sweeping everything into giant blue-and-white striped bags. Their voices floated up to him, carried along by the wind. Within minutes, the street was empty. Only the billowing plastic sheets tacked to the sides of the kiosks remained. There was a single crack, a shuddering drum roll and then the sky exploded. The tree directly outside his window groaned and creaked as the gusts increased and the first few fat drops of rain began to fall. Within minutes, the earth had given up its moist, hot smell. The rains had arrived. They were late.

He pulled the window shut. In the corner of the room the ceiling had already sprung a leak. It was supposed to be a five-star joint. He walked back to the bed, grabbed a towel from his bag and got into the shower. Time to get moving.

Ten minutes later, his dark blonde hair still wet at the neck and temples from his shower, he walked downstairs and into the hotel lobby. Dressed in a loose-cut, pale khaki-yellow suit with an open-necked white shirt and carrying an expensive briefcase, he looked like the sort of well-heeled, well-dressed tourist who had once, long ago, frequented the Freetown seafront. He was tall, well over six feet, the receptionist noticed as he walked towards her, and although the jacket and trousers hid his body, the impression was of a man of considerable speed and power. His movements were quick, neat, precise. His accent was faintly British, with an undertone of something else . . . hard to place. She wouldn't have known it anyway – to her he was simply another wealthy white man of the decent-looking sort you didn't see very much of any more around Freetown. But she noticed, as he paid for his room in cash, that his hands were broad and strong and that his nails were clean. He looked like a nice man.

'You not comin' back tonight?' she asked him as she counted out the bills.

'No.'

'Enjoyed your stay?'

'Yes, thanks.'

'Can I get you anything else? Anything at all?' She smiled coyly.

'Thanks, but no.' He slid the key across the counter. 'Another time, maybe,' he said, and walked off. Outside, an expensive-looking four-wheel-drive vehicle waited. A young man sprang forward as he approached and opened the door. She wondered briefly who he was. Freetown was full of white men in sunglasses and suits these days. But not many of them had nice, clean fingernails. She fixed a smile on her face and turned to the next guest.

'Enjoyed your stay, sir?' she asked automatically. She could see Fouad, the hotel manager, watching her closely from his spot in the corner of the room. That was the other thing about Freetown these days – everyone constantly watching everyone else. She wondered briefly if they ought to change its name. *Ain't nothin' free about it. Not any more.*

Inside the air-conditioned vehicle, Simon clicked open his briefcase and took out a sheaf of papers. He flicked through them quickly, mentally preparing himself for the meeting that lay ahead. It was at least a four-hour journey from Freetown to the town of Kono through some of the most inhospitable bush he'd ever known. As they left the city behind, climbing into the hills that fringed the capital, the Land Cruiser began to rock and sway as it clambered over what remained of the road. The last time he'd been here, scores of little children would run out after the cars as they passed through the outlying villages, laughing and waving. Not any more. No one smiled in Sierra Leone these days, least of all the children. He looked out of the window at the thick, lush landscape they were travelling through. Giant bouquets of thick, furry bamboo and the monotonous green screen of forest that ran along the roadside rushed at them as the vehicle bounced its way northwards. In the front seat the driver and the guard who'd been sent to pick him up exchanged a few words every now and then in Criou, which he did not understand. The African language he spoke was very different from the rapid-fire, staccato language spoken in these parts. He could feel the cool steel of his gun pressing against the small of his back. He tried to relax. He had the plans in the briefcase on his knees, a gun in his hand and a set of instructions from Jim Harte – everything he needed to get the job done and the contracts signed.

Some time later, after crossing a bridge guarded at both ends by unsmiling young men with guns hanging casually from their shoulders like handbags, they broke through the last of the carpet forest; now, the beginnings of the savannah grasslands rolled out before them. There was an old army building of some sort a few hundred yards away. The driver cut the engine and they sat there in the abrupt silence after the banging and shaking of the past four hours on the road.

'We wait,' the bodyguard said in answer to an unspoken question. Simon shrugged. As long as he was back in Freetown in time to catch his plane back to London that night, he didn't mind. He didn't fancy spending a single hour more than was necessary in this damp, humid place in which it was no longer possible to tell friend from foe. A small bird hopped on to the bonnet, pecking irritably at the silver badge before flicking off, darting left and right, then disappearing into the hazy, white sky. Presently a figure emerged from the building, arms slung loosely around a gun which he carried across his shoulders. The driver powered down the window and shouted something to him. A second later the response came.

'Come.'

'Let's go.'

They opened the doors and got out. The heat was incredible, like a furnace blast that sucked the moisture straight out of your skin. Even through his jacket he felt the cool metal of the gun turn warm. They walked across the dusty clearing. It was silent. A figure lay sleeping along a bench on the veranda, swathed in cloth, despite the heat, only the dusty yellow-pink of his soles visible. They walked up the steps to where two young men were waiting in the shadows of the main entrance. They were ushered inside. The gloom of the interior was sudden and profound, like walking into ink. It took a while for his eyes to adjust. There was an old school table in the middle of the room, and four chairs. Sitting astride one of them, chair turned backwards, with a cigarette in his mouth, was the man Simon had flown five thousand miles to meet. He looked Simon over slowly.

'Good of you to come all this way, Mr Carter,' he said, smiling to reveal a row of white, even teeth.

Simon nodded. 'Helluva ride.'

'Let's hope it's worth your while.' Simon didn't answer. He pulled the briefcase on to the table. *May I?* he gestured at it with his hand. The man nodded. Behind him, in the gloom of the interior, Simon could sense the attention of the others in the room. He pulled the first set of papers out of the manila envelope and passed them over. The man snapped his fingers and a fluorescent battery-operated lamp suddenly appeared. It cast a ghostly, whitish glow around the two of them. He read in silence, occasionally wetting the tip of his index finger as he took another sheet. It was just as hot inside the building, despite the gloom. Simon could feel the sweat running down his back. He thought longingly of the damp, misty fields around Harte's country home in Gloucestershire which he'd left the previous week. It felt like another planet.

'All OK?' he asked the man a few minutes later.

'Yeah. S'good. We both sign?'

'Indeed.' He reached into his jacket for a pen. *Nice and slow* — he drew it out and held it up. Someone laughed. He handed it over, allowing his companion the courtesy of first signature.

Ten minutes later it was done. The signed documents were in his possession; handshakes all round and he was out, walking towards the car. Fifteen minutes after that they were crossing the river, now swollen with the rains, and preparing to plunge into the canopy of the forest once again. With any luck, within the next few hours he'd be in the departures lounge at Lunghi Airport and then he'd be gone. As if he'd never been. He touched the briefcase lightly, as if for luck, and closed his eyes.

61

Caryn looked at her watch and yawned widely, bringing tears to her eyes. Two o'clock in the morning, New Year's Eve – and she was all alone. Nic had begged her to come to a party in

Chelsea but she'd declined. She wanted to spend her first New Year's Eve ever in her *own flat* alone, listening to her *own* music, making her *own* plans. Outside she could still hear the occasional thump and whistle of a firework going off, or the drunken shouts of party goers making their way up the street. She was inside, in her brand-new, practically empty flat. She looked around again and again at the freshly painted white walls; the stripped and varnished floorboards; the fitted kitchen running along one side of the living-room wall; the few pieces of furniture that were hers: a worn-out sofa that one of Brian's friends had given her, a desk that had been a present from Nic, two chairs, a bookcase, a few bits and pieces from the flat in Baberton House that had been home for the past twenty-odd years. Not much, perhaps, *but it was all hers*.

She stretched her arms above her head and yawned again. She still couldn't get over it. Her own flat. Bought, if not quite paid for. Nic and Tory thought she was mad – a *mortgage*? At the tender age of twenty-five? But Caryn was adamant. She'd never owned anything of value in her entire life, and certainly nothing worth fifty-six thousand pounds. But, as the very nice young man at the building society had explained to her, fifty-six thousand pounds spread over thirty years wasn't such an awful lot of money to make sure that the little, one-bedroom flat just off St Charles Square was hers. Short of failing to make her monthly payments, no one could take it away from her. She didn't know how to explain to either of them that that alone was worth more than the asking price. Brian was fifteen now – old enough to look after himself. Not surprisingly, he'd been the one to suggest it. Not buying a flat of her own, as such, but moving out. Getting on with her own life. He could stand on his own two feet, he told her gently. He was fifteen, Owen was back at home. Alice was the same – no better, no worse. 'Me and Owen can take care of her,' Brian said, grinning at her. 'Christ, you've done it for long enough.' She looked up at him, suddenly shy. And then smiled. Of course he could. They'd both been taking care of Alice for years. *Ooh, steady*, she cautioned herself, waving a hand in front of her face as if to ward off the tears. *Stop*. Sitting on her own on New Year's Eve with half a bottle of wine in the fridge was an open invitation to tears, and she'd had enough of those.

She got up and wandered over to the window. In a few hours dawn would break over the city and 2003 would begin. There was something magical about new beginnings, she thought to herself, looking out over the grounds of the Victorian hospital across the road. A fresh start, a closing-off of the old debts and the beginning of something new. Clean. Hopeful. In a year's time, where might she be? The year that was just ending had brought with it some pretty unimaginable changes – her new flat, her new job, new responsibilities. Six months after she'd started at Lighthouse Productions she'd won a promotion; six months after that, another. Now, a year and a half into her new career, she was the Assistant Director, in charge of almost anything they threw at her, from organising the daily call sheets, if they were filming in-studio, to finding four hundred extras on a day's notice. She *loved* her job – and everyone at Lighthouse seemed to love her. It was run by two men, Martin Gilman and Rupesh Patel, who'd been at school together and the whole place couldn't have been more different from Crystal Vision if they'd tried. No trendy East End offices, no gleaming, white computers and glossy wooden floors; no wine bars just across the road and certainly no leggy receptionists in off-the-shoulder Prada. The atmosphere at Lighthouse was tough, uncompromising and unsqueamishly down-to-earth. In their own words, 'a no-frills production company working to produce high-quality film and television for distribution'.

Well, there certainly weren't any frills; Caryn could vouch for *that*. There were six other people, working flat out in a grubby little warehouse on St Anne's Road, sandwiched between Holland Park and Ladbroke Grove. As well as Martin and Rupesh there was Gita, the location manager, Dave, in charge of sound recording and Jeff, the production manager. Gita was German; a tough, take-no-bullshit, highly efficient manager of whom Caryn was secretly almost afraid. Jeff was a New Yorker – fast as lightning, impatient and utterly absorbed in his work.

Dave was nerdy and rather sweet; when she first got the job, he'd made it abundantly clear that he liked her but the memory of having a relationship – if one could call it that – with someone in the same office was enough to put her off for life. She'd turned him down in the nicest way possible. And Katie, of course, the part-time administrator who handled everything that Caryn didn't. There was none of the subtle 'us and them' atmosphere between the staff that Rowland had thrived on. Caryn supposed it was due to Martin's unusual background – Oxford, then the army, then a merchant bank, probably just as his father had done before him. But somewhere in his mid-thirties, he'd suddenly realised what he wanted to do for the rest of his life. He'd thrown caution to the wind and started again. He still had that no-nonsense, 'let's-all-get-stuck-in-together' air that she'd always associated with soldiers – a tough, stocky man who looked as though he'd come out of the womb with a rugby ball in his hand.

He and Rupesh couldn't have been more different. Sweet, funny Rupesh with his dreamy, dark brown eyes behind glasses, furry lashes magnified by the convex sweep of the lens. He'd studied graphic design and then 'discovered sound', as he put it. He'd done just about every degree and course in sound production available and his dreamy, artistic air hid a ferocious technical competence that put the few other sound engineers she'd known to complete shame. Rupesh *loved* sound. *All* kinds of sound. Music, singing, humming, chatter, background noise, white noise, whispers, echoes . . . all of it. His computer held over fifty thousand samples and he was forever making little tape-recordings of noises that caught his fancy, to be used later in the editing process which Caryn occasionally watched. At Lighthouse, she wasn't a director in the creative sense of the word, like Martin was, but if she didn't do her job properly, he couldn't do his. In her wildest dreams, she couldn't have imagined that a year and a half after turning her back on Rowland, she'd be here. Shouting at cameramen; cajoling sulkily bored extras; pleading with the authorities for more time; dealing with officials; checking that everything was on time and within budget. When they were filming, either on location or in the studios, she strode around, clipboard in hand, making sure everyone was where they were supposed to be; that the scripts had been delivered, the dialogue coach was on hand, the caterers had been organised. It struck her sometimes, like a blow. *This is me. This is my life, now.*

She turned away from the window. Enough reminiscing for one night, even if it was New Year's Eve. There was just the one, tiny, *teeny* little thing that bothered her from time to time but she tried hard not to think about it. She wanted to start the new year looking ahead, not behind. Best not to think about it at all.

62

Simon arrived just after eleven p.m. The party was in full swing, the sounds of music and laughter mingling easily with the popping of champagne corks. He shouldered his way in through the packed hallway, avoiding the coats and bags on one side and the tightly packed groups of people on the other. He hung up his coat and scarf, squeezed past the last clutch of guests at the door and broke through into the kitchen. After six weeks in the dense rainforest, surrounded by jumpy guards, batting huge insects away from his face every other minute and pushing his way through foliage that *breathed*, London's wide, bustling streets and the damp, fresh cold came as a delicious shock.

'Drink?' someone asked, holding up a bottle of red wine. He looked across the table. A woman with short, dark hair in a tight red dress was looking at him archly, red-tipped fingers curled loosely around the glass that she held to her face. 'Are you a friend of Maddie's?' she asked, her smile provocative, beguiling.

'Thanks.' He took the glass she offered. 'No, I'm not.'

'So who d'you know here, then?' She took a sip of wine and looked at him. Her gaze was bold and predatory.

Simon sighed. After a week in Freetown, he'd had enough of predatory. 'Alison Graeme,' he said shortly.

'Ooh, you're one of Ally's boys,' she said, moving closer.

'Er, no. Just a friend.'

'Oh, *goody*. Just a friend . . .' He suppressed the urge to push her away. It was what he disliked most about parties – bold, drunk women. Drink had made her ugly, too.

'Simon! *Si*-mon!' Someone yelled at him from across the room. He turned, relieved. It was Alison. He pushed his way past the drunk woman, not bothering to excuse himself, and joined Alison at the far end of the room.

'Simon,' she grinned, obviously pleased to see him. 'You came! Didn't think you would.'

'Yeah. Sorry I'm a bit late. Fell asleep. I only just got back.' He kissed her on both cheeks.

'You're here before midnight, darling, that's good enough. Come, I want to introduce you to a few people. How long're you in town for? And where's that *gorgeous* brother of yours?'

'New York,' Simon said, ducking through the doorway. 'I'll see him next week. I'm only here for a couple of days.'

'Too bad. Well, tell him we all miss him,' Alison said, threading her way through the crowd. 'It's been *ages*. Oh, hel-*lo*!' She stopped in front of a small clutch of people struggling to carry on a conversation above the noise. 'Simon, this is Jamie. Jamie, Simon's one of my oldest friends,' she purred, pleased to have brought them together. 'From university. We go *way* back. And this is Nic . . . she's also—'

'Ally!' someone interrupted her, grabbing her round the waist. Simon watched in amusement as Alison was dragged off, presumably to meet someone else. She turned a mock-helpless face towards him as she allowed herself to be carried away. He shook his head, smiling, and turned back to the person she'd half-introduced him to.

She spoke first. 'Hi, I'm Nic. Sorry, I didn't catch your name.'

He stared at her. Tall, perhaps half a head shorter than he was; sleek, glossy shoulder-length dark hair; beautifully shaped brows over slanted, hazel-brown eyes; cheekbones you could open a bottle of beer on. She was wearing black. Her hair slithered over her shoulder as she tossed it back. He could almost feel it in his hands. Her handshake was firm and quick. 'Simon,' he said, recovering quickly.

'A friend of Ally's, obviously,' she said, smiling faintly, as they watched Ally being led on to the dance floor.

'Yeah.' He hesitated. 'And you?'

'Same. Funny, I've never seen you at any of her parties.'

'I . . . I work overseas,' he said, trying not to stare at her. His mouth suddenly felt dry. 'I'll just . . . I need a drink. What can I get you?'

'Glass of red, thanks.' She held out her almost empty glass.

'Back in a sec.' He turned and headed for the kitchen. He saw the woman he'd encountered in the hallway kissing someone else. He was safe. He smiled and picked up two glasses of red wine.

'Cheers,' he said, handing one to Nic. He took a sip. After six weeks of nothing but lukewarm Star beer, the taste flooded his palate pleasurably.

'Cheers,' she said, clinking her glass to his and glancing down at her watch. 'Ten minutes to go. You got here just in time.'

'Yeah. I overslept. I've only just got back.'

'From . . . ?'

Before he could answer, Alison appeared, interrupting them again. 'Come on you two, get over here! We're going to watch the fireworks from the roof. Come on!'

'Better do as the boss says.' Nic smiled at him. He caught his breath. Pearly white teeth; a wide, generous smile that lit up her face. She was gorgeous. He had to steady himself. It was the wine. And the jet lag.

They moved on to the roof terrace overlooking the Thames with the rest of the group. There were fireworks going off in every direction. The sky exploded in one magnificent burst of colour and light after another. Everyone began the countdown.

Ten. Nine. Eight. He looked down at Nic. She was smiling, her glass held against her lips. *Seven. Six. Five.* She looked up at him. Her smile was open, sunny; her gaze even in the dim night light was clear and direct. He felt something turn inside him, a sudden bolt of pleasure. He bent his head with a boldness that surprised even him, and kissed her. 'Happy New Year,' he murmured, breaking away a few moments later. Her lips were warm and soft. He had to suppress the urge to bend his head to hers again. Her expression was hard to read. He held his breath for a second, gauging her.

'Happy New Year,' she replied softly. They stared at each other.

'Would you . . . how about some more champagne?' he asked, unable to bear the tension. He wanted to do a hell of a lot more than just kiss her.

She nodded. 'That'd be nice.' Her voice was low and husky. There was something in it, something he couldn't quite place. The faintest trace of something . . . not strong enough to be an accent, but something at once wonderfully familiar and yet mysterious. He touched her arm, just above the elbow, and turned to go back into the house. He wanted to know more — unusually, for him.

It took him a while to make his way through the crowd to the kitchen. The flat was heaving. He had almost reached the fridge when he felt a hand slide round his waist. It was Alison. She grinned up at him. 'Aha! I caught you,' she shouted above the racket.

'Doing what?' he smiled down at her.

'Snogging Nic Harte,' she laughed. 'I should've known you two would hit it off. Mind you, she's pretty hard to resist. Jim Harte's daughter, no less!'

Simon felt the blood drain from his face. He stared at her. 'Jim Harte? Are you sure?'

''Course I'm sure! I've known her for ages. Funny, I'd have thought you two . . . what's the matter?'

'Al.' Simon tried to keep his voice steady. 'Do me a favour, will you?' He grabbed her arm and propelled her backwards into the hallway.

She looked up at him, the smile gone from her face. 'Sure. What is it?'

'I've got to go. If Nic . . . if she asks about me, will you just say you've no idea where I went?' He hesitated. 'Look, I know it's a lot to ask, but will you just say you don't know anything about me? Don't tell her where I'm from. Please. Nothing to do with her. I can't tell you any more than that. It's complicated.'

Alison regarded him steadily. 'Fine. I won't. But are you all right? You don't look—'

'I'm fine. I promise. I'd better run. I'll call you when I'm next in town.' He gave her a quick hug and then turned, hoping against hope that he wouldn't run into Nic Harte before he made it out the front door. He grabbed his coat and scarf and quietly left. Once outside, he leaned against the wall for a second, breathing deeply. His heart was racing. He'd just kissed Harte's daughter. Jesus Christ. How was *that* for a laugh?

63

Bloomin' Stories had taken over her entire life. Just over a year and a half on and it still felt as though she'd barely got a grip on it. For every successful wedding or corporate event, there was a disaster waiting to happen. She still couldn't think of Midland Bank without remembering their private banking launch earlier in the autumn. A complete and utter catastrophe. She'd spent weeks planning it – rich, autumnal colours, browns, russets, golds . . . she'd ordered two hundred Cambria Plush orchids, flown over from Thailand at considerable expense. They'd spent the whole night before the launch arranging them artfully around the room in beautiful, cream porcelain vases. The orchids were stunning; dramatic, blood-red, arching gracefully over the vases, their dark green, waxy leaves giving shape and edge to the arrangement. When she switched off the lights just after midnight, everything had looked wonderful. Mr Threlfall, her father's banker and the man responsible for giving Bloomin' Stories the business in the first place, had taken a quick look earlier that evening. 'Very impressive,' he'd said, giving her the thumbs-up. The normally austere reception hall on the ground floor of the elegant building on Fenchurch Street had been completely transformed.

It was Mr Threlfall who rang her at nine-thirty a.m. the following morning, panic in his voice. The heating had gone off during the night and every single bud had fallen off. In place of two hundred rich, colourful plants there was nothing but wilted green leaves, dead flowers and bare stems. The presentation was due to begin at ten a.m. She'd lost *that* client.

A week later, the VAT man appeared.

Someone coughed discreetly. Tory looked up, dragging herself abruptly back to the present. A young man was standing before her holding a large bunch of blue delphiniums. Her first impression was that he had the kindest face she'd ever seen. She wasn't sure why she thought it – he wasn't smiling or anything – but it was there, in his dark brown eyes, his eyebrows and in the way they turned up slightly in the centre, giving him an endearing, perpetually enquiring look. He had short dark brown hair, cut in that fashionably rumpled way of thirtysomething-year-old bankers and City types; a beautifully cut suit, faint stubble underneath the remnants of a holiday tan . . . she stopped herself, uncomfortably aware she'd never done this much thinking about a poor customer who'd probably only popped in to buy flowers for his wife. Or girlfriend.

'Hi,' she said breezily, tying a piece of raffia around a bunch of dahlias and putting on her most professional smile. 'Can I help you?'

His voice was fabulously deep and baritone. '*Oui* . . . yes, I'm looking for some flowers,' he said. 'This *is* a flower shop, *non?*' He grinned at her. He was French. The sound of the language brought on an onslaught of memories that made her legs go weak. She was glad she was sitting down.

'Yes. So it is.' Her cheeks were on fire.

'So . . . yes. I would like some flowers. These, I think.' He held out the bunch. 'I took them from the bucket outside. It's OK?'

She forced herself to answer as lightly as she could. 'For someone special?'

'Ah. *Pourquoi*?'

Tory smiled quickly. 'Oh, nothing . . . it's just that we always have a little story behind the flowers. On a card.' She reached across and pulled a sample card towards her. 'Like this one.'

He took the card from her. *Verbenas. The Victorians used to tie a chain of white verbenas around the neck of a sickly child in the hope of a cure.* He handed it back. 'Ah, zat's very nice. So what do these flowers say?' He pointed to the delphiniums.

Tory quickly rifled through her stack and pulled out the right card. 'The name means "little dolphin" in Greek,' she read. 'Because of the shape of the bud.' There was a short, uncomfortable silence.

'Hmm. Little dolphin . . . *non* . . . she's not a dolphin,' he grinned. Tory was aware of a sharp pang of disappointment. So they *were* for a wife or a girlfriend? 'Too . . .' He searched for the right word.

'Fussy?'

'*Oui, c'est ça.* Something *plus simple.*' She loved the way he mixed French and English. It made her pulse race.

She slid off the stool and walked over to her display counter. 'These are lovely,' she said, picking out a still-dripping bunch of Ecstasy roses. 'They smell gorgeous and they'll last for over a week.'

'Ah, *oui*, that's it. *Parfait.*'

She swiftly wrapped them in her trademark brown paper with a pink foil and a string of raffia, then selected the right card. '*Blossom, my darling, blossom, be a rose/of roses unchidden and purposeless, a rose/for rosiness only, without ulterior motive;/for me it is more than enough if the flower unclose.*' She frowned. Where on earth had her father found *that*? 'Well, this is the card that goes with the Ecstasy roses,' she said, handing it over. 'It's a poem. By D.H. Lawrence, apparently.'

'Ah. *If I were the moon, I know where I would fall down.*' Tory looked at him blankly. 'Also by D.H. Lawrence. A novel.' She had to laugh. He said it with such a straight face. She was rewarded almost immediately by a smile of such genuine warmth she almost took a step backwards.

'I . . . I'll just dip these in water,' she stammered, 'wo-won't be a moment.'

Five minutes later, he was gone. Tory stood at her table, staring after him. Oh, well . . . she shrugged the thought off. He'd come in to buy flowers for his girlfriend. And that was that. Pointless to think about him at all. In the meantime, there were other, far more urgent issues at hand. Like whether or not they would *ever* break even, never mind turn a profit. Bloomin' Stories was only just managing to stay afloat. It was tougher than she'd ever imagined. She had everything to lose and everything to learn. Yet every time she felt like throwing the towel in and calling it a day, she remembered the look on her father's face the day they'd taken on the lease – pride, trepidation, nervous anticipation . . . his face had been a register of her own. And somewhere in the midst of the emotions that flitted across it, she'd seen something else, something that had died in her family the night Susie failed to come home. Hope. It was that, more than anything else, that kept her going. The hope that one day, some day, the pain would lessen and life could, and should, go on. *That* was the reason she couldn't quit. Today, too, for the first time ever, she'd felt an attraction to someone who had nothing to do with Susie or the past or her efforts to escape it. What a pity he already belonged to someone else.

After his third visit to the shop in almost as many days, the penny finally dropped. The young Frenchman wasn't buying flowers for his wife or his girlfriend – he had come into Bloomin' Stories to see *her*. Tory wasn't sure what to say.

'Say yes,' he said simply. 'Dinner, that's all. I promise you. I don't ask for anything else. *Rien*.'

'It's not that.' Tory had to laugh.

'Then what is it?'

She hesitated. 'I don't know you,' she said finally.

'*Et alors?* How will you get to know me if you don't accept to come out with me?'

Wiz me. Her head was swimming. His logic was faultless. She took a deep breath. 'OK,' she said finally. 'OK, yes, *j'accepte*. Let's have dinner.'

He was delighted. 'You speak my language! Beautifully. *Impeccable*.'

'Hardly.' Tory laughed. 'A few words, that's all.'

'It's enough. It's a start. I will teach you *every*thing,' he declared in that dramatic, Gallic way she remembered only too well. 'I'm Luc, by the way. Loïc, actually. But you can call me Luc.'

'Tory. Victoria, actually. But you can call me Tory.'

'You see? Already we have something in common.'

Over dinner that evening she found out that he was indeed a banker; he worked for Credit Suisse, was on his second placement in the City. He came from a small village outside Bordeaux; both his parents were farmers. The flowers were for his mother, he grinned. 'Just in case you were wondering. It was her birthday. First time to London.'

'Me? Oh, no . . .' Tory lied. And then blushed to the roots of her hair.

He was gallant enough not to comment. 'I think she would have preferred the . . . how you called them? The little dolphins?'

'Delphiniums.'

'*Oui*. The roses were a little . . . *de trop*. She worries about the cost of such things.'

'You should've told me they were for your mother,' Tory said, hiding behind her wine glass. Luc's charm was almost palpable.

'But then you would not have wondered about me.'

'I didn't.'

'Ah, *oui*.'

On their second date, the following weekend, she found out a little more. He was thirty-one. He lived alone in a small flat in Battersea. He was passionate about football and he'd had two serious relationships. 'Don't you want to know about them?' he asked, after it became clear she wasn't going to ask.

'No. Not particularly. Why?'

'But *all* women want to know. About the last one, and so on.'

'Not me.'

'*Vraiment*? But I want to know things about *you*.'

'You *do* know things about me,' Tory said carefully.

'Yes, but not the details.'

'The details aren't important,' she said, accepting his hesitant caress along the side of her cheek.

'Of course they're important. How else will I get to know you? I mean, yes . . . I know you have a successful business and you are smart and talented, and *très belle*, of course . . . *oui*, I know all of that. But what about the *details*?'

Tory was quiet. She wasn't prepared for this. She'd been drawn to the lightness in him, partly, she supposed, because it was what was lacking in her. But what she hadn't guessed at was his openness, the generous, uncomplicated way he had of offering himself up completely, even after only a couple of dates. She could not be like that. She wasn't sure Luc could handle what she called the heavier side of things. Like her.

'Well,' she said slowly, 'there's not much to tell. I mean, I grew up in London, in Fulham . . . near where you live, actually. I still live with my parents. I ought to move out, I know. But it's complicated.' She was silent for a moment. Then she took a deep breath. 'I used to have a sister. She was murdered when I was sixteen. I don't get along with my mother. I think sometimes she would rather have my sister alive, not me. Those are some of the details, as you call them.' She lifted her head and looked at him steadily, almost defiantly.

Luc was staring at her with such distress in his normally open, sunny face it was almost comic. 'Well,' she murmured, bending her head to her plate again, 'you did ask.' Many men would have been put off. Not Luc, it seemed.

They left the restaurant together, not speaking. He seemed to understand instinctively, without asking or saying, that the next moves were hers to make. 'Where would you like to go?' he asked, starting the car.

Tory took another deep breath. 'Battersea?' she asked, almost shyly. The hand that touched her knee was warm. He kissed her, and it was a promise of something else to come.

He was quiet when he made love to her, as though nothing in the world could distract him. He was gentle, too. Tory kept her eyes open throughout, as if she had to remind herself of who he was. He brought Thierry to mind, of course, with the whispered endearments in French; he was the first since then. But Luc was nothing like Thierry. Thierry was a skilful, practised lover, nothing honest or spontaneous about him. The man lying beside her was very different. For a moment afterwards, when he yielded completely and sank back into her arms, a sweet, hot sensation stole over her, the closest she'd ever come to orgasm, not that she minded. She craved instead the warmth, the sensation of being held, caressed, loved. Luc had warmth – plenty of it and he *shared* it. She lay beneath him, her chest rising and falling to the calm, steady rhythm of his own breaths. A small noise struggled in his throat; his hand stirred slightly, as if he couldn't quite settle, and she covered his hand with her own. She could *feel* him smiling. She thought briefly of Caryn and Nic. She wondered what they would say.

64

Caryn carried her cup of tea over to the sofa and settled herself down. It was almost nine p.m. on a dark, rainy night – which made it marginally more acceptable to still be at work. Instead of . . . well, what? She smiled ruefully to herself. Nic was still moping over the inexplicable disappearance of some man she'd met at a New Year's Eve party and Tory was uncharacteristically wrapped up in some man she'd met in the shop – she, on the other hand, hadn't met anyone – which was why she was at home on a Friday night, working.

She sighed and picked up the notes Martin had thoughtfully left on her desk. He wanted to adapt a play that had already been performed at the Soho Theatre, a character piece of some sort. The budget was minuscule. They wouldn't be able to build sets, Caryn thought, making another note in the margins. *No sets.* Someone – probably her – would have to start scouting around for a list of possible locations. She felt a quick pull of excitement. Although she wasn't technically responsible for things like location or castings, it was up to her to begin the process of putting them together, which she loved doing. She skimmed through the working script and began visualising possible scenarios. It was a play about dating in London; four different couples with four very different sorts of issues. She warmed to it immediately. Much of it could have been written with her in mind – except, of course, she wasn't dating anyone. She began to separate out the tasks and draw up lists for each. Casting calls, locations, scriptwriters, technicians, rehearsals . . . in the coming weeks she and Martin would work closely together to get the major decisions out of the way so that the actual shooting was done as quickly and efficiently as possible. Martin had come to rely on her, or so he said. Caryn saw problems ahead of time, long before anyone else did. That saved time – and money, of course. And saving money made Martin very, *very* happy.

65

Mat spread the sheets out in front of him, taking care not to upset the system he'd devised for filing the various aspects of the life he'd spent the past few months uncovering. What had started out as a simple two-month investigation had turned into three, then four, then five. He was surprised he'd been given the time off, to be honest, but as his investigation deepened, his curiosity rose and in the end, he couldn't have set it aside even if he'd wanted to. DiAngelo was patient. *Just get me everything there is to know about him*, he said repeatedly. *I don't care how long it takes.* Well, six months, in the end. For all of that time he'd worked alone on a single, utterly absorbing story whose outcome even he couldn't have predicted. What was DiAngelo going to do with the information? he wondered. He'd declined to meet Mat during his investigations – he duly signed off the travel receipts and the expense accounts without even batting an eyelid. And God knew, in the past six months he'd been almost everywhere. New York, London, Harare, Johannesburg, Kinshasa, Lomé, Freetown . . . he'd criss-crossed the Atlantic the way some people moved between the five boroughs of New York. It hadn't been easy. On one memorable occasion, trying to get from Dakar to Praia, a journey of some six or seven hundred kilometres, he'd had to fly the six thousand-odd kilometres back to Paris, then down to Lisbon, wait for six hours and *then* board another four-hour flight to Cape Verde. It had taken him two full days to travel six hundred kilometres. But worth it. What he'd uncovered on that trip alone had more or less made up the bulk of his report.

The door to the conference room opened and DiAngelo strode in, followed by two men, one of whom he recognised. 'Mat, good to see you,' DiAngelo said warmly. They shook hands. 'I've asked a couple of people to join us,' he continued. 'Don McCormack, whom I don't think you've met, and Winston Freedland. *Sir* Winston, I should say. You Brits and your goddamn titles.' He smiled. Mat tried to hide his surprise. Sir Winston Freedland? What was he doing here? He was the owner of a clutch of British newspapers, including the *FT*, *WED*'s direct competitor. What was going on? 'I'll explain properly afterwards,' DiAngelo said, reading his expression. 'But for now, we can talk freely. Don't hold anything back.'

'No problem.'

'Ah . . . Leonie . . .' DiAngelo looked up as Leonie entered, carrying a tray of coffee and bagels. 'How'd you guess? I've a feeling we're gonna be here for a while.' Mat's hand went instinctively to his tie. There weren't many things that made Matari Ndava nervous – this meeting, however, was one of them. He still wasn't sure what exactly was going on.

'OK, gentlemen. Let's begin,' DiAngelo said after the last coffee cup had been cleared away. He leaned back in his chair, folded his hands behind his head and looked expectantly at Mat. 'Floor's all yours.'

Mat got up, cleared his throat and powered up his laptop. He brought up the first slide on the big screen and turned to the three men. 'I've divided the report into three distinct areas. First, the background on RhoMine, most of which I'm sure you know already. Then I'll talk briefly about the geopolitics of Southern Africa as a whole and lastly, the detailed dossier on Jim Harte himself. I'll make sure you all have copies before the meeting's over.'

Sir Winston leaned forward. His considerable bulk was squeezed into one of the more comfortable seats, although he looked anything but. His chubby fingers played idly with a pen, but his light blue eyes were alert and watchful. Despite his bon viveur reputation, Mat knew, there was very little Sir Winston would miss. 'Make it snappy, son,' he said, a touch condescendingly. 'I've a plane to catch.'

Mat ignored him. Like many a tycoon, Sir Winston rarely missed an opportunity to remind those around him of his status. He heard DiAngelo's barely suppressed sigh of irritation. 'Part of Harte's success, of course,' he continued smoothly, 'has been the turnaround of what was a relatively obscure mining company into the global conglomerate that RhoMine currently is. Much of what's in the report has been covered almost exhaustively by other people, particularly after his bid for the London *Telegraph*. As I'm sure you're all aware, he's spent the past few years dodging allegations of tax evasion and money-laundering, which the UK government has spent a considerable amount of money trying to make stick.' Mat paused. 'He's a remarkably complex man. Initially, at least, I assumed – like everyone else, I imagine – that his life story more or less followed the known facts.' He looked at each of the men sitting opposite him. There was a noticeable tension in the air. 'Actually, Jim Harte's story couldn't be further from that truth. His business dealings – if you discount tax evasion claims – are actually relatively straight-forward, but only if – and it's an interesting point – you understand the man behind the corporation.'

'How d'you mean?' McCormack asked, frowning. 'Oil, manganese, bauxite, diamonds . . . throw in a couple of car dealerships and a few banks . . . it's too disparate. Why so many disconnected ventures?'

'Well, here's the thing. On the surface of it, he seems like an ordinary chap. Yes, he's got more money than most, but he's a stand-up guy, as the Italians would say. Membership at all the right clubs. Homes in the UK and Zimbabwe, a place in the Alps, the holiday home in the Bahamas . . . it all adds up, am I right?'

'Where're you going with this, Mat?' DiAngelo asked, a little impatiently.

Mat put up a hand. 'Hear me out. Harte subscribes to an image, if you like, of a certain kind of man. But – and here's where it gets interesting – Jim Harte *isn't* that sort of man. Here's what we *think* we know. British, born in the early thirties, went to Rhodesia at the age of nineteen, worked for a couple of local, British-owned firms until he bought his first mine, Kanyemba, at the age of twenty-three. In 1970 he married an English girl, Jane Gough-Miller, daughter of Lord Gough-Miller, in London. He had two sons with her; they now run different parts of his business. The eldest, Patrick, married Sir James Barclay's daughter, Annette, a couple of years ago. Jane Gough-Miller died a few years later – it's rumoured she committed suicide, although nothing's ever been proven. Shortly after her death, he married Sarah Parker, a schoolfriend of Jane's from her English boarding school. They had a daughter, Nicola, who's now in her twenties, I believe. Sarah Parker died in 1977 in a hunting accident at their home in Chinhoyi.' He saw the three men exchange a quick glance. 'Again, there were rumours – foul play, he was having an affair, *she* was having an affair . . . but again, nothing stuck.'

'Well-connected young women, the pair of them. And both dead?' McCormack raised an eyebrow.

'As I said, there were rumours, but nothing's ever stuck. In 1986 he married his third and current wife, Molly Crenshaw. He and Molly have one young daughter, currently at school in the UK. As I said earlier, this much we know.' He faced the men who were listening intently. 'Now, this bit's taken longer than I thought to get to the bottom of but I think we've managed to put together a fairly accurate picture of what we *don't* know.'

'You say "we",' McCormack interrupted. 'I thought you worked alone on this?'

'In terms of *WED*'s involvement, yes, I worked alone,' Mat replied, 'but you can't get this level of information on your own.'

'And there's no risk of any of this . . . er, *investigative* work being linked back to us?' DiAngelo asked, more to appease McCormack, Mat noticed, than any concern of his own. He wondered why. The three men sitting in front of him were a very different breed from the man he'd spent the past six months researching. None of them, not even DiAngelo, had the stomach for a fight. Years of good salaries and better bonuses, year on year, had made them soft, comfortable, well fed. They were no longer hungry for it. Jim Harte, it seemed, was different. And Mat now knew why. He'd started out hungry. Literally.

He switched on the projector and dimmed the lights. Puzzled faces looked up at the screen. It was a map of West Africa. He pointed to a tiny group of islands lying off the coast of Senegal. 'The Cape Verde islands. Discovered by Alvise Cadamosto for the Portuguese in the fifteenth century. They have an interesting position, both geographically and culturally. A major stopping-off point for European and American trade routes, from the eighteenth- and nineteenth-century slave trade to South African Airways flights on their way to Europe. As you know, SAA were banned from flying over African airspace.'

'Where is all this going, Mat?' DiAngelo interrupted irritably for the second time. 'All very interesting, I'm sure, but you were asked to compile a dossier on Jim Harte, not on the history of West Africa.'

'I'm just giving you a bit of the background,' Mat said mildly.

'But to what?'

'To where Jim Harte was born. *This*, gentlemen – not the Home Counties or the Midlands – is where Jim Harte is from. If you'll just bear with me, I believe it holds the key to most of the decisions he's ever made.'

There was silence in the room. 'Cape Verde?' McCormack muttered. 'That's ridiculous. He's *English*. Rhodesian at the very least.'

'Well, actually, no; he's neither. Jim Harte's real name is James Habib.' Three mouths dropped open even further. Mat was enjoying himself. 'He was born to an Anglo-German mother and a Lebanese father in an internment camp on the island of São Antão in the Barlavento chain of Cape Verdean islands. The Habibs were on their way from Swakopmund in the German colony of south-west Africa to Düsseldorf when the Second World War broke out.' He paused. He had their rapt attention. He took a swallow of water and continued. 'They were on board the vessel *Mandelstam*, which ran into difficulties just off the coast of Senegal. The crew took to the lifeboats and put ashore in Banjul, which, of course, was British. There was apparently some confusion as to what to do with them until someone suggested sending them to Île St Louis, just north of Dakar. The French had an internment camp built on the island during the First World War. When the Vichy government came to power, the prisoners were moved to Cape Verde. James Habib was born on the ship that ferried them to São Antão. He spent the first eight years of his life in Mindelo, the country's second-largest city. Both his parents died on the island. In 1948, two years after the end of the war, he was shipped out to a maternal uncle in Portsmouth. The boy was more or less brought up by the camp's commanders.'

'This is absolutely *extraordinary*,' Sir Winston said, leaning back in his chair. 'Why hasn't any of this come to light before?'

'Well, my view – if you'll allow me to speculate – is that it's more to do with what we all would like to see in him, than anything else. I mean, the information's there, if anyone cares to look.'

'Explain what you mean.'

'Put it this way. You all remember the fuss over the Al-Rahmani brothers?' Everyone nodded. 'When they first appeared in London, it was assumed they'd come from money. An old Egyptian shipping dynasty, wealthy homes around the world . . . that sort of thing. It made them "all right", so to speak – members of the club. When the story broke on their backgrounds, everyone was shocked. If I remember rightly, their father was a goatherd. But when the dust settled, it turned out that the brothers themselves had never said any of it. There wasn't a single public statement or record by either of them to say they'd been to Eton or their family had pots of money. It was all a combination of rumour, innuendo and what people wanted to believe. I think Jim Harte's another example of the same thing. He *looks* like an English country gent, he *sounds* like one, he's got the money . . . we've all filled in the rest. All of us.'

'Are you saying,' Sir Winston suddenly found his voice, 'that Jim Harte is nothing more than a jumped-up refugee Arab? That it's all a sham?'

Mat winced inwardly. 'No, not at all. What I'm saying is, here's a man without much to lose. He's a loner, always has been. He practically brought himself up. *And* he's a chameleon. He speaks six languages, apparently all of them equally well, although you'd never know it. He's got a British passport, courtesy of his maternal grandfather, but he's spent his entire life outside of every single community he's ever been placed in. As far as I can make out, he spoke German with his mother, Arabic with his father, French with the authorities and Portuguese with the people around him. I presume there'd have been some pretty vicious anti-German sentiment in Britain in the 1940s, when he arrived—'

'You presume correctly, young man,' Sir Winston said, interrupting him. He glanced at DiAngelo, an eyebrow raised in admiration.

'I'm presuming, therefore, that he'd have become adept at hiding who his parents had been, the fact that German was his mother tongue, et cetera. He became, in effect, what people wanted to see. A young Englishman. I think becoming what others want to see is something he's done all his life. Perhaps even subconsciously.'

'And you think that's why he's had such spectacular success in southern Africa?'

'Well, from what I've gathered, he makes unusually clear-headed decisions. He's not weighed down by ideology in any form. He was one of the first whites to engage with ZANU, back in the seventies when no one thought they had a chance in hell. He's been close to them all – Mugabe, Nkomo, Muzorewa . . . the lot. He's got an uncanny nose for a winner, which, I suppose, is a trait you'd develop after years in an internment camp. He's someone who sees the world in very clear terms – profit or loss. That's it. The rest of it – religion, nationality, race – I can see how none of those things might mean very much to a man who's never really belonged anywhere or to anything.'

'And his family? You said his sons are running part of the empire. What do we know about them?'

'There's not much to know at the moment. Harte obviously keeps his family under close wraps. The eldest one, Patrick, runs the dealerships, which supply vehicles to the entire region. It's not a hundred per cent clear how Harte got the distribution rights quite so neatly sewn up but if you want me to find out, give me another couple of months. The second son, Shaun, runs the safari businesses – lucrative, but probably not strategically important.'

'He's got a grown-up daughter, you said?'

'Yes, Nicola. I found a couple of pictures of the sons but nothing on the daughter. I think it's safe to assume she has no direct influence or interest in RhoMine.'

'I don't believe it,' Sir Winston breathed. 'Extraordinary.'

'Everything I've said today is laid out in the report,' Mat said, realising he'd been talking for over an hour. 'There's just one last thing that I wasn't really able to crack and, I have to admit, it leaves me slightly worried.'

'What's that?' DiAngelo said sharply.

'It's to do with diamonds. As you'll read in the report, diamonds have historically been one of the mainstays of Rho-Mine's profitability, if not total output. They own three of the largest mines in Zimbabwe and a couple more in Zambia but there's a company that I *think* is linked to RhoMine that's started doing business in Sierra Leone. Ordinarily there'd be nothing unusual in that if it weren't for the fact that the mine they're operating – Kono – is in the heart of RUF territory. I won't go into much of an explanation about Sierra Leone now – we can do that at a later date – but it's rebel-controlled, which means that, technically, the West isn't supposed to buy diamonds within its borders. Security on the mine is being provided by a company called Baseline International, which is listed in the Caymans as a subsidiary of Global Strategies. They, in turn, are the operators of the Beira oil pipeline, and the pipeline is owned by—'

'RhoMine,' Don McCormack interjected, nodding thoughtfully. Mat nodded. 'I don't know if this means anything yet, except that the conflict in Sierra Leone is getting worse, not better, and that someone is making a killing bringing stones out of the country. On the surface of it, more stones in the market-place drives the value of diamonds down, not up . . . which is bad news for De Beers and everyone else, including RhoMine. On the other hand, Sierra Leone's a very rich country and diamonds aren't its only valuable resource. *If* Harte is linked to this – and it's still a very big "if" – it means he's backing the RUF to win. From what I've seen over the past six months, Harte isn't in the business of backing losers. Just something to think about, gentlemen. Have a good afternoon.'

66

'Estelle? You're not listening to me!' Mrs Devereaux frowned at her, exasperated.

Estelle snapped out of her daydream. 'Sorry. I . . . I was just thinking . . .' she mumbled.

'You're not paid to *think*, Estelle. Not to put too fine a point on it, darling, you're paid to fuck and you simply haven't been doing enough of it lately. I can't keep turning clients down, my precious. Fabien's called twice this week already. I had to give him Tamsin, for crying out loud.' She looked at Estelle closely. 'What on earth is the matter?'

To her horror, Estelle felt a hot tear suddenly start to make its way down her cheek. She brushed it aside fiercely. It was the word 'precious'. That was Gloria's word for her. She hadn't heard her mother's voice in years. Another tear followed. And then another. 'I . . . just—' She jumped up, unable to staunch the flow and ran across the cream carpet to the bathroom at the other end of the suite. She shut the door behind her and leaned against it, breathing deeply, tears coursing down her cheeks. She didn't understand what was happening to her. It wasn't *like* her. Not at all. Ever since the night when she'd heard Mr Khoury's colleague refer to her as a whore with that special pitch of contempt in his voice, she'd found herself dwelling on things. Her life and what it had become. The choices she'd made. The men she fucked. All of a sudden, the drive and determination that had propelled her out of Arcadia and into glamorous, fast-paced London just wasn't enough. Opening her legs – and her mouth – for the men who could afford her seemed pathetic, not ambitious. Sordid, not smart. She couldn't understand it. She had everything – a beautiful flat, a chauffeur, clothes, jewels, shoes. She accompanied men on holiday to places she'd only ever read about in the glossy magazines that occasionally made their way to Harare. She'd flown in private jets, stayed in private villas on private beaches. Why wasn't it enough? She'd made it. Of course she'd made it. So why this awful, aching emptiness? She took a deep breath and tried to control herself. Mrs Devereaux was worried. Pretty soon her worry would turn to anger. Estelle couldn't go on avoiding jobs. Mrs Devereaux had worked far too long and far too hard to build up her client base and, as every girl who worked for her knew, there were half a dozen other girls just *itching* to sign up. Estelle was one of the most popular girls on her books, but that meant nothing. She'd have to watch it if she wanted things to stay that way. Whatever else anyone might say about her, Estelle wasn't stupid. She blew her nose, wiped her cheeks and took another couple of deep breaths. She *had* to get it together. She had no bloody choice.

Sally Devereaux looked at Estelle closely as she emerged from the bathroom. Silly girl. What had happened? Had she fallen in love? Was that it? It happened from time to time, despite her best efforts to ward it off. There was even one girl – back in the beginning before Sally had learned what to do about such things – who'd married one. Karen Jones-Smythe. Back then, of course, she'd been plain Karen Hammond from Warrington. Pretty, though. Now she was a bona fide socialite with homes on four continents and a husband who *still* rang Sally Devereaux every once in a while. It didn't stop Karen from blushing on the odd occasion she and Sally ran into one another. Sally didn't like such situations. They blurred the boundaries she'd worked so hard to erect. Clients and girls; services and fees; favours and expenses. That was the sort of stuff she knew about. The other stuff – love, marriage, babies – she cared nothing for. It wasn't for her. *Or* for her girls. It was why she was successful. Men didn't frequent her business in order to find a prospective bride.

Christ, they came to her to get *away* from their brides. So when a girl as beautiful and valuable to her as Estelle Mackenzie kept putting clients off, claiming headaches, stomach aches, period cramps, migraines, nausea, *anything* . . . well, there were only two possible reasons. One, she was pregnant and two, she'd fallen in love. Both, as far as Sally was concerned, were equally distasteful. Although at least she could *do* something about the former.

'Are you pregnant?' she asked Estelle as soon as she'd sat down opposite. Estelle's face registered genuine surprise. So it wasn't that.

'No. Of course not.'

'So what is it?' She saw no point in beating about the bush.

Estelle hesitated. She looked at Sally with those astonishing blue-green eyes and then sighed. 'I . . . I guess . . . I'm just missing . . . I miss home,' she said finally, twisting her fingers nervously around each other. Sally was surprised. She'd never once heard Estelle even mention home, wherever it was.

'Where's home?' she asked, not entirely without sympathy. After all, the girl was only in her twenties. She suddenly thought of her own daughter and was alarmed to feel a lump in her throat. No point thinking about *her*.

'Zimbabwe,' Estelle said after a moment. Sally's mouth dropped open. She might as well have said 'the moon'.

'Your parents live in *Zimbabwe*?'

'Just my mum,' Estelle said, blowing her nose.

'What about your father?' Sally asked, her eyes narrowing.

Estelle did her best to shrug nonchalantly. 'He . . . he left before I was born. He lives here, I think.'

'I see.' Suddenly, the girl's erratic behaviour was starting to make sense. 'You've never met him?'

'No. I thought about it sometimes, when I was a bit younger. I thought I might try and find him.' She twisted the ring on her finger nervously.

'Well, why don't you?'

Estelle looked up at her in surprise. 'How?'

'Oh, Estelle. It's not rocket science.' Sally got up and walked over to the dresser. She opened her Dior handbag and took out a packet of cigarettes. She lit up, blowing the smoke away from her face. 'Anyone can be found. That's not a problem. If that's what's really eating at you, then I can help. You're one of my best girls, Estelle . . . no, you silly girl. Don't start crying again, for God's sake. I can't stand snivelling girls.' She regarded Estelle calmly. '*Finding* your father's not the difficult part.'

'What is?'

'It's what happens afterwards. Once you've found him. Then what?'

'Then . . . well, nothing,' Estelle said, still twisting her fingers round and round.

'Hardly,' Sally said dryly. 'You've spent the past twenty-odd years fantasising about a man you've never met who, in all likelihood, hasn't been thinking about *you* . . . it's painful stuff, Estelle. What if he turns out to be—'

'At least I'd *know*,' Estelle interrupted her, a touch defiantly. 'At least I wouldn't still be wondering—'

'Fine.' Sally cut her short. She walked over to the console beside the window and pulled open a drawer. She took out a small silver case and flicked it open. 'Here,' she said, flipping through a number of business cards. 'Call Phil Johnson. That's his number. Tell him I sent you. I'll deduct his charges from your earnings. Which means, darling Estelle, that you'd better pull yourself together, get back on top of things and start *earning*. Do what I pay you to do . . . *and* what you're so damned good at.' She smiled at her. 'You're costing me money at the moment, darling. And you *know* how much I hate to spend what hasn't been earned.'

A week later, having worked almost every night since her conversation with Mrs Devereaux, Estelle found herself sitting opposite a man who looked more like a dentist or a family doctor than a private investigator. He sat facing her across a green leather-topped table, fingers pushed stiffly upwards in a 'V' in front of his face, tapping them occasionally against his lips as he listened to her rather disjointed story. He said very little as she spoke, occasionally frowning as though a fact she'd mentioned didn't quite fit.

'So . . .' he said, drawing out the syllables as he spoke. 'This . . . Basil Mackenzie, you say, worked in what was then Rhodesia in the sixties. You've no idea for whom?'

Estelle shook her head. 'I just know he was a mining engineer.'

'I see.' He opened a drawer and pulled out a pad. 'Was he Scottish?'

Estelle shrugged. 'Yes, as far as I know.'

'Not much to go on, I'm afraid.' He looked at the copy of her birth certificate which she'd given him. *Mother: Gloria Cecilia Turner. Father: Basil James Mackenzie. Date and Place of Birth: 13 February, 1978. Salisbury, Rhodesia.* 'All right. Give me a month or so. I'll need to do some looking into things, probably do a spot of archive work. You say you don't know whom he worked for?' Estelle shook her head again. 'Well, that part's not altogether impossible. Easier than you think, actually. There weren't that many mining outfits in Rhodesia in the sixties. Leave it with me.'

Estelle stood up. She watched his eyes travel up the slender length of her body. She pulled on her leather gloves and picked up her smart little Gucci bag. 'Thank you, Mr Johnson,' she said, the warmth slowly returning to her voice. The knot of tension in her stomach was beginning to dissipate. For some reason, she trusted him. If anyone could find a man named Basil Mackenzie, Phil Johnson could. She felt better just knowing it.

'My pleasure, Miss Mackenzie. I hope you find what you're looking for.'

'Me too.'

That night, sitting astride a suitably grateful Fabien, she was so full of gratitude towards Mrs Devereaux and so hopeful that the question that had been gnawing at her for the past few weeks would finally be resolved that she made love to the poor man as she never had before, bringing him to the point of orgasm not once, but *three* times, seeing in his anguished, astonished face a look of such pure desire that she had to close her eyes. It was happening to her, too. Nothing to do with him, however. She clambered off him after three-quarters of an hour of the most intense sexual pleasure either of them had ever experienced and lay beside him panting, trembling with the aftershocks of her first ever climax. She was shaking from head to toe. Fabien could barely even speak. She was, he told her, nibbling at her, pushing the damp hair from her neck, 'the best fucking thing in the world'. He was blissfully unaware of the pun.

67

'What's this?' Tory picked up the envelope and looked questioningly at Luc.

'Open it and see,' he said, popping one of the pepper wheels she'd been slicing carefully into his mouth.

She slid her finger under the flap. A ticket fell out. Air France. CDG–MHE. First Class. 'Mahé? Where the hell is Mahé?'

'Seychelles.'

'You've got to be joking.'

'*Jamais.*'

The ring sat snugly in its box on the inside of his jacket. There was a moment's unease as he went through the metal detectors at the airport and was asked to empty his pockets, but Tory had already passed through in front of him and was drifting towards the duty-free shops. The official who asked him to open the box was sympathetically discreet. 'Good luck, mate,' he winked as Luc slipped the box back in his pocket.

'*J'espère,*' he winked back and moved off. 'Hope' seemed a rather weak description of the emotion surging through him at the thought of what he was about to do. He'd spent a fortnight looking for the right ring – emerging from the shop dazed each time after the obligatory half-hour sales patter. Solitaires, emerald cuts, baguettes, tapered baguettes, brilliants, radiants, princess cuts . . . he'd previously only ever noticed a diamond by its size. Now he understood size was the least of it. He eventually settled on the Barion cut, a beautiful, rectangular-shaped stone with sixty-two facets, producing the same fiery shine as the more traditional brilliant, the sales lady said, but with a modern twist. She smiled at his obvious appreciation. A little bit like Tory, he wanted to tell her, though she couldn't have known it. He was aware of how rash it would seem to everyone else, especially his mother – how long had he known her? Two months? Nearly three? Long enough. He'd known from the first time he walked into her shop that he would ask her to marry him, ridiculous as it sounded. He'd known from the moment he set eyes on her.

A few hours later he peered out of the window into the thick, empty blackness below. Tory's head lay heavily against his shoulder; she was fast asleep. They were somewhere above the Gulf. The cabin was almost silent. In First Class, the flight attendants seemed to glide, not walk, down the aisles – a discreet glance here, a pause there . . . anything and everything to make the lucky few who could afford it ever more comfortable. He stretched his long legs cautiously, not wanting to wake her. He looked around him. It was a very, very long way from the farm he'd grown up on just outside Périgord to the First Class cabin of AF391 on its way to what the brochures described as 'the last paradise on earth'. The only son of poultry farmers, he'd won a scholarship to a prestigious Catholic boys' school nearby and never looked back. He'd left everything behind: the farm, the small lake at the bottom of the hill where he'd scrapped in the holidays with the sons of other farmers who went to the local lycée. After high school he'd gone to Paris, to the École Polytechnique and from there to the European MBA programme at FNAC. Now, aged thirty-one, he was earning more money in a year than his parents had made in the past twenty, and the woman sleeping beside him was about as far away from the women he'd grown up around as it was possible to be. Yes, he'd come a very long way from home.

His mind went again to the box in the left pocket of his jacket. He'd never met anyone quite like Tory. There was a toughness in her that he'd never encountered in a woman before, not even his mother. At times he thought she was afraid of nothing. To have come through what had happened to her sister . . . he was speechless with admiration. And yet there was a fragility about her that made his heart ache. She was funny, too, in that dry, English sort of way that he'd come to appreciate. It sometimes felt as though he'd been waiting for her all his life. After almost ten years of working in the mercurial, quicksilver world of high finance, he'd learned one thing. When you stumbled upon a winner, you grabbed it. With both hands. His own hand went again to the box in his jacket. Tory was a winner. Anyone could see that; him most of all.

They landed just before noon to the sound of the sea lapping against the shore and the overhead crying of circling gulls. Stepping out of the aircraft, Tory felt the weight of the past eighteen months slide off her shoulders, dissolving instantly in the turquoise water surrounding them on all sides. She felt dizzy just looking at it. They were a thousand miles from the nearest landmass, the captain had told them just before landing. The beauty of the place was hard to take in. The sky was a dazzling, iridescent shade of blue, hovering somewhere between cobalt and turquoise, not a single cloud in sight. The neighbouring island of La Digue, which was where they were headed, loomed on the horizon, a thickly carpeted swell of green hills and sandy coves. She clutched Luc's arm in excitement. Even though all she'd ever heard about the Seychelles was how beautiful they were, she still couldn't quite get over how true it was. Beyond beautiful, beyond anything she'd ever seen. Even when their passports were stamped with the imprint of a giant *coco-de-mer*, the island's most exotic plant, she still couldn't get over it.

They had an hour's wait in the small airport lounge offering a tantalisingly nearby view of the beach, and then they boarded a smaller plane to fly them to La Digue and to the villa on the beach that Luc had rented. The little plane circled the island once before coming to rest on a small, tarmac runway. Tory's mouth hung open as they took in the semicircular beach, the Anse Source d'Argent with its snow-white sands and giant, gently sculpted boulders that popped out of the clear blue water.

A member of the hotel staff was on hand at the tiny airport bungalow. Ten minutes later, they were seated in a blue wooden cart, drawn by an ox, winding their way down towards the beach. An *ox*? She stared at the humped back of the placid beast as it tugged them slowly towards their destination. London was almost impossible to recall. Less than twenty-four hours earlier she'd been standing on the Circle Line, grabbing on to the overhead strap with both hands and trying not to inhale as the carriage rocked and swayed and her face was thrust against someone's armpit. They passed a few brightly painted old plantation villas – banana-yellow, baby-blue, deep lilac – all colours were intensified in the tropical light; the whole island shimmered. Some of the flowers growing wild by the side of the road were so spectacular she almost reached out to grab them. Luc shook his head, smiling at her.

'*Après*. You can do that later,' he murmured drowsily against her ear. 'Let's get to the villa first and . . . rest,' he said, nudging her meaningfully. Tory slapped his hand playfully. The cart in front of them carrying their luggage and the hotel guide, a cheerful young man who'd introduced himself as Pras, veered to the left and they ambled down a sandy lane surrounded by coconut trees . . . and then suddenly they were there. The villa, a beachfront building that looked vaguely Indonesian in style, had wooden shingled roofs turning slightly heavenwards at the corners and pale green and ochre pillars supporting the veranda over a steep cliff that plunged straight into the sea.

'Welcome to the Desroches Resort,' Pras said, smiling. Their luggage was unloaded quickly and efficiently by a team of equally smiling young men and Pras led them into the villa. Inside was no less impressive – dark wood panelling set off by white, starched linens and vivid primary-coloured accents like the silk cushions on the daybeds and the paintings on the walls. 'If you require anything at all,' Pras was saying, 'just ring the bell. Your cook will be along shortly to discuss your menu for the week. There are towels and an assortment of products on the veranda outside and the pool is for your use exclusively.' He smiled at them, bowed deeply, and then turned on his heel and left. Tory's mouth still hung open. She walked outside – just as he'd said, there was a magnificent, deep blue infinity pool just below the veranda, which overlooked the sea.

'This . . .' She turned to Luc, eyebrows knotted together in a frown, 'is for us? Just you and me? Just for the two of us?'

'*Oui.*' Luc smiled at her. 'I hope you like it.'

'Like it?' She turned to look at the view – the deep blue of the pool was mirrored by the sky and the wide open sea that stretched to the cloudless horizon. The beach lay in a perfect crescent before them, powdery white sand and swaying palms. There was no one about. The paradise below was entirely theirs. She stretched her arms above her head, basking in the feel of the sun on her arms. In the distance, across the yawning, rippled surface of the sea there was a single island and in the foreground, the curved, pointed bow of a dhow, ploughing its way across the water. 'Oh, yes,' she murmured, half to herself. 'I like it. I like it very much.' She turned to Luc, who was watching her, an amused expression on his face. 'Swim?' she said, grinning. 'Or would you like to . . . rest?'

'Both,' he said, unbuttoning his shirt and walking into the bedroom. 'We can do both at the same time. As the man said – it's all ours. There's no one else here. We can do,' he said, winking at her as he shrugged off his jeans, 'anything we like.'

Clouds, absent from the sky during the day, suddenly appeared before sunset, clustered together at the edge of the horizon to provide a blazing backdrop to the sudden death of the sun every evening. From their veranda overlooking the pool, Tory and Luc had an unbroken view all the way to the edge of the world, as Luc called it. About halfway between the beach and the edge of the world was a small rocky outcrop, named Silhouette

Island, and after their first spectacular sunset, she could see why. At a quarter past six every night, the colours of the rocks changed from dark green to dark grey and then to black. Silhouetted against the sinking sun, it was a perfect interruption in the silvery-black shimmering surface of the sea as night descended.

After three glorious days of snorkelling, swimming and sleeping beside the pool, she felt as though she'd been there for ever. She could barely recall London, and the smell of damp leaves in the courtyard behind the shop.

She picked up her wine glass and turned to Luc. 'D'you know, I think I could quite happily stay here for the rest of my life,' she murmured, twirling the delicate stem between her fingers. Below them, moving in a quick, straight line across the horizon, was a canoe. Blackened against the sun, the two stick figures inside it alternately raised and sank their paddles. She watched their progress for a minute or two, then turned back to Luc. He had a rather strange expression on his face and was jiggling something in the palm of his hand. 'What's the matter?'

He turned to her and slowly took the wine glass out of her hand. 'What you said just now . . . about life,' he said with an odd, nervous catch in his voice, 'there's something I want to ask you. *Maintenant*.' He stopped suddenly.

Tory frowned at him. 'What?' she asked. It wasn't like him to be tongue-tied.

'The thing is,' he said, suddenly getting out of his chair and kneeling beside hers. Tory looked at him in astonishment. 'I . . . *voilà* . . .' he said, opening his palm to reveal the little black velvet box. Tory stared at it. Her heart started to accelerate. 'And . . .' he continued, fishing in his pocket for a rather crumpled piece of paper. He shook it with his free hand and began to read in a rather stilted voice. '*In Ancient Egypt, it was believed that the vein of love ran from the ring finger directly to the heart. Placing a diamond, with its enduring power, on that finger was seen as the ultimate way to connect love with eternity.*' He looked up at her. He hesitated for a second and then suddenly the words came tumbling out. 'Will you marry me?'

Tory gaped at him. She opened her mouth to say something – anything – but nothing came out. She looked at the ring – a beautiful, rectangular-shaped stone set in a simple platinum band – and then at Luc's face, brows knitted together nervously. She swallowed. Her mind was whirling. They'd only known each other a little over three months – it was absurd! People didn't get married after three months, did they? The diamond winked at her; she reached out gingerly to touch it, as though afraid it might suddenly bite. Luc was still on his knees. Out of the corner of her eye she could see the watery green-blue light of the pool, its surface catching the fiery reflection of the citronella braziers that dotted the garden and beach. Just look at the trouble he'd gone to, she thought to herself, almost distractedly. He'd bought the tickets, paid for the holiday, bought the ring . . . he'd done all of that and she'd had no idea what he was planning. When had he thought about it? She stared at him. He'd just asked her to marry him. She was holding the ring in her hand. Luc was still on his knees . . . she had to say something. Quickly. She could hardly say 'no'. Luc was wonderful; he was charming and kind and funny . . . what more did she want? The thoughts flashed through her mind as she watched herself lift the ring out of the box and slide it on her finger, admiring the way it caught the light. In the same state of distracted disbelief, she watched herself look down at Luc, take his tortured face in her hands and kiss him. She heard the word coming out of her mouth as though it'd been spoken by someone else. 'Yes.'

Much later, when the villa was shrouded in darkness and Tory had finally fallen asleep on his chest, Luc lay awake listening to the symphony performance of the crickets outside and the distant but persistent lap of the waves against the shore. It had been a roller-coaster of an evening. For a few awful minutes as he'd knelt there at her feet, he'd been sure she would refuse. It hadn't really occurred to him that she would be anything other than delighted – a little surprised, perhaps, a little emotional, certainly . . . but he hadn't been expecting the confusion that was written all over her face when he opened his palm. He was shocked. Tory's normally blank, carefully composed face was a mass of contradictions – fear, surprise, uncertainty . . . it was written all over her in a way he'd never expected to see. When she'd said 'yes', of course, her face had righted itself, becoming the beautiful, calm, rather watchful face he'd studied for the past six months. In that moment, she'd slowly come back to herself. But the glimpse of something else had unnerved him. It wasn't the sort of question one returned to – once you'd asked a girl to marry you and she'd accepted, you could hardly keep asking, 'Are you sure?' It didn't seem right, somehow. And of course, afterwards, when she'd seen the expression on *his* face, she'd tried very hard to put things right. She was just surprised, that was all. He'd caught her by surprise. Of course she wanted to marry him – who wouldn't? She'd teased the good humour back into the situation and they'd gone to bed, making love with a surprising ferocity that brought tears to his eyes, not hers.

He shifted his body so that she was lying next to him, not on top of him, and put his arms round her. She stirred very faintly then sank back into sleep. In the moonlight he could just make out the white light of the diamond on her finger. He began to stroke the smooth skin of her shoulder and felt his excitement grow at the thought of what he'd just done, what he'd just asked of her. He slid a cautious hand in the space between her arm and the sexy, rounded curve of her hips and lower, his fingers burrowing into the silky softness between her legs. She was awake now, her body twisting itself to meet his. 'Tory,' he mumbled incoherently as she grabbed hold of him, pulling him on top of her, into her. *Je t'aime.*' Her reply was lost as he brought his head down and covered her mouth with his.

68

Caryn stared at the stack of CVs in front of her. After three late nights of sifting through them, tossing out the ones she thought were unsuitable or just plain awful, she'd managed to whittle the stack down to fifty. By the end of the day, it would have to stand at twenty. She picked up her pencil and started going through them once again. Eight actors were required. Four couples. The auditions were scheduled for Saturday morning. It was Tuesday. By Wednesday morning, she would have to have the twenty best. It was all in her hands. She was nervous – it was the first time she'd ever done it – but Martin had handed the task over to her without even batting an eyelid. *He* obviously thought she could do it, even if she didn't. She began the task of crossing names out all over again.

On Saturday, exactly as planned, she, Rupesh and Martin were sitting in a damp, fusty assembly hall, watching twenty young hopefuls going through their lines. Martin had quite specific ideas about the four couples – faces, voices, mannerisms and so on – and whenever he came across someone who fitted the bill, he made a note. Then whenever he came across someone whom he hadn't originally considered but whose performances were strong enough to persuade him to rethink a character – those too were noted and put to one side. At the end of the day, he still had a shortlist of fourteen names. Six would have to go.

By nine o'clock that evening, after fierce discussions, he'd made his choices. It fell to Caryn to let the lucky eight know.

'I'll be as kind as I can,' she said, half-jokingly, picking up her bag. She yawned, utterly spent. It was almost nine-thirty. They'd been in the hall since eight that morning with only a couple of short breaks.

Martin looked up. He and Rupesh were still arguing over the last lucky girl. 'What for? They're actors. They're used to rejection,' he said, grinning.

'Still . . . it must be hard. Can you imagine being turned down week after week?'

' 'Course he can,' Rupesh laughed. 'Rejection's his middle name. You ever seen him with a girlfriend?' he asked Caryn.

She hesitated. 'I—'

'There you go,' Rupesh said, turning back to Martin. 'He's used to it. That's why he loves dishing it out.'

Caryn threw Martin a helpless smile. 'See you tomorrow,' she said, turning to go. Speculating about Martin's love life was the last thing she wanted to do. Or hear about. She was still far too wary for that.

Martin looked up, grinning. 'Night, Caryn. And thanks for today. You were great.'

'Oh.' The unexpected praise brought a little colour to her cheeks. She hurried out of the hall before Rupesh could comment.

Shooting began a week later. Martin had broken down the scenes into a nine-day shot list, with an additional day for the outside London scenes. As always, money was tight and there was no room for wastage. Caryn had been to each and every one of the four locations so many times in the week prior to the start of filming that she was beginning to feel at home. There was the trendy loft apartment off Hoxton Square for couple number one, Matt and Naomi; the cramped, messy one-bedroom flat on the Finchley Road for couple number two, Bertram and Denise; the wide open spaces of the Greenwich Observatory gardens and a tiny Greenwich café for the third couple, Sue and Joe, and finally, the most exciting of all, a twenty-second-floor flat in the Barbican for couple number four, the yuppie duo Jane and Dave. Martin's list of demands was unusually long. There was a lot riding on the film, and he wanted to get absolutely everything right. They'd decided to use different lenses for different scenes. Caryn had spent the morning at the hire shop next to Euston Station making sure they had all the right equipment to hand. The assistants staggered from location to location, laden down with Sonys, Canons, Arri lenses, tripods . . . Caryn wandered each day amongst them, soaking up the terminology. She was a keen learner. It was exhilarating. Even Katie was involved, running from second-hand shops to department stores to get exactly the right accessory or prop that Martin thought they would need for the scenes. He was fanatical about detail – if there were cut flowers in a vase on the table, they had to be the *right* kind of flowers. Flowers that Jane, the high-flying lawyer living in the Barbican flat, would choose. Caryn was glad to be able to call on Tory for advice. Martin, notoriously hard to impress, was impressed.

'For Christ's sake, Meredith . . . you're having an *argument*,' she could hear him shouting at one of the actors. 'You don't have to *throw* anything at him but I need more emotion than this! Come on . . . you're angry with him, remember? Think about what he's just *done*!'

Caryn smiled and wandered back to the set. Money was tight and time was money – it was crucial that they got it right as close to the first time as possible. Mind you, she thought, glancing over at the actress who'd just been yelled at by Martin – even if you did get the part, it wasn't always fun. She wasn't sure she'd care to be on the sharp end of his tongue. She'd lost count of the number of times they'd shot and reshot the scene with Meredith and the actor whose name she could never remember – she had grown so used to calling him by his screen name. Two more days of shooting and then the editing would begin. Rupesh was busy at work on the score; there were a couple of classical tracks for which she would have to arrange the licences and then, fingers crossed, they would have a final tape. There would be a wrap party at a Soho bar the following week with all the cast and crew . . . and then it would be on to the next project. And hopefully the next one after that.

'Say you'll come. Please.' Nic's voice was at its most beguiling.

'But I won't have anything to wear,' Caryn protested, wedging her phone between her chin and her shoulder as she attempted to continue typing as she talked. 'I've never been to a party like that before and—'

'All the more reason to come. And you can wear whatever you like. You've got an LBD, I know you have. I've seen you in it.'

'A what?'

'A Little Black Dress. Oh, say you'll come . . . go on. Tory won't. Ever since she got engaged—'

'Nic, I *can't*. We're in the middle of production,' Caryn interrupted her, signalling to Katie to pick up the other phone. 'I'm working flat out. I've got two new locations to source, there's the actors to audition; it's just a bit hectic at the moment. Any other time, honestly.'

'Please? For me? It's only an evening.'

'Oh, all right,' Caryn sighed. It was hard to resist Nic when she really, really wanted something.

'Thank God! I was *dreading* going on my own. It's not till next Saturday anyway. You've got ages to get yourself ready.'

'Thought you said Zoë was going with you?'

'That's like being on my own. She won't deign to talk to me, you know. Not while she's surrounded by millionaires and models.'

'Oh, Nic, it sounds awfully glamorous,' Caryn said dubiously.

'It won't be. I'll pick you up – round about seven p.m., OK?'

'Yeah, I suppose so.'

'It'll be fun, I promise.'

Nic put down the phone, relieved. She'd actually received two invitations to the opening of the new De Beers shop on Bond Street – one addressed to Nicola Harte and the other to Nicola Parker, courtesy of RhoMine and *Gossip!*, respectively. She'd propped them both up beside the fridge, glancing at them occasionally, nervously. She hated going to parties on her own. Zoë was going, of course. 'It'll be a working night for you,' she said, 'see who's out and about, listen to the gossip, catch up on the news. That's what we're famous for, darling,' she trilled, her hand going automatically to her Rolodex for a list of stylists, wardrobe consultants and personal shoppers. *She* wasn't going to be working on the night of the party, that was for sure.

Nic made herself a cup of coffee, suddenly restless. Caryn's job sounded amazing, she thought with a pang of envy. She remembered how worried Caryn had been when she'd first applied for it – all that fuss about not having a university degree. Caryn was adamant. Without one, she'd be relegated to making coffee for ever. Why not just make it up? Nic remembered how surprised she and Tory had been. Caryn Middleton was just about the most painfully honest person they knew. Caryn Middleton was prepared to *lie*? But it had been the right thing to do, she saw that now. And anyway, Caryn was cleverer than anyone Nic had ever met. If it would help get her through the door . . . It wasn't as though she wouldn't be able to do the job once she'd got it – it was just a matter of *helping* her get it. They'd all put their heads together and thought up a suitably obscure degree at UCL. Sociology was exactly the right sort of vague course that no one really understood and would be unlikely to question her about. She'd done fantastically well – she'd been promoted a couple of times. Proof, if it were ever needed, that sometimes you had to bend the truth a little in order to get on. Christ, she should know all about *that*. She was a Harte, for crying out loud. Jim Harte's fortunes were built on bending the truth – and pretty much everything else besides.

69

After the intense build-up to his report, the aftermath was disconcertingly flat. DiAngelo instructed him to do nothing, say nothing. Everything went quiet. For the first time in his life, Mat found himself at a loose end. DiAngelo seemed reluctant to put him on to anything new; he'd been more or less out of the office for half of the year. He sat at his desk watching others get on with the stories of the hour. It was frustrating. He was still officially on 'special assignment', although the assignment seemed to have ground to a complete halt. He didn't like not having anything to do. In fact, he was dreadful at it. Even Leonie began to wish he'd stayed at home.

'Take a vacation,' DiAngelo told him after his second week. His tone indicated it wasn't a suggestion.

Mat looked at him warily. 'For how long?'

'Oh, two, three weeks. You deserve it. You're gonna need it. When we come back with Plan A you're going to be very busy.'

'Plan A?'

'Yup. We're working on it. And there will be no Plan B.'

'OK, boss.'

And that was it. He had three weeks at his disposal to go anywhere he wanted. But where? The question nagged at him. After having spent the past decade working almost night and day, there weren't too many people around with whom he could spend a couple of days, let alone three weeks. He tapped the TV remote against his thigh. Well, there really was only one option. As much as he disliked going back to the city that held so many painful memories for him, he really couldn't think of anywhere else to go. After all, there was no knowing whether the person he'd left the city in order to get away from was still there. She'd have moved on, surely. She always did. Besides, there were other people in London. He'd go and see his parents and his sisters, hang out with Simon if he was around. He had no idea where Simon actually was – the last phone call had been a few weeks back . . . somewhere in the Congo. He picked up his messages fairly regularly, though, and Mat still had the key to Simon's Battersea flat. He picked up the phone, dialled Simon's number and left a message.

At about four that morning Simon rang back, the shrill, insistent ring catapulting him straight out of sleep. He fumbled for the phone. 'Simon? It's four o'clock in the morning!' he growled.

'Sorry, *bru*. Just picked up your message. I'm here for a couple of weeks at least. Come on down. I can't believe you're actually taking a holiday. What happened? They fired you?'

'Don't sound so happy about it. No, I didn't get fired. I'm on holiday, that's all. I'll get a ticket tomorrow morning. Should be there by Saturday.' His mouth was dry – probably the result of the whisky he'd downed before going to bed.

'Excellent, *bru*.'

'I've got keys – you still live there, right?'

'Every once in a while.' He could hear Simon chuckling as he hung up the phone. He rolled over. It was strangely peaceful in the dark. Eight floors below he could just hear the early morning traffic; the garbage trucks whining steadily as they pulled in and out; taxis honking; the occasional shout. Yes, a few weeks in London would be good. The curtain over his eyes thickened and within minutes he was fast asleep again.

It took him barely half an hour to pack the following morning; he stopped by the office to pick up a few things and by late afternoon, he was in the back of a yellow cab speeding towards JFK. He made his way to the executive lounges. The long flights back and forth over the past few months had racked up a healthy number of air miles – time to get something out of the work he'd done. He ordered a coffee and picked up a newspaper. As he drank and read, he felt some of the tension of the previous few weeks begin to lift. Despite his apprehension about going back to London, he found himself looking forward to seeing the family, Simon – to having time off. Twenty days without a single meeting, interview, deadline . . . unbelievable. If he could just focus on the fact that relaxation was *good* for him . . . well, he might actually enjoy it. He was so used to the cut and thrust of the features floor – phones ringing, people talking, shouting, laughing, the pace and the frantic working before deadlines. It was hard to imagine that for the next three weeks he'd have none of it. Just the relative peace and quiet of Simon's Battersea flat and a couple of days at the Ndavas' Hampstead home.

'Sir?' He looked up. A pretty brunette in the uniform of the BA ground staff was smiling at him. 'Flight's boarding.'

'Thanks.' He picked up his bag and made his way to the gate.

London was just as he remembered. At seven a.m. in the haze of early summer, the streets were calm and orderly. As the cab nosed its way through the traffic heading into town, he leaned back in the seat, listening with half an ear to the radio, enjoying the cool, measured tones of Radio Four. It was a welcome relief. New York was the most dramatic city he'd lived in – from the exaggerated verticality of the skyscrapers to the honk-and-swerve tactics of drivers, everything was bigger, faster, louder. The streets were a battle zone between cars, cyclists, pedestrians – even the steam hissing from below the surface had to fight its way out. London, by contrast, was calm, measured. It soothed him just to watch. Simon's flat was on Petworth Street, nestled between Chelsea and Battersea Bridges. After years of living in hotel rooms and rented flats, he'd surprised everyone by buying it suddenly, and then promptly leaving it half empty.

The taxi dropped him off and disappeared down the road. It wasn't yet eight. He slid the key in the lock and opened the door. The smell of fresh paint still hung in the air. He jogged up the stairs to the door of Simon's flat and knocked before opening the door. There was no answer. The flat was pretty much as he remembered it. There was a raincoat slung over the top of the living-room door; muddy running shoes in the hallway; the smell of coffee and burnt toast in the air. Simon must have just stepped out. He tossed his bag on the spare bed and walked into the living room. There were piles of magazines and newspapers stacked up on the floor beside the sofa which, presumably, had once been plump and comfortable but was now squashed out of recognisable shape. There were dishes in the kitchen sink in the corner and half a piece of uneaten toast on a side plate on the dining table. He was suddenly hungry. He sat down on the squishy sofa and picked up a book that was lying there. One of the murder-mystery stories that Simon liked to read. He put it down. He hadn't read fiction in almost ten years. He closed his eyes. Despite having slept almost all the way from New York, he was tired.

★

He jerked awake. A door had slammed, somewhere in the distance. He lay for a second in the drowsy suspended state between waking and sleep and then the door burst open.

'You're here!' Simon slung the carrier bags on to the table and walked over. He punched Mat lightly on the arm – his standard greeting. 'I just went out to get some milk and the papers.'

'I just got in,' Mat said, struggling up from the couch. 'I could smell the toast. Figured you hadn't gone far.'

'Let's get some breakfast. There's a café round the corner.'

'Sounds good to me.'

Ten minutes later they were sitting beside the river, waiting for their orders to arrive.

'So, what's new?' Mat was the first to ask. Despite his tan, Simon looked tired. And, if anything, even more wary than he had when they'd last seen each other in New York.

Simon shrugged, lighting a cigarette. He blew the smoke out slowly. 'Not much.'

'Where're they sending you these days?'

'Here and there,' Simon said vaguely. He looked away. Mat knew better than to press the issue. He'd never fully understood Simon's career progression. He'd started out as an analyst, testing for the presence of certain types of trace minerals in soil samples that might indicate the presence of oil. That much Mat understood. It was well paid, straightforward. He seemed to be doing well, moving quickly up the promotion food chain. But then he'd switched from oil to mining, and that was when the foreign travel had really begun. Every other month it seemed he was in a different country, although doing essentially the same thing – testing the earth to see whether it could yield a profit or not. In the early days of their careers, they'd joked about it. Simon got his hands dirty whilst Mat kept his clean – in the figurative sense, of course. 'What about you?' Simon asked, steering the conversation away from him.

'Well, it's been a weird start to the year,' Mat said, stirring his coffee. 'I've spent most of it doing something quite different. I shouldn't say too much about it but I've been doing some investigative work, not reporting.'

'Into what?'

Mat hesitated. 'This goes no further, OK?'

'Sure.'

'I've been looking into RhoMine's CEO, Jim Harte. It's interesting – *he's* interesting. I've never met him but I'd like to. Never thought I'd say *that* about the guy.' He glanced at Simon. Simon looked slightly stunned. 'What's the matter?'

'Huh? Oh, nothing. Just thinking about . . . about something else for a second.'

Mat hesitated. 'Simon, is something wrong?'

Simon looked the other way. He shook his head. 'No. Everything's cool.'

'You sure? You seem a little worried,' Mat said delicately.

Simon hesitated. 'It's nothing. Just . . . you know how it is. Bloody women.'

'Anyone special?' Mat was surprised. It wasn't like Simon to let a woman get him down. That had been his department, not Simon's.

'Nah. She's . . . with someone else. But it's cool. Plenty more where she came from,' he said firmly. His expression was blank.

'Absolutely,' Mat murmured. He felt a surge of affection for the tall, rangy man with the deep tan and green-brown eyes whose face he felt he knew better than his own. As far as he could recall, Simon had never fallen for anyone the way Mat had. Tanja. Even now her name still caused him pain. He stopped himself. Simon would get over it. You just did.

70

Caryn tied the belt on her wraparound dress and took a quick, nervous look at herself in the mirror. She'd had her hair cut the week before and she still wasn't sure about it. It was the first time since the age of about ten that she'd had a fringe. Cut squarely across her forehead, the ends curling in underneath her chin. 'Suits you,' the stylist kept reassuring her. 'Honestly.' Caryn wasn't convinced. Her small, heart-shaped face stared back at her uncertainly. She turned slowly. She'd decided against her little black dress and at the last minute had gone out and bought something new. It was pale blue, of a clingy jersey-like fabric with a small pleated detail at the neckline and the sleeves. She carefully fastened a pair of earrings and stepped back. She looked grown-up. Sophisticated, in spite of the fringe. She picked up her bag. Nic would be there any minute now. Why, she asked herself for the umpteenth time that evening, had she allowed herself to be talked into going? A party to celebrate the launch of a new range of diamond jewellery was *so* not her sort of thing.

Nic was wearing black, of course. She looked every inch the glamorous heiress, though she'd probably have thumped Caryn if she'd said it. Her long dark hair was parted in the middle; she was wearing the most enormous pair of silver hoop earrings and a long, thin silver chain that disappeared into her cleavage. 'You look great,' Caryn said as she slid into the back seat beside her. For once, Nic was using her father's chauffeur. Caryn still found it hard to get used to – this time it was a silver Mercedes that smelled brand new. It was a complete mystery to both her and Tory why Nic didn't have a boyfriend. She was fabulously rich, fabulously beautiful and *nice* . . . an almost unheard-of combination. She went out on countless dates which never led to anything but whenever you asked her, she just shrugged and mumbled something about it 'not being quite right'. What,

Caryn wondered, was the problem? Not that *she* could talk, she reminded herself quickly. Since Rowland she'd been out once or twice with nice, perfectly harmless young men she'd met at office functions or once, with an actor who'd been rejected at one of Martin's auditions, but nothing had ever come of it. Deep down, her feelings about men were still unclear. She hovered between the helpless repugnance that thinking about Dave Humphreys brought on and the helpless desire that Rowland managed to ignite. Two extremes, both helpless, she thought to herself wryly. No bloody wonder she didn't have a boyfriend.

'Why so glum?' Nic asked, as they swung past the American Embassy on Grosvenor Square. 'You've hardly said a word!'

Caryn sighed. Nic could be awfully sharp-eyed at times. 'Oh, nothing,' she said, a touch defensively. 'Just thinking.'

'Don't. Let's just go and enjoy ourselves. You look scrumptious,' Nic laughed. 'I like the fringe, by the way.'

'Do you?' Caryn put up a hand to touch it. 'I'm still not sure.'

'Well, let's do a head count tonight, then make up your mind.'

'Head count?'

'How many heads turn as you pass them by.' She leaned forward to speak to the driver. 'Thanks, Carl, this'll do. I doubt you'll get any closer.' She looked down at Caryn's shoes. 'Can you walk in those?'

Caryn giggled. 'I've no idea. I only just bought them.'

'Come on,' Nic said, opening the door. 'And there was me thinking I'd dragged you out against your will. New haircut, new dress, new shoes . . . you've been looking forward to this all week. Admit it!'

Caryn scrambled after her, unable to protest.

'Where's this party again?' Mat asked Simon, picking up his jacket.

'New Bond Street. Come on, *bru*. It'll be fun. Supermodels galore.'

'And that's supposed to make me want to go?'

'When was the last time you went out with a supermodel?' Simon asked, flicking out the collar of his shirt from under his jacket.

'I haven't yet had the pleasure,' Mat said dryly.

'Well, then. Something new. C'mon, let's go.'

Mat gave a short, half-exasperated laugh and followed him downstairs. He'd had to go shopping that afternoon to buy a new suit – it hadn't really occurred to him to bring the sort of clothes he'd normally have worn to an event like this. Armani. Black, worn with a very fine light woollen sweater underneath. He looked at Simon. In his tan linen suit he looked every inch the Marlboro Man. He grinned reluctantly. Despite himself, he was half looking forward to it. It had been a long time since he'd had a night out. Amongst many other things, including Tanja, it was something that belonged to his past. He winced. Would it ever stop hurting?

Simon flagged down a cab at the corner of Petworth Street and they jumped in. 'New Bond Street, please.'

'Right you are, sir.'

The driver stopped at the corner of Brook Street. 'Doubt I can get you much closer than this,' he said, shaking his head. The other cars inching their way towards New Bond Street were obviously heading to the same place. Mat couldn't remember the last time he'd seen so many luxury cars at the same time. Mercs, BMWs, Jaguars, Bentleys, as well as the odd Ferrari and even a white Lamborghini. He raised an eyebrow. 'All the best places,' he murmured.

Simon snorted. 'It's fine. We'll walk from here.' They both got out. It was a pleasantly mild summer evening; a few late shoppers dawdled along, clearly curious about the event taking place halfway down the street. As they approached, Mat could see a thick velvet rope cordoning off the entrance. Enormous bouncers stood with watchful eyes as guests showed their invitations to an exquisite creature dressed in shimmering black who duly checked and then waved the chosen few in. Simon fished two invites out of his jacket. The girl parted her shiny red lips, murmured something in greeting and they were through the doorway.

It took a while for his eyes to adjust to the dimmed lights inside. There was a fountain – of all things – in the centre of the room; the soothing sound of trickling water mingled delightfully with the mellow jazz and the murmured conversation. Giant black-and-white photographs of a diamond-clad Iman hung from the ceiling. He saw Hugh Grant and his voluptuous girlfriend, Liz Somebody-or-other, in one corner, Kristin Scott Thomas, looking as languidly glamorous as ever, in another – Samuel L. Jackson, Tom Cruise, Nicole Kidman . . . Simon was right. Celebrities and supermodels galore. He raised one eyebrow as another exquisite creature, this time in shimmering white, approached them with a tray of drinks. 'How the hell did *you* get an invitation?' he murmured to Simon as he accepted a glass.

'Actually, I'm meeting someone here tonight,' Simon admitted, a touch sheepishly. 'Just a quick one. It shouldn't take long.'

Mat glanced at him. What sort of meeting could he possibly have in a place like this? And why hadn't he mentioned it before? Something wasn't quite right; he could sense it. As if on cue, a short, rather portly man in a suit appeared at his side, accompanied by two men whom Mat immediately understood to be bodyguards.

'Mr Carter?'

Simon turned round. 'Mr Khoury.' He nodded curtly at him and then turned back to Mat. He touched him lightly on the arm. 'Back in a bit. Enjoy yourself,' he said, not quite meeting his eye. The two of them walked off and Mat was left standing with the bodyguards, slightly irritated at having been dragged out to the party and then dumped.

'Mat! Mat Ndava!' Someone called out to him from behind. He turned round. A bearded man in an ill-fitting suit was smiling broadly at him.

'Rick. Rick Burnett. We worked together at the *FT* a couple of years ago . . . don't tell me you've forgotten?'

Mat looked at him blankly. He had. 'Hi. Sorry, didn't recognise you,' he lied.

'Yeah, it's the beard. No one does. What're you up to these days? Read your article on Bokassa the other day. Bloody good. You're based in New York?'

Mat nodded, allowing himself to be led into a conversation, his mind already drifting back to Simon and the strange turmoil he seemed to be in.

'Is that Hugh Grant?' Caryn squealed, unable to keep the excitement from her voice.

'Mmm. And there's Liz,' Nic pointed her out. 'And over there's Juliette Binoche. Ooh! There's Iman . . . God, doesn't she look *incredible*?'

Caryn gaped at her. Iman was wearing the Gross Domestic Product of a small country round her neck. De Beers officials and bodyguards hovered anxiously around her like butterflies. 'She's so *thin*!' she breathed. 'Like a twig!'

'They all are. I wonder where Zoë is . . . I'd better make sure I find her. She'll accuse me of missing all sorts of things if I don't let her know I'm here.'

'Champagne, ladies?' A gorgeous waiter in a crisp white shirt and gloves balanced a tray in front of them. 'Enjoy the evening,' he murmured, his eyes lingering on Caryn for a second before he walked off.

'You see?' Nic said triumphantly. 'I *told* you it suits you!' Caryn hid her face behind her champagne flute. 'Oh, good, there's Zoë. I'll just nip over and say hello. You'll be all right here for a sec, won't you?'

'Be quick. Don't you dare leave me!'

Nic turned and collided with another guest whose champagne glass immediately went crashing to the ground. She cursed and turned brick-red. The glass was quickly swept up by a waiter who rushed over, a damp linen napkin was produced; everything was quickly dealt with. Apologising profusely, and still red with embarrassment, Nic beat an exit and made her way over to where Zoë was standing, unfortunately with the ultra-chic editor of *Glamour*, Marianne French.

'Was that *you* causing all that commotion, darling?' Zoë asked in her honey-smooth voice as Nic walked up.

Nic glared at her. Since when had she ever been 'darling'? 'Er, yes,' she said shortly.

'It's the shoes, I bet,' Zoë said, looking down at her feet. 'Never mind, darling. You just need a bit of practice.'

Nic was just about to reply when a man walked past, cutting across her line of vision. Her eyes widened. She honestly couldn't remember when she'd last seen such an incredibly beautiful man. He cut through the main hall walking towards the exit, his body moving with a sexy, graceful swagger. Her mouth dropped open.

Zoë and Marianne obviously agreed with her. 'Mmm,' Zoë drawled, her eyes following Nic's. 'Who's *he*?'

Nic quickly closed her mouth and turned back to them. 'No idea,' she said shortly. The last thing she wanted to do was compete for attention with Zoë.

'Di-*vine*,' Marianne breathed. The two women winked at each other. Their expressions were almost comical.

'I . . . well, just wanted to say hello,' Nic said, gesturing in Caryn's direction. 'I brought a friend with me tonight—'

'Oh, no date? Never mind,' Zoë smiled at her. 'Just make sure you get me some gossip. Marianne's girls are working the floor. Don't want to be caught sleeping now, do we?'

Nic mumbled something incomprehensible and made her escape.

Mat, having made his own escape from Rick Burnett, was on his way to the toilets when he noticed the tall, striking, dark-haired girl standing next to a woman in a dress of a truly horrendous shade of purple, even in the dim light. She'd noticed him, too – he could feel her eyes on him as he crossed the floor. To his slight disappointment, she'd disappeared by the time he came out a few minutes later. He looked around for her and spotted her talking to a petite blonde girl, standing in the corner by one of the display cases. He was contemplating what to do next when the shorter, blonde girl walked away, obviously in the direction of the toilets. He grinned. It wasn't the sort of thing he normally did, but . . . what the hell? He was on holiday. Simon was nowhere to be found. He collected a glass of champagne and walked over.

'Model or mate?' he asked, disconcerted to feel his heart starting to beat faster. She was stunning. She was tall, almost the same height as him. He glanced down – high heels. Sexy heels.

'Sorry?' She looked straight at him, her eyes impossible to read. Was it his imagination or was there a faint smile playing around the corner of her lips?

'Just wondered if you were a model,' he said, laughing inwardly at the lameness of his introduction. She wasn't even wearing any jewellery. 'Or someone's girlfriend. Sorry . . . I don't normally do this.'

'And what are you doing?' She folded one arm across her midriff and held her glass of champagne aloft. There was definitely a smile playing around her lips. She was bold, as well as flirtatious. He liked that.

'Trying to chat you up.' He might as well be honest. She looked the sort to appreciate it. 'But you didn't answer my question,' he said slowly, looking straight at her.

'Neither, as it happens,' she said, tipping her head back and draining her glass.

He watched her finish it. 'Another one?' he asked, amused.

'Why not?'

'Back in a sec. Don't disappear.'

'Hurry, then.'

Nic watched him cross the floor and catch a waiter's attention. She couldn't take her eyes off him. His skin was the colour of dark, bitter coffee. He had dark, thick brows, almond-shaped eyes, high, wide cheekbones and a beautifully shaped mouth that seemed to be permanently tilted in a smile. She dragged her eyes away from his face and found herself staring at his legs instead. *Be cool, Nic*, she cautioned herself. He had a lovely, deep voice . . . a slow, perfectly proper English voice overlaid with the faintest hint of American. She prayed Caryn would stay in the toilet for just a little bit longer.

'Here you go,' he said, coming back with a fresh glass in his hand. 'I'm Mat, by the way.'

'Nic.'

'So what *do* you do?' he asked, taking a sip of his champagne. 'If you're not a model.'

'As little as possible,' she laughed. 'I work for a magazine. I'm supposed to be working tonight. That's my boss over there,' she said, pointing with her glass in Zoë's direction. Zoë had noticed the two of them, she saw with a little jolt of satisfaction.

'Ah,' he murmured. 'An . . . unusual dress, don't you think?'

'It's Miyake.'

'And it's supposed to look like that?'

'Well . . .'

'No, don't answer that. I don't want to be held responsible for rude comments about your boss.'

'What about you?'

'What about me?'

'Are *you* a model? Or someone's boyfriend?'

He laughed. 'Neither, though I suspect you're only being kind.' He seemed about to say something further when Caryn suddenly appeared. Nic could feel herself blushing. Caryn looked at the two of them, her eyes widening slightly.

'Oh, there you are,' Nic said quickly to cover her confusion. 'This is . . . Mat, isn't it?' She knew damn well what his name was.

'And you're . . . Nic?' His eyes were smiling. He didn't miss a thing.

'Yes, and this is Caryn.'

'Hi, Caryn.' They shook hands. There was a short, awkward silence. 'Well, I'll leave you guys to it,' he said, looking straight at her. 'It was nice to meet you.'

'Oh, yes . . . er, you too.' She wanted to tell him to stay but didn't know how.

He turned to go, then hesitated and turned back. 'Listen,' he said in a low voice, obviously for her ears alone. 'Like I said, I don't normally do this but I'm in London for a couple more days . . . if you feel like grabbing a coffee or a drink, give me a ring.' He pulled a card out of his pocket and scribbled down a number. He handed it to her.

She felt the heat rush into her cheeks. She took the card and turned it over, not even looking at it, trying not to smile. 'Can I?' she gestured towards his pen. He looked a little surprised but handed it over. She scribbled her number on the back of the card and handed it back. 'Now you'll have to call *me*,' she said. 'Ball's in your court, Mat.' She winked at him and walked off. Caryn quickly ran after her. He was smiling, she knew. She could *feel* it.

Simon's smile was held so tightly in place he felt it might crack. He'd spotted Mat as soon as he came in, talking to two women. He'd been about to cross the floor to join them when she turned her head in profile and he realised with a jolt who it was. He turned away immediately, aware of a great surge of irritation sweeping over him. Of *all* the bloody people! He should have *known* she'd be there. And why the fuck was Mat talking to her? He gave a short, annoyed laugh. It was bloody obvious why. She was gorgeous. Same reason *he'd* talked to her – kissed her, actually. He stood near the entrance, watching them. Mat handed her something – a card. Nic Harte took it, scribbled something down and then handed it back. Her number, no doubt. Mat slipped it inside his jacket. He could hardly bear to watch. A few moments later, the two girls walked off. When it was clear they weren't coming back he stepped forward and touched Mat lightly on the shoulder.

Mat turned round and grinned at him. 'Hey, you're back. How'd your meeting go?'

'Yeah, fine. Look, I'm not feeling so good,' he lied. He tapped his forehead. 'Headache. I don't know what brought it on but it's pounding. You stay, if you want, but I think I'm gonna head home. Sorry to be a party-pooper.'

''Course you're not. Come on, let's split. Nothing much

happening here anyway,' Mat said, frowning. His face was full of concern. Simon had to look away. They pushed their way out of the store and through the crowd gathered at the entrance. A few flashbulbs went off half-heartedly but no one was aiming at them. Mat jogged ahead and picked up a taxi on Oxford Street, turning down Brook Street to pick him up. As they pulled away, Simon's head really did start to pound. Seeing Nic Harte again had brought on a rush of blood to the temples. Seeing Mat talking to her had brought on something else. Something he'd never thought himself capable of.

71

He could hear the toilet flushing and then the sound of the shower being turned on. Mat's jacket hung on the back of one of the dining chairs. Without giving himself another second to think, he crossed the floor and slid his hand into the inside pocket. His fingers touched the card. He drew it out, stared at it and then slid it into his own wallet. He glanced at his watch. It was almost midnight. He poured himself a glass of water and swallowed two aspirin. He switched off the lights and walked into his bedroom, trying not to think. Next door, he could hear Mat getting ready for bed. The floorboards creaked; there was the sound of the wardrobe door being pulled open and then shut again, then the faint beep as he picked up the phone, probably to check his messages in New York. His heart started to beat faster as he heard him cross the floor, open the door and then walk into the living room. He strained to hear – had he gone to get his jacket? There was nothing for a few minutes, then he heard the gentle, careful click of the door being shut . . . and then silence. He peeled off his own clothes, too tired to shower and his head too muddled to think clearly. He lay down, waiting impatiently for the aspirin to take effect. His heart was thudding quietly.

Mat was also awake, trying to work out what on earth he'd done with the card she'd given him. He distinctly remembered putting it inside his jacket pocket. Had he dropped it somewhere? He could hardly start tearing the place apart at midnight, especially with Simon not feeling well next door, but he was agitated. It wasn't like him to lose things, especially not something like that. He'd put it into the right-hand pocket of his jacket; he was sure of it. On the way home in the taxi he'd slipped his fingers in a couple of times, touching it, a reminder of an unexpectedly pleasant evening. He'd liked the look of her, at first, and then he'd liked her. She was surprisingly cool. *Ball's in your court.* She hadn't even looked back as she walked off. How many women could pull that off? And now he'd gone and misplaced the bloody card. He grimaced. The first woman he'd seen in years who'd so much as piqued his interest and he'd gone and lost her number! He didn't even know her last name. He didn't know anyone else at the party so how, if he really had dropped the bloody thing, was he going to find her again? No, it had to be somewhere in the flat. He'd had it when he got out of the taxi, he was sure of it. He'd pulled his wallet out, brushing Simon's hand away when they pulled up in front of the house . . . could he have dropped it then? He was almost tempted to go outside and look right there and then, except it was well after midnight, he didn't have a torch and he'd wake Simon up . . . no, it *had* to be somewhere in the house. He had a sudden recollection of her dark eyes, her face, half-hidden behind the distorted curve of her champagne flute. He felt his pulse quicken. He wanted to know more. He *had* to find that damned card.

'You feeling better?' he asked Simon the following morning as Simon emerged from his room.

'Yeah, don't know where it came from. But it's gone. Sleep

well?' Simon asked, glancing quickly at the dining table. Mat's jacket was gone.

'Not really. The weirdest thing . . . I was talking to someone, at the party, I mean. She gave me her number, wrote it on the back of one of my cards. The damned thing is, I can't find it.' He gave an impatient half-laugh. 'I even went outside this morning to see if I'd dropped it on the pavement but I couldn't find it. I must've lost it in the taxi or something.'

'Annoying,' Simon said, his voice carefully light. 'Still, plenty more where she came from, I'm sure. As you're always saying,' he added hastily, seeing Mat's frown.

Mat nodded, clearly distracted. He poured himself a cup of coffee and took the bundle of papers he'd bought over to the window. It was going to be a quiet morning, Simon saw. Whenever he was upset, Mat simply withdrew into himself. He sighed. He shouldn't have done it, for all sorts of reasons. Just as when they were kids, he hated seeing Mat upset. Even more so when he was the cause of it. Unlike Simon, Mat rarely lost his temper. Slow to anger, quick to forget – that was Mat. Simon's polar opposite. There had been quite a few occasions when they'd settled things the old-fashioned way, with a proper, fists bared, no-holds-barred fight. Patience had lost *her* patience, she'd reprimand them whenever she came upon them scuffling in the dirt. Back then, it had been the quickest and most efficient way to settle their disputes. Once the fight was over, they would both invariably feel ashamed and then it was a matter of minutes, for Mat, at least, to regain his equilibrium. Longer, for Simon, true, but it worked. It had been years since they'd fought in that way, though. Years since they'd argued about anything other than politics, which, of course, everyone argued about anyway. They'd never seen eye to eye on Mugabe, which they both agreed was fine. Mat was a football fan, Simon favoured rugby . . . that too was fine, and somewhat historical: rugby, in southern Africa, was a whites-only sport; soccer was the game of the African masses. Fortunately for both of them, they'd never been interested in the same girl. Simon had always had a string of little beauties around him, right from the start. Throughout high school there had always been three or four competing claims to being Simon Carter's girlfriend, almost always simultaneous. Of the two, it was Mat who was more cautious with his heart.

And then, of course, he'd had it broken by Tanja Petrovitch, the daughter of the Russian ambassador, whom he'd met at boarding school in England. They'd gone out for seven years, all through university. And not once, in all that time, had she ever told her parents about him. When push came to shove and she had to – well, she shoved. Mat. Right out of the picture. Took up with someone else, an English guy who worked at the same bank – English in the way her parents would have understood and approved of. And that was it. Shortly afterwards, Mat moved to New York and the whole thing was history. Or so Mat said. Last night was the first time in years that he'd seen him even *remotely* interested in someone.

He turned away from the window and picked up his jacket. 'I'm just popping out to get some fags,' he said, avoiding Mat's eye. He felt like shit. He *was* a shit. How could he even think about doing this to his own brother?

72

Estelle sat with her knees pressed tightly together and her hands clenched across her lap. She could feel the diamond ring that one of her besotted middle-aged, overweight clients had bought her digging into the palm of her left hand. She was waiting for Phil Johnson to call her into his office. He'd said it would take about a month, but it was now closer to three. She felt herself to be close to breaking point with the tension of the long wait. The secretary looked up and smiled sympathetically at her. 'He won't be long,' she said, gesturing towards his office. 'There's just someone in with him at the moment.'

Estelle ignored her. She couldn't have spoken even if she'd wanted to. Her throat was absolutely dry. She tried unsuccessfully to quell the nerves in her stomach. Finally, just when she couldn't stand it any longer, the door opened and a large woman in a floral suit emerged, followed closely by Phil Johnson.

'Ah, Miss Mackenzie. Won't be a moment,' he said, seeing the floral lady to the door. 'Do go in. Cup of tea?' Estelle shook her head impatiently. She got to her feet and almost ran into his office. 'Have a seat, have a seat,' Phil said, coming in behind her and shutting the door firmly. He settled himself in opposite her and regarded her thoughtfully. Estelle's heart was thudding. It wasn't possible to tell from the expression on his face whether he had good news for her or not. Although *any* news would be good, she thought to herself quickly. Anything at all.

'Did you—'

He held up a hand to ward her off. 'First things first,' he said, pulling at the corner of his moustache. He opened a drawer and pulled out a buff manila file. 'I need to ask you a few questions—'

'Just tell me. Did you find him?' Estelle interrupted him. She could hear her own breathing, raspy and shallow.

He sighed. 'I did. It's a little more . . . complicated, shall we say?'

'Who is he? Is he still alive?'

'Very much so.' He brought his hands up under his chin. 'I found Basil Mackenzie. He lives in Oxford—'

'Can I see him?' Estelle broke in excitedly.

He shook his head. 'Not advisable, I don't think, Estelle.' He drew in his lower lip. 'Basil Mackenzie is certainly alive but he's not your father.'

Estelle stared at him, her eyes widening. 'He's not?'

'No. I haven't asked him to provide a DNA sample, admittedly, but I think he's telling the truth. No, Basil Mackenzie isn't your father, I'm afraid.'

Her lip quivered dangerously. 'Then who is?'

He hesitated. And then he mentioned a name.

Estelle almost stopped breathing. She stared at him. 'It c-can't be,' she stammered finally. 'He's . . . it's impossible. He's not my father!'

'Your birth certificate shows Basil Mackenzie listed as the father. But it's a copy. When I requested the original – which was why the whole thing took a little time – something else emerged. You were born in Zimbabwe before 1980, my dear, which means that all births, marriages and deaths were recorded by the Colonial Office and kept at Somerset House, here in London. So . . .' He opened the file and pulled out a single sheet of paper. 'This is a copy of the original lodged at Somerset House. I think you'll agree it's not quite the same as the copy you hold. The father's name has been changed. That, my dear,' he said, pointing at the copy on the table between them, 'is your father.'

Estelle stared at the birth certificate. She was aware of a great wave of emotion building up inside her, a slow burn in the pit of her stomach, spreading like fire through her entire body. Her fingers began to shake. 'Are you absolutely sure?' she asked, her voice turning steely with anger.

Phil Johnson nodded. 'About as sure as I can be.'

She was silent. Then she picked up the new copy of her birth certificate and held it up. 'May I keep this?'

'You may. Mrs Devereaux has settled the account so it's all yours. Oh, and this too.' He handed her the copy she'd given him at their first meeting.

'Burn it,' Estelle said firmly, and got to her feet. She folded the new birth certificate neatly in two and slipped it into her purse. She looked down at him. 'Thanks for your help,' she said softly.

He seemed about to say something, but didn't. She opened the door to his office and walked as steadily as she could down the corridor, ignoring the startled glance of the secretary, focusing on a single thought. Gloria had lied to her. Why?

73

How quickly everything changed. Less than a week ago, she'd been filled with optimism. Pure, shining, radiant optimism – the kind that got you out of bed in the morning with a smile. The kind that made the day ahead shine – the sky was bluer, clearer; the sun was golden and warm. Everything seemed possible, suddenly. She'd gone home the night of the party, a secret smile playing around the corner of her lips, driving Caryn round the bend. Nothing had happened – he'd done nothing more than ask for her number. And yet . . . everything had. Ridiculous to think that she'd spent a total of five minutes in his company. She couldn't explain it to Caryn and she couldn't explain it to herself. Mat. She didn't even know his last name. But she would, soon. He would call; they would arrange to meet and she'd see for herself just what it was about him that had stirred her so.

But he didn't call. The same optimism that had transported her to such dizzy heights brought her back down to earth with the swiftest, cruellest, hardest bump. By the morning of the fourth day after the party when it was clear that Mat was not going to call, Nic was on the floor. She was furious at herself. She'd spent a total of *five minutes* with the man? Good-looking or not, charismatic or not, she barely knew him. She'd barely even met him. One glass of champagne, five minutes of silly banter and flirtatious glances followed by a minute's worth of scribbling phone numbers . . . why, oh, why had she tried to play it so cool? Ball's in your court? He'd *dropped* the fucking ball. Why, oh *why* had she given it to him in the first place?

She sat at her desk at home and tried to concentrate on the piece Zoë had asked for. It was already a day overdue. Zoë's 'Kiss 'n' Tell' column in *Tatler*, their sister magazine, was avidly read by socialites and those desperate to *be* socialites every week – few people in the publishing industry would have guessed that it was actually written by one of Zoë's subordinates. Nic hated doing it and she especially hated having to write the way Zoë did: hard, brittle humour and stinging, bitchy one-liners. To tell the truth, she'd barely noticed who was at the damned party. She tried to recall what Liz Hurley had been wearing – very little, in all likelihood. She sighed. Her life was a series of 'whys' – *why* had she allowed herself to be bullied into writing 'Kiss 'n' Tell'? *Why* didn't she just leave *Gossip!* and do something more challenging with her life? *Why* was she so bloody weak-willed about everything? And *why* had she given him back his card without even looking at his name? Because she'd been trying – too hard – to be cool. The phone rang suddenly, shattering the uneasy silence. She took a couple of deep breaths before picking it up. Please let it be him. *Please* let it be him.

'Hello?'

'Hi, it's only me.' It was Caryn. 'Are you all right?'

'Yeah.' Disappointment washed over her. There was a short silence. Then, 'No.'

'What's wrong?'

'He hasn't called,' Nic wailed, unable to stop herself.

'Oh, Nic. Look, why don't we go out to dinner? Just you and me—'

'But what if he calls?'

'Nic. You've got an answering machine. He'll leave a message if he's that keen. And if he's not, forget about him. You know the rules. Come on, let's go out.'

'OK,' Nic sighed. At least going to dinner would take her mind off what felt like the most crushing disappointment of her life. 'Where?'

'Mezzo,' Caryn said firmly. 'And wear something nice. You need cheering up.'

Nic put down the phone, her heart still pounding. Caryn was right. Forget him. What was wrong with her? The only two men she'd met in the past year that she'd liked and they'd *both* turned out to be duds! It just wasn't fair. She looked at the phone for the umpteenth time. No, he wasn't going to call. She was sure of it. She would probably never see him again.

PART SIX

74

London, England, 2004

Tory pushed the pile of receipts and expenses away from her and stood up. It was a beautiful Saturday morning but as usual, here she was, cooped up indoors, going over finances. She had the entire weekend to herself – Luc was away on a business trip; surely she could find something more interesting to do? She couldn't remember when she'd last had a morning to herself. The shop took up almost every spare moment of her time and the little that was left over was spent with Luc. Her mother had long ago decided to lay down the law where her own husband was concerned – weekdays, yes; weekends, no. He rarely came into the shop on a Saturday. She walked over to the windows overlooking Canonbury Square. It was a glorious June morning. The sky was wide and blue; the sun was out. She pulled a face. When was the last time she'd been shopping? Just for herself? Just for fun?

Ten minutes later she ran down the stairs, slammed the little gate behind her and walked towards Upper Street. She loved her new flat. She'd been in it all of six months and now she couldn't imagine living anywhere else. It was on the fifth floor – no lift! – and the floors sloped a little but she loved it. Luc had helped her with the paperwork; without his subtle encouragement, she'd probably still be living with her parents on Hortensia Road. She wondered what would happen after they were married. It had been over a year since he'd proposed – the last and only time, in fact, they'd been on holiday together. The wedding had been postponed several times. Luc's mother died unexpectedly; a promotion at work; Bloomin' Stories finally began to turn a corner earlier that year . . . they both worked such ridiculous hours and there never seemed to be time to sit down and plan anything. They would do it soon; they *ought* to do it soon, just not at that very moment. Tory could practically hear her mother's voice as she explained to neighbours and friends why it was that they hadn't actually tied the knot. *Oh, you know what young people are like these days. It's all work, work, work.*

She bought a coffee at the little Italian café on the corner of Canonbury Lane and strolled along in the sunshine, stopping every now and then to look in the windows. It had been ages since she'd been shopping for clothes. These days, she practically lived in her working uniform of jeans and a T-shirt or sweater, much to everyone's irritation. Nic had warned her only the other day that she was in danger of turning into a bohemian hag, whatever *that* was. She grinned and walked into Monsoon.

Twenty minutes later she walked out with a beautiful cream linen coat, a navy and lime spotted silk scarf and a pair of gorgeously impractical, high-heeled strappy sandals. She was bemused. How on earth had she been persuaded to buy them? Where on earth would she wear them to? She hurried out of the shop, clutching her bags in giddy excitement. A few seconds more in there and she'd have walked out with a wedding dress. She walked towards Canonbury Square through the back streets, admiring the elegant townhouses and pretty front gardens, enjoying the unfamiliar feel of sun on her face. Just as she was walking up Alwyne Villas, someone came down the front steps of one of the houses and opened the little gate. She was still smiling to herself and for a second as their eyes met, it occurred to her that he probably thought she was smiling at *him*. She looked away quickly and continued walking up the road, but was aware as she did so of a strange build-up of tension behind her, as if something silly were stuck to the back of her head. She stopped. Something cold ran up her spine, prickling the fine hairs at the nape of her neck. She spun round. Recognition hung by a thread. 'Rob?' Her heart slammed into her chest.

'Tory?' He was rooted to the pavement. His face was white.

'Wh-what are *you* doing here?' Tory asked, the cold suddenly turning to heat and spreading rapidly across her face.

He passed a hand over his face. 'I live here. Up there.' He jerked his head towards the house he'd just come out of. 'I just got back. Couple of weeks ago. What are *you* doing here?'

'I . . . I live here too. Just up the road.'

'You're kidding. Christ, Tory. How . . . how are you?'

Tory looked at him. He looked the same, only older. He'd filled out; he'd lost the rangy, slightly awkwardly put-together look he'd had when she'd last seen him. Dark brown hair cut short and already greying at the temples; the same grey-blue eyes; six o'clock shadow on his face and chin. His face was harder, edgier than she remembered. Of course it was. It was more than ten years since she'd seen him last. He'd disappeared soon after the funeral. He'd gone to another school, just as she'd done, an attempt to escape the status that had been thrust upon him. For a while his mother kept in touch with Tory's parents. He'd gone travelling for a bit. Thailand, Vietnam, Laos . . . he just wanted to get away, his mother said. The last she'd heard was that he was living in Peru or somewhere equally remote. Since then, nothing.

And now he was back. 'I'm . . . I'm OK. It's nice to see you,' she said hesitantly, unsure whether to hug or kiss him – or neither.

'Yeah, you too,' Rob said, still looking dazed.

Tory bit her lip. 'Would you like to come up for a coffee or something? If you've got time?'

He swallowed. 'Sure. Why not? Sorry. I still can't get over it. You look so . . . different. All grown-up.'

'Well, it's been a while,' Tory said, smiling a little. 'You look the same, though.'

'Yeah, I suppose so.' They stared at each other uncertainly.

'Come on. I'll put the kettle on,' Tory said, shifting her bags to the other arm.

They crossed the street together in silence, both stunned by the improbable coincidence of meeting.

'Nice place,' Rob said, looking around the walled garden as they walked in through the gate. 'Pretty.'

Tory nodded. 'Yes, I like it. It's . . . quiet.' She opened the downstairs door and led the way up the five flights of stairs. 'Sorry, it's a bit of a hike.' At last they reached her flat. 'Mind your head,' she said, opening the door. Rob was over six foot.

'Wow, Tory, it's really nice,' Rob said, looking round.

'Living room's in here,' she said, trying not to sound too pleased. It wasn't a particularly large flat but she'd decorated it exactly the way she wanted. After having lived at home with her parents for so long, she'd been anxious to make her mark on her own space, in her own way. 'Have a seat. I'll be back in a sec.'

'These are beautiful,' Rob said, looking at the dark brown spiky flowers she'd placed on the dining table. 'What are they?'

'Actually, they're sunflowers,' Tory said sheepishly. 'I pulled the petals off when they started to get ragged. I always think the centres are just as lovely.' Rob looked impressed. Tory felt a comfortable release of feeling inside her, as if something pleasurable had burst, spreading its warmth throughout her body. 'I still can't believe it,' she said slowly. 'I can't believe you're standing here. In my living room.'

'I know.' Rob smiled faintly. 'It feels weird. Almost as though I'm not really here, if that makes sense?'

Tory nodded. 'Yeah, oddly enough, it does.' She turned and walked down the corridor to the kitchen. 'How d'you take your tea?' she called out, then remembering. *Milk, one sugar.* The memory hit her suddenly. The three of them, sitting in the kitchen at Hortensia Road, Susie pushing the biscuit tin away from her. She was always on a diet. She almost doubled over in pain.

'You OK?' Rob spoke suddenly from the doorway. His voice was hoarse.

Tory nodded. 'I'll be fine in a minute,' she gasped. 'It just . . . it just hit me.' He said nothing. And then she felt his hand on the nape of her neck. His touch was cool although his fingers trembled a little; she could feel them, fluttering above the bone that was the start of her spine. It was oddly calming. They stayed that way for a few minutes, neither speaking, until the wave of pain subsided and her breathing returned to normal. A few minutes later she was able to stand up and make them both a cup of tea. She even managed to put a couple of biscuits on a plate. She followed him back into the living room, the pain lightening just a fraction with each passing minute. A fraction, nothing more.

They chatted for a while, filling in some of the blank spaces that had opened up since they'd last seen one another. He was a photographer, he told her. Something he'd just sort of picked up on his travels. He'd done a book about Vietnam, one of the first travel books about the place, which had sold unexpectedly well. Another commission had come in to do a book on Chile, then one on Peru. Now he was doing a book on Buenos Aires. He'd decided to rent a flat in London as a kind of stopping-off point in between travels. His mother was getting on; it was nice to come back every once in a while to the same place. He hadn't wanted to come back to London for ages, kept putting it off. 'I just . . . didn't want to,' he said slowly, looking at his hands. 'But now I'm here, it's not so bad. How about you?' He glanced up at her.

'Oh, me? Well . . .' She stopped, aware that she was blushing. She didn't know how to describe the business without sounding boastful. 'I started my own business. A flower shop. My dad and I run it together,' she said finally.

He was quiet for a while. 'I always knew you'd do something special, Tory,' he said at last. 'You were always the artistic one—'

'Me? No, *I* wasn't,' Tory said automatically.

'Yes, you were. You just didn't see it.' He looked at her for a moment. Then he stood up. 'Thanks for the tea,' he said, picking up his jacket. 'It was nice to see you.'

'You too.' They stared at each other for a second, then he leaned forward and kissed her gently on the cheek.

'Take care of yourself,' he said, shrugging his jacket on. She nodded, not trusting herself to speak. And then he was gone.

75

Estelle looked at the two outfits the sales girl had laid out for her. She hesitated. The black and white houndstooth jacket and short skirt were classic Chanel . . . discreet gold buttons, the white stitching visible along the hems . . . she shook her head. Too boring. It was the other suit – by Dior – white linen, a knee-length skirt, with dark blue piping along the collar and plunging neckline. 'That one,' she said briskly, pointing to it. Classy. Exactly the way she wanted to look.

'Very good, madam.' The sales girl began the lengthy process of folding and wrapping the precious garments.

Estelle took a quick look at herself in the mirror. Her skin was an even deeper shade of honey, thanks to regular sessions at a tanning shop in Kensington. She wanted to look her absolute best. Her stomach was trembling with nerves. It was impossible to believe that it had taken her almost a year to organise the meeting, planned for the following day. Without Mrs Devereaux's help, she'd never have managed it. Men like Jim Harte simply didn't meet people he didn't know, much less twenty-something-year-old women who wouldn't say what their business was about. It had been scheduled twice; twice he'd cancelled at the last minute. Each time, organising the next meeting had taken months. Her stomach gave a lurch. She'd thought about nothing else for months on end, going over again and again what she would say, what *he* would say – the tears, the smiles, the hugs . . . everything. At long last, she'd found him. Deep down, she'd always known she was destined for something other than the measly, penny-pinching life Gloria had offered; now she knew why. She *was* different. She was a *Harte*, for crying out loud. Mackenzie? She'd get rid of that nasty appendage as soon as she could. *Why* had Gloria lied to her?

The sales girl approached her, bearing her outfit in a shiny white box. Estelle only just managed to suppress the little thrill of excitement that ran through her. Soon *all* her outfits would come from places like this. She could see the girl appraising her, taking in the endlessly long legs, tiny waist and long, glossy hair, wondering who she was. Well, after tomorrow they'd all know. Perhaps it would be in the papers? Or even on the news? Her stomach gave another lurch. 'Just send it round this afternoon,' she said imperiously, picking up her bag. 'It's on account. Mrs Devereaux.' Six hundred pounds' worth of designer clothing. Soon she'd be wearing triple that. Each and every fucking day.

'Of course, madam.' If the girl recognised the implications of an account held by Sally Devereaux, she made no sign.

Estelle swept out of the store in a cloud of perfume. She walked up New Bond Street towards Christian Billington, her hair stylist. She'd have her highlights redone, a manicure and pedicure and a massage to relax her. And then she'd go home, take a long, scented bath and prepare herself for tomorrow's meeting. The most important meeting of her entire life. She could hardly bring herself to think about it. In less than twenty-four hours, her life would change. She was no longer the daughter of a coloured worker from Bulawayo and an unknown and absentee white father – by tomorrow afternoon, the world would know her as a billionaire's daughter. She smiled to herself. No wonder she'd always had a taste for the finer things in life. As it turned out, they'd been hers all along.

'Oh, Jim—' Mrs Callaghan stopped him as he was on his way out the door. 'Don't forget you've got a meeting at three.'

Jim looked at her, irritated. 'Who with?'

She glanced at his diary. 'It's with a Miss Mackenzie. I don't have her first name. A Mrs Sally Devereaux set it up. You agreed to it, remember?'

Jim sighed. He didn't. Who the hell was Sally Devereaux? He looked at his watch. 'I'll be back in an hour,' he said, picking up his coat and his hat. 'Tell her to wait if I'm not back. What's it about?'

Mrs Callaghan shrugged. 'Mrs Devereaux wouldn't say exactly. But she's been trying to set it up for months. You've cancelled twice already.'

'All right. I'll be back later.' He opened the door and walked down the corridor to the lifts, his mind already discarding the information and racing ahead. He was unusually agitated. No one knew it – least of all his partners and shareholders – but there was trouble afoot. In the way of such things, it had started so bloody innocuously. For several years RhoMine had been running a highly profitable pipeline of illegal diamonds through a defunct mine in eastern Guinea, close to the Sierra Leonean border. Officials had been paid off, routes established, flight plans organised, the works. For almost three years straight, they'd been seeing record profits coming out of that unknown corner of the continent – just the way Jim liked it. The stones were flown out of Sierra Leone, usually under the cover of darkness. An hour later, the plane touched down in Côte d'Ivoire where they were packed into boxes, relabelled and then reshipped, arriving in Brussels and New Delhi with the original provenance lost somewhere along the route. Through a labyrinth of ownership, RhoMine controlled more than sixty per cent of shares in Consolidated Mines, the official owners of the Kanyati mine in Guinea. It was an operation that suited everyone – from government ministers right down to the idiots who paid over the odds for a diamond ring. Jim had never had occasion – or the desire, frankly – to visit the mine at Kono, or anywhere else along the godforsaken route. As long as the profits kept rolling in and RhoMine's share price kept going up, everyone made money; everyone was happy.

But – and of course there was a fucking 'but' – the recent coup in Sierra had increased the pressure on them to pay off the mine officials and ministers. It was typical – a few assholes in high places had become greedy. They wanted a greater share of the spoils. It was costing Jim a fortune in bribes, not to mention airline fuel, to keep sending suitcases of cash out to places he'd never heard of – Kambia, Kabala, Makeni – and certainly never wanted to see. And then the bloody United Nations had slapped sanctions on the country, making things even *more* difficult. As if he didn't have enough on his fucking plate. Even filing a flight path these days was a complicated, tortuous affair. Manning was fed up; Ogilvy was fed up . . . and now he was, too. It was almost too much fucking hassle. Except that the mines were producing some of the finest diamonds coming out of Africa and Jim was a pragmatist. Sooner or later the war in Sierra Leone would come to an end. He hadn't backed the RUF for nothing. The coup in March had resulted in a shaky power share between the RUF and the newly formed Armed Forces Revolutionary Council. Jim shook his head. When would they learn? Revolutions were bad for business. They were certainly proving bad for him. Rumours had begun to surface in the British press – as they usually did whenever RhoMine was about to announce a major deal. The net result, of course, was that share prices and investor confidence were dropping, not the sort of climate best suited for his latest venture – copper. A handful of mines were being dangled in front of his nose by a pack of businessmen, always asking for more. Guess who was leading the pack? Klaassens. He'd had the feeling he'd run into him again. Klaassens' pale blue eyes and soft sneer came back to him. *'Is that how you see it, Mr Harte?'* he'd asked him almost twenty years earlier. The little prick. Yes, it fucking well *was* how he saw it.

He pushed open the door to the tiny Italian restaurant on Gutter Lane. He smiled to himself as he walked in. *Gutter* Lane? How appropriate. That was where he'd bring Klaassens if his suspicions turned out to be right. He had a meeting with someone who would confirm it. 'Gordon,' he said, holding out his hand. 'Good of you to come.'

76

For the second time in twelve months Estelle sat outside the offices of a man who had the power to turn her world upside down, and was once again forced to wait. The battleaxe of a secretary who'd buzzed her in kept looking at her, as if she couldn't quite believe her eyes. Well, let her look. She was well worth a second glance. Did the old cow have any *idea* how much her suit had cost?

'He does know I'm coming, doesn't he?' Estelle asked her finally when fifteen minutes had turned to twenty.

'Oh, yes. He shouldn't be long,' the woman answered, barely keeping the curiosity from her voice. 'He did say to wait.' Estelle was silent. Her stomach was lurching, her heart was thudding and her palms were sweaty.

Ten or fifteen minutes later – she'd lost the ability to measure time – somewhere in the corridor outside she heard footsteps and a man's voice. Her stomach gave another, violent lurch. 'Ah,' the battleaxe said, lifting her head. 'I think that's him.'

The door opened and a tall, tanned man swept in. He stared at her, frowning. A look of incredulousness swept over his face. Estelle thought she might actually be sick. The secretary looked from one to the other, almost comically. Estelle found herself staring at the face she'd been scrutinising in photographs for the past twelve months, searching for resemblances not blotted out by time, or gender or race. She was acutely aware of the sound of her own breath, rising and falling in her chest. How could she have missed it? How was it possible she hadn't recognised him? *If I want to have sex, a whore's the last person I'd choose.* Waves of shame and horror washed over her, making a mockery of the Dior suit, the cloud of expensive perfume, the carefully painted nails and made-up face and her crocodile-skin bag. She opened her mouth but for the first time in her life was unable to speak.

Jim was the first to recover. He strode across the floor and opened the door to his office, ignoring Mrs Callaghan's glowering looks. 'Miss Mackenzie?' He gestured impatiently to her to enter. She got up rather unsteadily and walked towards him. He shut the door on Mrs Callaghan's unspoken question and turned to face her. There was no mistaking it. She was the whore Khoury had brought that night, a year or so ago. What the hell was she doing in his office? He walked over to his desk and sat down. She was undeniably beautiful – the most beautiful girl he'd seen in a very long time – but the question of what she was doing opposite him, given where he'd seen her last, still hadn't been resolved. 'What can I do for you, Miss Mackenzie?' he asked smoothly.

She stared at him for a second then gestured to the chair. 'May I?'

'Go ahead.' He wished she'd get to the point.

She sat down gracefully and opened her bag. She took out a packet of cigarettes and a manila envelope. She pushed the envelope across his green leather-topped desk and leaned back without saying a word. She tapped a cigarette out of the packet with her red-tipped nails and lit it. She looked at the envelope lying on the desk between them. He made no move to take it. 'Aren't you going to open it?' she asked.

He frowned. There was something in her voice . . . an accent of some kind? He shook his head.

'Not until you tell me what this is all about.'

She was struggling to contain something; he could tell. The cigarette, the direct-yet-coy gaze, the way she folded one slim leg across the other . . . she was playing for time, gathering herself. They continued to stare at one another. Finally, when he thought he couldn't stand the sight of her blue-green eyes on his for a second longer, she held the cigarette away from her and opened her mouth. A single word came out.

A shudder ran through him. Jim shook his head as if to clear it. He'd misunderstood. His eyes slid from hers, down the length of her neck, taking in the expensive suit, the white linen against the honeyed tones of her skin, the jewellery . . . he brought his gaze back up to meet hers. 'What the fuck did you say?'

She looked a little taken aback. But she kept her cool, he had to give her that. 'I'm your daughter.' Her smile wasn't pure. Jim felt something inside him snap; a hot, liquid rage suddenly flooded his mouth.

'What the *fuck* are you talking about?'

'It's all there,' she said, pointing with her lit cigarette towards the envelope. 'That's my birth certificate. I got the original. It's all there. My mother was Gloria Turner. She worked for you in—'

'Get out.' Jim felt the words tear at his throat. 'Is this your idea of a joke? Get out. Now.'

'I'm not joking,' the girl said, stubbing out the cigarette. Her voice shook. 'I promise you. I hired a private detective. That's my birth certificate. It's the original. I—'

Jim picked up the envelope. He slid a finger under the flap and pulled the sheet out without looking at it. His eyes still on her, he walked around the desk to the shredder. A second later, the metal teeth began their noisy work. The girl had gone pale under her tan. Her composure was slipping. When the document was thoroughly shredded, he switched the machine off. He walked back to his desk and picked up the phone. 'Listen to me, you little whore.' His voice was steely. 'If you don't leave right now, I'll call the police and have you arrested. Do you have any idea who I am?'

She stared at him, all composure gone. 'You're my father,' she said, her voice shaking.

'You're not listening to me. I have two daughters and believe me, you're not one of them. I don't know who the fuck you are. I've never heard of Gloria whatever-the-fuck-her-name-is and I'm warning you, if you're not gone from my office by the time I finish dialling, you'll be spending a couple of nights in a place you'll wish you'd never seen. Now, take your grubby little envelope and your cigarettes and get the *fuck* out of my offices. Go!'

She took a step backwards, stunned by the rage in his voice. She was trembling from head to foot. 'I—'

'GO!'

She opened the door and fled.

'Who on earth was that?' Mrs Callaghan asked as soon as he opened the door. He'd waited a full five minutes to bring his breathing under control.

'Mind your own business,' Jim snapped, grabbing his coat and hat. He slammed the office door behind him. He was shaking.

He ignored the lift and ran down the fourteen flights of stairs to the basement. His Bentley was parked in the corner; the chauffeur was enjoying a cigarette with a couple of the other drivers by the stairs. He saw Jim approach and hurried over.

'Sir?'

'Studgrove,' Jim barked at him. 'Now!'

Estelle ran all the way down Cheapside, ignoring the looks of passers-by stunned to see a woman in a white suit running in her high heels, her hair flying out behind her. She ran until she simply couldn't run any more and would have fallen had a gentleman in a bowler hat not stopped and grabbed her as she slipped. 'Hey!' he exclaimed, catching hold of her arm. 'Careful. You'll get yourself run over if—'

She was crying, her breath running away from her in huge gulps. 'L–let go of me,' she gasped, wrenching her arm out of his. 'Leave me alone!'

'Calm down. *Please*,' he said, obviously upset at the sight of her distress. 'You practically fell into the path of that bus!' Estelle stumbled against him and dropped her crocodile-skin bag into a large, muddy puddle. The gentleman bent down to retrieve it. He pulled it up, dripping, and whipped out a handkerchief. 'Oh, dear. Your bag. It's soaked!'

'It d–doesn't matter.' Estelle couldn't get the words out. 'Just l–leave me al–alone, please . . .'

A small group of people had gathered around them. 'Is she OK?' someone asked. Estelle suddenly felt a great weariness sweep over her.

'She's fine,' the gentleman said, sensing she was simply too exhausted to continue. 'She looks like she's had a nasty shock. She needs to get home, I think.'

'Look at that bag,' someone else whispered. 'Is it Chanel?'

Estelle leaned against the wall, feeling the pain and hurt spread like fire through her veins. She felt dizzy, as if the edge of the world was tilting away from her. She allowed herself to be helped into a cab, heard herself give the driver the appropriate instructions and even managed to turn and thank the man in the bowler hat who stood at the side of the road as they pulled out, waving frantically as if she were a friend. She closed her eyes. That morning, getting dressed to meet Jim Harte, hope had run through her like sunshine. Life was all lightness and possibilities. Now everything had changed.

77

On the drive down to Studgrove, Jim felt the tightness inside his chest intensify. Of course he'd known it – as soon as she opened her mouth and he'd caught the flattened vowels of his adopted country, he'd felt something clutch at his insides. She'd been barely a year old when he saw her last. How could he have seen her at Khoury's and not known? He felt bile rise in his throat. Her silk dress – he couldn't recall . . . was it red? Purple? – just waiting to slither down the length of her incredible body. He almost retched. He powered down the window and began breathing in huge gulps of air. He couldn't breathe fast or deep enough. Estelle Mackenzie was his daughter. The memory of the last time he'd seen Gloria rose and there wasn't a damn thing he could do about it.

He was thirty-eight then. Gloria, the pretty, dark-skinned maid who'd worked for them was barely twenty. He couldn't have said when he first noticed her. She had that silent way of gliding around the house, cleaning, dusting, washing – doing whatever Sarah had set her to do. Sarah was hopeless in the house; hopeless in the task of keeping the servants under control. They lied, stole, cheated, took advantage of her hopelessly English-schoolgirl ways. She was no match for the likes of Learnmore, Williams and the other one . . . what the hell was her name? Mary? Maria? They ran rings around her. But Gloria was different. God-fearing, respectable, from one of those old, coloured families who'd fallen on hard times, she knew her

Bible and her place and there'd been no trouble with her at all. Until that one night he'd come home drunk and in a foul mood after visiting Jane's parents, who still believed he had something to do with her death. Nothing could persuade them otherwise. She'd decided to take her own life – *he* certainly hadn't decided it for her. She was weak, that was the problem. Weak, just like her father.

He'd stopped off at Dirk Teunissen's place on the way home, full of rage. Three whiskies later, he'd reluctantly made his way home to Avonlea. Sarah had long since retired to bed. Gloria was in the kitchen, preparing a sandwich and a glass of whisky for him. It wasn't her fault, the poor girl.

She crept soundlessly into the room, bearing his drink in her hand. The fire was on; it was July and the ground outside was frosty. It reminded him a little of England. He held out his hand. His fingers touched hers; there was a sudden, electric shock of recognition and the knowledge that he could do anything to her – anything at all. He practically owned her, for crying out loud.

He drained it in one fiery gulp. 'Get me another one,' he growled, his temper still ruffled by the meeting he'd had. She brought him another whisky and again, their fingers touched. 'Take off your blouse,' he said, a tremor of aggression and lust running straight through him. She complied silently. She did everything in silence.

When he was finished with her, she got up quietly, buttoned her shirt and slipped out of the room. He found it oddly comforting. After that, he visited her once, sometimes twice a month. Always back there, in the servants' quarters. They said very little to one another. There was something soothing about the girl with skin the colour of coffee, huge, dark nipples like copper pennies and a quiet, dignified demeanour that never slipped, not once, not even when he asked her for things that would have made Sarah blanch with disgust. It went on for two, three months . . . ? And then she told him she was expecting a child. Not that she wanted anything from him, she said. It was just . . . well, she wouldn't be able . . . for a while at least. Until after the child was born. Oh, he needn't worry. His wife would never know. She would send it to her parents, down south in Bulawayo.

But when the time came, she couldn't bear to be parted from her. The child stayed in the quarters, mostly hidden from view. There were so many servants coming and going in those days, and besides, Sarah would never, ever have ventured down there. It was dirty, she said. They lived like animals. Yet they clean your house, Jim wanted to throw at her. You trust them enough to leave your daughter with them day in, day out. She's always down there, you know . . . down there where it's dirty. But he didn't. He kept quiet because he was afraid.

And then, there was that awful night when Gloria was in the kitchen with the baby and Sarah came home early. Nic had been about two. The baby's features, revealed by a certain cast of light, made her parentage clear. Sarah knew right away. He came home to hear the screaming — Sarah throwing things at Gloria . . . anything . . . a pot, a plate, the salt cellar, the copper pans. And Gloria, all the while, standing there patiently, abuse raining down on her. Sarah saw him come in and made a wild dash up the stairs to the study where she knew he kept his guns. He lunged after her, just missing her foot. Nic was in her cot at the foot of the stairs, screaming her head off. Fortunately the boys were at a friend's house for the weekend. Sarah went racing up; he picked himself up and threw himself after her. This time, he caught her by the ankle, catching her off guard. She staggered against the banister, twisting her whole body round, trying to shake him off. Nic was still screaming. Gloria was silent, watching them. He made a grab for the other leg and that was when it happened. There was a terrible creaking groan, the sound of wood being splintered and then she fell, tumbling through the broken banister, head first on to the stone floor. He would never, ever, as long as he lived, forget the sound her head made as it hit the floor. The sound of her skull breaking. Gloria turned then, pressing the child to her shoulder, and walked out. He was left there with the pool of blood spreading outwards across the floor, seeping into the cracks. There was absolute silence in the kitchen. He looked over to where Nic was lying in her cot — unbelievably, she too had fallen quiet. There was something in her eyes . . . ridiculous, of course, but he'd never been able to shake it. She knew. She knew what he'd done. He'd never been able to stand the sight of her since.

And Gloria? She extracted something from him, then. Basil Mac-kenzie, one of his mine managers, agreed to register himself as the child's father. It had cost him dearly. And it looked as though it would cost him still. He had no idea what the girl who'd come forward now, after all these years, knew.

78

Luc was talking to her. His mouth was moving and she could feel his eyes on her, but her mind was elsewhere. She pretended to listen, but all the while she was thinking of something else. Some*one* else. It had been just over a fortnight since she'd bumped into Rob and she could think of nothing else. She could conjure up at will the exact, heart-stopping sensation of hearing his voice and the way it dragged buried memories straight to the surface. She'd stood in front of him, arms hanging helplessly at her sides, unable even to speak. She remembered clearly the sensation of falling, followed by the equally powerful sensation of having to hold on.

'Tory?' Luc's voice was petulant.

She forced herself to listen. 'Sorry . . . what?'

'Which one?' he said, exaggeratedly patient. He rustled the newspaper.

Tory's mind had gone completely blank. 'Er, sorry. I wasn't listening. Which what?'

'Film. Which one d'you want to see?'

'Oh, I don't know . . . whatever you want.' She had the feeling she wouldn't be paying much attention to whatever film they chose. Her mind was too full. It was full of Susie and Rob and her and Rob and she couldn't stop thinking about either of them. It was all horribly mixed up. Her mind was a kaleidoscope of images – Rob, when she'd first met him: a gangly, rather spotty-faced teenager whom Susie brought home from school one day. *This is Rob.* That was it, no further introduction necessary. Susie was thirteen – *far* too young to have a boyfriend, or so her parents said. But Rob simply hung around until everyone in the family just got used to him and then it seemed as though there'd never been a time when he wasn't there. Susie's boyfriend. By the time she was fifteen, everyone thought it was such a relief that she'd chosen Rob. By then, of course, he'd lost his spots and his adolescent awkwardness and the two of them looked as though they'd been made for each other. Rob, tall, dark-haired, handsome – and petite, pretty Susie. Both clever, both sporty, both popular . . . the perfect match. When they did start sleeping together, Tory was the first person Susie told. She told Tory everything. Tory *knew* Rob – almost as well as she knew Susie. He'd been the big brother she'd never had. He helped her with her homework, gave her a lighter when she started smoking in secret, dispensed advice on the boys who were beginning to flock around her. He'd told her to avoid James Taylor but he thought Matt Cramer was OK. She'd trusted him enough to tell him things she hadn't told anyone, not even Susie. But when it happened, he dropped out of her life without even a backward glance. And now he was back.

She got up and walked quickly from the room. The memories were threatening to overwhelm her and she didn't want Luc to notice. He looked up as she passed, but he was so absorbed in the all-consuming question of what film to choose that he didn't see her at all. There was something else, too, that ought to be remembered – but that didn't bear thinking about. She just couldn't bring herself to think about *that*.

79

She stared up at the building. For a week now, she'd walked past the house every morning on her way to work, dawdling at the bus stop at the end of the road, hoping to catch a glimpse of him.

But nothing. She wasn't even sure he was there. He might be on a trip. In Peru or some other exotic location. She knew which flat he lived in – Flat C – his name was printed neatly on the buzzer at the entrance. *Rob Holden*. But she couldn't just drop in on him, could she? She looked up at the house again but there was no movement from behind the shutters. It was a quarter past nine. She'd been standing there for almost fifteen minutes. Her father would be angry. They had two weddings to plan for the coming weekend and without Tory there would be no floral display. She could sense his irritation with her. Three times in the past week he'd caught her gazing dreamily out of the window and she knew it alarmed him. The last time she'd been given to such bouts of dreamy inactivity was in the year following Susie's death when she'd closed herself up, just as they all had, emerging sporadically to do things that they didn't understand – like Thierry de Courcy and the whole Paris escapade. Even the floristry, as well as it had turned out, had been hard for them to accept. She could see it in her father's eyes that he was worried she'd suddenly go off the rails again, as her mother put it. She blew out her cheeks. Well, she could certainly see how it might appear that way to the casual observer. Standing in front of a man's house at nine a.m., waiting desperately for a glimpse of him – she was *mad*.

She shoved her hands into her pockets and turned away. Stop it, she said to herself fiercely. Just stop it. But it was easier said than done. Every time she thought about Rob Holden, something sweet and painful burst inside her, and she could no more control it than she could her own imagination. Which, of course, was running wild.

'I know, I know . . .' She put up her hands in mock defeat as soon as she walked into the shop. 'Sorry I'm late. I overslept.'

Paula, the part-time assistant who worked in the mornings, looked up. 'Oh, it's OK. We've had a slow start. There's someone to see you downstairs. He's with your dad.'

'Who is it?' Tory sighed.

'Dunno. But your dad knows him. Rob? Bob? Something like that.'

Tory froze. 'R–Rob?'

'Yeah, I think so. They went downstairs about twenty minutes ago. Shall I get you a coffee? Are you all right? You look a bit pale.'

'No, no. I'm fine. I'll just go down,' Tory said weakly. Her palms were clammy. She almost ran down the steps.

'Tory . . . at last!' Her dad was on his feet. She saw by the reddened eyes and nose that he'd been weeping. She was afraid to look at Rob. She was afraid she would burst into tears herself – of a different kind. 'Look who's here! Can you believe it? He just walked in – unbelievable coincidence! I can't believe it. I just can't get over it!' She swallowed. Rob obviously hadn't told him they'd met. Something was happening; she could feel herself being pulled towards it without fully understanding what was going on.

'Tory.' Rob got up. He hesitated, then kissed her on both cheeks, his hands gripping her forearms tightly. This time, the touch was warm. Something else was passing between them that had nothing to do with grief and the memory of Susie. His eyes were searching hers, looking perhaps for some recognition of the strange torture he seemed to be going through . . . she swallowed. Yes, she signalled silently. She was going through it as well. She saw that he understood, and slowly his grip relaxed.

'Rob,' she said, amazed at her own calm deception. 'I don't believe it! It's lovely to see you. How are you?'

'Really well,' he said quietly, and she understood he meant it.

'I've asked Rob to join us for dinner on Friday,' her father said, discreetly blowing his nose. 'Why don't you bring Luc along? We'll make it a proper . . . *family* night,' he said, his voice catching on the word.

Tory winced, something cold and liquid spreading through her. 'I . . . I'll ask him,' she said faintly.

'Who's Luc?' Rob's voice sounded strained to her ears.

'Oh, he's Tory's fiancé. Lovely man, really. We couldn't have asked for nicer, could we, Tory? You'll like him, I'm sure. Oh,

Gilly'll be *so* pleased to see you, Rob. I can't tell you. Won't she, Tory?'

Tory wasn't listening. Her mind was spinning ahead. Luc was the last person in the world she wanted to bring. In fact, she thought, sick to the stomach for even daring to voice the thought – even to herself – Luc was the last person in the world she wanted to see right now. Ever since she'd bumped into Rob, there was only one person in her thoughts. It had happened so fast. And yet, paradoxically and in ways she couldn't explain, it felt as though she'd been waiting for it – for him – all along. Rob had always been there. Right from the start. No wonder she was having difficulty remembering Luc.

'But where's Luc?' her mother cried as soon as she opened the door and saw only Tory standing there. Tory sighed. It was her mother's favourite refrain. *What – only you?*

'He's in Zurich, Mum. He's sorry he couldn't make it. Nice to see you,' she said a touch sarcastically. She came in and set the bouquet of lilac, summer peonies and white hyacinths down on the table. Their pungent, heady aroma immediately filled the air. Her sarcasm was lost on Gilly.

'You too, darling,' she said automatically. 'Oh, that's a shame,' she said, drying her hands on her apron. 'We were so looking forward to seeing him.'

'Yeah, well. Next time.'

'Dad's just opening a bottle of wine. Rob's not here yet. I think we said eight, didn't we, darling?'

'He's always late, don't you re—' Tory stopped suddenly. Her mother flinched, as though she'd been slapped. 'Sorry,' she said quietly. 'I wasn't thinking. I'll see if Dad needs a hand,' she said, fleeing the kitchen.

Her father was wrestling with a bottle of wine as she came in. She saw that he looked suddenly tired, older. A wave of remorse flowed over her. She'd been so wrapped up in herself lately that she just hadn't noticed anything else. 'Here,' she said, walking quickly over. 'Let me do that.'

'No, no . . . here it comes . . . oops!' He staggered, spilling a few drops on to the carpet. 'Oh, dear.'

'Don't worry, I'll get some salt,' Tory said, turning to go back to the kitchen. At that moment, the door bell rang. Her stomach gave a lurch.

'I'll get it!' Her mother practically ran down the hallway.

There was the sound of the door being opened; she heard her mother gasp, stifling a sob and then suddenly, there was silence. She waited uncertainly for something or someone to appear. Then she heard the footsteps coming slowly towards her.

And then suddenly, there he was. He stood in the doorway, filling it, both physically and with his silence which seemed louder than anything he could have said. He seemed to be waiting for something, some sign from either of them of how to proceed. How to walk into the living room that he once must have known better than his own; to take a glass of wine just as he'd done a thousand times before, cuff Tory very lightly on the chin, huddle with her over the choice of a record, perhaps, or a video . . . just as it had always been. But everything was different now, and not just because Susie was no longer there.

Tory thought her feelings must surely be written across her face. Surely he must notice? He didn't. He came in at the sign made by her father and didn't look at her, not even when he came to say hello. He looked everywhere but. Tory felt the hard knot of disappointment begin to tighten inside her. He talked to her parents, but not to her. Not once. He spoke to her when forced to, but his attention lay elsewhere. She didn't exist. It was clear to her that whatever connection had been made the day they bumped into one another on the street, he'd abruptly severed it – in pretty much the same way he'd severed the connections with all of them in the days following Susie's death. But why had he come to the shop? And what was he doing here, in her parents' home, sitting opposite her and looking as though he wished to be anywhere else on earth but here?

The air in the car was so tense it crackled. Tory shifted gears automatically, her mind stumbling ahead of her, trying to think of something to say. The meal had passed in almost total silence between them. Not once had he asked her anything, addressed a comment to her . . . even *looked* at her. She was both angry and hurt, and if it hadn't been for her mother practically forcing her to offer him a lift – *but you live so close to one another. That's marvellous!* – she'd have driven off and left him there. Marvellous? Was her mother *blind* as well as stupid? If it wasn't for the fact that he looked so bloody unhappy, not just disinterested, she'd have turfed him out at the nearest Tube station.

They came down from the A40 on to the Marylebone Road. She usually loved this view of London, the BT Tower lit up in blues and reds ahead of them, the soft yellow lights of the Landmark Hotel to their left, past the park. She turned left at Regent's Park and took a short-cut through Camden towards Pentonville Prison. He seemed about to say something, then lapsed back into silence.

'When's your next trip?' she asked finally, unable to stand it any longer.

'Huh?'

'You said you were going away again soon.'

'Oh. Yeah. Morocco. I'm doing something on Fez.'

'Oh.' Tory wasn't quite sure where or what Fez was. 'It must be interesting,' she said after a moment.

'Yeah.'

She drew a deep breath. What was the matter with him? It was almost as though he was angry at her – but for what? They were almost at his front door. She pulled the car up and didn't bother with the handbrake; her foot was on the clutch, ready to shoot off as soon as the door closed behind him.

He opened the door and got out. He held on to it and leaned into the car's interior. He was obviously dying to run off. 'Look—' he began, but Tory didn't let him finish.

'No, *you* look, Rob,' she said angrily, her foot still playing with the clutch. The car rolled slightly backwards. She put her foot on the brake and turned to him. 'I don't know why you're so angry with me. I haven't *done* anything. If you don't want to see me again, ever, that's fine. *I* didn't ask you to come to the fucking shop. *I* didn't invite you to dinner. I'm sorry that we bumped into one another and I'm even sorrier that we're neighbours. But don't worry, I certainly won't be knocking on your door any time soon – as a matter of fact, I won't *ever* knock on your door. So let me put your mind at rest. You don't have to—'

'Tory—'

'No, I'm not finished. That was the most fucking embarrassing evening of my entire *life* . . . sitting there with my parents and you acting as though you can't stand the sight of me. Well, you know what, Rob Holden? I can't stand the sight of *you* either! I wish I'd never bumped into you! In fact, I wish we'd never *met*!' And with that, she dropped the clutch and the car jerked forwards. He had no option but to let go of the door and jump back. She sped up the road, turned the corner and tried to find a parking spot through her tears. Five minutes later she found one, reversed the car badly into it and got out, slamming the door. She walked back up Canonbury Lane and turned left into Alwyne Villas. And there, standing outside the gate to her building, was Rob.

'Look, Tory,' he said as she walked towards him.

'Just leave me alone!' she hissed, holding on to her key tightly. 'Just—'

He grabbed her by the elbow. 'No . . . you've got it all wrong, Tory,' he said, his voice low and urgent.

She tried to yank her arm out of his hand; there was a short, rather embarrassed scuffle and then, without any warning or change in pitch, she found herself pressed against his chest. There was no time to think; no time to protest, even if she'd wanted to. Everything slowed down suddenly. The hand holding her wrist slowly loosened its grip. She felt it slide along her arm until it came to rest at the elbow, the painful grip turned to caress. She opened her mouth to speak but her words were lost as he leaned forward and kissed her.

She wouldn't think about it. Not now. She wouldn't think about the raw, urgent madness that had brought them from the pavement outside her house to here . . . Rob, pausing in his lovemaking to ask her – *what is it?* She had no clear idea of how they had got to this stage, those final, almost savage moments of pleasure. All she could remember was the moment when the unbearable anger in her dissolved, merging instantly into another, different kind of passion, one that had lain just beneath the surface of her emotions since, it seemed, for ever. His face above hers, features distorted with the sweet intensity of his feelings. She had the extraordinary sensation of having been allowed into a place in him that he had kept hidden, sealed off from everyone else. She wasn't prepared for it – for the force of his entry or for the way he sank into her arms afterwards. She turned her face away from him, afraid he would see her tears.

She watched him running his tongue along the edge of the paper, expertly sealing the roll-up held gently between thumb and forefinger. He was wearing Luc's dressing gown; through the half-open 'V' made by the thick strip of dark blue piping that disappeared into the folds of his lap she could see the dark brown hair of his chest and the pale, almost delicate skin beneath. She pulled out a chair and sat down, her chin cupped in her hand, waiting for him to finish. He smoked quietly, blowing it out towards the partially open kitchen window. There were a thousand and one questions she wanted to ask, a thousand and one things she wanted to say, starting with the most obvious. *What now? What happens next?*

'What are we—'

'I don't know, Tory,' he interrupted her quickly. 'I can't tell you. I need time to think.'

'But I—'

'Don't.' He reached across the table and took her hand. 'I don't know what this is,' he said, stubbing out the small cigarette he'd rolled. 'And I don't even want to ask. I need to sort my head out. There's too much going on up here,' he said softly, tapping his forehead. 'And right now, I can't think past when I'm going to see you next.' Tory's heart lifted ridiculously. Her breath was coming faster; her whole body was suffused with a tender ache of longing. His hand slid inside the wide sleeve of her dressing gown, trailing over the thin skin of her shoulder. He pulled his chair closer to her as his hand continued its gentle exploration of her collarbones, tracing the line of the silver necklace that lay flat against her chest. He brushed it aside, turning the palm of his hand to cup her breast. Desire rose in her immediately; she stood up, shrugging off the dressing gown and knelt in front of him. It was her turn to slide her palms along the hard muscles of his thighs, feeling the dark hair ridge underneath her skin as she moved towards him. She leaned forward and felt his whole body shudder as she took him into her mouth. He wasn't the only one unable to think past tomorrow. In fact, she couldn't think beyond the next few moments or the sensation of absolute, utter stillness that had finally settled itself on her – but warily, like some capricious, exquisite bird, ready at any moment to take off again. It was the most unsettling state of suspended disbelief. As if it was all going to end at any moment. Nothing mattered beyond the feel of his hands in her hair or the slow, rhythmic shuddering of his body. 'Tory.' His groan broke the silence and hung, like the lingering scent of tobacco smoke in the air, a closing punctuation mark to all that had gone on before. Except of course that this wasn't the end. It was only the beginning. But of what?

80

It still gave her the biggest thrill in the world to walk up the steps of the art deco building that was the headquarters of *ArtWeekly* in Camden and flash her ID card at the security guards. *Nic Parker, Assistant Features Editor.* She knew next to nothing about art; no matter. She'd been at *Gossip!* churning out trivia for so long she'd forgotten what it was like to be proud of her own work. To submit an article and actually *value* the feedback. To *care* what her editor thought – to care full stop. As usual, it was a late-night conversation with Caryn that had done it. She'd told her about her plans to leave *Gossip!* and apply for the position at *ArtWeekly*. 'You don't think it's mad, do you?' she'd asked her nervously.

Caryn raised an eyebrow. 'Mad? No, of course I don't. The only thing that's mad about it, Nic, is why it's taken you so bloody long.'

Nic looked out of the window. 'I know.' She fiddled with her coffee cup for a moment. 'I . . . I can't explain it. I don't know why—'

'You're scared. You're scared that you'll fail,' Caryn said quietly. 'I know what that feels like, believe me.'

'Do you? I look at you and Tory . . . you've both got proper careers, proper lives. Me, I feel like a complete failure half the time. I don't even know what I'm doing at *Gossip!*' She gave an embarrassed laugh.

'Just do it, Nic. Send in the application, get the job. Just do it.'

She did. *And* she got the job. Writing articles on art wasn't quite what she'd had in mind when journalism had first occurred to her but surprisingly, she was good at it. Or, to put it more accurately, *she* was surprised. No one else seemed to be. As the deputy editor said in an aside to one of the staff writers one day, the difference in tone of their features since Nic Parker had taken the job was remarkable. She had the right combination of sunny charm and steely determination. She had a knack for disarming the artists she was sent to interview and coming back with the sorts of details that readers loved to hear. Yes, everyone wanted to know what had happened when Patrick Madison left his agent, but wasn't it also interesting that he'd left his wife at the same time? Nic Parker brought a human dimension to the stories that made them both readable and enjoyable. The hints had already started dropping – she could find herself in line for the editor's job if he wasn't careful. Nic, totally unused to any kind of praise, was speechless. Daft as it seemed, it was Mat's face that popped into her head whenever someone said something kind. Ridiculous, really. She'd talked to him for five minutes almost a whole year ago but there had been something appraising in his eyes when he spoke to her that had nothing to do with her dress or the fact that her cleavage was deep and wide. No, he'd talked to her in a different way and although she couldn't work out exactly what it was, she couldn't shake the feeling that he would have approved of the direction her life had taken since they'd met.

She shook her head as she walked up the stairs. Crazy. Ridiculous. She didn't even know what he did. For all she knew, given where they'd met, he might have been a dilettante, as she was, a playboy, perhaps, a lightweight. But somehow, in some odd, unidentifiable way, she doubted it. *She* was the lightweight, not him. But that was changing. About bloody time.

81

'Oh, there you are, Tory! Something just came in by courier,' Paula shouted as she disappeared down the stairs to her office. Tory looked up, her pulse immediately racing. 'It's on your desk.'

She pushed open the door, wondering what it might be. Something from Rob? She picked up the envelope and tore it open. It wasn't from Rob. It was a new order. She looked at it for a second, stunned. It was from the editor-in-chief at *GQ*, the just-launched men's magazine. They were hosting the *GQ* Men of the Year Awards at the Royal Opera House and Bloomin' Stories had been chosen to do the flowers. She put it down carefully. She ought to have been thrilled. God knew they could do with the business. She knew that her mind simply hadn't been where it should. It had been six months since she'd slept with Rob for the first time, and despite the guilt she could think of little else. The impossible question of what they were doing and how long it could last hung over their every encounter. She couldn't stop herself. Whilst they were making love his face had a kind of openness; at times she thought she could see right into him, through the barriers and layers he'd carefully erected to protect himself. She understood all of that because she'd done the same since the day Susie died. Every time he came to her, there was the first layer to be peeled through, sloughed off. She recognised it straight off. He began in his remote, untouched state and ended by letting her into a place that in every other circumstance and with every other person he kept guarded and hidden. In those moments she felt herself to be perfectly at peace. But afterwards he began to shut down, shut her out. She ought to have seen then at what odds they would be. He taunted her, unknowingly perhaps, with something she could never have: him. When she tried to express this – her sense of being shut out – he resisted and withdrew further. And yet the more he withdrew, the more she pursued. It was becoming more and more difficult by the day – no, by the hour – made even more complicated by the fact that he was so seldom there. He dropped out of sight for weeks. Peru, Hong Kong, LA. And then he would show up, unannounced, and she would spend the next few days working out where and when they could meet. She told no one, and it made it all the harder. There were days when she thought her head and her heart might explode.

And then there was Luc, of course. If he noticed that something was amiss, he chose not to say. But he *had* to know. Tory shook her head in both exasperation and astonishment. It was impossible not to. Just as it had been at that awful, first dinner with her parents, it had to be written all over her forehead. All over her body, surely? She seldom wore the ring he'd given her, claiming it was too precious, too heavy, too special . . . anything to stop herself catching sight of it, the brilliant, flashing light cutting through her like a knife. He had promised her a long engagement – as long as she wanted or needed – and now, after almost eighteen months, they hardly ever spoke about it any more. Not about the engagement, not about the wedding, not about *them*. How could he not know?

She looked at the computer screen, aware it was beginning to blur. She plucked a tissue from the box and blew her nose. Her father would be in any minute now and it would be a mistake to let him see her cry. One kind word from him and she feared the whole thing might come tumbling out. Six months of bottling it all up, lying awake at night, her heart thick in her chest, her breath coming in shallow gasps for fear of waking Luc. The situation was taking its toll.

She picked up the letter from GQ again and forced herself to concentrate. The event was less than a month away. She would have to send a reply, draft a proposal and order whatever flowers she needed, all within the next few days. She took a deep breath, steadied herself and began to type.

82

Caryn scribbled quickly as Martin outlined the new project – a documentary about diamonds. He was in full flow, animated and excited, relishing the prospect of raising funds, travel, making contacts. Caryn smiled. The start of a new project was always exciting. Even Martin was smiling. Martin rarely smiled.

Finally he stopped. 'So – what d'you think?' He looked at Caryn expectantly.

'I think it's great. Lots of travel, though. It'll be expensive.'

'These sorts of projects always are. But I think we can find the money. You don't think it's too remote, do you? I mean, we're talking about places most people haven't heard of – Sierra Leone, Congo, Angola.'

Caryn considered the question carefully. She'd come to understand that however baffled she was by the fact, Rupesh and Martin genuinely valued her opinion. The fact that Martin rarely asked for it made the question that much more important. 'No,' she said slowly, 'but it might help to have the story narrated by someone that the audience can identify with . . . you know, a sort of Indiana Jones-type character. I know it sounds a bit cheesy but someone charismatic, an adventurer-type. D'you know what I mean?'

'Actually, I think I do,' Martin said, nodding. 'Good idea. Doesn't have to be someone well known – in fact, the opposite, probably. Make it more believable. But it needs to be someone the audience feels they can trust. I like it. Yes, I like it. Caryn, you're a bloody genius.'

'It's your idea, Martin. Not mine,' Caryn protested, blushing.

'Woman, can't you ever just accept a compliment?' Martin grinned. 'Right. Let's get the ball rolling. I need to speak to a couple of scriptwriters. Can you see who's on our list? Let's get a meeting set up. Give me a couple of days to work on a draft and see if I can come up with someone. I can really see this beginning to take shape. I think we could be on to a winner.'

Rupesh and Caryn looked at one another and grinned. When Martin was on top form there was no one quite like him. The opposite was also true, but this was certainly more fun. 'OK,' Caryn said, getting up. 'I'll set it up for Friday. Rupe, have you got a moment? I need to go over the budget for *Stormchasers* before the accountants come in on Thursday.'

'Be right there, boss.'

Caryn smiled. It still gave her a thrill. *Boss*. It wasn't true, of course, but it was nice to hear it.

A few days later, however, she found herself sitting opposite them, sincerely wishing she'd never voiced her opinion. 'I can't,' she said, shaking her head. 'I just can't. I've got no experience. I—'

'What are you talking about? Come on, Caryn. Of course you can do this. It's just a preliminary meeting. I don't actually know the guy. He's a friend of a friend but he'd be perfect, apparently. He's a mining engineer, works in all the countries we're looking at. He's perfect, or so she says. You just need to be able to persuade him to do it, that's all.'

'Me? Why me? I've never done anything like this before!'

'Since when has that ever held you back?' Martin asked, setting his chin obstinately. Caryn recognised the look. 'Ninety per cent of what you do here you've never done before, Caryn. Just have a drink and a chat, flirt with him a little if you have to. Just get him to agree to meet me. This was your bloody idea in the first place, remember?'

Caryn's heart sank. She knew it had been a bad idea to get too closely involved in the project. She took a deep breath. 'All right. Fine. I'll meet him, but I'm warning you . . . I'm no good at this sort of thing. He'll probably take one look at me and . . . and—'

'And what?'

'Nothing,' Caryn said reluctantly. The last thing she wanted was an argument with Martin – he would win, of course. 'Fine. I'll do it. But I'm not promising anything.'

'Good girl.' She shook her head in exasperation as Martin sauntered off, whistling. *She* was supposed to meet with this contact of Martin's and persuade him to sign up to the project? How on earth was she supposed to do that?

'So who is he?' Nic asked later that evening.

'I don't know. Some guy called Charlie. He's a mining engineer, whatever that is. I'm supposed to meet him tomorrow evening at the Dorchester and persuade him it's a good idea. How the hell'm *I* supposed to do that? I'm really only the bloody office manager, you know!'

'Oh, don't be so wet. Weren't you the one telling me the other day to stop being so afraid of everything?'

'Another thing I should never have said,' Caryn muttered, smiling to herself.

'Of course the most important thing,' Nic said, ignoring her, 'is the little question of what you're going to wear.'

'It's a business meeting, not a date!'

'Makes no difference. And besides, why d'you think Martin asked *you* to go?'

'What d'you mean? You don't think he'd . . . no, surely

not?' Caryn asked, alarmed. The thought hadn't yet occurred to her.

'Wouldn't put it past him,' Nic said darkly.

'How do you know? You've never even met him!'

'Ah, but I know his type,' Nic said dryly. 'It runs in the family.'

The following Tuesday, she found herself sitting nervously in the lobby of the Dorchester in a plain black linen dress, a red scarf round her neck – Martin's idea: *it'll make it easy for him to spot you* – and an empty Bloody Mary in front of her. It was almost four; no one had yet approached her. She was on the verge of ordering another one when she noticed a man sitting to one side, half obscured by the curtains. She knew immediately it was him. He was watching her – how long had he been there and why hadn't she spotted him? He got up and walked towards her.

'Caryn Middleton?' He towered over her. Caryn smiled nervously and he lowered himself into the seat beside her. He held out a hand.

'Hi. Yes, I'm Caryn. Thanks for coming,' she said, hoping she sounded more professional than she felt. Charlie was younger than she'd imagined – and a hell of a lot better-looking, too. Not that she had any idea what a mining engineer ought to look like, she reminded herself hastily. He was frowning at her.

'Haven't we met before?' he asked, obviously trying to place her.

Caryn shook her head. She'd definitely have remembered meeting him. 'No, I don't think so. I'm sure I'd have remembered you.' She blushed immediately. 'I mean . . . no, I doubt we've met.' He looked at her for a second, then rummaged in his pocket for a packet of cigarettes and offered her one. She shook her head. He lit up, still frowning and looked at her empty glass. 'Another?' Caryn nodded gratefully. A waiter glided silently over. Charlie looked like the type whom waiters obeyed. 'Two Bloody Marys,' he said, and turned to her. 'So . . . what's this project you've come to talk to me about?'

'Oh, right. Yes, I brought the project outline,' she began hurriedly, opening her briefcase.

He shook his head. 'Just give me a quick rundown. In your own words.'

She glanced at him. His tone was languid but there was nothing laid-back about his stance. She tried to think of who it was she'd met once before who had the same watchful, slightly wary look. She couldn't remember. She took a deep breath and began to outline the project, bearing Martin's hastily scribbled note in mind. *You've got to seduce him – not literally, of course, but with the project. He's the perfect lead for this. I'm counting on you, Mrs C.*

As she spoke, he studied her discreetly. There was something familiar about her, although he couldn't quite place her. Petite, thick blonde hair falling over one eye, curling around her neck, a few loose hairs on the fitted tweed jacket she wore. He glanced at her legs. High-heeled shoes, a nice dress. Nice. No wonder they'd sent her. He watched her mouth open and close. Lovely, well-shaped lips, not too much lipstick. Blue eyes. He'd warmed to her as soon as he saw her with the empty Bloody Mary on the table; she was nervous. He couldn't have said why but he liked that. She was young, too. Dammit . . . he'd seen her somewhere before. *Some*where. He frowned impatiently. It wasn't like him to forget a face. Especially not one as pretty as hers. She finished speaking and sat back, clearly exhausted by the effort. He gauged she'd been up all night memorising the lines. He looked at her. 'So . . . risky stuff.' It was a statement, not a question. 'What's in it for me?'

Caryn looked at him uncertainly. He certainly didn't waste time. 'Money?' she offered hopefully.

'How much?'

She hesitated, then mentioned a sum. He chuckled. 'Too little?' she asked anxiously.

'By a pretty long shot,' he smiled. He took a sip of his drink and then leaned forward. 'You're going to be filming in places where we might not come out alive. I admire your nerve – it's an interesting subject but these aren't exactly Club Meds you're talking about, you know. And I certainly wouldn't do this for the sort of money you seem to be offering. No, it's not money I'm after.'

'Then what is it?'

He lit another cigarette, playing for time. He rather liked watching her. There was something very pleasing about her. He had the impression she was someone who worked well under pressure. 'Make me an offer.'

She blushed immediately. 'What sort of offer?'

'Think of something. Something I might want.'

She stared at him. He could tell she was both embarrassed and slightly bewildered. 'I don't know you. I've no idea what you might want,' she stammered.

There was a second's carefully held pause. 'Let's see,' he said, astounded at his own response even as he formulated it. 'Have a drink with me. Later tonight. I've got a couple of things to do. I'll meet you somewhere.' She was speechless. 'I'll take that as a "yes", shall I? About eight?' He stood up. She scrambled to her feet. Even in her heels she barely reached his shoulder. 'Have you got a mobile?'

'Er, yes. Shall I . . . d'you want the number?'

'That would be logical.' He scribbled down her number. 'Where's good to meet?'

'The Outsider,' she said suddenly, looking just as astounded as he felt. 'It's a bar on the corner of Holland Park and Ladbroke Grove. I live just around the corner.'

'How appropriate. See you there, then. I'll ring you if I'm going to be late.' He winked at her and walked off.

As soon as he'd disappeared through the doors, she rang Martin. 'He wants to meet me for a drink later on,' she said, hoping the rush of excitement she felt wasn't evident in her voice. She wasn't about to tell Martin he'd taken down her phone number, either.

'How's he seem? Interested?'

'Um, it's a bit hard to tell . . . but yes, I think so.'

'Atta girl. Where're you meeting him?'

'The Outsider,' she said, hoping he wasn't about to say he'd join them. He wasn't. 'Cool. Well, you've got my number. If you feel at any point that it's not going the way you want, give me a ring. I don't want you to feel pressured, Caryn.'

'It's a bit late for that,' she said indignantly.

'You know what I mean. Be careful, won't you? From what I've heard, he's a bit of an operator.'

'Thanks,' she muttered and hung up the phone. Typical Martin – he'd made it sound as though it were the most important task of her entire professional life . . . and then he'd told her to watch it. Of course the man she'd been sent to meet was an operator. It was written all over his admittedly handsome face. Why did he want to meet her later? Why couldn't he have just said 'yes' or 'no' right there and then? More to the point, though . . . why had she agreed to it?

83

Estelle lay on her bed, slowly smoking one cigarette after another. The joint she'd had earlier to calm her down was beginning to wear off, but although Jody had kindly left her a little stash of blow, for once she didn't feel like it. She had other things to think about – other than getting high enough to be able do what Mrs Devereaux required of her.

It had taken her a good few months to get over the shock of it all. *I have two daughters and believe me, you're not one of them. I don't know who the fuck you are.* He was lying, of course. She'd seen the tiny, barely perceptible tremor at the corner of his eye. She knew because she did it too, unwittingly. An advantage he hadn't foreseen, of course, when he casually passed on his genes. She stubbed out her cigarette and swung her legs out of bed. Her mind was quite clear. She knew exactly what to do.

She wasn't going to go to pieces as Mrs Devereaux had feared. Oh, no. On the contrary, Jim Harte's denial had strengthened her resolve, not weakened it. Mrs Devereaux had underestimated her. So, too, had Jim Harte. If he thought for one second that she was going to curl up and die just because he'd been too ashamed – or scared, embarrassed . . . what the *fuck* was the difference? – to admit to a relationship with his maid that had had *consequences*, he was mistaken. He would pay for this. Jesus, she would make him pay. Revenge – or the thought of it – flowed through her like an electric charge, a secret savagery that made her fingers tremble and her heart beat faster. She was no Gloria. She was also cleverer than he thought. Going after him would be a mistake. Trying to get at him would probably only result in her own destruction and she had no intention of doing *that*. No, she had to get at him through something – or someone – else. *I have two daughters*. Well, what better place to start?

She picked up the phone beside her bed. There were a few things she needed to find out before she went any further. And this time, she knew exactly who to call.

84

It wasn't just that he was good-looking and it certainly wasn't his talk – there wasn't much of it. He was skilled at letting her do the talking. No, it was the fact that his charm was physical in a way that she'd never encountered before. It was there in the sun-bleached, tousled mess of his hair; the way he kept raising a rough hand to plough through it, the deep lines made by his grin which was steady, and quick. He seemed oblivious to his own powerful physicality. His appeal was rough, not smooth – it was nothing like the urbane, polished sophistication of Rowland, which was pretty much all she could compare it with.

'You remind me of someone,' she said recklessly, after her third glass of wine. He looked at her over the rim of his glass.

'Really?' he murmured, already disbelieving.

'No, it's true. You probably won't know him – not that *I* know him,' she added hastily. 'He's my best friend's father.'

'Who's that, then?' His tone was teasing.

'Jim Harte. I've never actually met him but— What's the matter?' He looked as though he were about to spit out his wine.

'N . . . nothing,' he recovered quickly. 'Just an . . . odd comparison, that's all.' There was another expression in his face, now, that she hadn't seen before. Not just wariness – he was the most wary person she'd ever met – but something else. She struggled to read it. Suspicion? Yes, that was it. He was looking at her suspiciously.

'D'you know him?' she asked hesitantly.

'No.' He swallowed the rest of his wine and stood up suddenly. 'Look, sorry to run out on you like this,' he said, grabbing his coat from the back of the chair. 'But I've just realised I've got to be somewhere else.' The disappointment was like a blow. She looked down at her feet. 'I'll . . . I'll give you a ring,' he said. 'About the project. I've got your mobile.'

Caryn still couldn't speak. She didn't trust herself to look up at him. What had she said? He touched her lightly on the shoulder, put down his empty glass and disappeared. Just like that.

Her eyes were burning. She pushed her half-full glass away from her, stood up and pulled on her coat. What had happened? she wondered, bewildered. Had he just been stringing her along the whole time? And she, stupid as she was, had walked straight into it. She pushed open the door to the pub and stepped outside. A gentle summer rain had begun to fall. There was no sign of him. *It's your own fault*, she kept repeating to herself as she walked back up the hill. *Your own stupid fault.*

He jogged down Holland Park, furious with himself for not having recognised her. Of *course*! He'd seen her standing next to

Nic Harte at the De Beers party. He'd been so shocked at the sight of Mat standing next to her that somehow he hadn't quite registered her friend. Idiot! He slowed down, aware that his heart was pounding. *Idiot.* He turned the collar of his jacket up against the light drizzle. He kept seeing her small, heart-shaped face, the curve of her cheek against the pale blue of her blouse, eyelashes dark and feathered against the porcelain skin. She'd tried to hide it, of course, but his abrupt departure had shocked her. He wasn't flattering himself. She was disappointed. After all, why else had she agreed to come out for a drink? She had to have known he liked her. He *did* like her. For the first time in a very long time, he was genuinely conflicted. By the time he reached the Holiday Inn at the roundabout, his breathing was beginning to return to normal. So what if she knew Nic Harte? She didn't know his name – not his real name, at any rate. She probably suspected he knew more about Jim Harte than he was prepared to let on, but in his line of business, pretty much standard operating procedure, was it not? He stood by the side of the road, his hand going almost of its own accord to the mobile phone in his pocket. A taxi drove by, its yellow light splashing past as it reflected in the raindrops. He almost raised his left hand but his right kept fingering the phone. He pulled it out of his pocket and stared at it for a second, then he pressed the little green button. Caryn's number was the last number he'd dialled. He listened to the ring tone, his heart beating unusually fast.

Caryn was almost at her door when the unfamiliar buzzing in her pocket signalled an incoming call. She pulled the phone out awkwardly, wishing she knew how to turn the ringer down. 'Hello?'

'It's me. Charlie. Sorry about just now,' he said without preamble, his voice soft and deep. 'Look, I know this might seem a bit sudden, but are you on your way home? Can I come over?'

There was no mistaking the question. She hesitated. What was she letting herself in for? She took a deep breath. 'OK,' she said finally, knowing even as she said it that she'd crossed an invisible line.

'Where d'you live?'

'St Charles Square. Two streets up from the Tube station. Number 42. Top flat.' She swallowed. 'Charlie, I . . . I'm not . . . I don't really do this sort of—'

'Me neither. I'll be there in ten.' He hung up the phone.

She ran the last few yards, her stomach already in knots.

He stood in the doorway of the living room, looking surprisingly ill at ease. The rain was beginning to beat heavily against the windows. She didn't know what to do so she opened one of the cupboards and took out a bottle of brandy. 'Drink?'

He shrugged. Why not?

She busied herself with getting the glasses and rinsing them. She turned to find a dishcloth and felt his hands come to rest lightly on her shoulders. She hadn't heard him cross the room. He turned her round to face him, taking the glasses from her hands and putting them carefully to one side.

'I—' Caryn began, her whole body trembling.

'Shh.' The hands moved from her shoulders to the smooth skin of her throat, fingers trailing across the sensitive hollow and sliding downwards. Caryn thought she might actually melt. His fingers were rough on her skin; they trailed across the thin cotton of her shirt, deftly unfastening a button or two, and then there was the warmth of his touch underneath the clothes, the lace . . . she gasped. His mouth, as he left a trail of warmth across her neck and cheek, was urgent, the soft thickness of his tongue a surprise. He lifted her easily, turning her round to face him, her legs sliding easily around his waist. She couldn't believe what was happening. She couldn't protest – she couldn't even think. All that mattered in the world was the sweet rush to the finish and the deliciously heavy feel of his body slamming into hers.

He was sitting up in bed, enjoying a cigarette. Caryn came out of the bathroom, too shy to meet his gaze. 'You don't mind, do you?' he murmured, indicating the smoke. She shook her head. She hesitated. What was she supposed to do next? Slip into bed beside him? If so, what should she do with the towel wrapped so tightly around her that it threatened to cut off the circulation under her arms? He solved it for her. 'Come here,' he said, tugging at the edge of the towel. He unwrapped her slowly, forcing her to turn around until the towel dropped to the ground and he patted the space beside him. Her bed, if not her side of it. She sank down gratefully. Their eyes met; he grinned and a strange, unspoken ease was suddenly established between them. She was moved by him, by the tanned, weatherbeaten body with its apex of dark, tufted hair springing from underneath her white cotton duvet cover, spreading across his chest, ending just beneath the throat. His body was scarred in places. Surprised at her own boldness, she traced the nick in his cheekbone that led across his cheek, stopping just before his left eye. She said nothing, but he was moved to answer. 'A fight. Long time ago. When I was a kid.'

'I can't imagine you as a kid,' she said suddenly, again wondering at the easy intimacy that had sprung up out of nowhere. It was bewildering. Just as he was. The whole situation, in fact, was nothing less than a mystery. Briefly she wondered what Nic would say.

'What's funny?' he murmured.

'Nothing. Well, it's . . . it's just . . .' She giggled suddenly. 'I don't know why I expect you to believe it but I've never done anything like this before,' she said, burying her face in a pillow. Her cheeks were on fire.

'You've never had sex before?'

'No, of course not. I don't mean *that*. I mean, well, we've only just met!'

'And?' His voice was teasing.

'And so . . . I don't know; it's a bit quick, don't you think? A bit sudden.'

'I prefer not to think that.'

She turned towards him. 'Your name's not Charlie, is it?' she asked on a hunch.

He blew out a cloud of cigarette smoke before answering. 'No, it's not.'

'Well, what is it?' she asked.

He took another drag and looked at her, the expression in his green eyes totally unreadable. 'The less you know about me the better,' he said after a moment.

'Why?'

He stubbed out his cigarette and turned to her. 'Less complicated.' He traced the curve of her cheek with the back of his fingers. Caryn was silent, moved by the unfamiliar caress. She had no idea how to respond. Or what to think.

85

Revenge. It consumed her. It was what she thought about last thing at night; it slapped her into wakefulness first thing in the morning. But it was also what saved her. It took a while to track down the two Harte girls. The *legitimate* daughters. The younger one, Jessica, was too young to be of any real use. She was fifteen and at school somewhere in England. No, it was the older one she wanted. Phil Johnson gave her the facts. She used her mother's maiden name professionally – Nic Parker, not Nic Harte. She was a year and a half older than Estelle; she'd studied English at university in London and had been working for several years as a columnist at *Gossip!* magazine from which she'd recently resigned. She was now a features editor at *ArtWeekly* and was enrolled part-time on a course at the Institute of Journalism. She was single, living alone in a flat in Primrose Hill that Harte had bought her. She had two close friends – one, a producer at a film company in west London, the other the owner of a moderately successful flower shop off Oxford Street. Those were the facts. He could find out more, take the investigation to another, deeper level. She just had to say what she wanted, or needed, and when.

Estelle put the typed report down carefully, a thrill of excitement running through her. So, she now knew where Nic Harte lived; she knew where she worked and she knew who her friends were. It was a start. She lit a joint, watching the blue smoke rise lazily towards the ceiling as she contemplated her next moves. She had to be very, very careful. She'd seen the rage in Jim Harte's eyes – she understood instinctively that he would stop at nothing to get rid of someone who caused him irritation – or, worse, shame. He wouldn't think twice about destroying her. Stories about Harte were difficult to come by – what little there was out there was enough to convince her. She would be playing with fire. She gave a tight little smile. She recognised it about him because she recognised it in herself. Just as he was prepared to go the distance in whatever venture he pursued, so was she. He'd met his match. He'd *made* his match, literally. She stubbed out the joint and stood up. The image of his face as he shredded her birth certificate in front of her came to her suddenly; her fists clenched involuntarily. The *bastard*. God, she would make him pay.

86

'You wouldn't happen to have a light, would you?'

Nic looked up. A girl was standing in front of her – a stunningly beautiful girl in skintight white jeans, high-heeled sandals and a flowery, summery top. Certainly not the type that usually hung around the student bar. 'Er, yeah . . . sure,' she said quickly. She fished a lighter out of her pocket and held it up. The girl bent down and cupped her hand – long, tapering fingers, nails in a deep burgundy shade . . . *definitely* not your average journalism student.

'Thanks,' the girl said, straightening up. She was holding a package in one arm. It looked heavy. She looked around her, obviously lost. 'I've been wandering around this place for the past half-hour – I think they've got the address wrong. This is Southampton Road, isn't it?'

'No, Southampton *Row*. Southampton Road's a little further up, just by the law courts. Who're you looking for?' Nic smiled at her.

The girl glanced down at the package. 'The Eastman Dental Institute.' She tapped it with a long, burgundy nail. 'Don't ask me what's inside . . . weighs a bloody ton.'

'Oh, I know . . . they're on the corner, next to the ITN building.'

The girl looked blank. 'I don't know where anything is,' she said, blowing away a cloud of smoke. 'I've only just come to London. They sent the wrong person out, I tell you.'

'Where from?' Nic asked. There was a faint, almost familiar accent in the girl's voice.

'Zambia. Southern Africa.' She smiled and shook her head. 'I know what you're going to say, believe me – I don't *look* Zambian. I've been here almost a month and that's all anyone ever says!'

Nic smiled at her in genuine delight. 'What a coincidence. I'm from Zimbabwe! I get the same thing all the time.'

'You're *Zimbabwean*? Wow! I must've guessed it, somehow, don't you think? A fellow African!'

Nic felt a sudden rush of warmth for the beautiful stranger who'd just approached her. It had been so long since anyone had referred to her as African. 'I'm Nic, by the way,' she said, holding out a hand.

'Estelle.' She shifted her package to the crook of her arm and shook her hand.

'Here.' Nic pushed her bag off the seat next to her, quickly making space. 'Are you on holiday?'

Estelle shook her head. 'You know how it is,' she said, lowering her voice. 'Came in on a tourist visa. Don't we all?

But I'm doing the odd job here and there. How about you?' She smiled at Nic conspiratorially.

'Well, my mother was English,' Nic said, half-apologetically. 'I've got a British passport.'

'Ah. Lucky you. Nic, eh? Isn't that a boy's name?'

'Well, it's Nicola, actually. But no one ever calls me that.' She looked down at Estelle's heels. 'They're lovely,' she said, admiring them. 'But a bit impractical for pounding the pavements.'

'I know.' Estelle followed her gaze. 'But I figure I need all the practice I can get.'

'Practice?'

'I'm trying to get into modelling.' Estelle gave a short laugh. 'You know how it is back home,' she said again, drawing Nic pleasurably back into a world she'd long since abandoned. 'Everyone says it'll be so easy, you'll make it, go all the way to the top . . . all that crap. Once you get here, though, it's a whole different story. I can't tell you the number of people who've let me down.'

Nic was instantly sympathetic. 'I know what you mean,' she said eagerly, though in truth she didn't. 'But I could give you a couple of contacts, if you like. If you need them,' she added hurriedly, not wanting to sound arrogant. 'I used to work for *Gossip!* magazine. I know a few really good photographers.'

Estelle turned her enormous blue-green eyes on her. 'Really? You'd do that? You really mean it?'

'`Course I would,' Nic blushed. 'It's no big deal, honestly.'

'Gosh, that's so kind of you. Who says we Africans don't help each other out, *ay*? I'll give you my number. Here . . .' She fished her mobile out of her pocket. 'What's yours? I'll ring you and then you can save it.'

'Good idea.'

'Wow. This really is my lucky day,' Estelle said, snapping her phone shut. She got up, grinding her half-smoked cigarette under one spiky heel. She picked up her package. 'I'd better get moving. Nice to have met you, Nic. Thanks again.'

'Oh, same here. I *will* call, I promise. I know this one photographer who'd be perfect for you,' Nic said quickly.

'That'd be cool.' She turned to go.

'Hope you find the building,' Nic called after her. She noticed how everyone in the canteen turned to look at Estelle as she sauntered out, her heels clipping smartly across the floor. What legs. Nic had never seen legs like those before. Neither, it seemed, had anyone else.

Estelle smiled in satisfaction as she exited the Institute and promptly chucked the package in the nearest bin. Easy. Ridiculously easy. Christ, if she'd known how easy it was to get information out of people, she'd have done it herself instead of paying Phil Johnson. A single phone call to *Art Weekly* had given her the day on which Nicola Parker attended her part-time course at the Institute of Journalism and two calls to the Institute had resulted in class times. She'd been to the Institute on the day she knew Nicola Parker *wasn't* there to figure out where and how to bump into her and what excuse to give; it couldn't have been simpler.

Getting the girl's phone number too was easier than she'd ever dared hope. Pathetic, really. One look at her face and Estelle had known exactly how to play her. African, my arse, Estelle grinned to herself. Nicola Harte was about as African as she was. Barely, in other words. The last time she'd been in Africa, Estelle had taken a long, hard look around her – and left. She wanted no part of the hopeless poverty which was all Africa ever meant to her. Poor little rich girl Nicola Harte, desperate to be liked. She almost felt sorry for her. Almost. Getting under the skin of the Harte family was going to be a whole lot more interesting than she'd imagined. Fun, too. *I could give you a couple of contacts, if you like*. She clenched her jaw. Lady fucking Bountiful. Did she think Estelle wasn't capable of making her own? *It's no big deal*. Yes it *is* a big deal, Nicola Harte. Watching you fall is going to be one very big deal indeed. You and the rest of your family. She turned the corner and stuck her hand out for a cab. Pounding the pavements? Not bloody likely. A cab swung round and pulled up beside her, the driver leering at her in the obligatory fashion. She yanked the handle open and climbed in. Step one was complete.

Nic was as good as her word. She rang a couple of photographers she'd worked with at *Gossip!* and by the weekend had a list of five or six names to pass on. She rang Estelle the following Monday and was mildly disappointed when her answering machine kicked in. She left a message, feeling for the second time the pleasurable pull of Estelle's flattened vowels on the tape. 'Hi, you've reached Estelle. I can't get to the phone right now. Please leave me a message.' She was oddly glad she hadn't told Estelle her real name. Of course Estelle would know the name Jim Harte . . . *everyone* in Southern Africa knew the name Harte. She didn't want Estelle to make any assumptions about her. Making friends in England was one thing; making friends at home was another matter entirely. Now, for the first time in years, the two worlds had collided.

She realised with a small jolt that she no longer knew anyone who'd known her back then. Back in Chinhoyi. For years that part of her life had been closed off, buried, dead. She'd successfully reinvented herself as Nicola Parker; no need for the other, earlier Nic to surface. Yes, Caryn and Tory knew who she was, but only in the most peripheral, abstracted sort of way. Neither had ever been to Africa, much less Zimbabwe, and certainly never to one of the Harte estates. For them, Africa and Jim's role in it were nothing more than a shadowy backdrop to Nic's life, present only in the odd turn of phrase or Jim's face on the news. The strange thing was, Nic realised, she too had bought into the story. She didn't think of herself as Zimbabwean any more. It was easy not to. Disbelief was the most common reaction when anyone asked her where she was from and she didn't know a single Zimbabwean, black *or* white, outside of the visitors who sometimes came to Eaton Square. So when Estelle appeared one day, out of the blue, her voice was an echo from another kind of past, one to which she did not often admit. No wonder she was pleased to see her. She brought her back to herself.

87

Mat rode the elevator up to the seventy-fifth floor, his heart racing. For over a year he'd been waiting for the call that would explain why he'd been pulled off his regular assignments and asked to rummage through Jim Harte's past. He'd come back from London in a foul mood – entirely due to the issue of the lost card – to find himself stalled by the very men who'd revved him up in the first place. DiAngelo was cagey; time wasn't right, wasn't sure what Sir Winston's plans were, legal issues to be resolved . . . he'd listened with less and less patience to the growing list of excuses as to why everything had suddenly gone quiet. In the end, sensing the futility of his questions, he'd pushed the whole thing to the back of his mind and tried to get on with the other, more mundane reporting that was the stuff of his working life. And now that was all about to change. Again.

Half an hour later he exited DiAngelo's office, his head reeling. Six weeks. In six weeks' time he was to deliver the article that would finish Jim Harte off. The instruction had come straight from the horse's mouth – Sir Winston Freedland. In six weeks' time, RhoMine would hold their AGM. Mat's article was timed to come out a few days earlier. Share prices would fall through the floor and the game, for Harte, would finally be up. It was time to bring him down. Sir Winston's own words. Apparently. He descended the floors to his own office, unable to think straight.

It took him just under a month to come up with the first draft, which he showed to DiAngelo one evening over dinner. DiAngelo read it through in silence and handed it back. *Keep going*, he said. 'And make sure every fucking thing checks out. He'll crucify you if you get it wrong. You won't get a second chance.' Mat listened and said nothing. DiAngelo was right. Again and again during the course of his investigations, he was reminded that Jim Harte genuinely believed himself to be above the law. In spite of his own distaste, he couldn't help but wonder at the sheer nerve of the man – he'd taken a failing, insignificant mining outfit in Rhodesia and in less than thirty years, built it into the biggest, most expansive conglomerate – outside of South Africa, of course – on the continent. It had made him rich, if not exactly popular. Mat presumed correctly that he'd racked up enough enemies to bring him down. But there was an equal number of men whose interests were so intricately bound to the fortunes of RhoMine that its destruction was out of the question. Somewhere between the two positions Harte was protected, or he protected himself. What was he? English? Arab? German? Businessman, crook, thief? Or simply the smartest, most pragmatic man left standing when everyone else had disappeared? Doing business in Africa, Mat knew, was not for the faint-hearted. Especially not on the scale that Jim Harte did.

Two weeks later, it was done. He rode up the elevator for the second time, his heart still racing. 'Ah, Mat.' Richard DiAngelo looked up as he walked in. 'Good to see you. Sir Winston'll be joining us in a minute.' Mat nodded, his throat too dry to speak. Leonie entered, carrying a tray of coffee and bagels. She looked a little tense, as though she too could sense the drama waiting to unfold. She placed the tray on the table and quietly withdrew. Seconds later, Sir Winston arrived. 'Morning, Richard. Mr Ndava.' He pronounced the name fluently. 'Right, let's get started. You've something for me, I hope?' He rubbed his hands in anticipation.

Mat tapped the six-page article out of its plastic folder and slid it across the table. 'Sixth draft,' he said. 'We're hoping it's nearly there.'

There was silence in the room as Sir Winston quickly read through the article, punctured only by the rhythmic chewing and swallowing of the two older men as they devoured the smoked-salmon bagels and finished the pot of coffee. Mat could neither eat nor drink. At last Sir Winston finished, gathering the six loose sheets and carefully tapping them into line. He took off his glasses, pinched the bridge of his nose and said, quite clearly, if a touch nasally, 'This'll do it. Scum of the earth. Typical Arab, if you ask me. Can't trust 'em as far as you can spit.'

Mat winced. It was neither true nor relevant. He felt a sudden tremor of dislike for the bloated, red-faced peer sitting opposite him, his expansive girth swaddled in expensive fabric, shrouded in a cloud of cigar smoke. Sir Winston's title was hereditary, not earned. Ten minutes in the real jungle of the corporate world and he'd be dead. 'It's a little hard-hitting in places,' he said cautiously, avoiding Sir Winston's eye. He'd no desire for him to see the faint contempt in his own. 'But given the overall tone, I think it's appropriate.'

'Oh, absolutely. The harder the better. I want to run it a fortnight on Monday – two days before their AGM.' He looked up. He smiled. Mat was struck by the venom behind it. Obviously the two men had crossed paths somewhere along the way and from the personal interest Sir Winston was taking in it, Mat had the feeling he'd come off the loser. 'I want every single shareholder to walk into that meeting with only one thing on his or her mind – getting rid of him. The oily bastard has to go.'

'So, are we agreed?' DiAngelo asked. 'We go to print?'

'We do.' Sir Winston got up heavily. He held on to the article as Leonie was dispatched to find his coat and hat. DiAngelo helped him ease his bulk into it. 'Stick that in there,' he ordered him, gesturing towards his briefcase. DiAngelo's eyes met Mat's for a second, a faint question in them. Mat nodded imperceptibly. Technically, he supposed, Sir Winston owned it. Though it would have been polite to have been asked. Although *politesse*, in all likelihood, wasn't Sir Winston's forte. 'Good day, gentlemen,' Sir Winston said, settling the brim of his hat. He leaned on his stick and was shown out of the room. There was a stunned, relieved silence after he'd gone. DiAngelo was the first to recover.

'That went pretty well, don't you think?' he asked Mat, nodding slowly.

Mat shrugged. 'It's done. That's the main thing.'

'Yeah, but you're not. I need you in London this week. And

the next. I want you to cover the fallout at the RhoMine AGM.'

Mat raised an eyebrow. 'Into the lion's den,' he murmured. DiAngelo grinned.

'Rather you than me. But you can take care of yourself, I figure. Probably better than I can. Besides, it's your territory. I can't stand the place. Crap food. Terrible weather.'

Mat smiled. 'One gets used to it,' he said diplomatically.

'Does one, now?' DiAngelo's expression was gently teasing. 'Good job, Mat. This'll up your asking price.'

'Are you offering me a raise?'

'Now you *know* I'd never do anything quite so reckless.'

'I do.' Mat picked up his own satchel and notes. 'London it is. I'll let you know when I've arrived.'

88

Tory got out of the cab carefully – in her tight, silk shift dress and impossibly high heels, she had to concentrate hard on staying upright. Any sudden movement to the left or right could well result in a fall. Perhaps the shoes had been a mistake? Nic's idea, of course. 'You can't go to the *GQ* awards in *those*,' she'd declared, rejecting one pair after another as Tory dragged them out of her wardrobe. 'What's the matter with you?' Tory shook her head impatiently, just wanting to get the whole process over and done with and get back to the awards. She'd been up since five a.m. with three of her helpers, getting all the flowers to the Royal Opera House and putting together the arrangements – the last thing on her mind was shoes. But she held her tongue and tried to concentrate on the matter in hand – getting dressed – managing, for once, not to think about Rob. Nic was in a frenzy of excitement. Tory hadn't been able to face the thought of an evening with Luc, pretending to be in love, and had asked Nic to come along instead. She had to leave a couple of hours early to make sure everything was as it should be with the flowers; Nic would follow later. Now, as she walked up the steps to the front entrance, blinking as the odd flashbulb went off by mistake, some inexperienced paparazzo thinking *she* was a celebrity guest arriving hours too early, she was glad she'd listened to Nic and made the effort. At least she didn't look as if she'd stumbled upon the event by accident.

She climbed the stairs to the magnificent ballroom on the first floor and pushed open the door. Even though she'd been there since seven a.m. that morning and the ballroom was no surprise, she gasped as soon as she saw the displays, their angular, almost architectural shapes emphasising the long lines of the room, casting striking shadows against the specially constructed silk screens that were hung strategically from the ceiling. She'd worked with one of the Opera House's top set designers and the result was fantastic. The giant bouquets of purple and orange bird-of-paradise flowers and spiky, ornamental cherry blossom radiated outwards from the long central bar towards the edges of the room. The centrepiece, hanging directly above the stage, was a complex, beautifully arranged and sculpted canopy of red anthuriums, yellow foxtail flowers and striking green and white orchids, flown over specially from Thailand for the event. On the stage they'd placed giant round glass bowls filled with creamy arum lilies and green bells of Ireland. It had taken her ages to compose the entire look. She'd taken a week-long course in *ikebana*, the ancient Japanese art of flower arranging, and it showed. She loved the new bouquets — unlike the techniques she'd learned at Cecilia Fry's, *ikebana* was about simplicity and discipline, stripping things back, clear symmetry and structure. The course had been unbelievably soothing, allowing her to focus on something other than Rob or the mess she'd got herself into. For the first time she'd used branches, leaves, grasses, mosses and the difficult-to-grasp concept of stillness and emptiness in an arrangement. It was masculine without being hard or stark; beautiful without being pretty. The flowers had drama, passion, composition. Just the sort of backdrop an event like this needed.

'Looking good,' Mark Ennis, the editor-in-chief of GQ sang, gliding past with the guest list in one hand and a marker in the other. He looked harried, like a man with an event to organise. Tory smiled, pleased by his obvious appreciation.

'Fab, Tory, darling.' Someone else came up to her, cooing. It was Diana Etherton, one of the coordinators. 'Colours are just di*vine*!' She pulled an official-looking clipboard from under her arm. 'Now, I need to talk to you about seating,' she said, a touch pompously. 'Such a shame that *divine* fiancé of yours couldn't come, isn't it? Never mind, you've got a friend coming so you won't be on your own. I've put you next to Pippa Grainger – from *Elle*. You remember Pippa, don't you?'

Tory was saved from answering by the arrival of someone clearly of infinitely greater importance and Diana sailed on. She walked over to one of the tables and inspected the centrepiece. They'd spent hours on the individual arrangements – no two tables were the same and with eighty tables to fill, Tory had stretched her imagination to breaking point. Keep it simple, she'd instructed herself over and over again. Let the flowers speak for themselves. Arabian chincherinchee, aspidistra leaves, sandersonia, yellow foxtails and those wonderfully complex, delicate paphiopedilum orchids echoing the ones in the suspended canopy above the stage. Some of the arrangements looked good enough to eat. She checked the water levels – everything looked fine. She could breathe. Relax. She looked at her watch. Almost an hour to go. She would take a quick walk outside and have a cigarette to try to calm her nerves. She tweaked a stem here, adjusted a bloom there and then headed for the door.

She found a spot on the terrace, away from the dozens of people scurrying around checking lights, sound equipment, microphones, place settings . . . hard to believe in less than an hour the likes of Ewan McGregor and David Beckham would swan up the red carpet. She lit a cigarette and stared at the ground. It was her biggest commission to date, not just in monetary terms. The press and contacts that would surely follow were just what Bloomin' Stories needed to take things to the next level of profitability. And judging from everyone's reaction so far, she'd pulled it off. She ought to have been pleased. It should have been the most exciting night of her life. But it wasn't. She hadn't heard from Rob in almost a fortnight. She stared disconsolately at the ground. After years of indecision and drifting, she'd finally settled down – she had a new flat, a successful business, a loving fiancé and a sixty-two-carat ring sitting at the back of a drawer at home . . . and all she could think about was when Rob would next call. The worst of it was, though – she couldn't stop even if she'd *wanted* to. Somehow Rob had got under her skin. No matter how hard she tried, she couldn't get rid of him. Or the aching longing that being with him produced. It was all a horrible mess. And sooner or later, it would all go horribly wrong.

She wandered back into the ballroom, stopped by one of the tables and picked up one of the elegant menu cards. *Crab rémoulade with a cucumber salad; seared quail salad with a mango salsa; poached canon of lamb in an Asian-style broth.* What was a rémoulade? Or a canon of lamb? She put the card down and looked around. Waiters were beginning to emerge from the preparation room at one end of the hall. On the stage, the acousticians and technicians were running through last-minute checks – every so often a loud 'squeak' escaped from the PA system. 'Testing, testing . . .' Someone kept tapping the microphones. She stood to one side, rather enjoying watching everyone else's last-minute panic now that her own job was done.

89

The taxi dropped him off as close to the Royal Opera House as it could get. He got out and fought his way through the scrum of photographers, emerging on the other side, cursing DiAngelo as he climbed the stairs. He'd been asked – no, *instructed* – to attend the ceremony at the last minute. The journalist who normally covered *WED's* Lifestyle and Entertainment pages had called in sick – was there anyone else in London who could replace him? Mat took the call, his irritation rising with every second. He couldn't have been less interested in the awards ceremony if he'd tried. Still, he reasoned as he was shown into the packed ballroom, Simon was out of town – what else did he have to do on a Friday night, alone in London?

He showed his invitation card to the scantily clad girl directing people to their seats. 'Matari N . . . N . . . Indava?' she said, bravely attempting his name. He nodded.

'That's me.'

'Super. You'll be on table twenty-four, over there in the corner. Enjoy the evening!' She flashed a too-perfect white smile and quickly turned to the next guest.

He wound his way across the floor, trailing a group of already merry guests. Everyone was in a party mood. After so long on his own with only his laptop for company, it was a little disconcerting to be around so much noise. He took a quick look at his fellow diners as he sat down. A motley group. They ap-peared not to know each other, either, which was just as well. To his left was a pretty brunette in a dress that looked as though it had been spray-painted on and to his right a woman in a yellow dress that matched the flowers on the table and little else. He steeled himself for a long, dull evening of chit-chat, reminding himself not for the first time that he was glad *he* didn't have to cover Lifestyle and Entertainment. What did the event unfolding in front of him have to do with either life *or* entertainment? He looked around the room. It was almost obscene. The amount of money spent on the flowers alone would have paid off the national debt of any number of small Third World countries. He glanced at the ridiculously poised canopy above the stage. It stretched a full six or seven metres, trailing foliage and flowers in all directions. He just hoped it wouldn't come down on anyone's head.

International Man of the Year. GQ Woman of the Year. Lifetime Achievement. Most Stylish Man. GQ Inspiration. He followed the awards, one after the other, in stunned disbelief. What was the difference between the *Armani Mania Man of the Year, GQ's Most Stylish Man* and *GQ's Inspirational Man*? Was it an honour to be named *GQ Politician of the Year*, as Jack Straw seemed to think? He'd never seen anyone look quite so delighted to hear his name yelled out loud. Who were all these *Radio Personalities*? He recognised a few of the editors who were also up for awards – Simon from the *Independent*, Martin Newland from the *Daily Telegraph*, Paul Dacre from the *Daily Mail*. They too looked absolutely delighted to be in the hot, crowded and unbearably loud room, rubbing shoulders with the people they wrote about – usually in damnation. He kept having to remind himself to shut his mouth. He could honestly say he'd never seen anything like it.

'What's happening to the orchids?' Nic whispered to Tory, pointing as discreetly as she could towards the centre of the table. In the striking green glass bowl, the tall, thin head of the paphiopedilum orchid was arching slowly towards the white linen cloth. Tory bit her lip, worried.

'I don't know,' she confessed, glancing nervously around. It was bizarre. Across the room, one by one, the heads were beginning to droop. She felt her hands begin to go clammy. It was only half past nine – the event was scheduled to run until midnight at least. At the rate the flowers were wilting, they'd be horizontal in the next half-hour. She couldn't understand it. She'd checked everything – water, humidity, smoke, heat . . . the supplier had assured her they would last long past the evening itself. The bowl in front of her was beginning to look truly ridiculous – one long, thin green stem flopping under its own weight, the delicate green and white striped petals slowly turning waxy and yellow. It was only the orchids, too. The rest of the flowers looked splendid. Clearly the orchids were responding to something they hadn't thought of – but what? She fought down a rising sense of panic. What was the best way to tackle the situation? She looked around again. Six hundred-odd people, now decidedly merrier than when they came in . . . well, there was only one thing for it. She would have to figure out a way to remove the orchids from the centrepiece without causing too much of a stir. Once they were gone, the arrangements might look a tad empty, but at least they'd look *alive*. The plant in front of her looked as though it were gently expiring, sighing, laying its fucking head down to rest. She grabbed Nic's arm. She'd had an idea. She and Nic would have to remove every single one in the next fifteen minutes or so otherwise the pictures in tomorrow's press would be fatal. The presenters were busy pulling names out of envelopes, the whole crowd was agog with anticipation; no one was paying any attention to the flowers – she had to act, and act fast.

'Help me out,' she hissed, pushing her chair back. 'We've got to get the orchids out of the displays. Come on. You do the tables at the edge of the room; I'll do the ones in the middle. I'll get one of the waiters to help us. Smile as you're doing it . . . say something about too much cigarette smoke, or something. Come on!'

Under cover of the buzz generated by the announcements, Nic moved swiftly from table to table, plucking out the offending flowers with as little fuss as possible. A few drops of water, a quick, guilty smile . . . *no, it's the smoke* . . . and she moved on to the next. No one paid much attention. She stole a quick glance at Tory, moving awkwardly in those ridiculously high-heeled shoes. She wished she'd never suggested them – hobbling from one table to the next with an armful of wet, dying orchids was hard enough in practical flats. Hobbling along in six-inch black patent heels was another. No wonder Tory was beginning to panic. Nic recognised the signs. 'Oops, sorry . . .' She dropped a couple of spots of water into someone's lap as she pulled out yet another dying flower. 'Sorry about that. Here—' She produced a napkin with a flourish. She could feel his eyes on her cleavage as she bent towards him. She moved on as quickly as she could.

There was a woman making her way around the edges of the room, Mat noticed, pulling flowers out of the bowls. A waiter hovered behind her with a black plastic bag, held discreetly aloft. Something had obviously gone wrong. He looked at the flowers on his own table – wilting, definitely. He suppressed a grin. He too felt as though he were wilting. Keeping the conversation going with the woman in the hideous yellow dress was proving more difficult than he'd ever imagined. She talked a lot but said nothing – or at least nothing to which he could reasonably respond. His eyes followed the flower woman as she edged her way around the room. Her back was to him – she was tall and slim, dressed in black. She said something to the waiter and then turned, making her way across the floor towards the last group of tables, including his own. She leaned across to pull out a flower and he suddenly caught sight of her face. He almost choked on his drink. An electric jolt of recognition flowed through him – it couldn't *possibly* be? Was it her? Nic? He stood up abruptly, cutting the woman in yellow off in mid-sentence and pushed back his chair. She hadn't seen him. He strode quickly across the room, still unable to believe his eyes. It *was* her! Around him, the tension in the room was building as one particularly important award was being announced. He was dimly aware of the two hosts fawning around each other in mock affection on the stage as they pulled open the prized envelope and made their announcement. 'And the award goes to . . .' There was a gasp from the audience as Pierce Brosnan stood up to a wave of thunderous applause. Nic paused for a moment to look at the stage and Mat moved swiftly towards her, his heart thudding. And then it happened. There was a noise like a thunderclap, an awful creaking, groaning sigh and the whole spectacular canopy he'd noticed earlier swayed precariously – once, twice . . . people began to scramble away from the stage. Brosnan looked wildly around him, wondering what the hell was going on. Someone shouted, 'Look out! Oh, *Jesus*!' Someone else screamed. And then the entire edifice simply collapsed.

They met in the lobby, shepherded there by harried security guards and event organisers, each looking more worried than the last. The awards were being filmed live; in the pandemonium that followed the collapse of the canopy, the stars were torn between the urge to run for their lives and the thought of being caught on camera looking anything less than perfect. Nic came through the door, an orchid still in her hands, looking more worried than panicked. He stepped forward. She saw him and stopped, incredulity spreading over her face.

'What . . . what the hell are *you* doing here?' People pushed and jostled their way past her, heading for the stairs.

'Nic. Christ, I *thought* it was you. I wasn't sure—' He stared at her. She was exactly as he remembered: cool, beautiful, a touch haughty, even with her mouth hanging open. He shook his head, as if he couldn't believe his eyes.

'What are you doing here?' she repeated, shaking her head as if she couldn't quite believe her own eyes.

'I just got into town. Look, can we go somewhere? Just for a couple of minutes. I owe you an explanation—'

'You don't have to explain anything,' Nic said, the haughtiness he'd so admired returning swiftly to her face.

'No, really. I . . . it sounds lame, I know, believe me, but I lost your card. Honestly. I've spent the past six months trying to work out where or how I dropped it, and I'd no idea how to get in touch with you. I don't even know your last name!'

Nic looked at him, oblivious to the sound of people streaming out of the ballroom behind them and the frantic attempts to lift the fallen canopy off the stage and get the show back on the road. It was on the tip of her tongue to tell him to get lost – as if she'd believe a story like that . . . but she didn't. She looked him straight in the eye, her eyes searching his face. He didn't flinch.

She saw, with relief, that he was telling the truth. 'Parker,' she said slowly, the corners of her mouth lifting almost of their own accord. 'Nic Parker.'

He held out a hand. 'I know this is hardly the right place or time,' he gestured to the chaos erupting behind them, 'but I can't afford to miss the chance. Can we go somewhere? Can I take you out?' The loudspeakers were announcing a return to the ballroom.

She shook her head. 'Not tonight, I'm afraid. That's my best friend in there. The one who was helping me get rid of these.' She held the dead orchid aloft. 'Or the other way round, actually. She's the florist. It was her canopy that just came down. I've a feeling she'll be needing a hand.'

'Tomorrow's chip paper,' Mat said, smiling faintly. 'Tell her that. No matter how bad it seems.'

Nic nodded. 'It was her first really big event,' she said grimly. 'What a thing to happen.'

'So when *can* I see you?'

'Friday?'

'Just tell me where and when. I'll be there this time. Promise.'

Nic looked at him, considering. She gave him the name of the little Italian restaurant at the end of her road. 'You don't know how lucky you are,' she said, tossing a backwards glance over her shoulder at the pandemonium behind them. Tory would be hysterical by now. 'You're getting a second chance. I don't normally do second chances, you know.'

'I know.' Mat's voice held a smile.

'How?'

He shrugged charmingly. 'I can tell. You're not the type. But you're also unpredictable. That's what I like about you.' He grinned at her and then turned and walked off. This time it was Nic who was left in the middle of the foyer, wondering if she'd just imagined the whole thing.

90

He opened the glove compartment, slipped his hand in and pulled out the gun. A 7.5 mm Beretta. He held it loosely in his hand. It was a beauty: cool, smooth metal, made heavier by the silencer. This was to be a quick, clean job. His target would be in the shower for less than five minutes; he had three minutes at the most to get in, do the job and get out again. He sat in the car waiting for the phone call. It was unbearably hot; sweat was trickling down his back. He waited, his whole body tense, one hand on the gun, the other on his phone. Outside the cicadas continued their evening chorus; the palms overhead rustled every once in a while when the ocean sent forth one of its long, languorous breaths. The windows were down; a gust of fragrance from the lime trees on the other side of the hedge brushed past his nostrils. He could hear the high-pitched, irritating whine of a mosquito hovering somewhere above his left ear. He swatted at it. Suddenly the phone vibrated in his hand, its blue light illuminating the interior of the car for a fraction of a second before he picked it up. He listened intently for a moment and then switched it off.

A few minutes later he saw the small gate to the side of the house swing open. He got out of the car soundlessly, slid the gun into the waistband of his trousers and disappeared through the gate. He nodded to the man standing beside it and walked across the gravel, his soles crunching lightly as he moved. He walked around the back of the house as he'd been directed. Again there was a side door waiting open. He entered the house, waited a moment to make sure there were no other noises and then ran lightly and silently up the stairs. He turned left at the landing and walked all the way down the corridor to the master bedroom at the end. The door was slightly ajar; through it, he could hear the sound of running water and the rattling hum of the air-conditioner. He walked across the terrazzo floor towards the bathroom.

It was over in seconds. There was a soft 'phut' from his gun, the force of the bullet lifting the man in the shower clear and sending him thudding against the tiled wall. A single, neat shot. As he fell, his arm caught the shower nozzle, knocking it off the pedestal. It wriggled in front of him, sending blood and water splattering against the plastic curtain. He slid the gun into his waistband and exited the house just as he'd come, in silence.

Ten minutes later he was back on the freeway, heading towards the airport. He replaced the gun and the phone, parked the car where he'd been told and picked up his bag. Within the hour, if he were lucky, he'd be sipping a gin and tonic in the Business Class lounge before boarding the flight. He walked quickly towards the terminal building, his body slowly beginning to relax. In and out in less than three minutes, just as he'd said. Pity all his jobs weren't as clean.

'So where is he now?' Martin asked petulantly.

Caryn shook her head. 'I've no idea.' It was true. He'd left her flat just before dawn that night with a quick kiss — not that she'd tell Martin *that*, of course — and that was it. She hadn't seen or heard from him since. He had a couple of things to do, he said. He'd be gone for a bit. He hadn't said whether he would call her or not, or whether there was to be anything other than the single most exciting night of her entire life . . . not his, she assumed practically. He seemed like a man who was used to the sort of quick, easy intimacy they'd shared. Unlike her, he'd probably forgotten all about it.

'But you were supposed to set up a series of meetings, Caryn,' Martin said, running his hand through his hair. A sure sign of agitation. 'We've got nothing. Not even a single recorded sentence.'

Caryn held out her hands. 'Well, he said he'd call,' she lied. 'I think the first meeting was just—'

'Just what?' He was looking at her oddly.

'I . . . I don't know . . . maybe he just wanted to check us out?' she offered.

'Check *you* out, more likely,' Rupesh muttered. Caryn could feel her face was on fire.

'All right. We sit tight for a bit. Wait for him to come back to us. But if he hasn't phoned by the end of the week, I'll have to call in a couple of other contacts. This is too important a project to screw around with.'

Caryn nodded. She didn't trust herself to say very much. What she'd done was so out of character that she didn't even know how to think about it, much less what to say. She gathered her notes and her phone and escaped to the sanctuary of her own desk, hiding her face behind the computer screen. She had plenty to do – there was absolutely no reason for her to stare dreamily into space, torn between the hot, pleasurable recollection of the night she'd spent with him, and the unbearable ache that came with knowing she'd probably never see him again. Not only had she sent him running in the opposite direction, she'd probably scuppered the project as well. Katie, who sat opposite her, looked up several times as if about to ask her if everything was all right, but there must have been something in Caryn's eyes that forestalled the question. By four that afternoon, Caryn decided she couldn't stand it any longer. She picked up her coat and bag, pleaded a headache and left early.

The flat was still and quiet, a welcome relief from the clamour in her head. She looked at her answering machine. No, not a single message. She fought the irrepressible urge to burst into tears and sat down on the sofa. It wasn't even five p.m. The evening stretched in front of her, endlessly. She was rarely home before seven p.m. these days, and it felt odd to be walking down Ladbroke Grove with teenage schoolchildren still on their way home. She switched on the TV. Anything to take her mind off things. The last of children's afternoon television was playing; she sat, slightly stunned, through the closing credits of *Teletubbies* before curling up. She covered her legs with her coat and before long, she could feel herself drifting off into sleep.

The phone shattered the quiet. She leaped up, her heart hammering. 'Hello?' Her mouth was dry and her head was thick. She peered at the clock on the wall. Ten past nine. She'd been asleep for nearly four hours!

'It's only me,' Nic said breathlessly. 'Were you expecting someone?'

'N–no, I was just . . . I just fell asleep.'

'Oh. Well, I have got the most incredible—' Caryn's doorbell sounded suddenly, interrupting her.

'Hang on a sec; someone's at the door,' Caryn said, putting down the phone. It was probably a wrong flat. It often happened. She pressed the buzzer. 'Who is it?'

'Me. Can I come up?'

Her heart almost stopped beating. She ran back to the phone. 'Nic? I've got to go. I'll call you later,' she hissed, not even waiting for an answer. She slammed down the phone and ran to the door. She glanced at her slightly dishevelled appearance in the mirror . . . smudged mascara, a thin red welt down her left cheek where her hair had stuck to it. Couldn't be helped. She could see his shadow through the pane of frosted glass in the door. She hurried down the stairs and opened it.

He stood on the doorstep, looking at her uncertainly. 'Hi.' He ran a hand through his tousled hair. He looked far less cocky and self-assured than she remembered.

'Hi.' She held on to the door frame, suddenly shy.

'I was just passing,' he said, though they both knew it was a lie. 'Is it a bad time?'

She shook her head, trying not to smile too broadly. 'Come in. I was just . . . well, I fell asleep, actually.'

'Did I wake you up?'

'No. A friend rang. I'll call her back later.' She led the way into the sitting room. They stood in the centre of the room, facing one another, both awkward.

'I'll make—'

'Can I—' They both spoke at once. He grinned, giving way.

'I'll just put the kettle on,' Caryn said, turning before her flaming cheeks betrayed her. She fled into the kitchen. Just as he'd done the last time, he followed her in. She filled the kettle with water and plugged it in. She turned round. He was peering at the photograph she'd stuck to the fridge door. It was of the three of them – her, Alice and Brian – taken the previous summer. They were standing, a little stiffly, in front of Buckingham Palace, of all places.

'Your family?' he asked, looking quickly at her.

She nodded. 'That's my younger brother and my mum.'

He prised the photo off the door, holding it up against her face. 'You look like her.'

'Yeah, well . . .' she stopped herself in time. 'Have you got any?'

'What?'

'Brothers and sisters?'

'No. There's no one.' His tone was short. There was pain behind the voice, she noticed.

The kettle whistled suddenly, breaking the tension. 'Tea or coffee?' she asked brightly.

He replaced the photo and turned back to her. 'Neither, actually.' He crossed the space between them, taking the kettle from her, setting it aside. She felt herself being drawn into his embrace; his shirt prickling pleasurably against her skin. It smelled of sun, of warmth and good aftershave; she buried her face against his chest. He slid a hand under her chin, forcing her to look up at him. His eyes were green flecked with hazel, she noticed almost distractedly; his jaw and chin were covered in a two-day stubble. A small sound escaped his throat, as if he were trying to speak, but she reached up, standing on tiptoe, wrapped her arms round his neck and pulled him closer, as if trying, by force, to draw him in. She was prepared for his roughness and his obvious strength, but there was a quiet vulnerability in him that she'd sensed in the few minutes he'd been in the house and it knocked her completely sideways. He took her breath away. He picked her up easily but this time at least he took her to bed.

'Where did you go?' Caryn asked suddenly. He'd been asleep himself for a blank, quick second and the sound of her voice brought him abruptly back to himself. 'You've got a tan.'

He ran a single finger along the slender line of her back, across the sharp nudge of her ribs until it found the warm, fullness of her breast. He touched the nipple, feeling it harden against his fingertip. She stirred gently in protest at his evasion. She was no fool. 'Have you been abroad?'

He was suddenly wide awake. He reached for a cigarette from the small bedside table and lit it, watching the smoke rise in gentle coils. Hesitantly at first, he began to talk. About the meeting in Freetown. About his decision to accept another contract. About the payments.

She listened, not interrupting him once. He had never spoken like this to anyone. 'You're going to get into trouble,' she said, propping herself up on an elbow and taking the cigarette from him. She took a long, slow drag. 'Aren't you?'

He looked up at her, at the pale, creamy skin of her face, very lightly freckled; at the blue eyes with their fringe of darker lashes; the small, but surprisingly full shape of her breasts and the taut, flat line of her belly that disappeared into the sheets. In the light drifting in from the street outside the window he was struck by her rare combination of delicacy and strength. He turned so that his face was pressed against the tiny cup at the base of her throat, his arms going around her small, compact body. She'd dabbed a spot of perfume there earlier in the day. Now, many hours later and after the sweat of lovemaking, the perfume was mingled with the scent of her own body. He lay still, not moving, breathing in and out, as if he might take the scent of her down, deep down into his lungs.

'I'm already in trouble,' he said at last, and began to kiss her.

91

He was sitting at the bar when she walked in. He seemed different – bigger than she remembered. The thigh that supported him as he half-leaned, half-sat on the bar stool was powerfully curved and athletic. He was wearing black, as she was. An elegant man, she thought to herself, taking in the details at lightning speed. His hair was cut very close to his perfectly shaped head and he had a small, neat goatee, a thin upper lip and a fuller, more sensual lower lip. His eyes were jet black and his brows were thick and dark. His skin was the colour of deep, dark cocoa. A beautiful face. He smiled and the whiteness was sunlight.

'Nic.' He slid off the stool.

'Mat.' She stood before him, presenting herself, palms up. They both laughed.

'I got here half an hour early,' he said, pulling the sides of his lovely mouth downwards. 'Just to be on the safe side.'

'As you should,' Nic said, sliding into the seat next to him. They looked at each other. She couldn't explain it – there was a lightness and a kind of grace about him that she warmed to immediately. They clicked. Just as they'd clicked at the party.

'What'll you have?' he asked, holding up his own glass of red wine. 'It's good. Barolo. A ninety-five, I think.'

She pulled a face. 'Impressive.'

'No, it says so on the bottle,' he said gently, pointing.

She blushed. 'Er, I'll have the same,' she said to the barman. 'Make it a large.'

'So,' Mat said when her glass had been poured. 'Here we are. Finally.'

'Finally. I'd just about given up on you, you know,' she said, taking a sip.

He raised his hands, culpable. 'I know, I know. I still don't know how I could have lost it. I went mad looking for it.'

'And I still can't believe we bumped into one another again like that. I very nearly didn't go to the show. I just went to support Tory.'

'Ah, the hapless florist. How is she?'

Nic pulled a face. 'Well, suicidal the morning afterwards. But you're right. Tomorrow's chip paper. What were *you* doing there? D'you know . . . I don't know anything about you. What do you do?'

'I'm a journalist. I work for *WED*; it's an economics journal, based in New York.'

Nic's mouth fell open. 'You're kidding?'

Mat shook his head. 'No. Why?'

'*I'm* a journalist. I'm the features editor at *ArtWeekly*.'

It was Mat's turn to look surprised. They looked at each other. Nic, for once, was dumbstruck. Fortunately the waiter interrupted them. Their table was ready.

He liked her even more than before. He remembered her as a little wary, possibly even aloof. This time, she was open and unguarded. The wine brought out a flirtatious lightness in her; it deepened her smile and brought out the blush in her cheeks. He found himself unable to take his eyes off her. She saw it, and her attraction was magnified. He fiddled with the stem of his wine glass as she talked. She was telling him about her course at the Institute. It had reminded her of school at first, everyone rushing past, too busy to chat, feeling as if she was the only person who didn't know where everything was, how to get to the library, where the canteen was. He grinned. It was the same for him, too, when he'd first come to England, he said.

'You're not English?' she asked.

He shook his head. 'No. I went to school here but I'm Zimbabwean, actually. What's the matter?' he asked. She'd begun to choke.

She shook her head, reaching for a glass of water. 'N–nothing,' she stammered, her face suddenly bright red. 'Something must've gone down the wrong way.' She took a huge gulp. 'It's f . . . fine.'

'You sure?'

'Yes, I'm fine.' She coughed. 'You were saying?'

'I went to school here, and then to university and then I left for the States. I've been there almost ten years now.'

'D'you like living in America?' Whatever it was that had caused her to choke seemed to have gone.

He considered the question. 'I used to,' he said slowly. 'When I first arrived. You know what New York's like – the pace, the people, the buzz. But now, I don't know. I'm—' He stopped, suddenly aware of the fact that it had been a very long time since he'd talked to anyone the way he now talked to her. 'I'm restless, I guess. I need to move on. Do something different. As a matter of fact, I—' He checked himself. He hadn't spoken to anyone about the work he'd been doing over the past year – and with good reason, too. He was surprised he'd even felt the need to tell her. 'No, it's too boring to talk about work. Tell me about you.'

She shrugged. 'Nothing much to tell,' she muttered, bending her head to her plate. He was puzzled. In a flash the openness he'd sensed in her was gone, replaced by the same wariness he'd detected the first time they'd met. He wondered what had brought it on. Was there something in her background she was reluctant to talk about? He decided not to press her. It was their first date, after all. He was due to leave for New York in just under a fortnight's time, which meant there'd be time enough to see her again – assuming she wanted to, of course. He experienced an unfamiliar pang of nervousness. He very much wanted to see her again. She was an odd combination of toughness and fragility, confidence and apprehension. At times her face was completely open, painfully naked. He could almost track her thoughts by looking at it. And at other times a mask slid into place, composed and wary. She'd been hurt before, he guessed . . . but not in an ordinary way. No, there was something deeper. He realised he longed to know what.

Nic bent her head, aware his eyes were on her in a way that made her uncomfortable. Why had she lied? Or at least decided against telling him the full truth? He was *Zimbabwean*? She still couldn't get over it. Of all the bloody places. How could she possibly tell him who *she* was? She was desperate that this encounter – whatever it turned out to be – shouldn't be tainted by her father or his reputation. She wanted him to like her. She had no way of knowing whether the fact that she was Jim Harte's daughter would make him want to run a mile or get closer. She didn't *want* to know. She didn't want to be judged either way. So she kept quiet. Later – if there was to be a later – she would explain. For the time being, she would say nothing.

He was good company. If he sensed there was something wrong, he chose to ignore it, telling her instead a bit about his life in New York. As he talked and ate, she found it hard to keep her eyes off his face. There was something about him that made her want to reach out and touch him. Just to make sure he was really there.

To her great disappointment, after he'd walked her down the street to her flat, he made no move to kiss her – or even touch her. She was certainly too shy to make a move herself. They stood for a moment under the street lamp, hands in pockets.

'I had a really good time,' she said, wishing he would *do* something. Ask her out again. Take her hand . . . touch her cheek. Anything.

'Same here. Are you—'

'Yes.' She didn't even wait for him to finish. They looked at each other and laughed. 'Sorry,' she said, blushing. 'What were you going to say?'

'You seem to know already,' he said, still chuckling. 'So? Are you free on Sunday?'

'Well, I've already said "yes",' she laughed. 'And yes I am. What did you have in mind?'

'Anything. Nothing. I'd just like to see you again.'

She looked down at her boots. 'Me too,' she mumbled.

'Sorry, didn't catch that.' She looked up at him. He was still smiling. 'I'm teasing. I'll call you tomorrow,' he said, lifting a hand and brushing a strand of her hair away from her face. She felt as though her whole body was on fire. 'See you,' he said, leaning forward and giving her a quick peck on the cheek. She watched him walk down the street, her stomach churning with nerves and desire. She had never wanted anyone – anything – quite as badly as she wanted him. At that moment, she would have given anything to feel the touch of his lips on hers or the weight of his arm around her waist.

92

Tory lay in bed at two o'clock in the afternoon, unable to stop crying. Next to her were the balled-up remains of half a box of tissues. It had been one of the worst weeks of her life. Starting with the fiasco at the Royal Opera House and ending with the fight between her and Luc the previous night. She felt as though her whole life was falling apart. She could no longer concentrate on anything important and it was beginning to show. Or, as Luc had flung at her, it had been showing for quite a while. Longer than she thought. The tears welled up in her eyes again as she remembered his face, white with pain and fear. He knew something was going on. He *had* to know. How could he not?

In the weird, twisted logic of the way her mind worked these days, the triangular web she'd spun around the three of them – herself, Luc and Rob – took her mind off the catastrophe that had been the GQ awards. She'd gone home that night long after everything had been cleared up and order restored to the show, unable to think about anything other than seeing Rob. Her first thought as the canopy crashed to the ground wasn't her business, her reputation or even – she winced – whether or not anyone had been hurt. Her first thought, of course, had been Rob. She wanted nothing more than the temporary haven of his arms. It was Rob to whom she would turn. Not Luc. Not Nic, who had hovered by for the remainder of the evening. Not her father. No, it was Rob. Only Rob. The strain of the deception was slowly driving her mad. No wonder Luc had stormed out. She struggled to remember exactly what had happened.

She'd been in the kitchen, cooking. He'd come in from work, slung his briefcase on the hallway floor and burst into the kitchen with a bottle of her favourite wine. She ought to have been pleased. It was a lovely gesture – the sort of impulsive, thoughtful thing that Luc did well. He came up behind her, wrapped his arms round her, presenting her with the bottle and planting a kiss on the back of her neck. It was the kiss that had done it. She flinched, as if she'd been hit or slapped, and she felt his body stiffen with the rejection. She moved away, carrying the pan of onions or whatever it was she'd been frying, to the sink. He stayed where he was, the bottle of wine dangling uselessly in his hand.

There was silence for a few minutes. She could feel the tension emanating from him but she was too scared to turn round. It was comical, really. There she was, standing at the sink with a pan full of half-cooked onions, unable to move. He stood in the middle of the room with a bottle of wine in his hand and a look of hurt on his face, no doubt . . . but what could she do? It had been a reflex, an automatic gesture of the kind that, in the end, betrayed. Everything about Luc set her teeth on edge and the worst part of it was that she knew it wasn't his fault – but she didn't care. It was as if she were attuned to a different frequency and her body showed it. It had been weeks since they'd made love. The thought of it made her queasy and Luc, of course, knew it. She could see him struggling to understand. She could feel him making excuses for her – she was tired, busy, worried, stressed about the awards ceremony and everything that had gone wrong. She could practically feel him going through the list of excuses a woman could make, lying beside him at night, her whole body stiffened against the possibility, accidental or otherwise, that their skin might touch or that he'd put out a hand or a leg to caress her in anticipation of something more, something else. She was going crazy. That was what it felt like. A kaleidoscope of tortured, conflicting emotions – lust, anger, shame, fear and the most intense desire she'd ever experienced . . . only not for him. Not for the man she was going to marry. 'I don't understand,' he said, lifting his shoulders helplessly. 'I don't get it.'

In the end he'd stormed out. He would be back. She would force herself to apologise, make an excuse, any excuse, he might even cry a little . . . *that* brought tears of shame and remorse to her eyes. She couldn't stand to see him cry. She would kiss him, they might even make love if she could bring herself to do it . . . and the whole, horrible cycle would begin again. The only person who could end it was Rob. If he said the word, she would end it in a flash. Call off the engagement, suffer everyone's disappointment, including her parents', which seemed to be the biggest hurdle of all, but she'd be safe in the knowledge that the person who mattered most to her in the world loved her. Wanted her. But deep down, in that dark, lonely place where she'd buried the sorts of things she didn't want to confront, including the one dark, horrible secret she couldn't even bring herself to *think* about, she knew it wasn't going to happen. Rob wasn't going to stay. He couldn't even bring himself to say when they would next meet, or when he would next call. Rob could no more commit to her than she could admit to the secret that was killing her.

She lifted the pillow, aware that she was finding it difficult to breathe. She lay in bed, tears rolling down her face and a heaviness at the bottom of her heart that wouldn't go away. Just wouldn't budge.

93

'Where are we going?' Nic asked in delight. He'd arrived, exactly as promised, at ten o'clock on the dot. In a dark blue BMW sports car with the hood down. It wasn't exactly warm but at least the sun was out. She almost clapped her hands in excitement.

'To the beach,' he said, pulling away from the kerb and swinging the car round towards the main road. 'It's a bit of a trek but it's one of my favourite places in England.'

'Where?'

'Norfolk.'

'Norfolk? That's *miles* away,' she said happily. She'd have gone to Wales if he'd suggested it.

'Two hours,' he said, looking at his watch. 'If we're lucky

we'll be there before lunch. Are you warm enough?' he asked, glancing at her.

'I'm fine.' It was true. Happiness, she was rapidly discovering, had its own warmth.

'There's a blanket on the back seat if you're cold.'

'I'm fine. Is this your car?'

'No, it belongs to my brother. He's away at the moment.'

'What does he do?' she asked, suddenly hungry to know more about him.

'He works for Shell. He's into minerals and things,' he said, switching lanes smoothly, heading towards King's Cross. 'He's usually overseas. I never quite understand what he does. What about you? Brothers and sisters?'

'There's four of us,' she said carefully. 'Two brothers and a younger sister.'

'And what do they do?' he asked, mimicking her question.

'My sister's still at school. And my brothers . . . work for my dad.'

'And what does he do?'

'He's a . . . a farmer,' she said, turning her head. She was blushing fiercely. It was partly true.

'Ah. A farmer's daughter. You don't look like a farmer's daughter,' he chuckled.

'Oh? And what do they look like?' She could feel his attention on her as they waited at a stop light.

He laughed. 'You've got me there. I've never met one, to be honest.'

She felt it again – that sudden, almost painful stab of attraction. What sort of women did he know, had he met? 'So I'm the first,' she murmured. 'Lucky me.'

He touched her knee lightly. She was glad she was already sitting down. 'Ditto.'

She couldn't speak for the bolt of pleasure that flowed right through her.

The car ate up the miles to Cambridge. In no time, he branched off the M11 and headed on to the A11, then again on to a series of smaller roads until she saw they were heading towards Swaffham. She'd never been to that part of England before; the countryside was flat and rolling in the late morning sunshine. At Fakenham he turned on to a tiny road in the direction of Holkham. She'd never heard of it either. 'Where are you taking me?' she asked again.

'You'll see. We used to come here all the time when I was at Cambridge.'

Again she was gripped by an irrational jealousy. We? 'It's beautiful,' she said carefully, looking out at the field only just beginning to come into green. Some of the trees were sprouting their first blush of leaves; others were still stark and bare against the flat landscape.

'It's peaceful. Wait till you see the beach.'

They parked the car at the side of a bumpy lane that ended in a thicket of trees. There was only one other car in sight. A closed-up kiosk selling ice-cream and hotdogs stood forlornly at the entrance to a shingle path that led into the trees. She looked around. The sun was out but there was a mist that made it difficult to see beyond. He took a blanket and a small bag from the car. 'Come on,' he said, holding out his hand. She slipped her own into it. His fingers closed around hers; the feeling almost brought tears to her eyes. She couldn't remember the last time someone had held her hand.

They walked along the path in silence. The shingles gave way to a wooden boardwalk that led them through the thicket. There was a slight incline and then, suddenly, the trees fell away and the beach was before them. She stopped; it was breathtaking. A line of low, grassy dunes broke the view to the sea, which was perhaps half a mile from where they stood. To the left and right the golden, damp sand spread itself in an arc, as far as the eye could see. It was low tide; hundreds of glistening rivulets scored the sands, running towards a bigger channel that had cut its way through the dunes and ended in a small marshy lake just in front of them. 'Come on,' he said again, tugging her forward. 'This isn't even the best bit.' She allowed herself to be pulled along dreamily, avoiding the streams and the patches of sodden sand until they reached a stream that was wider and deeper than the rest. He turned to her as if to ask something, but she'd already bent down to roll up her trousers. She kicked off her shoes and waded out in front of him, barefoot, squealing at the cold. He watched her, grinning, and then did the same.

'Yep, you really are a country girl,' he said as he stepped on to dry ground at the other side. 'Most girls I know would've demanded a lift.'

'You couldn't carry me,' Nic protested, laughing.

'Oh yeah?'

She looked at him. There was a smile playing around the corner of his mouth and a mischievous look on his face. She hesitated for a second, then broke into a run just as he made a grab for her. She ran towards the dunes, her hair whipping around her face, her shoes dangling from her fingers, laughing so much she could barely see where she was going. He caught up with her easily. He was also laughing. There was a second's hesitation and then his arms went around her. He'd dropped the bag and the blanket on to the sand; there was nothing between them. His chest was warm and solid. She pressed her face into his neck, her hands already finding their way across his back. His kiss was gentle at first, lips soft, almost tentative. She opened her mouth, feeling his response through his entire body. She yielded entirely; he could have asked for anything and it would have been his.

It was he who broke away, coming up for air. He held her face in both hands, turning her head this way and that, very gently, as if he couldn't quite take all of her in. Wordlessly, they fell into step again, his arm wrapped tightly around her waist. They clambered up the first row of dunes and stood on the peak, the splendid blue line of the sea receding before them.

'Good spot?' he asked, his voice very close to her ear. She nodded. He slung the bag to the ground and opened out the blanket. The mist was beginning to lift; overhead, broken only by the flapping of gulls and the perfect, in-step formation of a triangle of migrating birds, the thin blue sky was beginning to show. She looked down at him crouched at her feet, spreading out the blanket. From the bag he produced a bottle of white wine, two plastic cups and sandwiches. She began to laugh. He was unlike anyone she'd ever met. 'What's funny?' he asked, patting the ground beside him.

She sank, cross-legged, to the ground. She wrapped her arms around her knees and turned her face towards him. 'You,' she said, still smiling. 'You think of everything.'

'Once a Boy Scout,' he said, fishing in his pocket for something. A penknife. He flicked it open and selected the corkscrew.

'Were you really a Boy Scout?' she asked curiously.

He shook his head. 'No. But Simon was.'

'Who's Simon?'

He poured them both a glass of wine. 'My brother. Well, not in the biological sense. He's an orphan. His parents died when he was quite young. He's lived with us since I was a kid, although my parents never formally adopted him.'

'That was good of them,' she murmured, taking a sip. 'Where are they now?'

'In Hampstead,' he grinned, leaning back. 'My dad made quite a lot of money in Zimbabwe, back in the eighties, but he decided to leave. We were both at school here when he made the decision. He just turned up one day and said we wouldn't be going back.'

'Gosh.' Nic couldn't think of anything to say that wouldn't involve more explanation than she was prepared for. No wonder she felt so at ease with him; their backgrounds were more similar than anyone might have thought. 'So you've never been back?'

'Oh, sure. I go back pretty often. So does my dad. He still has business interests out there and I go to see my *gogo*.'

'Where does your *gogo* live?' she asked, realising too late that she'd made a slip. How would she be expected to know what a *gogo* was? She felt herself blush all over.

He picked up on it, of course. 'D'you know what a *gogo* is?' he asked, rolling over on to his stomach.

'Er, yes. A friend of mine – she's from Zimbabwe,' she stammered. 'She always used to talk about hers.'

'So I'm not the first Zimbabwean you've met?' he said. 'Pity. I was looking forward to teaching you a thing or two.'

She felt herself blush even harder. 'Like what?' she whispered, sliding herself down until they were lying side by side, not touching, their faces close. He didn't answer, but turned sideways to let her in. They lay on the blanket, the tall grasses on either side protecting them from the wind, and began to kiss one another, slowly at first, then with steadily mounting passion. The beach was completely deserted, the only sound the occasional cry of a seagull or the whistle of the wind. This time it was she who broke away to bury her face in the smooth, warm hollow of his neck, her mouth tingling and electric from his lips. They lay together not talking, just touching. She felt as though she'd never before experienced such peace.

Suddenly the silence was broken by the shrill buzz of a phone. He swore softly under his breath and reached into his pocket. 'Didn't think there'd be any reception here,' he muttered as he pulled it out. 'Richard?' he spoke into it. A warm flush of silly relief spread through her. A man. He was talking to a man. He got to his feet suddenly, his whole body tense. She watched him move away, listening intently to whoever was on the other end. He climbed up the dune behind them. Just looking at him produced an unspecified, all-over desire in her – the dark blue V-neck pullover he wore did little to disguise the finely tuned, almost perfectly sculpted body beneath. His legs in his black jeans were strong, perfectly shaped – he had the same, rugby-player build of her brothers but with more grace, less bulk. She rolled over on to her back, staring at the sky. She wondered what the call was about. She couldn't hear him any more, just the sound of the wind skimming across the surface of the sand.

The sun was out. She closed her eyes, basking in the unfamiliar feel of warmth on her face. In a second she was seventeen again, back in Chinhoyi at the end of the summer holidays, listening to the shrieks coming from the pool, dreading the thought of leaving again. She breathed deeply. Listening to Mat, unable to respond properly for fear of letting something slip, she'd found herself reluctantly thinking about home

– Avonlea . . . about her life back there. For so long she'd simply sloughed it off; she'd pretended to herself and to everyone around her who mattered that she didn't belong there any more and that there certainly wasn't anything about it she missed. But the ease with which Mat talked about slipping back and forth, visiting his *gogo* in one breath and his life in leafy Hampstead in the other . . . she understood instinctively that he'd managed what she never had – a state of grace between two worlds, not quite belonging to either but comfortable in both. That was what he was offering her, she realised suddenly. A way to be both. She sat upright, disturbed by the intensity of longing thinking about him had suddenly produced. She had the sudden, clear sensation of rushing towards something that was bigger and more powerful than anything she'd ever felt – a brief flash of illumination into something she could only dimly grasp. Without even being aware of it, he was offering her a truth about herself. She took a deep breath, dangerously, inexplicably, close to tears.

He switched off the phone and swore violently. He could feel his heart hammering against his chest. He crouched down for a moment, trying to regain his composure. As soon as he'd seen the call was from DiAngelo, he knew that something had gone wrong. He couldn't remember the last time he'd taken a call from him on a Sunday afternoon. He scooped up a handful of loose sand, letting it trickle between his fingers. Jim Harte had got wind of what was coming. Klaassens, the man whom he'd spoken to over the phone only a fortnight ago in Casablanca, was dead. He'd been shot at close range in the shower – a supposed burglary gone wrong. The body had apparently only just been discovered because the villa he'd been staying in was flooded. Richard said the authorities thought he'd been dead for a few days.

He stood up, suddenly remembering where he was and who was waiting for him on the other side of the dune. He felt something inside him tighten at the thought of her. He'd seen it again and again that day as they drove towards Holkham. They seemed to understand each other without words, without speech. It was extraordinary. The only other person with whom he shared such a deep, unspoken bond was Simon. Ridiculous as it sounded there was something about Nic that reminded him of Simon. He couldn't put a finger on it, but it was there. She got him. Like no one else had, or could. Why was that? He shoved the phone back in his pocket and began to walk back towards her. He cursed DiAngelo and Jim Harte and the whole fucking circus. He would have to be back in London that night for a meeting with Sir Winston. Klaassens was the man on whom the entire story depended. He was the one who'd gone after the truth, and now he was dead. A chill ran down his spine that had nothing to do with the cool, early-afternoon breeze. He realised, as he climbed over the dune and saw Nic lying on her back, her eyes closed and her hands clasped loosely above her head, that he wanted nothing more in the world at that moment than to be near her, inside her . . . it was years since he'd felt such longing. Not since Tanja. And the fact that he could say her name, even to himself, was an indication of just how far he'd come.

They were both quiet on the long drive back to London. The mist that had burned off partially by the open sea was rolling back in over the countryside by the time they neared the outskirts of Cambridge. DiAngelo's phone call had spoiled what had otherwise been the most enjoyable day of his life since . . . well, since he could remember. She was sensitive to the change in his mood, seemingly content to listen to the assortment of CDs that Simon left in the glove compartment, turning her head to smile at him when he put his hand on her knee, the only reminder of the extraordinary surge of feeling that had swept over them both back there. He liked that about her; there was a quiet generosity in her that he responded to. Tanja would have been a completely different story. Tanja *was* a completely different story, he reminded himself. She'd eaten away at him in a way that had attracted him at first – he'd mistaken her passionate, obsessive interest in everything he did, said or thought, as a sign of the strength of her feelings. It came to him later – much later – that it was simply the way she was. She couldn't ever let anything be. She was dramatic in a way that he later understood to be the source of her unhappiness; she was desperately, obsessively insecure. She had no sense of proportion; everything was overblown. Living with her had been a long, sometimes tedious, sometimes frenetic, roller-coaster ride.

Nic, he sensed, was constructed entirely differently. Again it came to him that there was something about her quiet sensitivity that made him think of Simon. They were both watchful but not predatory, operating on instinct when they had to, accustomed perhaps to being at the whim of others over whom they had little control. Simon's biological father had been a dreadful bully. He wondered briefly if in Nic's case the same applied. He tightened his grip on her thigh. She responded by covering his hand with her own. Her touch was light, not possessive. Just enough pressure to acknowledge his claim. He found himself smiling, despite the raging whirlwind of thoughts going round in his head.

He dropped her off just before five, apologising for having ruined the day. She leaned on the car door, her hair wonderfully tousled from the sea breeze, touching his forearm which was resting on the door. 'Don't be silly,' she said quietly. 'It didn't ruin anything. It was really special.'

He hesitated. 'I've got to go into a meeting in a couple of hours. I don't know how long it'll last. If it's not too late, can I call you?'

She straightened up and flashed him a cheeky grin. 'Ball's in your court,' she said, reminding him of the first time they'd met. 'You know where I am.'

He watched her walk up the path to her door. She was wearing a pair of those loose cargo pants that all the girls were wearing that year and she'd pulled a white sweater over the grey tank top she'd worn at the beach. A great ass, he noticed, grinning to himself. She turned at the door, gave him a quick smile and disappeared inside. He'd been right the first time. Cool. But with a surprising, hidden warmth. Self-possessed. It was perhaps that, more than anything else, that attracted him, drawing him in. He realised, as soon as he turned the car round and headed back up the road alone, that he missed her. Already.

Sir Winston's London home was on the top floor of a handsome ochre-and-white brick building on Dacre Street, next to St James's Park. After rushing back to Simon's for a quick shower and shave, Mat made it back across the river for seven. A doorman rode up in the lift with him, face carved from stone. He was ushered in by a uniformed maid who took his bag and jacket. From the enormous living room there was a magnificent view of the Houses of Parliament and, just to the right, of the river. He was shown through to the study, where two other men he didn't recognise were already seated. All three had tumblers of whisky and ice in front of them.

'Ah, Mat. You're here. Sorry about dragging you away from your Sunday. Richard said you were up in Cambridge.' Sir Winston eased himself out of his leather chesterfield and held out a hand. In the other he held a fat, pungent cigar. The room reeked of wealth.

'Er, yes. Holkham.'

'Splendid, splendid.' He turned to the other two men, who were eyeing Mat with frank curiosity. 'I suppose you must know that part of the world quite well?' he continued smoothly, talking to the other two. Mat nodded. 'History. King's,' Sir Winston said as an aside, puffing on his cigar.

'Really?' One of the men looked up, a fleeting expression of surprise on his face. Mat ignored him. He'd been through the little rigmarole too many times to remember. It was boring.

'And you are . . . ?' the other man looked at Mat suspiciously.

'Oh, haven't I made the introductions?' Sir Winston said, putting down his glass. 'How remiss of me. I do apologise.' Mat was silent. Sir Winston knew damn well he hadn't introduced him. He'd seen how much Sir Winston had enjoyed the look of surprise on their faces as he'd walked through the door. *I'm a maverick too*, he seemed to be saying. *I know all sorts of people*. Mat sighed. This too was a well-known rigmarole. 'Mat's the author of the report you've just read,' Sir Winston said smoothly. 'He works for Richard DiAngelo in New York.'

'Oh. I see. Well, excellent report, Mat,' the sandy-haired one said. 'I'm Barry French. Senior Counsel at Matherby's.'

'Company lawyers,' Sir Winston interjected. 'And that's Tom Roberts. Senior partner at Shearson's.' Mat shook hands with both men.

'Have a seat, Mat,' Sir Winston said affably. 'Whisky? Single or blend?'

'Single, please.'

'Good man.' He ambled over to the console and poured him a generous measure. 'Richard's filled you in, I take it.'

Mat nodded. 'Thanks,' he said, taking the glass.

'Tricky situation,' Sir Winston said, raising his own to his lips.

'Not necessarily,' Mat said after a moment. The three men looked at him expectantly. 'I mean, it's a little out of character for Harte – well, from what I know of him. He's obviously rattled. Can I speak candidly?'

Sir Winston nodded. 'Absolutely. Anything you say here is off the record.'

'Harte's panicking. Klaassens was obviously a hit and it's clear Harte was afraid of what he'd go on to expose. From the point of view of the AGM, however, it's a silly mistake. The papers are going to be full of it – a *supposed* connection, even if it can't be proved. It's spectacularly bad timing, if nothing else. But he ordered it. Question is, why?'

'Share prices are going to nosedive,' Roberts interjected smugly. 'The shareholders are nervous. Understandably so, if you ask me.'

'Harte's got one last trick up his sleeve,' Sir Winston said irritably. 'And that's the reason I've called you all here.'

'Which is—?'

'The Duke of Rothermere. Second cousin to the Queen. He's bringing out a full statement of support for Harte on

Thursday. Nicholas Oliver at *The Times* rang me this morning. They're planning on turning the whole fucking story round, making it seem as though he's being persecuted. A witch-hunt. Orchestrated by the Establishment. We've always had it in for him, or at least that's how he sees it. Whatever, it'll buy him the time he needs. The majority of his shareholders are so greedy and gullible they'll buy whatever Rothermere says. He's royalty, after all.'

There was silence in the room. Even Mat was surprised. How the hell had Harte managed to pull it off? How on earth had he got to the Duke of Rothermere, whoever he was? He was beginning to have an inkling of why he'd been asked to the meeting. A few minutes later, his suspicions were confirmed.

'You've got ten days, Mat. Find out whatever it is that Harte has over that bastard Rothermere and let me have it. I'll be at my home in Cape Town over the next couple of weeks. Richard'll know how to get hold of me. I want that man stopped dead in his tracks.'

94

Caryn woke first, pulled out of sleep by the radio alarm, set as usual to the Sunday-morning news. She heard the familiar two-tone chime and was just about to reach across the body of the man next to her when he caught her hand and gently pushed it away. So he wasn't asleep? She glanced at him nervously. It was the fifth time he'd slept over at hers, and she still couldn't get used to the sight. Or the touch, or the scent or anything about this complicated, complex man who still hadn't told her his real name but didn't seem unduly bothered by the fact. She felt his hand slide across her stomach, coming to rest on the tender skin just above her groin, sending palpitations of desire coursing through her. She lay beside him, her whole body tensed and waiting, but his hand didn't move. The plummy voice of the newscaster washed over them but she wasn't really listening. She had fallen, hard. The fact that she knew so little about him was driving her insane.

'In a statement issued today by Moroccan police, it was confirmed that the body of a man found in a rented villa in Casablanca yesterday was indeed the body of Herman Klaassens, the man at the centre of the allegations of corruption and fraud against RhoMine CEO, Jim Harte, that are threatening to spark a leadership challenge amongst RhoMine shareholders at the company's AGM next Monday. Harte's lawyers . . .' She stiffened and then sat bolt upright. 'That's Nic's father,' she said incredulously. She gathered the sheet to her naked breasts. 'That's Nic's dad. I didn't know he was in trouble—'

'People like that are always in trouble,' Charlie murmured drowsily. 'It's what they do.'

'Poor Nic,' Caryn said, sinking back into the pillows as his hand pulled her back down.

He ran his palm over her nipple, already hardening in pleasure. He gripped her arm, bringing her easily round so that she lay on top of him. He entered her slowly, his eyes never leaving her face. 'Poor nothing,' he murmured, moving his hips to meet hers. He slid a hand down her back, his fingers digging into the soft flesh of her buttocks as he rose and fell, his breath coming quicker and quicker. 'They get exactly what they deserve,' he whispered, pushing against her one last time, sending them both over the edge.

It was some time before she could speak again. Something in his voice had disturbed her, but it was all caught up in the exquisite pleasure of the moment and she couldn't really focus on it. She was left only with the draining sensation of her climax and the feeling that something, yet again, wasn't quite right.

He left just before lunchtime. She was getting used to the leaving signs – not just the physical ones. There was the slow withdrawal from her as he steadied himself to meet whatever it was that awaited him outside her flat. The high, passionate emotions that he revealed whilst making love seemed utterly alien to the quiet, focused person who left with a quick brush of his lips against her cheek and no word as to when, or if, he'd be back.

'Are you . . . will you be gone for a long time?' she asked, unable to stop herself. He paused in the act of lacing up his boots.

'Maybe,' he said carefully. 'It's hard to say. Why?'

She paused. 'Just . . . just wondering,' she said lamely. Although she hardly knew him, she sensed that pushing him was not a good idea. Not unless she wanted him to go. Permanently.

'I'll give you a call,' he said, standing up. His tall, broad frame filled her doorway almost entirely. Even when he was still, there was a palpable air of moving energy around him. And when he was gone, it was hard to believe he'd ever been.

She nodded, trying desperately hard to play it cool, to keep a lid on things, especially her emotions. 'See you,' she said, getting up from the table. She heard the door click gently behind him – and he was gone. She took the remains of their breakfast into the kitchen and stood at the sink, watching him cross the street, his duffel bag slung across his shoulder, hands in his pockets, until he disappeared from sight. She filled a glass of water from the tap and stood there, sipping it slowly, for a long time.

95

After her first meeting with Nic Harte, Estelle found it hard to focus on anything else. She still couldn't get over how easy it was going to be. Nic was flattered by the attention, hard as it was to believe. She'd felt a momentary surge of dislike for her as soon as she saw her – but that had quickly disappeared to be replaced by a strange sort of contempt. At first Estelle was surprised . . . astonished, even. Of all the traits she'd expected to find in Jim Harte's daughter – her *sister*, she kept having to remind herself – doubt wasn't one of them. Aside from the open admiration she was used to when women encountered *her*, she'd seen a strange longing in Nic's eyes to please, to be liked, accepted. Where had that come from? If she'd thought to find any sibling resemblance, there was none, or at least none she could see. The girl obviously took after her mother. Although – she frowned as she brushed her teeth – wasn't there something, perhaps, some faint resemblance around the eyes? She tried to recall Nic's face. She intended to become close to Nic Harte. *Very* close. So close, in fact, that she would be the last person Nic would suspect. She smiled again. Revenge, she was beginning to find out, was a purer, more satisfying emotion than she'd ever suspected. In fact, it was downright difficult to distinguish it from love. She spat into the sink with force.

She walked over to the dressing room and flung open the door. She had a lunchtime appointment with Jean-Claude, a new client whom she'd met twice before with slightly unusual tastes. He liked to look. That was all. Estelle didn't mind. In fact, she quite enjoyed the elaborate ritual of getting dressed in order to be undressed and admired. She'd gone shopping at Agent Provocateur the day before and staggered out with more bags than a woman could possibly carry. She'd spent half the evening organising and stowing the exquisite purchases in her wardrobe. Pleasurable beyond belief. It helped ease the tight ache that had lodged itself permanently in her chest ever since she'd run out of Jim Harte's office.

For today's meeting she selected a red corset with a discreet little frill at the bust, and fourteen – she counted them – mother-of-pearl buttons down the front. It would take Jean-Claude a while to undo them all, she thought, amused. Red cami-knickers? Or black silk? She chose the black. They were cut high across the bottom – she slid them on and swivelled to admire her rear view. Not a dimple, despite the fact she'd never set foot in a gym. Finally, a pair of fishnet hold-ups. She'd always disliked the whole stockings-and-suspenders nonsense . . . all that fumbling around whilst all they really wanted was to take them off. She bent down and pulled out her favourite pair of patent black high-heel pumps. Perfect. She almost clapped her hands in glee. Jean-Claude would *die* . . . well, hopefully not literally. She'd heard from Olga, one of the newcomers to the fold, that it had happened to her once . . . *not* a pleasant sight. Or weight, she'd added coyly, sending everyone into a fit of giggles.

She took everything off, laying the items carefully on the bed. Time for a shower and a proper, full English breakfast. She'd have Petko stop at the Ritz. With any luck she'd be back from her afternoon appointment by four p.m. Plenty of time for her to work out what to do next. It had been almost three weeks since their first meeting – just the right amount of time for the boundaries between them to have been subtly established. Nic had rung a day or so later and Estelle had deliberately ignored the call. They would meet on *her* terms, not Nic's. That was the first rule. By now, she knew, Nic would be disappointed and unsure. Had she rung too early? Was Estelle too busy? Why hadn't she rung back? Yes, she smiled to herself as she stepped into the shower. Nic Harte was asking the questions and she, Estelle Harte, had the answers. Estelle Harte. She repeated the name out loud, savouring the taste and feel of it on her tongue.

Nic was sitting on her own in the canteen, ostensibly going over her notes from the morning's lecture but having difficulty concentrating on anything other than Mat, when someone flopped down in the chair opposite. She looked up. It was Estelle. She was surprised and pleased to see her. Estelle smiled at her.

'Hey,' she said breezily, 'how's it?'

Nic was suddenly overcome by the greeting. It was exactly what Shaun and Patrick said to her on the odd occasion they met or spoke over the phone. *Howzit?* 'Oh, hi,' she said, trying not to stare or sound too pleased. A pale pink halter-neck silk blouse, tight blue jeans and heels. Silver hoop earrings dangled from each ear. It was impossible not to stare. The girl had *style*. In buckets. 'Did you get my message?' she asked, oddly nervous. Estelle was regarding her indulgently.

'Yeah. Sorry I didn't call back. I had to move out. I've been staying with friends. Well, you know how it goes.'

'Oh. Wh-where are you staying now?' Nic was embarrassed. Having nice clothes didn't necessarily mean she had a lot of money. Or *any* money, for that matter.

'With another friend. Actually, he's a photographer. He's going to take some shots,' she said happily, lighting up. 'Thanks for the numbers, by the way. I'll give them a ring. Anyhow, I was just passing by,' she said, waving the smoke away from Nic's face. 'Just thought I'd drop in and see if I could spot you.'

'Oh. That's nice of you. Actually, today's the only day I'm here. I'm at work the rest of the week.'

'Oh? Where d'you work again? Didn't you say last time? A fashion magazine or something?'

'No, *ArtWeekly*. I'm the features editor,' Nic said shyly. It still sounded strange to her ears.

'Wow. Sounds impressive. Listen, I was just thinking. What're you doing on Friday night?' Estelle asked suddenly.

'Er, nothing,' Nic said, pleased.

'How about meeting up at the 101 Club?'

'The 101 Club?'

Estelle looked at her in surprise. 'Don't tell me you don't know what the 101 Club is. You've never been?'

Nic felt her cheeks turn red. 'No—'

'I thought *every* Zimbabwean knew about it.'

'Er, no. I guess not . . .' Nic gave a short, embarrassed laugh. 'I don't know many – *any* – Zimbabweans in London, actually.' She thought of Mat; a sweet, sharp thrill ran through her. Perhaps she should ask him to come along?

'You don't know any other Zimbabweans? You're kidding, right?'

Nic felt her cheeks get even hotter. 'Um, no. We . . . well, we left a while ago. My dad keeps pretty much to himself . . .' Nic said lamely.

'God, you haven't *lived*. They play the *best* music. D'you like to dance?'

'I . . . well, yeah. I guess so.'

'So let's go on Friday. You'd really like it, I'm sure.'

'Why not?' Nic said, suddenly feeling rather reckless. 'Where did you say it was?'

'In the basement at the High Commission.'

'Er, where's that?'

Estelle stared at her. 'It's in Trafalgar Square. Next to South Africa House.'

'Oh. Can I . . . could I bring someone along?'

' 'Course you can. Who?'

Nic's blush deepened. 'Just someone I met recently. Actually, *he's* Zimbabwean. But he doesn't live in London.'

'Black? White?'

'Er, black, actually.'

Estelle raised an eyebrow but said nothing. 'So, Friday, then. He'll think it's really cool, I promise you. Meet you there?'

'Sounds good,' Nic said happily, a warm glow of pleasure beginning to spread through her. Mat would be impressed. She hesitated. 'Could . . . could I ask you to do me a favour?' She looked at Estelle quickly.

'Sure. What?'

'This guy that I'm bringing along. He . . . he doesn't know who I am. Could you . . . could you *not* tell him I'm from Zimbabwe too? I haven't really told him anything about me.' She gave a short, nervous laugh. 'I will. Soon. But just not right now.'

Estelle shrugged. 'No problem. It's none of my business what you tell him,' she said casually. 'Sure.'

'Thanks.' Nic wasn't quite sure how to take her response.

'OK, I'd better get a move on.' Estelle stubbed out her cigarette and stood up. 'Aren't you working?' Nic asked, getting up herself.

'Oh, no. I gave up *that* job. It was shit. Something better'll come along soon. See you Friday.' She fluttered her fingers at Nic and walked off, a dozen pairs of eyes watching her unbelievably pert bottom in those skintight jeans and those legs that never seemed to end.

★

It was just getting better and better, Estelle thought to herself gleefully as she walked away. A man on the scene — recent, by the sounds of things, and already she had something to hide. Well, Nic Harte's secrets were her weapons. Already she could see how easy it was going to be to reel the bitch in. This man, whoever he was, was in for a little surprise. She was aware that the line separating Jim Harte from his daughter was already beginning to blur. She'd started off thinking he was the one she wanted to punish — oh, she didn't care *how* she did it, but *he'd* been the target, not Nic. She would use Nic to get to him; that's the way she'd planned it. Now, however, things were beginning to change. There was something about Nic — the cool haughtiness that gave way almost immediately to pathetic doubt — that set her teeth on edge. Sitting there with her expensive leather bag and her groomed and polished fingernails . . . *she'd* never had to do what she, Estelle, had done. She'd never gone without, never had to worry about a roof over her head or putting food on the table. She'd had everything Jim Harte's money could buy whilst she, Estelle, had none. Nothing. No, Nic Harte would never have to open her legs the way she'd done; never have to endure someone's fat, pudgy hands clawing at her clothes, slobbering over her breasts, forcing himself on and into her . . . she stopped, suddenly aware she was almost running. She slowed down, avoiding the curious glances of passers-by until her breathing had returned to normal and the flush had receded from her cheeks.

96

Mat was busy; she could hear it in his voice when he rang. He was guarded about what he was doing. He was working on something important but he couldn't really say much more. It would be over in a couple of weeks. There was a slight pause.

Might she like to go somewhere with him, perhaps, when it was over? Could she take time off? Nic had to hold the receiver against her chest for fear of shrieking with joy.

She told him about the 101 Club on Friday night. She heard his slow, deep chuckle. 'Yeah . . . sure. Haven't been there in years. How do *you* know about it?'

'Oh, this friend of mine goes all the time,' she said airily, grinning to herself. Estelle was right. He thought it cool. Then she felt a sudden pang – Estelle was gorgeous . . . he wouldn't . . . would he?

'Male?' he asked, reassuringly brusque.

'No, a *girl*friend.' She laughed. 'Shall I meet you there?'

'Sounds good. Ten?'

'Perfect.'

Almost as soon as she'd put the receiver down, the phone rang again. She picked it up, smiling. 'Miss me already?' she asked teasingly.

'Nic?' It was her stepmother. Molly's puzzled voice came down the line. Nic nearly dropped the phone.

'Molly? Sorry, I thought it was someone else.'

'Who?'

'None of your business. What d'you want?'

Molly gave a silly, theatrical sigh. '*I* don't want anything, Nicola. It's your father. He's got an important meeting next week, Monday. He's asked for you all to be at the house that morning. Shaun and Patrick are flying over.'

'Next Monday? I can't. I've got college on Mondays.'

'It's not a request,' Molly said, pausing meaningfully. 'You're to look your best.'

'Why?' Jim had never asked her to attend anything.

'I don't know why,' Molly said huffily. 'We've all got to be there, that's all. Jessica's coming up from school.'

Nic sighed. 'All right. What time?'

'We've all to be there by nine.'

'Fine.' She put the phone down before Molly could say anything further. Nineteen years on and there was still no one who could wind her up like her stepmother. She wandered into her bedroom. Look her best? What did that mean? A suit?

Mat was getting nowhere. It was as if a wall had been erected around Edward Howard-Spencer-Stewart, the twelfth Duke of Rothermere. The unimportant details – who had preceded him, what his other titles were, where he went to school, whom he'd married, and so on – all of that was readily available and easily accessed. There was nothing in his background that would suggest why or how he'd developed a business relationship with Jim Harte. Money? Mat was sceptical. The duke was ranked ninety-fifth in the previous year's *Sunday Times Rich List*. There was always the possibility that his association with RhoMine had helped put him there, but Mat doubted it. Harte himself was ranked further down the list. It didn't make sense. The Duke of Rothermere had been married three times; two of the marriages had produced children. A girl and two boys. None of those seemed in any way to be connected to the Hartes. So what was it? It didn't help that Richard and Sir Winston were constantly on the line. *What have you found? Any leads? Step on it, Mat – we're running out of time.* Each time he put down the phone more exasperated than before. He knew he was running out of time. But what could he do? The connection simply refused to come.

It was on his third day in the British Library, going through the minutes of a series of previous RhoMine AGM meetings, that something caught his eye. He read through the minutes twice, made a few notes and picked up his bag. As soon as he was outside the building, he rang an old contact, a former professor of his at Cambridge. By three that afternoon he was on a train heading north, on his way to meet him.

Professor Nathan Schmidt was as he remembered; a little older, now completely white-haired, but possessing the same genial, gentle smile which masked one of the most formidable intellects Mat had ever encountered. His work on the Roths-childs, the great banking dynasty, remained one of Mat's favour-ite historical reads. He welcomed Mat into his rooms in Bodley's

Court, one of the oldest parts of the college. It still smelled exactly the same, Mat thought as he followed the now elderly Fellow through to his study. From the sash window he could see across the lawn to the river.

'Tea, Matari?' Professor Schmidt asked, picking up a little brass bell on his desk. Mat smiled. Professor Schmidt had never called him Mat. *Why should I? It's not your name.* He'd spent many an afternoon in the exact same spot on the other side of the enormous but tidy red-leather desk, listening, arguing, debating . . . he was suddenly twenty again, in awe of the man sitting opposite.

'That would be nice, sir.'

'So . . .' Professor Schmidt said when the departmental secretary had closed the door behind her. 'What's this all about, hmm?' His voice still carried with it the faintest trace of Vienna, where he had been born.

Mat gave him a quick outline of what he was looking for. He pulled his notebook out of his bag. 'There was something . . . I noticed in the minutes of one of the early RhoMine AGMs back in the eighties – a purchase was mentioned. A copper mine in Zambia. It seems Harte was so convinced by the engineer's reports that he bought out the other two competitors who were also bidding for the rights. But he didn't have the money. He went to Kleinworts, the investment bankers, whom he convinced to make the loan. I noticed that Edward Howard-Spencer-Stewart was a non-executive director of the bank at the time. He's not related to the Kleinwort family in any way and I just wondered . . . isn't that a little odd? I seem to remember in one of your lectures you saying that the reason banks like Rothschilds, Warburgs and Kleinworts were so successful was because they rarely let outsiders in. The only true family banks left standing, you used to say. So it struck me as a little strange.'

Professor Schmidt nodded. 'Correct. But, if my memory serves me right, Spencer-Stewart is *married* to a Kleinwort. I think you'll find that his third wife is the eldest daughter of Marguerite Herzog – second or third cousin to Nathan

Kleinwort. He would have been given the directorship on the basis of that marriage, I suspect.'

Mat nodded. 'But how did Harte get involved? How did he persuade Spencer-Stewart to back him when no one else would? And how did he get away with not paying it back?'

Professor Schmidt sighed. 'There's always a reason.' He picked up his cup. His hand shook a little but otherwise his voice was steady and clear. 'Again, if my memory serves me right, one of Marguerite's daughters was from a previous marriage.' He frowned, trying to remember the details. 'Spencer-Stewart adopted her, I believe, when he married her mother. Her name . . . it'll come to me in a moment . . . yes, Molly Crenshaw. I don't believe she ever took the name Howard-Spencer-Stewart. At least, not officially.'

'Jim Harte's current wife,' Mat said slowly, incredulously. 'Molly Crenshaw.'

'*Ja, ja.*' Professor Schmidt drained his cup. 'She does make a lovely cup of tea,' he said fondly. 'She's new.'

Mat grinned. In his younger days, Nathan Schmidt had been known to hurl teapots at the back of departing secretaries. He was particular about his tea. Mat put away his notebook, glad he'd made the journey. There was more to the relationship between the Duke of Rothermere and Jim Harte than met the eye, but at least he now knew where it had begun. 'Professor, I can't thank you enough,' he said, getting to his feet. 'And it was good to see you.'

'Ah, *ja*. One last time before I kick the bucket, *hein*?' He chuckled and leaned back in his chair. 'Likewise, Matari. I had always hoped you might come into the fold, one day,' he said, waving his arm at the room stacked with books and the gardens beyond the window. 'To teach, research perhaps? Always thought you were wasting a perfectly good mind out there. The *business* world. Hmph.'

'Oh, it's not so bad, sir,' Mat said, picking up his coat. 'It has its moments. Next week, for example.'

'One last thing, Matari.' Professor Schmidt looked up at him. His blue eyes, almost hidden by his white, bushy eyebrows, were twinkling. 'Might be relevant, I don't know. Harte's second wife, Sarah Parker, had a godfather. Someone rather well connected. I believe you've already met.'

'Who?' Mat paused.

'Your boss. Sir Winston Freedland. I've been keeping an eye on you, you see. I've a feeling the whole thing's going to get rather nasty. Have a safe trip back, won't you?'

He wrote for almost fifteen hours straight, pausing only to eat and drink, occasionally stretching his legs. When he was done, he emailed the draft straight to DiAngelo and then went to bed, whereupon he slept for another fifteen hours, emerging dazed but rested into the sunlight of a Friday afternoon. He was meeting Nic that evening. Simon was away – he vaguely remembered him saying he'd be back at the weekend. Where was it he'd gone? He couldn't remember.

He left the flat and walked down Petworth Street to Battersea Bridge Road, then cut across the side streets to Battersea Church Road. He bought the papers, had lunch in a small café on the square and relaxed for the first time in months. Professor Schmidt was right – things had taken a deeper, more vengeful turn. The earlier admiration he'd felt for Jim Harte had disappeared. A less scrupulous, more calculating image was emerging in which Harte seemed to stop at nothing. Murder, fraud, theft – and now marriage. All three of his wives had provided something other than the usual romantic obligations – from what he was beginning to understand of the man, he hadn't a romantic bone in his body. Yes, it was going to get ugly. He finished his sandwich and stood up. He wasn't sure which meeting made him more nervous – his date with Nic that evening or Monday's showdown at the Ritz.

'Why don't you come with me?' The words left his mouth before he could stop them. He wasn't sure who was more surprised – Caryn or him.

'Come with you?' Caryn repeated woodenly.

'Yeah. I'm only going for a couple of days. Three, four at the most. I bet you've never been to Cape Town before—'

'I've never been anywhere before. Apart from England. I've never even been to Scotland.'

He stared at her. 'What are you talking about?'

'I've never been in an aeroplane before. I've never been anywhere.'

'Holidays?'

She pulled a face. 'Never been on one.'

He began to laugh. 'That is . . . that's unbelievable. Well, in that case, you've *got* to come along. I can't believe you've never left the country.'

'I . . . I don't have a passport,' she stammered, excitement already beginning to build in her chest.

'Doesn't take long. Give me your documents and I'll get someone to sort it out.'

Caryn looked at him incredulously. Just like that. *I'll get someone to sort it out.* She knew she ought to stop, slow down, protect herself . . . but how did you protect yourself from someone like Charlie? How could you? He was extraordinary. She knew next to nothing about him – Christ, she didn't even know his real name! – and yet there was something so utterly capable and reassuring about him that anything could happen, literally anything, and she understood she'd still be safe. Not the sort of safety she'd taught herself. There was nothing of the careful planning, steady employment, always making sure she had enough to cover the odd uncertainties that life threw up, about him.

Just the other day, Brian had rung asking if he could borrow a hundred pounds to go to Glastonbury with some of his school-friends. She couldn't explain to anyone how proud she was that he always had her to turn to, safe in the knowledge that she'd never let him down. Brian had her, Alice had her . . . everyone depended on her, and most of her energy and drive went into making sure their trust was never displaced. She'd never had anyone to depend on herself. That possibility seemed about as remote as going on holiday – and yet now, in the space of less than five minutes, this man with whom she was having the strangest, most complicated relationship of her life was offering both. No strings. He asked for very little from her and occasionally offered something back.

'H-how much d'you think it would cost?' she asked timidly.

He laughed again. 'No, you idiot. I'm paying. I'd hardly invite you on holiday and then make you pay. Christ, what sort of person d'you think I am?'

'But—'

'Look, it's really no big deal,' he said, yawning. 'If you want to come, the offer's there.' He stood up. 'I'd better get moving. I've got a meeting in an hour. I need to be in Cape Town by Wednesday. If you do decide to come, we'd need to get moving.'

'I . . . I'm coming,' Caryn said, scrambling to her feet. 'What d'you need?'

'Birth certificate, I think. I'll ask Jenny to give you a ring.'

Jenny? The name sent a tremor through her. Who was Jenny?

'OK,' she said in a small voice. She couldn't help it. He gave so little away.

He smiled, as though he'd read her mind. 'Travel agent. She handles that sort of stuff for me.' He picked up his rucksack and walked to the door. 'See you.' And he was gone again.

Outside, walking back down Ladbroke Grove, he couldn't quite believe what he'd just done. He'd asked Caryn to come with him. Had he *completely* lost his mind? He shook his head, trying to clear it. Everything was topsy-turvy. His world was starting to slide. He'd told Mat he'd been gone for a couple of weeks. After his last job, he ought to have returned to London, to his own flat. He just couldn't face Mat. He'd checked into a hotel instead. He'd started sleeping with the young assistant director of a company who were doing a film about blood diamonds. No one had any clue who he really was. No one on the project knew his name. Not even Caryn. Worst of all, he'd grown to like her. *Really* like her. She was easy to talk to, comfortable, not prying. She seemed happy enough to take whatever it was he felt he could give. But what *could* he give her? What could he give anyone? He shook his head again. He was treading on very thin ice.

He stuck his hand out for a cab. He was due to meet Harte's lawyer, Ogilvy, at his club in thirty minutes to go over the details of this latest job. He had a feeling he wasn't going to like it.

It took Jenny less than forty-eight hours to organise a passport. Caryn stared at the burgundy cover in disbelief. Getting a week off work was easy – in the three years she'd been at Lighthouse, she'd never really taken a break. A couple of days here and there, *never* a week. Filming on *Blood Diamonds* was due to end with Charlie's interview on Sunday. Martin was pleased with the way it had all gone. She deserved a break, he said. Where was she going? Somewhere nice, he hoped. Caryn mumbled something about Spain and hurried out of the room before anyone could ask her anything further. Charlie would pick her up at five on Monday; their flight was at eight. The following morning they'd be landing in Cape Town, literally at the bottom of the world. She was so excited she couldn't sleep. He'd asked her not to tell anyone, least of all her best friends. He mumbled something about it being highly irregular to take friends along, but she simply couldn't keep it to herself. She told Nic instead that she was going to Cape Town for work. Nic was suitably impressed and delighted and gave her a long list of must-sees and must-dos. Tory was equally impressed, and said she'd give anything to come along. Caryn dashed out at lunchtime and ran all the way up the road to the shops along Notting Hill. She'd never been shopping for holiday clothes before – by the end of her lunch break she had no fewer than two swimsuits, three long, floaty kaftan-type garments, a new pair of jeans and several T-shirts. 'But it's winter out there,' Nic pointed out when she rang her later that afternoon. 'It'll be freezing.'

Caryn refused to listen. Winter or not, it would be warmer than here, she insisted.

'Don't say I didn't warn you,' Nic said dryly. 'Where are you staying?'

'Um, I'm not sure. Martin knows,' Caryn said, turning bright red. She hated lying.

'Well, send us a postcard, won't you? And wish me luck.'

'Why?'

'My *date*, silly. I'm meeting Mat tonight.'

'Oh, yeah. Good luck.' She hung up the phone, smiling, and glanced at the calendar on her desk. In three – no, four – days' time, she would be on a beach somewhere outside Cape Town, having flown across Europe and Africa, basking in the sun. She had to bite down on her lip to stop herself from squealing out loud.

Estelle raised one long, soapy leg out of the water, admiring its shape and form. She'd cancelled her client that evening, begging the beginnings of a cold, and had been in the bath for almost an hour, soaking and soaping herself in preparation for the evening ahead. She intended to cause the maximum damage possible with Nic Harte and her date. Nothing too obvious . . . she didn't want to scare Nic off. Just a little bit of mild flirtation – enough to make sure he noticed her, no more. She wanted him to remember her when she took her next step, whatever that might be. Her plans for the Harte family would take a while to mature. She intended to be there to witness the whole, spectacular crash. She felt her stomach tensing in anticipation. She hauled herself out of the water, wrapped herself in her thick terry-towelling bathrobe and walked barefoot to the dressing room. Nic Harte was hardly ugly – she'd have to put some effort into making sure she looked twice as good as her.

By nine-thirty, she was ready. A pair of faded blue jeans, a long-sleeved silky top with a plunging neckline; black, high-heeled stilettos and a thick, black choker at her slender neck. Her hair was piled high on her head; long, wavy blonde tendrils fell across her face and cascaded down her back. Smoky eyes, scarlet lips . . . the works. She looked hot. Nic Harte's date, whoever he was, wouldn't be able to keep his eyes off her. That alone was bound to ruin her night.

She picked up her purse, blasted her neck and cleavage with

one last squirt of Mitsouko and switched off the lights. She ran down the stairs, making sure no one else in the mews was looking – she was supposed to be lying in bed, rubbing her chest with Vicks – and walked quickly across the cobblestones. A minute later she was in the back of a black cab, speeding towards Trafalgar Square.

The club was just beginning to warm up as she pushed her way through the crowd gathered at the bar. Heads turned as she strolled past. Most of those present wouldn't have known that she was just another pretty coloured girl from Arcadia. That aspect of her had been buried long ago. A few looked at her curiously; her clothes alone made her stand out from the crowd. The 101 Club was a favourite haunt of Africans from almost every part of the continent, not just Zimbabwe – not that Estelle had been there often. Jonathan Marimba had brought her once or twice when she'd first arrived. To her, regardless of how she'd sold it to Nic Harte, it was a place that reminded her of something she'd rather forget. Too cheap, too loud . . . too African.

She peered at her watch in the darkness. It was almost ten-fifteen. Nic Harte and her mystery Zimbabwean would be there any moment. She pulled out her lip gloss, touched up her lips and ordered a rum and Coke. The barman slid the glass across the counter, his eyes silently appraising her. She ignored him and turned back to look at the already crowded dance floor. The music was beginning to warm up as well. Old, barely recognised favourites – Makeba, Dibango, Yvonne Chaka-Chaka and Brenda Fassie. She sipped slowly, the pulsating beat sliding into her veins along with the jagged crystals of ice and the smooth, syrupy warmth of the rum.

'*There* you are!'

She swivelled round on her seat and nearly choked. Nic had indeed arrived, followed by a tall, *extremely* good-looking man. 'Hi,' she said, quickly recovering. 'Thought you'd never get here,' she said, flashing them both her widest smile. She saw, with an immediate flash of annoyance, that he wasn't as impressed as he should have been.

'We got held up at the door. Seems like the whole world's trying to get in.' She turned to look at the man standing next to her. Even in her heels, he seemed to tower above them both. 'This is Mat,' she said, not without a touch of pride. 'And this is my friend Estelle.' She presented them to each other, her date and her friend, willing them to like and appreciate one another. Estelle, with her nose for such things, saw straight through to the fervent hope that they'd get along.

'Hi, Mat,' she said, giving him another high-wattage smile, wondering if she'd perhaps misread him.

'Hi.' He held out a hand. Estelle took it, unnerved by the tiny flicker in his eyes that let her know she hadn't. She saw at once that he was someone she would have to be on guard against. It irritated her enormously. His hand was strong and firm. She resisted the temptation to let her fingers rest within fractionally longer than was necessary. He would have to be won over. Slowly. Still, she liked a challenge. It gave her a certain pleasure.

'What're you drinking?' Estelle asked Nic, making a point of *not* looking at him. She turned towards the barman.

'What've you got?' Nic asked.

There was a shift in tempo as the music segued from highlife into makossa, followed by an immediate shout of appreciation from the dance floor. It was a heady, exhilarating beat. Estelle began to move to it, aware of several pairs of eyes watching her hungrily. She was a good dancer, always had been. Nic Harte certainly wouldn't be able to compete. 'Rum and Coke,' she answered, raising her arms above her head. Someone whistled. The barman noticed her and murmured something in Shona. She smiled to herself.

Nic turned to Mat. She was unsure of herself, Estelle noticed. It was almost endearing. The girl who had everything, unable to order a drink. Someone came up to Estelle, beckoning to her to come forward, into the crowd. She shook her head, laughing. She could feel her hair coming loose, tumbling across her shoulders. She shook it again and felt it fall down her back. She was enjoying herself. But when she turned to look back at Nic and Mat, they'd turned their backs on her and were talking to each other, their heads so close they were almost touching. Estelle felt as though she'd been slapped. She stopped dancing abruptly. The night wasn't quite going according to plan – and it hadn't even begun.

Later, Mat watched Estelle leading Nic on to the dance floor, obviously enjoying the attention. He turned back to the barman. They struck up a conversation in Shona, Mat enjoying the feel of the syllables on his tongue. He rarely had the opportunity these days. 'Pretty girls, eh?' the barman said, nodding in their direction.

Mat smiled. 'I don't know the blonde one,' he said. 'She's Zambian, I think.'

'Na, she's from Arcadia, man. One of those real light-skinned coloureds. She used to come in here a couple of years back with a guy from home . . . what was his name? Marimba. That's it. Jonathan Marimba. You know him?'

Mat shook his head. He frowned. He was sure Nic had said she was Zambian. He watched the two of them dancing. Nic danced well, he noticed. None of the 'look-at-me' posturing of her friend. There was something about Estelle he didn't like. She was too watchful, far too aware of herself – as if she were out to get something. But what? He looked at the two of them. She'd raised her arms above her head again in that silly, artificially sexy way. Nic had the grace to look embarrassed but he could see she was enjoying herself. It was probably a whole different universe for her. He looked around. It was good to be back in the 101 Club again. He hadn't been here for years. Not that it had changed much. It was as dark and crowded and noisy as ever. He'd heard it said that there were thousands of Zimbabweans in New York but he'd met very few. London was different. Outside of Harare and Jo'burg, there were probably more of his countrymen per square foot here than anywhere else. Simon would have enjoyed the evening, he thought suddenly. He grinned. In fact, Simon would probably have enjoyed Estelle. She was much more his type. Hard, dangerous, all surface. Just the sort of woman Simon liked. He looked at Nic again. Suddenly he wanted to be alone with her, away from the thumping music and the blue-green eyes of the girl who watched her constantly – he couldn't tell why.

'Where'd you meet her?' he asked, trailing his hand down the gentle convex curve of her spine. He watched the skin shudder lightly. They were lying on her bed, a half-finished bottle of beer on the bedside table and the flung-aside tangle of their clothes on the floor. He was spent. The faint green glow of her bedside clock showed it was just past four a.m. It had been almost two before he'd been able to drag her out of the club and away from that irritating girl, Estelle. There'd been no question that he wouldn't come back to hers; she was tipsy and marvellously affectionate. He kissed her in the back of the cab, her mouth warm and wet, the faint tang of whisky and a tequila shot still lingering on her breath. Once inside the flat, they didn't make it past the living-room floor. He could still see and feel her face above his, eyes squeezed tightly shut as pleasure washed over her, her whole body trembling as she came. He felt himself hardening at the thought.

'At the Institute,' she mumbled, her voice muffled by his body. He cupped the firm flesh of her buttocks, sliding his hand down the back of her thigh. 'Why?'

'No special reason,' he murmured, continuing his lazy exploration of her body. 'The barman thought she was Zimbabwean, not Zambian. You did say Zambia, didn't you?'

'Yeah, that's what she said.' She pulled her face out from underneath his arm and rolled over. 'It's funny. You sound like Caryn. She doesn't like her either.'

'What d'you mean?' His hand wandered up the flat plane of her stomach. Her skin was taut and sleek. The blunt edge of her nipple caught his attention; he traced it with his forefinger, back and forth, gently teasing her. He heard her catch her breath. She didn't answer.

Nic woke first, her mouth dry and her head pounding. She turned cautiously to the right and saw him, the colour of his skin standing out like a blow against the white sheets. He slept as she did, on his back with a hand flung outwards, as if in surprise. She slid her legs away from his, taking care not to wake him, and stood up, picking up her dressing gown from the back of a chair. She needed a drink, the bathroom and some aspirin, probably in that order. She tiptoed to the kitchen and opened the fridge. A glass of water and two tablets in hand, she walked to the window and looked out. The sycamore tree in the garden below was just beginning to bud; spring was in the air. She held the glass against her lips but did not drink. She stood there, lost in thought, her mind going over the events of the previous week, returning again and again to the same niggling point – she ought to tell him who she really was. After all, what was the worst that could happen? She didn't hear his footsteps behind her, but when his arm slid around her waist and she felt his warm breath against her ear, it felt like the most natural place in the world to be, protected by the circle of his arms. Yes, she ought to open her mouth and say it. *I'm Zimbabwean too. My name is Harte. Nicola Harte.* But she didn't.

97

She was dreaming. Everything about the journey – from the taxi out to Heathrow, being whisked through the lines as he showed their tickets and passports and another gold card that seemed to open doors wherever they went – was dreamlike. The flight was delayed; he took her to a lounge where they drank champagne and Caryn couldn't eat any of the delicious-looking snacks they kept being offered for fear of being sick. She had never been so excited in her life. He kept looking at her as if she amused him. She probably did.

'If we're going to spend the next ninety-six hours with each other,' he said unexpectedly, leaning towards her, his expression, as always, unreadable, 'I suppose I'd better tell you my name.'

She looked at him, her eyes widening. She'd grown so used to calling him Charlie she wasn't sure she could manage anything else. 'What is it?' she asked warily.

'Simon. Although that's not the name I'm travelling under.' He tapped the dark blue passport in his hand. *Republic of South Africa*. She looked at it nervously.

'Oh.' She didn't know quite what to say. Simon? She looked at him again. Yes, it suited him better than Charlie. But was it true?

'Yes.' Yet again, he seemed able to read her mind.

'Simon,' she tested it out on her tongue. 'Simon what?'

He chuckled. 'Easy now. Can't give *everything* away. Not just yet.' He glanced at her quickly, as though he couldn't quite believe what he'd said. There was a moment's awkwardness between them. 'That's our flight they're calling,' he said suddenly, standing up. He looked down at her. 'Coming? Or shall I leave you behind, now that you know who I am?'

'I don't think I'll ever know who you are,' Caryn retorted calmly, getting to her feet. She ignored the look that flitted across his face. 'Ready when you are, boss,' she said sweetly. She saw he was unsure how to react. They walked towards the departure gate in slightly uneasy silence.

The flight was long and surprisingly uneventful, considering it was the first time she'd been on an aeroplane. The seats in Business Class reclined all the way back; it was a little like being in a hotel room, she thought, albeit one that trembled every once in a while. She grabbed Simon's forearm through one particularly bumpy spot. He glanced at her but made no comment. After a few minutes she withdrew it, embarrassed.

After dinner, which she could barely eat for the butterflies still circling around in her stomach, he pulled his briefcase on to his lap and began to read a stack of typewritten papers he'd brought along. Caryn dozed fitfully for the next few hours, waking every once in a while with a start, unable to recognise her surroundings. 'Probably somewhere over Egypt,' Simon murmured absently in response to her question. Later, it was Sudan. Zaire. Congo. Unfamiliar names, unknown countries. Much later, a smudge of pink on the horizon suddenly blossomed into a flaming dawn; the cloudless sky threw up waves of red and orange, proudly announcing the arrival of a new day. She slid the shutter closed again and the cabin was plunged into darkness. Illuminated by the overhead light, Simon looked as though he hadn't slept; a fierce frown of concentration was etched on his face as he read through the endless stacks of paper. He glanced at her briefly as she got up to go to the toilet but said nothing. When she returned, her hair brushed and face washed, he touched her arm as she passed in front of him, but again said nothing. Her skin burned with his off-hand caress.

The plane banked sharply as they began their descent into Cape Town. Caryn slid open the shutter again and pressed her nose against the glass. She had never seen anything quite so spectacularly beautiful. Simon pointed out the majestic peaks of the Twelve Apostles standing out in sharp relief against the azure sky. He showed her other landmarks – the flat-topped Table Mountain, Lion's Head, Agulas Bay, Hout Bay, Muizenberg Bay. She listened to him in open-mouthed silence.

'Did you . . . have you lived here before?' she ventured to ask as the plane began its slow descent towards the airport. He shrugged.

'On and off,' he said quietly. 'A long time ago.'

She decided against asking him anything further. There was a gentle bump as the plane hit the tarmac and then, all at once, they'd arrived.

They were amongst the first passengers off the plane; it took remarkably little time to clear customs, Caryn following Simon's lead all the way. An unsmiling young black man in sunglasses met them at the exit. He and Simon nodded at one another, but did not speak. He led them towards a black Range Rover with darkened windows. There was another man behind the wheel; a blond, close-cropped head turned briefly as they got in. He and Simon exchanged a greeting in a language she didn't know or understand and the car pulled smoothly away from the kerb. 'Where are we going?' she whispered to Simon.

'To see someone,' he said, pinching the bridge of his nose. 'I've got a quick meeting; you can get some sleep if you like. You look tired. You hardly slept at all on the flight.'

Caryn turned to look out of the window, oddly touched by his concern. The area around the airport couldn't have been more different from the view at six thousand feet. Hundreds upon hundreds of squatter-like shacks, surrounded by barbed wire and open sewers; tiny, windblown huts of twisted, cast-off metal and plastic sheeting – *this* was Cape Town? She craned her neck as the car peeled off the main freeway and began to climb the hill. Now the houses were larger, leafier. Within minutes they were above the flattened landscape below – the bay spread out before them; the mountain rose on the right . . . an imposing, graceful set of buildings nestled at its foot announced itself as the University of Cape Town. They skirted the mountain, leaving the city behind. The freeway snaked through a wide, beautiful valley; there were farmsteads all around, beautiful, tree-lined roads leading up to whitewashed, gabled houses. It was another world from the one she'd seen just outside the airport. They turned off the freeway and drove up the steep side of a hill, brushing through trees that hung down, almost touching the road. At a small sign that read 'Groot Constantia', the driver swung the car to the left and screeched to a halt. An armed guard lifted the boom and they crunched on to a gravel track. There were several guards milling around the lane, all wearing dark sunglasses and holding their automatic rifles at hip level. She stared at them; they looked impassively back, not moving. Where the hell were they going? she wondered, as they bumped their way down the dirt track. Whoever Simon was meeting was someone who obviously took no chances with surprise visitors. She had the feeling that their every move was being scrutinised, somewhere and by someone none of them could see.

At last they pulled up in front of a charming farmhouse; the guns and security apparatus leading up to it suddenly seemed shockingly out of place. A spray of climbing roses ran over the small wooden entrance gate, twisting into a canopy overhead. Giant, whispering trees shaded the house from the sun; in the distance she could hear dogs barking.

'Come on,' Simon said to her, opening his door. 'We're here.' She scrambled out of the car after him. Where? she longed to ask. Their bags were quickly unloaded and she followed the three men into the farmhouse.

'Hi, Simon.' A man came forward to greet them. He raised a questioning eyebrow at Caryn.

'Friend of mine,' Simon said shortly. 'Is he here?'

'Yeah. Come straight through. He's waiting for you.' He looked at Caryn again. 'Is she——?'

'Yeah.' Simon interrupted him. 'Get someone to show her the way, will you?' The man nodded and turned on his heel. 'I'll be back later,' Simon said to her. 'Danny'll be back in a moment.'

Caryn nodded wordlessly. A couple of seconds later a young girl appeared. 'Please come with me,' she said, adding something in an unfamiliar language to the man who was carrying their bags. Caryn followed her out of the kitchen and across a pretty, cobblestone courtyard to an outhouse. She pushed open a heavy wooden door and they stepped into a small guest house. Caryn looked around her in surprise. There was a small, blue and white kitchen with a large wooden table and chairs; a living room with a fireplace and beyond that a door which presumably led to the bedroom. 'Please let me know if there's anything you need,' the girl said, walking towards the front door. 'Dinner is at eight.' And before Caryn could ask her anything further, she disappeared, shutting the door silently behind her.

Caryn stood in the middle of the kitchen. She suddenly felt tired and quite overwhelmed by their arrival in a place she neither knew nor understood. Was it a hotel? A guest house of some sort? Who had Simon gone to meet? She pushed open the door to the bedroom and stood in the doorway, looking at the enormous four-poster bed, the thoughts spinning round and round in her head. She had to lie down. She kicked off her shoes, sank into the soft, feather duvet and pulled the blanket that had been laid across the foot of the bed across her shoulders. It was cool, almost chilly, in the darkened interior. She'd assumed Africa would be hot. The sun was shining but in the shade the temperature was hardly warmer than the early summer they'd left behind. She closed her eyes. It was hard to believe that less than twenty-four hours earlier, she'd been in her flat in Ladbroke Grove, packing. She could hear the dogs barking, far away, and the sound of a tractor or a motorbike buzzing in the distance. A bird chirruped outside the window and then everything was quiet again. Her breathing was loud and sonorous in her ears. She slid into sleep.

The man he had flown six thousand miles to see studied him discreetly over the top of his coffee cup, a curiously effeminate, floral porcelain cup-and-saucer affair that didn't suit him. He balanced the cup with his little finger held aloft in an exaggerated gesture of politeness. It set Simon's teeth on edge. He wanted to get in, do the job and get out again as quickly as possible. There wasn't time for the peculiar little social niceties that this man seemed to enjoy.

'Danny here'll drive you there and back,' he said, the metallic, guttural quality of his voice grating in Simon's ears. 'Shouldn't take you more than a couple of hours. I hear you brought someone with you?'

'Yeah.' Simon didn't elaborate.

The man smiled. 'That's good, Simon,' he said benevolently. 'High time, too, I don't mind telling you.'

'Is that it?' Simon half rose to his feet. The last thing he felt like doing was discussing Caryn – or anyone else, for that matter – with the man he'd only ever known as 'Colonel'.

'*Ja*, that's it. You're good to go. You've got everything you need?' Simon nodded. '*Goed*. Well, I doubt I'll see you again this time round. I'm leaving for Maputo this afternoon. Enjoy your stay, Simon. Danny'll get a message to me when it's done.' Simon nodded again and walked to the door. 'Oh, and Simon,' the Colonel called out to him as he reached the door. He turned, his hand already reaching for the handle. 'Not too clean this time, hey? Last time was a little *too* professional, if you know what I mean.' He smiled.

Simon pulled open the door and shut it quietly behind him. Danny and Sipho, the men who'd met them at the airport, were watching him impassively. He ignored them and walked through the kitchen to the guest house. He remembered Caryn and his pulse quickened. What was she thinking? he wondered. He pushed open the bedroom door and saw her, lying on her side with her legs drawn up to her chest and her thick blonde hair spread across the pillow. He locked the door behind him and quietly crossed the floor to the bathroom. He took a shower, tension sloughing off him with the steady, powerful stream of water cascading down his back. He dried his hair roughly with a towel, wrapped it around his waist and walked back into the bedroom. She hadn't stirred. He lifted the blanket and slid into bed next to her, his heart beating fast. Her small, firm body was the reassurance he sought, unknowingly, perhaps, that all would be well. He put his arms around her, drawing the scent of her hair deep into his lungs. She stirred and turned towards him, releasing the trapped warmth of her body and drawing him in. Quickly, and without words, he moved inside her, the small, inarticulate sounds of pleasure that came from her already familiar to him. The strange emptiness that had been with him for as long as he could remember suddenly ceased, dropping away. He was secure, at last, against the falling terror that had somehow become his life. He made love to her fiercely, burying himself in the pleasure she afforded, steadying himself against the thing he had agreed to do. This would be his last job, he thought to himself, watching her face underneath him through the furry thickness of his lashes. The very last one.

98

His mobile phone dragged him out of sleep. He cursed, flinging back the covers, and stumbled towards the living room. He rubbed his eyes and looked at his watch: seven minutes past six in the morning. Who the hell was calling him at six a.m.?

'Hello?'

'Mat?' It was Leonie Frith, his PA. He felt the hairs on his neck start to prickle. A horrible sense of premonition broke over him.

'Frith? What's the matter?'

'Oh, Mat. I'm sorry, I didn't know . . . I didn't want to call but—'

'What's happened?'

She drew in a deep breath; he could hear her fear down the long-distance line. 'I've been sacked, Mat. It happened this morning. They've locked me out.'

'Who sacked you? What're you talking about?'

'DiAngelo.' She began to weep quietly. 'He asked me to leave straight away. He locked me out of my office. I'm in the lobby—'

'Leonie,' Mat broke in, his heart racing. 'Where *is* DiAngelo? Can you get him on the phone for me?'

'He . . . he's not taking my c-calls,' Leonie sobbed. 'H . . . he's in his office with the other managers and—'

'Leonie, when did you last do a back-up?' Mat interrupted her again, his mind racing ahead.

'On Friday. I took the disks home, like always.'

'Frith. Listen to me.' His voice was calm but urgent. 'Go home, get those disks and take them straight to my bank. You've got the safety deposit-box keys. Put the disks in it, go back home and wait for me. I'll get the next flight out to you.'

'Mat—' Her voice was tremulous.

'Don't panic, Frith. You just make sure you get those disks to the bank. We'll talk later. Don't worry. We'll sort this out.' He hung up the phone and stood for a moment at the window, watching the watery dawn break over the park. Despite the early-morning chill, he was sweating. Things were suddenly about to get a whole lot more complicated. Why hadn't he seen it coming? He'd been suspicious of Harte from the beginning. After his conversation with Professor Schmidt, he'd been surprised at the lack of activity from the Harte camp in the run-up to the showdown. Now he understood why. There wasn't going to *be* a showdown. That was the whole point. That was why Harte had been so quiet – he'd been planning his pre-emptive strike. But even Harte wasn't *that* quick. Someone had to have told him about the article. There was only one person who'd seen it. The very person who'd locked Leonie out of her office. DiAngelo. He should have been disappointed; he wasn't. Nothing much surprised him any longer. Perhaps he'd been around the sucking mud of big business for too long.

He turned and walked towards the bathroom. He had a sudden urge to call Nic. She was the only person whose voice he longed to hear. He blew out his cheeks. No, better not. She had a deadline, she'd told him. Some article that had to be handed in by the end of the day. He'd call her later on, once he'd sorted out a ticket. He turned on the shower and stepped inside. He felt strangely calm.

Nic fastened the button on her skirt and twisted it around, smoothing it down. She glanced at herself in the mirror before shrugging on her jacket. She looked demure, professional – wasn't that what Molly wanted? Her hair was pulled back into a neat pony tail; her skirt and jacket were smart, tailored and she fished a pair of red slingbacks out of her wardrobe . . . perfect. She picked up her bag and keys and closed the door. She'd no idea why she'd been summoned to Eaton Square, but at least she'd have the chance to see Shaun and Patrick. And Jessica, of course. She unlocked her car door and slid inside. With any luck, she'd be there in plenty of time. She pulled out of her parking spot and joined the tail-end of the morning rush-hour traffic.

She had to park on Elizabeth Street, a couple of minutes' walk away from the house. An unusual number of cars were double-parked along Eaton Square and the adjacent streets. She locked the car and walked down the street. As soon as she rounded the corner, her heart sank. There were at least a dozen photographers standing around, leaning against the railings, smoking. They watched her curiously as she ran up the steps towards the front door – not for the first time she thanked her lucky stars that her father had always been so adamant about keeping the family away from the press. None of the waiting photographers knew who she was. She pushed open the door, wondering what the hell all the fuss was about. She could hear her father's voice booming out instructions to someone on the phone and yelling out something to Molly at the same time. She hurried towards the sitting room on the first floor.

'Jessica!' She walked over to the sofa where her half-sister was sitting, still in school uniform. 'When did you get here?' she asked, bending down to give her a hug.

'About an hour ago. Manning drove me up from school. I missed lacrosse practice. What's going on?' Jessica asked, her blue eyes wide with questioning.

Nic shook her head. 'I've no idea,' she said, looking around. 'Are Shaun and Patrick here?'

'Yeah. They're upstairs.'

'I'll be back in a sec,' Nic promised and quickly walked out of the room. She ran upstairs to the bedrooms on the second floor. Shaun came out of his, a grim look on his face. 'What's going on?' Nic asked, kissing him quickly.

'Press announcement,' Shaun said briefly, holding up a stack of papers. 'Dad wants us around when he makes it.'

Nic's heart began to race. 'Why?'

He shrugged. 'Dunno. Just said it's important we're all here.'

434

'But what've *we* got to do with it?' Nic protested. 'It's nothing to do with *us*.'

'Well, not with you, but Shaun and I are board members, remember?'

'But—'

'Oh, *there* you are!' Molly exclaimed, coming down the stairs, her hair still in oversized rollers. 'I thought you said you'd be here early?'

'I'm here now, aren't I?' Nic said, scowling. 'Would someone mind telling me what's going on?'

'Your dad's just bought the Riverbrook Group,' Molly said, obviously relishing the fact that Nic didn't know. 'Didn't he tell you?'

Nic stared at her. The Riverbrook Group? 'The *Sunday Times*? The *Daily Star*?' she asked incredulously.

'Mmm. The biggest group of newspapers and magazines in the world. Isn't it *exciting*?' Molly said, looking for all the world as though she actually read any of the papers or magazines within it.

'But why?' Nic was still incredulous. What her father knew about the press and running a media empire could fit on the back of a postage stamp. He *hated* the press.

'Don't ask *me*,' Molly said gaily, continuing on her way down the stairs.

Nic turned to Shaun. 'Why on earth would Dad want to own a bunch of newspapers?'

'So he can control what gets said, of course, you idiot,' Patrick said affectionately, coming out of his own room. He hugged Nic. 'You should understand that, of all people. Some hotshot Zimbabwean journalist in New York's been writing the biggest load of crap about him. He got hold of a copy of the guy's article last week. It was the only way to stop it being published. We haven't seen it but Ogilvy says it'll sink Rho-Mine if it ever gets out. Not that any of it's true, mind you. The journo's obviously been paid to write it. The AGM's been cancelled but the announcement's going to push the share prices up, which buys everyone a bit of time.'

Nic listened to him, her mind whirling. 'A Zimbabwean journalist?' she said, the blood rushing to her head.

'Yeah. Mat somebody-or-other—'

Nic thought her legs might give way beneath her. 'Mat?' she said weakly.

'Yeah. Matari Ndava. He works for *WED*. Well, he *used* to work for them. He was sacked this morning. Hey, where are you going?'

Nic didn't reply. She ran down the stairs, her mind in complete turmoil. She passed Jim on the way down, Ogilvy hot on his heels.

'Where the hell d'you think you're going?' he growled as she rushed past.

'I . . . I forgot something,' she stammered, her face immediately turning a fiery red.

'Well, it'll have to wait. We've got half the world's press outside. I'm about to make an announcement—'

Nic took a deep breath. 'No,' she said as calmly as she could. She put out a hand and touched the handle. 'You'll just have to manage without me.' She pulled open the door.

'The hell we will—' Jim put out a hand to stop her, his face darkening, but it was too late.

She stepped outside. The assembled photographers leaped into action; there was a startled pause and then the cameras started clicking. Nic pushed her way through the men who'd gathered on the front step. 'Who is she?' she heard someone yell. 'Dunno. I think she's the daughter—' someone else shouted. 'Where's Harte? What's going on?'

She clattered down the street in her heels, her heart thumping, not even caring who was behind her. She yanked the car door open and threw her bag inside. A couple of photographers had followed her; she started the engine and swung wildly out, narrowly missing them and peeled off, her tyres squealing as she accelerated. She fumbled in her bag for her phone – she *had* to talk to Mat. She dialled the number awkwardly, praying she wouldn't run into a policeman. It went straight to his answering machine. She almost flung it across the seat. She turned up Park

Lane, heading towards Marble Arch, unable to think clearly. Mat had written an article about her father? Was that why he'd sought her out? Her whole body was tense. Was *that* the reason they were together?

99

Mat landed just before six p.m., thanks to the time difference between London and New York. He took a cab from the airport straight to his apartment. He was tense but his mind was absolutely clear. Harte had thrown down a challenge but even *he* must know there was no way to keep the story from the papers indefinitely. He was playing for time, that much was obvious. But Sir Winston wouldn't have sold the Riverbrook Group without a fight – tired and bloated as he was, the old bull wasn't about to see his life's work disappear into the hands of someone like Harte who couldn't tell a tabloid from a broadsheet. No, Harte was going to have the most monumental battle on his hands and he knew it. He *had* to know. He wasn't the sort of man to go into something like this without being reasonably confident about the outcome. This was one battle he wouldn't win – at least, not easily. So why had he entered it?

He ran up the stairs and opened the door to his apartment. He felt the sudden release of tension as he surveyed his almost empty home. He checked his messages – still nothing from Nic, despite the half-dozen he'd left on her mobile. She must have switched it off; he did that sometimes when he needed to work. He pulled a quick face; it was past midnight in London. Why hadn't she called him back? He threw his bag on the couch and walked into the bathroom.

A quick shower and a cup of strong black coffee later, he pulled the phone towards him and began the long, laborious process of establishing what damage had been done and what his next moves might be. Frith was at home, waiting for his call. She picked up the phone immediately. She was understandably upset – she'd been employed at *WED* for nearly a decade, after all – but she'd done exactly as he'd asked and everything he'd written over the past year and a half had been deposited in his safety box earlier that day. They made an arrangement to meet for breakfast the following morning.

He hung up the phone and turned on the television, looking for something to take his mind off Nic and why she hadn't rung. As he'd suspected, the takeover of the Riverbrook Group by RhoMine had sent all sorts of shockwaves running through the industry. He flipped between the business channels, seeking a more in-depth analysis of the situation and its likely outcome. CNN featured an earlier shot of Harte's London home. He paused. '*Reporters gathered outside the Eaton Square, London home of Jim Harte this morning*,' the newscaster was saying. '*An announcement by Harte was expected at ten o'clock local time . . .*' There was a shot of the front door being opened and closed and the tall, unmistakable figure of a girl hurrying down the steps, her hand raised to ward off the photographers. He stared at the screen. '*Nicola Harte, Jim Harte's eldest daughter, was seen hurrying away from the family home minutes before Harte and his lawyers—*' He felt the wind leave his body as though he'd been punched. Nicola Harte. Nic. Jesus. Of course.

100

Caryn lifted a hand to shade her eyes from the blinding strip of bleached sand that stretched out in both directions, a beautiful, unbroken curve, bracketed by the mountains on one side and the shimmering, liquid blue horizon on the other. The beach was almost empty. Behind them, the dunes hid the road and beyond that the makeshift homes of the township that came almost as far as the shore. They were at the edge of the continent, Simon told her, pointing to the strip of mountains that jutted out into the blue. 'The end of Africa. Beyond that's Antarctica.' She followed his finger. It was hard to grasp. Ladbroke Grove might as well have been on the moon for all its relevance to the three days they'd spent here. They were due to fly back the following evening. She shivered, suddenly cold in her borrowed sweater and shorts.

A man jogged past with a large black dog. She watched them, the only figures on the crescent of sand. The man bent down and picked up a stick, throwing it into the water. The dog bounded happily after it. She looked down at her bare feet as they walked, her footprints disappearing almost as fast as she made them. 'Why did we come here?' she asked Simon suddenly. 'Why did you bring me here?'

He didn't answer for a while. He walked along, his hands shoved deep in his pockets, a frown of concentration on his face. She looked at him – at the weathered, sun-toughened skin with its perpetual, dark blonde bristles and the darker brown of his lashes and brows. His face and body had a wild, tough beauty that he did his best to disguise, strange as it seemed. She looked at the scarred, hardened body that her fingers knew almost as well as her eyes; the hazel-green eyes that seemed to be perpetually searching for something or someone she couldn't see; his rare smile. She was moved by him in ways she couldn't express. When she did try to express it, however tentatively, she saw immediately how quickly he withdrew. There was an angry shyness, a strange distaste for her small gestures of appreciation – he seemed to want nothing more from her than he himself was prepared to give. Very little, it seemed. Most of the time he remained closed to her. Walled off. Guarded against. It touched her all the more. There was a quality in him that she'd only just begun to glimpse and she wanted more, of course. 'Why did you bring me here?' she repeated, watching warily for signs of his retreat.

To her surprise, he didn't retreat. 'I don't know,' he said

finally, picking up a stone and sending it skimming across the surface of the sea. 'I . . . I just did.'

'Are you glad I came?' she asked, aware of the thumping sound of her heartbeat in her ears.

'Are you?' he deflected the question neatly.

She looked out at the sea. 'Of course. Who wouldn't be? It's incredible here. So unbelievably beautiful.'

'There was a river near where Mat and I grew up—' Simon said suddenly, and stopped. He ran a hand through his hair.

'Who's Mat?' Caryn asked, surprised at the unexpected piece of information.

He turned to look at her. There was a strange, faraway expression in his eyes. He seemed about to speak and then, maddeningly, stopped himself. 'It's a long story,' he said eventually. 'I'll tell you some other time.'

Tell me now! Caryn longed to cry. But she knew what happened when she tried to cross the thresholds he'd so painstakingly set between them. She bent down and picked up some stones of her own. They turned to face the sea. In a few minutes, they would return to the car he'd rented and drive out across the Cape Flats to the airport. By seven that evening they'd be gone, flying back through the night to Europe. And then what?

Something had changed between them in the past three days that she couldn't quite put her finger on. There was a new wariness to Simon that was different from the casual, off-hand manner he'd shown her before. She didn't know whether to be pleased. He was quiet, just as he'd always been, but she'd caught him looking at her once or twice when he thought she wasn't paying attention. There was an intensity in his eyes that she hadn't noticed before. Did it have anything to do with her? Or was it to do with the strange nature of whatever it was they'd come all this way for? He'd said nothing about why they were here, naturally. He'd been gone two or three times apart from the brief hour or so he'd spent with the man he referred to as 'the Colonel' when they first arrived. On their second day, the two men who'd picked them up at the airport came for him and he disappeared for the morning. He came back at lunchtime and found her in the paddock behind the vineyards, watching the Colonel's collection of sleek, Arab horses. He said nothing but there was something in the way he looked at her that gave her to understand he was pleased to be back, standing next to her in the winter air watching the horses at rest.

They'd spent the following day at the Waterfront in the city, no different from the hundreds of other tourists who walked up and down its length, drinking crisp white wine and eating seafood in the shadow of Table Mountain. And then today, he'd dropped her off at Tokai Beach that morning, telling her he'd be back in an hour or so. And now they were heading back to the car and he hadn't said a word about why he'd come. She sighed. She somehow doubted he ever would.

He looked at his watch. 'We'd better get going,' he said, picking up a last stone. He looked at it for a second, then slipped it in the pocket of his jeans. 'Traffic'll be bad at this time of the day.' She nodded. On impulse, she slipped a hand into his. He stiffened for a brief second, but at least he didn't move away. They walked hand in hand, just another couple, towards the huts that signalled the beginning of the beach.

The car smelled strongly of alcohol and the sharp, acrid scent of sweat when he opened the door. She wrinkled her nose.

'Sorry,' he said, powering down the windows as soon as he started the engine. 'Had to give someone a lift.' The cool sea air rushed in as they rolled towards the exit. 'It'll clear in a couple of minutes.'

'Who on earth was your passenger?' she giggled, fishing out a handkerchief and holding it to her nose. He didn't answer. She turned and looked back at the beach. She wished she'd thought to bring along a camera. In a few hours, she knew, it would be hard to believe it had ever existed. 'Thank you for bringing me here,' she murmured as he swung the car on to the main road. 'It's been amazing.'

'You liked it?'

She was quiet for a moment. 'It's very beautiful,' she said carefully.

'But?'

She turned to look at him. 'But it's a bit . . .' She stopped. 'I don't know . . . it's a bit *unreal*, somehow.' She looked out of the window again. 'I mean, there's all this,' she waved at the view of the bay disappearing behind them. 'And then there's this.' She pointed at the groups of street children rushing up to the cars as they stopped at the traffic lights. 'And I can't get the picture of the houses on the way to the airport out of my head. It's too *extreme*. I mean, *I'm* poor. Christ, you should see where *I* grew up. But this . . . this is different. I don't think I could ever live here. It's too much. It's wrong.'

'Perceptive little thing, aren't you?' Simon said as the car surged forwards again.

'Little?' Caryn asked indignantly.

'No, I don't mean it like that.'

'Well, how'd you mean it?'

He was quiet for a while. 'You surprise me, sometimes,' he said slowly. 'That's all. You understand things that most people don't. Or won't. When I look at you,' he turned his head briefly to look at her, 'I see someone prim and proper. *English*, in the way I always wanted to be—'

'You're not English?' Caryn was surprised.

'No.'

She turned to look at him. 'So where are you from? Here?'

He hesitated, then shook his head. 'No. I'm from Zimbabwe.'

'*Zimbabwe?*'

'Yeah. Like your friend. Nic Harte.'

'Nic? Do . . . do you know her?' she asked incredulously.

'No, not exactly,' he said slowly. 'Look, I know this is all a bit sudden and probably quite weird. Can we talk about this later? In London?'

'But you can't just drop a thing like that into the conversation, Simon. It's not *fair*,' Caryn said, aware of her own anger suddenly beginning to mount.

'What's fairness got to do with it?'

'Everything! You can't just drop bits and pieces of information when you feel like it,' she said hotly. 'It's just—'

'What?' There was a warning edge to his voice.

Caryn bit her lip. She'd been seeing – if that was the word to use – Simon for almost six weeks and it was the first time she'd let him know what she *really* thought, not what she dared to show. Oh, well. She'd done it now. Might as well go for broke. 'You never tell me anything about you. Until a few days ago I didn't even know your name. Maybe this is the way you do things. Women, I mean. But *I* can't. I can't bear the secrecy and the way you . . .' She swallowed. 'The way you control everything. It's not—'

'What you want? What you're used to?'

Caryn nodded. 'It seems wrong, somehow. As if you're just—' She stopped, aware she was pushing him into a territory he neither wanted nor understood. 'Playing,' she said finally. 'Playing with me. With us.'

'Us?' There was genuine surprise in his voice.

She turned to look out of the window. It was hopeless. He would never let her in, never let his guard down. 'Forget it,' she shook her head. 'Forget I ever said anything.'

'Fine.'

'OK.'

And that was that. An uneasy silence developed between them, Caryn determined not to let him see just how much he'd upset her or what it had cost her to speak. With a composure that surprised even her, she went through the departure formalities with a pleasant if distracted air, at the same time resolving to end the silly relationship as soon as they got to London. It wasn't even a relationship – you couldn't call it that. How she'd wound up in South Africa with a man whose name she wasn't even sure of was almost beyond her. What was she doing? It would only lead to trouble. Which seemed to be the sum total of her experience of men anyway. Rowland. Simon. What was wrong with her? She picked up a couple of magazines and a paperback novel at the news stand before boarding the flight. If she wasn't going to talk to him, she'd better have something to do during the long flight back home.

As before, Simon led her into the Business Class lounge to wait for their flight to be called. If he noticed her off-hand manner, he made no comment. *Fine. Two can play at that game,* she thought to herself, answering his question about whether she'd like something to drink or not with exaggerated politeness.

He brought two glasses of wine over. 'Sure you don't want something to eat?' he asked. 'It'll be a while before they serve dinner on the flight.'

'No, thanks. I'm fine,' she answered, pulling her magazines out of her bag.

He looked down at her. She forced herself to continue reading. Every now and then, she'd noticed, there was an innocence to him that she found hard to resist. Like now. She saw that he was unsure of himself; her coldness had caught him off guard. But it would be a mistake to look up, to surrender. She turned the page, her whole body tense with the effort of ignoring him. He sat down next to her. 'Look,' he said suddenly, turning to her. 'I'm sorry. I shouldn't have said anything—'

'It doesn't matter,' she said lightly, glancing at him. 'Really.'

He looked even more uncomfortable. 'It's just . . . it's complicated.'

'Simon,' she said, holding up the magazine as if to ward him off. 'It's fine. I told you. You don't have to explain anything to me. I mean, it's not as if we're having a relationship, or anything. This is just a fling. Nothing serious. You said it yourself.'

'It's not that,' he said softly. He seemed to be struggling with something. 'It's not what you think.' He stopped. And then went on suddenly. 'There are things I'd like to tell you. Things I *ought* to tell you. But I can't right now. There's no reason on earth why you should believe me, I know. I will tell you what's going on. Just not right now.'

Caryn swallowed. There it was again. The almost painful

vulnerability she'd glimpsed in him before. She didn't trust herself to speak. He caught the look in her eyes and, to save the situation, he leaned across and kissed her.

101

Estelle watched the six o'clock news that evening with a growing sense of disbelief. The newscaster was talking rapidly. '*The controversial Zimbabwean businessman Jim Harte has made a dramatic purchase of the Riverbrook Group, whose media holdings include the* Sunday Times. *The previous owner of the Riverbrook Group, Sir Winston Freedland, has just died of a heart attack after being surprised by a gang of armed robbers at his holiday home in Wynberg, Cape Town. Sir Winston's death opens the way for Harte and his team . . .*' She stared at the screen. '*Since the announcement yesterday, Rho-Mine shares have risen dramatically . . .*' The image cut away to a picture of Jim Harte standing outside his magnificent London home. He couldn't possibly have looked more smug. She watched his mouth open and close as he congratulated everyone who'd been involved in the negotiations over the past few weeks and expressed his utmost sympathy to the family of the recently deceased.

She stabbed the 'off' button on the remote angrily. Things were *not* going according to plan. Jim Harte wasn't suffering. He wasn't rueing the day he'd met her and he certainly wasn't yet full of remorse. If anything, life seemed to be getting better and better. There he was, the proud new owner of a bunch of newspapers, standing in the hallway of his beautiful house in Eaton Square, smiling widely, his arm round his wife. That bitch of a daughter of his had just been filmed running down the steps of her house. It ought to have been *her*, Estelle. It ought to have been *her* home; *she* should have been included in the picture of the happy family. She was part of the family. She should have been the one standing there, smiling prettily for the cameras, not sitting in the dark watching them all rise to even greater prominence whilst she sat alone, unacknowledged, uncared for. A tidal wave of anger and resentment rose rapidly in her chest. She had to take things to the next level, quickly. Hit them whilst their fortunes were rising. It would make the fall just that bit sweeter. But she had to move fast. It was time to bring the Hartes to their fucking knees. She bit her lip in excitement and winced as the metallic taste of her own blood filled her mouth. Pain? She hadn't felt a thing.

Mat sat in the dark, the telephone held loosely in his hand. Midnight in New York, dawn in London. Six messages, all from an increasingly desperate-sounding Nic. He brought the phone up to his lips, lost in thought. She was Jim Harte's daughter. Why had she concealed it? Why? He ran over their conversations again and again in his head. He ought to have guessed; she'd dropped enough clues. The way she'd never given him her full name; the fact that she knew so much about Zimbabwe . . . she knew what a *gogo* was, for Christ's sake. She'd known, all the time they'd been together, who he was, hadn't she? He hadn't hidden anything from her. She'd pretended to be a farmer's daughter. An *English* farmer's daughter. Why?

He looked at the phone again. He needed to talk to Simon. He was the only person in the world who would understand, but he had no idea where he was. It was over a month since he'd spoken to him. Another measure of how quickly he'd lost his head. Hardly a fortnight went by without one or the other calling, checking in, just seeing how things were. Now a whole month had slipped past without his noticing. He dialled Simon's mobile. Unsurprisingly, it went straight to answer phone. He left a quick message and stood up. It took every ounce of self-discipline not to pick up the phone again. If there was one thing he'd learned over the years, it was to do nothing. To let things lie for a while. The answer of what to do and how to respond would surely come to him. Right now he craved only silence. He wasn't sure he could bring himself to speak to Nic. He lay down on his bed, fully clothed. Sleep would not come easily, he knew. He had the disturbing sensation of falling, falling into something he couldn't quite grasp. For the very first time in a long, long while, he was unsure of himself. Nic had confused him. Deliberately? Surely she wouldn't have stooped so low? He closed his eyes, waiting for sleep to overtake him and extinguish his doubts.

He met Leonie the following morning as planned. She was already waiting for him at the restaurant. She looked tired and drawn. He sat down opposite, the anger rising immediately in his chest. 'I don't know what to say,' he said, shaking his head. 'Why you had to get it in the neck as well—'

'I would've resigned anyway,' she said briskly. 'I wouldn't have stayed.'

'Thanks, Frith,' he said, looking at her closely. 'I appreciate the vote of confidence. Really. But it's not fair. This had nothing to do with you.'

'I think Richard always knew where my loyalties lay,' Leonie said wryly. 'I'm not unhappy about it, I have to say. I can't imagine staying on if you weren't there. I mean, the others are perfectly nice and all that but you and I . . . well, we get along, don't we?'

Mat smiled. Leonie Frith certainly wasn't one to show her emotions easily. It was true. They *did* get along. And he couldn't imagine his working day without her, either. 'So, what do we do? I'm taking this . . .' he tapped the envelope of disks she'd brought along and placed on the table between them, 'straight back to London. Mark Davies'll jump at it.'

'He's been after you for years,' Leonie smiled. 'Of course he'll jump at it. At you, too.'

Mat nodded slowly. 'The strange thing is, though, Harte *must* know that. He knows I'll just take it elsewhere. Yeah, it's bought him a couple of days and his share price has gone up, but I can't help thinking there's something more to come.'

'Like what?'

He shrugged. 'Dunno. I wish I knew. Then I'd know how to

react.' A smiling waitress suddenly appeared. He was starving, he realised. They ordered and then he turned back to her. 'Look, taking it to Davies at the *Observer*'s all very well and good, and yes, he's probably going to offer me a job, but what about you? It's a lot to ask, Frith, I know. You've got your whole life here—'

'I'm coming with you,' she said simply but firmly. 'That's the whole point. I *don't* have a life here.' She looked down at her hands. 'After Norm died. Well, there's really only been work, you know. And without you around . . . I don't know . . . it just won't be the same. I'm not a young girl, Mat. Maybe it's time for me to go home as well. And if there's a job waiting at the other end, well, it'll make things simpler, that's all. But I'll manage, either way. You don't have to worry about me.'

Mat looked at her. He felt a sudden rush of affection for the prickly, fiftysomething-year-old woman who'd worked side by side with him for nearly ten years. It was just as she said – he couldn't imagine a working day that didn't include her. He reached across the table and touched her forearm, rather surprised by his own boldness. His smooth, dark skin was an interruption on her pale, freckled forearm. She stared at his hand, as if she too were struck by the contrast, and then pushed back her chair suddenly, mumbling something about the toilet and practically ran from the room. He was touched. An hour later, he walked back to his apartment, his head considerably clearer. In one area, at least, he knew what he had to do. He turned up Chambers Street, heading home. He needed time to think.

Nic put down the phone, trying hard not to cry. It had been almost thirty-six hours since she'd pushed her way past her father and run down the steps, her only thought that she had to get to Mat before he heard the news about her any other way. She'd failed. The fact that he hadn't returned her calls was proof. She stared at the floor. She had to do *something*. She *had* to get Mat to talk to her. She had to explain to him why she'd lied. But how? Her phone rang suddenly. She grabbed it with both hands, almost dropping it. It wasn't Mat. It was Estelle.

'What's up?' Estelle asked immediately, sounding concerned. 'You sound like you've been crying.'

Nic couldn't hold back her tears any longer. 'I've done something really stupid,' she blurted out, past caring what Estelle or anyone else thought.

'What? What's going on?'

'It's Mat. Oh, God. I'm sorry, Estelle. I don't know why I'm blubbering to you about it. You've probably got a hundred and one other—'

'Hey, it's OK. Tell me what happened.' Estelle sounded so genuinely worried that Nic's tears began to flow afresh. Within ten minutes, she'd spilled the whole story out. 'What'm I going to do?' she asked, reaching shakily for a cigarette. 'He won't return my calls. He probably hates me. He hates my father, I know he does. So do I. I should've been straight with him. I should've been straight with *you* but I—'

'Where does Mat live?' Estelle interrupted her. 'Normally, I mean.'

'I don't know. New York, I think. I don't even know if he's still here. I must've left him twenty messages on his mobile but—'

'What's his last name?'

'Ndava. Matari Ndava.'

'Maybe I can help,' Estelle said, her voice suddenly rising in excitement. 'Just hang in there. I'll call you back.'

'How—?' Nic's heart surged. But the line was already dead.

Three hours later, Estelle rang back. The three longest hours of Nic's life. She sounded triumphant. 'Two hundred and forty-seven West Jay Street. Eighth floor. He's in New York. He left yesterday.'

'How the hell did you find out?' Nic was flabbergasted.

'Oh, I have my ways,' Estelle giggled. 'A friend of mine knows him. They were at university together, or something.

449

Anyhow, the point is – he's in New York. When are you going?'

'Going?'

Estelle sighed. 'Nic. What are you waiting for? If he won't pick up the phone . . . well, you'd better get your ass over there before some other girl moves in!'

'D'you really think I should go?' Nic asked tremulously, her mind already beginning to race ahead.

' 'Course you should go. What a dumb question!'

'Now?'

'Absolutely. Now, what can I do to help?'

'Oh, Estelle,' Nic began to cry again. 'I don't know how to thank you—'

'Don't be silly. Look, I know we've only just met, but you're a really special person, Nic. I can tell. I know we're going to be best friends. I can feel it. Just you wait and see. Now, give me your address. I'm coming over. Get a ticket. I'll help you pack.'

'What a *lovely* flat!' Estelle exclaimed as soon as she walked in. 'It's absolutely beautiful!'

Nic looked up from where she was flinging clothes into a small suitcase. It was horribly expensive but she'd found a seat on a flight leaving at eight p.m. that night. 'It's a bit messy,' she mumbled, embarrassed. 'I didn't have time to clean up—'

'Oh, I bet you've got a cleaner,' Estelle laughed. 'Rich little heiress like you.'

Nic glanced at her nervously. There was an edge to Estelle's voice that she hadn't heard before. *That* was why she hated telling anyone who she really was. The name Harte always conjured up the sort of luxurious lifestyle she'd always been careful to avoid. 'No, I—'

'Oh, I'm only teasing,' Estelle smiled. 'I bet all your friends are *totally* jealous. Now, what're you wearing on the flight? Let's see. No, that's definitely out,' Estelle said, reaching across the bed and plucking a shirt from Nic's hands. 'And *that's* not going, either.'

'But—' Nic protested, looking bewildered.

'Girlfriend, do you want him back or not?'

An hour later, she was done. Estelle had taken charge of everything. She'd organised her wardrobe, called a cab, taken down Caryn's and Tory's numbers with a promise to call and let them know she'd be gone for a few days; she would call *ArtWeekly* the following morning and let them know there'd been a family emergency . . . everything Nic could think of. 'Who's going to look after your plants?' she asked as they trooped down the stairs. 'D'you want me to do it?'

'Oh, no,' Nic protested. 'That'd be asking far too much, Estelle. I couldn't possibly—'

' 'Course you can. I don't mind at all. Honestly. It's not like I'm doing anything much during the day. I mean, I'm not working at the moment. It's no trouble at all.'

'Are you sure? It's an awful bother. I don't even know where you live. You might have to travel miles to get here.'

'Oh, no. I'm staying at a friend's place. It's not far, don't worry. You've got enough on your plate. Just leave me the keys and I'll keep an eye on things whilst you're gone. You never know – he might sweep you off to the Bahamas or something,' she giggled.

Nic's heart gave a sudden, painful lurch. 'I doubt it,' she said glumly. 'It's not his style.'

'Well, you just concentrate on getting him back. Forget about everything else and don't worry about things at this end. I'll make sure everyone gets your messages and your place'll be sparkling when you get back.'

Nic felt a sudden rush of tears. 'I know it's all I ever seem to say these days,' she said, gratefully handing her suitcase over to the cab driver, 'but thanks again, hey?'

'Like I said. What're friends for?' Estelle grinned. She slapped the roof of the cab. 'Get this girl to Heathrow as fast as you can!'

The driver sped off, wheels squealing as he turned the corner. Nic looked back but Estelle had already disappeared. She leaned back in the seat, her heart thudding steadily as she thought of what was to come. All she could think about was Mat. Seeing him. Explaining to him. *Being* with him. The rest of it – family, work, even Tory and Caryn – simply fell away.

Estelle stood in the doorway of Nic's living room, her chest tight, fingers clenched with rage. It was a mess, true, but even the scattered clothes and books couldn't hide its moneyed, easy elegance. She looked at the comfortable couches, the pale wooden dining table and upholstered chairs, the bookcases, expensive television and stereo in one corner of the living room, an upturned pair of high-heeled shoes, white Armani jeans and a silk Hermès scarf slung over the back of one of the chairs. All this. For free. For nothing. For being Jim Harte's daughter. Everything in Estelle's little luxury pied-à-terre had been paid for – Christ, she was *still* paying for it – nothing had come for free. All those years of fucking anything and every-thing Mrs Devereaux threw at her, with no end in sight. She wasn't like Pandora or Marie, two of the girls who'd been smart enough to save their money and get out of the game. Pandora now ran a successful lingerie shop in Knightsbridge, bankrolled by a customer who'd had a soft spot for her. Estelle saw her occasionally when she went into the shop herself, attracted by a vision of independence that she just couldn't seem to achieve for herself.

She'd made money in the years she'd been working for Mrs Devereaux, but she never seemed to save any. Her closets were full of clothes and shoes, handbags, beauty products, jewel-lery . . . the sorts of silly things that, once bought, became almost worthless. Where was she to go with six Balenciaga gowns and the latest bag from Prada? Nic's wealth was different. She understood that immediately. Understated, valuable, eter-nal. Her flat was full of the sorts of things Estelle admired in other people's homes: heavy, silver-framed photographs of Nic in her ballet outfit; winning a rosette at a local gymkhana, coming first in the swimming races at her exclusive Harare school. She wandered over to the antique sideboard and picked one up. It was a woman she didn't recognise but who looked a little like Nic. She turned it over. There was no inscription. Nic's mother, perhaps? She set it down. There was one of Jim on horseback. Estelle stared at it. He was handsome in the way of old movie stars from the fifties and sixties . . . tall, upright, proud. She pushed it away from her abruptly.

She wandered into the bedroom. The bed was unmade. She looked at the crisp white sheets and the silk throw lying carelessly on the ground. Nic's dressing table was almost bare, unlike Estelle's. There were no pots of the latest skin creams from Chanel and YSL, no magic potions or products guaranteed to make you glow. A blue tub of Nivea cold cream and an open tube of lipstick. The Body Shop. Ugh. She put it down again, wrinkling her nose. She pulled open one of the drawers. A few pieces of jewellery – again, nothing that Estelle would ever wear. Cheap but striking. Definitely not Estelle's style. She shut it again.

She was enjoying herself, wandering through the evidence of her half-sister's life. In the second bedroom that Nic used as a study, there were more books than Estelle had ever laid eyes on. She flicked through the titles . . . nothing of interest. Nic's laptop lay, still open, on the desk. She pulled open a drawer. There were several large notebooks inside. She lifted one out. Diaries. Her eyes widened. She looked at the spine. 1996. There were at least a dozen others, neatly aligned. 1985, 1986, 1987. She picked them out, one by one, and took them into the living room. She picked up the notebook titled 1981 and began to read. The life of the girl she resented more than anyone else in the world was slowly being unfolded before her, allowing her to step right in.

The phone rang suddenly, shattering the silence. Estelle almost dropped the notebook. She looked up, dazed. The clock on the wall said it was eight forty-three p.m. She stared at it in shock. She'd been reading for almost five hours straight. She was late! She'd forgotten all about her booking that evening. In a panic, she jumped up just as a man's voice came on the answering machine. 'Nic? This is Mat. I'm coming back to London. We need to talk. I'll stop by tomorrow morning around lunchtime. I did get your messages but I needed some time to think. I'll see you tomorrow.' He hung up. There was a brief burr of the dialling tone then the machine clicked off. Estelle ran to the kitchen, grabbed her bag and fished her own phone out of it. She punched in Petko's number, told him she'd be half an hour late and ran out the front door, almost forgetting to lock it. She was due to meet a client at a Mayfair restaurant at ten. If she was late, Mrs Devereaux would be on her like a ton of bricks. She hailed a cab on Regent's Park Road and clambered in, sweating. Her heart was racing. If Mat was back in London, it meant Nic would surely be on her way back soon. And before she got back, there was something Estelle needed to do.

Mat read the draft through one last time, made a couple of notes in the margins and slid the entire thing into an envelope. He got up, took his plate and cup to the kitchen and washed up, mentally checking off the things he needed to do before leaving for the airport. Again. He looked around – the place was mostly empty anyway. He'd cleared out the closets and packed most of his stuff into a couple of cardboard boxes that he'd left in the hallway. Mrs Saitowitz from the apartment on the second floor could have the spare key; the following day, Jerry, a friend from Harvard, would move in for a couple of months, just until he'd decided what to do. It had taken Mat less than twenty-four hours to put his New York life away. A measure, perhaps, of how temporary it had been all along. He turned off the tap, dried his hands and looked at his watch. It was almost five. Time enough for a quick shower, finish the last of his packing and then call a cab to take him to the airport. Simon had rung back; he was back in London and would meet him the following morning at Heathrow. He took a deep breath. What he had to say to Nic had to be said face to face. Any other way was cowardly. It was one thing he was not.

Half an hour later, he was ready. He heard the cab blow its horn outside. He picked up his suitcase, scribbled a note for Jerry and opened the door. One last look? No, he shut the door firmly behind him. He walked down to Mrs Saitowitz's apartment.

'You leavin' already?' Mrs Saitowitz said as she opened the door, a cigarette dangling permanently between her lips.

''Fraid so, Mrs S.,' he smiled. 'Thanks for taking care of the keys. Jerry should be here tomorrow morning.'

'Well, I ain't going nowhere,' she said, taking them from him. She pulled her multicoloured housecoat around her. 'You have a safe flight, now.'

'I will. Thanks again.'

'Sure.' She closed the door. He ran down the last flight of stairs, his bag banging awkwardly against his legs, and pushed open the main door to the street. The cab was waiting. He slung his bag into the boot, jumped in and directed the driver towards JFK. He leaned back. It was hard to believe that less than thirty-six hours after arriving, he was heading back.

Nic peered at the building. 'Yes, that's it,' she said, stuffing the piece of paper back in her bag. She pulled out a handful of notes. 'Can you wait for me, please? I just need to make sure he's there.'

'You're payin', lady,' the cab driver drawled. 'Ain't no thing.'

She pushed open the door and stepped out. It was boiling hot in New York, even at seven in the evening. Sweat was trickling down her back, although that had more to do with nerves than temperature. She felt sick with anticipation. On the flight over, she'd been unable to sleep a wink. She'd sat bolt upright in her chair, too nervous to eat or drink, watching reruns of American sitcoms until she thought she might scream.

She ran across the road and scanned the entrance for signs of a bell or a buzzer. There was nothing. She stepped back and peered up at the façade. His apartment was on the eighth floor. She knocked as loudly as she could on the main door, hurting her knuckles in the process, and waited. Nothing happened. She rapped again, as loudly as she could. Her heart was racing. Across the road the cab driver peered suspiciously out at her.

She was just about to take off her sandal and hammer on the door again when she heard the squeak of a window opening.

'Bell's broken, honey. Who you lookin' for?' A red-haired lady with a cigarette hanging out of her mouth looked down at her.

Nic looked up gratefully. 'Mat Ndava,' she began nervously. 'I think he's on the eighth floor?'

'Oh, you just missed him. He's on his way to London. I thought you were comin' tomorrow. You're Jerry?'

Nic felt dizzy. She stared up at the woman. 'To London?' she croaked.

The woman nodded. 'Say, you OK there?' Nic stepped back from the door. Her head was spinning. She put a hand to her mouth, afraid she might really be sick. 'You OK?' the woman repeated.

Nic forced herself to look up. She nodded. 'I . . . I'm fine. It's just . . . I've just come from London,' she said, tears threatening to overwhelm her. 'I've been trying to get in touch with him for the past couple of days and I . . . I thought—' She stopped, aware she would burst into tears if she said anything further. 'I'd better go,' she said quickly. 'Th-thanks.'

'No problem.' The window scraped back upwards. Nic walked across the road to the cab, defeat seeping out of her pores. What now?

'Where to, lady?' the cab driver asked, starting the engine.

'Back to the airport,' she said, fighting back the tears. She would get on the next available flight back home. Surely Mat would call her if he'd gone back to London?

An hour later, her face streaked with tears, she turned away from the ticket sales desk and asked someone to show her the way to the nearest hotel. She wouldn't be able to get on a flight until Saturday morning. Two whole days away. For one wild moment she even thought about calling her father to see if Manning could pick her up – but she hadn't spoken to him since Monday, when she'd run out of the house, and it was probably fair to say sending Manning over to New York to get her would be the last thing on his mind.

She walked into the lobby at the airport Hilton, checked into a suite which, at nine o'clock in the evening, was all that was available. She didn't even bother to unpack. She lay down, still in the jeans and not-so-crisp white shirt she'd left London in some twelve hours earlier, and cried herself to sleep.

All through the interminable evening spent sandwiched between two fat businessmen, Estelle's mind was elsewhere. One of them had a hand on her knee; the other's eyes were firmly glued to her cleavage. She sipped her champagne, oblivious to their obvious appreciation and their meaningless chatter. She felt a million miles away. She *was* a million miles away. Nic's diaries, written sometimes in painstaking detail, every single day for nearly twenty years, had given her a long, hard look at a life that should have been hers. The ballet lessons, the ponies, the Sunday-afternoon *braai* by the pool at Avonlea; the trips by private plane, shopping in New York, skiing in Gstaad, winters in the Bahamas. So *what* if her stepmother had been mean to her? The sheer scale and luxury of it all blew that little consideration right out of the water. Whilst she and Gloria had lived in Arcadia, where meat was only ever served on Sundays and even then at the largesse of the Cunninghams. Gloria walked the six miles to work every single morning whilst Nic and her stepmother were chauffeured by plane and car around the world. She burned inside.

She felt her companion's hand slide further up her thigh. She wanted nothing more than to get the man back into his hotel room, fuck or suck his brains out, whichever he preferred – both, if she had to – and get Petko to drive her straight back to Primrose Hill. She had things to do. As for those two friends of Nic's . . . she felt her chest tighten angrily. They'd better watch out as well. She'd read what Nic had written. So Caryn thought she was false, did she? She had *no* fucking idea.

102

To say that he was surprised to see the girl he'd met at the 101 Club standing in the doorway of Nic's flat was putting it mildly. He stared at her. It was midday. She was wearing a silk nightdress he recognised as Nic's – her nipples stood out clearly against the thin fabric. He took a step backwards. She was waiting for him as he climbed the stairs to Nic's front door, her arm draped provocatively above her head.

'I . . . I'm sorry. I thought . . . Is Nic in?' he asked, confused. What the hell was she doing there? In Nic's nightdress?

'Oh, hi, Mat,' she said, chummily familiar. 'No. She's gone away for the weekend. I think she'll be back early next week. I just got up—' She yawned delicately. 'I was just making some coffee . . .' She stood back, her body silhouetted against the light coming in from the windows behind her. 'Would you like some?'

'No, thanks,' he said shortly. 'I guess . . . well, I'll stop by early next week, then,' he said, half turning to go.

'Shall I tell her to give you a ring? They didn't say where they were going—'

'They—?' He stopped.

She put a hand to her mouth. 'David. Her boyfriend. Didn't you meet him that night, at the club? Oops,' she smiled prettily. 'Have I put my foot in it?'

He stared at her. 'David?' he repeated woodenly.

She pulled a coy face. 'Forget I said anything,' she said archly. 'Are you *sure* you wouldn't like a cup?'

'Quite sure.' He turned and bolted back down the stairs. He yanked open the front door and slammed it shut behind him. *David. Her boyfriend. Didn't you meet him at the club?* So his suspicions about Nic Harte were confirmed. He was shocked at how much it hurt.

Estelle watched him leave, a small, satisfied smile playing around her lips. She'd seen from the way his eyes widened that her little slip had hit the mark. He wouldn't be back, of that she was quite sure. She knew a thing or two about her countrymen. This one was proud. Arrogant, too. She could see it in his stance; the wary, slightly aloof eyes, the way he held himself. No, the comment had hit home and there was no way *he'd* hang around. All she had to do now was make sure Nic didn't go after him and she had a pretty good idea how to do just that. She shut the door behind her. She pulled her hair into a pony tail, wriggled out of Nic's nightdress and pulled open one of the drawers. She found a pair of sweatpants and a T-shirt and pulled them on. She'd better start clearing the place up – she'd just had a text message from Nic to say she'd be arriving the following day. She wanted the flat to be absolutely spotless when she got back and if there was one thing Gloria had taught her, it was how to clean a house.

Three hours later, the place was sparkling. There wasn't a surface left that hadn't been polished or shined to within an inch of its life. The floors were spotless, the cushions plumped; even the dishcloths had been washed, dried and ironed. Nic would be heartbroken, but she'd sure as hell be appreciative. And that was what she wanted. Her job over the next couple of months was to make sure Nic remained that way. She would be the best friend she'd ever had. Forget those other two bitches – from now on, that role was hers. She pulled off her clothes and walked naked to the shower. She opened her white make-up pouch and took out a bottle of perfumed shower gel. Nice as Nic's flat was, with its power shower and soft, fluffy white towels, she drew the line at products from Boots.

After an exhausting six-hour flight from JFK, Nic arrived back at Heathrow at seven on Sunday morning, seventy-two hours after she'd left it, airport delays notwithstanding. She hadn't slept a wink on the flight over; by the time they landed, her stomach was tight with nerves and there were unhappy dark circles under her eyes. She caught a cab from Heathrow and leaned back against the seat, utterly drained. In the cold light of the past couple of days, haring off to New York seemed the silliest, most childish thing to do. London was damp and muggy after the heat and blue skies of New York, but the grey heaviness in the air exactly matched her mood. There was little traffic on the way into the city and within an hour, she was outside her door. She pulled her bag out of the boot, paid the driver and disconsolately trudged across the road.

103

Jim put down the phone, poured himself a glass of his favourite whisky, Lagavulin, and walked over to his desk. He sipped it slowly, savouring the fiery peat taste at the back of his throat, feeling it burn its way down into his body. He sat down, placing the tumbler to one side, and brought his hands up to his chin. Freedland was dead. Britain's most influential group of news-papers was now firmly in his control. RhoMine share prices were at an all-time high. On paper, at least, he was worth several billion dollars. Not bad for the penniless orphan who'd dis-embarked in Portsmouth in 1948 with nothing other than a letter of introduction for an uncle whom he'd never seen and subsequently hated.

He picked up the glass again. All through the four-hour-long AGM, he'd sat by silently, watching Ogilvy and Butcher give a wholly false rendition of RhoMine's accounts for the year just ended. Share prices up, stocks rising, capital reserves strong, future looking good. That was the stuff they liked to hear. At times like these, he mused, the ends justified the means. His board members – greedy, self-aggrandising, self-serving bastards to a man – were swept along by their own avarice. In their ex-pensive pinstriped suits that did nothing to disguise the ambition in their paunches, they listened and believed what they wanted to believe. Jim had neither sympathy nor pity for them. The English, he mused, were masters of the art of studied disinterest. He gave a short laugh. At one point in the meeting, someone had raised the issue of corruption – some minor annoyance over the large amount of cash reserves that RhoMine kept in a Swiss account precisely for the payment of bribes and sweeteners that Harte claimed were fundamental to doing business in Africa. If news ever emerged . . . the man turned to look at Jim, his hooded eyes slowly blinking. Jim stifled the impulse to reach across the table and grab him by his starched lapels. Corruption? The idiot had no idea. Every single man at that table was corrupt, he wanted to say. *Including you, you fat prick. Corruption is both fundamental and necessary to the way the world operates, not just in Africa.*

He sighed. That, in the end, was the difference between him and them. *He* knew what it took. Every single dirty deal, every compromise, every time you stomached what you thought you couldn't, ever. Every transaction contained within it, however hidden, a little 'something' for the men who made it happen. Without it, nothing worked. In some places the little 'something' was transparent – take the deal they'd just done over the copper mines in Mozambique. Everyone at the table, palms open. In others, like the Riverbrook deal, it was buried under layers of secrecy, shredded memos, numbered accounts and muted conversations. But it was still there. In some ways, that was why he'd been attracted to Africa in the first place. In Africa it was all there, on the surface, in every handshake, every conversation, every meeting. In Britain it had taken him a decade to work out how to say it, how to do it, when and where to make the payments. And that, in the end, was what it all boiled down to – payments. Who got what, when and how much. Occasionally, however, like now, a fly in the ointment threatened to upset the smooth running of things. That fucking young reporter, Mat Ndava, was one such fly.

Jim had been aware for some time that there was someone out there asking questions, digging up the sort of personal information he'd always been so careful to keep hidden. It had taken him a while to find out who he worked for and why he was so interested. Again, of course, it had come down to a payment. The pathetic, grateful DiAngelo was only too happy to turn over what he'd managed to glean, but DiAngelo's boss was a different matter. In one of those awful twists of fate that life liked to throw at you every once in a while, DiAngelo's boss had turned out to be one of the few men who couldn't be bought by Harte, not at any price. Winston Freedland. Sarah's godfather. Would you *believe* it? Sarah's family had never been satisfied with the explanation of her death – right from the beginning they'd asked questions. Nothing that proved anything, of course. The whole saga had been played out endlessly in the British media. Yet another reason to want the old bull dead. The Brits had never quite forgotten the way Freedland had gone after him in the press. It was easy to see where their natural sympathy lay. After all, Freedland was one of them. Eton, Cambridge, City. The smooth, Darwinian process expected of young British males of a certain class and age. Jim was not of that class – never would be, it seemed. Freedland was the insider, Harte the outsider . . . and that would never, ever change. Well, Freedland was dead and he, Jim Harte, was alive. Very much so.

He sipped the last of his whisky slowly. Buying DiAngelo had bought him the necessary time to push the Riverbrook acquisition through, but that was about it. A little time, that was all. Ndava would simply take the story elsewhere. He was a smart, ambitious young man. Unthinkable that he hadn't kept copies of his work and that he wasn't, at that very minute, working out where to take it next. Jim set down his glass, smiling to himself. But Matari Ndava, however clever he might be, hadn't yet met someone like Jim. He picked up the phone and dialled a number.

'Gordon? It's Jim. I need to talk to you. It's about that son of yours . . .'

104

Martin made a few last-minute adjustments to the way he'd framed the final shot and leaned back in his chair, yawning. It was almost nine o'clock and the three of them were looking at the rushes before the hour-long documentary could be pronounced complete. Rupesh had the headphones on. Caryn was sitting a few feet away, her mind anywhere but in the room with them. She watched Simon's silhouetted face fade from view and then the list of credits began to roll.

'Well, what d'you think?' Martin asked them both. 'Caryn?'

Caryn came back to earth with a bump. 'Sorry?'

'What's the matter with you?' Martin asked, irritated. 'Your head's been in the clouds ever since you came back from holiday. Next time you ask to go on one, I'm going to say no.'

'Sorry,' Caryn said guiltily. 'It's just late, that's all—'

'Yeah, well, the quicker I can get an opinion on this, the sooner we can go home,' he said tetchily. 'That last shot – any good?'

'I think it's fine,' Caryn said wearily. 'It's great.' She stood up, aware that Martin's eyes were on her. 'I've got to go home, Martin. I'm exhausted.'

'OK. Let's finish this up tomorrow morning. I want to bike it over to the Beeb before lunchtime.'

Caryn nodded, too tired to speak. She stopped by her desk to pick up her bag. She fished out her phone – four missed calls, three of them from Nic. The fourth call was from Simon. A friend of his was arriving the following morning. He had to go to Heathrow to pick him up. He'd ring her later.

She closed the phone slowly. Something had happened between her and Simon on the trip to Cape Town. She wasn't sure what had caused it, but their relationship – if it could be called that – had slipped into a deeper, more unexpected gear. For a moment she remembered the first time she'd seen him in the lobby at the Dorchester, striding across the floor, six foot two of rugged, sun-bleached charm with a laid-back nonchalance that pulled every female eye towards him. It was hard to reconcile that man – to think he'd told her his name was Charlie! – with the wary, troubled man who slipped from her bed before dawn every morning, or who issued invitations to fly halfway round the world at the drop of a hat. Simon was a mystery to her. She knew next to nothing about him. No, less than nothing. He'd handed her a few, random straws – he'd grown up in Africa; he'd lived in London for a while; he had no family. But beyond that, she knew nothing. And yet, despite his carefully constructed reticence, there were moments when they were together when she had the sensation of suddenly and unexpectedly having been allowed in. In his most private moments, he gave her the tiniest, most fleeting glimpse of the deepest, barest parts of himself that she couldn't walk away from. She'd told no one about him; neither Nic nor Tory had ever seen him. They never went out anywhere together where they might be seen. It had crossed her mind once or twice . . . was he married, perhaps? But deep down, she knew the subterfuge had nothing to do with anything as conventional as a marriage. He had other reasons to hide. She glanced at the conference room. Martin and Rupesh were still bent over the screen. She sighed. She'd lost the appetite for it, somehow. All she wanted to do was go home and wait. Wait for him to call.

He pressed the buzzer just before midnight. Caryn slid out of bed and ran to the door. His mouth was warm and tasted of whisky. 'You've been drinking,' she murmured. He didn't answer. His neck was warm against her face. He kissed her again, his hand holding her head gently, his tongue seeking some sort of answer to an as yet unasked question. He slipped his other hand under the thin silk of her nightgown, fingers sliding over her skin, bringing out the goose bumps along her arms. He pulled her hips towards him; he was already hard. Caryn felt the slow burn of pleasure begin to travel its way up her body. She pulled his head down roughly, her lips brushing the day-old stubble that lay beneath the sandpapery texture of his cheek. She couldn't have enough of him; it ended, as it always did, with them on the living-room floor, as if waiting any longer was too exquisite a pain to endure.

Afterwards, lying drowsily together in bed, his face illuminated by the ghostly blue of her bedside clock and the irregular burn of his cigarette, he placed his hand on the tender skin of her groin, stroking it lightly, and turned to her. 'What if,' he said slowly, as though testing the words on his tongue, 'I asked you to come away with me? For a while, I mean.'

Caryn's eyes flew open. 'Where?'

'Somewhere. Anywhere.'

'Leave London, you mean?'

He nodded. 'Yeah. Go away for a bit.'

She was quiet for a while. 'I couldn't just leave,' she said slowly. 'I mean, there's my job . . . how would I manage?'

'You mean money?'

'Yes. I've . . . I've always worked—'

'I have money, Caryn. Money's not an issue.'

'It is for me, Simon. I've never had any. Whatever I have, I've worked for it. And then there's my family. My brother. And my mum.'

'Where are they?' he asked quietly. 'You never talk about them.'

'Well, you don't talk about yours,' she said, propping herself up on one elbow.

'Nothing to talk about,' he said evenly, stubbing out his cigarette. He rolled over to face her. 'Could you? Leave?'

'Where would we go?' she asked, her breathing slow and even.

'Where d'you fancy?'

'Somewhere warm. Where you grew up? I've always wanted to go to Zimbabwe. You know, from the way Nic talks about it—'

'No, not Africa. Africa's finished for me,' he broke in. She heard him fumble for another cigarette. 'Anywhere but Africa.'

'I don't know. I've never been anywhere. Apart from Cape

Town. And Colchester. And I certainly don't want to go *there*.' Caryn smiled.

'Is that a "yes", then?' he asked quietly.

Caryn took a deep breath. The words drifted lightly away from her, as though spoken by someone else. 'Yes. Yes, I'll go with you.'

He left very early in the morning, when the pale, watery light was just beginning to filter through the blinds. From the tangle of bed sheets, she watched him as he pulled on his jeans and buttoned up his shirt, the naked body that was now so familiar to her slowly disappearing as he became a stranger to her once again. He leaned over and kissed her, hard, and then stood up, collecting his things. As usual, he left without saying a word. Caryn heard the front door shut quietly behind him and the soft tread of his footsteps on the stairs. And then he was gone. She stretched her arms above her head, yawning. She glanced at the bedside clock. It was five-thirty. She rolled over, stretching her legs, and nudged something off the bed. She slid an arm out of the bed and groped for it, wondering what it was. It was his wallet; it must have fallen out of his back pocket as he got dressed.

She stared at it, then switched on the light and turned it over in her hands. It was a dark brown leather wallet, scuffed and worn in places. He'd obviously had it for a long time. Her heart was beating fast. She flipped it open. There was the usual stack of credit cards on the left-hand side. She pulled one out. A platinum American Express card. *Simon Carter. Member since 1988.* She stared at it. A visa card in the same name. On the right-hand side were a number of business cards. She hesitated. She was snooping, wasn't she? And it was wrong of her, she knew. But he told her so little. She'd just agreed to disappear with him and she didn't even know his last name. She drew her knees up to her chest, the wallet held loosely in her hand. Well, now she knew it. *Simon Carter.* She had the feeling she'd heard the name before, somewhere. But where? She flipped open the wallet again. A hundred pounds or so. Some US dollar bills; a twenty-rand note from the Cape Town trip and – she tugged the note out, looking closely at it. Fifty Maltese lira. She had a vague idea where Malta was. A job? A recent holiday? There was a business card tucked behind one of the twenty-dollar bills. She looked at it. *Matari Ndava. Senior Staff Writer, WED.* A New York number. She felt the hairs on the back of her neck stand up. She turned it over. *Nic. 0207 284 2312.* It was Nic's hand-writing. She knew it as well as she knew her own. Suddenly she remembered where she'd heard Simon Carter's name before. She swallowed. She was no longer sleepy. Nothing made sense.

Simon stared at Caryn. She was crying, her face red and blotchy from what seemed like hours of sobbing, and for the first time in his life, he wasn't sure what to do. He sighed. It had been three days since he'd left his wallet at her house – so *stupid* ! – and even though she'd handed it back to him without a word, he knew that there would be recriminations. Impossible to believe she hadn't gone through it. Of course she had. He'd wondered briefly to himself if he hadn't subconsciously left it at hers on purpose – it was one way of bringing things out into the open that he'd never dared voice before. He ran a hand through his hair. 'Look, Caryn. I told you before . . . it's complicated.'

'How is it complicated? Just tell me the truth, Simon. Who *are* you?' She brushed aside her tears angrily.

He shoved his hands in his pockets and looked down at her. She was angrier than he'd ever seen her, but there was some-thing oddly comforting about her too. She *cared.* She cared *about him* – it was written all over her face, the frown drawing her eyes together in an expression of concentration. It had been years since he'd seen anyone so passionately interested in . . . well, in *him.* Absurd, perhaps, but true. He liked to keep the world at a safe distance, at arm's length, away from himself, his true self. He was disturbed not only by the questions she was asking but even more so by the responses they'd generated in him. He turned away from her and walked over to the window. He opened his mouth to speak, to say something in his defence, but nothing came out. He stood looking down at the street below, at the odd couple walking past, an elderly woman walking her dog, stopping every few paces to chivvy it along. It was a fat dachshund of the sort you hardly saw any more these days. Suddenly his head was spinning. There was the soft 'tick-tock' of the clock Caryn kept on the mantelpiece and the muted sound of the radio in the kitchen, background noises that were different from the droning sound in his head. He shook it impatiently. There was a clamouring that he couldn't get rid of, a sharp, insistent tug towards an imagined scene that he'd buried for so long. He shook his head again. He could hear Caryn's breathing, a harsh, angry sound, followed by the sound of his own heartbeat.

All at once he was ten years old again. Cycling down the road towards the farmhouse, his wheels spinning and sending up clouds of the red dirt that lay on the surface of the earth in the barren place his parents had chosen to make their home. *Mukiwa! Mukiwa!* A group of children ran alongside, giving half-hearted chase until their thin spindly legs tired and they slowed down, receding into the distance as he pedalled furiously along. *White boy.* That was what they called him – what everyone called him, from Moses, the itinerant farmhand his father sometimes employed, to the guards at the new army camp just outside Filabusi. *Mukiwa.* White boy in Africa. It was an Ndebele word that everyone used to describe people like him, even the Shona. The fact that this particular *mukiwa* spoke Shona as well as anyone else made no difference. But the jeering children on the sides of the roads weren't to know that. The only person who didn't call him that was Mat. Mat called him Simon and talked to him as though he were no different from himself.

His hair was still wet; he and Mat had been swimming in the river. He'd been teaching Mat how to swim. Swimming was perhaps the only thing he could do that Mat couldn't. At least not yet. At his school in Nyanga, the whites-only school, there was a swimming pool, of course. At Mat's school, the local school for blacks, there wasn't. But that wasn't the only difference between them. Mr Ndava, Mat's father, was rich. Simon's father, Douglas Carter, wasn't. A reversal of the usual roles.

Mat's mother, Mrs Ndava, was warm and soft and always had something for him to eat when Mat took him home. His own mother barely remembered him. All she cared about was Cookie, her fucking dog, and where the next bottle of brandy was coming from. Simon hated the dog. A low-slung, over-weight brown dachshund. He had never taken Mat to his house. He would have been – how to put it? Ashamed? Afraid? Ashamed of the squalor and the desperate way they lived; afraid of what his parents would say. Mat was the only person in the world about whom he had anything even remotely approaching affection or feeling. He hated his parents, he hated the dog and the farmhouse with its peeling walls, the floor that never got swept and the cupboards that contained nothing that didn't come in a glass bottle. He hated the sound of his father labori-ously counting out the measly sums of money he brought home on market day in exchange for whatever he'd managed to coax out of the stubborn, unyielding earth. Sometimes, when he came home empty-handed, it was Simon who bore the brunt of his rage. Mrs Ndava, when she saw him, would cluck her tongue and put some sort of homemade paste on the most recent and open of wounds. He sat stiffly under her hands, unused to the feel of contact of that sort, until it was over.

He heard it on the radio. In his mind's eye, he saw the dog. It would have been blown apart like a sausage that had split its skin. He was sick, then. Standing in the yard, spewing out the *sadza* and peppery goat stew that Mrs Ndava had fed him. But there was relief, too.

He turned away from the window. Caryn stood in the kitchen doorway, arms wrapped protectively around herself, the strain of the past few days etched clearly across her face. He was moved by her in ways he couldn't describe. He reached for her, aware of a great tension suddenly breaking in him, clouding his eyes. He kissed her fiercely. Then he began to talk.

She watched him sleep, his body finally relaxing as he sank lower and lower into the depths of slumber. They'd been talking for almost six hours, she noticed, glancing at the bedside clock.

It was dark outside. She felt a sudden fierce wave of tenderness for the man who slept with his arms wrapped around her, even in sleep, as if he couldn't quite trust her to be there when he awoke. She closed her eyes but some part of her mind kept returning to the sound of his voice. She could almost picture it – the dilapidated farmhouse; the bare cupboards; the sound of bottles clinking as they were taken up, drained, and put aside. It was her childhood, too. That terrifying sense of the edge of the world, just waiting for you, an unpaid telephone bill or a final rent demand away. The whole world poised, waiting for you to fall. Yet hers was nothing compared to his. He spoke of things she could only dimly grasp at. Simon was the perpetual misfit, the odd one out. He would never belong to the Ndavas in the way they belonged to each other; their way of being together, as a family, was so different from the culture to which *he* belonged, however reluctantly. The bonds that held the Ndavas together – duty, respect, a quiet admiration – were at odds with the image of the sort of family he longed for. A cheerful, bustling, pie-baking mother and a calm, pipe-smoking father who took you fishing on Sundays . . . *that* was the imaginary family he'd grown up with, culled from English schoolboy novels and the vague memory of those white childhood friends he'd had before Mat walked into his life. Patience Ndava, politically active, a strict disciplinarian, a cook, yes, and many other things besides – she fed, clothed and talked to him, but she wasn't the mother of the storybooks or childish dreams. Mat didn't seem to expect it of her, or his father, Gordon. He was happy with them in a way that Simon could never be. There were times when the gulf between their worlds yawned, tugging at the bonds of friendship they'd formed. It wasn't his fault; it certainly wasn't the Ndavas'. They cared for him the way they cared for Mat. *You are my son. That's it. That's everything.* He'd grown up with Gordon's refrain in his ears and it was true. But it wasn't enough.

He stirred in his sleep; a small noise escaped from his throat as his body moved and settled again. Caryn bent her head to kiss the dark blonde hair on the crown of his head. She wasn't sure what would happen next. Simon was entwined with Mat and

Nic and her father in ways she couldn't even guess at. It was so far removed from her own life and upbringing that she hardly knew what to say. For the time being it seemed enough that she was there, holding him, listening without judgement. For how long, though? Even she, with absolutely no experience of the sorts of games that were being played out across continents and alliances, could see that it was more complicated than she could possibly imagine. This was not the time for confession and absolution. What had happened – what he, Simon, had done – went far beyond that. She slid her body down until she was beside his. She was empty, unable to summon any sort of answer. She lay there in the dark, her breath coming faster and faster. It *was* another world he described. Perhaps that was the point?

105

Mat walked down the long driveway of his parents' home, away from the house. His head was reeling. He'd walked into the living room and seen his father with a rare glass of brandy on one of the sidetables, his hand occasionally giving a tremble – as if betrayed by the turmoil that must surely have been going on inside his head. He gave his own head a violent shake, as if to rid himself of the memory. He'd stormed out. He'd never before so much as raised his voice to his father – to either of his parents. It was not their way. Disagree, yes, by all means, but never publicly. Never in the open. But when Gordon had opened his mouth to ask – no, to *instruct* – Mat to drop the story, he'd been unable to contain himself. Something had burst inside him, then, from which there was no going back.

He yanked open the car door and got inside. His heart was racing. He peeled out of the driveway, sending a spray of gravel scattering behind him, beyond caring what his father or the neighbours thought. He headed south towards Battersea. There was only one person in the world he could talk to right now. Simon. He hoped he was home. He'd seen him briefly the morning he'd arrived but he'd been strangely absent since then. He wondered what it was. A woman, perhaps? Simon never said.

Half an hour later, he pulled up in front of the flat. He ran up the stairs two at a time, his whole body still coursing with adrenalin. It was as if he couldn't get his father's words out of his ears. *I work for Harte, Matari. I've been working for him for a long time.* There was music playing softly behind the door. Relief flowed over him as he slid his key in the lock. He opened the door. Simon was lying asleep on the couch, a newspaper folded across his chest. He opened his eyes slowly as Mat walked in.

'*Bru*,' Mat said, tossing the car keys on to the table. 'Am I glad to see you.' He walked into the kitchen and pulled a bottle of water out of the fridge. He twisted off the cap and drank straight from the bottle, wiping his lips with the back of his hand. He stood in the doorway. 'Is something wrong?' he asked, frowning slightly. There was a strange expression on Simon's face. An odd calmness, something he hadn't seen in him for a very long time. Simon shook his head. Mat put down the empty bottle and walked over to the couch. He sank into the chair opposite Simon and looked at him warily. Something had happened. Simon pushed himself up into a sitting position and picked up the packet of cigarettes lying at his feet. He lit one slowly, inhaling deeply.

'You look upset,' he said eventually, not looking directly at Mat.

Mat nodded, still frowning. A feeling of great distance came over him, as if he were looking at Simon from a long way away. He took his time in responding. 'I've just been to see Dad,' he said eventually, his breath leaving his body in a long sigh. 'He . . . we had an argument.'

Simon looked at him through the haze of cigarette smoke. 'About what?' he said carefully.

Mat looked away. It was his turn to flinch, as if something too intimate had been said aloud. He brought a hand up to touch the smooth, oiled near-baldness of his head, an oddly feminine gesture of self-consciousness. 'Fuck, I don't even know how to say it. All this time . . .' He broke off, agitated. He got to his feet. 'Simon. How d'you think Dad made his money?'

Simon looked away. Mat hesitated. There was the feeling as often happened between them that Simon knew what he was thinking; was thinking the same thing himself. 'Do you really want to know?' Simon said it quietly, less of a question than a statement.

Mat stared down at him. 'Don't tell me you knew? You knew about him and Harte? Don't tell me that, *bru*. Don't say it. *Please*.'

'Mat . . .' Simon's voice was strained. 'I think . . . there's something I need to tell you.' He got up suddenly and walked to the kitchen. Mat heard him opening a cupboard, heard the chink of a glass and of ice-cubes being dropped into it. He came out a few seconds later with a drink in his hand. Pale gold; a whisky, perhaps. He swallowed a mouthful, baring his teeth as the fiery liquid burned its way down his throat. 'I haven't been completely honest with you,' he said slowly, staring at his drink.

'Don't tell me,' Mat gave a nervous half-laugh. 'You work for the asshole too—'

Simon raised his eyes. There was a moment's hesitation and then the world as Mat understood it caved in. Simon nodded. 'That's the bastard of it, Mat. Yes, yes I do.'

PART SEVEN

106

Caryn carefully eased the car into the traffic heading south on Sepulveda, turned left on to Manhattan Beach Boulevard and then left again on to Highland. She drove slowly and carefully, remembering to do exactly as Simon said. *Indicate, check your rear-view mirror, watch the car in front of you at all times. If you hit someone from behind, it's almost always your fault.* There was a lot to remember. She'd finally passed her test but she still didn't feel confident enough to drive further than a few blocks away from the house.

She pulled up in front of the whitewashed, clapboard town-house with a view directly on to the beach and killed the engine. She stared up at the house. Even after four months she couldn't quite get over the fact that *she* lived here. Or that the little yellow car was hers. Or that Simon was inside. In fact, she found most things about her life these days hard to grasp. She could never have imagined she'd have the courage to leave Alice, or Brian, for that matter. It was Brian, in the end, who'd persuaded her she'd done the right thing. 'Go on,' he'd said to her, that last month in London. '*Live* a little, Car. I can take care of things.' She looked to the left and right. The houses in Manhattan Beach were a charming, eclectic collection of clapboard townhouses in bright, pretty colours – white, pink, blue, lemon yellow. It was about as far from Baberton House as anything she'd ever im-agined. She looked around her again, as if to make sure it was all really there, and opened the car door.

The cool winter air washed over her, salty and misty on her

skin. She opened the boot and took out the brown paper bags packed full of food. Through the narrow lane between the houses she could see the sea – wide and rolling – merging at the thin line of the horizon with the sky. California really was as everyone said – a dream. A surfeit of beauty and the good life, and now the good life was hers. She kicked open the gate and lugged the bags up the stairs. The house was on three levels: a garage in which Simon kept his car – a big black SUV that Caryn knew she would never have the courage to drive – then up a flight of outside stairs to the front door, which opened on to a large, sunny open-plan kitchen, dining and living room and finally, accessed via a spiral staircase, two bedrooms and a large terrace overlooking the beach on the top floor. It was enormous; three or four times the size of her London flat. For the first few weeks she'd wandered around it in a trance, unable to believe her luck. It belonged to a friend of his, he'd said, who was in Australia for a year or two. It was unfurnished and they'd spent a hilarious couple of days wandering around the furniture shops on Melrose Avenue, looking for stuff. But it was *theirs*, even if only on loan.

She pushed open the door; Simon was talking to someone on his mobile out on the terrace overlooking the beach. She smiled at him through the glass and began to unpack the groceries. That was the other thing about this new, crazy life she couldn't get used to. She, who had always worked for every single thing she owned or used, who'd never even taken out a loan for fear of being unable to pay it back – now she lived the sort of life she'd only ever associated with someone like Nic. Money meant very little to Nic. 'That's because you've always had it,' Caryn reminded her every time the subject came up. Not that you could ever accuse Nic of being flashy – the opposite, actually. But it was more her attitude towards money – she wasn't afraid of it, like Caryn, and she'd certainly never had to curtail a dream because of the lack of it. Caryn envied the easy confidence that having money brought; her move halfway across the world with a man she couldn't tell anyone about was the single most daring thing she'd ever done. There were nights when she woke up in a cold sweat at the thought of it.

There was so much about Simon that still remained a mystery to her. The precise nature of his business, the deals he made, the trips he took and the relationships he'd formed with people like the man they'd flown to Cape Town to see would remain closed to her, always. She'd understood that almost from the beginning. But it was part of the pact she'd made with herself if she wanted to stay – no questions other than those he was prepared to answer. And she did want to stay. She understood Simon in ways she could never explain. For all his sophistication and the secret source of his wealth, Simon *knew*, in the most profound way possible, exactly what it was to be poor and in that, they understood one another perfectly. She hadn't been joking when she told him he reminded her of Jim Harte – men without a past and prepared to do anything to secure their futures. Unwittingly, perhaps, Nic had prepared her for Simon in a way she'd never expected. She could no longer imagine her life without him. But there was a price to be paid – the argument with Nic when she said she was leaving was only the beginning. Could she bear to lose everything else as well?

She heard the grate of the sliding door opening and closing behind her. 'What's up?' she asked, knowing as he came up behind her and wrapped his arms around her that he probably wouldn't answer. She was right. He held her tightly, burying his face into her hair, breathing deeply. There were times it was he who seemed surprised by it all, not her. He held her sometimes as though he were afraid to let her go. She liked it, and yet she didn't. For all his need for her, there were things about Simon Carter she wasn't sure she could trust herself to know.

107

Tory unlocked the door to her office and shut it firmly behind her. It was quiet inside; upstairs she could hear the girls empty-ing and refilling the pails, setting the stock outside and sweeping up the debris of the previous day's sales. She leaned against her desk, breathing deeply, her fingers going automatically to the small white cardboard box in her jacket pocket. After a week of waking up with a metallic taste in her mouth and three days of bending over the toilet bowl, she hardly needed Boots to con-firm what she already knew: she was pregnant. That, despite the early-morning nausea, was the easy bit. She closed her eyes briefly. Everything was in such a mess. *She* was a mess. And now she was pregnant. Her head was swimming.

To say it couldn't have happened at a worse time was the understatement of the century. Bloomin' Stories was about to open a second shop, just off the Marylebone Road. Despite – or perhaps even because of – the disaster at last year's *GQ* awards, the resulting publicity had almost doubled her turnover. Profits were rising, people were beginning to take notice and orders were flooding in. She'd had to hire three new people in the past four months and when the lease on an existing flower shop just down the road from the Conran Shop had come up, it seemed too good an opportunity to miss – and so they'd jumped. Her father, naturally, was delighted. Nic was delighted. Caryn sent an enormous bouquet of California roses. Luc was thrilled. Everyone, in other words, was delighted – except Tory herself. And Rob, whom she saw less and less, which in turn only served to sharpen her desire. He was preparing to leave; she could sense it. All the signs were there. This time, perhaps, even for good. The thought of it was a constant, trembling refrain. She was conscious of going about her daily business with a fever-like dread burning below the surface of her skin. Soon it would end.

She ought to have been relieved; the madness of the past few months was drawing to a close. Soon she'd be able to return to her calm, ordered life, focus on her business and the future that lay ahead. Instead she could barely function. And now *this*. She withdrew the box from her pocket and stared blankly at it. It was bound to happen. Perhaps she'd subconsciously willed it? A missed pill here, a forgotten day there. It didn't take a genius to work out that sooner or later the whole thing would come crashing to the ground. After all, she'd done it before. What she was doing now wasn't so very different from Thierry. Only hers was the cuckolded partner, now. She winced. Poor, poor Luc. The worst thing about it was that she felt almost no shame. She couldn't have stopped herself even if she'd wanted to, which she didn't. It was as if there were two people living inside her – on the one hand she was a successful, capable businesswoman, living in a beautiful Islington flat with her equally successful, handsome fiancé and on the other, scarcely recognisable, she was the desperately insecure part-time lover of a man whom even *she* could tell was bound to her in ways that weren't altogether healthy, or even sane. Susie lay between them in all the muddled complexity her death had provoked and neither she nor Rob could pull away.

Minutes after meeting him that first time on the road outside her house, she knew there was something she could tell him that she'd never dared to tell anyone else, ever. It took her a long time to bring the subject up but once it was out, there was no going back. He'd listened to her confession without comment and the relief had simply overwhelmed her. She'd gone home to Luc that night, terrified that somehow he would see on her face what it was that had to be said. He hadn't. He hadn't even noticed. Somehow, in some strange, twisted way, that had justified the affair. Luc would *never* understand her. Even after their last argument, when it ought to have been clear to even the village idiot what was going on, he refused to see it. He'd come back, exactly as she'd known he would. He wouldn't leave; he couldn't. He didn't understand what had gone wrong, but he wasn't going to leave her. Not until they'd worked it out. Together. Tory, too exhausted to argue, was too feeble to resist. The relationship was far from good. Luc seemed to be waiting for something; some sign that the unhappiness into which she'd fallen would one day come to an end. He was deluding himself; they both knew it.

And now there was this. A child. Rob's child. What now? The desire to tell someone was overwhelming. Her hand hesitated over the phone. She picked it up and dialled.

She'd left the lights on, Nic noticed, as soon as she opened her front door. She frowned. She distinctly remembered switching them off as she left for work that morning. She was careful about things like that. She switched them off, puzzled. It was the second or third time something like that had happened. Once she'd found the faulty tap in the bathroom running, even though she distinctly remembered shutting it off. She tossed her bag on to the chair and walked through the flat, slightly unnerved. She pushed open the door to her bedroom, half-expecting to see someone sitting there. There was no one, of course. She stared at the bed, reassuring in its calm, perfectly made-up state. She was being silly.

She kicked off her shoes and glanced at her watch. It was almost nine p.m. She'd been working on an article all day – it had to be on Mark's desk first thing in the morning and she'd better get to it. He'd accused her more than once in the past couple of months of having lost focus. It was true. There were days when all she could do was stare out of the window wondering why and how it could have all gone so wrong. She walked into her study and switched on the computer. There was a faint, familiar scent in the room. She frowned, trying to place it. She hadn't noticed it earlier; what was it? The trace of a perfume – one of her own? She looked around her uneasily again, unable to shake the odd feeling that there was someone else in the room with her. But there was no one. The flat was quiet, the only sound the low murmur of the computer. She pulled the stack of notes she'd been working from towards her and looked on the desktop for the file marked 'Work'. She scrolled around for a second or two, wondering why it wasn't in its place, just underneath 'Hard Drive'. She stopped. Where had it gone? She frowned. It *had* to be there. She'd filed it away somewhere else by mistake, that was all. She began to go through her folders. 'Finance', 'Personal', 'Family' – nothing. She tried the 'Find' function and typed in the name she'd saved it under – still nothing. She was utterly baffled. She'd spent the better part of a week on the article – where the hell was it?

By ten p.m. she was no closer to solving the mystery. There was nothing for it but to start again and hope she could remember what she'd already done. She could have kicked herself. What the hell had she done with it? She got up to make herself a cup of strong coffee. As she passed her answering machine, the little green light was flashing. She suppressed the irrational hope that it might – however wildly improbable it was – be Mat and pressed 'play'. It was Tory. She sounded distraught. She grabbed the phone and pulled it towards her. The article would have to wait.

An hour later, she put down the phone, her head spinning. She'd listened almost without interruption for an hour straight. Tory was in a mess. That was putting it mildly. Hell, they *all* were. She longed to pick up the phone again and ring Caryn but of course, she couldn't. Thinking about Caryn produced the same painful ache that thinking about Mat did. At a time when she'd needed Caryn most she'd simply turned up one morning and announced she was leaving for LA. Just like that. Without a backward glance at anyone. It was the only time in two decades of the closest, most loyal friendship she'd ever known, that Caryn had done anything like it. She'd stared at her that morning, sitting in her kitchen, unable to grasp it. Why? Why now? Caryn had mumbled something about a new documentary, going off to do some research, but they'd both known she was lying. It had something to do with the man she'd secretly been seeing, but Caryn refused to say who he was. There were one or two terrible, bleak moments when Nic actually wondered – she could hardly bring herself to think about it – was it Mat? But Caryn simply wouldn't say. They wound up shouting at each other, Caryn slammed the door behind her and that was it. She left on a blustery November morning. One postcard, a month or so later, a hastily scribbled little thing that said almost nothing – and that was it. As if their friendship had never been. It was a betrayal of the harshest kind, and there were times when Nic wasn't sure which hurt more – Caryn or Mat.

If it wasn't for Estelle, quite frankly, she'd have gone mad. Tory was so wrapped up in the disintegrating drama of her own life that she'd been almost no help at all. She shook her head slowly. When had it all gone so disastrously wrong? In a few months' time she'd be turning twenty-eight. She would come into the trust fund that Jim had set up for each of his children, not that she particularly cared about the money, but it was a sign, wasn't it, of adulthood? Of maturity? She ought to be looking forward to her thirties, not mourning everything that had gone before. No, if it wasn't for Estelle, who'd become such a shoulder to cry on – the only shoulder to cry on, in fact – she'd have been lost.

She walked into her study, still unable to take it all in. Tory was pregnant, not by Luc but by her dead sister's boyfriend. She shivered. It was almost too creepy to be true. How could it have happened without her knowing? But she *had* known. Deep down. She'd known something was up for months. Tory had been withdrawn and silent, a throwback to their days at school. Nic had been so wrapped up in herself that she'd ignored the signs. A shiver went down her spine again. It was exactly the same accusation Caryn had flung at her. *It's not always about you, Nic.* Just thinking about it made her eyes smart with tears.

108

Estelle took a long, slow drag on her cigarette and looked at the envelope she'd just picked up from Phil Johnson. His invoice was discreetly attached. Fuck, he was expensive! It would take her at least two clients, possibly three, to cover it. Still, he was good and he delivered. The stack of information she now had at her disposal was growing daily. She knew everything she needed to know about Nicola Harte, her two 'best' friends – she thought the word with a sneer – and the little secrets they were all so desperate to hide. Who'd have thought it? She blew out a cloud of smoke. They had *everything* – money, security, family; they'd been to the best schools. What more could they have been given? And they'd *still* managed to screw everything up. She glanced back at the report again, a smile beginning to play around the corner of her lips. So Caryn Middleton also had something to hide. Well, well, well. Who'd have thought it? Little Miss Goody Two Shoes. She'd always disliked her. Always.

She stood up and stubbed out her cigarette. She had half an hour to get ready for a new client that evening and she needed to look her best. She had almost everything she needed to give Nic Harte the biggest shock of her life, but it wouldn't be enough. Destroying Nic's life was all well and good but however much she looked forward to seeing Nic utterly humiliated and her relationships with everyone around her in tatters, she'd quickly realised that it wouldn't make much difference to Jim Harte. He wouldn't give a damn. Jim Harte was preoccupied with other stuff, nothing to do with his family. She was no fool. He'd purchased the newspaper group to keep the lid on something and from the little Nic had said, it was clear that Mat Ndava was somehow involved. But she didn't understand why Mat hadn't just sold the story to someone else, whatever it was. Nic had hinted at some awful revelations that would drive the share price of the company he owned down . . . but what? The only person who could possibly know more than she did about the Hartes and their sordid past was her own mother. Gloria. And as much as she didn't like to think about Gloria, other than sending her money every month, sooner or later, she realised, she was going to have to ask her the question that had been tearing at her for the past year. *Why did you lie?*

She finished dressing and quickly swallowed an E just before

Petko was due to pick her up. She needed it to summon up the enthusiasm for the few hours of work that lay ahead. Within a few minutes of the tablet dissolving on her tongue, she began to feel better. A slow, pleasurable warmth that she knew would last for at least three or four hours, making everything and everyone around her just that bit warmer, was beginning to take hold. She quickly checked the container Eva had given her. Half a dozen left – enough for the rest of the week. More than ever now, she just couldn't manage without them.

Half an hour later, Petko dropped her off outside Black's, the exclusive members-only club in Mayfair. Every head in the club turned as she strode past. She was meeting a new client – Robert. He was a little younger than average, Mrs Devereaux had told her, the heir to some sort of family fortune. 'Be nice to him, Estelle. I want him back,' she warned. With the warmth generated by the tablet still coursing through her veins, that wouldn't be a problem at all.

'This way, madam.' Someone appeared, guiding her smoothly towards the lift. Members' rooms were on the top floor. She followed him in.

The lift opened out directly on to a plush living room. The lights were dimmed; there was soft music in the background. There were several groups of men sitting around the low sofas and leather club chairs being fawned over by clusters of very beautiful girls. It was all very discreet. She was ushered through the living room to a set of double doors and asked to wait. A few seconds later, someone shouted for her to come in. She took a deep breath, pushed open the door and walked in.

Her first impression was that she'd stumbled on to the set of a porn film by mistake. There was an enormous low bed in the centre of the room, dressed almost entirely in black silk sheets and leopardskin throws. The entire room was mirrored. As she stared at the man lying, semi-naked, in the middle of the bed, she could see her own reflection multiplied a thousand times in every direction, left and right. She had to bite down on her bottom lip to stop herself from laughing out loud. Robert – she assumed that was who he was – looked up at her from beneath a long, floppy fringe. Was Mrs Devereaux *kidding*? He looked like a teenager!

'Hi,' she said, trying not to smile. 'You must be Robert.'

He looked at her haughtily. 'Who're you again?' he asked, as if he couldn't quite focus.

Estelle walked over to the bed. 'I'm Estelle,' she said pleasantly, looking down at him. He was wearing a pair of tight silky black briefs and a thin gold chain . . . and nothing else. There was a strong smell of alcohol in the room and on the table beside the bed she noticed several packets of pills and the odd, tell-tale line of coke. She hesitated. In all the years she'd been with Mrs Devereaux, she'd never encountered anything quite like this. She wondered what he wanted. All her other clients were older men with very clear tastes, generally of the conservative sort. Not one of them, so far as she could remember, had been doing it for the first time or needed a line of coke to get on with the job. They were all men of class and power; there'd been nothing seedy about any of them. There was a suaveness to the whole thing that she'd come to expect. The sulky, bored young man in front of her was different. She sat down next to him.

'Did I say you could sit down?'

She looked sideways at him in surprise. There was an edge to his voice that she hadn't picked up on at first. 'No,' she said slowly, 'but—'

'Stand up. And take that fucking dress off.'

She got up slowly, her earlier pleasure evaporating rapidly. He was drunk, yes, but there was something else in his tone she didn't recognise. A strange kind of menace. She unzipped the black evening dress and stepped out of it. She stood in front of him in her tiny black lace thong and high heels and looked down at him, wondering whether to be openly defiant. He might be paying, but there were limits to how far he could push her. 'Anything else, sir?' she asked, with just a touch of sarcasm.

'Yeah. Get me a glass, will you?' He picked up the whisky bottle lying next to the bed.

Estelle looked around. There were glasses on a tray beside the door. She walked over and picked one up. 'Would you like me to pour it for you?' she asked, walking back to the bed.

'No. Yes.' He handed her the bottle. She bent towards him and was just about to unscrew the cap when he suddenly lunged out at her, catching her off guard. The blow landed on her cheek. She dropped the bottle, stunned and staggered back. 'Get back here,' he growled at her, pointing to the bottle, which lay on its side, spilling whisky over the sheets. 'And clean that up.'

Estelle's mind began to race. She couldn't very well run to the doors with nothing but a scrap of black lace covering her behind, but there was no way she was going to stay in the room with the young man who was rapidly turning into a nightmare. 'J-just give me a sec,' she said, bending forward to retrieve her dress. If she had to, she'd make a dash for it with it wrapped around her. He was quicker than her. He snatched it up and shoved it under the leopardskin throw, grinning at her.

'Not thinking of leaving, are you?' he asked, his voice suddenly silky-smooth.

Estelle swallowed. He was clearly nuts. 'Is there a bathroom here?' she asked, hoping her voice was steady. Her heart was pounding.

He shook his head. 'Come over here,' he said, more softly this time. She hesitated. 'Come on, I'm only teasing. Sorry about that,' he added, touching his own cheek. 'I get a bit carried away.' He giggled, a high-pitched, nervous giggle.

Estelle sat down gingerly on the edge of the bed. He pushed his hair out of his face. The childish gesture was oddly reassuring. She eyed him, slightly less nervously. Perhaps the combination of coke and alcohol – and whatever pills he'd been popping – had simply gone to his head? 'So. . .' she began after a minute. 'What sort of things do you like?'

He contemplated the question for a second, then pointed to his crotch. 'Suck me off,' he said, slurring his words.

Estelle took a deep breath. Perhaps that would calm him down. Send him to sleep. She bent her head and peeled off his satin briefs. His penis was limp and flaccid. He buried his hands in her head. As she took him into her mouth, she began to relax.

She'd yet to meet a man who could resist her skills. For a moment, he seemed to calm down. And then he started making the most terrifying noise she'd ever heard; a low, growling sound in the back of his throat. He had her by the hair, tightening his hold slowly. It felt as though he were trying to peel it off her scalp. 'You're hurting me,' she said urgently, raising her head. He shoved it back down again with such force she felt her teeth scrape against his pubic bone. She told herself not to resist, not to struggle, but she was choking. He was stronger than he looked. His hands were tight around her head and she could hardly breathe. The sound droned on, a rumbling, menacing sound which vibrated against her skull. She was absolutely petrified. She tried to lift her head again to scream, but his grip was too tight. She began to struggle, but it only served to excite him more. She could feel his penis thicken and lengthen, pushing against the inside of her mouth. She began to struggle in earnest, unable to breathe. He was laughing now. Finally, just when she thought she might black out, he released her, giggling hysterically. She scrambled backwards down the bed, past caring whether she ran out the door naked or not. He lunged after her, but this time she was quicker. She kicked him with all her might, hitting him in the shoulder, and grabbed the leopardskin throw, stumbling over her shoes. He yelled something indistinct, but she was already running towards the door. When the bottle hit her, she was almost halfway out – there was a sudden crack as it hit the side of her head and shattered against the door. She could see the horrified faces of the fully dressed people in the living room outside, heard the screams and then she pitched forward and everything went quiet.

There was a small gash where the whisky bottle had hit her, requiring two tiny stitches which the doctor had done for her at home. Mrs Devereaux sat on the edge of her bed, looking at her sorrowfully. On the dressing table was an enormous bunch of white roses – Estelle felt like hurling them out of the window. In addition to the pain of her wound – '*very* superficial, just a scratch, really, darling,' Mrs Devereaux kept repeating, as if that would somehow make her feel better – her entire scalp felt as though it was on fire. She wished she and Eva would just leave her alone.

'Will you be all right?' Eva asked, a worried look on her face.

Estelle nodded impatiently. Mrs Devereaux got up. 'I'll look in on you later this evening,' she said. If it weren't for the fact that her head ached and the inside of her mouth tasted and felt like cotton wool, Estelle might have found her concern touching. 'You just lie back and go to sleep. You need all the rest you can get. You poor thing. If I'd only known he'd turn out to be such a lunatic. Dreadful. You're lucky it wasn't worse, though, darling. It just doesn't bear thinking about.'

Estelle closed her eyes. She was still too angry to cry. It was yet another reminder of the bitter unfairness of it all. What had happened to her would never happen to Nic, living blissfully under the protection of Harte's name. She would never have to endure the sort of humiliation that she, Estelle, endured on an almost daily basis. She would never know what it was like to be *owned* by men like Robert Whatever-the-fuck-his-name-was, grabbing hold of her hair, shoving her face in his lap. She turned to the wall. No, none of that would ever happen to Nic Harte. Daddy would always see to that. Well, perhaps not. She would teach the Hartes a thing or two about humiliation. She was nearly there. A couple more enquiries to make, a few loose ends to be tied up – Jim Harte would live to regret the day he'd flung those words at her. *I have two daughters and you're not one of them.*

109

There was an annoying little refrain going round and round in her head and try as she might, she couldn't get rid of it. *It's my party and I'll cry if I want to.* She knew why she couldn't stop singing it. It was her twenty-eighth birthday in a month's time and at the rate she was going, she'd be sitting on her own, crying her eyes out, dreading the year ahead. It was depressing. Her twenty-eighth birthday ought to have been a time of celebration, not despair. Something to look forward to, not dread. They all needed cheering up, not just her. She had to do something. The thought flashed through her mind suddenly. A party. A special, no-expense-spared dinner party . . . somewhere beautiful, somewhere special, away from the humdrum of their daily lives. Why not? She would come into her trust fund shortly afterwards. The money was hers to do with as she pleased.

She stared at her computer screen, a small thrill of excitement finally running through her. Why hadn't she thought of it before? It was time to hold out the olive branch to Caryn. She would invite her, and her mystery man, whoever he was, if he could be persuaded to come along. Tory and Luc, Estelle, Ally and her boyfriend Graham. There was Tina, the only person at *ArtWeekly* whom she considered a friend, and her boyfriend Julian; Steve, the photographer from *Gossip!* with whom she was still friendly. She'd think of somewhere nice to take everyone. Studgrove? Everyone knew she was Jim Harte's daughter; she might as well make use of the fact. There was also the apartment on the Boulevard Saint Michel in Paris. Jim hardly ever went there. It wouldn't hurt to ask, surely? A weekend dinner party in Paris sounded perfect. Suddenly buoyed by the thought, she turned back to her screen. Yes, a party. It would be her way of saying sorry to Caryn. She missed her more than she could say.

1 1 0

'Jim?' His secretary's voice interrupted his thoughts. 'It's Nic. On line two.'

Jim frowned. Nic *never* rang him. Ever. As he reached for the phone he was aware of a faint tremor of fear running through his hand. Ever since Patrick had told him she'd been with – whatever *that* meant – Mat Ndava, he'd been afraid to see her. He gave himself an impatient little shake. He'd have sooner died than admit it, but Nic was the only person in the whole world whose opinion of him meant anything to him. He knew it was low. Worse than low.

He cleared his throat. 'Nic? H-how are you?'

'Fine, thanks.' She was politely distant. She quickly outlined her request: she wanted use of the Paris apartment for a dinner party – her twenty-eighth.

'Sure. There's no one there.' He hesitated. 'D'you need . . . anything?'

'No, thanks. Just the apartment, if that's OK with you.'

'It's fine. When are we going to see you?' He surprised himself with his own question.

There was a second's hesitation from her, too. 'Soon,' she said evasively. Before he could say anything further, she put down the phone. He replaced the handset slowly. Nic's twenty-eighth. Twenty-eight years. He could scarcely believe it. Just look at what had come to pass.

Nic put down the phone and looked out of the window. There was a new hesitancy to her father; she'd sensed it immediately. She hadn't been back to the Eaton Square home since the morning she'd run out to find Mat. She wasn't sure she could bear it. Or him, for that matter. All was not well in the Harte empire. Patrick and Shaun were back in Harare, battling one fire after another. Jim was more frequently in London. His takeover of the Riverbrook Group hadn't gone quite according to plan. Nic shook her head in disbelief. Anyone could have foreseen trouble. Jim knew next to nothing about running a newspaper. The printers had gone on strike; senior managers and editors had walked out in droves; there were production problems, distribution problems . . . the list was endless. She knew that circulation was way down – it wasn't looking good, it had to be said, and now that it was known just who she was, it was beginning to affect her professionally as well. The phrase 'daddy's girl' had never sounded so hurtful. She heard it a lot these days.

'Daddy' had been on the front page of the *Guardian* the previous day – someone had casually (perhaps spitefully) tossed a copy on to her desk. Insider trading, corruption, scandals, bribery – it could hardly get worse. *Stop it*, she admonished herself sternly. *You've just started organising your birthday party to cheer yourself up!* She switched on her computer. Instead of concentrating on the task at hand she was sitting with her chin in her hand, moping. She pulled her notebook swiftly to her. She wasn't going to start her twenty-eighth year the way the previous one had ended. No way. She was made of sterner stuff. Wasn't she?

The two-tone beep signalling an incoming message dragged her smoothly out of sleep. Caryn sat bolt upright in bed, a shaft of bluish moonlight coming in through the open doors and laying a line upon the floor. She looked around for her phone. Beside her Simon's breathing changed in pitch but he slept on. A phone call in the middle of the night could mean only one thing. She slid soundlessly out of bed and walked over to the dresser. The blue flashing light illuminated the room in short, urgent blasts. She flipped it open. It was Nic. She felt a momentary surge of relief. At least it wasn't Alice, or Brian. *Just sent you an email*, she read. *Please say yes. I'm sorry. I miss you, love, Nic.* She closed the phone slowly. It was four-seventeen a.m. Typical Nic.

'What is it?' Simon's voice broke in on her thoughts.

She turned. He was sitting upright in bed, his naked torso disappearing into the tangle of sheets. He reached for his cigarettes. 'It's Nic,' she said slowly. 'She just sent me an email.'

'She sent a text in the middle of the night to say she'd sent an email? It couldn't wait until the morning?'

She sighed. 'We . . . we had a bit of an argument. Before I left.'

'I know.'

'You do? How? I never said—'

'Caryn. I'm not blind, you know.' He lit a cigarette and patted the empty space beside him. 'Come here.' She put down her phone and walked back to the bed. He drew her back down with one arm. His touch was tender. 'You're not the only one with secrets,' he murmured against her skin. His mouth sought hers out.

'It's not a secret,' she whispered, a wave of sweet helplessness beginning to sweep over her. 'Just a silly disagreement, that's all.'

'What about?' His voice was a warm breath in her ear.

She shrugged, turning herself into the crook of his arm. 'Oh, nothing, really.'

'Really?' His hand crept under the elastic of her pyjamas, cupping her buttocks as he pulled her on top of him. She shivered. He slid into her slowly, his whole body taut with pleasure. 'You sure?'

She couldn't speak. She leaned forward, letting her nipples graze his chest as he swiftly brought them both to the edge of an explosive climax. She forgave Nic the text. Just the text.

'It's her twenty-eighth birthday party,' she called out to Simon the following morning from the computer in the corner of the living room. 'She's having a party. We're both invited.' She held her breath.

He appeared in front of her. 'She doesn't—?'

'No, of course not,' Caryn reassured him quickly. 'I haven't said anything, I promise. But she knows I'm here with someone. Nic's not stupid, either.'

'I can't,' he said flatly. 'Don't ask me to.'

'But *why* won't you come?'

'Caryn.' His voice held an unspoken warning.

She sighed. 'What is it with you and the Hartes?' she asked, exasperated. 'Is it because—'

'Leave it alone.'

'Why? Whatever happened between you and Jim Harte must've happened a long time ago. Why can't you just—'

'Caryn!' She looked at him in surprise. It was almost the first time she'd heard him raise his voice. He looked angry. Worse than that – there was fear in his eyes. She backed away from what she couldn't understand. He ran a hand through his hair. 'Just . . . just forget it, OK? You go. Tell her whatever you like. Just don't mention me.' There was finality in his voice; nothing more to be had from him.

'I won't.' She turned back to the computer, wondering how to word a reply. Of course she would go. She missed Nic and Tory more than she'd ever thought possible. A weekend in Paris sounded almost too good to be true. She didn't even know the Hartes had an apartment there – was there no end to his wealth?

I I I

Planning the dinner party was the single most enjoyable thing she'd done in the past six months. Replies to her invitations came in almost immediately. To her immense relief, Caryn agreed to come, but without her boyfriend. He would be away, she explained in her email, but didn't say where. Nic studied the guest list. So far, eight people had confirmed. Caryn, Tory, Luc, Ally, Graham, Steve, Tina and Julian. And then there was the awkward question of Estelle. Caryn and Tory disliked her intensely, she knew. Neither had said so in as many words, but it was clear they didn't want her there. Both of them had met Ally and Graham over the years, and Caryn had met Steve a few times – there were no problems there. But Estelle was a different matter. Nic wasn't sure of the source of their uneasiness but Caryn's email was pretty explicit. *Does she have to come? She gives me the creeps.* What to do? Estelle could be rather irritating at times, granted, but she'd been there for Nic in ways that neither Caryn nor Tory had in the past few months. She bit her lip anxiously. Although, to be fair, both of them had more on their own plates than they could handle without taking on Nic's problems as well. That was the odd thing about Estelle, come to think of it. She never alluded to problems of her own. She seemed a hundred per cent focused on Nic – it was *that* that made Tory uneasy. 'I don't know the first thing about her, and neither do you,' Tory said to her later that evening. 'Don't you find that a bit odd?'

Nic shrugged. 'She's just . . .'

'Just what? Creepy?' Tory echoed Caryn's words.

'No! She's not creepy. She's just a good friend, that's all.'

'Well, she definitely gives me the creeps. Caryn agrees with me.'

'I know. But I can't not invite her, can I?'

'Why ever not?' Tory sounded surprised. 'Christ, you've only known her for a few months. It's not as if she's a long-standing friend. Not like some of us.' Tory's voice was suddenly playful. 'Oh, don't invite her, Nic. Please. It'll be awkward and you've said it yourself – we all need a bit of cheering up. *I* certainly don't fancy looking at her across the table all evening. Have a dinner in London alone with her if you must, but don't bring her to Paris.'

'All right. Fine, I won't. But we need one other person. Numbers are odd.'

'Well, invite someone else.'

'But who?'

'Nic Harte, d'you mean to tell me you only know eight people?'

'No, but it's got to be someone we all get along with.'

'Look, it's better to have the right kind of people at the party than the right numbers. If there's only nine of us, so be it. You can sit at the head of the table. Don't worry about it. Or get a round table.'

Nic smiled. Tory had a way of putting things. Fine. Estelle would be struck off the guest list. Luckily she hadn't mentioned the party or her birthday to her yet. Best to keep it quiet. She'd invite her to dinner when they were back in London. She hung up, wondering what all the fuss was about. Estelle, creepy? No, they misunderstood her, that was all. Perhaps it was, as Caryn had once suggested, a southern Africa 'thing'. Estelle and Nic understood one another in ways that she and Tory couldn't. Maybe. Or maybe it was just plain old-fashioned jealousy. Nic smiled suddenly. It was nice to be fought over. She couldn't remember *that* ever happening to her before.

The following weekend she left for Paris. It had been years since she'd been in the lovely apartment just off Boulevard Saint Michel. She caught an early Saturday-morning flight and by lunchtime was standing outside the apartment, the sumptuous gardens of Catherine Labouré behind her, sunlight filtering through the trees to the pavement below. It was late spring and Paris was in full, gorgeous bloom. She looked up at the building in delight. She'd forgotten just how beautiful Paris could be. She pressed the buzzer and waited. One of the many housekeepers employed by RhoMine would be waiting for her, Molly had told her, a touch defensively. Why hadn't she invited *them* to her twenty-eighth, her tone implied? Nic ignored her. She could think of nothing worse.

The door clicked open and Nic stepped inside the courtyard. It was exactly as she remembered it; a beautifully kept garden in the triangular patch between the elegant sandstone buildings, ornate wooden doors leading off the courtyard to the stairs and the smell of flowers in the air. She pushed open a second set of doors and entered the wonderfully cool stairwell. She climbed up the winding staircase to the second floor. The views were better from the top, she remembered Patrick saying once. And Jim's quick rejoinder – *ceiling heights are always better on the second floor. Remember that.* It was true. Madame Censier, the housekeeper, was waiting for her at the door.

'*Bonjour, Nicola,*' she beamed at her. '*Bienvenue. Ça fait long-temps,*' she said, smiling at her. Nic nodded. Yes, a long time indeed. She led her through the hallway into the sitting room. Nic looked around her with pleasure. High ceilings, tall French windows overlooking the communal gardens, elegant, under-stated furniture, gleaming oak parquet floors . . . she nodded vigorously. Yes, it would most certainly do. She turned to Mme Censier, smiling.

'*Parfait*,' she said firmly. It was indeed perfect.

Madame Censier nodded in satisfaction. 'Your father told us there will be nine of you?'

Nic nodded. 'Yes, they'll arrive early on the Saturday afternoon. The dinner party's that same night and then we'll probably leave on Sunday evening. I think there's enough room for everyone, don't you?'

'Oh, yes. We have six bedrooms, plus the study. And there's the library, too.'

'Fantastic. Now, I brought a couple of menu suggestions . . . shall we take a look together? Dad said you would help me with the caterers.'

'*Bien sûr*. Let's see what you have planned.'

By mid-afternoon, the formidably efficient Mme Censier had organised everything. A walking encyclopaedia, there was nothing she didn't know or know how to do. From which white wines to choose, to where to get the best Valencia oranges, she had it all covered. At four o'clock, mindful, no doubt, of Jim's English tastes, she excused herself from the dining room and returned fifteen minutes later with a tray of tea, English scones and fruit cake. It was all Nic could do not to laugh out loud. If only Jim's attention to detail in each of the houses he owned had been used in his business affairs, he wouldn't be in half the mess he appeared to be, she mused, munching contentedly on a fruit scone. She cast a quick eye over the wine list Mme Censier had drawn up – a mixture of Old and New World wines from a Châteauneuf du Pape 1996 to a South African Black Rock Chardonnay. The menus were equally impressive. Parmesan baskets with Parma ham and salsa; blue cheese and walnut salad; Moroccan spiced lamb; baked salmon with parsley and capers; whole baked sea bass with garlic and chilli butter and a magnificent selection of desserts from a patisserie around the corner – chocolate soufflés, lemon and raspberry tarts, white chocolate and strawberry parfait and an enormous selection of cheeses – as Mme Censier said, there was something for everyone. Nic's mouth was watering just reading the list.

She spent the rest of the day wandering through the apartment, listening to the radio and making sure she'd thought of everything. Music, food, drink, sleeping arrangements – in rather typical Harte style, she thought to herself wryly, she'd left nothing to chance. And then there was the little matter of what to wear. It had been Tory's suggestion to dress up. Perhaps not quite black tie, but formal nevertheless. She felt a sudden impatience for the clothes that hung in her wardrobe at home. She glanced at her watch. It was four p.m. The shops along the Boulevard Saint Germain would still be open. She grinned to herself. Why not? When was the last time she'd gone shopping for an evening dress? She grabbed her handbag and jacket and went running down the stairs.

She turned slowly in the mirror, unaccustomed to the image of herself as the sort of woman who wore evening dresses made of the sheerest jersey imaginable, falling in folds to her feet and held together under the bust by a baroque clasp. The salesgirl who'd singled it out from amongst the stacks on the rails smiled confidently. '*Très belle*,' she said firmly. '*Voilà*.' There was a moment of sadness as she looked at herself again – despite the fact that it was *her* birthday, *her* dinner party, *her* friends . . . there was no one there for whom the dress would be anything other than ordinary. No one special. *Nothing compares*. The Sinéad O'Connor song suddenly ran through her mind. Nothing would ever compare; that was the problem. It was ridiculous, really. After all, how long had they actually been together – a couple of months? Why couldn't she just get over him and move on with her life? It was obvious he'd moved on. Not a word since. Nothing. A resounding silence from the one man she'd do anything for. Anything he asked. Except, of course, he hadn't. She still found it hard to reconcile Estelle's image of him with her own. A player. A string of girlfriends. No one special. But Estelle had seen him, hadn't she? With her own eyes. Estelle knew about men like him.

In some ways, she supposed she ought to be grateful. It could have been worse, although some part of her dimly recognised the near-impossibility of the statement. *How* could it have been worse? That was the thing about it. However brief their relationship had been, she'd known from the outset that Mat would be different. It was hard for her to put into words exactly what it was about him that had captivated her so. It wasn't just his looks or the palpable evidence of his charisma, hard as they were to ignore. No, it was something deeper, something much more intuitive – an immediate recognition of a shared past that had nothing to do with the differences between them, obvious to everyone else except her and Mat. The irony of it all was that they were so much alike. If only she'd had the courage to tell him who she really was. Then it would all have made sense. Or would it? Perhaps he'd known all along – perhaps he'd been playing with her, just as Estelle suggested, hoping to get a better story, the insider's scoop. *That* was the supreme frustration about the way it had ended. A thousand and one questions still hung in the air, unanswered and unanswerable by anyone except her and Mat. The agony of it was, they probably never would be.

There was a lump in her throat as she handed over her credit card and watched the dress being packed away. A dress he would never see, nor care to. Caryn hadn't been joking when she said he would be hard to forget. She was wrong. It was impossible.

The following week, Estelle knew something was up. Nic, normally so eager and carefree with information, had suddenly turned coy. She was going away at the weekend, she told her, to Paris, but she didn't say why. Estelle's ears pricked up. She didn't want to appear too eager, but she was. Who was she going with?

'Oh, no one. I'm going on my own. I've . . . I've got some stuff to take care of, that's all. Just for the weekend. I'll be back on Sunday night.' Nic's response was lame beyond belief.

'Shame,' Estelle said, her mind racing ahead. 'I was going to ask you if you wanted to come out next Saturday night. Never mind, maybe the week after.'

Nic jumped at the invitation, as Estelle knew she would. 'Yes, definitely. I'll call you when I get back.'

She put the phone down, still thinking hard. Nic was leaving on Friday at eight a.m. Time enough for Estelle to get into her flat, snoop around a little and find out what was going on. The thought flashed through her mind – was she going to meet Mat Ndava? No, impossible. Nic wouldn't have been able to keep that little piece of information to herself. As much as she hated the girl, she had to say that the devotion she'd shown to the arrogant prick was touching. Estelle had never believed in love at first sight – ridiculous idea! – but Nic Harte was definitely smitten. Months later her feelings showed no sign of diminishing. Just what *was* it with that man? It was clear to her that for Nic, at least, *not* talking about him was by far the harder option. Estelle was sick to death of hearing about Matari Ndava. But she was canny enough to realise that she was probably the only person Nic confided in. That little bitch Caryn Middleton was too wrapped up in her own life to bother, and Tory Spiller was too busy screwing her dead sister's boyfriend. Between Phil Johnson and the fact that she still had a key to Nic's flat, there wasn't much about what went on in Nic's life that Estelle didn't know. She almost giggled aloud. She couldn't wait for the right moment to let it all slip out. The only question was when.

At ten-seventeen a.m. the following morning she had her answer. She stared at the computer screen in front of her, rage building in her chest until she thought she might explode. Nic's birthday the following weekend. A dinner party for eight of her closest friends in Paris. In yet another of the Hartes' beautiful homes. She sat in front of the screen, almost blinded by tears of anger. It was all there, in black and white. *Don't invite her, please. I can't stand her. She gives me the creeps.* And Nic's pathetic response. *OK. Tory said the same, by the way. I know she can be a bit irritating. Anyhow, she's not coming. I'll make up some excuse. You're right, I suppose, she doesn't really belong.*

She sat there for almost ten minutes, unable to move for the white-hot rage inside her head. She scrolled down the list of messages, not even sure what she was looking for. There was one from Nic to Caryn. *Something to tell you.* She clicked on it and scanned it quickly. Her mouth dropped open. It just got better and better. She clicked on Caryn's reply. For the next twenty minutes, she went through Nic's emails one by one, carefully noting anything and everything that might be of use. By the time she was finished with them all, there would be nothing left standing. Caryn, Tory, Nic. They all had something to hide from one another and from the so-called 'friends' who surrounded them. She shuddered. An almost sexual thrill of excitement ran through her. So Nic Harte was planning a twenty-eighth birthday party in Paris without her. Oh, boy. It certainly would be a dinner party to remember – in more ways than one.

She exited the programme, taking care to wipe out any traces of her presence, and stood up. The dinner party was planned for the second of May. She didn't have long to get everything in place. In her mind's eye, the scene was already set. Eight smug, self-satisfied 'best' friends, sitting around a beautifully laid dinner table, glasses in hand. She would walk in halfway through, accept a glass of wine or champagne, enjoy the looks of pained embarrassment on all their faces and then she'd let her little bombs fall, one after the other. Nic thought she was irritating? That she didn't belong? She had *no* fucking idea.

112

Nic scanned the arriving passengers anxiously. Caryn's plane had landed over an hour ago and there was still no sign of her. She swallowed the last of her coffee and was just about to walk over to Starbucks to order another when she caught sight of her coming through the doors that flew open and shut with every passing footstep. She chucked the empty cup in the bin and hurried towards her. It had been almost seven months since she'd last seen her – she was thinner, she noticed immediately. She waved and made her way through the throng that was gathered, pressing against the barriers. Caryn turned, spotted her, and gave her a smile of such relief Nic thought for a moment she might actually be crying. *She* certainly was.

'Nic!' Caryn pushed her way past a clutch of relatives crowding around a mother and newborn child. They hugged and for a moment it was as if the cooling of their friendship over the past few months had simply never been.

Caryn was the first to break away, stepping back shyly. They looked at each other, weighing up the changes.

'You look exactly the same,' Nic said, wiping her cheeks with the back of her hand. 'I half-expected you to come back all tanned and bleached-blonde. Like Pamela Anderson or something!'

'Hardly. I don't go to the beach that much.'

'Come on, car's over there. Tory can't wait to see you. I can't believe you're actually here! It feels as though you've been gone for ever. You've got to tell me *all* about it. God, I've missed you!'

'How's the job?' Caryn asked, steering the conversation away from herself. She hated lying to Nic, even by omission. Not for the first time she wondered just what the problem between Simon and Jim Harte was. He was absolutely adamant. Under no circumstances was she to tell Nic Harte who he was. None whatsoever. If she did, he'd walk. Caryn knew enough of him to know that he wasn't joking.

'Oh, it's fine. Heaps better than *Gossip!*, I can tell you! I'll show you when we get back to mine. I've got this month's edition on my desk. Here we are.' She opened the car door and helped Caryn stow her bags in the boot. 'I hope you brought something gorgeous to wear,' she said, smiling. 'I did. I can't even bring myself to think about how much it cost. But birthdays are special, right? It's not every day that you turn twenty-eight and I'm *determined* to have a good time.' Her voice was suddenly steely. There was a question lurking just underneath the surface of Nic's voice that Caryn longed to bring up. She couldn't. Mat. Nic had fallen hard – Caryn knew that you didn't just walk away from something like that without a backward glance. Yet she steadfastly refused to talk about it, hiding her pain behind a façade of cheerful chit-chat. Caryn wasn't fooled. She'd long been accustomed to looking beneath the surface of things where Nic Harte was concerned.

Although it was spring, the damp, cool air and grey skies were a relief after the blinding white light of southern California. Caryn gazed out at the lush, green countryside. She thought of Alice and Brian, whom she'd see in a very short while, and how much she'd missed them both. As they drove into central London, she had the very strong sense of her life coming back to her after months of hiatus.

Tory looked at her reflection in the mirror. She turned sideways, letting her skirt slide to the floor as she scrutinised her stomach. Still flat; the faintest hint of a swell, perhaps, but nothing discernible. She was nearly nine weeks pregnant, but no one apart from Nic and Caryn knew, or would be able to tell. She was no closer to making a decision about what to do than she had been when she first blurted out the news to Nic. A strange paralysis had taken hold; she rose each morning and went to work with the secret of her body hidden inside her, the fact of it surfacing every now and again as she went about her daily routine. *I'm pregnant.* Sooner or later she would have to do something. The sexless state into which she and Luc had somehow fallen would force the issue. Even if she'd wanted to, which she didn't, there was simply no way she could pretend to pass the child off as his. Soon she would begin to show; she had to do *something.* One way or another.

She pulled up her skirt, fastened it and stepped into her shoes. She had a christening to organise that morning. The irony of it wasn't lost on her as she picked up her car keys.

The Metropolitan Bar just off Piccadilly was the perfect setting for their reunion. Nic was the first to arrive, straight from work. She ordered a gin and tonic – *make it a double, please!* – and shrugged off her jacket. She flicked through the newspapers left lying conveniently on the table beside her. Jim was headline news – yet again. The police had found something that appeared to link him to Sir Winston Freedland's death. No details, as yet, and certainly no suggestion that he'd had a hand in it, but there was clearly more to come. Nic sighed. Nothing about Jim surprised her, although even she couldn't quite believe he'd have anything to do with murder. The memory of the conversation she'd overheard a few years earlier outside his study came back to her. *I don't want Simon Carter's blood on my hands.* She shivered, suddenly cold. Who was Simon Carter? she wondered. And what had he done for Jim?

'God, I thought the bloody day would never end.' She was interrupted by Tory, who flopped down in the seat next to her. She looked tired and drawn.

'You look like you could use one of these,' Nic said, pointing to her half-empty glass.

'Well, I would . . . but I can't.' She glanced down at her stomach. 'I shouldn't.'

'Shit, I forgot.' Nic pulled a face. 'Does that mean you won't be drinking at the party, either?'

'Well, unless I decide to . . . you know. It's only a week away, so no, I probably won't.'

'Won't Luc think it a bit odd? You haven't told him, have you?'

Tory shook her head. 'No. I still don't know what to do—'

'Gosh, why are you both looking so glum?' Caryn cried, throwing her bags on the table, interrupting them. 'What's going on?'

Tory hugged her tightly. 'You haven't changed a bit!' she exclaimed, stepping back to look at her properly. 'We were worried you'd go all Californian on us.'

'Not a chance,' Caryn laughed. She looked at Tory, then at her stomach. 'You haven't—?'

'I haven't.'

'So that's why we're looking glum,' Nic interjected. 'She won't be drinking at the party, either.'

'God, that'll be a first. Are you OK? How're you feeling?' Caryn asked.

'Lousy.' Tory shook her head. 'I'm sick most mornings, I can't concentrate, I'm moody – it's crap, actually.'

'Well, no change there,' Nic teased. 'You don't look any different. It certainly doesn't show.'

'Yeah. I've probably got another couple of weeks and then I'll have to do something.'

'D'you want it?' Caryn asked quietly.

There was a moment's awkward silence, then Tory looked away. She shrugged. 'I don't know,' she said simply, and it was the truth.

What kind of party was it going to be? Nic thought to herself, as she studied both Caryn and Tory. What with Tory's pregnancy, Caryn's secret lover and her having to hide the fact of the party from Estelle, they all had something to hide. Not the best start to the next decade of her life. Or theirs.

113

Jim listened to Ogilvy, his long-standing, long-suffering lawyer, with a growing sense of dread.

'She's got this . . . er, *idea*, somehow . . . that she's your daughter. I don't like it, Jim, I have to be honest. She's been asking questions. None too discreetly, I might add. There isn't . . .' he hesitated, then went on. 'There isn't any truth to it, is there, Jim?'

Jim was silent. He swivelled in his chair away from Ogilvy's pained expression and looked out of the window. From his vantage point on the tenth floor, the City spread itself out away from him. Rain was falling, drumming steadily against the window, sliding down the pane in blurry, quivering streaks. To say that he had worked hard to reach this point was the understatement of the century. He was sixty years old. His whole life had been about reaching this point, not just figuratively. He wasn't the sort of man who indulged in introspection, but Christ, he'd come a long way. He rarely thought about the past, seeing it largely as an irritating distraction from the present and the infinitely more important future, but the tenth floor of an elegant building just off Fenchurch Street was a world away from where he'd come.

There wasn't much about the camp in São Antão that he cared to remember. Hunger, mostly, and the bleak rise and swell of the Atlantic that stretched endlessly in all directions. He remembered misty mornings on the beach, the tide retreating and only the harsh sun flowing over the emptiness, watching the local women dressed in black garb, searching for crabs. With their voluminous robes tied around their knees, they had the profile of wading birds. Every now and then a wave broke over them, racing in a last gasp towards the shore, sending them laughing and shrieking back towards the dunes. He shook his head abruptly.

Across the gleaming mahogany table, Ogilvy was watching him nervously. Behind Ogilvy were half a dozen paintings of the sort a man in his position ought to have – captains of industry, board members long deceased. He didn't particularly care for them himself, but the people he'd hired along the way to paint a convincing portrait of him as a mogul of wealth and taste assured him – *everyone in the City has these sorts of paintings, Harte. Everyone.* It was a far cry from the corrugated tin and rotting concrete of the camp. Yes, he'd come a long way. That was all anyone needed to know. And now, if he understood it correctly, Ogilvy had come to tell him that the blasted girl who'd showed up in his office was more of a threat than he'd realised. It was all about money, of course. The types of questions she'd been asking – stupid, stupid bitch! – made it abundantly clear. She wanted money, recognition, revenge. In that order. Well, she'd get none. He hadn't worked himself almost to death over the previous half-century to give anything up, least of all to the illegitimate child of a fucking domestic worker. His jaw clamped shut of its own accord.

'Get rid of her,' he growled, swivelling round to face Ogilvy. 'I don't give a damn how you do it.'

Ogilvy stared at him. 'Get rid of her?' he echoed. 'How?'

'Oh, don't be so naive. Call Simon Carter. I don't care what he does or how he does it – I don't want to know. All I want to know is that she's gone. Permanently. Of course there's no truth to it. Fucking little gold-digger.'

Ogilvy looked at him uncertainly. 'Carter hasn't worked for us for a while,' he said carefully. 'I'm not even sure where to find him.'

Jim glared at him. 'Just do it, will you?' he said almost wearily. 'If that little bitch has her way, we're all going down. I don't know how much you've managed to squirrel away for yourself over the years, but I hope for your sake it's enough. If this ship goes down – and we go down with it – it'll be all over for you as well, Ogilvy. You'd do well to remember that. Now, where are we on the Inkati mines?'

The late-afternoon sun bore down on Simon as he sat in a deckchair on the terrace overlooking the beach. The air was fluid, bee-heavy. His pulse slackened in the steady warmth. Beside him a book lay unopened; a glass of beer stood sweating in the heat. He sat, suspended between wakefulness and sleep, overcome with a sweet lassitude under the hypnosis of the sun. The shrill insistence of the phone came to him from behind the closed sliding doors. He swore softly, half-intending to ignore it. But it might be Caryn. He got up and went to answer it.

It wasn't Caryn. It was Ogilvy, Harte's lawyer and right-hand man. One last job – yes, he knew Simon wanted out and that he'd sworn Freedland would be his last, but wouldn't he just consider this one? Relatively easy. A young woman. Harte was prepared to pay whatever he wanted.

'Forget it,' Simon said shortly. 'Not a woman. And how did you get this number anyway?'

'I have my ways. Oh, for God's sake, Carter. Since when did that bother you?'

'Forget it, I said. I'm not doing it. I don't care how much he's offering. I'm out, Ogilvy. I've told you.'

Ogilvy sighed. 'Look, Simon. I . . . I wouldn't be asking you if I didn't think—' He stopped abruptly. 'We're not sure who she is. She claims she's Harte's daughter – he denies it, of course – but we've reason to believe she's out to destroy him, one way or another. She knows a fair amount, I don't mind telling you. Including who you are. And who your girlfriend is.'

There was silence for a minute. 'What does my girlfriend have to do with this?' Simon asked quietly.

'She's close to Nic Harte. I've had someone follow her over the past few days. I've reason to believe she's planning something, but I'm not sure what. Look, if you won't do it, give me a name. Someone you trust. My neck's on the line here, Carter.'

'Yeah, well, you should have known it would be one day, Ogilvy. That's the deal, isn't it?'

'Give me a name.'

'Let me think about this. I'll call you back.'

'Don't leave it too long, will you? We're fast running out of options.'

Simon didn't reply. He hung up the phone and walked back to the sliding doors. The tough, glittering skin of the ocean danced in front of his eyes, rising and falling, rising and falling without end. He leaned his forehead against the cool glass and brought up an arm to steady himself. It had to be that girl Caryn had told him about – Estelle Something-or-other. It ought to have come as a surprise, but nothing about Jim Harte surprised him. There was no way in hell *he* was going to do the job – contrary to what Ogilvy thought of him, he did have *some* form of moral judgement, and bumping off a young woman was out of the question. But the fact that she knew about Caryn – now that worried him. How had she found out? He knew Caryn; she wouldn't have told Nic. He trusted her. So the girl had found out some other way. As had Ogilvy, and therefore Harte. He'd been careful to cover his tracks but, as he knew only too well, anybody could be found. It was just a matter of time.

Tiredness settled upon him suddenly. As always, in those moments when he felt uncertainty closing in, it was Mat he thought of and longed to see. But that too was out of the question. Their last meeting had made it painfully obvious. He still couldn't bring himself to think about his own betrayal, or what the discovery of what Mat's entire family had been up to might have meant to him, the most stubbornly principled person Simon had ever known. The fact that Gordon, his father, was in on it too simply made it worse. Mat would never forgive him; never forgive *them*.

It came to him as he stood behind the doors, watching the sea, that part of him wanted the girl, Estelle, to succeed where others had failed. He wanted her to bring Harte and his whole, corrupt empire crashing to the ground. But another part of him was afraid. He'd seen what Jim Harte was capable of – Christ, he'd done it for him often enough. He would never go down without dragging everyone else behind him. Jim Harte wouldn't hesitate and he certainly wouldn't think twice about sacrificing others in order to save himself. The knowledge had never bothered him before; now, things were different. Caryn had changed him. He couldn't imagine his life without her, nor hers without him. He could feel his breath coming in short, urgent gasps. If Jim Harte was in danger, so too was he. And if he couldn't bring himself to get Harte *out* of danger, then he had to find someone who would.

114

The dress was made of a thin, stiff silk, drawn tightly across the bust, following the curve of her waist and hips and stopping mid-thigh. She turned slowly, admiring herself from all angles.

Midnight blue, shot through with tiny gold threads, it fitted her like a glove. Her gold platform shoes were lined up neatly beside her bed; her overnight case lay open-jawed on the floor, waiting to be filled. Her ticket, passport and hotel reservation were safely in the YSL clutch an appreciative client had given her the previous Christmas. She was almost ready. Nic was already in Paris. Her so-called friends would be getting ready to leave; she would follow later that evening. Didn't want to run the risk of bumping into them at the airport. She peeled the dress off her body, folding it carefully between layers of tissue paper before stowing it in the case. She intended to cause a stir in all senses of the word, not just with what she had to say. She wanted every eye in the room on her when she opened her mouth. From the emails she'd read, she knew they would all be dressed up to the nines – well, so too would she. She couldn't resist a little smirk. She knew the contents of Nic's wardrobe inside out; unless she'd been shopping in the past few weeks, there was nothing in it that even came close to her little outfit from Chanel. She flipped open her jewellery box and selected a necklace, earrings and a wonderfully heavy ring to match. Everything was set. In less than twenty-four hours, everything about her life would change.

115

Mme Censier had to practically shove Nic out of the room so that she and the two girls she'd drafted in to help with preparations could actually get on with the job. Even when it was absolutely clear that she was neither wanted nor needed, Nic just couldn't resist peeking in every few minutes to watch the transformation taking place. Mme Censier was as good as her word; nothing was left to chance. The whole apartment had been cleaned and polished so that the furniture reflected in glossy pools beneath her feet. Rugs were swept, beds stripped and then remade with stiff white linen sheets and enormous, plumped-up pillows. Fresh soap and towels were in the bathrooms, a small dish of liquorice and a single rose beside each bed. Gigantic bundles of white lilies and heavily scented burgundy roses stood in buckets in the kitchen, awaiting Mme Censier's instructions as to where they should go. Nic hovered in the doorway like a child; she asked for and was granted the job of displaying the flowers in the cut-glass vases that Mme Censier laid out for her. The chef arrived at lunchtime; from the kitchen came the sound of banging pans and expletives. The wines arrived shortly afterwards, followed by the delivery of the desserts and cheeses.

Nic felt the excitement in her begin to build. The first guests were due to arrive shortly. Tory, Luc, Caryn and Ally had all flown together. She'd toyed with the idea of asking Jim if Manning could fly everyone down, but discarded it for fear of appearing over the top. She'd organised a driver instead to pick them up from Charles de Gaulle and drive them into Paris. There would be time for a drink and something light to eat before the second group arrived. She took a quick, last look at the dinner table – silver and white tableware; large, scalloped plates with a delicate silver filigree pattern; beautifully starched and folded white napkins. The crystal glasses sparkled, catching and throwing light against the two ornate chandeliers that hung over the table. It was perfect, exactly as she'd planned.

At a quarter past three she took a quick shower, changed into jeans and a blouse and wandered into the living room. She flopped down into one of the grey silk couches and turned on the stereo. For a second, unable to stop herself, she thought of Mat. She'd have given almost anything to see his slow, wide smile again or feel the rumble of his laughter deep inside his chest. She turned and buried her head in one of the pillows, overcome by a longing that was so intense it hurt. How could it be that such a brief encounter could have produced such depths of emotion? She heard his voice again: *A farmer's daughter, eh?* In her mind's eye she traced the outline of his features, the full, sensual mouth parting to reveal a flash of brilliant white, the ebony sheen of his skin, so different from her own – the uncanny sensation of knowing someone in the deepest sense of the word, no matter how little time they'd spent together. They'd never really spoken about it, not properly at least, but it was clear to her they were two sides of the same coin. Displaced, out of place, perhaps – a white African and a black European. Unlike her, he slipped in and out of the two worlds with grace. It was something she hadn't realised until she'd met him that she too longed to do. The fact of it and the realisation that he was gone from her made the loss that much harder to bear. She put up a hand to her cheek, aware that it was wet with tears. She heard the doorbell, and Mme Censier's answer. Her guests had started to arrive. She wiped her face hurriedly and stood up, forcing a smile to her face. Now was not the time for tears. That time ought to have passed. Long ago.

By seven that evening, the apartment was filled with the sound of laughter and conversation. Everyone had arrived on time; they'd been picked up at the airport as planned and brought through the city to the elegant, usually empty townhouse that had now come to life. At six, they'd all gone into their rooms to get changed and dressed for dinner. From behind the kitchen door, Nic could just make out the sounds of champagne corks popping and the oven door opening and closing as Mme Censier and her helpers prepared the trays of canapés and drinks. She put down the mascara wand and looked at her reflection. Her hair was up, twisted into a tight knot on the crown of her head and held in place with two antique wooden hair combs. She turned her head cautiously to one side. The long drop earrings Tory had given her for one of her birthdays dangled almost to the curve of her neck. She'd taken a few of the long-stemmed Harkney roses into her room and placed them on her dressing table. They were the colour of translucent ivory, their inner petals just tinged with blush pink. Their concentrated sweetness filled the room. She picked up the cut-glass bottle of perfume lying next to her and slowly removed the stopper, dabbing the liquid at her wrists and the base of her neck.

She stared at her reflection, reading the complete language of her face. She hardly recognised herself. She was twenty-eight. In a few minutes she would rise from the dressing table, fasten the silver-heeled shoes she'd bought especially for the occasion and stand up. There was a growing sense of apprehension, a strange awareness of the need to pause and think. But about what? The dress was beautiful; the shoes, the earrings. Again, everything was just as it should be. She shook her head slowly from side to side. Stop it, she cautioned herself sternly. *Enjoy this moment. Don't think about what could have been. It isn't — and that's that.*

Tory looked lovely, despite the weight of the secret she was carrying inside her. The colour was up in her cheeks, an exceptionally pretty blush that rose from her cleavage and travelled all the way up her neck and face. Luc, too, was particularly handsome that night. They made a striking couple, Nic thought to herself, whatever their private drama. Caryn caught her gaze; they smiled at one another. Nic felt a swift and immediate prick of tears behind her eyes. They'd known each other for almost fifteen years; hard to believe at times. To her, it felt as though she'd known them for ever. There wasn't a single member of her family present for her birthday, despite the fact that it was being held in one of Jim's homes. In many ways, it summed up the state of her relationship with them. She looked around her — eight of her closest friends were present; the wine and champagne had started to flow, music was playing softly in the background — it was perfect. She began to move amongst her guests. It had been a while since she'd seen some of them, and she was quickly lost in conversation, catching up.

Tory sipped her glass of fizzy water slowly, trying to focus on anything other than the slightly queasy sensation in her stomach that had started on the journey over from London and stubbornly refused to go away. Luc hadn't noticed anything; neither the fact that she wasn't drinking, nor the fact that she wasn't feeling her best. She watched him joking and laughing with the others; as always, she was struck by his physicality, his wild, almost careless streak of life that was at odds with his personality. He had a wonderful, deep colour that spread from his neck to his cheeks. In winter, his face was quick and rosy; in summer, he had the warm, sun-mellowed skin of fruit. His eyes were always lit up, as if he'd just been running, his whole body caught in a moment of splendid activity. Yes, he was a deeply attractive man. So what was wrong with him? She took another sip of water. It wasn't the time or the place to start thinking about what she'd done, or why. It was a time of celebration, not intro-spection. Now wasn't the time to start thinking about the past. But it couldn't be helped. The past was now present in her in a way that couldn't be altered, and sooner or later she was going to have to confront it. She looked at Luc across the room. He offered her everything; with him there was none of the doubt that Rob wrought. With Luc, she gave of herself in the assur-ance that it would be received, accepted, without question. His generosity was palpable, unlike Rob's. With Rob everything was measured, calculated, conditional. It wasn't often that she dared think about it, but the reasons behind why she couldn't shake herself rid of Rob were too dangerous to contemplate.

All of a sudden, standing there in the middle of the room at her best friend's party, the memories started to surface. The thing – no other word for it – with Rob had been a kind of madness, born out of her unspoken guilt over the last words she and Susie had exchanged that morning before she left for school. She'd never been able to rid herself of the feeling that she'd caused it. If Susie hadn't been so upset she probably wouldn't have gone to Bagley's that night, and she wouldn't have stormed off when Rob got there. It was her fault it had happened, and she had to live with it. But during the months she'd spent with Rob – if sleeping with him occasionally could be described as being 'with' him – she'd come to see another side of the man they'd both idolised, Tory from her outsider's position as the besotted younger sister. Rob was moody and unpredictable in ways that had nothing to do with her. Far from being the kind, gentle person she'd always thought he was, he was difficult and – hard as it was to admit to – downright manipulative. When he didn't get what he wanted, he withdrew into himself, walked away and no amount of coaxing could bring him back. He came and went when he pleased, answerable to no one but himself. When she'd first bumped into him, she'd assumed he had become like that *after* Susie's death, but the more she got to know him, the more she began to remember things, little things, that Susie had said. And now the painful memory of that last Friday suddenly surfaced and she was powerless to stop it.

She'd been in Susie's room, watching her put on make-up, fluff out her hair with her fingers in preparation for meeting Rob. She'd picked up the mascara wand Susie had dropped. She'd scuttled up to the dressing table next to Susie, shyly pleased that she hadn't yet been thrown out of the room. Susie's moods were legendary – one minute she was happy to have her younger sister sitting beside her, chatting as though they were friends, not sisters, and then the next she was fed up with her, bored by her, irritated by her. Tory had lived in perpetual worry of being rejected by her older, prettier, wittier sister. She'd brushed the tips of her own lashes with Susie's mascara and looked at the two of them in the dressing-table mirror. Susie – blonde, sparkly, fair. Herself, dark, olive-skinned, odd. Definitely not pretty, like Susie. She'd turned her head slowly, this way and that, pulled a face . . . smiled at herself in the mirror.

'*Here, give me that!*' *Susie had said, her irritation finally breaking through. She'd snatched the mascara wand out of Tory's hand.* '*Get lost, will you?*'

'*Why?*' *Tory remembered the whining sound of her own voice as if it were yesterday.*

'*Because. Just scram.*'

'*But why can't I stay? I'm only sitting here. I'm not doing anything, Susie, honest. I'll be quiet, I promise . . .*'

'*I said, scram!*' *Susie's voice had risen dangerously.* '*Why can't you just leave me alone?*'

'*But—*'

'*Get out!*' *It was almost a scream.*

'I hate you!' Tory shouted at her, scraping her stool back. Hot, angry tears were already forming in her eyes. 'I hate you!'

'Yeah, well, that makes two of us,' Susie said coldly, turning back to the mirror. 'And don't hang around downstairs waiting, either. I can't stand the way you mooch around Rob. Neither can he.'

Tory yanked on the bedroom door handle, her cheeks on fire with anger – and yes, shame. It hurt like hell to think about it. It was true. She fancied Rob. Everyone fancied Rob. But Susie'd got him. She'd had him ever since she set eyes on him. That was just the way it was with Susie. She got whatever she wanted. And although wild horses wouldn't have dragged the words from Tory's lips, she'd wanted him, too. But wild horses were no match for Susie – she'd seen straight through Tory's studied indifference whenever Rob was near. The thought of her and Rob laughing about it tore through her, winding her. 'It's not true!' she yelled, her hair falling over her face as she flounced out of the room. 'You're such a fucking liar. I hate you! I wish you were dead!'

Less than twelve hours later, she was. Tory had spent the next fifteen years wishing more than anything she could take the words back.

'What's wrong?' Luc's voice suddenly brought her back to herself. She jumped.

'Nothing.'

'You've gone all pale. You OK?'

'I . . . I'm fine,' she stammered, turning away. The last thing she felt like doing was talking to Luc. Even looking at him seemed to be the worst form of betrayal. She mumbled something about needing the toilet and disappeared. She wasn't sure she could even bring herself to look at her own reflection, let alone his face.

Caryn watched Tory stumble towards the bathroom. She caught a glimpse of Luc's face – concerned, confused – and winced inwardly. She wondered how he felt. It was clear to her, as it probably was to everyone else, that something was going on. She looked at the other guests, laughing and talking, busy helping themselves to canapés and topping up champagne glasses – why couldn't things be as easy for the three of them? Nic's bright smiles and cheerful expression did little to hide the occasional slip of the mask when another, deeper sort of emotion could be seen. Disappointment? Longing? She couldn't say. She took a sip of her own champagne, allowing her mind to wander into the sort of territory she'd steeled herself against. She didn't know what Nic knew about Simon; there were so many unanswered questions. Where had Simon met Nic, and why was he so adamant that Caryn shouldn't ask her? And why did he have the business card she'd found in his wallet? She remembered how upset Nic had been when Mat didn't call – had Simon taken the card from him and hidden it? Would she ever get to the bottom of the mystery surrounding Simon and the Hartes? It seemed unlikely. It also seemed unlikely that she would ask. The delicate balance that enveloped her relationship with Simon depended on her acceptance of things just the way they were. She wasn't sure she'd ever have the courage to change.

116

By the time the main courses were brought out, the dinner party had settled; everyone was having a good time. They'd all swapped seats a couple of times, conversation was flowing, even Tory had lost the haunted, hunted look on her face and was slowly beginning to relax. Nic saw Luc reach for her hand once or twice . . . perhaps things between them weren't as bad as she'd feared? She looked to her left and right – animated faces, smiles, laughter. All as it should be. She took a sip of wine, pleased at the way everything had turned out. In the distance, she heard the doorbell chime and, through the half-closed doorway, the sound of Mme Censier's voice. Someone had obviously come to the door. She frowned, wondering who it could be. A few seconds later, Mme Censier appeared at her elbow.

'Sorry to interrupt,' she whispered, 'but someone's here to see you. She's downstairs in the lobby.'

'Who?' Nic shook her head, puzzled. It was almost ten.

'She wouldn't say. A young woman – said she's a friend, that's all.'

'A friend?' Nic repeated, frowning.

'What is it?' Caryn asked, turning towards her.

Nic lifted her shoulders. 'Someone's downstairs to see me, apparently. She didn't give a name. Wonder who it is.'

'Shall I come with you?'

Nic shook her head. 'Don't worry.' She pushed back her chair and stood up. 'I'll be back in a second.'

The first thing she saw as she came down the sweep of the staircase was the long, graceful line of Estelle's legs. A sudden wave of panic swept over her, prickling the fine hairs at the back of her neck. 'Estelle?' she said incredulously. 'Wh . . . what on earth are you doing here?'

Estelle stood up, crushing the cigarette she'd been smoking under the heel of her foot. 'Just thought I'd drop by,' she said smoothly, the corners of her mouth lifting in a way that was anything but pleasant. 'Seeing as it's your birthday and all that.' She presented herself, palms spread outwards. 'Don't worry, I won't stay long. I hope this is all right,' she said, looking down at her dress and high-heeled shoes. 'Wouldn't want to embarrass you in front of your friends.'

'B-but . . .' Nic stammered, her face burning with a mixture of embarrassment and trepidation. 'I . . . how did you—?'

'Find out?' Estelle interrupted her. She smiled, a slow, glittery smile that made Nic's blood run cold. 'Oh, never mind that.' She looked up the staircase. 'Nice house. Didn't know you had a place in Paris too, Nic. Daddy buy it for you?'

'Estelle . . .'

'Party's upstairs, I imagine?' Estelle cut her off. 'So who's here?'

'Estelle . . .' Nic began again weakly. It was too late. Estelle was already walking towards the stairs. She brushed past Nic in a cloud of her signature scent. Nic felt sick. Everything had been going so well – what the *hell* was Estelle doing there? She turned and followed her, her mind racing. Something was about to go horribly wrong. She could feel it.

Estelle stood in the doorway, eyes narrowing as she surveyed the scene of cosy intimacy in front of her. Eight heads turned towards her; she saw Caryn and Tory exchange a glance. There was a sudden uprush of feeling inside her; how dare they gather without her? The simmering rage that had brought her from London to Paris was now hammering at her ribs. She suddenly felt as though she couldn't breathe. Behind her was Nic. Everyone seemed frozen; no one knew quite what to say. From the looks being exchanged up and down the table, it was clear no one aside from Tory and Caryn had any idea who she was. It was yet another reminder of her outsider status. She could feel the anger spreading through her veins.

'Estelle . . .' Nic began hurriedly, going to stand defensively behind her chair. 'I . . . we're just having a small party. I would've invited you, but—'

'Just for your closest friends, is it? But I thought *I* was one of your closest friends, Nic,' Estelle said, not even bothering to look at her. Tory and Caryn's eyes were fixed on her, waiting for her to do or say something. She noticed the way Tory held her boyfriend's hand – gripping it tightly as if in the face of something evil or awful – or both. 'Or did I get it wrong?'

'Look, Estelle,' Nic broke in quickly. 'Why don't . . . would you like to join us?' she asked hurriedly, avoiding Tory and Caryn's looks of surprise. 'We're just about to have dessert and—'

'How kind of you,' Estelle murmured sarcastically. 'Are you sure I'm not interrupting anything? Imposing myself on you?'

'No, no . . . not at all,' Nic said weakly, sounding anything but sincere. Estelle's eyes narrowed again. Everyone present looked as if having Estelle join them was the last thing they wanted – how dare they? They didn't even *know* her! One of the men stood up and offered her his seat. She slid into it gracefully, noting the quick, habitual look of interest from the man sitting opposite as her skirt opened to reveal an expanse of thigh.

'Sorry to gatecrash the party,' she murmured, accepting a glass of wine from a girl in uniform who'd just come into the room. 'Only just heard about it.' She lifted her head and looked across the table at Tory. Tory's expression was one of stunned disbelief. 'Having a lovely time, are you, Tory?'

'Yes, thanks,' Tory said frostily. Estelle looked away. Stupid cow. She'd soon wipe that snotty expression off her face.

'And you're . . . ?' Estelle turned to the man who'd given up his seat.

'Steve. I used to work with Nic. Sorry, I didn't catch your name.'

'Estelle. I'm a friend of Nic's. Well, not in the *inner* circle, obviously,' she smiled again. 'But still, we're pretty close, wouldn't you say, Nic? Or at least *I* thought we were.'

'We thought we'd keep the numbers even—' Nic's voice trailed off uncomfortably.

'And how're you, Caryn?' Estelle looked at Nic contemptuously and then turned to Caryn.

'Fine, thanks,' Caryn said shortly. She turned her head to talk to the man sitting next to her – a deliberate snub.

'That's nice to hear,' Estelle said sarcastically, flashing her a smile. 'Back from LA?'

'Er, yeah.' Caryn gave Nic a quick, nervous glance.

Estelle noticed it immediately and smiled inwardly with satisfaction. *Oh, yes . . . she's told me all about you. I know all about you, Caryn Middleton. Sitting here as though butter wouldn't melt in your mouth.* 'Enjoying it?' Estelle asked, enjoying her discomfort.

'Would you like something to eat, Estelle?' Nic broke in hurriedly.

'Wine's fine,' Estelle snapped, holding up her glass. She

certainly didn't want their leftovers. She turned back to Steve. 'So. Are you *also* a journalist? Nic's got a thing for journalists, hasn't she?'

'Estelle!' Nic said, rather too quickly. 'I don't think—'

'Oh, relax,' Estelle snapped, draining her wine. She held up her glass, signalling to the waiter. A bold, brittle rage was slowly making its way up her body. 'Delicious,' she murmured to no one in particular.

Caryn surveyed Estelle from the other side of the table, seething with rage and an unspecified nervousness. There was something in Estelle's gaze that she flinched from. She couldn't *believe* the girl had had the nerve to show up uninvited – how on earth had she found out? And now that she was here, what the hell did she want? She looked stunning in her midnight-blue silk dress with her honey-coloured hair cascading down her back and those smoky, made-up eyes. But she looked dangerous, too. There was something hard and predatory about her that made Caryn's hair stand on end. Neither she nor Tory could fathom what on earth Nic saw in her. Was it the fact they were both from Africa? What the hell else could it be? There had to be *some* reason why Nic liked her so. Oddly enough, they even looked alike. It had taken her a while to see it – Estelle's features were usually hidden under layers of make-up and accessories – but every once in a while, the likeness between them emerged. Something in the eyes, perhaps . . . and those high, wide cheekbones. She glanced at Tory. She too was looking at Estelle with barely disguised irritation. Caryn sighed. It had been a wonderful evening up until Estelle's sudden arrival. Damn her, she thought to herself angrily. Why couldn't she just fuck off back to where she'd come from?

A few seats away from Caryn, Tory was also watching Estelle nervously. She'd stared at her in disbelief as she sauntered across the floor to join them, tossing her hair over one shoulder, making a beeline for the men in whose eyes she knew she'd find the most appreciative welcome. Even Luc couldn't keep his eyes off her. She glared at him and was mortified to see Estelle's slow smirk. She studied her profile as Estelle talked and flirted. Nic had said something about an accident – she'd had to go to hospital for stitches – but looking at her now, her hair falling in soft waves down her back, she'd never looked better. Tory had to suppress the urge to pick up a bottle of wine and either smash it over her head or tip its contents down her throat. Estelle set her teeth on edge like no one had ever done before.

'*Qu'est-ce qu'il y a?*' Luc murmured, noticing her agitation.

'Nothing,' Tory said shortly.

'Who is she?' He jerked his head imperceptibly in Estelle's direction.

Tory shook her head. 'Just some friend of Nic's. I can't stand her.' She looked up and was disconcerted to find Estelle's gaze on her, almost as though she'd read her lips. A cold, nervous tremor ran through her. She had the sudden, dreadful premonition that something was about to happen – but what? What could Estelle possibly do to her? Or anyone else? She pushed back her chair suddenly. There was a cold, metallic taste in her mouth; she dimly recognised it as fear. She was being ridiculous. What on earth was there to fear?

'What's the matter?' Luc looked at her, concern in his face.

Tory's head felt distinctly woolly, even though she'd had nothing to drink. 'I . . . I'm not feeling so good,' she muttered, pulling her pashmina around her shoulders. She was suddenly cold. 'I think I'll just go outside for a bit. Get some fresh air.'

'Shall I come with you?' Luc was already halfway out of his chair.

Estelle's eyes flickered over the two of them. There was a moment's carefully held silence before she opened her beautiful mouth. And then everything happened at once. 'Leaving?' Estelle asked, playing with the stem of her wine glass. 'So soon?'

'No, I'm just—'

'Are you all right?' Nic broke in hurriedly. 'Something wrong?'

'Oh, I doubt it,' Estelle said lazily. 'You know what it's

like . . .' She turned her head to look at Tory. 'In your condition—'

'Condition?' Luc put a hand on Tory's shoulder as if to protect her.

Tory suddenly felt faint. 'I'm fine,' she snapped, turning away.

'Of course you're fine. You ought to be blooming, or isn't that what they say? I know the first three months—'

'Estelle!' Nic's voice held a desperate note of warning.

'What condition? What is she talking about?'

'*Nothing*,' Tory hissed, hurrying towards the door. She felt nauseous. How the hell . . . ?

'You didn't know?' Estelle turned to Luc, spreading her hands before her in a slow gesture of disarming surprise. 'Oh, I thought you'd have been the first—'

'Estelle! Stop. Just stop.' Caryn got to her feet. 'It's bad enough you barging your way into Nic's party but—'

'Shut your mouth,' Estelle turned to her. 'Who asked *you* anything?'

'Oh, Estelle,' Nic broke in anxiously. 'She's only—'

'Only what? Sticking her nose in where it doesn't belong?'

'Hang on a minute—'

'Listen—'

'Hey, everyone! It's Nic's birthday, remember?' Steve interrupted them, trying to calm the situation that had erupted almost without warning.

'Let's all just have another round of champagne, shall we?' Ally joined in, picking out a bottle from the ice-bucket. 'It's almost midnight. Let's have one last toast.'

Estelle turned her head slowly, her eyes flickering slowly over the group. She looked at them contemptuously – their bright, eager faces, buoyed by drink and the warmth of friendship from which she'd been excluded. *Oh, don't invite her.* She wasn't good enough. Simple, in its own way, as that. All that mattered now was getting even.

'A toast?' she asked, her voice sounding dangerously sharp, even to her own ears. 'Yes, let's have a toast. To old friends . . .

what d'you say, Nic? Old friends and new ones, too, of course. Only—' She stopped and cocked her head to one side. Nic's face was fixed on hers. 'The thing is—' She stood up. 'I'm not really a *new* friend. No, not new. And not a *friend* exactly, either.'

'What the fuck are you talking about?' Caryn interrupted her angrily. 'If you've got something to say, Estelle, then bloody well say it. If you haven't, then why don't you just fuck off back to where you came from and leave us the hell alone?'

'Oh, you'd like that, wouldn't you, Caryn?' Estelle said, rounding on her. 'That'd be *your* way of dealing with things, wouldn't it? Pretending. That's what you do, isn't it? You pretend.'

'What the hell is going on here?' Steve asked, looking from Caryn to Estelle and back again. 'Is there something I'm missing?'

'All sorts of stuff,' Estelle said, smiling slowly at no one in particular. 'Nic knows, don't you, Nic? And you, Caryn. You know exactly what I'm talking about. I know you'd prefer to pretend nothing's wrong, of course. That's the way you like to do things, I know. '

'Look,' Luc broke in suddenly, breathing quickly. He looked from one girl to the other, his face a mask of confusion and worry. Tory remained where she was with one hand on the door handle as if too petrified to move. 'I don't understand what's happening here.'

'Of course you don't,' Estelle said sweetly. 'You'd be the last person to know if *she* had her way—'

'Estelle!' Nic's voice rang out sharply. Her face was suddenly white. 'That's enough.'

'Says who? *You*?' Estelle gave a short, nasty laugh. 'As if you're in any position to decide what's enough. You have no idea who you're dealing with, Nic. No fucking idea.'

'Look, everyone, let's all just calm down for a minute.' Graham tried to inject a note of normality into the conversation. 'There seems to be some sort of—'

'Oh, shut up.' Estelle took another mouthful of wine. Her

pulse was racing. Nothing could have stopped her now. 'I've no idea who *you* are but you haven't got a clue who these people are.' She pointed a finger at Caryn. 'Little Miss Goody Two Shoes. D'you want to know what she's been up to?' She barely glanced at Caryn, who was staring at her with a mixture of incredulity and hostility. 'She's supposed to be your best friend, Nic. Your *best* friend! I bet you don't know who she's been seeing behind your back for the past year, do you?' She laughed mirthlessly. 'No, I bet you don't. Does the name Simon Carter ring a bell with anyone?' She stared at them. Nic's face had gone deadly white. Caryn looked as though she would faint.

'Simon? Simon Carter?' Ally broke in suddenly. 'Simon from university?' She looked at Nic, obviously confused.

Caryn put a hand to her throat. Her mouth trembled, as though she couldn't get the words out fast enough. 'Wh-what the hell d'you think you're playing at?' she said through gritted teeth. 'Why don't you just leave?'

'Leave? Oh, no. I'm not finished here,' Estelle said, her chest heaving. 'Not by a long shot.'

'Get out.' Tory's voice broke in on them from across the room. Everyone turned to look at her. She too was breathing fast. 'Just get out. No one wants you here, d'you understand? You're not welcome.'

'D'you think I give a damn what *you* think?' Estelle barely even looked at her. 'Who the hell d'you think you are? You're in no position to talk—'

'Estelle, *please* . . .' It was Nic. She sounded close to tears.

Estelle ignored her. She opened her clutch bag and took out her small silver cigarette case. There was absolute silence from the guests gathered around the table as she shook out a cigarette and lit it. She blew the smoke out carelessly in Tory's direction. And then she continued. 'I mean, you've got a secret or two of your own, haven't you, Tory? Pretty obvious, wouldn't you say?'

'What the hell is going on here?' Luc's voice was strained. Tory was holding on to the door as if for dear life.

'What's the matter, Tory? You don't like it when the spotlight's on you?'

'You little bitch!'

'*I'm* the bitch? Me? Oh, no, you're wrong. I mean, sleeping with your dead sister's boyfriend is one thing, having his child and trying to pass it off as your fiancé's another thing altogether. No, I'd say *you're* the bitch here, not me.' Estelle blew another cloud of smoke towards Tory. Tory's face was as white as a sheet. Luc looked from Estelle to Tory and back again, his face slowly crumpling with the awful recognition of the truth. Estelle smiled to herself. It was going better than she'd dreamed; one by one, her bombs were hitting home. She turned her head and looked Caryn in the eye. 'And as for you,' she said slowly, almost lazily. 'I give you the creeps, do I? Well, nowhere near as much as your boyfriend does. Have you any idea who he is? What he does? Why don't you ask Nic who he is?'

Caryn stared back at her, guilt and confusion written all over her face. 'Who the hell are you?' she finally spat out. 'What the hell do you want from us?'

'Nothing. Nothing at all.' Estelle regarded her coolly. 'No, let me rephrase that. I don't give a shit about you,' she said, pointing her cigarette directly at Caryn. 'And I certainly don't give a shit about *her*.' She looked Tory up and down. 'I hated you both from the first time I set eyes on you.'

'So what are you doing here?' Caryn asked, her voice trembling. 'Who are you?'

Estelle took a drag on her cigarette. Every eye in the room was on her. She looked at Nic. 'Ask her,' she said flatly. 'She knows.'

Everyone turned to look at Nic. She spread her hands helplessly in front of her. 'I don't know what you're talking about, Estelle. I don't. I don't understand what's going on.'

'Oh, I think you do,' Estelle smiled. 'You'd have to be blind as well as stupid not to have figured it out by now.'

'Figured *what* out?' There was a note of desperation in Nic's voice that thrilled Estelle. At last she had Nic Harte just where she wanted her.

'Why don't you ask your father?' Estelle regarded her calmly. 'He'll tell you who I am.'

'Wh-what are you talking about?' Nic whispered. She sat down suddenly, as if her legs couldn't quite hold her up. 'Why . . . what's my dad got to do with this?' Her voice was shaking almost as badly as her hands. 'You're making this up . . .'

'A liar as well as a bitch?' Estelle gave a short laugh. 'That'd be convenient, wouldn't it? No. You ask your father who I am. He'll tell you. And then you tell him that I know everything. Every last detail. You want to know what happened to your mother? *I* know. A hunting accident? I don't think so.'

Nic's face was completely drained of colour. No one else in the room dared say a word. Estelle looked around the table triumphantly. She could see from the look of hurt on Nic's face that she'd scored the sort of hit from which there was almost no recovery. She stubbed out her cigarette, swallowed the last drop of wine in her glass in one gulp and stood up. She surveyed the frozen, fearful faces around her. Luc was staring at Tory as if he'd been slapped. Caryn's face was contorted in a mask of shame and confusion. And Tory couldn't look at anyone, not even Estelle.

She'd won. No need to go further; she'd won. Her heartbeat was a deafening roar inside her head; the blood was racing through her veins. There would be no going back, not now. She'd done exactly what she'd come to Paris to do. She'd blown a hole in the Harte family, wide and deep. It was impossible they would recover. She almost felt sorry for Nic. *Almost*, but not quite – Nic was only now having to face what she, Estelle, had faced every day of her life for the past twenty-eight years. No one had bothered to tell Estelle the truth about who she was. Gloria, Jim Harte, Basil Mackenzie . . . none of them had had the nerve or the courage to tell her who she really was. She'd had to find out the hard way and even then, when the evidence was staring them all in the face, they'd denied it. Jim Harte had tossed her aside in pretty much the same way he'd tossed Gloria, once he was finished with her. Gloria had never had the strength or courage to confront him, but here was her daughter, come to confront them. From *her* there could be no running away.

She ignored the housekeeper and yanked open the door. Her heels made a high-pitched clattering sound as she ran quickly down the stairs. She felt almost light-headed with the relief of having brought something out of her that had been lying dormant, in wait. She'd pulled it up, thrust it out of her body and thrown it in their faces – she relived the thrilling sensation of watching where and how her words had found their mark. At the door to the courtyard she stopped and turned to cast one look back up at the elegant, moneyed townhouse. Inside they would all be trying to recover; Tory, holding on to the door and avoiding her boyfriend's eyes; Caryn looking everywhere but at Nic; and Nic – again, the sharp, almost animal thrill of revenge ran through her – Nic's haunted, drained face staring at her, unable to take it all in. Nic knew. Of course she knew. Impossible not to. Which of the revelations would have shocked her the most? Estelle pushed open the heavy wooden door. It wasn't her business any more. She'd done what she'd come to Paris to do. All she had to do now was wait. Nic would run to her father; soon Jim Harte would contact her and the whole, satisfying business of negotiation would begin. She suppressed another small smile. She'd won. Just as she'd predicted.

She turned left and made her way towards the Boulevard Saint Michel. Her hotel room was waiting, just as the rest of her life was waiting – fresh, moneyed, clean. A clean start. She hurried past the groups of people coming out of the restaurants that lined the road; women in expensive dresses and clouds of sweet-smelling perfume, the men with cigars clamped between their teeth, hands lightly on the tanned shoulders of their wives and mistresses as they ambled along the pavement, heads turning as she passed. Ahead of her was the discreetly elegant canopy of the Hotel Palais. She stepped inside the lobby. Inside it was all golden, soft light and the faint murmur of the piano in the bar. Soon, she thought to herself with glee, she would own homes such as the hotel she'd chosen. Perhaps Harte would give her the Parisian flat? She'd rather liked it! She had an uncanny, fleeting glimpse of herself all those years ago, sitting in the lobby of the Hilton, watching Sally Devereaux sip her tea. *I want to be like that.* That was what had gone through her mind; exactly that. *I want to sit here and look as though I could afford to own this place if I wanted. I want people to notice me, envy me.*

The lift doors opened and she walked inside. A second later a tall man with dirty blonde hair stepped in, his eyes going over her in the customary way. The blood was up in her cheeks; her eyes were sparkling. He didn't smile, but there was something in his eyes that gave her to understand he'd noticed her. She pressed the button for the sixth floor. She felt, rather than heard, his movement behind her. Nothing noticeable, just the faintest pressure as his hand brushed the small of her back. He was good-looking; she'd noticed that immediately. Was he . . . ? She turned her head slightly, momentarily caught off guard. He was looking straight ahead, his face completely blank. She glanced at his composed, expressionless profile. Yes, he *was* good-looking. And no, he couldn't have touched her. She'd imagined it. She almost smiled to herself. The lift moved smoothly upwards. A split second later she felt the sting of something along the length of her forearm – a tiny prick, almost like a mosquito bite. She lifted her arm to touch it, protectively. They glided upwards in silence. And then it hit her. She heard herself gasp as the wave of dizziness came over her; the sound was very loud in her ears. A single noise that seemed, for a moment, not to have come from her own throat. And then there was nothing. Nothing at all.

117

As soon as the door slammed behind Estelle, Nic felt her legs give way. She sat down hard in the chair, staring blankly at the remains of the dinner party before her. No one said a word;

there was an unspoken, tacit agreement that they all needed to recover from the dread Estelle had left behind her. Tory walked unsteadily out of the room. Luc watched her go. Caryn's face was turned away from her, towards the wall. In the taut bulge of the muscles in her neck, Nic registered that she was crying.

'Wh . . . what shall we do?' Ally finally spoke. Her voice was tight with anger.

Nic shook her head wearily. 'Nothing,' she said at last. 'I'm . . . I'm really sorry. I don't—'

'*You're* sorry?' Steve was incredulous. 'Who the hell was *that*? What've you got to be sorry about? She just waltzed in here and fucking ruined—'

'I think I'd better go and see Tory,' Nic mumbled, getting up from her seat. The last thing she wanted was sympathy. She opened the door, ignoring Mme Censier's stricken face. The dinner party had been ruined, of course. No one quite knew what to do, least of all the kitchen staff. They hovered in the doorway, unsure whether to clear away the plates or bring out fresh ones. Nic ignored them and walked through the apartment to the bedrooms. She hesitated for a second, then tapped on the door. 'Tory?' she whispered. 'It's me. Can I come in?' There was a muffled sound of assent from within. She pushed open the door. Tory was sitting on the edge of the bed, one hand curling protectively around her stomach. The look of pain and fear in her eyes was almost palpable. Nic's heart turned over. 'I . . . I'm sorry, Tory. I don't know what to say. I just don't know what to say.'

Tory looked down at her hands. There was silence for a few moments. 'Nothing to do with you,' she said finally, echoing Steve. 'It had to come out somehow.'

'But not like this,' Nic said, moving to sit beside her. 'Not like this.' She hesitated, fearing something – a rebuke, a turning away, accusation.

Tory shook her head slowly. 'No, I suppose not. But it's out now. I can't explain what happened, Nic. I . . . I don't know why I did it. Rob, I mean. It was like a . . . a madness. I just couldn't stop myself.'

'What about Rob?'

Tory shrugged, turning her head towards the window. 'He's leaving.'

'Does he know?'

Tory shook her head. 'No. I can't bring myself to say anything. Sometimes I wish I'd never bumped into him, but there are times when I can't imagine not seeing him again.'

'Do you have to?'

'What?'

'Tell him,' Nic said flatly. 'Does he have to know? Does he have the right to know?'

'I . . . I don't know what you mean,' Tory said hesitantly. 'Of course he does.'

'Tory, listen to me. Luc loves you. No, let me finish.' Nic held up a warning hand. 'After tonight, who knows what'll happen? Who knows what he's thinking right now? But *you've* got to decide what you want to do. Not what Rob wants, or what Luc wants – the only person who can make a decision about your future is *you*. No one else. If you want to keep the child, then that's what you're going to have to work out between you and Luc, and you and Rob, if that's what you want. But it's your choice, Tory. No one else's.'

'But—'

'No "buts". This is it, Tory. It's your life, not theirs. Figure out what *you* want to do, then do it.' She got up from the bed, suddenly and strangely energised. A feeling of calm determination had come over her as soon as she'd seen Tory's dejected face. It was as if in talking to Tory she was also talking to herself. She had no idea where the words had come from. *Figure out what you want to do, then do it.* She looked down at Tory, a small smile playing around the corner of her lips. 'You'll be fine,' she said softly. 'You're stronger than all of us put together.'

'No, I'm not—' Tory began, almost automatically.

Nic held up a hand again. 'Take it from me,' she said, walking towards the door. 'You're stronger than you think. And now I'm going to bed.'

'Are you all right?' Tory asked suddenly, looking up at her.

Nic nodded. 'I think *she* thought I'd just crumble,' she said, tossing her head in the direction of the front door. 'But she hasn't got a clue. We're all tougher than we think.'

'Nic . . .' Tory seemed about to say something, then hesitated.

'What?'

'I don't say it often enough, and I should, I know . . .'

'What?'

'Thanks. For everything. For being there all the time. You've never judged me, not once.'

'Who'm I to judge?' Nic said lightly, opening the door. 'Forget about me, Tory. This isn't about me. It's about you. Now get some rest. I'll knock on your door in the morning before I leave.'

'You're leaving? Where're you going?' Tory looked at her in alarm.

'There's something I should've done a long time ago,' Nic said cryptically, and then shut the door.

118

Gordon Ndava looked up as the maid ushered a young woman into the room. He stared at her. In the background, he could hear Patience, his wife, opening and shutting cupboard doors as she began preparations for Sunday lunch. He was the first to recover. 'Good afternoon, Nicola,' he said, getting up from his favourite chair by the window. 'Do come in.' She was taken aback, he could see. Probably wondering how he knew her name. He had the uneasy premonition that the uncertainty of the past few months was about to be brought to the fore. He and Mat hadn't spoken since the day he'd admitted he too worked for Jim Harte. Here was Harte's daughter in front of him; he had an inkling why she'd come. 'You won't remember me, I'm sure,' he said, motioning her to one of the sofas. 'But I've visited Avonlea many times. Oh, when you were much younger,' he added, smiling, trying to put her at ease.

'You've been to Avonlea?' she asked, sitting down as he bid her. There was bewilderment in her eyes. 'You know my father?'

'I *work* for your father, Nicola. Or at least, I used to. Yes, I visited your home many times. You were usually away at school. Like my sons.'

'Is . . .' She cleared her throat nervously. 'Is Mat here?'

He shook his head. 'No,' he sighed heavily. 'I'm afraid not. Is that why you've come?'

She looked down at her hands. 'Yes.'

'I see. I didn't know you two knew one another,' Gordon said. He studied her discreetly. Things were slowly beginning to make sense. 'How long have you . . . er, known each other?' he asked delicately.

'Not long. I didn't know that . . . that it was all connected, you know. I didn't know who he was.'

'And I assume he didn't know who you were, either,' Gordon said with a sigh.

She shook her head, still staring at her hands. 'I knew he was from Zimbabwe,' she said quietly, after a moment. 'But I didn't tell him *I* was, too. I was afraid he'd—' She stopped.

'What?'

She twisted her hands awkwardly. 'I don't know. That he'd think . . . that he'd look down on me.'

'Look *down* on you?' Gordon was genuinely surprised. 'Why?'

'Because . . . because of being . . . well, I'm white, aren't I?'

Gordon looked at her, shaking his head. 'I didn't bring my sons up that way, Nicola,' he said quietly. 'Don't you know who Mat is? You must have met Simon, surely?'

She looked up. 'Simon?' she asked, momentarily puzzled.

'Simon. Mat's brother. Simon Carter.'

She stared at him. 'Simon *Carter* is Mat's brother?'

'Ah, so you've met Simon?'

'Just once, at a New Year's Eve party years ago, but I didn't know they even *knew* each other. I've just found out that he works for my father as well. Mr Ndava, please tell me what's going on. I feel like I'm in some kind of strange dream. Nothing makes sense any more. She also said that . . . that—' She stopped, her voice breaking. There were tears in her eyes.

'Oh, my dear . . . no, please don't cry!' Gordon got up, agitated. He looked anxiously at the door. Patience was much better at this sort of thing, although it had been years since they'd had a tearful girl on their doorstep – it was generally Simon who brought those sorts of situations about, never Mat. Even then, he'd never quite known what to do or say. 'I'll just get my wife.' He hurried towards the door. 'I'll be back in a second,' he said, pulling it open. He hurried down the corridor to the kitchen. 'Patience!' he hissed, pushing open the door. '*Kurumidza! Musikana we kwa Harte aswika. Ari kuchema!*'

Patience put down the frying pan she was carrying and looked at him, confused. '*Ani?*' Who?

'Nicola Harte. *Kurumidza! Handizivi kuti ndoita seyi naye.* I don't know what to do with her. She's crying.'

Patience untied her apron strings. '*Ari kuitei pano?*' she asked, hurrying after him.

'I don't know why she's here. Something to do with Mat.'

'Oh.'

They entered the sitting room together. The girl had tried to compose herself but at the sight of Patience, she burst into tears again. Gordon shook his head as Patience went over to comfort her. What was happening? What had happened between her and his son?

The resemblance between Mrs Ndava and her son was so striking that it simply brought on a fresh wave of tears. Nic found herself pressed against her shoulder and the tenderness with which the older woman held her was more than she could bear. It was the last thing she'd expected to do – and the last people with whom she'd expected to share the turbulent events of the past forty-eight hours – but, within minutes, she found herself opening up to them in a way that was wholly unfamiliar to her. In that respect, Gordon Ndava was more like his son than he perhaps realised. He listened to her without comment, his forefinger pressed into the soft pad of his cheek, waiting patiently for her to finish. He said nothing, but his eyes were both kind and soft. Impossible to believe they were strangers.

'Not strangers, exactly, Nicola,' he demurred gently. 'We are all far from home.'

Home. That word again. 'I don't know what to say,' she whispered eventually, after the storm of weeping had passed. 'I feel so silly, coming here like this . . .'

'Well, where else should you go?' Gordon asked, still regarding her almost indulgently. 'But I have to tell you, my dear, that I don't know where Mat is myself. It's been over two months since we last spoke. Things aren't good between us right now, I'm afraid.'

'Is it . . .' Nic could hardly bring herself to speak. 'It's not because of my father, is it?'

Gordon sighed. He got up. Nic saw the warning look that flashed quickly between him and his wife. He passed a hand across the back of his neck in a gesture that brought Mat immediately to mind. She winced. 'My son,' he began heavily, 'sees the world in black and white. Good and bad. Right and wrong. He always has, even as a little boy. Oh, in other ways he's tolerant. But not in this way. Myself, it's not so simple, I don't mind telling you.'

Patience drew in a sharp breath, apparently warning him. 'No,' he quickly said in Shona as an aside to her. 'Let me finish.' He turned to Nic and spread his hands. 'No one gets to where your father is without dirtying his hands, Nicola. You must know that. Where we come from . . . you know how things are. So much blood has been spilled, there's always been something for us to fight over. And your father is a fighter, if nothing else. A good one. Not always fair, I grant you, and not always clean. But who is? He wouldn't be where he is if he had been. And neither would I.'

'Gordon,' Patience broke in. 'That's enough. She doesn't need to hear any more. Enough.'

'No, she needs to understand.' Gordon held up a hand. 'The education you've both had . . . all *three* of you have had. Mat, Simon, you . . . how d'you think that was paid for? The homes, the cars, the holidays, the *security*. Everything on a plate, when and where you want it. My God, when I think of where *I* came from – where Patience and I grew up – what we had, compared to what we've been able to give you! None of you have ever been hungry; you've never had to go without . . . wanted for nothing. *Nothing,* I tell you!'

'But we never asked for it!' Nic burst out, fresh tears forming in her eyes. 'I didn't *ask* to be rich.'

'But you are, my dear. As are my sons. The best of everything. There's nothing Mat or Simon wanted that they couldn't have. But the bottom line is, Nicola, it came at a price. It's the price we paid – your father and I – so that *you* wouldn't grow up the way we did. D'you know, your father once told me he was in his twenties before he went to sleep on a full stomach. I've never forgotten it. Like me. That's why we understand one another, you know.'

'I don't understand. How's that possible?'

Gordon regarded her thoughtfully. 'Do you know anything about your father?' he asked gently. 'Do you know where he came from? What he's done to get where he is?'

'Gordon . . .' Patience's voice was concerned.

'Answer me, Nicola. What do you know about your father?'

Nic wiped her tears and looked at him uncertainly. 'I . . . I don't know. Not much, I suppose. He never said much about himself . . . about his past, I mean. I just assumed—' She stopped, painfully aware of how inadequate her response must sound. 'He never talked about it.'

'Did you ever ask?'

Nic looked down at her hands. It took her a few minutes to find her voice. 'I never wanted to know, I suppose,' she whispered finally. 'I just—'

'Don't judge him. You don't have that right. Neither of you.'

Nic nodded slowly. There was a tightness in her chest that made it difficult to breathe. Suddenly her father's face appeared before her and she realised, not without pain, that she hardly ever thought about him. Not in the way Mr Ndava was asking. He was right. She knew next to nothing about the man she called her father. 'Mr Ndava,' she asked finally, looking up at him. 'I need to find Mat. Will you help me?'

119

The doorbell rang, interrupting him. He looked up from the computer, frowning. It was just past ten o'clock on a Sunday morning. He wasn't expecting anyone; there were few people who knew where he was. The bell rang again, loud and insistent. He sighed and stood up. The tiny cottage in Dorset to which he'd fled after that fateful morning when he'd finally understood the extent of Jim Harte's influence, was so far removed from everyone and everything he knew that at times he found it hard to believe in the existence of the world outside. It belonged to an old contact of his from his *FT* days. *It's yours*, he'd said to Mat several times as they discussed the stories they'd never followed or the leads they'd omitted to chase. *Any time you need it*. Well, the time had finally come.

He'd driven away from the house on Kemplay Road that morning, his whole body tense with the shock of finding out that his father and Simon both worked for Jim Harte. Always had. Always would. It had taken him less than an hour to throw a few clothes into a bag and jump back into the car. Four hours later he was pulling into the overgrown driveway. He'd unpacked in less time than it had taken him *to* pack and he'd been working non-stop ever since. He was three-quarters of the way through the book he'd always intended to write. The book that would blow the lid off the whole, sordid RhoMine affair. It was also the book that would finally bring Jim Harte down.

The doorbell rang again. He got up and walked across the small living room, still frowning. He yanked open the door. It took him a few seconds to register who he was staring at. His mouth opened in protest but she held up a hand, warding him off. 'What the—?'

'Mat, I—'

'How did you . . . who told you I was here?' he asked sharply, to cover the confusion he felt at the sight of Nic Harte standing in the doorway of the one place in the world he was sure no one would find him – not until he was ready, at least. He saw the look of pain flit across her face and it was all he could do to keep his arms by his sides. Time had done nothing to diminish the sheer physical pleasure seeing her had always brought. He stared at her, unable to believe his eyes.

'Can I come in?' she asked finally, lifting her shoulders almost helplessly.

He stood back to let her pass. The scent of her hair curled around her as she walked through into the tiny living room. His whole body was taut with conflicting emotions – surprise, anger, disbelief and yes, desire, too. 'How did you find me?' he asked, struggling to keep a hold on his feelings.

'Your father.'

'You went to my *father*?'

'Where else should I have gone?'

'How did he—?'

'He has his ways,' Nic said, shrugging off her coat and placing it over the back of the single, upholstered chair. He couldn't take his eyes off her. There was a calmness to her movements that astounded him, partly, he supposed, because he himself was anything but. 'It took almost a week. I—'

'It's fine,' he cut her off abruptly, again more sharply than he intended. 'I don't want to know. You're here.'

'I'm here.' She said it simply. There was no trace of coquetry. It was one of the things he had always liked about her.

'Why?'

Her gaze was direct and frank. There was a small, taut fold of skin at the corner of her eyes; slowly, as he watched, her expression changed, the fold sank away. Her eyes were the same cornflower blue, staring at him out of the time they'd spent together. 'How could I *not* come?' she asked, turning the palms of her hands upwards. The gesture was disarming. He felt his emotions begin to slide alarmingly. Nic Harte. She hadn't been in the room ten minutes and he was already beginning to lose his grip.

'Where's your boyfriend?' He heard himself ask the question, his voice unnaturally loud in the silence curling around them.

'There isn't another boyfriend. There never was. There's something I need to tell you, Mat. It's about Estelle.'

The thick, silky weight of her hair was the first thing he felt when he woke in the early hours of the morning. It lay spread across his chest, falling across his body, the ends tickling him faintly as they breathed together as one. His heart jammed blood into his veins. Outside he could hear the birds beginning to stir; the short passage of time that brought him to consciousness was measured by her breathing. Nic stirred softly, her hand going out automatically, even in sleep, to feel for him. He felt again the wonderful soft weight of her body against his side and ran his hand slowly down the base of her spine, his fingertips prickling pleasurably under the satiny smoothness of her skin. A small sound escaped from the confines of her throat; a tiny, half-whimper, half-protest, as his hand began another kind of exploration, his body already hard and taut with a hunger for her that the past few hours had done nothing to assuage. His hands tingled with the feel of her body. She rolled over fluidly and he felt himself slowly drawn into her, the anger and bewilderment that had blown up inside him the day he'd arrived on her doorstep to hear she was with another man dissolving as his body dissolved in hers.

He began to make love to her again, fiercely, pushing against the unspecified fear that was slowly rising in him. It was easy to believe, lying in the lumpy double bed beside her, that everything that had happened in the past few months could be pushed away, set to one side against the strength of feeling that existed between them. It could not. What had been said and learned could not be undone; his father, Simon, RhoMine, Jim Harte – the realisation that he was hopelessly in love with the daughter of a man who represented everything he abhorred couldn't be avoided. Jim Harte had tried to destroy him. He'd spent the past two months dreaming about his revenge. When the idea of the book had come to him, he'd seized upon it with a sense of relief. It was what had been driving him ever since – the notes, the research, the hours spent on the phone and in front of the computer. He was meticulous, just as he'd been trained to be, and as the story unfolded, so too did his sense of satisfaction at a series of wrongs slowly being put right. But Nic's unexpected appearance on his doorstep had changed everything. He was no longer sure of himself and that, for a man as principled and steadfast as he believed himself to be, was torture. He lay beside her, his heartbeat slowly returning to normal, and thought about what to do.

There was absolute silence in the room as Nic finished reading. She put down the page, her whole body still. She couldn't bring herself to look at Mat. He knew more about her than anyone else – more, it seemed, than she did. He stood by the kitchen window, watching her calmly, saying nothing.

'How . . . ?' She gestured weakly at the stack of sheets she'd just finished reading.

He pulled the corners of his mouth down. 'It's not that difficult, Nic. You of all people should know that.'

'But when? All this . . . it's years of work, Mat. How long . . . ?' There was a question she didn't dare ask.

He answered it for her. 'Nothing to do with you. I swear it. Christ, I didn't even know who you were then. Nicola *Parker*? It took me a while to get over that one.'

Nic looked back down at the manuscript. Six hundred-odd pages that held the key to who her father was and to most of her own life. She turned her face towards her palm, covering her mouth. 'You can't do this, Mat. Not because of *my* father but because of yours. Because of Simon.'

He turned away from her, looking back out over the fields now in the first flush of spring. The morning light was cool and clear. 'There's something I once read,' he said slowly. 'A long time ago. In school, in fact. I've always kept it at the back of my head, somewhere, one of those things you read somewhere that *says* something to you, jumps out at you from the page. It's from Shakespeare. One of the sonnets.'

'What?'

'*You had a father. Let your son say so.* It meant something to me back then. It still does. It was one of the things *I* had and Simon didn't. I was proud of my father, Nic. He knew . . . *things*. How the world worked. How to negotiate with people, manoeuvre, get things done. I didn't know anyone else who could do what he did . . . and look where he'd come from. It's different for you . . . for whites, I mean. You've always been wealthy—'

'That's not true,' Nic broke in, gesturing towards the pages in her lap. 'Not if this is anything to go by. That's what your dad said to me. That they understood each other.'

'I'll bet,' Mat said bitterly.

'No, it's not like that.' Nic was astounded to find herself defending him. 'He said they both knew what it was like to go to bed hungry – something you and I have never had to face. I don't condone what they've done, Mat, not for a second, you've got to believe me. But you and I . . . we wouldn't *be* here if it weren't for them. For what they've done. It almost doesn't matter.'

'But that's just it!' Mat turned back to face her. His expression was genuinely pained. 'It *does* matter! Of course it matters! Have you any *idea*—'

'Yes. Yes, I have.' She tapped the manuscript again. 'It's all here. In black and white. You've done your research, Mat. Nothing's been left out. It's all here. Where he came from, where he's been, who he had to screw to get where he is. My mother . . .' She stopped, took a deep breath and then continued. 'I think I knew all along that something was wrong.

He—' She swallowed, her voice thickening painfully. 'He couldn't stand me, you know. He couldn't stand to be near me. I thought it was Molly, or the fact that I was a girl. Or that I was stupid, ugly . . . oh, I can't tell you how many reasons I tried to find for the way he was with me. I've spent most of my life wondering what it was I did wrong.'

'And now?'

She looked up at him. 'Guilt,' she said simply. 'That's what it was. He couldn't look at me because he was guilty. I understand that now. But it was an accident, Mat. You said it yourself. You wrote it. Here.' She stabbed the manuscript again. 'Whatever else he's done, he didn't do *that*.'

'How the hell can you just sit there?' Mat asked incredulously. 'He killed your mother, Nic! It's your *mother* we're talking about! Not some stranger—'

'I never knew her. I was two when she died, Mat. I don't even remember what she *looked* like.'

'That doesn't change the facts.'

'No, but it changes the way I feel about it. Look, I didn't come here to plead his case or to beg forgiveness for things I didn't even know he'd done. I don't care what he's done, don't you understand? I came here because of you, not *him*. I came here for myself . . . for us.'

'But that's exactly it!' Mat took a step towards her, bending down so that his face was on a level with hers. There was an anger of the kind she'd never heard before in his voice. 'It *does* matter! We are who we are, Nic. I know it, you know it. Jesus, the whole world knows it!'

She stared at him, the dreadful question blocked in her chest struggling to assert itself. *So what now?* She opened her mouth to speak but nothing came out. What now? She saw that he understood. He turned away from her and stared back out over the fields. There was tension in the set of his broad shoulders underneath his woollen pullover. He put out his forearms and leaned against the sill, his back to her. She waited, her breath coming in short, shallow exhalations, measured against the thudding of her heart. His voice, when it finally came, was quiet. 'I would do anything for you, Nic Harte. I mean it. I've never—' He straightened up and turned back towards her. There was bewilderment in his face. He turned the palms of his hands upwards in a gesture of near helplessness. 'I've never felt this way about anyone before. Believe me. But this . . .' He spread his hands. 'This is different. Don't ask me not to do this. Anything else – but not this.'

There was a wrenching upheaval of emotion inside her that pushed her to her feet. She could hardly look at him. The words were out before she could even think about them. 'Then you'll have to do this without me, Mat. I *can't*. He's my father. I can't just stand back and watch you bring him down. I just can't.'

'Your choice, Nic.' Mat's voice was cold.

'What're you going to do? Go after them all? My father, yours, Simon? Hell, why stop there? You could get my brothers, too . . . Molly, Jessica? Me, even. You could get us all, just like that!' She snapped her fingers, hot angry tears suddenly flooding her eyes. 'There's Estelle, too . . . you know you never liked her. This is your chance!'

'Stop it, Nic. You're being ridiculous. This isn't about revenge! Is that what you think? That I'd go to these lengths to—'

'To what?' She interrupted him again. 'You're going to destroy everyone because you've got a grudge against my father? I'm not my father, Mat.' Nic was screaming now. 'None of us is! We didn't ask for any of this. I've got no more control over what he does than you do! Who *cares* what he's done? Why can't we just forget it all and walk away? We could go anywhere, do anything. We don't have to have anything to do with it – with them.'

'You're asking me to run away?' he asked.

'Run away, move on, whatever you want to call it. Let's just get away from all this . . .' She waved her hands dismissively. 'From this . . . this *shit*. Let's just *go*! Get out!'

He shook his head. 'No. Running away's not the answer. Not for me.'

'Then what is?' Nic's heart was lodged firmly in her mouth.

He pointed to the manuscript. 'That. I will bring that bastard down if it's the last thing I do, Nic. I'm sorry. I can't just sit back and watch him get away with it again. This isn't just about us, for Christ's sake.'

'So what *is* it about?'

'Greed. Corruption. Power. You know . . . the stuff you and I are supposed to expose. Isn't that why you became a journalist? Our first obligation is to the truth, remember? Maintain independence from the stories you cover? Or doesn't that apply when it's your family we're talking about?'

'Don't patronise me!'

'Then don't act like you don't know what I'm talking about!'

A thick, angry silence wrapped itself around them. They stared at each other, neither willing to give way. Minutes ticked by. Mat's mouth was set in a tense, stubborn line. She could hear her own breath, and his, pacing out the seconds to the inevitable showdown.

It was she, finally, who turned away, picked up her bag and walked out. Sunlight bounced off the chrome wheels of the car as she walked towards it; the early-morning haze was beginning to burn off. She unlocked the door and got in. She placed her shaking hands on the steering wheel, hoping against hope that he would open the door after her, run out on to the pebbled driveway and stop her. He did not. The closed wooden door of the cottage turned its blank, unseeing face towards her. She drove away.

120

It was chilly outside. Tory wrapped her arms around herself as she crossed the road to where Luc's silver BMW was parked. His face was turned in profile away from her. In the darkness, it was impossible to read. She hesitated for a second, then, heart thumping, she tapped on the glass. He turned slowly towards her, the remains of his cigarette still held between his fingers. There was an agonising wait as he looked at her through the smoky glass, then he slowly rolled the window down. They stared at each other.

Tory was the first to break the silence. 'You came back.'

He lifted his shoulders in the Gallic shrug that was so familiar to her it brought tears to her eyes. How could she have done it? she wondered to herself, staring at his face. How could she have walked away from the one person in the world for whom being herself was enough? Luc loved her. *Had* loved her, she corrected herself automatically, wincing. What was wrong with her that it hadn't seemed enough?

'Here, get in.' Luc leaned across and opened the passenger door. Tory hesitated, then walked around the car. Her heart was hammering. She slid into the seat beside him, not daring to look at his face. They both spoke at once, suddenly urgently.

'I can't—'

'It wasn't—'

She turned to face him. In the dim light of the car's interior, there was pain etched into every line of his face. Her hand went out automatically to cover his, guilt and shame washing through her as the words came tumbling out. 'I didn't mean to hurt you, Luc, I swear. I don't know what came over me. I . . . I can't explain it.'

'Try. You never give me a chance, Tory. *Jamais*. You keep everything locked up, here.' He tapped the side of his head angrily. 'I know there are things . . . things you don't want to talk about, but if you can't talk to *me*, well, who else can you talk to?'

Tory felt the hot slick of tears on her cheeks. She fidgeted with her hands. 'I know,' she whispered. 'I just . . . I didn't think. It's all so mixed up, Luc. You can't imagine—'

'How can I imagine anything when you say *nothing*?' he burst out. 'Have you any idea what it's been like these past few months? Living with someone who won't even *talk*?'

'I—'

'Sometimes I get the feeling you'd rather I disappeared and left you alone,' he went on bitterly .

'Don't say that,' Tory whispered, wiping her cheeks furiously with the back of her hand. 'Please don't say that.'

'*Mais, c'est vrai*, Tory. Whether you like it or not. It's true. You don't even look at me any more. You look straight through me as though you wish I were dead.'

The sound escaped from her lips before she could stop it. 'Don't. Don't ever say that.' She began to cry. 'That's what I said . . . to *her*. To Susie. The d-day . . . the morning she died. I said it. I said *that* to her. I—'

'Tory, what are you talking about?'

'I wished she were dead!'

'Is that . . . ?'

'I said it! I said it!' She began to weep, shaking her head from side to side. 'That morning we had an argument and—' She stopped, unable to continue. She heard Luc swear softly under his breath, in French, then all of a sudden, his arms were around her, pulling her towards him. He pressed her against him so tightly her breath went still inside her. He said nothing, just continued to hold her, the weight of his body squeezing the mixture of grief and guilt out of her until there was nothing left. Just the feel of his arms and the whispered sound of his voice in her ear. 'I love you, Tory. Why can't you see that? Why isn't it ever enough?'

121

In the cool dark of the bar, two men sat talking. Behind them, bathed in the bluish light of the stage, a girl sang softly into a microphone. Her voice was smooth and rich; the notes she held seemed to go on for ever. Simon gripped his beer – his third so far – and steeled himself against the unaccustomed wave of loneliness that burned over him like a fever. He fished in his pocket for a cigarette. 'How come you always run out when you need one most?' he said to the man sitting opposite.

'Here . . .' The man slid something across the table.

'Thanks.' Simon pocketed it, aware that his attention was only peripherally on the conversation they were having.

'Everything OK?'

'Yeah. Of course.' Simon forced a quick smile to his face. 'Everything's cool. It's all taken care of.'

'Fine. Look, I gotta run.' The man pushed back his chair and stood up. 'You sure you're OK?'

'Absolutely.'

'OK. Well, we'll be in touch.' He strode away from the table without looking back. Simon watched him go. The girl's voice broke over him, smoky and low; close to the stage, a table broke out in appreciative applause. He was sweating, despite the air-conditioning. It was time to leave. He tossed a couple of dollar bills on to the table and stood up. Caryn. She was on his mind all the time now, when it should have been on something else.

Half an hour later, he swung the SUV on to the pavement in front of the house. He sat for a moment or two, looking out at the rapidly emptying beach, watching the fat-bellied sun sinking slowly across the flat line of the sea. His fingers drummed a blind, impatient dance on the steering wheel. He killed the engine, ran lightly up the steps and opened the door. The house was as quiet and lonely as it had been when he'd left that morning. He tossed the keys on to the counter and walked to the sliding doors. The vast blue sky was slowly being emptied of light; he stood behind the glass, his hand going out automatically to unlock the latch that would push the doors open, but stopped midway. He fished in his front pocket for a cigarette and stuck it almost angrily between his lips. Try as he might, he couldn't shake the feeling that something was about to happen – but what? Caryn was due back any day now; he ought to be pleased. So why this dreadful premonition that he wouldn't see her again?

122

'Here.' Caryn handed her a tumbler full of dark gold liquid. 'Your teeth are chattering.' She watched as Nic took the glass and downed the small measure of brandy in a single, swift gulp.

'Did you know?' Nic's question needed no qualification.

Caryn looked away. 'Yes,' she said eventually, slowly. 'But not at the beginning.'

'How long?'

'A while.'

'How long?' Nic repeated the question.

'Almost a year,' Caryn said reluctantly. 'Look, Nic . . . I'm sorry, really I am. I should've said something, I know. As soon as I knew who he was. I didn't even know his real name for a long time. But by then . . .' Her voice trailed off. 'I had no idea, you've got to believe me.'

Nic looked at her questioningly, then nodded slowly. 'Did you know about Simon and my father?' she asked, her voice thickening painfully.

'Not right away, no. After the film came out there were questions. It was Martin who first asked me. I think he's always known more than I have.'

'How come I'm always the last to know?' Nic asked angrily. 'How come everyone else figures it out and I don't?'

'Oh, Nic . . .' Caryn sighed. 'Sometimes you don't *ask*, you know.' She looked at her best friend almost sadly. 'You *must* have known about your father. Come on. You don't get to where he is without . . . well, without bending the law a little.'

'A *little*? Caryn, hiring someone to bump off your opponents isn't bending the law a little. It's—'

'I know,' Caryn interrupted her quickly. 'I know what Simon does; you don't have to remind me. Look, I didn't plan it, OK? It's not as if I *decided* I was going to fall in love with him; it just happened. He's . . . he's the most—'

'I know. I met him first, remember?' Nic looked down at her

empty glass. 'God, what a fucking mess.' She set the glass carefully on the side table. 'How did it all get so complicated?'

'Complicated times,' Caryn said, spreading her hands. 'Especially for people like you.'

'Like me?'

'You, Mat, Simon. Look at where you're from. With your history? It's no bloody wonder things are so complicated.'

Nic was silent. It was almost exactly what Gordon Ndava had said. 'Mat's absolutely adamant, Caryn,' she said finally, her voice dropping to a whisper. 'He's going to publish that book.'

'What else can he do?' Caryn asked, lifting her shoulders. 'If it were me—'

'Would you do it? Destroy your own father?'

Caryn looked away. It took her a while to speak. 'From what you've said,' she began carefully, 'he's never been much of a father, has he? Yes, he's looked after you financially and all that, but what about the other stuff? Not that *I* know anything about that, mind you. I can't even remember what my dad looks like, but I'm not blind, Nic. You never say much – that's not your way, is it? – but we both know how it's been.'

'But he's still my father,' Nic cried out. 'That's got to mean something, hasn't it?'

'Does it?' Caryn shrugged.

Nic stared at her. 'But if I don't have him,' she said slowly, 'if I don't have my family – who *do* I have?'

'Oh, Nic. You'll always have your family—'

'I mean it, Caryn. There's no one else. Shaun and Patrick both work for my dad, you know that. If he goes down, they go down with him. What'll happen to Jessica?'

'Nic,' Caryn broke in gently. 'Your father isn't stupid. They'll be taken care of no matter what happens to him. He's too clever to let anything happen to them.'

Jim's sleek black Mercedes stood at the kerb. The driver was nowhere to be seen. Nic walked up the steps and opened the front door. The sound of Bach floated down the stairs from her father's study on the first floor. She walked up the second flight of stairs and paused outside the door, listening for the sound of voices. There was only silence. For once, it seemed, he was alone. She tapped once, twice on the door and then pushed it cautiously open.

Jim was sitting in his favourite leather armchair, his back towards her, his fingers moving almost imperceptibly to the closing strains of what Nic recognised to be the Well-Tempered Klavier. She stood in the doorway, suddenly unsure of herself. What had she come to say? A small, nervous sound escaped from her throat. Her father turned slowly in his chair.

'How long've you been standing there?' he asked, his voice expressionless.

'Ju-just a couple of seconds,' she stammered.

'What d'you want?'

'There's something I need to tell you,' she said, coming into the room. She closed the door behind her and leaned against it, trapping her shaking hands behind her back. 'It's about Mat Ndava.'

He looked at her, frowning a little. 'What about him?'

She glanced at his face. He looked tired, suddenly, and old. A sharp stab of pain lodged itself below her right rib. She was aware of how little she knew about him – how little she knew him. When was the last time she'd properly looked at him? 'Mat's been doing some research,' she said carefully. 'On you.'

Jim let out an exasperated sigh. 'Let me save you the embarrassment, Nic. He's writing a book. He's been digging around in the past. Tell me something I don't already know.'

'It's potentially quite dangerous. For you, I mean.'

Jim gave a short, humourless guffaw. 'How's that?'

'Well, he's found out about certain things. To do with RhoMine and . . . and stuff.'

'So?'

Nic stared at him. She was finding his apparent nonchalance hard to fathom. 'I thought . . . I just thought that you might want to know,' she said lamely. 'In case—'

'In case what? Your bloody boyfriend decides he's going to write a kiss 'n' tell memoir and drive our share prices down?

Come on, Nicola. Tell me I've taught you more than that. Please.' Jim shook his head impatiently at her.

Two angry spots of colour appeared on Nic's cheeks. 'First of all,' she said hotly, 'he's not my boyfriend, and second, I came here to warn you. I thought you'd want to know, that's all.'

'Mat Ndava's been a bloody thorn in my side for the past few years, Nicola. Don't you think I saw this coming? I've known that young man for most of his adult life. I've always known it would end up this way. I'm fully prepared, young lady. Fully prepared. Let him bring it on.'

'Wh-what are you going to do?'

Jim looked at her closely. He shook his head in disbelief. 'What? D'you think I'm about to get him killed?' He laughed shortly. 'Is that what you're afraid of? Is that why you came here?'

'No, of course not,' Nic lied, knowing her reddened face would betray her. Fear clutched at her insides.

'Is that what you think of me?' Jim asked incredulously. 'D'you really think I'd go to those lengths?'

'You've gone to them before,' Nic said, her heart thudding wildly. She had never before spoken to her father like this. 'I know all about Simon Carter and—'

'You know nothing,' Jim interrupted her, waving his hand dismissively at her. 'Trust me. You know nothing.'

'I know right from wrong,' Nic said angrily. 'I know you've broken the law sometimes. I know you've done things that . . . that you shouldn't have. Mat said—'

'*Mat* said? What the hell do you and Mat know about anything?' Jim cut her off peremptorily. 'This has nothing to do with you and your precious Mat! Jesus *Christ*! If that young man had any idea what's been done to put him where he is—'

'We didn't ask for it!' Nic suddenly shouted at him. She could feel her throat thickening again, though this time with anger, not with tears. 'Don't try and tell me that this was all done for our benefit. That's bullshit and you know it! Don't you dare pretend you did all this for us!' The look of fury on Jim's face ought to have silenced her, but Nic was beyond caring. 'You don't give a damn about us . . . about any of us! We're only useful to you when—'

'What on *earth* is going on in here?' The door burst open. Molly stood in the doorway, a look of bewilderment on her face. 'Nicola! How dare you raise your voice—'

'Oh, for once in your goddamn life, Molly, why don't you just belt up!' Nic rounded angrily on her. 'Stay out of this! It's got absolutely nothing to do with you!'

'Don't you speak to me—'

'Shut *up*!' Nic screamed. She turned back to face her father. Tears of pure rage were coursing down her cheeks. 'I'm sick to death of listening to your bullshit and being treated like some bloody nuisance you can't wait to get rid of. I'm *sick* of it, d'you hear me? All the lies, the crooked deals, the corruption. I've had enough!'

'*You've* had enough?' Jim bellowed at her, rising from his chair at last. His face was as dark as thunder. 'Let me tell you exactly what those lies have bought you,' he spat out. 'That nice little flat you live in, all those private schools you got thrown out of, the nifty little sports car. Who d'you think pays for all that, eh? You think all of that falls off a tree?'

'Of course I don't! I'm not stupid! But why d'you have to go about it this way? Why can't you earn a living *within* the law, like everyone else? Why d'you think you're above it?'

'The law? Whose laws? You don't know the meaning of the word,' Jim growled, holding up a hand to ward off Molly's outraged voice. 'You see?' he rounded on her suddenly. 'I should never have let her go to university. I knew it was a bad idea, right from the start!'

'You didn't "let" me,' Nic screamed. 'I *earned* it! I worked my ass off to get my degree. This has nothing to do with it! I'm talking about corruption and—'

'Let me tell you something about corruption,' Jim roared. 'Corruption is what makes the world go round, my girl. Corruption is the reason why you didn't grow up in a tin shack with nothing in your belly but hunger! Have you ever gone without? Have you ever lacked for *anything*? Food to eat, a place to sleep, a home to go to? Have you?'

'That's not all there is to it! What about love? What about a *proper* family? What about honesty and . . . and respect for each other?'

Jim threw up his hands in disgust. 'Respect! You want to talk about *respect*? Without money there *is* no respect! Have you ever had respect for a pauper?'

Nic took a deep breath. She was shaking from head to toe. Molly stood in the doorway, looking in astonishment from one to the other. Jim's face was beetroot red; his fists were clenched. In that moment, she was fully, horribly aware of the smouldering rage that simmered just below the surface of the man she'd been afraid of her whole life. Mat was right. What her father projected wasn't strength; it was the opposite. It was weakness that drove him, and fear. A terrible, haunting fear of failure, of poverty, of his past – of the truth. An incredible weight was suddenly lifted from her shoulders. *She* wasn't afraid. On the contrary. She had never felt so sure of anything in her life. 'You've got it wrong, Dad,' she said, struggling to bring her voice under control. 'Respect isn't about *money*. It's not for sale. You earn it but you can't buy it. Not from me.'

The tension in the room was palpable. For a few seconds, no one spoke. Jim's face was contorted in a mixture of rage and confusion. Molly began to cry. And then Nic turned and walked slowly towards the door.

'Just where d'you think you're going?' Jim spat out as she reached for the handle.

'As far away from here as I can,' she said without turning round.

'You won't get very far,' Jim shouted after her as she let the door close behind her. 'Go on, run after that boyfriend of yours . . . see how far *he* can take you.' The door closed on his voice. Nic opened the front door and walked down the steps. The Mercedes was still parked outside the house; the driver had returned and was sitting in the front, reading the paper under the street light. It was nearly dark. He looked up as she passed but didn't recognise her. He was new; he probably wasn't even aware his employer had a daughter. She shoved her hands in her pockets. It was suddenly chilly, but she scarcely felt the cold. She was burning inside, but not with anger. For the first time in her life, she was free. Free to do whatever she wanted, go wherever she wanted . . . be whoever she wanted. At that moment, there was only one place in the world she wanted to be. But that option was closed to her, now. That much was painfully clear.

123

Simon leaned back in his chair, stifling a yawn. Across the desk, a frown of intense concentration on his face, his barrister read to the end of each page before setting each one carefully aside. They'd been sequestered in Graeme Lessor's chambers for the best part of the day. He looked out of the window; the spotlessly manicured lawns stretched away towards the rose-covered wall at the far end of Lincoln's Inn. Within the cloistered halls an air of calm, unhurried judgement prevailed. He watched as a gardener cut a swathe across the grass, pruning shears in hand. There was something about the neat little world of hushed voices and measured tones that set his teeth on edge. Lessor coughed discreetly. Simon turned to face him.

'Hell of a gamble,' Lessor said without preamble. 'Don't quite know how the judge is going to take it.'

'Best I can do,' Simon said evenly. 'It's all there.'

'Indeed.' Lessor tapped the thick sheaf of papers. 'It's just that we don't go in for that sort of thing here. Under normal circumstances.'

'Yeah, well. Circumstances are what they are, I guess.'

'Quite. Well, Mr Carter. Leave it with me. I'll be in touch again as soon as I've managed to secure an audience with his lordship.' He rose from his chair. Simon followed suit. The two men shook hands and Simon walked out of the room. His fingers brushed his mobile phone lying in his pocket. He had to steel himself against the urge to pick it up and dial Caryn's number. It had been over a week since he'd spoken to her; she wasn't the type to question his frequently inexplicable absences, but this time it was he who felt the need to call, to explain, to hear her voice. But he couldn't. Not until he'd worked it all out. He stopped and lit a cigarette, cupping his hand against the stiff breeze. He drew the smoke down into his lungs as though trying to chase the longing out of his body. Once Lessor had negotiated the terms of his plea bargain, he would be free to do whatever he liked. But not until then. If he talked to her now, he wouldn't be able to stop himself telling her what he was about to do. For the time being, until he was sure it would all go according to plan, he had to stay silent. And to do that, he had to keep away from her, as hard as it was. If it all worked out, there would be time enough to explain. He couldn't keep the corners of his mouth from turning upwards. If it all worked out, they would have all the time in the world.

124

It was almost five by the time she finally pulled up in front of her flat. She got out of the car and quickly walked up the stairs. She paused for a moment at the door. It was hard to believe it had only been a week since the night of her birthday party. A week ago she and Caryn had been lying on the bed, watching Tory shake out the creases in her dress. Despite everything they'd been through in the last few months, Nic had genuinely thought the party signalled a new beginning for all of them. Instead, all their old ghosts had come back to haunt them, even the ones she wasn't aware of.

She pushed open the front door, half-expecting to see Estelle sitting on her couch, going through her things. She still couldn't get over the shock of realising Estelle was her half-sister. Estelle was family. She understood now why Estelle had sought her out. She felt hunted, almost trapped, and not just by Estelle. *This* was the flip side of her life – the shadowy half-truths and outright lies; the deception and the awful, aching dread that whatever lay beneath the surface of the privileged life she'd led was worse than anything she'd previously imagined. Mat was right. *This is who we are.* But she *didn't* know who she was; that was the problem. Everything had been turned upside down in the space of a week, and she no longer knew what or who to believe. Jim wasn't even English; she knew next to nothing about him. But Gordon Ndava was right – she'd never asked. Somewhere, somehow, perhaps she'd always known? Perhaps subconsciously she'd decided it was better *not* to ask?

She slung her bag over the back of a chair and sank down into the sofa. Mat's face immediately floated up through the mist of hurt and confusion. She closed her eyes, tracing the exact map of his features in her mind. His expression was watchful; the black eyes that absorbed all gazes, including hers, were wary. She felt again the sharp stab of pain that went through her every time she recalled his face. She would never again feel herself to be under his intense, intelligent scrutiny. She picked up a cushion and held it to her chest, feeble protection against the waves of loneliness and heartache that continued to break over her, wave after slow, retreating wave. There was nothing for it but to hold on and hope it would pass.

The phone rang, jerking her into wakefulness. Her heart gave a lurch; was it Mat? She shoved aside the blanket she'd thrown over her legs and stumbled towards it. 'Hello?'

'It's me.' It was Caryn. Her heart plummeted. 'You OK?'

'Yeah. No. I don't know.'

'Are you alone?'

''Fraid so.'

'Can I come over?'

'No, I . . . I just need to be alone for a bit. I'm OK, honestly. I—'

'Have you seen the news?' Caryn interrupted her.

'No. Why?'

'I think I'd better come over. I'll be there in half an hour.' And before she could do or say anything further, Caryn hung up. Nic sat still for a second, feeling the steady thump of her own heartbeat. What now? She picked up the remote control and aimed it at the television, almost fearfully.

125

There was no sound in the room, save for his own breath. He stared at the TV screen; there was a slow, cold dread working its way up his body, limb by limb. In a few moments, the phone would start ringing. Ogilvy, of course, and then the others. All looking to save their own skins. He turned his attention away from the screen and looked across the room. A handsome room, tastefully furnished in the pale, inoffensive quasi-corporate colours that Molly liked. Did he like it? He wasn't sure. He rarely asked himself that sort of thing. Molly, never happier than when she had an interior designer or a personal shopper in tow, had spent months decorating and redecorating the Eaton Square house until it finally resembled what she thought was the sort of house they ought to live in. It was expensive – oh, yes. And tasteful, he supposed. The right sort of paintings; carefully chosen artefacts of crystal, glass, ceramic – not an African mask or object amongst them. Molly wrinkled her nose at that sort of ethnic display. She was English, to the roots of her being. Zimbabwe, for her, was little more than the Home Counties with a better climate, cheaper staff.

And for him? He laid his hands, palm down, on the polished walnut surface of his desk. The wood was warm under his touch. He ran his fingers along the edge, feeling in its smooth solidity a reassurance of some sort – he had worked long and hard to surround himself with objects that spoke of wealth, as if hidden in the price of a chesterfield was the assurance that this – his gaze took in the large, calm study – would last. The journey from São Antão to Eaton Square was longer than anyone would think. He half smiled to himself. São Antão – how many years had it been since he'd thought of the place? Not that there was much to think about. The camp, the prefab house with the corrugated tin roof, the steady roar of the ocean and the constant growling in his belly – he'd tried to forget São Antão, not remember it. He'd almost succeeded, too. Funny, wasn't it? There was an almost perfect symmetry to the way it had ended.

Eighteen months ago he'd made a phone call to Gordon, asking him – no, *telling* him – to rein in his son. But it wasn't Mat who'd brought the house down; it was the other one. Simon. The one he'd trusted. The one who was like him, or so he thought. He'd understood that about Simon Carter from the very first time they'd met. He recalled their first meeting, Simon standing in front of him with that near-perfect calm and non-chalance. Fooled everyone, but not Jim. He'd seen beyond the studied indifference and the tight, closed-off handsome face and seen himself, twenty years earlier. The facts were remarkably similar – an orphan, a *mukiwa*, a genuine loner. Jim had acquired the necessary trappings that wealth brought – wives, children, homes – Simon Carter seemed neither to need nor desire the same and that, Jim understood immediately, made him capable of anything. Exactly what he required – at the time.

He turned back to the television. The coldness had worked its way up his chest but his face felt hot. Beyond the closed door he could hear voices. The phones were already ringing; soon the house would be full of people, including, no doubt, the police. He stared at the image of himself flickering dully across the screen. An old shot of him coming out of the board meeting a year ago when he thought he'd beaten Mat Ndava at his own game. Yes, it *was* funny. *The pen is mightier than the sword.* Which fool had said that? He'd gone to such lengths to prevent Mat

Ndava from having his say that it hadn't occurred to him anyone else could have done the same. Or worse, as it turned out. Carter had struck a plea bargain. In return for anonymity and freedom from prosecution, he'd told the authorities everything they wanted to know, and more besides. And from *that* there would be no escape. He wouldn't be able to buy, charm or force his way out of this one. Yes, it truly was the end. He passed his hand slowly over his face in a gesture of defeat. He could hear the doorbell and the sound of feet running down the stairs. Any moment now. *Any moment now.*

Epilogue

It took only a few minutes. A couple of questions, just as her lawyer said – how long had she known the deceased? What was her state of mind when she left the dinner party that night in Paris? Had she any reason to suspect the deceased wished to take her own life? *The deceased* – it was strange hearing the coroner talk about Estelle in those terms. *The late Estelle Mackenzie.* It made her sound elderly. She was only twenty-six – had been only twenty-six, she kept reminding herself. She was dead. A supposed overdose. There'd been a man with her in her hotel room. The man had long since disappeared, but there was evidence of drugs strewn all over the room. It was still hard to believe.

She answered the coroner's questions as best as she could. No, she hadn't known Estelle Mackenzie worked as a prostitute. No, no one knew who she really was until that night. In the aftermath of her death everything had come out; the whole edifice had started to crumble. It was Nic who'd borne the brunt of it. Jim Harte would soon be in jail. Molly and Jessica had gone to live in Studgrove, which was practically all that was left of the Harte empire. The beautiful home on Eaton Square was gone; Nic's flat, her car, her monthly allowance; the estate in Zimbabwe – all gone, swallowed up by legal fees and the claims of those who'd come after him. Jim Harte hadn't been quite as prepared as he'd thought. Nic's brothers were still in Harare, working for others, now – but at least they'd been spared a jail sentence.

The night Jim had been arrested, Nic had simply disappeared. It was almost six months since she'd last been in contact and Caryn had no idea what to do about it. *It's over*, she longed to tell Nic. *Me and Simon. It's finished.* But her phone calls had gone unanswered and her letters and emails returned – now there was nothing for it but to get on with her own life and put the past years behind her. She couldn't have stayed with Simon, not now – not after everything she now knew. He'd done the right thing, Caryn supposed. He'd turned Harte in before anyone else could, including his own brother, Mat. She alone knew the private agony and the extent of his shame – not just about what he'd chosen to do, but whom he'd done it *for* – and for what? Money? No, Simon had told her the last time they'd met. No, it wasn't about the money. It had never been about the money. Well, why, then? It took him a long time to answer and even when he did, she had the feeling it was something he would spend the rest of his life trying to figure out. Jim Harte was much more than an employer. To the young, impressionable and orphaned *mukiwa*, he was an answer to the riddle that had plagued him all his life.

'What's a *mukiwa*?'

That too, took him a while to answer. 'It's what the Ndebele call me,' he said finally, lighting a cigarette. He blew out the smoke across the top of her head. 'It means "white boy". White boy in Africa. That's me.'

'But you and Mat . . . that's what's always been so special about you. You don't think like that. You said it yourself.'

'Yeah, but the rest of the world does,' he said, reaching for an ashtray. 'Especially where we're from. I thought . . . oh, I dunno. Harte seemed to find a way, that's all.'

'A way to do what? Lie? Steal?'

He gave a short laugh. 'Yeah, that too. No, I meant a way to *be*. To be white. A white African. He didn't give a shit about anything. He just seemed so confident, y'know?'

'And you wanted to be like him?'

'I guess so. In that way, I mean. I wanted to feel like I

belonged. And I knew long before Mat did that Gordon was involved. It sort of made it OK, I guess. All in the family.'

And that was that. She'd left shortly afterwards and hadn't looked back. He was right in one respect: it *was* complicated. But they were the sort of complications she could do without. The months she'd spent in LA with him were enough to convince her that there wasn't a chance in hell she could live her life the way he did. She'd worked too hard and too long to give it all up to become the girlfriend of someone who had done things to and for others that Caryn couldn't even imagine. In the end, that was the distance that had come between them; not Jim Harte or even Nic. Life, insofar as she understood it, was simple. You worked hard, you took care of those close to you and you went to sleep at night with a clear conscience. Simon lived by another, different set of rules and she simply couldn't bring herself to be part of it.

Ten minutes later, the questioning was over. She was shown out through a side door and asked to wait for a few minutes. She took a seat near the window and tried not to think. Suddenly, the door opened again and the man who'd shown her in entered, followed by Nic. Caryn's heart slammed against her ribs. Nic looked straight ahead without blinking, as if she didn't trust herself to look left or right. *This way, please*, the man said, opening the door for her. She passed through without comment. The door closed behind them and Caryn felt the familiar ache of tears start up in her throat. Nic didn't want anything more to do with any of them – her, Tory, Simon . . . she'd closed the door on everything and everyone. Who could blame her? Under the terms of the deal he'd struck with the police, Simon had remained free of the threat of prosecution but he'd shopped them all – Harte, Ogilvy, the Zambians . . . everyone. Poor Nic. She couldn't imagine what it must be like to lose everything – family, fortune, friends *and* Mat, the one person she'd have given everything up for, anyway. And then to see

Caryn and Tory 'get away with it' – those were her words, weren't they?

Luc had taken Tory back, of course. There was no question he wouldn't treat the child as his own. And she'd gone back to Simon, or so Nic believed. But Simon had paid a price. He and Mat no longer spoke to one another. Closer than brothers for almost twenty years, but there was no way their bond could survive this. Who would have thought it would end up like this? She thought back to the day she'd first spoken to Nic Harte all those years ago. She could picture it as if it were yesterday. She'd tripped going through the doors and sent her file folder flying. She'd been scooting around on her hands and knees, trying frantically to pick up the papers when someone spoke to her. She'd looked up – it was Nic.

'Thanks,' she said awkwardly, taking them from her. 'I . . . I must've tripped . . .' she stammered.

Nic looked down at Caryn's shoes. 'I'm not surprised,' she said dryly. And then suddenly, they both giggled. 'I'm sorry,' Nic said finally, trying not to laugh. 'But they're just the—'

'. . . most awful shoes,' Caryn finished for her, shaking her head ruefully. 'I know, believe me.'

'Well, why d'you wear them then?'

'Because I haven't got any others.'

'Oh.'

'Well, thanks for helping me,' Caryn said finally. 'I'd better run. I've got French . . . well, so've you.'

'Oh, I don't think I'll bother today,' Nic said nonchalantly. 'I'm not in the mood.'

Caryn stared at her. Not in the mood? 'Er, OK. Well, thanks again.' Nic nodded and turned away. Caryn hesitated. 'You . . . you can borrow my notes, if you like. If you're not coming.'

Nic stopped and turned round. It was her turn to look surprised. 'All right. Thanks.'

'Bye.'

'Bye.'

That had been the beginning of a friendship that, if she was honest, had meant more to her than any other relationship she'd ever had. Nic and Tory were more than sisters, closer to her than any family member had ever been.

It was suddenly stuffy inside the cramped office. Caryn looked around to see if there was a window she might open. It was a low-slung, nondescript modern building with a row of impossibly high, horizontal windows, none of which looked as if they'd ever been opened before. She stood up, ignoring the look of irritation that the man who'd ushered her in threw her and walked quickly to the back door. She noticed someone standing to her left, just inside the portico. She turned, her mouth dropping open in disbelief.

'Caryn.' Mat nodded at her, the corners of his mouth going up in a smile.

'Mat. What are you doing here?' Her voice had gone high with surprise.

He tilted his head in the direction of the coroner's office a moment. He too looked older, thinner. His mouth and jaw were covered in an unfamiliar beard, but his dark, intense eyes and expression of wary confidence were exactly the same. 'Waiting for Nic,' he said simply.

'Does . . . does she know you're here?'

He shrugged. 'No.'

'But . . .' She opened her palms in a question she couldn't articulate and looked up at him. 'What about . . . ?'

The door behind them opened suddenly. They both turned. In the dissolving play of light as the sun slipped from behind a cloud, shone briefly and then disappeared again, Nic and Mat faced each other. The air around them seemed to draw breath, hold itself . . . Caryn turned away. There was a powerful surge of emotion struggling for release within her; she almost choked. Her left hand went automatically to the set of three engraved silver rings Nic had given her for her birthday, years ago. *Trust.*

Hope. Love. Her fingertips traced over the delicate lettering, confirming what, deep down, she'd known all along. *Trust. Hope. Love.* In that order.